BEAUTIFUL MONSTER

C.G Klein

For the Bungled and the Botched.

Text copyright © 2015 C.G. Klein
Cover design by C.G. Klein
All rights reserved

No part of this book may be reproduced, or stored in a retrieval system, or transmitted in any form or by any means, electronic, mechanical, photocopying, recording or otherwise, without express written permission of the author.

ᛉ Contents ᛊ

THE END

Chapter 1	3
Chapter 2	19
Chapter 3	32
Chapter 4	46
Chapter 5	59

ANGEL

Chapter 6	79
Chapter 7	93
Chapter 8	111
Chapter 9	126
Chapter 10	145
Chapter 11	154

THE RETURN

Chapter 12	171
Chapter 13	185
Chapter 14	199
Chapter 15	215
Chapter 16	232

SECOND JUMP

Chapter 17	253
Chapter 18	275
Chapter 19	293
Chapter 20	310
Chapter 21	322
Chapter 22	338
Chapter 23	356

BANISHMENT

Chapter 24	377
Chapter 25	387
Chapter 26	401
Chapter 27	416

REBIRTH

Chapter 28	432
Chapter 29	444
Chapter 30	460
Chapter 31	472
Chapter 32	486
Chapter 33	496

THE RESCUE

Chapter 34	515
Chapter 35	531
Chapter 36	545
Chapter 37	557
Chapter 38	573
Chapter 39	587
Chapter 40	601
Chapter 41	616

THE ROMANCE

Chapter 42	627
Chapter 43	639
Chapter 44	651
Chapter 45	664
Chapter 46	681
Chapter 47	699
Chapter 48	714

THE BEGINNING

| Chapter 49 | 719 |

THE END

Chapter 1 ଓଃ

Theo rises from the mist, pieces put back together with only memories of them once having been apart. It's the beginning of a new dawn, a new light, similar yet unfamiliar, orderly yet disorienting. Where is he? *Who* is he? And how did he get here? He searches his mind but has no answers. He looks up from the warm place in the grass where he slept so long and so peacefully. A quiet fog floats all around him. He can see a few feet in front of him and no further. The air is humid and scented with the most aromatic fragrances of lavender, tea roses and lilacs. All seems peaceful but from the haze comes a memory: an impact, fire, and people screaming. Then as quickly as it came, the memory is gone.

He rises on unsteady legs and feels like he hasn't been on them for a very long time. He has a sense of time passing but no recollection of it. He lifts his hands and the mist swirls around them, mist more like smoke but with no odor, swirling in little twisters in the wake of his fingers. He sweeps his hands around watching the patterns form and drift away, feeling very much like he's hallucinating, living the fantasy of a dream yet suffering the consequences of being fully awake.

Ahead of him, he hears a noise. He looks up and sees an orb of light passing through the particles of mist. The light sways this way and that, then gets bigger, and then he hears footsteps in the soft grass. The light takes a shape, grows shoulders, arms, hands, gets bigger, becomes a man. It's a man coming towards him in the mist and he is bright, giving off his own light source, glowing.

"Come, Theodore Duncan, we've been waiting for you." A hand extends out of the fog, large and gnarled and inked black with tattoos. The fingers are adorned with heavy silver rings.

The voice that greets him is grated, deep, almost growling. Regardless, he takes the hand because it is the only hand there. Those gnarled fingers close around his. The embrace is like nothing he's ever felt before. A warmness enters his body and fills him with euphoria. Suddenly everything is perfect, suddenly everything is going to be okay. He knows that wherever he is, as long as he follows this hand, he will be all right.

The man waves him forward and the fog begins to thin. Theo looks down at his feet and is surprised to see he is wearing sandals. He frowns at the long, white robe cinched at his waist. His skin looks very pale, but nothing in comparison to the hand holding his with the metal bands and the shocking black tattoos. Beyond that, he can see only the outline of a formidable shape leading him forward. The grass is soft with dew yet doesn't wet his feet. His steps seem light, almost weightless. Again, the memories come: twisted, churning metal, him tumbling inside a concrete dryer and fierce screaming filling his ears.

"Try not to think about it," the man says.

"Where am I?" Theo swallows hard, considering only one possibility. "Is this Heaven?"

They step out of the mist and come to the edge of a hill that overlooks a rolling meadow. He sees his guide clearly now. He's rowdy looking, fierce, a wave of slick black hair combed back over his head. He has long shady sideburns and rings lined up across his fingers like brass knuckles. Scripture and saints are tattooed down his arms and up his neck, a stark contrast to his angel white skin. And that's what he is, an angel. No better proof than the eagle like extensions rising from his back. Theo finds them almost grotesque to look at, not the feathery, dream-like apparitions he envisioned as a kid in Sunday school. These appendages twist from gnarled knuckles that protrude from his back. They are muscled and veined and the feathers are hard and pointed. They look like they must weigh three hundred pounds apiece.

"Is this Heaven?" Theo whispers again, his hand slipping from his guide's. The warmth goes with the touch and the absence of light makes him feel very cold. He focuses his gaze to a narrow, trampled path that zigzags down the steep hillside, then across a bridge and past a forest, towards a jeweled city gleaming between two mountain ranges. The city is a gathering of ancient buildings, temples, cathedrals, libraries, fountains and more.

"Follow me," his guide says, moving forward.

Theo does as ordered and it seems to trigger a memory of a life long ago where he always did as asked. And it was a happy obedience. He glances back up to the hilltop shrouded in tender mist. He can see nothing beyond it and remembers even less. Instead, he focuses forward to those massive wings sprouting from his director's back as they switchback down the hill single file. It's only then Theo feels the weight of his own back and a downwards thrust with each step he takes. Reaching over his shoulder, his hand brushes thick muscles and bone protruding from the flat plains where his shoulder blades used to be. His fingers quickly retract and he doesn't investigate further.

They continue down the path trampled neat with sandals and bare foot prints until they reach the valley floor. There, a generous meadow is tucked between two treed mountain ranges. All around him are grasses so green, waters so blue, skies so high and clear that he can hardly believe any of it is real. Deer graze beside the path, even if people pass just feet away. They don't jolt or run. There is no fear here. He feels it too. A safeness. A quiet bliss. Even the woods, which seem dark on approach, are open and full of light as they enter. In the trees, he sees a group of girls gathered in small clearing, looking like little fairies, like pixies in the rising bloom.

"Is this Heaven?" he asks again, stuck like a broken record. He can think of no other relevant question to ask considering the peculiarity of the situation.

The burly angel throws an intense look over his shoulder. "Not quite. Heaven's just a step or two away. You are on *The Reserve*."

"The Reserve," Theo repeats, his eyes moving densely forward. He should ask more questions but he's so dumfounded by the rapture in front of him that he can think of nothing relevant to say. And he is being nagged by an unknown terror lurking behind him. Something behind the mist, something awful, frozen in his memory like a glacier beginning to thaw, chips of memories breaking off as the huge block begins to crack.

After they leave the forest, Theo sees a field walled off to one side. It catches his interest as something foreboding and secluded among the welcoming grasslands and bright, cheery gardens. Behind the metal gates, monitored by angels that can only be described as guards, he sees hundreds and hundreds of tiny pools filled with water. They extend as far as he can see, dotting the landscape all the way to the edge of the horizon. Ponds reflect across the vast plane like upturned coins. There are statues perched all around the pools, statues in odd poses, all hunched over and leaned slightly forward.

"What is that?" he asks, staring but feeling like he shouldn't.

"The Field," his guide replies with no further explanation.

"The Field?" Theo whispers, glancing back but a rise in the road now impedes his view. Strange, a place so locked away in paradise, hidden behind high walls and secured gates. It draws his curiosity but only momentarily until the next wonder distracts him all over again.

They cross a covered bridge spanning a slow moving, meandering stream. Down in the cut banks, he can see a group of angels gathered around a row boat. They seem to be in deep discussion over something. And then more angels down past the bridge walking with books tucked under their arms. And further ahead, a pinnacle on the horizon, an ancient holy city. Theo sets his focus there now, turning away from the meadows rich with buds and blooms, wild berries and fruit trees, and even from the gazes of young angels looking curiously in his direction. There is something grand about the city, monolithic, central. It stirs him, revives him, fills him with an excitement unparalleled by anything else on his journey thus far.

"What's the Reserve?" he asks, still following along on the narrow path, still staring in amazement at the animal-like appendages sprouting from the man's back in front of him. He had an image of what an angel would look like, but this is so literal, not wistful or magical, but a man with moles and broken fingernails and boney, feathered wings. And such a beast of a man too, so commanding, so intimidating. So unlike anyone he would ever associate with in life. And that's when he realizes it, for the first time he contemplates the fact that he might actually be dead.

"I'm Veddie," the angel says and slows when the road broadens so they can walk side by side. The city is just ahead, stepping up the mountainside making it appear more impressive and intimidating from their low vantage point. The road grows wider, roughhewn cobblestone changing to smooth polished marble. They approach a triumphal archway marking the entrance to the city. It stands ten stories high and six feet thick carved in painted concrete and rustic travertine. Columns of Composite order thunder up to creation where winged figures of Victory raise their hands to the sky. Closer to the ground, two stone warriors on horseback eternally greet all who pass through the portal of the Victory arch. Written on the entablature of the arch is a phrase in Latin.

"What does it say?" Theo asks, pointing to the words as they pass beneath.

"Borne up to Heaven on the back of an eagle, we pass through thee."

Theo stares up breathlessly, nearly knocking down another angel leaving the city. "Sorry," he whispers, feeling foolish and wonder struck.

A magnificent road proceeds onward, a columned thoroughfare busy with bustling angels. The city follows the contours of the landscape, heading down to the left towards an emerald port and up to the right towards a precinct of temples. He can see the turrets of a large cathedral at the edge of the horizon surrounded by temples and garden courts, squares and plazas. Staring up, he's shocked when the sunlight is suddenly blocked by a stone arch covering the street. They pass through a long tunnel, the walls and roof decorated with carvings depicting religious narratives and conquests. It appears to be lit from within, but Theo sees no source of the light. Amongst the art, there is also verse carved into the walls. His eyes skim over the phrases as he passes, catching pieces here and there.

'For he will give his angels charge of you to guard you in all ways.'

'Praise be to God who created the Heavens and the Earth. Messengers with wings - two or three or four...'

'Praise ye him, all his angels; praise ye him, all his hosts.'

Again they pass by too quickly and he finds himself struggling to keep up. Now they enter a street that seems to divide the lower half of the city from the upper half. It leads straight from the city gates to an old forum that frames an ocean port. Beyond the port, he can see an aqueduct, a light house, and distant mountain bluffs.

"Come this way," Veddie says. "This is the street of steps."

Theo turns from the main boulevard and follows Veddie up a set of stairs that seems to never end. It meanders up the hillside, stopping at various plateaus which offer them prospects of their gained elevation. Glancing back, it's a glorious view over the city and back towards the meadow. The misty hill is just a distant shroud now but he gets a better view of the mountains that surround them and their snow-capped peaks sitting just above the clouds. Ahead, the view is more provoking but still very much obscured. He gets the sense that the higher they go, the higher the order. Houses get bigger, more wondrous, and opulent. Gardens become larger and more elaborate. And at the highest point is that glorious cathedral that seems to crown the city, its peaks challenging the very mountains surrounding it. At this point, he can only see glimpses of it, nothing of the cathedral herself, but something about that sight draws him towards it. He longs to go there, feels pulled there by an urgent calling.

Clearing the street of steps, they enter into a high boulevard between the edge of the city and a swiftly moving river. To the left, there are municipal buildings, open classrooms, and towering libraries. To the right, a rugged mountain terrain is broken up by the occasional domed structure. The street they are on appears to be the hub of the city. Everywhere are angels, walking, talking, and seated on benches. Everyone looks at him as he passes. Everyone smiles and says hello.

"You see, Theodore, paradise is just up there," Veddie points in a general direction. "Folks call this place *The Reserve*. It's somewhere in between life and death."

"But....but what...?" Theo stammers.

"It's where the dead are processed and the elite remain behind to get trained."

Theo thinks about that statement for a while as their walk through the mystical city continues. They walk past residences with open windows and doors. He spies internal gardens and beds on rooftops and baths open to second story balconies. Each of the houses has a name on the lintel accompanied by a symbol. The house of Jacob. The house of Thomas. The house of June. Everything is open, grassy paths travel straight into the homes, through the heart of the house and out into the back gardens. There is not even glass in the windows. No need in a place where there is nothing to lock out. All of it is splendor beyond anything he's ever seen before, so grand, so perfect. He's overwhelmed to the point of tears. The emotional response seems to open an unwanted doorway. Suddenly there's panic. He feels something hit his face. Then an urgent moment as the glass implodes and his hand is torn from the wrist. He grabs for his arm suddenly certain there will be nothing at the end of it.

"I told you not to think about it." Veddie says, glancing back.

"Can you read my thoughts?" Theo whispers incredulously.

Veddie chuckles, a deep hearty sound that resounds over all the voices on the street. "No, son, just your face."

Theo swallows hard, feeling like he might be sick. "Where are we going?"

"Judgment."

Theo remains silent for the remainder of the trip. Worry dulls his curiosity. He lowers his eyes and resumes his journey down more dark passages. He can't remember anything, not who he is, where he lived or what he was doing with his life. He feels empty with no memories or past to stimulate his emotions. He longs for an opinion, for an experienced thought, for some indication of the man he used to be. All he has is that one horrible event that seems to have brought his life to a screeching halt.

He suddenly steps into water and the shock brings him back to the present. He is standing between two crystal lion sculptures with water roaring from their mouths. The sound is deafening and he wonders how he couldn't have heard it on approach. Veddie is ahead of him on a street flooded with rushing water. More like a river rushing down the street though the water is only a few inches deep. Mist rises from the water and the air is cool and crisp. On either side of the street are rows of weeping willows that are so encased in dew that they appear transparent. The water continues to the end of the street, in quick rapids, to a stone archway that is too dark to see into. Theo stares at the huge yawning mouth and suddenly he is very uneasy. Judgment.

Veddie looks back at him darkly and Theo picks up his pace. Water swirls around his feet and saturates his sandals. The hem of his robe is pulled forward by the current, pulling him toward that dark portal. Even from half a block away, he can hear the cavernous rush of water as it feeds that gaping mouth. Was he good in life? Was he moral? Was he true? He doesn't remember. It's as if he is facing someone else's judgment and he just has to hope that they behaved themselves on his behalf.

They come to the portal, pass beneath its ominous archway, and step down a dark, poorly lit stairway. Water rushing down into the dark abyss threatens to take him off his feet. The stairs are sharp and steep and Theo fumbles for a handrail. The temperature drops as they descend the dark staircase. He can see his breath in the dwindling light.

"Stay close," Veddie says coolly, his breath drifting back around his head.

"How far is it?" Theo gasps as he steps down into knee deep water. It's shockingly cold and dense. They continue through the flooded passageway with no light at all. And in that darkness, Theo begins to see the end. It was a car. He was hit by a car. And someone else was with him. He doesn't know who. He sees a bumper in his face, in his mouth. He runs his tongue quickly over his teeth to see that all the bones are all still there. There was fire and blood and he went one way and his hand went off in another direction.

Though the water is cold, he becomes very hot and flushed and finds himself dashing cold water over his face to cool down. He was in a vehicle when he was hit. He was driving someone home. Someone who was very bad. Someone he was warned not to spend time with. And that's all he remembers as they leave the passageway. They enter a large cistern the color of gold, the walls lined by monstrous pillars. The pillars are five feet thick, their orders submerged. The room is a pool of glimmering water, the vaulted rooftop reflecting the still waters below. Unlike the finely crafted architecture he's seen thus far, these pillars are roughly hewn, with obvious breaks and cracks where large blocks were stacked on top of each other to form the cylindrical markers. The room is reverently silent, the drip of condensation the only sound.

"Come this way," Veddie says in a much softer voice than he was using above. He continues down the main apse, not bothering to lift his robes as they travel through the water. There is an energy in the room, a weight, a presence that causes Theo to walk slightly hunched. The hallway is an illusion of shadows. Reflections make the hall appear to continue on forever both horizontally and vertically. Amongst the pillars are of statues of saints. First, Raphael, the angel of man, immortalized by artist's hand as a young and vibrant warrior armed with sword and arrow. Next, the midday archangel, Michael, wisdom, purification, the master of the energy of balance. Then Gabriel, the angel of love and Heaven, beautiful and effeminate. And lastly Uriel, angel of earth, angel of night, powerful, dark and mysterious. But as they continue, there are more. Angels he's never heard of before: Uzziel, Ithuriel, Zephon, Abdiel, each looking as fierce as the last. While the sight of familiar archangels comfort him, the unknown ones make him uneasy.

Tearing his eyes from the fearsome statues, Theo notices tapestries hanging from some of the pillars. They document sacred lists: Seven Spiritual Words of Mercy, Seven Capital

Sins and their Contrary Virtues, Seven Gifts of the Holy Spirit, Zorostrian Seven Archangels, Military ranks of Postexilic Angels, and Duties of the Ordained. Again, he finds himself struggling to take it all in when he notices that they are nearing the end of the passage. At the end, two angels are seated at an elevated table. Behind them the wall is made of water and all around them are monumental stacks of gilded books. Theo's chest tightens at the sight of them. All he can think of is the bad man in the car beside him. Who was this man? And why was he driving him somewhere? It doesn't sit well that this is his only memory of his former self.

Veddie stops at the foot of the platform and bows his head. Theo gently lifts his eyes to see two dark-skinned angels, each with identical brilliant blue eyes. One is male and one is female, though there is very little to distinguish their sex. Their features are so similar that they could be siblings or even twins. Their bodies are equally slender, finely adorned, their wings of bronzed gold. Their hair is like silk, braided in wreaths of living blossoms. And from each of them is the same warm, glowing aura, not so much a physical light as a feeling reached standing in their presence. Theo exhales a quiet breath, returning his gaze down. His knees tremble just to be near them. These two hold his future in their hands.

"Mannkar. Nakir," Veddie says addressing each one in turn as he rises out of the water to the first step leading up to the elevated platform. "I present to you Theodore Duncan."

Theo looks up, eyes wide and lost. He's not sure if he should kneel or bow. He feels like he should do something. The twin angels take out a book and written across the cover is his name: *Theodore Duncan*. They open the book and each begin to read, the one on the right reading the right page and the one on the left reading the left. With very serious looks on their faces, this activity continues for what feels like hours. They turn each page in unison, their eyes moving back and forth like synchronized swimmers. Though the water falling behind them should be deafening, the room is deathly silent. Theo stands until his legs cramp, until he feels he might pass out and tumble back into the water. And when he feels like he can take no more, they close his book with a resounding crack.

"Church Militant," they reply in unison.

Veddie bows and takes the book from them. He turns back the way he came, and once again, Theo follows like an obedient servant. His heart is beating out of his chest. Church Militant? What does that mean? It sounds good but he can't shake his unease. The water seems heavier and more cumbersome as they return the way they came. He finds himself frustrated, irritated, and extremely exhausted. His robe seems to weigh a thousand pounds as he stumbles and trips through the dense water.

Veddie stops, Theo's book clasped beneath his arm. "Are you all right?"

Theo hangs his head like a disciplined child. "What does it mean? What does Church Militant mean?"

"Frankly, it means you're in," Veddie says, moving forward. "Come along. No time for waste."

Theo shudders a bit, relieved, but no less anxious. He glances at that book tucked beneath Veddie's arm. The volume of his life. His achievements. His failures. Everything that he used to be that is still somehow lost to him. When will he remember his life? Will he ever remember it?

They return the way they came, the streets now bustling with busy students, books clung to their chest rushing this way and that. The trip to the cistern has left him in shambles. Theo struggles with his robes now heavy with water, trying to wring them out as Veddie continues his relentless pace. He also wrestles with an overwhelming feeling of unworthiness after being in the presence of the angels of judgment. Sure, he is Church Militant but what does that really mean?

Veddie turns down another street in the disorderly labyrinth that is the Reserve. Here, the walkway less busy, lined with two story offices and long rows of ancient maple trees. They enter an archway and walk into an open courtyard where tables are set up with students lined around them. All of them are fresh faced and nervous, new arrivals like himself, fidgeting anxiously with their wet robes and fingering awkwardly at the new appendages on their backs. Each is accompanied by an angel with a Life book beneath their arm.

"Come on," Veddie says, cutting to the front of a line. He shoulders the student being served aside and leans across the table. "Papers for Theodore Duncan."

The man seated behind the table, a smaller angel with dark shoulder length hair and a neat trim beard gives Veddie a disapproving look. He looks as if he might refuse but then rummages through his files and gives Veddie what he requested. Veddie snatches the papers away and directs Theo off in another direction. He barges to the front of every line and is quickly served ahead of all the others, though no angel is as resistant as the man behind the first table. It seems as if Veddie is important here.

As Veddie collects items, he passes them to Theo. Theo takes the increasing pile, suppressing his complaints. He's never been more exhausted in his life, or at least the short life he can remember from his birth on the misty hill to the place he stands now. While waiting for Veddie to push himself to the front of another long line, he spies a paper placed on the top. It says:

7:00am - Breakfast and Orientation with the First Years
8:30am - Auras and Circles of Light in the Atrium with Ryder
10:00am - Beginning Animal Auras in the Meadow with Lila
11:00am - Prayer and Meditation in the House of Raphael
12:00pm - Lunch and Meditation in the Fountain Court
1:30pm - Library Tours and Introductory Book of Life
2:30pm - Advanced Gospels under the Archway
3:45pm - Public Bible Studies in the Forum
5:00pm - Supper and Discussion
7:00pm - Angelology and the History of the Saints
9:00pm - Hymns and Praise at the Courtyard of Saints
10:30pm - Campfire Songs and Lights Out

Theo exhales a long held breath as Veddie continues to interrupt and offend his way through the orientation. What is happening? He really doesn't know. He supposes this schedule means that he is staying on the Reserve instead of continuing on to the afterlife. Church Militant seems be a call to guardianship, but he cannot be entirely sure. Veddie has explained nothing, as if this is information he should already be aware of. He just died; he feels like he should be resting, mourning, processing, not racing around picking up school books and schedules. He glances anxiously at the man who met him on the hill, his only contact in this new life. When is he going to explain what is happening to him?

Finally, for the first time since he woke up in the mist, he and Veddie sit down. Or rather, Theo sits on the steps of the main library while Veddie paces on the plateau below. Theo is quickly learning that Veddie is demanding and not to be trifled with. He's forceful, straight forward, and Theo can see that people here are in awe of him. Who Veddie is to him or what he's exactly doing here, is still a mystery to Theo. Little has been offered in the way of explanation and even less in sympathy or encouragement.

"You *are* dead," Veddie says bluntly. He takes out a cigar and lights it, then holds it between his heavily ringed fingers. "The Reserve is training grounds for guardian angels. Here, we educate you and prepare you for service back on earth. I am to be your mentor. Each mentor is specifically chosen for each student. Your education will begin first thing in the morning."

Theo misses most of Veddie's speech after the words: *you are dead*. Of course, Theo knew it but to actually hear the words is shocking. He can hardly believe it's true.

"You see, chosen people, the ones that serve and obey, the deserving and righteous remain at the Reserve to act as guardians over the ones back on earth. It is a voluntary service, you are not required to take the post, but few refuse and fewer leave it once they've joined. It is a great honor to serve as a guardian. Orientation, tomorrow, will explain more of this. I only take the best of the best Theodore, only the finest. Don't worry about your friend from the accident; he's in a coma right now but he'll wake up soon and your death will be a turning point in his life. It'll settle him down, grow him up, and turn him towards a more righteous path."

Theo cringes at the mention of his passenger, this bad man he was transporting who was apparently his friend. "So I am dead?" he stammers, still struggling to accept the first statement.

"Yes, that is what I said."

"But I don't remember my life."

"Some do. Some don't. You may not ever remember the life before this one. What happened down there isn't important. Your real life begins now. Do not dwell on the past. The past merely formed the man you are today. The rest is inconsequential."

Theo hunches forward over his heavy pile of books but does not expect comfort from Veddie. His mentor is a no-nonsense kind of man. Somehow, he thinks, once he gets his feet under him that will suit him perfectly.

"What should I do now?"

"Sleep tight. Things will be clearer in the morning."

Sleep tight, Theo does not. He sits rigidly in his assigned bed in the large circular dormitory, listening to the uneven breath of a newly dead's restless sleep. He's in shock, waiting for something to switch on in his head and have this all make sense. His life is a murky underwater memory, and his family, if he had any, he can't even recall. He has no sense of himself alive and no sense of himself dead either. Veddie left him on the library steps and Theo sat there for the remainder of the day. Strange to sit for so long and not be hungry or thirsty, not have any of the old bodily restrictions he used to have. Without routine he feels adrift. He hopes tomorrow will bring more clarity.

"Terrible, isn't it?"

Theo jumps at the sound of a voice nearby. In the dim light, he sees a boy in the bed next to him.

"I'm Eric," the boy says extending his hand over the headboard.

Theo shakes it. It's the first time he's touched someone since Veddie led him from the mist. It feels oddly real and makes him realize how real he still feels. He's no disembodied spirit drifting around, he has a body, weight, presence. He's breathing. His heart is beating. He still has blood in his veins.

"Theo," he replies, dropping his hand back to his lap.

"Your first night here?" Eric asks.

"Uh-huh." Theo looks at the silhouette of the boy so much like himself. He's young, maybe seventeen, if age means anything up here. He's of smaller stature and wingspan, fair-haired with light skin and teeth so white they shine in the dark.

"I didn't sleep for three days after I got here. Did they put you straight into school?"

"Tomorrow," Theo replies.

"They like to keep you occupied, keep you moving. It's the best way, really. You don't want to sit around and think about your death too much. That will just drive you crazy."

Theo shifts uncomfortably on the feathered appendages. They have joints and knuckles in them, like a huge spider clutched to his shoulders. He just can't get used to the feeling of wings. Lying on his back they bunch up like bags of marbles underneath him. Turning on his stomach, they spoon him like an uninvited bedfellow.

"How long have you been here?" he asks the boy.

"I died four months ago. Do you remember anything yet?"

Theo sighs, so tired, yet not willing to succumb to sleep. "I sort of remember how I died. I think I was in a car accident. I think there was someone with me."

"Is he here?"

"No, I guess he survived." Theo states what he's been told.

"Listen," Eric says, leaning closer like he's telling Theo something he shouldn't. "If you're going to remember, you'll do it in a dream. If it takes longer than a couple days to happen, then you're not going to remember at all."

"Why wouldn't we remember?"

"I don't know. Some people remember and some don't. You might remember your life and not your death. Or your death and not your life. I guess it'll be the one that's the most important. My friend Evangeline has been here for years and she still doesn't know how she died."

"Do you know how you died?" Theo asks the boy.

Eric groans and rolls his eyes. "I choked on a grape."

Theo laughs, then covers his mouth as the sound echoes all over the domed room. "Sorry," he says afterwards.

"Don't worry. I'm used to it."

A grape. He supposes people die in all kinds of way. Stupid, ironic, poetic or unjust, it's all the same in the end.

"Try and sleep. It might help."

Theo settles in bed remembering Veddie's last words to him. Sleep tight. Things will be clearer in the morning. Seems like there was more meaning in those words than he realized.

Chapter 2☙

Morning comes painfully early. Theo opens his eyes to the sound of bare feet on stone floor padding past his unpleasantly public sleeping arrangements. The sun is just up, cutting diagonally across the dormitory through large rose windows, tinting the floor with a kaleidoscope of colors. Groggily, his eyes travel up the soaring vaults to the frescos that line the ceiling. Epic battles greet his tired eyes of gods and saints and all the rest. At this early hour, it just seems too much to absorb.

He sits up, rubbing his face. The boy in the bed beside him is gone. It seems too early to be up but all around him students are on the move. Unlike a normal university setting, first years vary greatly from the very young to the very old. They are here on the first year of their death. It is the only thing they have in common right now.

Theo rises and neatly tucks his bed back in order just like he used to back home. That's when he realizes that he remembers home. He straightens up with a gasp. He is Theodore Duncan, the only child to Andrew and Dianna Duncan. He lived on an estate on the outskirts of town, born to an affluent and influential family. He was devoutly religious, not only as a child, but as teenager as well. He was not just religious but educated in the church, dedicated to it. He was smart, well-liked, determined and straight forward. He attended only the best schools, had only the best things, but he was never spoiled. He was taught that important things in life had to be worked for, things like education, morals, even health and happiness. He had a good life, an easy life. Before he died, he was a student in university studying in religion and theology. He wanted to go overseas and work with the needy, build churches and aid in global despair. He had a friend. His name was Buddy. Buddy wasn't like his other friends; he wasn't well off or particularly well educated. He was someone that Theo's parents considered crass and a bad influence. But their differences seemed to amuse Theodore. Buddy was in the car when they crashed. They were driving home from a Halloween party. Buddy was dressed as a half black, half white Michael Jackson. Theo was dressed, quite ironically, as the devil. They were hit by a dump truck and he died instantly.

The dream that returned his memories was fierce and arousing. He didn't just remember the events of his life, but experienced the very essence of his existence. He was headed for greatness when a ten ton dump truck abruptly put an end to all that. The single-minded direction of his life suddenly derailed. He sees it so clearly now. He had a whole list of things to do tomorrow, then Friday and then the weekend was completely booked. Death didn't fit into his schedule.

He sits back down on the edge of the bed, feeling dizzy. How can any of this possibly be real? He thinks he might be in shock. To go from a reality he recognized for twenty-four years then be thrust into another world that he simply must accept and move on from? How is he ever supposed to get used to this?

Theo follows the crowd towards orientation. There is a buzz amongst the students; he can hear it though hardly anyone is speaking. They are all new arrivals like himself, fussing with their wings, itching at their pinching sandals, and stumbling around gawking at the grandness of their surroundings. And, for once, he blends right in with them. In his life before this one, he was something set apart. Rich, successful, driving only the best cars, going only to the best schools. He was top of his class, admired by both students and faculty. It's unsettling just to be another face in the crowd. To have all his advantages taken away. And yet he feels a growing excitement as well. A new adventure, a new beginning. And here, in the place he's been trying to reach all his life.

"There'll be speeches, then your first teacher will take you on a tour of the Reserve."

Theo looks to the side to see Eric, the boy from last night, falling into step beside him. He's much younger in the light of day, maybe only fifteen instead of seventeen.

"Speeches?" Theo says, returning his gaze forward. If he has any advantage in this crowd, he's of bigger stature than most of the others and can see clear over their heads. They are walking down the main street in the lower section of town heading towards the old forum, the one by the ocean. It's just a large, open gathering space surrounded by columns. There is a raised stage at the end where several podiums are set up as well as a long table at the back.

"This is your first time here?" Theo asks Eric.

"No, I came my first day but I still come all the time."

"Really, why?"

"You'll see." Eric takes him by the arm and pulls him forward. "Hurry, we want to get a good spot."

Theo stares up at the stage, nervous with anticipation. So little has been explained to him about his new life and Veddie is nowhere to be seen. The courtyard is now full to the brim with freshly dead faces. He and Eric are up near the stage, the crowd spanning back several blocks. Further back, some have climbed up pillars and onto distant rooftops to get a better look.

"We'll meet the elders," Eric says over the murmuring crowd. "The higher level guardian you become, the brighter you are. Some angels are so bright, you can't even look at them."

"How many levels are there?"

"Nine."

Theo bounces nervously on his heels. "So...we're meeting angels?"

"Not just angels. The founding angels as well as the elders of guardians. Maybe if we're lucky, we'll even see an archangel. Though I wouldn't count on that. They are pretty busy. Whatever you do, don't look the any of them in the eye."

"What?" Theo turns to the boy. "Why not?"

"Just don't. They don't like to be challenged."

Theo swallows hard, looking back over the crowd. There's a disturbance near the back. A wave of excitement rushes up to the front and everyone turns around to see. Even from a distance, Theo's breath is taken away. A procession of warrior angels is approaching up the street. Unlike the fresh faced first years that fill the courtyard, these angels are darker, fiercer, some in swords and armor.

"But...what will happen if we look? I mean this is Heaven, right? We can't actually be hurt here," Theo whispers, feeling a hot flush come to his face

Eric shrugs. "I don't know. That's just what I've been told. Haven't really had the urge to disobey."

Theo turns as the procession enters the forum. The crowd parts, students quickly dropping their head in a show of respect. In size, the warriors are larger than the newly dead with considerable wingspans, harder faces, thicker skin, their clothes more decorated, their eyes more determined.

"Don't look," Eric says, elbowing Theo.

Theo drops his head but curiosity gnaws at him. How can he not look? How can he miss an opportunity like this? "Who are they? Do you know?" he whispers.

Eric glances up and then quickly back down. "Of course I know. This is Malik, the angel who guards the gates of Hell."

Theo's eyes widen and he is unable reign his gaze back in as a battle weary angel stomps through the crowd in heavy steel boots. His wings are iron grey and one has a chunk missing near the top. He wears a chest plate and a helmet with silver horns and his eyes are completely black, no whites at all. He appears to be steaming or leaving a trail of smoke in his wake. He is three times the size of a normal man, looming, intimidating, awe-inspiring. Theo holds his breath as he nears, lowering his eyes to a mid-level range. But from his peripherals, he keeps watch as the warrior angel passes smelling of sulfur and wood smoke. Theo shudders and feels like he might faint. It's like leaning too far over the guardrail of a powerful waterfall, feeling the rush, the fear, the queasiness sucking him downwards. Except this is a man, not even a man, the angel who guards the gates of Hell.

Theo's eyes rise to see the next one, his heart racing and eager for more. All the other new arrivals have their eyes firmly fastened to the ground. They seem to know what to do and yet he's been told and he can't seem to obey. He's surprised at his disobedience. He was never so defiant in life. He always played by the rules. He did exactly what he was told. And yet, he's getting a rush from his insubordination. A thrill.

"Will you quit looking?" Eric thumps him in the arm and then quickly glances down the divide in the crowd to the next approaching champion. "That's Ridwan. He guards the gates of Heaven."

Unlike the angel of Hell, Ridwan is brilliantly lit, adorned in precious stones and metals, his face smooth and shining. His skin is bronze and his hair is gold. He is in a kilt with heavy boots, wearing a chest plate and a shield and sword. He's not as large as the first angel, but his presence is just as powerful. Theo is unable to lower his gaze before Ridwan takes notice of him. Never has he been in the presence of such power. It's like crossing eyes with a cougar in the forest. Ridwan's gaze is a quick sharp warning that he swiftly obeys. He drops his eyes and keeps them down until the remaining angels have ascended the stairs. Then, while they are at a safe distance away, he discreetly continues his investigation. The angel of Hell is, ironically, seated next to Ridwan, the angel guarding Heaven. Next to them are the angels from the cistern that gave him his judgment. The dark twins with the bright blue eyes. He can't remember their names. Next to them is something so engulfed in light that he has to shield his eyes. This one is more awesome and frightening than the last four combined. At least that's until he looks at the next one, a woman, dressed very much like a Viking warrior with red curly hair that extends outward in gravity defying proportions. Her presence is alien, otherworldly, and absolutely terrifying. He looks down, trembling, and cannot look up for a very long time. Not until he hears a voice he recognizes.

"Praise be to God who created the Heavens and the Earth. For God has power over all things."

Theo looks up and sees Veddie at the podium.

"That's Veddie," Eric says quickly with as much trepidation as he did about the angel from Hell. "He's the newest warrior and one of the elders."

Theo looks up at his mentor in amongst the warriors. No wonder Veddie pushed his way to the front of the line yesterday; no wonder everyone quickly submitted to his every wish. Veddie has station here and Theo had no idea how important he was until this very moment. Even amongst the battle-scarred and nebulous creatures that occupy the table behind him, Veddie still holds his own atmosphere of power and intimidation.

"You are angels now, be sure of that. And here, at the Reserve, you will acquire all the tools necessary to return to the battle below. As you were once helped, so you will help others in return. Do not be overwhelmed. Do not be afraid. Nothing can harm you here. And if you should decide to move on, Ridwan…"

The mentioned angel rises.

"…will help you continue your journey through the gates of Heaven. But until then, we angels, we guardians and warriors reside here at the Reserve.

"What you have entered into is a glorious institution dedicated to the education and elevation of art, religion, music and, of course, guardianship. Trust in your mentors. They have been chosen for you for a reason. Rely on your fellow students for support and companionship. Why the Reserve, you must be asking yourselves, why not straight to paradise? Because you are all chosen for your special skills and abilities as qualified candidates for our guardianship program. Here you will train, study, and live as you work your way through levels of the Light. Congratulations, first years. Your journey has just begun.

"I am Veddie. Dynamic Authority, elder and warrior angel. The house of Veddie patrols the forces of darkness, governs the rise and fall of nations, and is in charge of all religions. I am the Powers: the sixth level of nine celestial hierarchies. You too will be assigned a rank and may work your way up as high as you wish. Not all posts are easy ones but all are in need. Malik will confirm that."

At the end of the table, the angel who guards Hell chuckles deeply. Theo looks up at him again, into his empty black eyes. He is not even man anymore, but something risen beyond. As soon as Theo sees him, he knows what he wants to be. He wants to become one of the angels sitting atop this stage, one of the elders that secure so many fearful gazes. He wants to be side by side with Veddie and the others. If fills him with delicious hope. Suddenly there is a future. Suddenly he can see it.

A church service follows with the sharing of communion. Other angels are introduced, so many he'll never remember them all. And doctrines are spoken, also so numerous that they pass right over his head. It's amazing and overwhelming, almost too much to take in. He feels like he's in some fantastic dream and before he knows it, the ceremony is over.

"That's why I go all the time," Eric tells him as the crowd disperses. "You'll never get tired of it and you'll never really absorb it all. Different warriors come all the time. And maybe one day, you'll even see an archangel."

"Have you ever seen one?"

"Up close?" the boy replies. "Not yet. But I keep hoping."

Theo looks back at the empty stage where the warriors lined the table. He knows his future now. And he can hardly wait to get there.

Before first class, Theo finds his way to Veddie's house. He takes out his map, turning it one way and then another. He's not even sure where he is right now. Finding his way to the House of Veddie might be a difficult task. He leaves the dorms and enters the street that spans from the Victory gates to the ocean forum. From there, he climbs the street of steps and returns to that bustling thoroughfare that runs along the bank of the river. He passes by the big library, now able to marvel at the structure in a way he wasn't able to yesterday. The sheer size of the architecture is something to be admired. Angels appear like ants next to columns. Statues rise to impossible heights. And everywhere there is water supplied by an underground cistern that spans the entire city. It comes to the surface in reflective pools, fountains, and out of the overflowing urns of cherubs. Beautiful excess in a place where there is all supply and no demand.

Worried about the time, Theo steps up his pace. He goes down two dead end streets before realizing he is holding the map upside down. Finally, turned around in a stone garden, he asks for directions and makes his way to Veddie's doorstep. The house of Veddie sits on two stone platforms above street level, each platform spanning the width of the house and sprouting marvelous gardens of well-tended shrubs over its ledges. The building itself is nearly half a block wide, its main entrance surrounded by a lush and looming terrace. The columns that extend from one end of the house to the other appear like a large gapped-tooth smile gleaming down at him. Mounting the stairs, he arrives to the top with a view over the city towards that glorious cathedral. He stops just for a second to admire the magnificent sight but then urgency stirs him forward. Veddie is waiting. He does not want make a bad impression on his first day.

He turns and enters through the gates, passing on a walkway between two crystal blue reflective pools. Each pool has a three tiered fountain in its center that sprinkles down into the clear, calm water. After that, he enters a marble hallway with three arched portals on each side. Through the gaps he glimpses a large internal courtyard with a symmetrical hedge design and a fountain flowing in the middle. It's surrounded on all sides by the stone walls of the house which are completely shrouded in flowering vines. Veddie's house is no less grand than the man himself and Theo can't wait to get his new life started.

Coming to the main forum, he finds a dozen students already gathered. Unlike the students he currently bunks with, these boys are mature, more distinctive, and smartly attired. They are all fair haired and of considerable height and stature. Though they are still dressed in white robes, it's the details that sets them apart: the subtle trim to their hems, a gold emblem at the breast, and a sash threaded with silver.

Even their books appear more opulent, with fine script across the front and pages edged in gold leaf.

"Come sit," Veddie says, directing Theo to the bench where his students are seating themselves beneath a stone relief of the archangels. "I'd like to introduce you to my students and my students to you. I keep a small but excellent group here. I believe you will find them a suitable intellectual match. I want everyone to meet Theodore Duncan. He is our latest recruit."

Theo sits down receiving curt greetings and stiff handshakes from them all. Once again, it looks as if he has fallen in with the distinguished ranks. That pleases him. He feels like he was born for greater things and that he died for them too. He's pleased his superior abilities are being properly recognized in the afterlife.

"You will learn the duties of the ordained," Veddie says, moving to the podium at the center of the room. Even in his own home, he is distinguished above the crowd.

"Munus docendi," the students reply. "Munus sanctificandi, munus regeni."

Theo glances around as the boys speak in unison. Is he supposed to be joining in?

"The seven gifts of the holy spirit," Veddie continues.

"Wisdom, understanding, counsel, fortitude, knowledge, piety, and fear of the lord."

"And the three powers of the soul," Veddie finishes.

"Memory, intellect, and will," the boys finish in turn.

Theo clutches his books, feeling overwhelmed and confused. Has the lesson begun? Is he supposed to be replying with the rest? He doesn't like feeling of being left behind. Veddie moves from the podium and begins to pace. Theo watches him nervously, worried the change in disposition is because of his lack of response.

"Do you know the orders of the angels?" Veddie asks harshly, glancing at Theo.

Theo's eyes widen when the question is directed at him. He does know, but his memory is shaky right now. He just recalled his personal life this morning; he certainly hasn't remembered his entire education yet.

The boy beside him pipes in, "Seraphim, Cherubim, Thrones, Dominations..."

"Authorities, Powers, Principalities, Angels, and Archangels," Theo finishes, a hot tear of sweat running down his back. He blurted out the response without thinking. He's not even sure if it is correct.

"Excellent," Veddie says, pleased. "Then your memory has returned?"

"Well, some of it," Theo stammers.

"And your death memory, has that returned as well?"

"Uh, a little."

"Good, excellent. I expect great things from you, Theodore Duncan. I hope that you will not disappoint me."

"No, sir," Theo replies, though feels his reply is on shaky ground. Veddie is extremely demanding and, worse yet, teaches with little direction. Theo is getting the impression that he is expected to know the answer before it is taught to him.

"Good, then I will tell you what I have told the ones that came before you. These are the rules we guardians are governed by as proclaimed by the Roman Catholic Church. These rules are as follows: Angels have a beginning, but they cannot perish: they remain everlastingly the same."

Theo takes out his pen and quill and begins to write.

"Number two: Angels are not subject to the laws of time.

"Number three: Angels are completely superior to space, so they could never be subject to its laws.

"Number four: Angelic power on the material world is exerted through the will.

"Number five: Angel life has two faculties - intellect and will."

Theo quickly scratches down the rules, content to be back in a role he understands: student and teacher, authority and obedient.

"Number six: an angel never goes back on a decision once taken.

"Number seven: angels have free will; they are capable of love and hatred.

"Number eight: angels do not know the future.

"Number nine: angels may influence another created intellect but not another created will."

Theo finishes writing, looking up, eager for more. The other boys, though they must know this, still listen in quiet rapture as Veddie dispenses the rules.

"This will all be common knowledge to you soon enough. You will learn, as you become a guardian, the limits and reaches of your celestial abilities. There are three things we ask of you here, three things we demand and expect you to obey: voluntary poverty, entire obedience, and perpetual chastity."

Theo exchanges a secret smile with himself. Of the two, he has already mastered in his former life. He supposes the one he will have to address is the vow of poverty.

Veddie nods in approval. "Boys, I need a little time alone with my new student."

Theo walks alongside Veddie as they cross the forum to the courtyard in the center of the house. It's nature strictly organized, not a leaf or flower out of place. It centers around a grand fountain where three angels each struggle to hold their urn higher. In the corners of the yard are statues depicting a likeness of each of the four archangels. Though Theo has recently learned, there are many more than the four he knows.

They stroll around the stone pathway under a warm and perfectly placed sun. Even from the gardens, Theo can hear Veddie's students exchanging heated theological discussions. He's completely revived now and amazed at how vibrant he feels. He can smell the flowers, feel the scented air in his lungs, the heat of the sun on his skin. He feels just as alive as he did before he died. Maybe even more so.

"You are better this morning?" Veddie asks in his usual gruff, short manner. It seems like more of a statement than a question. Like his feeling better is expected.

"Yes," Theo replies quickly.

"It will be overwhelming but you'll adjust. With your considerable standing and education, you'll be at quite an advantage here. However, your education must begin at level one. Since you know the celestial hierarchy, then you know the nine levels that you'll need to work through before you can stand amongst us. But I have no doubt you will obtain those goals."

Theo beams with pride, pleased that Veddie understands how lofty his goals have become. "Yes, sir, I am determined."

"I know that. And I know that you are eager to forge ahead but you must be patient. There is a reason for the pace we travel here. Some of the lessons you will know, a lot of it perhaps, but there still is plenty to learn. You brought your schedule?"

"Uh, yes," Theo quickly pulls it out.

Veddie skims down the list but doesn't appear to be reading it. "Classes take place six days a week and, of course, a day of rest on the seventh. At the end of each semester, you will *jump*, as the students like to call it. Jumping merely implies descention, you will go to earth with your level assignment and when that assignment is completed, you progress to the next level. Do you understand?"

"Yes, sir," Theo replies keenly.

"My students are here to support you. I see you're still in general housing; I'll have that fixed as soon as possible. I want to see you lodged amongst my students and closer to the temple district. You'll spend most of your time studying there. My students have a lot to offer you and, you'll see, are a superior breed in and amongst themselves. As a mentor, I will be here as much as I can but with my duties as an elder, I will be abroad a great deal of time. The reason I select the students that I do is because I know they will function well without me and will need little in the way of guidance. My students come to the table already prepared."

"Yes, sir, I am ready," Theo says, now tremendously excited. He was a determined and strict student in life; he will be the same in death. He wants very much to prove himself to this fearsome and powerful man.

"Good. The first day will be less structured than your regular schedule. Some of the students need more time to adjust. You'll meet in your first professor's home and he'll give you a campus tour and answer any questions you might have. Who is your first teacher?" Veddie looks down Theo's schedule and frowns. His face turns red and his lips recede inwards. He seems very angry. Theo stares up at him worried he did something wrong.

"This will not do." Veddie exhales and paces back and forth a few times, his tattooed hands in fists. He slows and faces Theo, coming to an unsettled conclusion. "All right, go for your tour. I'll have this resolved as soon as possible." He passes the schedule back and then stomps away.

Theo stares densely as a furious Veddie leaves him standing alone in the courtyard. He looks down at the schedule. His first teacher's name is Daniel Ryder.

Chapter 3 ❧

The House of Ryder. Theo stands outside the building with a better understanding of why Veddie was so upset. Unlike Veddie's grand palace, Ryder's house is on the lower side of town, very near to the forest, and partially shaded under the permanent shadow of the nearby mountain range. It is ground level and he can see straight through the front door to the tangled, unkempt courtyard at the rear of the house. There are weeds growing up the front columns and the open windowsills are teaming over with thirsty, neglected plants. And it's loud. He can hear the ruckus from out on the street. Unlike Veddie's church like stillness, this place sounds like a local pub.

Bracing himself, Theo enters the building. The main entrance is a tenth the size of Veddie's and there are shoes scattered all over the floor. He sees cobwebs in the corners of the dusty room and the main fountain has a layer of scum floating on it. No glorious waterfalls here, the fountain sends up lazy streams of water in random directions like a kid spurting water through a gap in his teeth.

Theo steps down from the entrance to the main level, actually lower than the street. He sees water lines a few feet up the wall as evidence of previous flooding. An ivy plant leans forgotten in one corner with a stack of dirty plates beside the base. And there's a sort of a yeasty toe smell to the whole place that makes Theo feel nauseous.

Keeping his shoes firmly in place, he enters a narrow hall to the right and comes to an opulent room modeled after an Indian brothel. Here, students are scattered everywhere, seated on plush pillows, lounging on the floor, and hanging off the ends of couches. They are in the throes of a great laughing fit and there must be fifty of them crammed in the small room. He can't tell teacher from student or if this Ryder person is in amongst them.

"Is this the House of Ryder?" a girl asks, coming behind him with the same look on her face that he must have.

Theo shakes his head. "I guess."

The girl looks down at her schedule, troubled. "It says I'm supposed to meet here for a campus tour."

Theo nods. "That's what I'm here for."

"Campus tour?" a voice calls from inside.

Theo looks in and sees someone he recognizes right away. The dark haired teacher who gave Veddie the squirrelly look when they cut in line at registration. All the other teachers, when interrupted, gladly gave over the information Veddie requested, but this one seemed eager to challenge him when they met. And this Ryder, as Theo sees him now, is just half the man that Veddie is. Thin, geekish like science teacher looking hippy Jesus with long dark hair and a short trim beard. His robes hang over his slender body, his sleeves too long for his arms, his hems grubby at the ends. He is sprawled in amongst the students in the most ungraceful way.

"Down the hall," Ryder says, pointing. "You are too early."

Theo turns away, displeased, unwilling to wait for any further direction. He leads the girl down the narrow hall and peaks in the next door. As he opens it, he spies a long, slender leg stretched out on an examination table. He gasps, surprised, and pulls the door shut quickly. Frazzled, he continues down to the next door where he finds a room full of dirty linens piled up around a wash bin that looks like it hasn't been used in years.

"Let's just wait in here," the girl suggests, pointing to the room across the hall.

Theo takes a seat in another unorganized space. It appears to be Ryder's study. His books are jumbled in the shelves, stacked on windowsills, and even fashioned as stools around the central table. There's a bird flying around the low ceiling sending anxious feathers raining down all over the room. Theo sits down uneasily, cringing every time the bird flies over. Down the hall, there's a shriek of laughter followed by rowdy applause. Theo glances at the girl; they seem to share the same concern.

It's well past nine when the groups finally breaks apart. There are still only two of them waiting in the room. The crowd seems to linger in the hall forever, laughing and shuffling around, but soon the noise dissipates and a disheveled Ryder appears in the doorway. Theo dislikes him instantly. There's something about his manner, the informal way he carries himself, his untidy appearance that rubs Theo in all the wrong ways. The man is undisciplined, too casual, too muddled for Theo's stringent standards.

Ryder glances inside the room, returning the same look of condemnation. "Yes," he says, his hazel eyes fixing smartly on Theo. "One of Veddie's, I presume."

Theo frowns. He thinks he's just been insulted.

"And the lady," Ryder steps in and warmly offers the girl his arm. "You, my dear, are in the wrong room."

The girls blushes and takes his arm with a smile. They walk out together. Ryder tosses Theo a look before he's out of sight. "Coming, hero?"

The remains in the room, fuming. Who does this puny, little (he checks his schedule) Ascensions teacher think he is, anyway? He considers just leaving but his strict and obedient manner won't allow him break out of an assigned schedule. He takes comfort in the fact that Veddie knows who this Ryder is and is doing something to fix this problem. Until then, he supposes, he will just have to put up with it.

   He turns down the hall and joins the group that stands in the dilapidated courtyard. The garden is filled with students so this must have been the place they were supposed to meet. Ryder's sparse directions sent him and the girl into the wrong location. He looks around the garden area in displeasure. It's not even a full courtyard; the back wall is adjacent to another building. And it's a disorganized mess, most of the plants are brown and dry from neglect. The sun seems seedier on this side of town too. It's lower in the sky, angled into his eyes, and too hot and humid. And there are over thirty students jammed in the small enclosure with Ryder standing up on the fountain above them. The whole scene annoys Theo to no end.

"Yes, yes," Ryder says, "First years, new arrivals, I assume you slept well last night?" Theo remains unchanged as a chuckle passes through the crowd. He supposes Ryder is referring to the awakening most of the students experienced during the night. The recollection of their former lives. Regardless, the joke does little to lift Theo's mood.

"I realize that this must all be very disorienting. My name is Ryder. Mentor to some of you. Others, I don't know." His gaze travels past Theo, a slight glimmer in them. "So first we'll begin with an introduction. My name is Daniel Ryder."

Theo rolls his eyes. *You already said that, buddy.*

"I am the head of Light and Ascensions department but you, of course, don't know what that is yet. You will, soon enough. Anyone who has visited my office also knows I dabble in the Chemical Arts as well. Call me Ryder. No one calls me Daniel. I'm sure you all have questions. I'll do my best to answer them." Just then, he loses his balance and almost falls back in the fountain. The students giggle but Theo is only aggravated by the teacher's blundering behavior. How did he get paired up with such a fool?

"To start with...you *are* dead. Be sure of that." The statement brings a number of reactions from chuckles to jeers. "That's right, every last one of you. Some of you will remember the moment it happened and some of you may never recall. Of course, when you are ready, you may consult the Book of Life if you like, but that time is far from now."

"What is the Book of Life?" Theo says, raising his hand, feeling insolent and impatient. "Why can't I read it now?"

"Yes? Theodore Duncan? And just as expected, such an eager little disciple. The Book of Life is your story, a living documentation of your life. You saw your book during your judgment but now your volume rests in the main library and can only be accessed when your mentor deems it's time. Don't be in a rush to read it. After all, who really wants to know the truth about themselves, anyway?"

Theo drops his hand, getting more annoyed, surprised he can still get annoyed, being an angel and all.

"So, guardians," he continues. "You have wings but you cannot fly. At least not in the physical sense. You are what we like to call the zeros, newbie's, fresh from the grave as it were. The shock of death is still upon you. Yes, I can see the bewilderment in your eyes. The wonder will dissipate. Not to worry." He lifts up a thin yellow book and indicates he wishes the group to follow. All the students scramble to pull out their own copy, all but one.

"There are seven levels of guardianship attainable. As of this moment, you will begin training for your level one. Things will become clearer throughout the day as you meet with all your instructors and begin to get a feel for your surroundings. What we will concern ourselves with right now is getting you oriented.

"Every person has a Light, it's what makes them alive, a soul, a circle, an aura that surrounds their being. Some people's Lights are small and some are large, it all depends on their place in life, their experiences, and their strength of spirit. This Light goes where they go, it affects the people around them. As a guardian, you are caretakers of the Light. Firstly, you will be assigned a charge. A charge is a person on earth who is in need of your services. As a guardian, it is your responsibility to maintain your charge's Light, to help repair it, and to help it to develop.

"Guardians progress by levels. Levels come between one and nine, though guardian angels only reach as high as seven, seven being the most extreme charges we take on. Seven guardians are few and far between, taking a life's work to achieve. Angels in the eight and nine arena are a whole other matter indeed. These are the archangels and warrior angels, like Malik and Azrael. I'm sure you all took a peak at them during orientation, even though you were warned not to. Not many will reach the level of the warrior angels, not many want to take on that kind of responsibility. For now, concern yourself with guardianship. Level one charges are for trainees only because they have the largest and most predictable auras to work inside of. So think about auras. Who can give me an example of a level one Light? Of someone, of something that might embody a level one aura?"

"Babies?" a girl offers, tentatively raising her hand.

Ryder points at the girl and says, "Exactly. For example, a sick child or a child with a disability would need a guardian. A child is innocent and unaffected and their Light is very large. Plenty of space to move around in. Other examples?"

Theo scowls in agitation. When are they getting to the tour? He has no interest in what this teacher is talking about, and he blames the teacher for that.

"Yes, in the back?" Ryder calls.

"Um...animals?" another student offers.

"Exactly! Exactly what I was looking for," Ryder exclaims. "Animals have the largest and most consistent auras on earth and as level one trainees, you will each be assigned an animal as your first charge. Your assignment is not necessarily to change the animal's aura but to get a feel for your environment. Babies," Ryder points to the girl, "are level two."

Someone down near the front raises their hand. "If I'm guardian over a family pet, will I see the family as well?"

"Good question. I'm glad you asked. No, auras are very specific. Although you may cross paths with another's aura, it will be too brief to get any sense of it. Think of an aura like a hula-hoop radiating out from that person's center. You can only see what's inside that persons, or that animals, aura."

"But what's outside the aura?" another girl asks.

"Darkness," he replies.

That brings Theo's attention back up to Ryder. Darkness?

"Not to worry, there's little chance of stepping outside an animal's Light. They could encompass all of this city. You'd have to be fairly determined to get lost outside an animal's aura."

"But if someone does step outside the Light?" someone else asks. "What happens then?"

"Angel's get lost outside the Light. You'll learn more about that in your level two training. You can be rescued. Most angels get left behind in the bathroom when their charge suddenly leaves and locks them inside. If you do happen to get lost, stay where you are and don't wander about. The further away you get, the harder you'll be to find."

"Have you ever lost an angel permanently?" Theo asks, without raising his hand.

Ryder locks eyes with him, giving him that challenging look that he gave Veddie at orientation. "From time to time."

The tour begins. While students pile up eagerly behind Ryder, Theo follows begrudgingly behind. Even though this is content he should be learning, he doesn't want to be learning this information from Ryder. He keeps hoping Veddie will swoop in and rescue him, reassign him to a more professional tutor but rescue does not arrive.

They return to the main library and approach its two-story façade. Pillars stand in pairs across the front entrance, framing statues on pedestals between them. A riser of steps takes them up to the main landing. Though the outside is archaic, the inside is in complete contrast. Bookshelves seem to defy gravity rising three stories high around them. About two thirds of the way up is a catwalk that gives access to the higher levels. Along the lower level, ladders help students find what they need. Light seems to explode in from every window, making what should be a dark space, brilliantly lit. In a central area are long rectangular tables and private study areas near the walls. A fireplace burns in one corner. But the thing that catches Theo's eyes most keenly is the black spiral staircase that runs up to a second story riser locked behind solid steel gates.

"What is that?" he asks, interrupting Ryder as he explains the ins and outs of library circulation.

Ryder looks up and the rest of the student's gazes follow. "That is the Book of Life section."

"So why is it locked? I mean if my Book of Life is up there then shouldn't I have access to it?"

Ryder turns and puts those challenging eyes on Theo again. His expression is surprisingly dark. There's something about him that makes Theo uncomfortable, nervous even, though he would never let the scrawny Ascensions teacher see it.

"Like I said earlier, you may think you are ready to face the truth about yourself, but you are not. Everyone has a way they believe they are perceived but that is rarely the truth. Your mentor will know when it's time, if it ever is."

Theo scowls, unsatisfied but silenced for now. Maybe other people have things in their lives they can't face but there is nothing in his earthly life that would come as a surprise to him. His life was pure and true; he was hard working and dedicated. Maybe this Ryder can only see in the world what he sees in himself but Theo knows he could face his book right now without a single thread of doubt.

The tour continues. They're taken through a market square where vendors exchange goods. Food is not for survival, just for interest or pleasure. They see the arts building, study hall, and amphitheater. They pass through endless fountain courtyards, beneath yawning archways and overflowing gardens. In the higher levels of the city, an acropolis of buildings and temples rest just beneath the towering arches of the cathedral. This is where most of the teacher's offices and administrative buildings are located. Down the hill where the street of steps is located, there is a mixture of domestic and public facilities. A pantheon is down by the river. A domed observatory across the river. The meadow leading back to the misty hill is free for exploring and so is the ocean port and the river beds. The two places that Theo is really interested in seeing, that being the cathedral and the Field, are skirted around and questions about them avoided.

At ten o'clock, he's finally set free, released to his second professor, Lila: Animal Auras instructor. He could not be happier. That is until he encounters the rapture faced nymph with lavender braided in her hair and rose petals sewn into her hems. She is gushing over with uber happiness, steering students through the meadow exclaiming about every feathered or furry creature that crosses her path. Her instruction meanders this way and that, often going off in the most inexplicable directions. She talks about rabbits and kittens and crickets, goes on and on about the glory of their Light, about the color of it, the smell of it, the shape of it. Her voice is unbearably high and she animates everything she says with exaggerated arm gestures. Theo is just as annoyed with Lila as he was with Ryder. If this is the slow pace Veddie was telling him about, he's not going to be a significant guardian for at least two dozen years. There are no textbooks; nothing is being written down. Lila calls it life experience. Theo calls it experience wasted. He leaves the class with a throbbing headache, longing to break from the group and return to the House of Veddie for some more stimulating education.

Prayers and meditation start next. A full hour in a small, musty temple spent listening to other students' nose breathing with their hands upturned on their knees. Theo just stares out the window at the angels bustling by to their important destinations and at the glorious cathedral calling to him towards grander things. Veddie said the first day would be unstructured, but this is frustratingly slow.

Lunch and debate follows. Theo partakes in neither. Instead he roams the cobblestone streets, seeking the towering cathedral. But no matter how many turns he makes and how far he walks, he never seems to get closer to it. He gets caught in dead ends, in courtyards, and storage rooms.

"How do I get up there?" he finally asks a few passing angels. They give him a queer look and giggle: *leaving so soon*? Frustrated, Theo sits down on a stone bench in a quiet alley. He's so angry, he's fuming. Veddie said angels were capable of love and hate but how can he harbor such hostility if he's in paradise? He can't seem to settle his nerves. Maybe it's just the shadow this morning's stimulating ceremony has cast over the rest of the day. Nothing could compare to it. Meeting the angel who guards Hell perhaps had set his sights too high for the remainder of the experience. Still, he wants to get started at something. Meditation, relaxation, and crickets are not his cup of tea. He's fiercely excited to begin a serious education.

After lunch, relief. Gospels with Veddie and delivered in such a fiery and determined way as to bring the class to their feet by the end of it. His mentor far outshines the rest. This is the one he'll learn from. This is why Veddie was chosen for him. He's joined by Veddie's students, a fierce and resolute lot who continue outside the classroom with more apt conversation. He leaves them remorsefully and rejoins the herd for more elementary bible studies. He's spent by the end of the day, spent and disappointed. He skips the celebration around the fire and searches around the compound until he finds higher level classes in session. Even though he has no understanding of the subject, he loiters outside and soaks in the lively conversation.

The House of Veddie is empty that night, quiet as a tomb, no students and no mentor inside the compound. Theo returns to the dorm hoping there might be a note transferring him but his bed is undisturbed. No word about transfer from Ryder's classes either. Looks like he'll be attending Auras and Circles of Lights as scheduled tomorrow morning. He lies down on his bed and stares up at the portal in the roof. There are little to no lights on the Reserve, only the lanterns that the angels carry around. Now that the sun has set, the dorm is completely black. Students are stumbling in, back from the celebration, giggling and reeking of campfire smoke. Eric thumps down in the bed beside him, then turns over and taps his headboard between them.
"I didn't see you at the fire."
"I didn't go," Theo replies bluntly. He sounds gruff like Veddie. He likes that.
"Oh? It was a good time. You should've come. It's a great way to meet people."
Theo exhales, rolling his eyes in the dark. It occurs to him that he's already met the people that he needs to know here. It seems harsh, but that's exactly how he feels.
"How did you like orientation?"
Mention of orientation revives him. "It was amazing. Do you know who the other ones at the table were?"
"Sure," Eric says, lowering his voice to a whisper as students settle down to sleep. "That big one at the end was Malik. He guards the gates to Hell."
"Yeah, you told me that this morning."
"Did I? Okay, um…Ridwan was next."
"Gates of Heaven, yup."

"Okay, who was next? Oh, Mannkar and Nakir. They're the two who judge you when you first come in. The brother and sister."

"Twins?"

"I guess. I don't know. I mean they look like it, right?"

"Yeah, they do." Theo shifts his arms behind his head still staring up at the roof. It is too dark to make out the portal at the center of the ceiling or the artwork that surrounds it anymore.

"There's a white one, really bright? That's Spenta Mainyu. That's the Holy Spirit."

"What?" Theo sits up now, looking at the boy though it is too dark to see him. "He's an angel?"

"Of sorts. I mean once you reach that level, I guess you kind of stop being human, you know?"

"How many orientation ceremonies have you gone to?"

"Oh, as many as I can. You can get up before classes and attend every day with the new arrivals if you want."

"Really?" Theo knows exactly what he's doing tomorrow morning.

"Now the one next to him, that's the one you want to be careful of. She's the redhead…"

"Oh yeah, I remember her."

"Scary right? Like pee your pants scary."

"Yeah, that's the one."

Eric sighs rolling onto his back. "That's Azrael. She is the angel of death."

Theo opens his mouth but nothing comes out. The memory of her is vivid. The sight of her scared him stiff. He was shaken for minutes on end after seeing her. And was unable to even skim his eyes in her direction afterwards.

"Veddie was there too. I mean he's not a full angel yet, but he's an elder. I think he's a level six or something."

"Yeah, we've met," Theo states proudly.

"How do you know Veddie?"

Theo smiles, feeing satisfaction when he says, "He's my mentor."

"What?" Eric turns over on his front, clunking his head on the headboard as he does. "You're one of Veddie's students?"

"Mmm-hmm," he replies with a satisfied smile.

"What are you doing here, then? I thought you guys had a special dormitory in the temple district?"

"I guess I'm waiting to be reassigned."

"Yeah, Veddie's students get all the good stuff. Private baths, gardens and everything. Wow, I can't believe you're one of Veddie's."

"Who's your mentor?"

"I'm with Jacob. He's one of the history professors."

Theo closes his eyes with a sigh, finally feeling exhausting setting in. "Do you have any classes with this Ryder guy?"

"Ryder? No, I haven't heard of him. But there's so many professors here, you'll never sort them out."

The next morning, Theo is up with the sun. Long before any first years have even stopped dreaming, he's down in the forum ready for the show. He has new hope today, hope that yesterday was just death's equivalent of jet lag and this morning he'll be back to his normal, eager self. The sun is just rising and the platform is being prepared by worker angels. Theo lurks near the stage, determined to be front and center when proceedings begin, not just so that he can see them, but so that they can see him as well, to take notice of him and be ready to receive him when he rises to their ranks.

Theo catches an elbow in the side and turns to see Eric. "Oh hey."

"You're here early," Eric says with a grin.

"I didn't want to miss it."

"Did you hear the rumor? The archangels were in town this morning."

Theo looks back towards the town. "Are you serious?"

"It's just a rumor. Maybe they'll come to the assembly," Eric says, his attention drifting away.

Students gather and the procession of warriors begins. Theo has placed himself in such a manner as to be right near the stairs when angels ascend the stage. Knowing what's to come, he's even more excited than yesterday. This time he wants to really see it, to absorb every detail of the experience. This is his destiny. He is going to become one of them.

He lowers his head but not his eyes for the angel who guards Hell. Malik comes in like before, his body steaming, battle scarred, and world weary. This time, he proceeds with two massive crows flying behind him. His face is drawn down with hard lines and there is a scar from his right eye to his chin. Though his eyes are completely black, Theo notices they have a spot of white at the very center that move in the direction he's looking. Anytime that spot moves his way, Theo quickly focuses on the ground. Next comes Ridwan. He arrives as fresh as the first spring breeze. There is something dynamic, youthful, and vital about him. Again, Ridwan meets his eyes, this time with the slightest nod of acknowledgement. This time Theo is able to hold the gaze and even timidly respond to it. This is the one Theo wants to be like, the one he relates the most to.

Next come Mannkar and Nakir. They are identical copies of each other, exotic, almost Egyptian in their dress and skin color. They are neither fierce nor intimidating but they hold a quiet power between the two. Church Militant was the verdict they gave him. A good ruling in all regards. He wonders what a bad ruling is. What happens to the ones who were less obedient in life?

Next comes the Holy Spirit. Inside the shimmering light that surrounds it, there appears to be the form of the man but Theo cannot look in its direction for more than a few seconds at a time. The light is blinding and scorching hot as the creature passes by, humming loudly like he is standing next to an electricity plant. Eric called him by a name, but Theo can't remember what it is. The Holy Spirit, walking right past him, he can barely breathe.

The one that comes after is scariest of the lot. Eric called her Azrael, the angel of death. She is wildly beautiful but in a terrifying way. Her hair reaches nearly her waist, though the majority of it floats around her like she's underwater. She has a thick iron band around her neck and similar bindings around her wrists. Her breasts are bountiful, barely contained, her hips swelling widely outwards. Theo's breathing increases as she nears. He is excited and aroused in a way he's never experienced before. She sees him and he looks down, but not fast enough. Her eyes swivel to his, piercing rubies, so light they are nearly transparent. They lock on his and he finds himself frozen and unable to move. She continues walking but her attention is on him now. She seems to thrust her chin forward to challenge him and Theo falls to his knees. A few students lean down to help him but quickly retreat as Azrael gets closer. She stops in front of him. The assembly is now completely silent.

"Rise, child," she leans down and whispers into his ear in a sweet and sultry voice.

Theo rises on trembling legs. He keeps his eyes down, which focuses his gaze on her full and luscious breasts. They rise and fall as she breathes, a web of veins pumping hot blood across their ample mounds.

"Why do you look at me?" She breathes hot across his ear. "Are you not afraid of death, child?"

Theo's eyes shiver closed and blackness comes upon him. For a minute he is falling, falling, and then he gasps in a breath and sees he has collapsed in the aisle. Azrael has moved up the stairs and the next warrior angel is approaching. Theo pushes out of the way but cannot get his feet under him. Not until Eric grabs his arm and pulls him back up to standing.

"What are you doing?" he whispers angrily. "Did you look at her?"

"I couldn't help it." Theo says clasping his shaking hands to his front. Now that it's over, it was the greatest rush of his life. His heart is pounding. He has sweat all over. And her voice in his ear was sweeter than Heaven itself. He's wild with excitement, with defiance, with adrenaline. It was a rush like no other. Day two has not disappointed.

Chapter 4ୡ

Theo sits down in Ascensions class. This will be his first lesson with Ryder. He wishes Veddie would hurry up and transfer him. He can hardly stand to be near the fumbling teacher. And fumble he does. Ryder enters the classroom and stumbles up the steps to the stage. He drops his notes, his quill, and then his notes again before he makes it safely to the podium. "Right," he says, once he's gotten himself settled and turns to face the class. They are seated in the ruins of an old theatre, no roof, with clouds gently passing overhead. Though this is unlike a normal classroom setting, he's at his usual place. Front row center. His books are open, his pen poised over the page.

"Angels have a beginning, but they cannot die: they remain everlastingly the same." Ryder turns to the board and picks up a piece of chalk, drops it, and then picks it up again.

Theo huffs out an impatient sigh. Dawn was thrilling but mid-morning is waning once again.

"Angels are not subject to the laws of time," Ryder says while he writes. "What does that mean? Can anyone tell me?"

"We don't age," someone calls out.

"Exactly. Angelic power in the material world is exerted through the will. Do you understand what that means?"

Theo opens his book and sighs as the debate continues. Veddie already went over this. Theo has the rules written neatly across the front page of his notebook. There was no need to explain their meanings; he knew that Theo would understand.

"Angels have free will; they are capable of love and hatred. That is self-explanatory. As well as, Angels do not know the future; they do not know the mysteries of space. When they say an angel may directly influence another created intellect but cannot act directly on a created will, that means that the intellect rules here, not the fist. You can only influence through the will. That is applicable both on the Reserve and back on earth. When they say angels are completely superior to space and cannot be subject to its laws, they mean..."

Theo retraces the lines of his notebook thinking about Azrael. He doesn't know what possessed him to look at her this morning. As soon as he saw her, he just lost all his senses. He supposes death has that effect on people. He's pleased, though, that Ridwan saw him and even nodded. He has no doubt he'll be coming back to orientation for more, even after what happened with Azrael today.

Ryder's chalk suddenly screeches across the board. "Stop," he says.

Theo looks up, thinking the order is directed at him and his obvious lack of attention.

"These are the rules of the Roman Catholic Church!" Ryder shouts.

Theo is taken aback. He wasn't expecting such a roar from this meek looking professor. Ryder puts down his chalk and manages to descend the stairs without incident. He walks right up to Theo's desk and rips out the page he wrote the rules on.

Theo gasps, staring up at the raven haired teacher in horror.

"No rules," he says, while waving Theo's notes around. "We have been given free will for a reason. As a guardian it is imperative that you make decisions for yourself. No one religion rules here. They are all broken off pieces of a complex system. Do not concern yourself with the aspirations of others. This is not a race to the finish line. There are many ways to achieve success on the Reserve. It is time to start thinking for yourselves. Destroy this." He crumples up the paper and then indicates that the rest of the students do the same. "Tear it up."

Slowly, one by one, students begin to tear out their carefully written notes and crumple them. Ryder nods as he turns to Theo's desk, locking eyes with him. Theo angrily returns the gaze. "Point taken!" Ryder shouts, causing Theo to jerk back in his desk. "Today, Theodore Duncan looked right into the eyes of Azrael, the angel of death, knowing that this action is strictly forbidden. What we have here is a true free thinker. Let none of the rules apply to him. This boy is a shepherd; he is no sheep."

Theo's jaw clenches and he snatches the crumpled notes back from Ryder. He presses the paper flat and returns it to his notebook

Ryder sets his challenging eyes on Theo and says, "Time to start your education."

The next day goes the same as the first. He's just doing time until Veddie frees him from this unchallenging curriculum. Meanwhile, Ryder talks about Auras, about essence, about the breadth of Light and the influence of meditation. But it all remains just that: theories and concept. When is there going to be action, actual work done? Lila continues her dream journeys about crickets and butterflies. They spend an hour in a field watching the deer graze. You can see their Light if you concentrate hard enough, she tells the students. One by one, students gasp in amazement. Theo just stares back at the glorious cathedral, at the guardians bustling around on important missions. It just seems like he's going nowhere. To his disappointment, Veddie's appearance in the gospel class was just temporary. Another flighty teacher takes his place. And the gospels are old news to him; the bible already studied end to end. He feels like he should be at a higher grade already, not muddling around in the primaries with the zeros.

Some classes are okay. Object Negotiation catches his interest. They gather in the Courtyard of Saints while the teacher explains that the only thing back on earth that will be real is him. Think of earth as a sculpture, he says, every object, every leaf, every door, every obstacle in your path is carved from the same stone. You cannot open doors. You cannot travel through walls. You cannot even pick up the smallest leaf. Think of it this way, he says, you are not so much as walking *in* the grass as *on* the grass. When you are down there, they are the ghosts. An angel's power is from will alone. This is your only influence. You cannot touch or move anything.

First Jump classes also keeps him focused. It's like skydiving, his professor explains, you actually travel through the atmosphere on the way down to earth. The Field he spied on his way to the city is the entrance. The pools located there are portals to the living. Each pool is the entrance to one person's soul but beneath the water, it is much more complicated. In the Field, thousands upon thousands of souls are waiting to be rescued. A charge is assigned, not chosen. Once taken, the assignment is permanent and must be seen through to the end. First Jump is just a testing ground. Animal auras are used so one can get a feel for the Light. But you must be prepared. It can be very overwhelming the first time down. And each charge can take years or even decades to complete.

Along with Object Negotiation, are countless theology and Angelology classes. There are hundreds of holy messengers each with their own special duties and accomplishments. Not all are as well-known as Azrael or Ridwan. There are many in the shadows, all a part of the whole. Asha, the angel of right. Israfil, who awakens the dead. Lilith, queen of the night. He has to learn ranks of the Islam, the angels of Zoroastrians, the Postelexic Jewish angels. He has to learn the seven capital sins, the spiritual works of mercy, the conditions for mortal sin, the duties of the ordained and countless other doctrines that he spied on the pillars of judgment. Each religion holds some grain of the truth and yet none has captured it whole. It is his job, as a new recruit, to put the pieces back together. To find the whole truth as it was meant to be in the beginning before the people of earth began to pull it apart.

Sunday comes around again. His first week on the Reserve over. As he lounges in bed watching the sun lift in the sky, he feels cautiously optimistic about what lies ahead. There were a lot of adjustments to his new life this week, a lot of upsets and frustrations, but overall he's starting to settle in. This morning, he waits until he hears all the footsteps leave before he throws back the covers. He's used to privacy, his own bed, his own space. It's the one vow he knows will test him the most:

poverty. Still, promise of his own room among Veddie's elective will ease those pangs soon.

He gets up, straightens all the corners of his bed and then goes outside. A spring sun rises in the east and the courtyard outside the dorm is humming with songbirds. Being struck by an uncommon bout of spontaneity, he leaves the courtyard and decides to explore. He heads west to a sector he hasn't been to before. Here he finds a vegetable garden on the edge of the city where the river tumbles down the hillside into the meadow. A large basin has formed at the first fall creating a pristine wading pool. Benches line the edges of the pool and there is a place where it looks like campfires have been built. Trees adorn the yard and between them are woven hammocks. Though the sight is beautiful, as everything here is, it strikes him odd that there are no people around. In fact he's seen no people this morning at all.

Concerned, he turns back and takes the shortest route to the House of Veddie, once again, encountering no one. But as he climbs the steps to the terrace, he hears the familiar sound of his fellow students bantering. He finds them in Veddie's immaculately tended garden. As soon as they see him, they all look his direction and stop talking. Right away, he knows something's wrong.

"Where were you?" they ask. "Veddie is looking for you."

Theo experiences a pang of fear. "Why?"

"Mass?" one of the boys says, as if he should know better. "You missed service this morning."

"Service, but no one told..."

"*Theodore Duncan!*"

Theo turns to see Veddie standing under the garden archway. He's ten times as intimidating when angry. Theo's heart begins to pound and a nervous sweat breaks down his back.

"I didn't know that..."

"There is a ceremony at nine sharp every Sunday morning. I expect you to attend." Veddie raises his thick tattooed arms and crosses them over his chest. His eyes are dark and fuming.

"Yes, sir," Theo says, lowering his head. Behind him, he swears he hears someone chuckle.

"If you are unsure about something, then consult my students. You leave nothing to chance, do you understand? How do you think it looks to have a seat at my table empty during morning mass? You bring shame on the house of Veddie."

"Yes, sir, I'm sorry." Theo says, keeping his head bowed in submission. "I will be there next week."

"Good. And what is this I hear that you confronted the angel of death?"

Theo looks over his shoulder at the gathering of boys all staring back at him. There is mockery in those eyes, condemnation. He shouldn't have done it; he has no one to blame but himself but he feels a sharp stab of anger pass through him, regardless. This is his first week here. How is he supposed to know all the rules if no one tells him?

"Sir, I didn't confront her, I…" He sighs, dropping his head more. "I'm sorry. It won't happen again."

"Come with me," Veddie says, turning back into the house.

Theo follows along, hearing snickering behind him. He doesn't look back. Veddie walks him out to the front of the house and stands on the terrace looking down at the city below him. It's a beautiful sight but Theo cannot enjoy it.

"I'm sorry," he stammers.

Veddie sighs, lighting that cigar that he never smokes. He face remains gruff but his voice softens some. "You're having trouble in your studies?"

"No, sir, I…"

"I've had reports from several of your teachers that you've been inattentive. "

"No, sir, it's just…"

"I told you that the curriculum would be beneath your educational standing. I also told you that everything you learn is required, whether you feel like you know it or not. Everyone must start at level one. That is the way the system works here."

Theo stares down at his feet. He knows exactly what Veddie is referring too. Lila, gospel studies, meditation, Ryder's class, he has been inattentive and in some cases, disrespectful. He supposed that Veddie would understand aware his higher education level, but it seems his tutor is much stricter than he first anticipated.

"I will do better from now on, I promise." Theo says, now resolved to ace every class, no matter how foolish or simple he might think the subject.

"Good, now go back and join the group."

Theo leaves the House of Veddie, humiliated. He returned to the group but it wasn't the same as before. They seemed to shy away, not wanting to associate with him after Veddie scolded him. Somehow he's been labeled a black sheep and now the students have retreated in fear of being marked by him. He sat there, talked over and around, feeling more excluded than he ever has in his life. He can't understand what's come over him. He was such a good student in life; he was top in all his classes, never late or missed a day. And he was always surrounded by students, they looked up to him; he was always the leader in every group and very popular. How is it he's become a pariah in paradise?

He leaves, determined to go straight to his books, but in his emotional state, he doesn't pay attention to where he's going and finds himself lost in a part of town he's never been. He's surrounded by short, square houses all jumbled up together, the streets twisting this way and that. It's mostly storage areas and back alleys but he can't seem to find his way out. Frustrated, he begins to panic, running down the streets in hopes that haste will succeed where logic failed. But he keeps coming around to this same block with a broken fountain in the center, and each time he sees that fountain, his frustration grows.

"Damnit!" he cries, surprised to hear himself curse. In an attempt to gain some ground, he climbs up the side of a building and looks over the top. From there, he can see a man a few streets away standing in an alley. He quickly drops and follows the route. He comes to an old street overgrown with weeds. The buildings are crumbling and forgotten. Here, he finds an average looking angel of no great luminosity standing in long concrete alley that is sloping down towards a firmly locked gate.

Theo turns down the alley and approaches him. While Theo first thought he was standing idly by, he can now see that the man is guarding the gate at the end of the alley. The gate is firmly locked and behind it, there is only darkness. The man looks a bit edgy as he nears, gripping his spear tighter and glancing around nervously. Theo slows, standing much further away from the man than he normally would.

"I'm lost," he says, stifling his curiosity about the gate. "Do you know the way out?"

"Lost?" the man says.

"Yes, I've got turned around." Theo brings out his map but can't seem to find the place he's standing.

The man comes forward and points on the map. "You see you have to go down this street by the fountain or you'll keep going around in circles."

"Oh," Theo says, now understanding where he went wrong. He looks up and the angel returns his gaze a bit fearfully. He should leave now, but he can't help but ask, "What are you guarding?"

"This?" the man replies. "Oh, these are just the drainage vaults. They go under the city for miles."

"Drainage? Why do you have to guard them?"

"Well, we don't want anyone going in and getting lost."

Theo doesn't buy the explanation but suddenly Veddie's angry face appears in his head and he backs off. No more challenging, no more disobedience. "Oh, okay. Well, thanks for the help." He leaves unsatisfied but determined to put the incident out of his mind. From now on, Theodore Duncan walks the straight and narrow.

That afternoon, he takes his books and walks down to the old forum. The students are gathered by the port enjoying the sunny afternoon. There are a few seated at the edges of the park doing exactly what he plans to do, study. He finds himself a nice lonely corner and sets up his work for the afternoon. He is determined to earn back his mentor's admiration but before he can get started, he finds himself surrounded. He looks up at Veddie's group of supercilious scholars. They are each uncommonly fit, tall, with light hair and skin. Theo sharply remembers this morning's rebuff. While he is resolute in his quest to win Veddie back, he is less eager to prove himself to this bunch.

"Do not be angry at us," one says, he is the biggest blonde, his face is sharp and angular and his eyes the most brilliant blue. "We cannot oppose Veddie."

"And he will find out any improprieties," says another one. He is by far the shortest, with a cut of long sleek hair halfway down his back.

Theo sits down with his back against a pillar, looking up at them. He thought Veddie found out about Azrael on his own, but it seems that the boys are admitting that they tattled on him.

"Don't get us wrong," the third one says. He is not particularly distinctive in any regard, at least not in this group of contenders. "We've all wanted to do it. Look at her, I mean."

"I can't believe you did it," exclaims the first one. "It must have been very frightening."

"It was," Theo says, his desire for acceptance overpower his angry resolve. He's furious at the boys but he supposes their explanation makes sense. He would probably do the same if put in a similar situation.

"Meet us after supper tonight? Veddie should be satisfied that we snubbed you long enough," they say, nudging each other. "We'll be going up to the temple district to rub shoulders with the elite. I think you should want to be there."

Theo smiles, abandoning his grudge. "I'll be there," he says and then watches them leave together. He feels the weight of resentment lift off his shoulders. He was never a very angry person in life. It doesn't fit him now either. And the boys' explanation satisfies him. After all, Veddie is very demanding. They want to stay in his good graces just as much as he does.

Relieved, he opens a text book and rests back against a pillar. The sun is just right, warm but not too warm and without a cloud in the sky. Somehow everything has straightened out this afternoon. He is ready to start over in all regards. The first project being his studies. He reads a few lines but then a bird flies over and distracts him. He watches it sail over the afternoon bathers and on into the cove. Past it, is a small exit in the rock that appears to go out to sea. But on closer inspection, he sees only clouds beyond, just a hazy wilderness and nothing more. Is that the end of their world? There are no boats in the port. The rock walls are too steep to negotiate around to the opening. Swimming would be the only option, but to swim that far? He sighs, returning to his books. Concentrate, Theodore! He reads a couple more lines but then his minds drifts off to tonight's gathering. He's excited to be a part of the group again, to meet all the influential angels in the industry. Maybe Ridwan will be there. Sighing, he returns his focus to the page. He reads again, determined to extract every possible detail to memory but finds his mind wandering again. Why is someone guarding the drainage vaults? Why isn't a gate enough? Is there something below the city, or do they truly want to keep angels from getting lost? Concentrate, Duncan! He flips the page, hoping the next paragraph will hold his interest better. That's when he gets the sense he's not alone.

He looks across the forum. Sun baked blocks steam in the afternoon light. Water laps on the shore of the cove. There are a few students across the forum sitting against pillars like he is. Nothing has changed. He focuses back down, reads a few more lines and then gets the overwhelming sense of being stared at. This time, when he looks up, he sees the students across the forum looking at him. And some are coming up from the water, slowing as they near the plateau, all gaping in his direction.

"What, the…" Theo begins and then hears something behind him. He turns and sees Azrael crouched on the ledge above him. "Oh my god," he whispers, stumbling forward off the ledge. He turns awkwardly and falls onto his ass. Azrael rises up on the ledge where he was sitting, looking down at him. Then she jumps and lands with her feet on either side of his hips. She slowly crouches down until she is squatting over his outstretched body.

"What is it about this one that interests me so?" she says, reaching down to touch his face.

Theo squeezes his eyes shut, but that is no protection against her Light. He can feel it all around him, humming like a hive of hot, angry bees. Her fingernails graze his face leaving peppery scratches behind. Even though his eyes are closed, he can see a red glow behind them, like he is right up against the sun. He exhales a short breath, his hands clenched on his chest, his legs stretched straight out, his toes curled in.

"Not quite dead and yet not quite alive. The boy is fresh, he has a smell to him I enjoy very much. I wish for him to speak my name. I wish to hear my name on his lips."

Theo shudders and feels a wetness release between his legs. His eyes creak open for a second and his pupils' burn from what he's seen. She's so close but not quite touching, crouching over him like a predator about to devour its prey. She squats, her knees open beneath her metal skirt. And hidden in the shadows, the jewel of her womanhood, that dark forbidden place that caused all men to fall. His eyes flick up frantically. He sees her breasts spilling out over her breastplate, her skin an ocean of bronzed invitation. Her wings block out the sky, the sun, and it is so hot he can barely breathe.

"The boy will say my name. He will say my name."

Theo opens his mouth but only a short hiss comes out. Azrael lowers down until her face is directly over his. Her eyes are red wells, the irises turning, a kaleidoscope of lost souls orbiting inside them. Her lips drip with hot blood, parted, a split tongue darting out. Her nostrils are inflamed as she drinks in his scent. And her hair, a tentacle creature with a life of its own.

"Say it, boy, say it."

"Azrael," he whispers, with a sharp pain in his chest. "Azrael."

"Azrael," she repeats, running her finger along his lower lip.

Theo gasps and his tongue involuntarily darts out. The tip of his tongue grazes her long slender fingers and is instantly burned. He pulls it back in and clamps his mouth shut, turning his head to the side. He remains there, his whole body seized, and it takes several minutes for him to even realize that she has gone away.

Gasping, he opens his eyes and sees blue sky again. He's on his back, lying in a pool of his own sweat and urine. He feels like he's passed through rollers an old ringer washer, every bone broken, every organ compressed until it burst. He forces himself to sit up and his head swims as he does. Both his lip and tongue are dried and charred.

Becoming aware that he's being watched, he looks over and sees all the students from the forum now staring at him. His first fear is that Veddie will hear about this. The second is that the people around him will see that he urinated on himself. Worried someone might come over and check on him, he forces himself to his feet and stumbles away unsteadily.

Theo hides in the bathhouse behind the first year dormitory. Curtain drawn over his stall, he seeks solace in one of the few private places on the Reserve. The bath is oval in shape, higher in the back and carved from a single block of stone. The stall is lit by a single circular hole in the ceiling.

He crouches in the tub, robes and all. After escaping the forum, he fled down every back alley and remote garden path he could find. Seeing the dormitory courtyard full of students, he rushed around back and sought refuge in the baths. He would rather return sopping wet and pretend he fell in the river than explain that he peed himself during an encounter with Azrael.

He feels sick, his head full and throbbing. He can't go to the gathering tonight, not after this. He was already warned by Veddie just because he looked at Azrael too long. What will happen when his mentor finds out about this? All he can do right now is hide.

Theo's encounters with women on earth were few and far between. He had no particular interest in them; he was absolutely focused on religion and studies. Women were a distraction as far as he was concerned. He saw it time and time again as fellow students fell into the abyss of love and never returned. They lost focus of their dreams, their goals, even their good sense. But it wasn't just an emotional withdrawal, there was physical disconnection as well. He'd never met a woman who stimulated his interest. Women were too concerned about their looks, their clothes, their possessions. They were too focused on getting married, having children, and finding a house. He had more to achieve than material wealth. The whole concept was of no interest to him whatsoever.

Leaning forward and embracing his knees, his robes heavy and wet in the tub, he can't deny any longer that Azrael aroused him. Sexuality was a concept completely foreign to him on earth. The very act seemed uncivilized and dirty. At twenty-four years of age, he felt he had a certain mastery over that thing which drives most men mad. He was not a victim to his passions as other men were. But he cannot ignore the tension between his legs. Azrael has woken something he had hoped would remain in slumber.

Chapter 5☙

Vowing to regain his composure and standing, Theo turns his focus on education for the next few weeks. He immerses himself in his studies without coming up for a breath of air. In Object Negotiation he learns that guardians cannot descend from the Reserve or ascend from earth strictly from their own will, but they must use a conduit: water. Advanced jumpers can travel through a mist or even a reflection but beginners need larger bodies of water to succeed. He also learns that his charge, the man or woman he will be assisting, will also be as immobile and solid as any other object he encounters. The only thing real during descention will be himself. Ryder, though exceedingly annoying, is a wealth of information. Theo is surprised to learn that Ryder is just two levels below Veddie. He has a multitude of degrees and teaches several different courses, well into the advanced levels. It's from Ryder he learns that the statues he saw in the Field are actually guardians in descention. The body, now devoid of life, stays behind as the souls enters the pool. Guardian bodies will remain perched poolside for days, weeks, or even months, depending on how long their descention lasts. Even Lila has her moments, explaining the intricacies of Light, how it grows, how it fades, and proper ways to influence change. He remains steady and stays the course but does not go to the forum or to an orientation meeting again in fear he might be singled out by Azrael.

One morning, while the others are at orientation, Theo finds himself on a rooftop staring down towards the meadow he first arrived on. With a clear view to the misty hill, he can see new arrivals being led from the fog. Each one is accompanied by an angel but not all of those angels are mentors. In fact many of the angels here hold common jobs like clerks and librarians.

He watches the procession, a person here, a person there, all being led down from the hill, through the gates of Victory, and then up past the rooftop where he sits. Many of them stagger along, still in the throes of death, many of them wailing. From here, they are led up the maze of streets where they are taken to judgment. After judgment, some are taken towards the office district to receive their schedules and books. Some are taken up to Ridwan. But others return the way they came. They are led back out the meadow and their escorts return alone. Where do the ones that are rejected go? Do they meet Malik at the gates of Hell and continue their journey there? Though still curious, he's given up any extra-curricular curiosities like trying to gain access to the cathedral, the Book of Life section, or even the drainage vaults. From now on Theodore Duncan focuses on his studies. Still, he can't help but venture a glance to that glorious cathedral, the crown jewel of the Reserve. There are no church services there, no ceremonies, no gatherings. And no matter how hard he tried in the past, he never got close to the site.

"*Wondering about it, I suppose?*"

Theo jumps at the sound of a voice close to him, then physically jolts when he sees a disfigured angel lurking nearby. The man is deformed, his hands oversized, his knuckles bruised and twisted. His lower lip hangs long over his chin. When he smiles, his teeth are yellowed and terribly uneven. His skin is olive, his wings sagging and black.

"It is no cathedral," the dark angel says moving closer. "You can try to find it, but you won't. The only way there is by escort. One way in but no way back."

Theo rises, shuddering just being near to the creature. "Who are you?" he asks, rising to move several feet away.

"Why, David, of course. Certainly you have heard of me."

"No, I haven't."

"Oh, you will," he says with a smile that makes Theo want to run screaming into the hills.

"You said you know how to get to the cathedral," Theo continues, casually moving another step away. The angel is repulsive, dirty hair hanging in sweaty strings around his throat; his eyes are sickly and webbed with tired veins. His stained robes are tattered and worn around the edges. He looks homeless, but how can anyone be homeless in Heaven?

"Are you eager to go? For I can get you a ticket."

"A ticket where?" Theo says, spying the ladder he came up on, wishing he just stayed in the library. It seems like every time he goes off on his own, he gets in trouble.

"Why to Heaven, of course. Is it not what you seek?"

"I don't know what you're talking about," Theo says, taking another uneasy step towards the ladder.

"Gaze upon the steeples, young angel, but be in no rush to enter. For those golden portals are the gateways to Heaven."

Theo turns, his eyes lifting to the unreachable cathedral. He remembers asking someone for directions when he first searched the streets and alleyways for access. They seem to laugh at him and say: what's the rush? Now it makes sense. The cathedral is not a building but the gateway to Heaven. He stares up at the golden peaks in amazement. It's so hard to believe that he is in on the doorstep to paradise. No wonder he has been so drawn to it.

He turns back to respond but he's all alone on the rooftop. At the edge of the building, the ladder shakes as the dark angel descends to the street. Theo waits a few minutes, then takes the same path down.

Theo arrives at Lights and Ascensions. He opens his books and sets his pen on the page. Ryder comes in, his usual flustered self. Stumbling up the steps, dropping his books, and receiving his usual round of giggles.

"Mr. Duncan," Ryder greets with a sarcastic nod.

"Mr. Ryder," Theo returns with equal unpleasantness. Their dislike for each other has become a sort of game between them now. And no secret to the rest of the students in the classroom.

The raven-haired professor, who is rarely seen amongst the temple district gatherings, composes himself and takes out his chalk. "Enough of the Light, today we will talk of the Darkness."

Theo sits up, eager for more information. Despite his objection to the teacher, he is determined to learn, to ace his courses and make Veddie proud.

"There is no Light without Dark, and no Dark without Light. There could be no definition of an aura without a Darkness to define it. A level one guardian will probably never see the Darkness beyond a charge's aura. You could run for days trying to reach the edge of an animal's aura. But as you progress further on, get into higher levels, their Light gets smaller and so do the edges of your universe.

"Ask any guardian and he'll tell you in explicit detail his first experience falling outside the Light. I was level two. My charge was an Autistic boy. He fell down a flight of steps, broke his neck, and he died. I stayed with him until the very end, though I had the opportunity to ascend before it happened. I would not let him die alone and when he died, the Darkness overtook me. The only way I can describe Darkness is like standing naked on an anthill. It consumes you, pricks at every pore of you, fills your ears, fills your eyes, your nose, your mouth. I, of course, panicked. Instead of remaining still, I went into a frenzied sort of stop, drop and roll affair. It was like being on fire. You know what that's like, Mr. Duncan."

Theo narrows his eyes at the slight and nerdy professor. He was feeling a moment of compassion, even empathy for the queer professor as he recalled the sad story but then a taunt about his own untimely death has sent him in alternate direction.

Ryder tucks a thick curl of hair behind his ear. "The point is, it's important to retain a certain reverence for the Dark. It is not alive, not a living thing, just the experience of being outside the Light. It is the sensation of the absence of the Light. It can't hurt you but it can overwhelm you."

Feeling saucy, Theo thrusts his hand in the air. "Why can't we go in the vaults?"

Ryder turns and drops his chalk. "Excuse me?"

"I got lost a while back and I ended up at the entrance to the drainage vaults. There was this angel guarding it. He said we'd get lost in there."

"Then that's why you can't go in." Ryder answers, returning his attention to the board.

"But why a guard? Isn't a gate enough? If they tell us not to go in, then we won't go in."

"Really?" Ryder turns back around, approaching the front of the stage. Daily interruptions between the two have become the norm in Lights and Ascension class. It seems Theo enjoys interrupting as much as Ryder enjoys procrastinating. "Were you not warned about the angel of death?"

"I was." Theo sits back, folding his arms over his chest. There was no fallout from the encounter in the forum but he is still unnerved every time he hears Azrael's name. And he still avoids the orientation meetings in fear of her.

"And yet you disobeyed?"

"I didn't disobey," Theo replies smartly. "I was misinformed. I made a mistake."

"One of Veddie's students making a mistake?" Ryder counters. "Imagine that?"

Theo narrows his eyes at Ryder. Angry, he replies, "It just seems like there a lot of secrets around here. Why hasn't anyone told us that the cathedral is the gate to Heaven? Why do I have to find out from some dirty angel on a rooftop?" Theo sits back, satisfied by the shocked reaction from both the teacher and students.

"And who was this *dirty* angel, Mr. Duncan?" Ryder asks, now abandoning his lesson. He focuses his attention on the only boy seated in the front row.

"He said his name was David. This David guy told me about the cathedral."

"David?" Ryder repeats, going a bit grey. "Where did you see him? Was it down by the vaults?"

"The vaults?" Theo's eyes flicker up to Ryder. David said that Theo should know who he is and it seems that in some circles, he is known. But what does this have to do with the vaults? Feeling like he's gaining ground, Theo pushes harder. "He was all black and kind of deformed. His robes were dirty.

Filthy, really. There was definitely something wrong with him."

"Who is David?" someone asks behind him.

Ryder sighs, his lips turning inwards, his gaze locking with Theo's. "I shouldn't have said anything. If you have questions, you should discuss them with your mentor."

"But you're my mentor," someone else says.

Drumming his fingernails on the podium, Ryder seems to accept Theo's challenge. "All right, sometimes angels experience something that they cannot come back from. Sometimes angels lose their way. Some people will tell you that they are dangerous. I am here to tell you that they are not. We are angels but we are humans just the same. At least we on the lower levels still are. David is a fallen angel."

Theo raises his eyebrows, surprised by the honest reply.

"Not fallen like you think you know. The days of Heavenly crusades are long over. Iblis and his followers are defeated up here, though we still fight for control over the earthly domain. But there are ways to fall up here as well. And for those like David, who refuse to repent, they will remain forever lost to us. Don't think your journey here is absolutely secured. There are many hardships ahead, many challenges to face." Focusing just on Theo, he says, "You do not know everything about this place or the people who reside here. The Reserve has many miracles and mysteries to be uncovered, as well as its darker sides."

When class is over, Theo gathers his books, a bit unsettled about how the argument ended. It seems he was bested. Ryder doesn't play by the rules. He has no one to be accountable to. Theo has to worry constantly that Veddie will find out about his confrontations with Ryder, which have continued despite his vow to reform.

It seems as if Ryder is not finished with him either. As soon as Theo closes his books, Ryder says, "Mr. Duncan, please keep your seat."

Theo stutters while rising, looking around as the students casting wry glances in his direction. He slowly returns to his seat, though he will be late to his next lesson if he does not leave now. The class empties out, leaving him sitting all alone. Still, Ryder takes his time on the stage gathering up his things with a deliberate slothfulness that drives Theo mad. Finally he descends down the stairs and comes to stand in front of his desk.

"Is there something you're trying to prove to me, Mr. Duncan?" he states evenly.

Theo looks up into his teacher's eyes with as much animosity as he can manage and replies snidely, "Not a thing."

Ryder nods, his expression cool and calm. "I was wrong about you. Earlier in this semester, I called you a shepherd, but you are just a sheep."

The insult infuriates him. Ryder turns to leave but Theo launches out of his seat in pursuit. And just as he's about to catch him, Ryder swings around and shoves him against the side of the stage. Theo gasps as Ryder lifts him until his feet are off the ground and holds him there with a strength that seems to defy all odds. "Don't mess with me, Duncan. I've dealt with your type before. And if it's a war you want, you will lose."

Theo retreats to Animal Aura class, suddenly grateful for the easy spirit and simple manners of the flower child, Lila. He finds solace under a tree amongst the other students. He can't shake his encounter with Ryder, not just physically but emotionally as well. Ryder outmatched him and Theo could do nothing to stop it. He was utterly humiliated by the incident. His only consolation was that no one else was there to see it. Who does this Ryder think he is? And how could such a puny man overpower him? It occurs to him that physical size likely has no bearing on strength here. After all, an angel's powers are in intellect and will alone. But that would mean his will is inferior to Ryder's and he just can't accept that. No, he decides that he was caught off guard and that gave Ryder the advantage. His will is ten times the size of the Lights and Ascensions professor. He knows one thing for sure, he won't spend one more minute in Ryder's classroom. He'll go straight to Veddie's office and tell him what happened. Veddie will be furious when he hears about it and will transfer him immediately. Perhaps even go to Ryder and show him who the superior intellect really is. It thrills him to no end to imagine his mentor towering over a faint and frail Ryder and to imagine the geeky professor begging forgiveness in return.

Later that day, Theo walks up to the five story monument where most of the upper level teachers have their offices. Lined with brick and bordered in exotic stonework, the building is a piece of artwork in and of itself. Theo enters the front doors to the wide open lobby and takes one of the several staircases up to the higher floors. He enters a long, golden hallway lined with polished wood and potted trees and plants. At the end of the hall, a two story window is framed entirely in vines. From the window a clear view over the city and the misty hill that first brought him here.

He finds the door marked Veddie with a shiny, spotless nameplate. Even the doors are ornate with detailed carvings. No stone left unturned on the Reserve, no opportunities for embellishment overlooked. Theo taps lightly on the door, suddenly nervous about disturbing his mentor without an appointment. But after today, he feels like he has no choice. It's time to get Daniel Ryder out of his life.

"Come in," Veddie says in his usual, gruff manner.

Theo opens the heavy door and sees Veddie seated behind a wide marble desk between two shelves of leather-bound books. Quill pen in hand, he scribes onto a parchment, a muddy ink pot to one side, the cathedral in the window behind him. The office is grand and entirely deserving for someone like him.

"How are your studies progressing?" Veddie grumbles without looking up.

"Um...good," Theo says, nervously twisting his hands behind his back. It occurs to him, just at this moment, that he's had very little contact with Veddie in these past few weeks. He barely knows the man who is supposed to be his mentor and is still terribly uncomfortable around him.

"And your teachers are treating you well?" he says, continuing to write. "I hear your studies have improved."

"Um...yes, sir. I have been working very hard," Theo says nervously.

"So what is it, exactly, that you need from me? I am very busy, Mr. Duncan."

Theo takes a deep breath and says, "Well, um...Ryder."

Veddie looks up with guarded eyes, setting his pen aside. "You are having problems again?"

"No," he answers quickly, feeling his body tense up. This was a mistake. He never should've come here for something like this. But now that he's here, he can't let the incident with Ryder go. "It's just that, I was wondering when you were going to get that transfer through?"

Veddie picks up his pen and returns to his work with a heavy sigh. "The transfer is in the system but it hasn't been processed. We are very busy here. If you have not heard, there is a war going on below. We don't have time for the petty concerns of squabbling students."

Theo cringes, wishing he'd just left things alone. He turns towards the door and says, "I'm sorry. I'll leave."

"Sit down."

Theo looks back and sees Veddie indicating with one of his many ringed fingers to the chair across the desk from him. Theo sinks there quietly while Veddie finished his project. In time, his mentor sets the pen aside and sits back in his chair. The peaks of the cathedral are positioned behind him like a crown on his head. He looks more fearsome and intimidating than Theo has ever seen him.

"I heard you've had another encounter with Azrael."

Theo slowly closes his eyes, feeling like he's going underwater again. Azrael. What was he doing coming here and setting himself up for another scolding? "Yes," he says, lowering his head to a respectable level.

Veddie shakes his head, looking agitated. "You are in her sights now. That is unfortunate. Death takes what she wants, when she wants. I'm afraid she is used to having her way. You were warned what would happen if you confronted her."

"Actually..." Theo begins and then quickly stops.

"Actually, what?" Veddie says, narrowing his eyes.

Digging his nails into his palms, Theo replies much quieter. "I wasn't warned, sir."

"Warned about what?"

Feeling his frustration mounting, he says in a slightly louder voice, "You didn't tell me not to look at her. No one told me anything, so how was I supposed to know?"

"I thought I explained this to you. My students are there to educate you in these things. I can't be here to monitor everything you do. I have more important matters to deal with."

Theo glances up at him with cautious eyes. He doesn't know why, but Veddie's good opinion is life and death to him up here. "I don't mean any disrespect but I can't know what I don't know. I didn't know about Azrael. No one told me. How am I supposed to know the rules if no one tells me?"

"Do they have to?" Veddie challenges, looking at him like he's an idiot.

His dander rising, his heart rate increasing, Theo says, "Maybe they do."

Veddie stares at him for a very long time, his expression hard and unchanged. "Expect no favoritism from me. This is a journey you make on your own. You have been brought into the house of Veddie for a reason. Here, your only focus should be on your education. That is *if* you still wish to become one of us."

"Of course I do," Theo replies, feeling his face getting flushed.

"I am not your father; I am your mentor. If you are having some sort of emotional problem, then tend to it yourself. What we do here, we guardians, it is a serious matter. Don't be misled by Lila and her Animal Auras. Lives are on the line here. Ryder is a fool. It is a miracle he has progressed as far as he has and it is unfortunate that your first experiences here must be with him. But the semester is nearly half-way over. Next semester, you may choose your teachers."

"Yes, sir," Theo says, burning with humiliation. Veddie may not be his father but he's sure receiving a scolding like a disobedient child.

"And for now, you will stay in the first year dormitory. It seems to me that you have proven that you are not ready to join my dormitory. There is a certain level of decorum amongst my students and I can't have you disrupting that. And for the time being, you should not be seen in the temple district either, less you cross paths with Azrael. Be strong and stay focus on your studies. Once you get yourself back together, I will reverse these decisions. And I will speak to the elders about Azrael's behavior. I will not have her attacking my students."

Theo leaves another meeting with Veddie utterly humiliated. His mentor insulted him in every way possible. He did nothing wrong. Azrael attacked *him*. Maybe he did look at her once but he hardly sees how one look garnished so much retaliation from her. And he is at the top of his class in every subject he's attending. Even Ryder's class, even though the professor aggravates him so. And yet he receives no accolades. Worse yet, punishment. He was only going to Veddie to ask about a simple transfer that Veddie himself promised him. He hardly sees what he did to deserve such treatment.

He continues down the street and out of town. It seems like there is nothing he can do to please anyone anymore. He's so frustrated, he could scream. Though the day is over and the sun descending, sleep is far, far away. And the thought of returning to that first year dormitory, which has now become a prison to him, makes his skin crawl.

He crosses the river and continues into the forest. There, he hears familiar voices talking. Eric and a few of his peers are sitting by a fire. Eric calls Theo over. Even though he wants to be alone, Theo accepts the invitation and allows himself to be introduced to the crowd. He meets two girls and another male. The short brunette is Justine, Grace is a larger red-head girl, and Jack, a lanky, blond boy.

"Theo is one of Veddie's students," Eric boasts proudly.

"Really?" Grace, replies. "But aren't you in the dorms with us?"

"For now," Theo replies darkly.

"You look tired," Justine, comments. "You must have a lot of extra studies."

Actually, he doesn't. He's on the same, snail-pace as the rest of the drones. Being Veddie's student has brought him little advantage so far, except in status alone.

"Daniel Ryder is my mentor," Justine proclaims proudly. "I just love him. He's so amazing. I wouldn't want anyone else."

Theo grimaces, glad it's dark enough to hide his expression.

"Every night we gather at his house and we go over our lessons for the day. Or just sit around the piano and sing. Everyone is so nice. We eat and then play in the garden. Sometimes I don't get to sleep at all. But I'm never tired."

"No, me neither," Eric says. "Weird, isn't it? I mean, I sleep but I don't have to."

Theo finds that revelation surprising. He is exhausted all the time, hauling himself off to bed every night with a hundred bricks on his back. In the morning, his eyes are heavy sandbags, almost impossible to lift open.

"I've heard Ryder is fun," the blond boy comments. Theo has already forgotten his name. "I'm with Jacob though. I can go to him for practically everything. Even the stupidest stuff. And I have so many stupid questions. His door is always open. Even in the middle of the night. It's crazy." He leans in closer to the crowd and says in a lowered voice. "Sometimes I don't know how I got into the Reserve."

"Me too!" Eric exclaims. "I mean I wasn't exactly a saint in life or anything. I hardly did anything at all. I laid around all day, playing video games. I guess I was kind of disrespectful to my parents. I didn't know anything about religion."

Theo frowns, setting his hands in front of the fire, though they don't need to be warmed. Not religious? Are the prerequisites to guardianship so lax?

"No, me neither. I was such a bad student too," Grace says. "I failed everything! And now I'm an 'A' student."

"Me too," Justine exclaims.

Theo grits his teeth. They are top students as well? These kids who know nothing about religion and failed all their classes on earth? It upsets him that he's on the same level as people who were uneducated, lacking in religion, and, frankly, unworthy before they came here. He gave his whole life to religion and education. What was all his hard work and sacrifice for anyway? He receives no accolades here. All he gets are reprimands from Veddie for his trouble. It doesn't seem fair.

"Hey," Eric says to the others, "should we ask him to come with?"

Theo looks over at the impish blond boy who is the closest thing he has to a friend since he arrived on the Reserve. "Come where?"

The others look at him fearfully as if a student of Veddie might spoil all the fun.

"We're going to sneak into the Field, just to see what it's like. Do you want to come with?"

Theo pulls inward, his first impulse is to refuse. But then he considers it. After all, what has all his good behavior brought him anyway? He's been curious about the Field since he arrived. But if he were to get caught? Veddie would kill him after the reprimand he got today. Not to mention all his disturbances with Azrael. He just can't risk it right now. "I don't think I can. I should get to bed early tonight."

Theo lies in bed listening as beds squeak and students twitch. By far, this day has been the worst for him. Shot down by Ryder. Scolded by Veddie. And then left behind by Eric and his friends as they do the things he's been wanting to do since he arrived. He can't understand why his journey above has been so difficult for him. In life, he was the most productive person. Nothing ever got him down. He wasn't emotional or irrational. Other students seem to be having a great time. Why can't he get with the program?

It seems too early to sleep but he just wants to be unconscious. It seems like it's the only time he's at peace here. It bothers him that sleep appears to be optional for other students. He couldn't stay up past the curfew if he wanted to. He's often tired during the day as well. But as he's drifting off, he hears the crew from the campfire returning. They come scurrying in all out of breath and giggling amongst themselves.

"That was amazing!" they whisper. "Are you sure no one saw?"

They all bundle up near Eric's bed unaware that Theo is still awake. One of them even plops down on the edge of Theo's bed like he's not even there. He feels a horrible anger rising up in him. This tiny little square of the Reserve, his bed, is all he can really call his own. And he can't even keep people out of that.

"I don't think so," Eric says and then they all titter beneath their breath.

"It was so real," one of the girls says. "You could actually sense them as you walked by, like really feel it."

"I know, I thought I was going to cry. It was so…amazing."

"Incredible, right?"

Theo shuts eyes, wishing his ears had lids as well.

"What will happen if Jacob finds out?"

"Oh, he wouldn't care. He's so relaxed about that kind of stuff."

"Ryder says he snuck in before his first jump. He even told us where the hole in the fence is. He said that it would give us a better appreciation of what we're up against if we go in before our first descention."

"He actually said that?"

"Well, he told us not to tell."

"If so many of the teacher's don't care, why do you think they lock it up?" Eric asks the others.

"Because if you fall in a soul pool that has no guardian, then you have to take on that charge. No matter what their level."

"What? Why didn't you guys tell me that? You know how clumsy I am." Eric thumps his companion in the shoulder. "How do I even know which ones have guardians? I mean other than the fact that there were guardians standing in front of them all lifeless."

"Creepy, right?" the boy says.

"Jacob says the ones with no reflections have guardians," one of the girls says. "The ones that have reflections, those are the ones that are waiting for help."

"Wow, there were so many of them," the boy comments, "how can we get to them all?"

"We can't. Jacob says. "Most of them will never get help."

"Did you see that level seven section up by the tree?"

"I couldn't even go near it. It was so horrible. Can you imagine accidentally falling in there? You'd have to be that seven's guardian, no matter what."

"That's crazy. Can you imagine being forced to take on a guardian like that?"

Theo remains awake long after the rest of the students have gone to sleep. These kids aren't just pacing him, they are lapping him thanks to their mentor's help. He knows nothing about the Field. Veddie has only told him that when it's time to go, they'll go. And yet these kids are getting a plethora of information from their mentors. He's falling behind.

Angry, he throws back the covers and slips on his sandals. He should've went with the group, but it's not too late to go now.

It's like a meteor field after a rain fall. Thousands upon thousands of pools dot the hillside leading off as far as the eye can see. In between are a labyrinth of stone pathways, some dangerously narrow. Trees and flowers spring up here and there, with a bench or two in between. He couldn't find the hole in the fence, so he walked right through the front gate. Greeted a guardian walking by as if he was supposed to be there.

He hates to think that he's this much of a snob, but he needs to know that he's a little above the rest. Being assigned the same bed, the same clothes, the same classes, has taken away every advantage he had built up on earth. He wants to move quicker than the others. He wants special treatment because he believes that he's earned it. Surely the outstanding work he did when he was alive should mean something. And if Veddie won't recognize it, then he'll have to go ahead without his mentor's permission.

Carefully, he approaches the edge of a pool. It shows the reflection of a boy writing at a desk. He looks very sad. And Theo can feel the heaviness of the boy's emotions all around him. It's tangible like a scent in the air. He approaches another pool. A girl sits on the sidewalk with her hands around her knees. He feels her sadness, her loneliness, even anger, though has no indication as to what her situation is, just emotions. It scares him, the scale of the problems that wait out here. There's no sound in the Field, no birds, no voices, nothing. It's eerie and oppressive like a graveyard.

An idea begins to form in his head as he wanders amongst the lonely and the lost. An idea to prove himself to Veddie and the elders. If he falls in a pool, then that charge is assigned to him, no matter what. If he falls in a pool, he could bypass all these novice assignments and go straight to the real thing. He could pretend it was an accident. It seems lots of the kids are sneaking out here at night, some even with the permission of their teachers. Veddie would be mad at first but after a while he would be forced to recognize Theo's accomplishments. The more he thinks about it, the more it makes sense to him. He's so ready to begin and he already has the skills and training he needs. Maybe he doesn't understand all the basics it takes to be a guardian, but he is prepared in every other way. It seems ridiculous to be holding him back when there are so many souls in need. The more he thinks about it, the more convinced he becomes until he decides that this is the only way to get what he wants. Now he just has to find a soul suitable for his caretaking.

He passes by the reflection of a woman smelling a flower and then a baby in a cradle, each time getting a small sense of their troubles emanating up from their pools. The baby is sad; he is hungry. This woman is stressed; she needs money. He surveys one after the other until it becomes too much to handle. He finds his way to the safety of an old tree close to the edge of the Field and sits down on a wooden bench beneath it. Now he understands why the charges are assigned and not chosen. How does one pick one soul over the other?

They are all in such desperate need. Maybe their situations vary, but the pain is so real. He drops his head in his hands and takes a deep breath, beginning to doubt his decision. Is he ready for this? Then he thinks about Veddie's reprimand, about Ryder's smug face, and all of the other students pulling ahead of him. No, this is the right decision. He rises with a second wind and looks off to the left. A decaying stone path leads off into the dark, overgrown and neglected. The path has obviously not been used for a very long time. He walks cautiously down the center, feeling heavy emotions grow thick like fog. He clears some shrubbery and he comes to an image of an old man. The mood around the man is so horrible and so ugly that Theo recoils back. The man is sick, beating his kids, drinking himself to death. Shivering, Theo moves past him as quickly as he can. He comes to another. An old woman in adult diapers is yelling at her television. She is crass and rotted, her Light so foul it stinks. Feeling sick, he moves further down the path until he is near the edge of the fence and clear of them all. Leaning on the steel gate that surrounds the compound, he catches a glimmer of Light beneath the weeds. Leaning down, he clears away a thick blanket of weeds and twigs. A soul pool cowers beneath the debris, softly glowing from within. And in there, in a flowing red dress, is a girl dancing in the water. She's like a mermaid, her hands stretched above her head, her eyes lightly closed, her hair drifting all over. And her essence grips him like a hot fever, a power, a sensuality, a soul experience like none of the others. She is crying out in the most honest way he's seen so far, completely lost and forgotten in every way. He crouches down at the edge of the pool, watching her move. She's magnetic, electric, the essence of her soul, if repaired, would be the most beautiful thing the Reserve has ever seen. She is capable of great love, great devotion, great kindness. But her needs are unclear, her struggles complicated. It is not hunger or sadness or jealousy or despair. It's an emotion he has no explanation for. She is just in need of everything.

He sits down at the edge of the pool, angry that she is left in this overgrown place, forgotten down this dirty path with all these sickly souls. In fact, had he walked here during the day, he wouldn't have known this pool was here at all. It was only under the cover of darkness that he seen the faint glow through the reeds. He makes his mind up right then and there, this is the one he'll save and prove himself in the process.

He stares at the girl, the warm tangerine light emulating from her pool, pulsing as if sending out a signal to the guardians. *Help me. Help me.* I will, Theo thinks, and realizes, with a rush of excitement, that he's going to do it right now. The plan is not well thought out, perhaps impulsive, but he just can't imagine spending another day up here like he did today. As much as he hates to admit it, Veddie is holding him back. They all are.

He stares down at the water, a thin veil of liquid between him and her. All he has to do is touch it, just graze his fingers along the surface of the water and his fate is sealed. He experiences another surge of excitement. Finally, an opportunity to take his future into his own hands. To prove what he is capable of. To prove what he is worth. Reaching out tentatively, he touches his hand to the surface of the water.

ANGEL

Chapter 6 ☙

He begins to fall. Colors shoot past him like taillights on the freeway. Wind is tearing through his robes and pulling his hair out at the roots. He can't open his eyes; he's afraid his eyelids will rip from their sockets if he does. Descention is sharp and it's furious and he begins to panic. Maybe there's more to it than just touching the water. Maybe he can hit the ground. Maybe he can die. None of his classes ever mentioned anything about landing. He begins to thrash, trying to turn himself right side up. He's falling so fast that his lungs start to fold in. He passes through asteroid belts, through thunderheads, and waves of rain. His belt loosens and then his robes lift up over his head, and then they're gone. He reaches backwards, opening his eyes to sees his robes spinning away, as if they are the ones falling and he is the one standing still. He goes end over end, until there is no up or down, arms and legs out like DaVinci's Vitruvian man. He opens his mouth to scream but his mouth inflates like a balloon. He feels his chest expanding, his legs get smaller, his fingers breaking off. This is the end of him. He won't survive this. He closes his eyes and prepares to die.

Hands over his face, gasping for breath, Theo realizes his body has stopped moving. His heart is thundering in his chest and adrenaline charging through his whole body. His skin prickles from the fall, burning from exposure to the elements. He feels stiff and tight all over and is covered in a greasy sweat.

Breathing deeply, he begins to hear something. Slowly, and very fearfully, he lowers his hands to see he's in the passenger seat of a car. And seated in the driver's seat is the girl in red.

She's not in red now but there is no mistaking her Light. The feeling of her aura is all around him and is so much more intense than it was when he was above. For a second, he experiences euphoria. He did it. He's here. He has his own charge. Level one is an animal, level two is a baby, so the lowest level he could possibly be is level three. Veddie will have no choice but to promote him. He'll finally be above the level of the rest of the first years. And he'll be more equal with the rest of Veddie's students. But his moment of euphoria ends when he realizes he's naked, his robes lost in descention. He gasps, folding his hands over his lap, glancing nervously over at the girl.

It's very real. She is right beside him and yet is completely unaware of his presence. Her Light is an orb encircling them, just wide enough to illuminate the inside of the car and a foot or two past its interior. He can't see where she sees, not the horizon, or the lines on the highway, or any of the traffic she must be driving through. It's like being on a rollercoaster with only six feet of vision in all directions. A car passes on his side and the tail lights gale past him. He can even feel the pressure of the wind rushing past the car but he can see nothing past the Darkness.

Swallowing hard, he returns his attention inwards. He knows nothing about her, not even her name. He can't believe how real this is. He can feel the dash under his fingers, the seam of the seat pressed into his back, the leather cold against his calves. Like his teachers explained, the seat isn't soft, it's hard and ungiving like a stone park bench. Everything has the consistency of rock but still retains its original form. And he's no ghostly spirit hovering around her. He can feel the softness of his thighs as he cups his hands over his lap, feel his pulse racing inside his chest, even a nervous sweat running down his back.

He blushes, glancing over at her again. He's seated right beside her completely nude. Is this how he'll return to the Field? He'll have some explaining to do if he does. No one ever said 'hold on to your robes' during descention. Seems like it might be important information. He'll have to leave immediately, ascend at the first sign of water. He can't walk around like this. Well, he could. No one can see him but he just wouldn't be comfortable doing it. And he's done what he's come here to do. He's made this charge his own, established himself as a real guardian ready to begin some actual work.

He presses back in the seat as she suddenly accelerates. The roar of the engine shakes his thighs and sends little shivers up his spine. What if the car crashes? What if she dies and her Light goes out while he's here? How can they find him if they don't even know he descended? He should've thought this through better. Veddie will be so angry. What if they banish him? Can they do that?

He can't worry for long because the girl takes another corner and everything in the car shifts over to his side. He grabs for the dash as a water bottle breaks open across his feet. Water fractures across his toes like hundreds of tiny marbles. He cries out, hearing the squealing of the tires and smells the rubber left behind on the road. His heart is racing so fast. He never thought it would be this way. In the classroom it seemed so different, so clean, so idyllic. This is dirty. This is gritty. This is real.

The girl pushes the gas pedal to the floor and Theo can feel gravity pressing against his chest, his wings crushed against the stone seat. He returns his hands in his lap and looks over at her. She seems unruly, distracted, looking off to the side or over at him for long periods of time. He squirms when her eyes are on him, just empty pools in the dark car. It's thrilling like Azrael, that feeling of being completely under a woman's control. Who is the girl forgotten in the reeds? Why would the guardians leave her soul in such horrible company with the abusive old man and the woman in diapers? To look at her now, to be inside her Light, she seems brilliant.

She suddenly slams her foot on the brakes. Theo thrusts his hands forward to keep himself from hitting the dash. The car screeches to a stop, stationary but still running. Beyond her Light, he can see nothing. And there's something queer about the edges of her Light, it seems to be humming, wavering in and out like it has a life of its own.

"Fuck!" she cries. She opens the car door and takes off running, the driver's door yawning open. Theo watches her leave, momentarily stunned. And then he sees the Darkness coming. A black tidal wave rolls towards him, devouring everything in its path. It is a swirling leviathan consuming both land and sky, pulling down stars and trees into an endless dark abyss. It comes for him on the heels of a hundred thousand screams. It cracks the passenger mirror before Theo finally launches himself out the other side of the car and takes off in the direction the girl left. She's jumping a fence and is moving fast. Theo races after her. The Blackness crushes everything behind him in pursuit of his very soul. And with it comes an all-encompassing panic like he's never known before.

The girl is moving fast. He pumps his legs after her, a sweat breaking down his back. His nose is running, his eyes welling up, and now he knows he's in more trouble than he ever could have ever imagined. He turns down an alley and jumps over a dumpster, never looking back. He can't look back or else the Black will swallow him whole. He can hear footsteps everywhere and police sirens wailing in the distance. The girl cuts through the woods and into new shadows. Now the path is unlit and he can't tell the black of night from the Black in pursuit. His panic levels peak. He runs harder and faster than he has ever ran in his life, merges with the girl like tandem runners, penance for an impatient and foolish guardian. He thought Ryder was being colorful, that his descriptions were exaggerated but now he knows if he loses her, he will become lost forever. Not just lost, but succumbed, consumed.

They go through a park, down another street and then on and on. Theo gasps behind her, stumbling and tripping, feeling the limitations of his body, surprised he still has limitations. His wings are actually holding him back, heavy, lumbering, catching on ungiving tree branches and thorny fences. He is painfully aware of his genitals, unrestrained and jangling gleefully like half inflated party balloons.

Finally, the girl slows and begins to walk. Theo remains closely behind, the stench of his sweat mixed with hers. She walks a short ways on a dirt road. She turns at an approach and he hears a gate screech open. Now they are walking through a path in a grassy junkyard. He sees traces of things in the distance, metal hands reaching up to the sky, fabric rippling in the wind, and twisted machines meant for sinister things. He keeps close behind her, her Light still indistinguishable from the night. The long blades of grass scratch at him like steel spikes. His footsteps make no sound. She opens a door, hinges weeping in protest, and then they are inside a building. It is completely dark and he trips and falls trying to keep up with her, stumbling over unseen obstacles in his path.

Finally, she lights a candle and sets it on an old wood table. Theo can see no more than the table and chairs around it. The table is cluttered; the chairs from many different pairs. She sits now, her breath not nearly as ragged as his, dark wavy hair falling nearly to her breasts, her large hazel eyes framed in thick black lashes and her soft pink lips slightly ajar.

The girl opens her purse and turns it over, carefully spreading its contents on the cluttered table. He notices that her knuckles are bruised and swollen. She has scars on her arms, some old and some new. Her fingernails are ragged and uncut. Her forehead comes together in a hard line between her brows.

"Jackpot," she whispers, taking out a roll of cash. She places it aside and then takes out a credit card and snaps it on the table in front of her. He can see the card between them. The name on the card is Stacey. Somehow he thinks neither that name nor this purse belongs to her.

After rummaging through the purse, she puts her head down on the table and rests. Theo remains impatiently perched nearby unable to think of anything but escape. In the classroom, this all seemed pretty black and white. Come down to earth, hang out in your charge's aura, pray and meditated to help them in their healing process, then tap into some water and he's back above. He can't imagine praying right now or being able to concentrate on anything at all. He's so worried she might get up and leave and he won't be prepared. In fact none of the things he learned in the classroom seem practical in this situation. Descend through a pool. Ascend through water. But where's water? What if she lives in the desert or something? He doesn't have any sense of where he is except that he's inside a building. And since this charge wasn't assigned to him, he doesn't have any background information on her. He shudders, rubbing his bare arms. He never should have disobeyed.

A knock on the door brings both their heads up.

"Who is it?" the girl says. Her voice is lovely. It matches her beautiful hair, her wonderful lips. He's surprised at his attraction to her. He's never been attracted to anyone before.

"It's Bea, dumbass, let me in," he hears another girl call, her voice muffled.

The girl looks tired. She closes her eyes and returns her head to the table with a sigh. "Do I have to?"

"Come on, you bitch! Open this door!"

Strange, he can hear things outside the Light, but he can't see them. The sound is directional as well; he knows which way the voice is coming from.

"Just hold on." The girl rises and Theo backs a few steps away. He watches as she gathers up the purse and all the items on the table. He follows her off into another dark room. She opens a closet and shoves the purse on the top shelf, puts a shirt over top of it and then closes the door.

She returns to the main room and clicks on the light. Theo doesn't even see the visitor enter the door because he's so shocked when electricity illuminates the seriousness of her situation. "My god," he whispers, lifting his feet and staring down at the stained carpet. The floor is littered with laundry and muddy shoes, used paper towels and empty soup cans. He's in one of two rooms that look to be part of a house barely the size of a single car garage. A naked light bulb hangs from the ceiling of both rooms, the kitchen and living room separated by a half wall. The kitchen is a galley, apartment style, a walk through, assuming you could walk through it. Forgetting about the girls, Theo turns into the kitchen. The stove has the coil burners and the traps are filled with black, burned crusts. On top is a pot that looks like it's been rusted there for the better part of the century. He touches the old pan, tries to lift it but it's as if the two are fused together, the pot as heavy as the stove and no less mobile. There's a spoon beside the stove. He tries to move it with the same results.

He turns and he sees a sink full of soiled dishes left soaking in stagnant water. A moat of deflated orange bubbles circles the perimeter of the sink and there's something parasitic scuba diving in the murky water. The counter top is buried beneath open cereal boxes, empty egg cartons, and even a pile of broken glass. The floor isn't much better, an obstacle path of discarded items he has to negotiate around to get to the next room.

He turns the corner and trips on an empty plastic bag. He crashes to the floor harder than he can believe and then turns to see the crinkly plastic bag, its empty mouth yawning open as if laughing at him. He leans forward and touches the flimsy container. Like cement, even the smallest and lightest thing cannot be moved by him. It's astounding. And so is what he sees when he stands up and enters the room where two brunettes lounge across an uneven couch. Bea, the girl from the door, is Asian and about the same age as his charge. The couch they sit on has no particular color or style and is obviously missing the legs on the right side. The couch looks like it has spent the better part of its life outdoors. There is one cracked window in the living room and a console TV with knobs. And junk everywhere. Dishes stacked behind the couch. A pail sitting in the center of the room. And all sorts of things that should have seen the inside of a dumpster bin a long time ago. He's afraid to touch anything, even though logically he knows he can't catch a disease.

Theo looks at her again, like he's seeing her for the first time, this girl in red, nesting in her own filth. He can't see the beautiful side anymore. It's tainted now. He thinks of the woman in diapers and the man in his garbage. That's why she was with them. Because of this. This girl is filthy. No one with any self-respect could live like this. She's a thief and who knows what else. He thinks about the car and the rapid escape that followed, now certain that the vehicle must have been stolen.

"So what were you up to tonight?" Bea asks.

Theo turns his attention on them again, feeling like a pervert standing naked in the room. He moves behind one of the chairs feeling more secure with something in front of him.

"Nothing," the girl says. "What about you?"

"Usual stuff," Bea replies. She's thin and tall with straight black hair and large round glasses. She looks better off than the girl in red, at least she's dressed better. "Mom wants me at the restaurant more. I hate that old Sashimi hole. Everything I own stinks of fish as it is."

While the girls talk, his charge's Light becomes larger. Theo sees a hallway emerge down towards a bathroom. Water. He stands for just a moment, heart racing. If he ascends now, he could be back before Veddie even knows he was gone. That might even give him a few days to prepare his defense before the truth is found out. And now that he's been here, even for just for an hour, he can see how much he still needs to learn before he can care for his charge.

He follows the hallway, glancing at a bedroom devoid of all furniture except for a mattress on the floor under a medium sized window and a towel for a curtain. His attention quickly turns to the bathroom. The light is off but he can see a simple tub, toilet, and sink illuminated from the hallway light. The lid from the toilet tank is missing. The bath has a thick greasy ring around it with a few streaky finger marks down the side. The sink counter is cluttered with a forest of items from toothpaste to muscle rub, to pain pills and sanitary napkins. "Gross," he whispers.

He reaches for the sink taps and then thinks again. There won't be any water coming from the faucet unless the girl turns it on herself. Somewhat begrudgingly, he goes to the toilet. Beggars can't be choosers and if he has to ascend through toilet water, he will. But as he reaches the basin, he finds it void of any water, the same greasy ring around it that the tub has.

"Shit," he grumbles. He stands for a moment, paralyzed. No water in the toilet? What does he do now? He slowly exits the bathroom and returns to the hallway. There, he sees another closet yawning open, the clothes rack broken and tipped diagonally between the walls. There are parts of a broken shelf in there, a window blind stained with something that smells like peanut butter, and a pile of sopping wet towels sitting in a musty puddle. He grimaces, backing away and returning to the living room.

"So I have some news!!" Bea declares, clapping her hands together. "I've been asked to the prom."

"The prom?" the girl exclaims. "That freak show?"

"Don't you know it? I can hardly believe it myself. Did you think in a million years that either one of us would be going to the prom?"

"No, I didn't," the girl replies darkly.

"It's that new Arab guy. I think he's Arab, kind of brownish anyway. And he's pretty cute. He just came out and asked me. He said he liked me for a long time."

"And you want to go?" the girl asks.

"Yeah, I guess. I mean," Bea grimaces, "I don't want to be the only girl in town without a date."

The girl nods but her Light pulls in a little. Bea's phone rings. She answers and argues with the caller. She clicks the phone off with a whispered swear and says, "Mom wants me home now. Guess I better go."

"She afraid you'll get fleas or something here?" the girl snickers and Theo raises his eyebrows.

"Something like that. See you tomorrow? Maybe I'll scoop you up a date too."

"No, I've already got a date."

"What?" Bea turns on her heel. "You bitch, why didn't you say something. Who is it? Romeo?"

"Romeo?" she scoffs. "Are you kidding? I'm going with my shotgun. We've had this date planned for years."

Theo's mouth drops open but Bea only giggles. "Cool. Aim above my head, okay? We can go all Columbine on their asses. Just don't shoot Stacey in the boob while I'm near. I don't want to die from silicone shrapnel."

"You'll be the last one standing," his charge sings. "See you later."

"Okay, bye, Angel."

Angel? Theo looks over at her. Her name is Angel.

As soon as Bea leaves the porch, Angel snaps off the light plunging the two of them into absolute darkness. "Fucking prom," she whispers. She turns suddenly and walks towards Theo. He stumbles back and trips over the grocery bag again. Angel steps over him and goes to the picture window. She stands there, her hands in her pockets. Headlights sweep across her face and it's dark again. Theo stares in silence, feeling uneasy about intruding on her intimate moment. He supposes this will be the first of many he will be privy to.

Angel thumps her fist on the window and turns abruptly towards him. Theo pushes out of her way again even though he probably doesn't need to. Twenty-five years of mortal habit he supposes. He reluctantly follows her as she makes her way back to the bedroom, turns on a lamp and kicks her pillow on the bed. The mattress is obviously worn, has no sheets or order to the layers, no up or down, just a nest of twisted quilts, pillows, and laundry. Theo keeps to the perimeter as she paces, feeling very exposed in the lamp light. She scares him. A lot. With her sudden movements and erratic behavior, she is someone he would've stayed away from in life. Ironic, really, that out of all the pools he could've 'fallen' in, he decided to pick this one. He experiences a moment of anger. Not just at his stupidity but at this entire situation. This is his retirement from a short but heartfelt life of servitude? To be ridiculed and held back on the Reserve by his peers? To live in squallier down below with a dirty charge? He wishes he could just leave right now, escape through water and be back in the Field before daybreak. But there is no means for escape. At least for tonight, he's trapped.

Angel finally slows down. She goes to the corner of the room, turns up the carpet and lifts a floorboard. She pulls out a large journal, a white notebook, and a stack of papers. Retiring to the bed she spreads them around and takes out a pen. She lays on her stomach and begins to write in the journal. While she is still, Theo surveys the room. He spots a towel crumpled in the corner. Even if he had a towel to put around his waist he might be able to think clearer. He was never fond of nudity in real life, never spent any significant time naked, never even took a good look at his naked body in the mirror. He finds this situation incredibly uncomfortable and all he can think of is finding cover. But the towel, like everything else, is unattainable to him, like the marble folds of a Renaissance statue. There's nothing he can do physically in this world and it's more frustrating than he would've imagined. He sees the window across from him, reflecting everything in the room except for himself and experiences a moment of grief. He's dead. He's really dead. Not a part of this world anymore. And somewhere, out there, his body is six feet under, rotting beneath the ground. His family and friends are going on without him. His life is over. He looks down at Angel, scratching her pen across the paper. He turns back with a sigh. This is so much harder than he would've ever guessed.

Angel continues to write. She seems so peaceful and quiet now, deeply concentrating on her project. Why is she here in this place all alone? Where are her parents? Why is she living this way? He experiences a moment of sympathy for her. Is he really going to give up on this girl so easily? He hasn't even been here for two hours and he's already running away. This is what he wanted, isn't it? A challenge? What is Veddie going to say if he returns with nothing accomplished? Maybe he needs to stay longer and prove that he is worthy of this assignment. But then he sees the girl in her mess and wishes he'd never descended at all, wishes he were in his bed like the other newbie's safe in the clean confines of the dorm.

He notices the corner where the carpet is still turned up. One floorboard is set aside. He goes over and he sees a lot of things hidden beneath the baseboards. A radio, credit cards and stacks of CD's. Is this her stash? Where she hides all her the stuff she steals? With a sigh, he looks up at the window and his missing reflection. He's made a huge mistake.

Angel eventually falls asleep with papers strewn all around her. It looks like a literary crime scene, a creative maelstrom swept through and left her for dead. But it's just her and her mess of a life. Theo passes by the bed as he paces the room. Verses, prose, and poetry are strewn around like stepping stones. And they're hard like stepping stones too. He can walk right across them without causing a single wrinkle. He wonders if he should look and see what she's writing. It seems wrong but isn't that what he's here for? To find out who she is? To try and find ways to help her? If he had done this properly, he would've gotten her Book of Life, he would've known what her problems were already. But he doesn't know anything. It is something he had not considered when he entered the Field. Now he will need to find out about her in another way. At least until he gets back to the Reserve and reads up on her. He crouches down by the nearest sheet. It has a drawing, a sketch of a boy in blue pen. Beneath it in muddy script are the words:

For all the ones that I involved
And for Ambrose most of all
Forgive me
This time I decided to feed the monster.

He pulls back, looking at her. Who is Ambrose? And why does she need to be forgiven? And for what? Now more concerned, he crouches by the next sheet and reads another entry.

April the 17th,
Just seven months ago I was sitting across from one of the greatest guys I've ever met and I didn't even know it. I never expected this. I never expected him. Oh, I feel it coming on me. The fantasy that is my life. The rumors I write to keep myself alive. He's taken. In decency, I can't have him. I won't have him. Except inside my head and in between these pages. Then I'll have him all I want. He's going for a ride with me. For as long as that ride lasts, I suppose. Oh, the things we're going to do.

Oh obsession. Oh, how I obsess. He is on my mind today and there is no escape. I am a willing captive. My mind is a raging fantasy world and all I need are characters to fill the roles. And he is a character, therefore summoned into the fantasy. My imagination is a wild and untamed thing. It cannot be controlled. In denial and fantasy, all my dreams are possible. I want him. I want him. Like no one else. My obsession. Mine. And no one can take that away from me.

Theo runs his fingers over the words. She is in love with someone named Ambrose. He moves to the next sheet now curious to learn more. He finds a shopping list: lamp, curtains, pillows, topics of little interest. Then he sees another sketch partially obscured by an upside-down text book. It's a man with his hands over his head, and whatever is happening beneath that text book, he appears to be pretty pleased about it. Theo backs off from the sketch and spots a poem, visible only in pieces. The top half says:

Opening the door with a wrinkled wink
In their coffee-stained bathrobes
Clinging to a lipstick cigarette
They watch while you rummage through their busy basements
A lipstick cigarette
Burning down between bulging blue-veined fingertips

The latter half says:

This finish line is elusive
This one just dangles
Electricity with no circuit is all sparks
And I am Jacob's ladder.

Feeling weary, Theo retreats back to the safety of his corner. He is in way over his head with this girl, this woman in red. What he needs to do is focus on escape. Then get her information when he's back on the Reserve and deal with any punishment Veddie chooses to hand down on him. Then, he supposes, he'll need to decide what to do from there.

Near dawn, Theo jerks awake. The sun must be rising because the light in Angel's aura is beginning to brighten. The proximity of her Light is unnerving. Suddenly he longs for the expansive Light of a nice uncomplicated puppy. Something he can stroll around in. Breathe in. This morning, he feels older and more tired than he ever has, dead or alive.

Angel sleeps with her head where her feet were. She is a disheveled mess. Theo rubs his eyes, trying not to look at her. Her shirt has slipped off her shoulder and one of her hands is tucked inside it. Her hair is spread madly about the bed and her waking moans and mumblings are making him blush. He tries to pray, tries to keep his eyes away from her peeping pink flesh. But when he lowers his head, he sees himself dangling out like the tongue of a thirsty dog. It's obscene to have all his stuff out for the whole world to see. Even though rationally he knows the world can't actually see him.

Angel turns on her side and her shirt yawns open. Theo's eyes widen as he sees the swells between her breasts and her slowly rising stomach. He swallows hard and closes his eyes against the rising tide of his late blooming manhood. Why is this happening now? For his entire life he was nothing but focused. Why is it in death that he finds himself losing control?

Theo wakes up a second time and he's alone. He's sitting against the wall, holding his knees against his chest. Darkness is nipping at the edges of his toes. He crawls up the wall and scurries out of the room and runs into Angel leaving the bathroom. She's naked, her hands up over her head as she pins her hair back. Theo's eyes dash to her breasts, her belly button, the swell of her stomach, and quickly back up to her lips. They're face to face, his body facing hers, all their parts perfectly matched up. He pulls back as she passes him but can't help look back at the dimples above her rounded rump and sweep of dark hair brushing over her shoulders. Something more than dirty thoughts begin to rise and Theo rushes into the bathroom. He needs water. He needs escape. He's not equipped to deal with this. But when he gets inside, he remembers the inaccessible taps and the dry toilet. How he scoffed when the commode was suggested as escape. He thought: *as if I would ever do that*. Now he thinks, lid open, he would dive in head first.

Chapter 7 ∞

School. Theo cringes as they pass through the glass double doors of Angel's high school. It's like all his nightmares combined as he enters the hallowed halls of teenage angst completely in the nude. He had no choice but to follow Angel or else stay behind in the Darkness and wait for her to return. And he's not even sure that the place she stayed in last night was her home. Or what that was.

He loved school when he was alive. It was his home away from home. The pursuit of education was his whole reason for living. Pristine classrooms, stiff wooden seats, hushed libraries and lively coffee houses, long shiny hallways with groups of smartly dressed students, teachers scurrying about with personal computers and trusty clipboards. School bells and blackboards and art rooms and science labs. There was nothing he enjoyed more but now he darts as quickly as Angel does, feeling edgy and embarrassed at every glance that seems to linger too long. All these clothed people, safely secured in their pressed shirts and buttoned up jeans. What he wouldn't do for a pair of pants right now. A skirt, a loin cloth, even a thong would give him more comfort than this brazen nudity. He feels like a streaker, a pervert, a creep. He cringes as students brush against him, rushing to their first classes. He's all shrunken and pulled in, every part of him looking for a place to hide.

He glances at Angel. She's so obviously disturbed, dressed like a rag doll, her shoulders turned in, her hair unwashed. He seen these kinds before, scampering here and there, books clung to their chests, eyes digging into the floor. He'd never given them a first thought, never mind a second. He didn't even consider that there might be something wrong with them. He never really considered them at all.

"Hey, it's the shack rat," he hears someone call. Theo glances back but the slander is lost in the Darkness. Angel doesn't react at all, just keeps moving forward. At her locker, she finds her combination lock on backwards. She flips it up and opens the lock upside-down as if she's done it dozens of times before. Theo crouches beside her, trying his best to keep himself covered. A girl looks over at him and laughs. He knows she can't see him but he cringes all the same. Look at the naked guy in school. Weirdo. Peeper.

He takes a deep, shaky breath, possibly the first one taken since he descended last night. Was it only last night? It seems like an eternity ago. He's only been missing for a day, not even a day, maybe ten hours. How long will it take for someone to notice his absence? He wanted to return before Veddie found out where he was. Then he would have some time to prepare his defense. The longer he stays, though, the more likely his improprieties will be discovered beforehand.

A hand slams against the locker near Theo's head. A group of boys move in around Angel like buzzards around a desert kill. They're all dressed to the nines in tight jeans, snake-skin boots and shiny belt buckles. There were a lot of trucks in the parking lot. The volleyball team is called Longhorns. And Theo's seen more than his share of cowboy hats pass through the hall this morning, so he's probably somewhere redneck, rural. If only Angel would loitered beside a street sign or a phone directory, he might get a better sense of where he is. Not that it matters. He's not really here; the location of his charge is irrelevant. Yet the urge to orient himself is overwhelming. He wants to know what time it is, what day, what month, what school, what street. He has to keep reminding himself that this stuff isn't important anymore.

"Hey Angel," one of the boys says. "How're you doing, kid?"

Angel remains quiet, her head down.

A couple boys around him chuckle and call him Romeo. This Romeo is largest of the group, a big brute of a boy. He has thick black hair and wears a bomber jacket. The boy next to him is wearing a rodeo shirt. Romeo lifts the rim of his baseball cap and says, "I know you're hungry and all, little girl. I've got something for you to eat. But you have to get on your knees to get it."

Around him, Romeo's posse chuckles.

"Come on, I'll give you a cool hundred bucks, Angel. I know you need it. I don't pay all my whores, Angel, just you."

Angel doesn't answer him and pretends to be interested in something on the floor. Although she appears quiet and unaffected outwardly, inside her Light is burning. Theo can't make out specific emotions yet but he can feel the sickly tightness surrounding him. And the Light has pulled in very close. Now there is only him, Romeo, and Angel inside it. The other boys are no longer visible.

Romeo leans down next to Angel's ear and whispers, "I'd like to taste your filth."

Feeling his temper growing, Theo thumps Romeo in the chest. Or tries to. His hand recoils, his fingers wringing, wrist throbbing like he punched the side of a building. And now the other boys have moved close enough to enter her Light. Farm boys press up as close to him as they are to her. His worries for her start to wane as his own concerns mount. They're too close to all his exposed parts, denim rubbing against him, calloused cow hands grazing his naked skin.

"I have something warm for you," Romeo hums and laughter ensues. "Do you want to see it? I can show you right now."

His boys chuckle and Romeo reaches down for his belt.

"Boys?" A voice calls from outside Angel's Light. "Time for class, boys."

Romeo turns and nods at the person, perhaps a teacher or principle. Theo cannot see who Romeo is talking to. Then the boys all chuckle and leave.

Theo remains pressed up against the lockers long after the boys are gone. He was never bullied in school. He never realized how frightening it actually could be. He was so scared for himself while it was happening, so ashamed of his nudity, so appalled to have another man so close to his naked body. He was concerned about Angel at first but then his own fears paralyzed him in the end. And even when he tried to defend her, his attack was futile. *Angelic power in the material world is exerted through the will.* It makes more sense now than it ever did. He has no effect on the physical world around him but how can he defend Angel with his will alone?

Theo stands behind Angel's desk, his back to the wall. He challenges every eye on him that seems to rest too long. Crazy thoughts go through his head. Like maybe this is all a game, some sort of cosmic joke to make Theodore Duncan lose his marbles. Maybe everyone is in on it except for him. Maybe he's actually standing naked in school and everyone really can see him. Look at Theo lurking naked in school full of under-aged girls. Hunched slightly forward, he clasps his hands over his crotch and prays they will be near water soon.

In the radius of Angel's Light, he can see a few people around her. And from what he's seen so far, it's not exactly a diverse community she's living in. In fact Bea is the only person of any ethnicity that he's seen so far. The rest of the students are of the meat and potatoes sort. Country themes continue in the classroom. Theo notices posters on the walls feature weed control and tractor sales. Also nearby, an announcement for the prom for the end of July. So Angel is eighteen and close to graduating. It's the first real tidbit of information he's managed to collect on her.

"I had this crazy dream last night. It was so real," Angel whispers over her shoulder at Bea.

"About Ambrose?" Bea pipes in eagerly.

Again, Theo wonders about Ambrose, the one that appeared so frequently in her writing last night. Who is he? Is he a student here? A teacher? He sees no indication of anyone in her life other than Bea. Angel has talked to no one since Bea left last night. He hasn't heard the phone ring and Angel has remained silent throughout the day, even though she is surrounded by people.

"No. Not really. I dreamt there was this guy in my room."

Theo focuses back on the conversation, suddenly riveted. Does she mean him? But she can't see him, can she? He skims over the few people visible in Angel's small aura suddenly certain they all know he's here. Why didn't he just hold on tighter to his robes? His nudity is making the situation so much worse than it needs to be.

"Are you sure it wasn't Romeo? Fucking stalker. Probably peaking in your windows and jerking himself off."

"Yeah, probably. I wouldn't doubt it," Angel snorts.

"He's such a shit," Bea finishes. The conversation ends as the teacher enters the room but Theo's mind continues to race. She couldn't have meant him. He is not real. And a charge cannot see their guardian. That's impossible. They are not in the same worlds.

High school, so much different than university, with the clicks, the rivalries, and the petty animosities. And those things are escalated in a small community where there's no room for diversity. It's less about education and more about social order. Bullying is not what he imagined it would be. Angel is not openly or physically attacked, it's more of a quiet exclusion with sly cuts along the way. Other than Romeo, most people just turn their backs to her, pretend she's not there or that she doesn't even exist. And some just don't see her at all. It makes him feel guilty. He would have been counted himself among the not seeing, among the oblivious and self-centered. He would've never considered himself to be this way before coming here.

The class starts to shuffle around for a group assignment. Theo is forced to duck and dash as students screech desks into a new order. Now separated from her only peer, Angel focuses intently down on her books. She's in a group with three girls and one guy. The girls are mostly blond, big country hair, full blooming breasts, and a full coat of makeup. The boy is blond as well, a meaty country kid with a shaved head and a sunburned face. He wears a ball cap and his sleeves are rolled up past his elbows. Everyone in the group seems to be acquainted except Angel.

Oh my goodness, oh my goodness, the one girl keeps saying. She has a tiny cross around her neck and breasts like mountains where the small trinket is wedged between. She's obviously from money; Theo's from money and he knows all the signs. Her clothes are expensive and her purse is likely worth more than the stuff inside it. All the kids have smart phones and iPods, tablets and notebooks spread across their desks. Angel is the only one with just a binder and a pen.

"My daddy just bought the Vernon's place," the girl, who Theo now regards as Breasts, says.

"What's that, the five hundred acres?" the boy replies lazily. He's so blonde he's almost transparent. He has no visible eyebrows and his face is covered in carrot red freckles.

"Thousand," Breasts boasts. "And a cool million for the equipment to run the place. Daddy says I can tear the old farm house down and put a mansion up there after I'm done school. Course I'll hire someone for the land," she says, inspecting her nails.

"Who wants to drive a dirty old tractor? That's grunt work," another girl interjects. She's dressed in a pink jacket, her nails pink, her shoes pink. Pink, for now, Theo decides.

"Uh-huh," Breasts mumbles, her eyes an impossible blue. They must be contact lenses. Nothing on these girls appears to be authentic. "It'll be over five thousand square feet when it's done with the granite countertops and the imported hardwood floors I wanted. Oh, it seems like I've been shopping forever. Custom tile work has to be ordered. The taps cost me a thousand dollars alone. And don't forget the rainfall shower head with the LED lights in it."

"Ooh nice," Pink says. "I didn't know you were getting that."

"Of course! Now if only those stupid surveyors would hurry up. We can't break ground until those morons get finished. I'm so tired." Breasts feigns a swoon, picks up her phone and quickly texts someone. "Did you get the new truck?" she says in the direction of the boy.

"Platinum super cab. Could sleep like six inside," he replies. "Seventeen inch DVD and these fucking kick ass speakers in the back. Sweet ass."

"Did you guys hear about the Kicking Horse Saloon last night?" Pink says, suddenly animated. "Little Miss *Lohan* got picked up for a DUI again."

Angel drops her pen and everyone looks over at her. The mood in the group has suddenly changed. Theo can sense it but doesn't know what happened. Angel's Light pulls in around her, barely leaving him room to stand inside. He's forced to push up against the back of her seat, his head over her shoulder. He can no longer see any of the other kids, just hear them.

"I mean what's she thinking? Driving around drunk? She's gonna get someone killed," Breasts says.

"Right, hey? I mean at least I know my limits," the boy says.

"What kind of a fucking idiot gets behind the wheel that drunk? And everyone knows the cops are waiting outside," Pink says.

"Fucking cops," the boys grumbles. "They're never around when you need them. When there's something important worth investigating."

Theo frowns at the odd conversation. Bunch of redneck kids protesting drunk driving? The exchange seems forced, almost staged. And something is wrong with Angel. She is barely breathing, her body wound like a tight little spring. Her Light has become sickly yellow. He can smell the sweat running down her back, taste the salty anxiety in her aura. Their bond is growing quickly. He can feel the sway of her emotions now; it is already becoming more distinctive.

"How's the assignment progressing?" a teacher asks, passing by.

Angel glances to the side and her Light expands a little. The teacher taps her on the shoulder as he passes, discreetly so that no one else notices. It's enough to bring her back from whatever hell she'd stumbled into. Her Light expands out a little bit, enough for Theo to back up a step or two.

The girls all look up at the teacher with innocent eyes. *Very good*, they say, displaying their perfectly bleached smiles. And then they begin to work on the assignment they've gathered together for.

Later, after class, Bea catches up with Angel, bumping her shoulder purposely as she passes. "That was a ghoulish," she says. "I got caged up with Romeo *and* Stacey."

"Yikes," Angel says, though her tone remains bland, her Light tarnished. Theo's not sure what happened. Was it the kids at her table? Or was there someone else in the room that he couldn't see? He wishes he knew more about her situation. Going in blind has made this so much more difficult.

"Yeah, Romeo gets a text halfway through and Boobs McNastybitch tells Stacey that her group would be perfect if you weren't in it. Fucking cow, hey? She texted that right in front of you."

"She did?" Angel says, visibly hurt.

"Yuh, Stacey read it out in the group like I wasn't even there. She's such a nasty little cunt-muffin."

The day drags on at much the same pace. Except for Bea, Angel talks to no one and is approached by no one in return. The isolation is cruelly ironic in a school teaming over with students while this girl, obviously troubled, is left to wither in isolation. At lunch, down a long empty hall in the science wing smelling of formaldehyde and frog parts, Angel sits down at a bench beside a window that faces the brick wall of the next building. It's lunch but she isn't eating. In fact he hasn't seen her eat since he arrived yesterday. Is she anorexic? He can hear the hungry rumble of her stomach and can almost feel her parched mouth.

"Maybe you should go eat." Theo sits at the opposite side of the bench from her, wincing at the cold slats press up against his bare bottom. He never expected to be so worried about himself during descention. There is real fear and anxiety that he has to deal with on top of Angel's problems. She is his charge now until he finds some way to turn her life around. And she's troubled in ways that will take him years to work out. He stares across at the girl and tries to remember that feeling that drew him in. Whatever it was he felt standing above the pool, he does not feel it here. He acted on a moment of weakness, his own foolish pride goading him on.

Between them, Angel has a tattered book bag. She only occupies herself with its contents when someone is passing by. Otherwise she just sits and stares out the viewless window, sighing long and hard. What else is burdening her? He knows she's a thief and a pretty advanced one if that car they were in last night was stolen. And she is living in terrible poverty but what else? Theo seems to sense that there is a lot more going on here. He's noticed the scars on her arms and wrists. She could be suicidal, not surprising considering the way she's treated. The only attention she appears to get is from bullying. Where are her parents? How'd she come to be in this isolated place? He has so many questions and no way of getting them answered.

After lunch, Theo plods after his charge as they skirt around the backside of the school and knock on an unmarked metal door. He's not sure what he likes less, naked inside or naked outside. Outside, a large shiny sun blasts away all his shadows, illuminating his every crack and crevasse. Outside, cars are driving by, planes are flying over, and students are en-mass in the quad and parking lots, a multitude of curious eyes darting in his direction. He just can't get over the discomfort of his own nudity. Is he really so self-conscious that he can't be naked in a world full of blind people?

The metal door opens and a large woman with pleasant face and an apron appears in the doorway. "Just a minute." The woman returns with a Styrofoam container full of food.

"Thank you," Angel says.

"Anytime, dear," the woman says. "You take care now."

"Thanks." Angel replies quietly.

The woman turns and standing behind her is a guardian. He's someone Theo doesn't know but a guardian all the same. Theo stares at him with great big wide eyes. He's not sure whether to hide or to ask the man for help. Before he can decide what to do, the man retreats with his charge and the moment is over. He's not sure if the guardian saw him or not. If he did, he certainly did not acknowledge the fact.

It's a long and unpleasant day at school and Theo is relieved when they finally leave. They biked here. Well, she biked and he frantically jogged behind, all his parts jogging along with him. Now when they return to the stand, they find the bike has two flat tires, obviously tampered with. Angel just sighs and pushes the bike from the stand, the squeal of the flattened wheels causing chuckles around her. Spoiled country kids leaned up against their daddy's fully loaded pickup trucks getting their kicks from watching some poor girl push her only mode of manual transportation across the parking lot. It makes Theo furious. A fistful of anger grows inside him with each set of sniggering eyes that turns in her direction. She's done nothing to deserve all this. She just keeps to herself, bothers no one and yet there is a huge target on her back. For a moment, he just wants to kill them all. The rage washes over him like a torrential rain storm. Then, just as quickly, it fades to a quiet resolve. It's pointless to get upset. He can't do anything about it anyway. And he's not here for them; he's here for her.

They walk for nearly an hour until they reach the edge of town. Theo sees little in her Light but the cracks in the sidewalk and passing mailboxes. But even from his limited view, he can tell that they're entering the poorer side of town. Wrought iron fences and custom mail slots change to dented tin boxes and unpainted wooden picket fences. Soon, the sidewalk ends and a dirt road begins. They walk for another five minutes and then they are at her gate. She pushes it open with a screech and they tromp through overgrown grasses to the saggy front porch of that horrible little house. He sees it for the first time in the light of day. The house is pale blue with faded wooden siding. The porch is bereft of all color, nearly rotted straight through in places. The whole place leans a bit to one side. He wonders how the property has not been condemned.

Angel opens the door and then they go inside. Despite how he despises this place, Theo breathes a sigh of relief when they are back. Hard to imagine a day worse than the one he had today. He thought he had stresses in his life but nothing compares to this. In fact he never appreciated how good he had it until this very moment.

Inside, he sits on the edge of the tipsy couch, his legs aching and exhausted. He hates the feel of the rough pilled fabric against his ass, the smell of the unwashed dishes, and the visual chaos in general. He needs to sleep, to rest, but where?

And how? Before he can even consider it, Angel reappears in a blue uniform, picks up some keys and heads back out the door.

"What now?" he whispers, pushing off the couch. They go back out into the yard towards a truck that must be abandoned. But then he sees the keys swinging from her fingers. "Oh, you have got to be kidding me," he whispers. To his horror, he watches as she gets into the driver's seat of some late model, stone-aged, rust bucket and turns over the engine. It starts with a horrendous screech and black smoke billows out the back end. He climbs reluctantly into the cab, the vinyl seats sticking to his back, and stares at the cracked plastic dash, the ancient cassette deck, radio dials, pull vents and roll down windows.

"Come on," Angel whispers, putting the truck in gear and backing it out on the road. "Be good to me."

They drive silently side by side. The sun is going down. He can tell only by the changing light on her face, because her Light only illuminates the two of them inside the cab and a few feet out onto the hood. Beside him, Angel sits rigidly, her eyes constantly flicking to the dials on the dash, watching as the temperature meter rises higher and higher. Not long after they leave, a wisp of smoke begins to emerge from the vents.

"Come on, you fucker, not now," she grumbles and pushes the truck faster. Theo grips the armrest, staring at the smoke entering the cab. It smells like burning wires. This isn't safe. Again, he wonders what happens to him if she dies. A naked guardian found next to his underage charge. Might put a black mark on Veddie's perfect record.

The ride seems to last forever with mounting temperatures and increasing vent smog until she finally puts the truck in park and kills the engine. The old beast hisses like a space ship that has crash landed. They both exhale a sigh of relief that the ride has ended and leave the truck together. They seem to be in a parking lot, at least there are a lot of vehicles parked around them. Then a red car, rusty and dented, enters her Light. Angel smiles and runs her hand affectionately along its side. Theo frowns at the gesture.

Her limited Light is becoming aggravating to Theo. He is completely at her command. He can go nowhere but the places she goes. He can't get away from her in the bathroom, or bedroom, or even walking down the street. And he never knows where she's going. If she turns suddenly, he has to quickly correct himself else be lost in the Dark. God, how he hates the Darkness now. It's not the quiet peaceful black of a cold winters night, it's back alley dark, it's waking nightmare dark, humming, buzzing, cutting off the edges of the world around him, threatening to devour him at every misstep.

Angel turns and Theo stumbles to keep up. She comes to a door, accesses it by a key card, and then goes inside to a crisp smelling lobby. Chairs and tables pass by, a fridge and counter, and he hears the hum of other people nearby. Angel stops at the fridge and takes a lunch clearly marked: Jim. The next thing he knows he's in the women's locker room. Angel enters the shower room and passes by a row of lockers. She checks inside each one, rifling through jacket pockets and handbags. She finds a towel and shampoo. She also takes a purse and whatever loose change she can find. *Oh, Angel*, Theo sighs, now feeling more sorry for her than ever. This isn't about crime; this is about desperation. She has no food, no money. She's stealing just to keep herself alive. He never realized money could be so much of an obstacle. If food got low at home, they just went out and got more. If he ran out of money, he went to the ATM. Money was always there. He was never lacking anything. He never even considered what lacking would be like. Or that it would be as bad as this.

Angel enters one of the shower stalls, pulls the curtain closed and rummages through the purse. Like the night before, she takes cash and credit cards. She happily folds the paper money into her pocket without a pang of guilt. Then she sits on the stall bench and savors every bite of Jim's ham sandwich. Afterwards, she curls up on the tiny bench and naps for almost an hour. Theo sits on the shower floor and tries to rest too. His head is spinning. He can't even believe it's only been twenty-four hours since he came here. Time seems agonizingly slow. Do they know what he's done yet? Can they rescue him if he's unable to escape? Maybe they'll leave him here as punishment for his prideful disobedience. Without water or some sort of portal, he'll be stuck in this hellish existence forever.

The shower suddenly starts. Theo scrambles up against the side of the stall as water rains down. Angel steps inside. He was so lost in his own worries that he didn't even notice her wake and undress. Now she is directly in front of him, naked and wet. He jerks back and squeezes his eyes shut but she keeps brushing against him as she turns beneath the water. Her skin is hard and cold like all other objects he's contacted, but it does little to stave off his growing arousal. The water that rains off her body ricochets against him in hard little pellets. Like a shower of Nerds, he thinks madly. He feels the swell of her thigh and a whisper of her breast and it's making him more aware of every hair, every nerve, every exposed plane on his body. Worse yet are the soft sighs and mews from his oblivious invader. He sucks in his breath and pulls back tighter against the wall as if the mere deflation of his lungs will make his body more slender. He pinches his eyes painfully closed and keeps his hands in arrest against the sides of the shower wall. Don't look, he thinks, don't look. He died a virgin, twenty five years old; he never laid his hands on a naked women or himself for that matter. He never had the slightest sexual yearning. At least not until he took his vow of chastity in Heaven. Now, reluctantly aroused, he can't help but slip an eyelid open. And when he does, the other eye opens right after. Angel is in a state of absolute bliss, her eyes fluttered shut, her mouth slightly open, her hands up and cupping the water as it rains down. Theo swallows hard, his eyes following the rivers of water as they swirl around her breasts and drip like honey off their hardened tips. His eyes go down further, to the hollow of her waist, the hump of her hip bones, and to the folded intersection veiled in shadow below. Up his eyes return to her dimpled bellybutton, to the firm voluptuous swells of her breasts, to her plump open mouth and then up, up to the overhead shower and the rain coming down. He gasps staring upward at the rigid spray, feeling a pinprick of arousal deep inside his hips, an ignition point, the pilot light suddenly coming alive. The fire spreads swiftly, hurried, creating tension in his thighs, a tightening of his fists, and a thickening of his tongue. His cock inflates, the pressure mounting to the point of unbearable discomfort. He closes his eyes again, shuddering. Not this, not now. Please, make this stop. Someone find me, someone save me, someone get me out of here. He takes long, deep breaths, fists in angry dispute but he can't pull his creature back in. Turning his head to the side, he releases despite his reservations, expels in the shower down the side of her leg.

The water goes off and Angel steps into a towel with a satisfied sigh. Theo remains in the corner of the shower, shaking, his face flushed red and hot. He just came. On his charge. He feels sick, like he might pass out. He keeps his eyes away from her, like refusal to see her might assist in his denial. He can't believe what he just did. Could there be a worse crime to commit with his charge?

Angel dresses back in her uniform and returns the purse to its locker. Then she leaves the room. Theo follows, disgustingly aware of his body now. Sick, that's what he is, sick. And the worst part is that he can't even hide his shame. His cock is still out, raw and red. Blood still pumping riotously through its veins. Cupping his hands over it only stimulates the excited skin. For the millionth time, he curses himself for losing his robes during descention. He could've tried harder to hold on to them, cinched the belt or grabbed onto a slipping sleeve. Now he is in exile in the nude. He can't think of a worse possible fate.

He glances up as they pass through a crowd of men. He sees them watching her, their lips smacking like hungry wolves. Their dirty little creatures filling up with blood. He forces the shower out of his mind. Maybe it didn't happen at all. Maybe it's just a part of this horrible dream that has become his reality. He folds his arms tightly over his chest, matching Angel's hunched stance and quick pace. Why now? Why her? Whatever it is, he needs escape and fast. He keeps thinking about that guardian in the cafeteria. To the other guardian, he may have just appeared as a fellow guardian on duty, albeit nude. He should've done more to indicate his peril.

They turn into a side room where several people are gathered around a table. They all wear the same uniform as her. One sits on the far side of the table from the others. The boy looks up at her as she passes, not like the wolves just did but with a smile and warm affection. The smile is returned by Angel. She blushes and continues past him and picks a folder and a company cell phone. She returns to sit across from the boy.

"Where are you working tonight?" the boy asks her. He's wearing an ID badge around his neck with a name on it. Ambrose.

"In the trailer park," she groans, though is anything but unhappy.

"Don't get picked off by stray dogs," Ambrose jokes, looks down at his paperwork and then back up at her. "I do the school district today."

"Don't get picked off by stray bullies," she jests and he laughs. And then they both laugh.

Theo eyes the boy suspiciously. Ambrose seems uptight, shirt buttoned all up to his adam's apple, sleeves fastened all the way down to his wrists. Dark hair. Dark eyes. Beefy. Nothing to call home about. But Angel's whole demeanor has changed. Her Light has expanded to twice its size and now Theo can see the entire table and all the staff gathered here. There's an older man who looks like he hasn't been fully inflated and a guy who looks like he wishes Guns n' Roses were still together. One girl has frizzy yellow hair and fuzzy smoker's teeth to match. Angel and Ambrose are the only young ones in the group.

A voice comes in from outside the Light. "All right you jokers. I'm not paying you to sit around and gossip. Get to work!" Everyone at the table quickly grabs their belongings and heads for the nearest door. Angel does the same.

"Hey," Ambrose calls coming up beside her. He hands her the company phone. "You forgot this."

Angel smiles a bit. "Thanks."

"I'm not paying you to sit around and gossip!" Ambrose whispers in his best smoker's voice.

Angel lowers her head and smiles some more. "He's crazy."

Ambrose laughs and the two continue out to the parking lot side by side. Theo follows behind them. His dander is up. Who is this guy? This Ambrose? He walks very closely beside her, brushing his shoulder against hers as he moves. He's pointing out things on her schedule and she is all aglow. Her Light is huge now, the size of the whole parking lot and more. He can see all the cars and the grass surrounding the lot. Her Light seems to swell with the beating of her heart, moving in and out in soft waves. Theo turns his glare on the boy standing way too close to Angel as they exchange a warm goodbye. Angel gets in her truck and watches him leave. With a happy sigh, she exits the parking lot, truck smoking and leaking, leaving oil like a breadcrumb trail in case she loses her way. She is completely oblivious to her troubles now.

Angel reads utility meters, that's what he finds out when she gets to her destination. For hours she walks around the trailer park reading meters latched onto the outside of houses. Again, she talks to no one, just slips silently in and out of yards collecting numbers. Theo struggles to keep up with her. They must walk ten miles before they get back to the truck. Inside, Theo collapses, his legs burning, his exposed thighs raw and shouting in pain. Nude in the trailer park. Nude in the school. What an embarrassment. What a humiliation. When is this day going to end?

They return to the building and Angel's Light starts to waver. It's gets fuzzy around the edges and then moves in unexpectedly. It comes in so quickly that Theo has to snatch his arm to his side to keep it from being bitten off by the Dark.

"What's wrong?" he asks her. She has become very rigid and stiff. Her Light is sickly. She sits down in the meeting room and Theo has to stand snug against the back of the chair because her Light is so tight.

"There's been too many mistakes," the grizzled old supervisor yells. "Check your numbers before sending them in. This isn't brain surgery, people. Just read the meter, send in the numbers, and get your asses back here on time. Now get out of here."

Theo hears the sound of chairs screeching and bags being gathered. Angel hesitates though, fiddling with the edges of her clipboard. Her heart is beating very quickly. Instead of leaving, she returns to the bathroom and stares at the mirror, her breath short and fast.

"What's happening?" Theo asks. There has been no incident to warrant such a sudden mood change. He can't understand what is going on and why it happened so fast. Angel splashes some water on her face, then bolts from the bathroom. Theo rushes to her side, the Darkness clipping his shoulder. Angel returns down that grey hallway, then suddenly slows and walks up to the photo copier. She presses the copy button and takes out the empty sheet it produces. Glancing up, she presses it again and then takes the two empty sheets, folds them and then puts them into her pocket. Theo watches her, very concerned and confused, until Ambrose suddenly swaggers into her Light with a few copies to make of his own.

"Hey, what are you doing? Making copies?" he grins.

"No, I'm calling Baghdad," she replies snidely.

Ambrose rolls his eyes. "Out of the way, woman."

Angel steps to the side with a giggle, staring up at him like he invented both the sun and moon and placed them in the sky himself. "Are you working late?"

"Had a meeting with Scary," he says jamming the buttons with his stout fingers.

"And was it?" she asks.

"Was it what?"

"Scary?"

"Oh, yes indeedy," he replies with a brilliant white smile. Finished with his copies, they walk down the hall together. Angel's Light pulses in and out with her breath.

"Oh," he says, reaching in his breast pocket. "I picked up your paycheck. I thought you left without it." He hands it over to her and that's when Theo sees the ring on his finger. Ambrose is married.

Angel blushes and takes the envelope. It has some writing on it.

"Sorry, I wrote on it. I mixed it up with mine," he says, holding a door open for her.

"It's okay," she grins, stepping out into the parking lot.

Silence follows. Ambrose shuffles and then takes out his keys. "Well, I'll see you tomorrow."

"Okay, tomorrow." Angel sings. She gets in her truck and runs her fingers across the sentence he wrote on her envelope. It says: pick up milk. She smiles, gazing down the handwriting as if he's written down the three words she most wants to hear from him.

Chapter 8☙

Angel comes home that night on an absolute high, swooning over such a casual and insignificant encounter. It's the happiest Theo's seen her since he arrived. He hardly sees what this guy 'Ambrose' has done to deserve such affection. He's just anybody who happens to be slightly nice to her. It bothers him, this attraction she has for him. This guy is married. Why is she wasting her time with a relationship that can never happen? This can only lead to more pain and disappointment. And Ambrose seems to be leading her on, at least he's not doing much to stop her obvious affection for him. He seems to enjoy the attention with little realization of how fragile this girl actually is.

Theo trudges into the house behind her. He thought he was exhausted when they got back from school but now he is beyond tired. He glances at Angel's paycheck as she places it on the counter. Petty cash compared to what he used to spend. And for so much work? What a horrible life but Angel hums as she enters the house and tosses her few belongings aside. She turns on a lamp and lays down on her bed still in uniform. Theo lands on the floor near her with a sigh of relief. Please go to sleep, he begs her, quit moving, quit thinking, quit this madness and go to sleep. Angel grabs a few sheets of paper and begins to write. Theo sits down and hugs his knees, closing his eyes. As Angel writes, he hears her pen scratching against the paper, furious little pen strokes as she recants the events of today in her dog eared journal. And all of a sudden, he hears her voice inside his head. At first he looks over, thinking that she's reading aloud as she writes but is alarmed when he sees her still on her stomach composing silently in her notebook. He can hear the words she writes on the paper as if she is speaking them inside his head. He stares over at her, his breath up in his throat. Does the bond really happen so fast? He knew that eventually he would hear her thoughts, but he assumed that it would take weeks or even months. This is coming too fast and without his consent. He's not ready to deal with Angel's inner workings.

For Ambrose,

I've been needing to write you a letter but the words aren't coming out right. I have so much I need to say and I don't know where to start. I think you know I've been acting strangely. Maybe you don't know that it's related to you. I probably shouldn't be telling you any of this. I should put down this pen and walk away but I can't. I have no sense around you. I do the dumbest things when you're around. And I don't know how you feel about me at all. Do you hate me? Do you like me? I can't read you. Sometimes you make me so confused. I used to be so comfortable around you and now I can barely look at you.

So if I'm going to say it, then I guess I'll just say it. I have a crush on you. A big school girl crush and I just don't know what to do with it. You make me crazy. I act like a lunatic when you're around. You probably know. This is probably no surprise to you at all. I bet you can see right through me. You're different that way. You're watching the world the way I am. Studying people. Deciphering them. Seeing what makes their tick, tock. Do you see through me too? Have you discovered my tock? I hope not.

I know you're married. I know this is ridiculous. I know there is nothing to be done about this. Please don't think I write this letter to induce you into any impropriety. That is not my intention at all. I mean only to let you in on the secret so that I might free myself from it as well. Know that I adore you. I think the world of you. I'm so glad I know you. You are something special.

The words stop when her pen does and Theo stares at her a little short of breath. Like everything else down here, it was much more intense than he expected. She invaded his mind, took it over wholly, and he could think of nothing else, could hear nothing else but those words like a soft consolations to a forlorn heart. And her words were rhythmic, clear, and sweet. But the narrative stops as she rests her pen over the paper. He's relieved to realize that he doesn't hear her thoughts yet, only her writing. Still, the experience has him shaking, almost scared as she turns the page and begins to write again. Pen strikes paper and her words come swift and sultry. But this time her scratchings are harder, her concentration more intense, the message delivered to him with twice the force as she gives her first letter more of a lusty twist.

For Ambrose,

Meet me after work tonight. In the women's locker room. In the shower. I have something I need to show you. I have something I want to give you. Something I've never given to anyone else. Something I'll guard with my last breath. Me. I want to give you me. All I ask is for you in return. Just one night. Just one hour. Just one stormy kiss pushed up against the wall, just around the corner, just out of sight. Meet me after work is over. The water is hot in the shower. The steam we can make on our own. The building will be barren, the office our playground. Hunt for me. Search for me. Capture me in the utility room. We'll shake all the keys off their hangers. The warehouse is empty at night. The forklift is parked inside. We can use the roll bars for leverage. The windows are tinted in the coffee room. The possibilities are endless. You can put me on the windowsill. Shove yourself inside me as the world drives on by. No one will know. No one will suspect. Give yourself to me. Just one night. Just one hour. Just one kiss to remember in a searing blush when we catch sight of each other the next morning. Give yourself to me, Ambrose, to me.

Theo remains frozen on the floor, hands clutching his knees to his chest. He can only breathe in shallow bursts. The words, the passion, so intense as if he were thinking the thoughts himself. His whole world is spinning. He can't remember why he's here or where he's going. There's nothing but Angel and that pen.

Angel sorts though the nest of papers and journals on the floor and picks up a white notebook. This one is different from the other, pristine, in white vinyl and held together by a single clasp. She thumbs through pages and pages of what appear to be collections of short stories, each one only two or three pages long. This book intrigues him more than the others, makes him sit up and even lean forward a bit. It seems to have more importance than the stacks of sheets or the run down journal. Angel takes up the pen again.

I'm standing in a dark forest, naked. It's dark. It's night. The only light is where I stand. It exposes me completely. I can't see into the dark, but the dark can see me.

I lift my hands and vines come down to take my wrists. My feet are pulled apart at the ankles by eager roots. The air is cool on my skin as the vines begin to circle up my thighs and down my arms. Up and up, down and down, they come slowly, inch by inch, slithering round and round, over my calves, over my knees, under my shoulders and over my ribcage.

Theo turns away and begins to pray. Concentrate, Theo, concentrate. He can't be a party to this. He has to meditate, focus, and try to block her out. But as hard as he concentrates, the more her words carry on inside him, the White Book scratching away at his determination and control.

In the darkness, eyes watch me. I feel them on me from the man who spies on me, watches me and waits for me. Waits until it's time for him to join me. I shudder and I squirm, held captive by Mother Nature's lusty son. The vines rise up to my lips and leave dew on my hips. They tighten and pull me open, open so my watcher can see me clearly, see what I have to offer, what I want to give him, what I want him to give me.

Angel sighs and Theo can hear her free hand sliding across her body. Her pen keeps scratching. He closes his eyes and tucks his head between his knees, praying, praying that this is the moment rescue comes.

I'm pulled down to my knees, my legs drawn open, my arms up over my head. More tentacles move in. I breathe in little gasps, waiting for what's coming. Vines touch my back, move to the front, touch my breasts. Cold and wet like bony little fingers they twist and they knead, they constrict and contract. Beneath my open knees, the ground is crawling. Vines open my mouth, go inside, go down lower, touch my mound.

Theo grips his eyes shut, his hands clenched in prayer, his back bowed away from her. He can hear her soft little mewings. And he can't stop the fantasies of where her hands are going, of the girl in the shower and the water gliding down her body, that he is the forest god in the dark shadows watching. He can hear the bed sheets whispering, hear hands on skin sliding as that tempting little bud begins to expand deep inside his own hips.

My knees are driven up and open by fat juicy tree limbs, my feet begin to lift straight up, pulling my hips off the ground. My head falls back into the damp earth. I'm too weak. I'm too wet. The blood rushes to my head. Oily vegetation lifts my ankles until I'm nearly upside down, helpless and under the forest's control. It shakes me and shakes me and I come down all over. Run down all over. And I'm ready for more.

The vines disappear and I settled to the forest's bed. I lay there gasping and ready for nature's son to take over. I lay with my eyes closed and can do nothing more. My body is ravished, the ground wet from excitement. I feel something between my legs. I look up, delirious, and see a forest god kneeling between my hips. Between his legs is a dark spongy member shaped like a fist. The oily, wet tendon throbs and pulses with light. He is twice the size of a normal man, transparent in places, with a machine between his legs that could render me blind. He is earthy and beautiful, with dark eyes and dark hair. His wispy, ethereal hands lift my knees and position me for entry. I push up on my elbows and look at that thing he intends to put inside me.

Angel grunts and Theo sees the top of her uniform sail past him. Kneeled tensely nearby, unable to go any further than her Light allows, unable to escape her words because they are inside his head, he looks back. He swallows hard as he sees her body swollen and flushed with hot blood. Her nipples are hard, her breasts swollen, her hair spread wildly beneath her. He gasps and gasps again, his own forest god rising. He's never done it. He's never touched himself. Never had the urge. He was always too busy. Always working or planning or scheduling. He thought he was stronger than the rest of them, than his bad friend and all his pathetic jerking-off stories, but now he knows he was never really tempted. This is a whole new place never investigated, an examination of something left dormant inside him. He has no sense of the Reserve, of his schooling, or his dedication. He cares about none of it, just the taming of this burning hot monster that's growing inside him. He shifts on his knees. When he looks down, he sees it, larger, longer than before. It's begging him to touch it. Angry at himself, angry with his lust, he clamps his hand around the back of his neck and clings on to the last threads of his resolve.

Solid and veiny with a thick-skinned nut, green and velvety and possibly two inches across, I look down as he drives his hips forward and touches his tip to my blazing target. I bite my bottom lip and brace my arms back in the mud. He presses forward an inch and I cry out reaching forward as if to stop him. He shoves in another impossible inch. I collapse back and dig up handfuls of soil. Another inch and I kick back trying to escape but he holds me firm. Another inch. Another inch. Another inch and his hips finally meet mine. I'm full to the top with him, stretched to every limit I have ever imagined. He bumps me a few times, a few gentle nudges until I release oily lubrication and then the machine goes in motion. Slow, agonizing strokes bring our hips apart and back together again. He's splitting me in half with the most intense pleasure. I come. I come again. There is nothing anymore, no trees, no sky, no earth, no nothing. Just me and him, this forest god and his fist cock. My legs stretch out, my toes point to their limits as he pushes me past mine, thrusting, thrusting me right into the bowls of the earth. Harder, harder. Again, again. Our hips slapping, spanking parts. There is no time anymore, just muscles in motion. Just sensation and endless pleasure and me impaled on this enormous forest god, pushing and shoving until he thrusts me right off the ground. He lifts me up and plants himself inside me, puts seeds inside me and in orgasm we run together. Seeds plant me inside and grow out until we are one object fused together at the hips. I...

Angel gasps and tosses the pen aside. She rolls on her back and goes to work. She hides nothing. Does it all out in full light, no blankets, no shame, open windows, she doesn't care. Theo stares up under lowered lashes at her, his face burning hot. He's pent up in a way he never believed possible. There is only one way out of this. And the longer he watches her, the less he cares about the repercussions.

Swallowing hard, he focuses down. He drops his hand from his neck to his thigh. The close proximity drives his excitement levels higher. He moves his fingers around, listening to Angel's moans in the background. His extends his thumb out to graze the electric skin and it's all over from there. He grabs a big handful and rolls his head back. He whispers to his god in a way he never did before, pumping and pumping. His slated eyes go to Angel and suddenly he wants her to see. He turns towards her, rising on his knees and strokes himself in full view of her. Near her and under the eyes of god and everything, he lifts that swollen red core into the air. He heaves and hauls, clenching his teeth, his wings arched back until everything releases. He opens his mouth in a silent scream and spews out every worry and tension, every promise and every responsibility, falling back in a fiery haze of heavenly orgasm. He rains down on Angel in her own throws of passion, her hair tangled, her hands working, her mouth open. He shakes himself off, raising his eyes to the ceiling in absolute delight.

Theo sleeps all night and wakes up just before dawn. He simmers in a moment of quiet euphoria before he remembers the reason behind it. Then he quickly sits up and looks over at Angel. Only three vows to follow and he's already broken one. And broken it in a way never even considered possible by the elders. His eyes move to the dark window though the sun is rising and another day begun. His happy high fades to sickness now, disgust, shame, and disappointment. His first sexual experience should've been something meaningful and important. Not like this. He masturbated in front of a girl who was dreaming of someone else. The whole thing makes him ill. What will happen to him now? Can the guardians see him? Is there a record of his activities down below? Will Veddie find out? Will they send him away? And how will he live with himself when this is all over and done?

He glances over at Angel tangled in her bed sheets, both hands thrown over her head, her legs folded to form a perfect little 'V' between her hips. It happened so fast, the feeling came over him so immediate and so glaring. In the moment he didn't care about anything else.

Angel wakes up with a groan and an equally hung over look on her face. A glance at the clock has her swearing but not rushing. If she had something to do, she already missed it. Pulling on an oversized shirt and long baggy pants, she makes her way to the bathroom. Two days and he hasn't seen her bathe or even turn on a tap. She hasn't walked past a pond or crossed over a river. Not even lounged near a fountain. It's like she's doing it on purpose.

Her Light is relatively stable this morning, large enough to leave him some space. And he needs it today, needs to be as far away from her as he can manage. She's dangerous in ways he never thought possible before. While she gets ready for the day, he walks around her filthy apartment. Ryder talked about advanced escapes through glasses, droplets of water, even reflections. But he didn't get far enough in his lessons to learn how to do that.

He hears the front door slam. He runs to the door and shakes the knob frantically but it doesn't even rattle. She's left the house while he was lost in thought. Theo turns and sees the Darkness coming for him. It creeps across the living room floor and then into the kitchen. He rushes through the narrow galley, trips over the plastic bag, curses profanely, and then presses himself up against the bay window. Outside he can see that Angel has stopped in the yard and is filling a bucket from a hand crank water pump. She's not leaving. Still, if she walks out any further, he'll be swallowed whole. He watches tensely as she works the old pump jack filling a ten gallon pale of water. Then, with much relief, he sees her return to the house with the bucket. He looks over his shoulder and sees the Darkness retreating. That was close, way too close. He can't get complacent. He must keep her in sight at all times. Whatever's lurking in that Darkness, he doesn't want to encounter it.

He watches her struggle to bring the bucket inside, water sloshing over the sides. She sets the bucket on the floor catching her breath. Water. He launches towards it but she picks it up and struggles to carry it down the hall. Theo hovers behind desperately waiting for an opportunity to ascend. But before he can attempt anything, she empties the water in the back of the toilet and then puts the lid back on. Theo swears bitterly, thinking that he's never cursed so much in his entire life.

She returns to the pump and fills another bucket. This time he follows her outside. Bringing it back in the house, she pours some in the sink to wash herself, then sets it aside. Theo jumps at the pail. Finally, an escape. Glancing one last time at Angel, he dives his hands downwards but his fingers ricochet painfully off the water as if the surface were frozen. He pulls back his hands, shocked. It's no different than the plastic bag or the door knob but water is supposed to ascend him, right? Angrily, he tries again, concentrating, closing his eyes, even praying. But the water will not let him in. He swears again, staring helplessly down at his last hope for escape, gone. Why can't he ascend? Is there something he's forgotten? Some sort of password or incantation that needs to be spoken to activate the portal?

Angel pushes past him and back into her bedroom. Theo tries again and again but to no avail. All he had to do was touch the water in the Field to descend, so why isn't it working in reverse? He rises, a frantic desperation coming over him. He really is trapped here. And now there is nothing he can do but wait for rescue. And what if no one notices he's gone? What if no one finds him standing in that lonely corner of the Field? Will he be stuck here forever?

Theo follows Angel into the post office. She picks up a stack of mail, tossing nearly half in the garbage before she leaves the building. She continues on to the school, which is already well in session, and finds a bench outside the back of the building. There she opens bill after unpaid bill, three hundred, four hundred dollars mounting on each. Property taxes on a property not worth taxing, utilities on a house with no appliances, water with no plumbing, and so on. White bills have reminders on them, yellow ones have threats, red ones contain pending disconnections. Your account is in arrears, please pay now. Your payment is overdue, make a payment immediately. Pay by this date or legal action will be taken. Your account has been redirected to a collection agency. All this trouble for that worthless house and tiny plot of land. Again, he wonders where her parents are. She's barely eighteen and living all alone, at least as far as he can see. Why, he's twenty-four and still lives with his parents. And what a home he has, or had. His garage is bigger than Angel's entire house. And the bills? He's never given much thought to the cost of living. He supposes his parents pay all the bills but he's never seen the mail. He just buys stuff on credit and the credit cards get paid. He gets a car and drives it, puts the gas on the family account. Life costs him nothing. How much he took that for granted. He didn't even know he was taking it for granted. He remembers his bad friend grumbling over his never-ending cash flow. Must be nice, he'd always say, and Theo would just shrug like it was nothing. He never realized the toll everyday bills could take on the average person. And for Angel? He seen that check she got at work. It doesn't add up to a quarter of what these bills are. What a terrible, miserable life she lives.

During class, Angel makes a small grocery list. Adds it up and then crosses off half the items. Things like butter and milk; things that are pretty essential. Her whole grocery list adds up to about forty-five dollars. She seems happy to have it and tucks it away in her pocket with her stolen cash from the previous two days. Then she takes the bills and tries to add up minimum payments. Her limit appears to be three hundred dollars, three hundred and not even a third of that to feed herself, it seems criminal. She puts a hundred to gas and a hundred to electric, but that only leaves one hundred left for gas, groceries, insurance, and phone. She sets the phone bill aside along with its threats; she will have to let them disconnect it. She sets aside the house insurance; there is nothing she can do about that either. She adds up the numbers again. Eighty to the gas company, eighty to the electric, forty-five for truck insurance, which gives her one hundred and seventy five. Fifty to the water company, another forty to property taxes, leaves eighty-five left behind. She seems satisfied then remembers gas for the truck. She adds another thirty to the list. So that leaves fifty-five. She minuses the grocery bill and that leaves ten dollars of extra money. Ten dollars. Not much of an emergency fund. It depressing; it's depressing watching her do it and she looks equally as depressed while doing it.

At lunch, he follows her to the bank. She deposits her check and the stolen cash and begins to make her payments. Down and down the numbers go until Angel reaches the last fifty-five. Phone's still getting disconnected and house insurance is pending and payments made are simply down payments to keep the wolves at bay, not even close to clearing the mounting bills, late charge fees, fines for reconnection, and interest.

"I'll take the rest in cash," she says when she's finished and seems relieved that the whole ordeal is over.

The woman glances at her computer screen. "Oh and don't forget about bank fees. Because of last months bounced checks, there will be an extra seventy-five dollar charge taken from your account. You'll need to make another deposit by the end of the week to avoid further penalties."

Angel goes all red and glances back at the growing line behind her. Seventy five dollars? Might as well be a million.

"Can't be bouncing checks, dear." The cashier begins to count out Angel's cash but she waves it away.

"Better leave it in," she says and then walks away. Theo rushes to catch up with her as she leaves the bank in tears. She rolls her screechy bike away from the parking lot full of expensive sedans and SUV's and tosses the grocery list in the garbage.

"Christ!" Theo cries, so frustrated he could scream. Can't anyone give this girl a break? She's isolated and bullied and stealing just to get money for food. Meanwhile, the greedy utility companies snatch up every last cent she has. No water, no food, nothing in her house but a bed and a couch; she has nothing. He didn't even know poverty like this existed anymore. He's truly ashamed of himself. He thought he was a good person when he lived, but he never gave away anything, not to charity, not to friends. He just figured if you worked hard then you got what you deserved. Now he sees that some people are just lucky and some people are just fucked. And Angel is one of the unlucky fucked.

He is exhausted by the time they get back at school. Angel stops by the back door of the cafeteria for a hand out. A different woman comes to the door, one with a hard mouth and ugly face to match. No guardian with this one. "Sorry, we don't give handouts. If you want food, you pay like the rest of us." Angel goes away quietly but her eyes are brimming, her stomach grumbling. She retreats to the science lab hallway, opens her bag on the bench, and leans her head against the wall.

Theo sits while she quietly cries. Classes go out and people pass by with little concern. She's invisible to them. Would he have noticed her in his school? Or would he have walked by like the rest? He already knows the answer to that. He was racing so fast through his life that he never saw anyone but himself.

Romeo passes through Angels Light, a few friends behind him. He stops. "Go on without me." His boys chuckle and laugh and then continue down the hall.

"Baby, what's wrong?" Romeo lifts a knee and puts a cowboy boot on the bench between Angel and Theo. Angel keeps her eyes out the window. Romeo reaches over and pinches her arm, "Hey I'm talking to you, little sow."

"Get your hands off her," Theo punches Romeo and comes away gripping his hand painfully.

Angel shudders and her eyes turn to Theo. She looks straight at him, right into him, and Theo is sure she knows he's there. He whispers, "There are more places than this, more places you can go, more that you can be. Can't you leave here? Can't you go somewhere else? There must be some way out of here."

Angel just drops her eyes.

Romeo fingers the edge of the bills sticking out of her pack, then takes one out and opens it. He reads the phone bill and then sets it on her lap, running his hands across her thigh. "Don't worry about it, bruised Betty, no one calls you anyway."

Angel crumples down and covers her face as she breaks into more pieces. Theo rises up and kicks at Romeo, pushes him and spits at him with little effect.

Romeo shrugs and traces his fingers through her hair. "My offer still stands, little one. I can take care of that teeny, tiny bill. All you have to do is take care of me. Think about it." He struts away just as pleased as can be, leaving Angel in shambles. Theo drops back to his seat and covers his face as well.

"Hey! Hey, Angel, darling!"

As Theo and Angel are leaving for the day, a lady appears in the Light. She passes Angel a Styrofoam container and says, "Don't you worry about those old hags. There's always food for you as long as I'm working in the cafeteria. All right?"

It's the woman with the guardian! Theo lunges forward but Angel's Light is so small he can only see the guardian from the neck down. Can the guardian see him? Theo waves his arms around frantically yelling the name Veddie over and over again. I'm trapped here. I can't get out. Please send help. Please hurry.

"Thank you," Angel replies weakly, unable to even lift her eyes to see the woman. The woman turns away and so does her guardian.

"Come see me tomorrow," the woman calls after her.

Angel tucks the food away in her bag and returns to the bike stand to find both tires flat again. A few people burst out laughing and then big expensive pickups tear out of the parking lot leaving trails of hot diesel fumes in their wake. Angel leaves the bike there. With no money to repair the tires, it's a write-off anyway. She trudges along the sidewalk and out of the school grounds. On and on she goes, for blocks and blocks, her Light inching closer and closer. Theo just follows. No words of encouragement seem enough today. If only he were alive, the things he could do to help her. What a thousand dollars would do to ease her pain. Running water, a warm bed, a hot meal, all the things that most people take for granted.

"Hey girl, want to go for a ride?"

Theo looks to the side and sees the roll bars of an oversized truck slide into view. He can't see the driver and doesn't need to. It's Romeo.

"Get in. I'll take you home."

Angel keeps on walking. The truck pulls up again and the engine revs obnoxiously, sending plumes of exhaust into Angel's direction. The door slams and soon the slick teenager appears in her Light. "Aww, come on, you're not mad about that thing in the hall? I was just kidding around. Who cares if they disconnect your hard line? Just use your cell phone."

Angel keeps walking, but he continues to follow.

"Oh come on. No hard feelings, right? You're not going to be mad at me? Come on, I'll give you a ride home. Maybe I'll come in for a bit and we can do that thing we talked about earlier. What do you think? Just between me and you. The boys don't need to know. It can be our secret." He takes out a few crisp hundred dollar bills from a mighty stack of cash bursting from his leather wallet linked to his belt by a long silver chain.

Theo turns his head, disgusted. He notices a mangy old Rottweiler digging through the garbage in an alley. The dog looks up at him. "Attack," Theo whispers and the Rottie lifts its head. The dog bears his teeth and charges towards them.

"Holy shit," Theo cries, stumbling to get out of its way. The dog jumps over him, side-swipes Angel, and then clamps down on Romeo's thigh. Romeo screams and punches the dog in the head. The old mutt goes down with a painful yelp and then Romeo leaps on it and begins kicking the animal over and over again. Angel turns to see what's happening to the dog. Fear becomes horror and then outrage and then she attacks. Just like the Rottie, she hits Romeo from the side and he's sent reeling. He lands hard against his truck door and falls to the sidewalk for a few seconds before regaining his composure.

"Christ! Fucking Jesus Christ, fucking dog!" Romeo screams. "I'm gonna get my gun and shoot that fucking thing in the head! Mount his mangy, old head on the trophy wall myself." He wipes at the wet spot on his jeans, blood. He looks up as if ready to attack the dog again.

Something rises up out of Angel, a command Theo's never heard before. "Get out of here!! You leave him alone. Get the fuck out of here!" she screams and her Light erupts outward. It rumbles over Theo like a shock wave, out past the buildings, out past the city limits and all the way up to an endless blue sky. It erupts with such a force that Theo is blown to the ground. He lands on his back and stares up at the sky, wind knocked out of him, the edges of her aura suddenly miles away.

"All right, Jesus Christ, you two fucking deserve each other anyway. Couple of dirty, homeless bitches." Romeo gets in his truck, slams the door as loud as he can and the engine roars to life. He slams his foot on the gas and tears away leaving a strip of rubber and more black smoke behind. Theo sees the vehicle for the first time, jacked up, smoked windows, decals of smutty ladies outlined on his mud flaps and, to top it all off, metal bull balls hanging from the trailer hitch.

Theo pushes up to his knees as Angel rushes to help the dog. The wave of Light didn't just run Theo down, it went right through him, it baptized him. He experienced it, experienced her, what she was meant to be, what she could be if all this wasn't happening to her. Her Light is pure, blinding, powerful, and now hovering beyond the edges of the planet. He stares out at it trembling, shaking, in total awe of what just occurred.

Beside him, Angel drops down to help the dog. "Hey, are you all right? It's okay now. He's gone."

Theo stares out at her Light, dozens of miles wide. "Look at this," he whispers, rising and stretching out his arms. He swings in a circle, enjoying the freedom of movement, of space, and even sight. "Angel, look at this."

But Angel's focus remains on the dog. She helps him to his feet and takes him back into the safety of the alley. "I'll get you some help, okay?" she says. "I'll come back for you." She pets him and talks to him until the animal is calm again. Then she rushes to her pack, gets the Styrofoam container and gives the dog her food. She stands back, smiling, as the dog devours the only meal she was going to eat all day.

Chapter 9ଓ

On the way home, Angel takes a detour. She turns down a side street and walks and walks until the houses get bigger and the yards get smaller. She travels past gas stations and convenience stores and soon arrives in the parking lot of a grocery store. She pauses for a second, then goes inside. She takes a hand cart and walks through the aisles. She has no money, just the few remaining dollars the bank is going to withdrawal at the end of the month, so what is she doing? She tosses item after item in her cart while finely dressed women engrossed in digital contraptions pass by with carts brimming to the top with processed foods. Angel keeps grabbing things at random. She keeps glancing around and then back towards the door.

"Are you going to steal this?" Theo whispers, suddenly on edge. Would she just take a cartful of food and walk out? Surely she'd get caught. "Angel, don't. There has to be another way. Can't you go to the food bank or something?"

"*Hey, girl!*"

Both Angel and Theo jump as Bea appears behind them.

"Doing some shopping? Can I come with?"

"Um...I'm, uh...just about done," Angel says nervously, leaving Theo with little doubt as to her intentions.

"Cool, I was just stopping by for a few things too."

They walk around together but Angel's shopping spree is at an end. She's nervous now as they approach a busy checkout with more food than she has money.

"Can I put this in yours?" Bea asks obliviously, tossing a few items in Angel's cart. "Come on, it's like ten bucks. Isn't our friendship worth ten bucks? I'll give you a ride home. How's that for fair?" Bea prattles on completely unaware of

126

Angel's intentions. They're in line now; there's four more people until they reach the cashier. What is Angel going to do? She can't pay for the items she has in her cart. And now Bea is there, preventing escape. Angel is glancing up and then around, lifting her cart and putting it down again.

"Um," Angel begins. "This line is taking too long. I'll just go to customer service and meet you outside, okay?"

"Cool beans," Bea says. "Meet you outside."

Angel swallows hard and waits for Bea to leave the building. Her heart is beating so fast and loud, Theo swears he can hear it. Cher is playing on the overhead speakers. *If you could turn back time.* Angel looks at her wrist impatiently, checking a watch which she does not have. She pretends to be in a hurry and then glances over at customer service. Just one person there. As if deciding to opt for the shorter line, Angel excuses herself and sneaks around the person ahead of her, through the cashiers kiosk, and then on to customer service. Theo scrambles along behind her, his heart racing too. A few people glance her way, but disinterestedly. Theo notices the cameras at the door. They'll have a picture of her when she leaves. Is she really going to do this?

Angel gets in the line for customer service and as she does, leaves her cart on the floor. The old man in front of her returns a foot bath and then prattles on and on about the price of tires. Angel glances back to her abandoned cart. What now? What is she going to do?

"Next, please?"

Theo jerks his head up and then follows her to the check out.

"Yes, can I help you?"

"Um, yes, I was just wondering about jobs?" Angel asks. "Do you have any applications?"

Theo exhales. She's decided to take the high road. Thank god. She chats with the cashier in a friendly manner for a minute and takes the application and folds it into her pocket. She takes a few steps away and then turns back. "Almost forgot," she smiles and reaches back for her cart.

The cashier laughs. "Wouldn't want to forget that."

Angel grabs the cart and heads for the front door. It was all a ruse. She asked for the application then pretended she'd forgotten groceries as if she'd already paid for them at the cashier. The girl at customer service practically verified the theft. It's brilliantly bad. Angel takes the cart in hand and walks right out the front door, right out past the security cameras and the grocery store greeter. Having seen her in the line for customer service, the man assumes she's paid and waves her on by.

Theo comes out into the radiant summer afternoon covered in sweat. He feels like they pulled off a major bank heist, not just the theft a hundred dollar's worth of food. He's never stolen anything in his life. He feels nauseous, dirty and tainted after being pulled into another one of her sick escapades.

"Took you long enough," Bea complains behind the wheel of her mother's mini-van. "Got my stuff?"

"Sure did," Angel grins. "Got everything I needed."

At home, Angel takes her groceries to the table and spreads the items out one by one. She fingers pilfered treats as if they were coated in gold. Food, glorious food. She eats a bit of everything, savoring each precious mouthful and then packs the rest away in the fridge. After she eats, she cleans up a bit, gets laundry into one pile, empties the sink full of stagnant dishes and fills it with clean soapy water. She tosses the dishes back in the water but doesn't clean them.

Angel's Light comes in slowly during the night like a warm, setting sun, until it rests in a clean circle about twelve feet or so around her body. She falls into bed with her journal and rereads old passages she's written. While she does, Theo goes to the bathroom and stares at his empty reflection in the mirror, thinking about the Reserve and whether a rescue effort has begun at all. Soon after the writing begins, Theo is forced to abandon his own thoughts for hers.

When I was nine, I was camping at a lake with my family. They were just a few short feet away cooking supper inside the trailer. I was outside at the picnic table, alone, my usual sullen, solitary self. A man cruised along the side the campsite. He slowed, gravel snapping under his truck tires, his eyes like bulging, probing marbles. I will never forget that frightful face. The overripe skin, the undone hair, that thick grotesque mustache. He looked like a wanted poster.

WANTED:
white male
thick moustache
bulging eyes
into young girls.

I could feel his troubled stare from across the campsite. He slowed the truck to a stop across from me. It was a rusty red beater, Chevy or GMC, or something like that. He said nothing at first. Just parked and stared and gripped the steering wheel so tight. Suddenly the whole world was empty and I was all alone, the only one left in the world, and alone to battle him. If I didn't act quickly, I'd be on the back of a milk carton or front page news. Missing child; last seen with a bulgy-eyed, white male at local park.

He leaned out of his truck, reached his hairy hand for me, turned his palm to the sky, and called me forward with the come hither of a single pointed finger beckoning. I stayed where I was, fear rooting me deep in the earth. He said, "Come here girl, come here." I could hardly breathe. I knew if I went with him, I would never be seen again.

A voice was screaming inside my head. Move! Get away! Get inside! Do it now! I acted against my own regard. I moved ahead like underwater. I would have to get closer to him if I wanted to get back into the camper. The man watched me eagerly as I approached. He thought he'd gotten me. He thought he fooled another one. But I turned suddenly and bolted into the camper. I slid quietly into the nearest seat, my heart rapid and fragile as a hummingbirds wings. I silently celebrated my victory in shaken terror as I heard the truck move on by. The man would continue his search for a less obstinate, more obedient child. I never told. It was my fault. I shouldn't have been sitting outside where predators could prey on me.

Theo slowly returns to the bedroom. Angel has pages and pages of her work strewn all over the edge of the bed, poems and sketches, journals and even the dreaded White Book still out from last night. He's tried not to think of last night, and has managed successfully to avoid it throughout the day, but now it's quiet and there are no other distractions and he's back in his room where he boldly lifted his prick to Heaven last night. What unbelievable pleasure; what undeniable shame. He feels like he's losing himself. Maybe he's lost already. And if Veddie doesn't find him soon, who knows what he'll do next.

At fifteen, I was led astray. He was a supervisor at the food joint where I worked. Much, much too old to have an interest in me. He took me for a walk. I was sick and drunk, many senses impaired. He said he wanted take me to his place so we could watch a movie. We walked for blocks and blocks across the city. It was dark out, very late. He took me to his home. He got very drunk and then it began. He grabbed me and threw me around, tried to force me into his arms. I pleaded for him to let me go and when all else failed, I pretended I was going to throw up. Angry his needs were unsatisfied, he shoved me outside the door to fend for myself in a dark unfamiliar neighborhood, in the middle of the night, alone and completely vulnerable. I was nothing to him. Just another failed conquest. A fish he decided to throw back into the sea.

Angel settles back with a sigh, bringing the book to her chest. She's so lonely, so alone. He's never met anyone so isolated in his life. How many of them are there? These lost and lonely people? Hiding in their homes, in their basements, in the back of classrooms, thinking no one in the world cares whether they live or die? Wanting to love and be loved but having no way to accomplish that goal. It makes him very sad to realize that the world is such a hopeless place.

Angel opens the book again, looking very tired. Even though the passages are bringing her down, she continues to read.

When I was sixteen, a man came to me with a desperate plea. He had all this charity work he had to do for Mothers Against Drunk Driving and he needed my help. He brought boxes of those ribbons that you wear to support the worthiest of causes: M.A.D.D. I was so impressed. The man was an alcoholic. He had been most of his life. I imagined how he turned his life around as I eagerly folded the ribbons for him. I was so excited. But slowly, so slowly, my enthusiasm began to dim. Because what had changed him? Nothing that I knew of. There was no life altering moment that pushed him into a more positive direction. He was still behaving in the same way I always knew him to behave in. He was drinking and hiding it and had, on several occasions, had me in the car while doing it. I realized that I wasn't helping him with the project; I was doing his community service for him. No words can explain what happened inside me when

I discovered that he had been caught driving drunk again. And he was shirking off his community service off on me. His own daughter.

Theo sits down now, staring at her as she softly cries. The first mention of her parents, her father, and what a story to introduce the man who gave birth to her. He thinks of his own parents, of the things he used to regard as annoyances and intrusions, but tricking your own daughter to get out of community service? It's completely unfathomable to him. Where are they now, these delinquent parents of hers? Suddenly he wishes he could hear her thoughts and not just her written words. He has so many unanswered questions.

They sleep through the night. Angel sprawls across her bed and Theo curls like a faithful puppy at her feet. They don't wake up until it's nearly noon. Clearing cobwebs from their eyes, they take the day slow, get up for a bit and then sleep some more. In waking moments, Angel continues to tidy the house, brings in more water, and has three whole meals. She seems happier, her Light is larger, encompassing the whole house. It gives them space and Theo can go off into his corner for some much needed time away. He continues, though fails, in his attempts to escape. Water from the pail garnishes the same results. Still, he tries and tries again hoping he'll recall some detail from the classroom he's forgotten from before.

Night comes and so does work. Theo still struggles against time. He doesn't know if it's Tuesday or Saturday, January or June. He can only guess the time of day by the changing of the sunlight cast in her Light, and the season by the color of the grass beneath his feet. He's still dying for a few solid numbers. Nine-thirty on a Thursday afternoon, June the fifteenth. Anything to indicate some normalcy.

They make another frightful drive in the old truck to the parking lot of the utility company. This time Theo gets a better look at the grey two-story building, the nifty, clean lunch room and the women's locker. Today, Angel steals nothing, doesn't riffle though belongings, even passes by an open purse on the shower room bench. Missed opportunities, he supposes, thinking like her now. How badly she needs the money and yet sometimes she resists. She's still forty dollars shy for the bank and has no money for gas once this shift is over.

Ambrose is waiting for her when she gets to the meeting room, sitting alone at the other end of the table. A little apart himself. He's in his blue uniform, a few buttons open at the top but sleeves secured all the way down. His hair's a little spiky, messy, the way she likes it. He greets her and they sit down across from each other.

Theo pays closer attention to Ambrose's reactions, to the way he watches and responds to her. Knowing he's married changes everything. If he's leading her on…well, like Romeo, there's really nothing he can do about it, but if he could do something about it, he would love to get his hands on either of them. He's still naked, three days nude, still swinging his thing around the corridors and out in the parking lots for only the clairvoyant to appreciate. His concern over it is starting to dull; it's more of a nuisance than a disability.

"Did you get your route copies done?" Ambrose asks her with a sweet smile.

"Oh, I forgot," she says, looking up at him and blushing.

"Come on, we can do it before Scary shows up."

Ambrose walks back down the hallway and Angel follows him, her eyes on his broad shoulders, his ass, his hair, his hands. He stops by the photocopier and turns slightly to face her. He stands too close. He looks too long. "See, you take your appointments and fax them through the copier."

Angel raises her eyebrows and shrugs. "I don't know how to use the fax."

He chuckles and reaches for the buttons, his arm brushing against hers. "See, you press the buttons like this."

"Dur," she says in her best caveman voice. "I know how to push the buttons."

"Yeah, you push mine all the time."

"Funny. You never told me you were a comedian."

"Really? Thought you came to all of my shows."

He looks at her and she looks at him, their arms still grazing and the moment seems to last forever. Theo decides that this man does have genuine feelings for her, but why is he indulging them? He can't be married and have Angel too. That's not how it works. At least not in his world.

Angel drops her gaze and blushes a bit. Once finished, they walk back to the meeting room, both talking quietly. They converse in broken sentences, in private jokes that Theo doesn't understand. It makes him mad. Maybe even jealous. She's his charge now and his feelings towards her are getting muddled.

Ambrose's phone rings as they near the meeting room. "Hold on," he says and answers it. Hearing the voice on the other end, he turns away and begins to talk in a lower voice. But the caller on the other side speaks so loudly that both Theo and Angel can hear it.

"I was just down at the department store and I found these shirts on sale. I got two in the black you like and then three more for me and Jules. And I picked up a pair of jeans too and a new purse. It was a real great deal. Wait until you've seen all the great stuff I've got."

"Um..." Ambrose says. "I'm at work."

"I picked up a new dress and I was thinking I could wear it when we go for lunch with your parents on Tuesday. Oh and could you..."

"Sonya," Ambrose says firmly.

"But I was...I couldn't wait to..."

"I will call you back. This isn't an appropriate time."

"But I was..."

Ambrose hangs up the phone on his wife. It's extremely rude and Angel beams that he's chosen her over his wife to spend time with in this moment. Ambrose tucks the phone away and gently places a hand on the center of her back to ease her forward. Angel's Light quivers open and Theo just closes his eyes and looks away.

Angel drifts through the evening, walking impossibly long routes in a nauseating state of bliss. Theo just shakes his head and follows behind. This is a disaster waiting to happen; there's no hope for a relationship between her and Ambrose. He even calls her once on their work phones claiming he did it by accident, making a few jokes that cause her to glow for the rest of the evening. But when Angel gets back to the meeting room, Ambrose is sitting down at the other end of the table, surrounded by meter readers. They're all talking about something and laughing and carrying on. Angel comes in the room and slows, looks his way and then takes her normal seat at the opposite end of the table. Across from her, the other seat is painfully vacant. She glances his direction and quickly back to her hands.

"Hey Angel!" the girl with the yellow teeth calls. "You missed out on some fun."

Angel looks up and meets Ambrose's eyes briefly before turning her gaze to the woman with the frizzy hair and tapered pants.

"We all ran into each other for supper," the lady exclaims loudly. "Went down to that new place by the mall. Didn't we, Ambrose?"

Ambrose keeps his eyes away from Angel. "Uh...yeah."

"Good food," the withered old man comments. "Ate myself sick."

"Too bad you missed it," the girl cries and pats Ambrose on the cheek. "He's such a charmer."

Angel fidgets a bit, trying to remain calm. Ambrose called her around supper. He said it was by mistake and he must have meant it. He didn't invite her along with the rest of the meter readers for supper. She swallows hard, rises and carefully returns her things to the storage room. She walks calmly down the hallway until she's out of sight. There, she retreats to the bathroom, to an empty stall and waits there quietly until she's sure everyone's gone. Her face is cold and expressionless, but her Light is searing hot. Theo senses an eruption in the near future and is terrified for her, and for himself.

She leaves the bathroom long after everyone is gone. Walking down that long grey hallway, the supervisor calls out to her. "Don't you have a life, Angel? Get out of here. I don't want to see your face in here after shift is over."

The ride home is quiet. The walk to the house is quiet. It's the sort of silence that proceeds when you've lit a fuse and have run for cover, waiting for the bomb to go off. Angel goes to her room. She sits down on her bed and picks up a pen. She stares down at the empty pages very silently. Theo holds his breath, waiting for Angel to crack. He's scared of that pen now, of what's creeping out of her mind, finding its way down those wayward fingers, and landing on the surface of the page. She sets the pen to paper and the ink begins to flow.

I never write in true distress so feel the pain of my empty pages. I am so close to the edge right now and I don't have the strength to go on. I am so tired of being alone. If I fall, I pick myself up. And if I can't, then I stay down. And I stay down. And I stay down. And down is all I know anymore. The world doesn't want me. I don't want me. I can't do this anymore. I'm tired. The house is in turmoil. I hate this place but it's the only place I have. I have no money to leave. I have no money to stay. Just scraps of cash and I am trapped here in this place that I hate. That hates me. The world hates me. I am out of control. I am doing things I never dreamed I'd do. I'm taking things that aren't mine. Maybe it's time the world stops turning. Maybe it's time I end mine. This is the darkness. I am in the darkness now. Swallowed whole. Sometimes I just want to die. I just want to die.

Angel begins to cry, quiet pent up sobs with her hands up over her face. Theo rises intending to comfort her but she suddenly stands and throws her journal across the room. Something happens to her Light, it gets hot, wavy, and it starts to burn. It pulses with her breath and Theo retreats back. Angel breaks her pen in half and then turns against the wall, placing her head against it, her clenched fist planted against the surface. Then she pulls back her arm and punches her fist against the wall. Soft at first and then harder and harder until she is screaming through gritted teeth and leaving dents of bloody fisted fingers in the chipped paint. Afterwards, she slides down to her knees, spent, cradling her bruised hand against her chest and then cries and cries, the kind of full-out sobbing you do when you're all alone, when all is lost, when there is no hope for change, when there is no hope for anything, when death is the only escape.

She crawls back to the bed after, spent, picks up another pen and writes these four lines:

If I fall in the forest
Does anybody hear?

Picked apart by a thousand little creatures
Piece by piece, I disappear.

Theo lifts his head. He's sitting against the wall, arms around his legs, head on his knees. Angel isn't where he left her. She's on her back, staring straight up at the single naked bulb hanging from the ceiling. She's taking in short, shallow breaths, almost hyperventilating. It's strange, the way she focuses up, the way she breathes. He pushes off the floor and approaches to find her lying like a corpse inside a coffin, her hands folded high on her chest, and beneath her hands she clutches a knife. She holds it with the tip beneath her chin and the blade flat against her body. Her fists, one still bloody and swollen, clutch the handle with all her might. She stares up but sees nothing.

"Angel? Angel?" he cries, dropping to his knees beside her. What should he do? How can he stop this? Pray? That seems fucking ridiculous right now. She needs intervention. She needs someone to grab that knife out of her hand. But after so many failed attempts at interaction with this world, he knows what the result will be.

"Angel? Angel, please don't," is all he can come up with. His mind is spinning in a thousand different directions. He's worried she'll die. He's worried he'll die with her. He gazes at her pink lips dropped open, her swollen eyes staring up, her expression so harried and so blank at the same time. What's she thinking? Is she psyching herself up or has the decision already been made? It can't end this way but what can he do? He is the only one that can stop her but he cannot move her in any way. If only he knew what she was thinking. If only their minds were more closely linked, then maybe his thoughts could sway her decision. He knows that link will come. Maybe not soon enough for him to save his troubled charge.

Angel closes her eyes, squeezes them shut and a tear breaks loose. Her tense hands grip the knife and she takes another deep breath. Panicked, Theo reacts without thinking. He swoops down and presses his lips against hers. Angel sucks in a breath and Theo's eyes pop open. She's soft. Her mouth is soft and wet; it gives against his. He feels the warmth of her quickly exhaled breath. He can touch her skin and it moves against his. He pulls back in shock. Angel's eyes slowly close, her mouth partly open, her tongue gliding inside her mouth. She was real. He felt her. He presses his lips to hers again and Angel lets out a little whimper. Her tongue touches his and retreats back like a turtle's head. Her knife clatters away to the side of them. How can this be? He's dead. He's not real. And she shouldn't be real to him either. He touches her cheek, her face, her skin. He traces his fingers back in her hair, gets them inside, so soft, a woman's hair tangled in his fingers. Angel's hands rise up, they press to his chest, then grab the back of his neck and pull him down closer. Now they are both moaning, kissing and squeezing and touching. The Light comes in, gets intense, gets hot. Sweat forms on Theo's brow, down his back, down his neck. He's breathing fast and so is she. Her hands are going up, then down, down, down. They slip beneath his belly and reach between his hips. Theo jolts back and rolls off her, off the bed and onto the floor. His arm extends in the Dark. He pulls it back, screaming. Like a thousand insects laying eggs inside his skin. Gasping, he turns on his knees and looks over at her. Angel lies as if unconscious, her head hanging off the edge of the bed at an unnatural angle, her clothes are rumpled and dishevel. It looks like he raped her. Ashamed, he rolls away and draws his arms tightly around his body.

Angel's writing rouses him. He opens his eyes, sees the popcorn ceiling and hears the pen scratching. Maybe he *is* in hell. The devil is tempting him and is winning for sure. Angel is shuffling, moaning. Theo stares up at the naked dead bulb, the Darkness burning just past his left ear.

For Angel

Wait for me in the women's locker room. Get yourself wet before I come. I am so hard for you right now. Swollen and full and pointed straight up. Why don't you lie back on the bench and open your legs? Open them wide. I want to see you every part of you. The bench is a perfect kneeling height for me. Get wet in the shower so I can slide you back and forth across the polished wood. Then I'll take you outside into the lunch room while you're still moist. Oh, you're hot for me. Hot and wet and so very tight. A nice tight fit, that's what I like. Get up on that windowsill and open your legs. Hold on to something because I will make you feel this. Fuck, you're going to feel this. Come to the utility room with me. I'll cover you in cold keys, a hundred hands have touched these, and save just one to press inside. I'll unlock you and spill all your secrets across the utility room floor. I have a need to drive the forklift but only if you're at the wheel. I'll rev the engine for extra vibrations. All that grease makes for nice lubrication. I know how you like to get dirty. I'm going to make you filthy. Leave the elevator doors open so they can all watch us. I'll push my hips out while you move your lips in. Kiss me high, but, oh god, kiss me low. And when the tension is too much, I'll put you down on that elevator floor and fuck, fuck, fuck. Find something to hold onto because I'm coming inside. I'll ravage every part of you. I'll plant my seed inside you. I'll get you so wet that the shower will feel like a desert. Feel it, Angel, feel me. Inside you. I'm so hard for you. For just one night. Just one hour. Just a few minutes as the elevator comes between floors.

Theo groans and covers his face with his hands. She's doing it again. Touching herself. And this time it's his fault. He put his hands on his charge. He kissed her. Not just kissed her, took advantage of her. He's aroused again. In every possible manner. He can't move, doesn't dare to. It takes everything he has just to stay there and listen to her orgasm. He can't help but imagine himself orgasm with her. Inside her. His mind is going further than ever before. If her mouth is soft, then...but he doesn't dare think it. He can't go there. He has to get out of here. If escape doesn't come soon, then there's no stopping this madness. Her words are an infection. And he is dying to get sick.

They sleep through the better part of the morning then spend the afternoon lounging around the house. Angel is in a dreamy trance where she sits on the couch and stares right at him while her hand moves under her skirt. Theo doesn't have the strength to fight it anymore. He watches without shame. Touches all the places of his body he never dared to in life. Lies back with his legs open and hands behind his head. Lets the air get to it. Lets it breathe. Angel seems to feel it too. She writes nothing through the entire day even though arousal usually sends her straight for the pen. She seems lost in fantasy with him, the knife in her bedroom now as forgotten as his holy resolve.

She takes her journal to work that evening. There's a staff meeting before shift. Hair tousled and uniform unbuttoned, she saunters into the room and Ambrose's eyes shoot up to hers. He's back on their end of the table, buttoned up all tight and proper, his hands folded neatly over his clipboard. Angel sinks down in the seat across from him, says hello only with her eyes and then opens her notebook under the table.

I come in quietly. I say hello to no one. I keep busy and keep my head down low, filling out my time sheet and checking my schedule. I am in the meeting room, overcome. I've been crying most of the night. Playing most of the day. I am a mess. It's all coming out of me. I hate who I am when I want someone. I become weak, needy, clingy. I rise to a level of desperation that is pitiful even to myself. I feel like I'll die if I can't make Ambrose mine. It's too much. I hold my paper beneath the table and write. I scribble words, scream them in muddy ink across white pages to the dark and handsome man across the table, the cause of all this commotion.

Ambrose clears his throat, looking a bit nervous and uncomfortable. "Hey, did you…"

"All right, move your asses," the supervisor called Scary shouts. Theo does not even know his real name. "We got a staff meeting today."

Angel snorts and everyone looks over at her.

"You got a problem, missy?" he shouts.

Angel hangs her elbow over the chair looking back with challenge in her eyes. "Not particularly."

"Get!" he cries and everyone rises.

Angel tucks her pen into her journal and falls in line with the group. Theo glances back at Ambrose who's walking behind her. He's watching her, hard. Did he just get Angel so riled up as to accelerate this affair? What was he expecting? That Angel would come to him?

The group is led down the hall to another room with a black board and a semi-circle of desks around the room. Outside the windows, are utility vehicles all lined up in a row with company logos on their sides. The meter readers sit down amongst the other workers. Angel doesn't sit next to Ambrose but across the room from him. Theo stands behind her with his hands on the back of her chair glaring at the married man across the room. All the men are watching her today, oozing over her. *Hi Angel*, they sing as she passes, holding clipboards in front of their hips. She's leaking today, leaving a sticky trail of breadcrumbs and the dogs are hot on her scent. Her Light is around them all and they feel it. Angel lowers her hands beneath the table and writes some more.

I write his name in secret code right beneath his notice. Please, Ambrose, give me release. Free me from this pain. I need you to see me. Why can't you hold me? It's all I can do to restrain it inside. I'm a predator today. I'm prowling. Would he give in to me if I cornered him? What would I do if he cornered me?

I've never been loved or cared for. Just used and abused. All I know is lust. All I understand is sex. It's the only thing I think men and women come together for. It's the only language I can understand. And in everything he does and everything he says, I look for signs he's insinuating more. I try so hard to keep myself level but he's giving me so much to hold on to. So many long looks with those bedroom eyes. So many private moments he doesn't share with the others. So much attention on me. We're different when we are alone and I want to think that means something. I'm reasoning with myself every day. He is just a friend. He's married. He doesn't mean it that way. But my mind is a ticking time bomb and that time is ticking down. The closet door is creaking open and I've stuffed so much crap inside it; it's not going to stay in there much longer. It hurts so bad to see him and know that he is perfect for me and know that I can't have him. I'm tired of reasoning and restraint. God, he is so sweet, and so beautiful, and so real. I've been looking for him for so long, all my life, and he belongs to someone else. Why do I have to play by the rules? Why can't I have him too? Why am I always the one on the outside looking in? Why does everything have to be so fucking hard for me?

I perch myself on the furthest side of the room from Ambrose. I am trying so hard to hide it from him. I am trying so hard to make him see. See me, Ambrose, please see me. I hate my ridiculous games, my unreasonable feelings, my pitiable fantasies. I am just coping, not living, surviving, not thriving.

Angel sighs as the meeting continues. There are two men directing it, the angry supervisor and another one, a nifty looking blond one. Theo sees Scary for the first time in the light. He's dried up like beef jerky, his face angry even at rest. He and the blonde are lecturing about various going ons around the office. Most of the readers stare blankly ahead, except one. The steadfast brunette across the room whose eyes keep crawling up to her. Angel isn't returning the gaze but she seems well aware of it. Theo retains his protective position behind her chair scolding himself all the while. He should've never put his hands on her.

Twice a month we have these meetings. Warnings for the meter readers and safety for the entire company. In staff meetings, all the readers are brought together to be scolded for our goings on. Scary thumps around the table, a jack in the box ready to pop. He tells us how to tuck our shirts in. Rips out his shirt as a demonstration of how he imagines our slovenly appearance as we stumble around the city like drunken monkeys. "We gave you a uniform, we expect you to wear it," he tells us. Not just wear it, but wear it the way he wants it. Wear it! Wear it! He cries and points with his hairy donkey fingers.

Angel looks up with a smile. The one she calls Scary starts lecturing about vehicle safety and company policies. Spouts off a long and endless dialogue about how to do a proper circle check on your vehicle before entering it. Says that all employees are required to do these circle checks. He hands out clipboards with check-lists demanding that the readers verify all points before entering or exiting their vehicles. Things like checking beneath the vehicle for animals or children, walking around and inspecting for dents that might have been received while the vehicle was parked, checking to see that all the signal and brakes lights are working, things like that.

Nearby, the woman with the yellow teeth leans over and whispers, "Yeah, but what are we going to do with the rest of our spare time?"

Angel giggles and both Scary and Ambrose look over. Angel ignores them and then watches through the window as an employee enters the parking lot, jumps in a company vehicle and drives off, no circle check. Smiling, she focuses down on the paper.

In meetings we're served stale doughnuts and given exams on how to park. Should you park at an angle, across the sidewalk (next to the blind kids playing ball with their crippled grandmother) or over by the road in the designated spot where it's clear? We roll our eyes and giggle, but inside we are all insulted.

I never sit next to Ambrose at the meetings. I sit across the room or behind a few seats so he won't see me looking so much. I can't stop looking at him. He's a rare find. Call the archeology department, I've uncovered a new strain of man.

Last meeting, I sat behind him and watched him the whole time. Tapped my feet on his chair leg until he turned around and smiled. During the meeting, he teased his earlobe for minutes on end. Touched it and pinched it and kneaded his digits around the supple lobe of skin. I missed the whole meeting wishing I were an ear.

Angel pauses and sets the pen to rest in the binding of the book. Her bruised hand is wrapped. She's prepared to tell anyone who asks that she slammed it in a door.

When the meeting is over, the readers return to the meeting room for an extra lesson. They watch and they listen but Angel keeps on writing. From across the table, Ambrose reaches over and writes upside-down on her paper.

Writing a story?

Angel writes, *wouldn't you like to know.*

Kind of, he replies. *Is it about me?*

Theo raises his eyebrows at the presumptuous statement and Angel just blushes.

Maybe, she returns, *sometimes you're interesting.*

Only sometimes?

Angel reddens and smiles, her pen stalled on the paper. They look up at each other for way too long then Angel lowers her eyes and smiles again.

Chapter 10ꝏ

Angel returns home that night, lights a few candles and goes to bed in her uniform. Theo hangs by the door, his hand on the jam, his other hand on his hip. He is unbearably aroused. He can't resist her anymore. Doesn't want to. She wrote him off dozens of times in the last twenty-four hours and something has changed in him. A switch has been flicked. A new need risen and eager to be explored. And now that he's inside the sin, it feels amazing. Thrilling. Undeniable.

Angel finds a clean page and starts sketching out a poem. She goes through a few renditions before she comes up with:

Everywhere

I want you in tall grasses
Beneath a steamy morning dew
Crushed insects smeared across our backs
Your hand brushes off the ants
In waking sky, I see my breath
Pull the thick out from the roots

I want you in the cut banks
Where the snowy mountains scream
The earth, it buckles down below us
In an ancient act of process
Rocks converging, lifting higher
An ocean trench releases steam

I want you in a woodsy cabin
In the forest's dark and deep
A full moon pulls my tidal waters
Lift my knee and brace your feet

Leaves applaud, skin scratching rough walls
Something slithers down, it creeps

I want you in a summer squall.
Nature's fist baring down
Your windy hands, they twist and tip
A thunderhead between your hips
Blood spatter mud, hail, breaking storm
A bolt of lightning touches ground

I want you in the springs of bloom
Your sun kissed hair, your everything
Petals rain down in between us
Crushing daisies, tincture fragrance
Trees rise up like rigid soldiers
Press the thorny rose into us

Tired of her yearnings for the married flirt from work, Theo says, "Enough of him. Write something for me."

Angel smiles and eagerly opens the White Book. She scans down a list of potential locations, contemplating each option. The Elevator. The Lunchroom. The Locker Room. The Car. Utility Room. Wedding. Park. The Meeting Room. The Alley. The Church.

"I like the last one," Theo says from the door, raising his hands and running them back through his hair. "Write the church."

"Hmm," Angel sighs. "The church."

I kneel down at the front of the church with members of the congregation. A preacher dressed in white robes delivers communion while his alter boys follow with the wine. Their robes are open down the front.

The preacher offers me a wafer. I open my mouth. He sets the little circle inside. His fingers graze my tongue. He smiles at me and makes me a second and more brawny offering. I lower my eyes and open my mouth wider.

Theo walks around her as she writes, feeling wild, feeling crazy, completely undone. What's going to happen to him? What's going to happen when Veddie finds out? None of it really matters right now because he can taste it in his guts and primal release is his only option. Tonight he puts more than his hands on her.

The preacher blesses me while shifting his hips. I look up at him, my mouth open to all possibilities. My tongue slides up and over and then down and around. I suckle like a nursing pup. Eager for his next worshipper, he pulls away. He continues down the line with that cerise contribution. Instead of wafers, worshipers take the staff. Men and women all the same, close their eyes and lead with their chins, faces strained up in religious ecstasy. The altar boys come next. Wine runs down their bodies and we taste the blood of Christ off the bodies of his fucking disciples.

"God," Theo whispers, kneeling down beside her, his erection in full bloom. She's still dressed, still on her stomach but he's ready now. He places his hands on her back and is shocked when he finds her hard as a stone. Like the door. Like the yawning grocery bag. She is once again inaccessible to him. But what about last night? She was as real as if he were still alive. He kneels beside her, his body tight with tension. Touching himself isn't enough. He wants full interaction. He wants someone to take away his control. But she's impenetrable now, like sticking his cock inside the mouth of that plastic bag. He looks down at her, cringing as she turns over and begins to undress. Now it is torture where before it was pleasure. First she releases a few buttons down the front of her shirt and then she loosens the button on her pants. She pulls the pants down a little until he can see the tempting curve of her hipbone. Her Light begins to heat, move in, move closer. Theo is forced in until he is almost on top of her. He stares over her, salivating, as she holds the book over her chest and continues to write.

He sits in his confession box and I sit in mine. There is a window between us and a curtain before us and boy do I need to confess. All the sins I've committed today. All the ones I'm going to do tomorrow. I touch the screen between us, spread my fingers across the lattice and tell him all my riddles. He's bothered, I can tell. I ask him things; I begin to request. "Join me on the other side, child," he whispers. I enter the other curtain and he's there waiting. Waiting and ready with his organ pointed straight up to Heaven. A cold hard preacher's cock, so congested, so neglected. Deliver me, Father, I whisper. I hold his cross while he claims the right. Father, son and Holy Ghost, we celebrate a Roman holiday.

Angel closes her eyes with a hard, heavy sigh. She is dying to finish herself off, but the story comes first. She rolls back on her front and sets the book beneath her chin, her pen eagerly poised. Theo straddles her back and leans over her shoulder. He is naked and hard, his cock grazing the cold stony surface of her back, his chest heaving against the enduring lines of her shirt. He runs his tongue up the frozen rivers of her hair.

I am stretched over the altar. Wonton altar boys hold my legs open by the ankles. They're naked except their crosses and their collars. There are candles burning beside my ears, at either side of my waist, and one long, thin white tower burns between my legs. I can feel the heat dangerously close. I can see the wax slowly dripping down.

The Priest dips his hand in holy water and touches the wick. The light goes out with a hiss. He lifts the candle and signs the Stations of the Cross on my body. From nipple to nipple. From lips to hips.

Angel gasps and tosses the book away. Still straddled over her, Theo stares down at the undulating waves of a woman's body in heat. She shrugs her shirt off her shoulders and then tucks her hand down beneath her hips. She releases a soft sigh and then begins to work.

Theo wets his lips, his mouth desert dry. He's still straddled over her back. *Turn over*, he thinks eagerly, *turn over* and she complies. He moves down between her legs as she scissors her pants off her ankles. Then the shirt comes off too. Kneeled between her open thighs, Theo's eyes go down to that soft, yet impenetrable mound, to the moist hairs barely concealing what's swelling up beneath them. He wets his thumb and reaches down. He doesn't care if she can't feel it, he has to touch her. He presses his finger to the soft mound and it sinks inside. Angel cries out. Her hips thrust upwards. Theo's body rockets backwards. They both remain arched and frozen for a few moments and then Angel lowers her hips to the bed, gasping. And Theo lowers to his hands and kneels over her. Slowly, carefully, he touches the tip of her left nipple. She's soft, the skin crinkled, leathery and stiff. With a gasp of excitement, he traces his thumb across her breast to touch the other tip. Angel quivers with excitement, her eyes tightly closed. Theo moves the thumb back to the center of her ribcage, then up to her moist lips and into her soft mouth. Angel groans, her lips rising up around the thumb, her tongue circling the tip. With her own moisture as lubrication, Theo continues his journey towards the critical destination. He traces her saliva down, down between her collar bones, between her breasts, past her belly button, down between her hip bones, past the thin forest of glimmering hair, glides over her swollen folds and then disappears into the molten core. Angel rises with a horrific breath, pushes him back by the chest, her eyes two thin slits. "God," she grunts, legs up and open like in labor, her mouth dropped open. Slowly, she lowers back down with a soft sigh, legs falling open to either side of him.

Theo looks down at that roaring chasm, that doorway to his ultimate demise, swollen, slippery and eager for his entry. He's fully aroused now, risen from the dead, dynamite ready for detonation. He has no thoughts, no worries, no doubts. Now it is only about the sex. He braces his arms to either side of her and presses his swollen head to her scorching orifice. "Oh!" Angel cries, shoving her hips up and swallowing half of him in the process. The action sends Theo over the edge. In two short strokes, he digs down until he is all the way inside her, in her womb, chasm like hellfire burning and the devil's side seems so much sweeter. Fuck god and all his rules, all his rituals, and religions. Just let me fuck, fuck, fuck. He pulls his hips back until his shiny organ emerges, glimmering in the naked bulb light, quivering with her gratification, and then plunges down, down, down until she is full to the top, a hot line forged between them. Angel writhes in delight, every limb in motion, undulating beneath him as their bodies come fully together. Eager and engorged, Theo moves his hips down again, up again, each time with more vigor. Then in short, frustrated, edgy cuffs while her juices creep up his hips like rising flood waters. He clenches his fingers down on the mattress on either side of her, turning his eyes up to the Heavens. The only sound in the room are their frustrated grunts and succulent slick strokes as their rigid hips encounter. Angel cries, arching up and leaning her head back.

She slaps his ass hard and Theo goes over the edge. He hammers her in angry little divots, quicker, faster, until their hips meet mid-air and vibrate together. He explodes deep inside her, spends every last drop into her belly. They collapse down together in a hot heavy sweat with sticky love fusing their eager bodies together.

Theo wakes with a groan, Angel cold and hard beneath him. "Fuck," he grumbles, rolling off her and onto his knees. He's spent, he's dirty, and he smells like sex. He glances back at her, her legs thrown open, her skin rubbed raw in the most obscene places. He had sex with his charge. And the worst part was that she didn't even know he was here. She was probably thinking about Ambrose while doing it. Yet he couldn't rationalize with himself when the emotions overcame him. He has only himself to blame in weakness and temptation. He went into this with both eyes open. He had been anticipating the encounter all day long. Probably since the first time she took out the White Book. How cocky he was last night, standing in the doorway, goading her on. How indestructible he felt then, powerful, godlike in his own right. Now it's all crashing down on him. What he did was so much more than the previous nights. This will damn him for sure. This will banish him from the Reserve. But he could think of none of that last night. In those moments, his vision was so narrow. Angel, just Angel and sex, sex, sex.

He shudders and Angel wakes up. She wakes up with a heaving groan, sits up a bit, her hair like an eighties rock star. "Fucking what?" she whispers, reaching down between her legs. "What the hell?" There's blood down there. She frowns and touches the red spot on the blankets beneath her. She pushes up from the bed, walks right past Theo and into the bathroom, slamming the door and locking him outside. Theo stares down at that red spot in horror. That can't be what he thinks it is. Because he's not really here. No matter how real it seemed last night, he could not have broken her. It isn't possible.

Leaning against the locked bathroom door, he slams his head back a couple of times. He feels sick, more than that, something he's never felt before. Self-loathing. In one single act, he destroyed his life and permanently altered hers. What the fuck was he thinking? He stares up at the water stained ceiling and begins to understand why Angel punched the wall, why physical pain might be the only avenue of release because what he feels right now cannot be dealt with by meditation, prayer or therapy. It can only be released with pain.

Angel rests in bed and writes in her journal. Not the furious erotic writings that she usually produces but she quietly composes poetry and for once Theo is spared from her passions. She eats some of her stolen food, even attempts to clear the table and put down a nice place setting. She seems to eye the chair across the table as she does as if considering to set another plate down. For him? He's not a part of this world anymore but after last night, he's not so sure. Why was she solid one moment and then malleable the next? How is what happened last night even possible?

He watches her, now convinced that rescue will never come. He contemplates the idea of remaining her silent companion during the day and her secret lover during the night. Gone are the ambitions of angelic grandeur on the Reserve. Now he just wants to get his dick wet.

They settle back down to bed that night, Angel in bed and Theo sitting against the wall. He's terrified to move, to even think, in fear that it will get her roused and then who knows where they will end up next. Once could be justified as a mistake but twice could not be explained so easily.

"Honey, I'm ho-ome!"

Angel looks up. There's a voice from the kitchen, a male voice and the sound of feet. Theo rises, his heart in his throat. Something breaks in the next room. Then he hears Romeo say, "Look at this place! What a dump!"

"Shit!" Angel cries. The first thing she does is grab for her journal and all the poetry scattered around the bed. Handfuls of poems gripped against her chest, she rushes out into the hall. Theo sprints behind and glances back as they race into the bathroom. He sees Romeo and several other men standing in the living room. They're drinking and tossing the bottles to the floor.

"Angel!" Romeo calls. "We've come to collect our dues."

Theo sees him take a step towards the door and Angel slams it shut. Dropping her papers, she pulls a piece of wood from below the sink and braces it between the cabinet and the door. The wood is just the right length to fit between the two objects which makes Theo wonder how many times she has had to do this before. She takes a knife from the medicine cabinet and backs in the bathtub. As she does, Theo gets knocked back into the toilet. He falls ass end into the water and feels himself ascending. He starts swirling and lifting, the world around him becoming hazy and faded. His head drifts back and he feels himself begin to lift. Then he sees Angel cowering in the bathtub and thrusts himself out of ascension. He lands back on the floor with a hard thump. He can't leave her now. Not like this.

"Look at this fucking mess," Romeo slurs from down the hall. "You should hire yourself a maid, girl. Or, I guess in your case, *yourself*." All his boys laugh and feet thunder up and down the hall. The fridge is thrown open and ransacked of its few meager items. One of the boys is in the bedroom. "I found her panties," he cries. "Come and smell them."

"Let me see," another one cries and his footsteps lead in. He takes a big breath and they all laugh like hyenas.

Angel cowers in the corner of the bath, covering her ears, knife still in hand. Someone is walking around banging pots together, singing a drunken song. A window breaks. Something large drags across the floor and they hear jumping and then someone falls with a mighty crash. There are no windows in the bathroom. No escape.

"Oh Angel?" Romeo cries. "Stacey says hello. Stacey says she knows it was you who took her car. I didn't have to pay *her* a hundred dollars. Oh Angel, where are you?" He raps on the door and Angel's eyes go sharply to the cheap encasement. "You could call for help but," he laughs, "I guess you don't have a phone anymore." He bangs the door more aggressively while the others go on with their ransacking.

"Angel! I know you're in there! Come out and play with me. Is this hide and seek? You hide it and I see if I can find it? Come on, Angel, deals still on. I got the money. It's all here for the taking." A hundred dollar bill starts wedging beneath the door.

Angel closes her eyes and puts her hands over her head, curled up in the corner of her tiny bathroom while rich men's sons ransack her tiny, impoverished home. Theo is scared for her and for himself. This is more than teenage pranks, this is assault.

"Angel? Angel! I know you're in there." Romeo's voice gets softer, more menacing. "Oh, Angel, once I get in there we're going to have so much fun. You just wait and see. You're going to love it. And then you're gonna wanna give it to all of my boys after."

The chaos continues and with it an anger grows in Theo. So much suffering. So much pain. And what has she done to deserve it? Even the guardians have deserted her, leaving her pool neglected in the corner of the Field. Something inside him breaks, changes him. He rises from the tub. No more. If the guardians aren't going to help her, or her parents or teachers, then it will have to be him. Things are not exactly as he was told on the Reserve. He can affect things physically, and if it works with one thing, it can work with others. While Romeo continues to thrust his fists on the door, the wood brace turning with each strike, shivering and splitting, Theo charges the door and punches it with everything he's got. To his surprise, Romeo pulls away screaming.

Theo steps back, gripping his fist. It hurt, like punching a cement block, but this time he felt it move. Just an inch for him but Romeo obviously felt the effects much more directly.

"Fuck!" Romeo cries. "I think I broke my wrist!"

Someone throws something, a final crash and then angry male feet begin to exit Angel's home. Gasping, Theo stumbles back and falls in the tub beside Angel. Suddenly it's quiet, so very quiet. Just his breath and Angel's breath, both in speedy unison. What remains outside the door is unknown, scary surprises waiting to be unwrapped, the shambled remains of her already shattered home. Theo's gaze turns on Angel. She's glassy-eyed, arms gripped around her knees as she lightly rocks. One of her hands is still bruised and swollen. Her Light is coming in fast, roaring in. It's thin, scared, and fluorescent. It comes in around their shoulders and remains there shuddering, thin and blurred around the edges. It's so close that Theo has to keep his head lowered, almost against his knees to keep the Darkness from nipping off his ears.

Angel whispers something quietly and then picks up the knife she brought in the tub for protection. But now the protection she needs is from herself. She turns it against her wrist and Theo grabs it. "Angel, don't! Angel!" Where she was soft before, she is hard now, rooted to the tub like a hundred year old tree. The Light moves in more, buzzing intensely, scalping the top of his head. His keeps his eyes under it, like peaking below the surface of the water. He hears her thoughts come clearly into his head, this time without the involvement of her pen.

Do it. No one wants you. No one cares. It's time, Angel, it's time.

Theo covers to his face as she begins to cut. But he can't escape her thoughts, even her vision as she watches it happen, as she fantasizes about her death in her head. There is satisfying relief when the blade skims across the skin, when the blood is released. Spilled blood helps the demons escape, it helps to release the pain. She cuts again on the other wrist. Not through the veins, not yet, just nicks them and sees the blood slide with a cheerless satisfaction. She's building up her courage to open them wider, to put an end to the pain. In her head, she imagines herself found the next day, the whisperings around the school, Romeo with a shock of regret. Then with more pain, she imagines her body lying in this tub for weeks before anyone even notices she's missing. Imagines herself found in terrible a state of decay because there is no one to miss her, no one to care if she's gone. Her dark fantasies are unbearable. Theo whispers for her to stop but doesn't dare open his eyes. He can't tell the difference between her imaginings and reality; he can't tell if she's opening her veins or just thinking about doing it. Her mind moves so spastically. From school, to Bea, to Ambrose, and then finally her parents. She remembers the day they moved out of the house, her sister, her mother and father. They took everything of value, the appliances, stereo, bed sets, furniture, and left only the worthless stuff behind. Left the garbage and the clutter, and her, because that is what she is. Garbage and clutter. They blamed her for everything. Angel was the reason the family was in turmoil, not the drinking or the abuse or the poverty, it was only her fault. Blood spills like tears. There is no escape for her, only death. Only death. He sees blood running down her arms, pooling in the tub around them but does not open his eyes to see if it is really happening. He can't stop her but he won't watch her either. If this is the end of both of them then he supposes he got what he deserved. Not her though, her death will be totally unjust. He hopes Romeo will pay, that someone will press charges, maybe even manslaughter but he doubts it. Romeo will go on. The bullies will go on and no one will care about one girl's death. One tree falling in the forest.

Chapter 11☙

Theo slowly ascends towards the light. He has no body anymore; he is floating, flying, weightless, free. The Darkness is over and now there's only brightness and light. He's in a place that is safe and warm. He is back on the Reserve under the care of anxious guardians. His head rests against the breast of an angel and she is stroking her hand down his back in comfort. He can hear the slow beat of her heart, feel her warm blood pumping though her body. He is safe again, safe on the Reserve. But something is cold and wet, like a spill seeping through dry clothes. His feet are like icicles and his head is throbbing. The hand on his back begins to dig in, his ass numb, his bones aching.

Slowly he creaks his eyelids open and sees drippings like hot fudge melted over ice cream. Thick streaks trickling down a smooth white surface, opulent chocolate drips and he remembers going to the ice-cream shop with his parents and ordering food for all his friends and there were treats everywhere and happy ice cream smiles all pointed in his direction. But the memory fades and the chocolate drips turn red, long spikes like teeth on a gap-toothed comb. Slowly inhaling and exhaling, he looks up, follows the drippings until his eyes reach the lip of the tub to where an arm rests over the side. And scratched into the inside of that arm is the word: *dead*. He pushes back and sees Angel with her head rolled back and mouth partly open. She's cut both her wrists and on the inside of each arm is a word carved into her skin. *Dead* on the right and *Loser* on the left. Dead Loser.

Theo recoils. She's like a murder victim spread out beneath him, except her attacker came from the inside. She's sitting in her own blood and when he looks down, he realizes he's kneeling in it too. With continuing horror, his eyes rise to the wall behind the tub where Angel has written in blood:

Dead, I am alive. Beautiful Monster.

His eyes lower back down to her. She is still alive because her Light is still around him, though low lit and barely shining. But this is no life at all. Not for her or for him. It all seems to hit him right in that moment and he drops over his knees feeling frustrated sobs bubbling up his throat. She may be lost from her flock but he is too. Perched in some remote corner of the Field, looking like all the other guardians busy inside their missions. Except he is in exile and he is certain now that he will never get out.

Theo wakes with a start. Rises and finds Angel sitting up across from him, her head lowered, her hands running up and down the freshly cut wounds. He wakes after suffering through countless blood-soaked nightmares, only to be roused back into the real horror. He is no better than Romeo. He took advantage, used her for his own pleasure, took her virginity. He was supposed to be helping her but he can't do anything right. He could've left last night. He started to ascend and then stayed to protect her. What good did it do? She still cut herself. And now she's disfigured for life, however long that life might be. He sees words parked above her shoulders, painted on the wall like a speech balloon in a gruesome comic book. *Dead, I am alive; Beautiful Monster.* So much blood. So many streaks and smears and spots and handprints. It's on her hands, on his feet, marks sickeningly dark against the white tub. He brushes his hands against his thighs and a shadow flashes past his shoulder. He turns sharply but it turns with him. Reaching back, he finds his own wing, and brings it forward. He sees that his brilliant white feathers have all turned black.

"What the fuck?" he whispers, turning awkwardly so he can see better. His wings are all black now, the feathers dull and oily. He remembers the dark angel on the rooftop and how Ryder labeled him a fallen angel. Is that what he's become? A fallen angel?

"Angel! Angel!"

Both Theo and Angel look up from their bloody nest in the dirty bathtub. It's Bea's voice calling out.

"Fuck's sake! Cunt mother fuckers!" they hear her cry and then with more urgency. "Angel? Angel, where are you? Shit, Angel, are you all right?"

Angel looks at the door, wincing as her cut arms touch the cold porcelain tub. She's worried about being caught here in this state. Worried about what Bea would think if she knew she was insane. But the wood post is still blocking the door. Bea can't get in. Swallowing hard, she calls out. "I'm okay."

Bea knocks on the bathroom door. "Fucking shit-faced Romeo."

"Yeah, fucking Romeo," Angel replies, calmly. He can hear her coaching herself. Keep your voice steady. Make yourself sound normal. Don't let her see you like this. Make her think everything is okay. And even deeper inside, she's worried if Bea finds out she tried to kill herself that Bea will try and stop her before she's finished. The last thought frightens Theo. She's not finished yet?

"Did he hurt you?"

"No, I locked the door. He couldn't get in."

"You want me to call the police?"

Angel looks around at the bloody bath, worried she can't clean it before the police arrive. "No, they won't do anything anyway."

"Fucking Romeo. Cowardly little, ball sack. He deserves a nice itchy STD."

Angel manages a weak laugh.

"They did a real number out here. Not too much left. You want me to raid the garage and see if I can get some replacements?"

"If you want," Angel sighs.

"All right, I'll come back, okay. Angel, you really should call the police."

"I'll think about it, okay?"

"Okay."

Angel stays very still as Bea's steps fade away. Steady, she thinks, keep level, keep calm, don't give yourself away. But when she hears Bea's mini-van drive away, she loses it. She collapses over her knees, her face against the bottom of the tub and hurls out sob after sob right from the guts of her soul. She thinks hopeless thoughts about her utterly hopeless life. Theo hovers over her, hands outstretched, unable to comfort her. He feels hopeless too. A hopeless guardian, a fallen angel, who can do nothing to help anyone, not even himself. It feels like this is the end for both of them. She should just die and then he can die with her and then they can both finally be at peace.

Both hung over, eyes swollen and stained with blood, they rise from the tub. Angel gathers up her journals and they leave the bathroom, close the door behind them and then turn into the bedroom. Angel doesn't look at the house and Theo follows suit. They just stare at the floor in front of their feet until they stand at the bedroom closet. There, she swings the door open and gets inside. Angel slides down to her knees on the stiff carpet. Light streams in slats through the door giving her just enough illumination to write. Theo sits stiffly beside her, his feet braced against the opposite wall staring at the clutter littering the closet floor. Now he is one of same, more garbage cluttering her life. A fallen angel who raped his charge, took her virginity, not to mention his own. Sick, that's what he is, sick.

Angel takes her pen and scrawls in the slanted light. She writes:

Birds take my eyes
Carry them so high
That I cannot see
Animals come to me
Open me up
Make holes, make caves
Help me to die
Help me decay

Theo watches her, hears her words as she writes, feels the thoughts behind them, knows the pain of inspiration. Sometimes memories, sometimes just feelings, the grief is so precise, complicated, and multi-layered. Angel has been through hell, is in hell.

She writes:

Quietly, I live.
Quietly, I die.
She writes:
Father Provider is a Trickster Bastard.

She thinks about her father. He was a drunk and a bully. Everything had to be just one way and she never knew what would set him off. He thought rules were for everyone else but him. He thought he could drink and drive and get away with it. One day, he ran over a boy trying to cross the street. That's when the real trouble began but in her eyes, it started way before that. Her family was never right, never real. Nothing in her life has ever been real.

She writes:
Bottles in the kitchen
Bottles on the floor
Fathers in the bathtub
Itching no more.

She cries again, sleeps a little and dreams about life before the family left. Appearances were so important to her father. That they appear like the perfect family, that people on the outside thought that their lives were ideal. That no one ever knew that there were problems within. Her father was always the nicest to her when they were out in public, when the neighbors were around, when they were in church. The boy in the crosswalk changed all that.

Angel writes:

I cut myself so I can die
Little deaths
Everyday
Release the pain
And make it real
The hurt held hostage in my veins

This blood is real
This cut is real
I slide the blade across my skin
I see the blood
I let it slide
I slash and slash and slash again

My father's drunk
Cooking pig
In underpants, the smoke filled room
I cut and kill
He drinks and dies
Little deaths
Everyday

I pound my fist right through the wall
Break the knuckles, even more
I hate my face, my ugly head
My broken heart
I am so dead

I want to bleed
I want to die
To end the pain
Why even try
I trick, I sneak, I trick you all
No one gets behind this wall

My heart is split
It's broke
I'm done
I don't have anyone
I hide the truth, I hide myself
The smoke filled room, the burning stench

I cut myself so I can die
Little deaths
Everyday

She eases to the floor, pen in hand, and sleeps and bleeds and cries until there is no day and no night, no time in this world after her death. Everything stands still and yet goes endlessly on at the same time. Bea comes back. Raps on the bathroom door a few times. When it sounds like she might break it down, Angel calls,
"I'm in here."

"What? In where?"

"In the bedroom."

Between the slats of the closed closet door they see Bea walk in the empty room. The mattress has been stabbed and torn apart. Angel's blankets hang out the broken bedroom window. It smells like the boys relived themselves on the walls.

"In here? In where?" Bea calls out confused.

Angel sighs. "I'm in the closet."

Bea turns towards the door, reaching for it.

"Please don't come in."

"Okay." Bea stands outside the closet door. "My dad's pretty pissed. Says he's coming over in the morning and he's going to call the cops if he doesn't like what he sees. They gave me some stuff too. I know Romeo took all your shoes last time…"

Last time, Theo thinks, so it has happened before.

"…and pots and pans and everything. Listen, you can come stay with us for a while."

"Thanks. I just need some time alone, okay?"

"Okay, but I don't think you should stay here."

"Yeah, I don't care much for staying here either."

"Romeo's a major prick you know, a sergeant, really. You know that, right?"

"Yeah, I know," Angel sighs, barely listening.

"Okay, here's some clothes. I'll be back later, okay? Probably can't keep dad away for much longer either. You know how he is."

"I know."

Bea leaves and Angel thinks about all the stuff she's going to have to do before Bea comes back with her parents. She'll have to clean the bathroom and hide all her journals and find something to cover her arms with and then try to act like a normal person who isn't going to kill herself and a whole bunch of other people very soon.

The last thought stutters in Theo's mind. *Kill a whole bunch of other people?* What does she mean by that?

As if answering his unspoken query, Angel turns to a well-worn page of her journal. It's a center part, a two-page spread, with designs framing the edges in pen. At the top of the left page it says:

Save The Date.

Underneath, is a list of names. Some he recognizes, Romeo, Stacey, a bunch he doesn't. Some of the names are scrawled over again and again, almost breaking through the paper. On the other side of the paper is picture of a girl, anime style, dressed in a torn prom dress holding a ridiculously big gun in her hand. She's standing on a dismembered head. Beneath the drawing it says: end of the prom. She has clippings pasted in amongst the writing. Clippings of school shootings, pictures of the shooters, captions of why they did it, captions of what they did after they did it. School shooter kills twelve. Boy brings a gun to class. Shooter turns the gun on himself. Shooter crashes his car around a pole.

In hard lines across the top of the pages, retraced over and over, are three words:

Suicide is My Destiny.

Theo swallows hard looking over at her with a dense sweat spreading across his back. Is Angel going to shoot up the school at the end of the year? At prom? Then kill herself? This is so much worse than he ever thought it was.

Theo sleeps in fits and sweats, waking up gasping, squinting in the slatted light. This nightmare is endless, full of musty corners and gloomy revelations. Dreary, hopeless, no life at all. He heard once that poverty and depression kills more people than alcoholism or tobacco. He remembered scoffing at the report, especially the poverty part. What's poor? Just smaller than him with less complications. And depression? Takes some pills and see a psychiatrist. That's what he thought. He never envisioned this endless struggle where no advances can ever be made, where no opportunities appear, being trapped in one place and unable to escape, no breaks, no luck, no hope, no nothing.

They get up eventually. Angel dresses in a bathrobe and goes out to survey the damage. For Theo, he can only judge by her reactions because he can't see very far beyond her Light. Just bits of things scattered across the carpet, broken glass, bent frames, boot marks, and mud trails. The fridge door is open and everything is gone, even the ice trays have been snatched away. Her table is gone, the couch, the chairs, the TV, everything. She has no food, no glass in the windows, no front door. Theo's sorrow turns to anger, to an outrage that is becoming a frequent acquaintance of his. He imagines taking Romeo's cowardly neck between his hands until his vertebrae cracks. He imagines stabbing Romeo in the head, punching the knife in until he doesn't have a face anymore. He imagines himself standing over Romeo's lifeless body and how satisfied he'd feel to see that kid bleed to death. His heart races at the murder fantasy. Justice, finally, delivered by his hands and not by his god. Where is god? Who is this god? What kind of all-seeing power lets the weak go on struggling while the strong continue destroying? There is no order in this chaos, no fate in this device, no religion in this disharmony.

He follows Angel as she attempts to clear the blood from the bathroom. *Dead, I am alive* fades in streaks down the bathroom wall as Angel squeezes a rag over it. She cleans her devastation away and then returns to the bathroom sink. She takes a few things from the cabinet and closes the mirror. Theo glances up as her reflection comes into view. Behind her is nothing, no reflection, no evidence of him being here. She is all alone and that is all she knows. She cleans her wounds, those horrible words etched into her skin and bandages them up. Not for medical reasons but for shame. Afterwards she looks up at the only reflection she can see. *Disgusting*, she thinks, *can't even kill yourself right.*

Theo closes his eyes, his lips pulled back in a tight line. He's not sure how much more he can take of this.

Can't even kill yourself right. Can't even kill yourself right. Fucking loser. You deserve to die. Stupid. Stupid. Stupid. Stupid.

There's a sharp crack and crashing and breaking. Theo jumps back to find that Angel has punched the mirror and its broken shards now tumble into the sink. She hunches forward, her fist now bleeding, and he sees that deadly rubble gathered around the drain. She is ready for it now. This is the end. She can feel it. So can he.

"Angel, don't," he cries and grabs her shoulders from behind. She's soft again. Mobile and malleable. He pulls her down to the floor with him and wraps his arms around her from behind. "You are beautiful," he whispers. "Beautiful. Beautiful. Beautiful."

"No ugly," she whispers. "Ugly, stupid, deserves to die."

"Not you, this place, this place is ugly, stupid. You are beautiful. You are beautiful."

"No," she whimpers, hunching and bleeding, fighting to get free of him. "I'm finished. It's over. Let me go."

"Never. You stay with me. We are together. You are not alone anymore."

Angel shudders and her tired body breaks. She collapses forward. Theo rises and lifts her up with him. He carries her back to the safety of the closet. He can't open the door, so he sets her down and she does it for him. Inside they go and he indicates to a pen. "Write," he says. "Just write it, okay? Don't do it, write it."

Angel releases a long, shaky sigh and takes the pen and her journal and curls up against his chest.

This is the darkness. I am in the darkness now. Swallowed whole. I want to die. I want my death heard. I want it to rattle the world around me. I want them to regret. If they won't cry for me, then they will cry for themselves.

I am so close to the edge right now and I don't have the strength to carry on. Not again. Not one more time. I can't pick up the pieces and go on one more time. I don't know what to do. Everything is gone. I have nothing left. All I want is to make a new way, a new better life. Write, find love, get out of here and yet the whole world stands against me. I'm too tired to go on. I fuck up everything in my life. I am so tired of rejection, of constant disappointment. I just want to die. Please let me die. Fall into the quiet. Into the stillness. Let it all end. Let it be tonight.

"No, not tonight, Angel. Write about something else." Theo scolds and tightens his grip around her, holding the wrist that writes. "Write something better."

All I have is my pen and my stories, the company I keep to keep me alive. But it's not enough anymore. Why do I have to be alone? Why do I have to be strong? There is panic in me so painful. I'm so close to falling over the edge. I'm at the point where you've tipped too far forward and resigned yourself to the inevitability of the fall. I can't go on like this. I won't live a half-life like my dad. I'm pulled under, here again, in this cold and painful, isolated place and I don't think I can get out. And if I can't get out, I don't want to be here anymore.

"Stop it!" Theo grips her wrist and shakes it hard. "Write something else. No dying. You are not dying. Not tonight. Not any night. Not like this. Do you hear me?"

Angel whispers, "What does it matter?"

"It matters," he says. "To me."

A tear falls down Angel's cheek. She leans back against her fallen angel and stares out at the slats of fading light. "I need something real."

"It doesn't matter if it's real, it just matters how it makes you feel," he whispers. "Write about *him*, if it makes you happy, if *he* makes you happy. Do what you have to do, okay?"

Angel squeezes her eyes shut, thinks long, thinks hard and ever so slowly starts to transport herself to somewhere new, someplace safe. She takes her pen and writes:

For Angel,

I looked in my mailbox and was surprised to find a letter from you. I opened it up, all handwritten and folded. Everyone texts but you still write. I've always liked that about you. I didn't read it right away. I didn't want the others to see. I took it to my car and I was so curious. You always have something interesting to say, Angel. I love talking to you. But having a crush on me? I never figured myself as the crush-worthy type. More the pal around guy, more the let's just be friends guy. No one gets me like you do. We kind of get each other. I guess sometimes I catch you looking my way and I'd always wonder what you were thinking. But now I know your secret. It was me.

I like being around you. I like the way I feel when you're around me. You make me feel special. You hear to me like no one else does. And do you ever make me laugh. So clever. So beautiful.

Angel's pen falls away as doubts rise. Beautiful, she scoffs, she can't even accept it in fantasy. But Theo lifts her hand back up to the page. He begins to speak the words in her ear and as he does, she writes them down.

I've come to realize that you've had this horrible and unjust life and that you have been through so much suffering. Forget them, all of them. None of them are important. Only me. I am the only one that matters. *And you matter to me. I love your words. I love your heart. I love your mind. I love you.*

Angel falls asleep in his arms, and for once Theo feels like he's done something right. Maybe not the way a guardian should do it but the results are the same. She sleeps against him and dreams of Ambrose and her heart is full, if only when unconscious. *Keep dreaming of him*, he thinks, *I don't care.* Everything has changed. He's no longer the same person he was when he descended. He feels older, wiser, haggard and weary, but okay. They made it through today and he's grateful for that.

Mid-evening he wakes up to the sound of music. The closet door is open and Angel is out in the bedroom. She's cleared away a circle of debris and the floorboards are up where she usually hides her journal and papers. From there, she's taken out a stereo, plugged it in and the music is blaring. It's angry. It's coarse and screaming. And she's coarse and screaming alongside.

I guess Michael Buble doesn't cut it in a full suicidal rage, he thinks, regarding the music that he used to enjoy. He would listen to bands like the ones she's playing and think, why? This is why. To match the rage, to give it voice, to give it release. And he can feel her fury, hear her dark fantasies as she imagines herself standing up to Romeo just like she did in the alley not so long ago. She shouts it out, screams it out for all to hear. Neighbors be damned, Angel will roar tonight.

The next song is slow, sad, and Angel sinks down to the floor onto her knees, sinks into her hands thinking of Ambrose, thinking of loneliness, of him seeing her and her life for what it really is, of him seeing her struggle and throwing away everything for her. Of him seeing her. Of her being seen. She goes down and down with the beat of the song, her Light moving in closer and closer. Theo moves in with the approaching Darkness and joins her.

"Rise up, Angel," he says from behind. "You can dance with me."

Angel rises and dances in the arms of her fallen angel. Together they swirl and circle, her back to his chest, his arms around her waist, her hands over his. She turns her head back and kisses him and they kiss and they dance in dark fantasy for what seems like eternity. He is a fallen angel. He accepts his fate now, accepts that the elders have hidden vital truths, that everything in the Reserve may not be what it seems, that there may be things that he needs to discover on his own.

"This is not the end of you," he whispers over her shoulder.

Angel reaches up and runs a hand through his hair, smiles, eyes closed. "This is not the end of me."

He smiles too, his heart full of her, his hands full of her. She is so much to him now; he never imagined it could be this way.

But the next song comes on strong and Angel's Light changes. She throws back her arms, throws him off her, and her Light goes out to the edges of the room. She's on stage now. She's the lead singer and this is her song. She belts out the lyrics, lost in a music fantasy. Ambrose is there, front row, watching her. Romeo's outside trying to get in. The song is perfect. You will not destroy me. You will not take me down. She pumps her fist in the air and the fans rise up with her. Thousands cheer and she is a million miles away. It doesn't matter if it's real, it just matters how it makes you feel, she thinks and a smile spreads across Theo's face. He can see the fantasy too. He's in the crowd now, so real, the smells, the sounds, the lights, the magic. To live inside such a vivid mind as hers, he can't even imagine it. The song reaches its crescendo and Angel throws back her head for the finale. And then Theo sees her, against the rising sunlight, the Angel in the red dress dancing in her true spirit. Her Light explodes outward, hits him full in the chest and sends him flat on his back as it thunders out in seismic waves across the horizon to touch the face of the rising sun.

Angel turns the music off and takes her bare feet carefully through carpet debris and out to her tilty old porch. Her eyes are sparkling, her scars burning, an excited blush painted on her cheeks. While the world rises to screaming alarm clocks and bitter coffee, Angel settles down on the old porch swing and gives thanks just to witness another sunrise. That's what she still has. The sunrise. A morning star just for her. Theo sits down next to her basking in her Light stretched out from horizon to horizon. He can see the birds swooping miles up in the sky, the distant line of the city, and beyond it to a whole world of possibilities. They both sigh and he reaches his hand for hers, still warm, still soft as they sit together in the new hope of a new morning.

But then in that sun, so intensely bright, Theo sees something come out of it. A shape. A hand. A hand with five gaudy silver rings.

"I have to go," he tells Angel. "You stay strong. You remember me. I will be with you from now on. I will protect you. I am your guardian." Theo takes one last look at her then reaches for the hand in the sun.

THE RETURN

Chapter 12ଓ

"Get him to the tower!" Veddie shouts. Theo is rushed into town, a team of guardians at either side of him. His mentor is quick on the heels of his rescuers, barking out orders and waving his tattooed fists in the air. All around, students with gold leafed binders clung to their chests stop and stare as one of their own passes under the protection of the frantic brigade, robes stained in blood, wings and hair black as night.

"It's Theodore," they whisper and some follow as the busy procession continues through the city. Theo, barely conscious, stares up through squinted eyes at the brilliant sky. He can't remember who he is, where he is, or why he's here. All he can do is marvel as Veddie's heated face fills the sky, his words echoing through his head like cries in an empty cavern.

They enter a building and he's carried up a spiral staircase, then inside a small room where they place him on a bed. Theo's head floats back as a wave of dizziness overwhelms him. Nausea bubbles up his throat, then he rolls frantically on his side and throws up over the bed. Guardians sidestep and shout, trying to escape the carnage as he vomits again and again. His stomach purged, Theo drops his head back to his pillow and passes out.

Theo sucks in a breath, his first breath in what feel like a month. Light comes in next, a sunrise just past his eyes, and then tulip air and flitted wings wafting through an open window. His body feels tight and stiff like he's encased in firm bindings. His head is heavy, a hard, angry pounding rising up from a rigidly stiff neck. People are shuffling around him, talking and quietly whispering.

"I hear he was looking around the Field and fell into a pool."

"How did they get him out?"

"Emergency extraction. It's rarely been done."

"Poor boy, look at him. He must have been through so much."

Images start to rise with Theo's consciousness. Images of a girl in red, dancing in her blood. Then quick sharp flashes of her hot breasts, her soft cunt, his hard dick rupturing inside her. He moans and a flurry of activity gathers around him. He's waking, they cry, someone get Veddie.

More pictures. Blood slashing. Angry dogs. Dancing music. White bathtubs. Inside her. Inside her. The feeling of his rigid character concealed to the very hilt inside of her. Of her tenderness dripping in his furtive down. Glimmering. Trickling. An uncomfortable sweat encases him, his chest constricts. Angels. Fallen angels. Lurking in the corners. He's releasing and everyone is watching. Everyone can see his affection emerging. He shudders out a breath, becoming aware of the heaviness of his limbs, the realness of his breath, of a solid form beneath him. Where is he? Paradise or purgatory? In the shock and the panic, he hears Veddie's voice.

"Give him something to sleep. He should not be up yet."

His eyes crack open almost a day later to see he's in a round room with one gothic window overlooking the flower filled meadow and the misty hill he first arrived on. The roof is turret shaped with musty rafters crisscrossing between it. There is only one bed in the room, the bed he rests on, and a table at his side with a basin and some herbs and medicines on it. Two chairs are perched against the far wall with a short table between them. The room is brilliant with rising sunlight.

He sits up slowly, suffering the worst hangover he never had, head heavy, stomach churning, eyes red and weary. Activity accompanies his rising. Nurses bring him fresh food and rub his dry skin with anointed oils. They call for Veddie, for the elders, for the doctor. His room fills with fleeting caregivers, no one addressing him or talking directly to him.

He feels sick, dizzy, elderly with experience. His memories are twisted and unclear, vibrant and nebulous all at the same time. He's not sure what's real and what's not anymore.

"Leave me with him," Veddie says as he appears at the door. He lights his pipe and walks to the only window as the nurse angels quickly exit the room. Once lit, he holds the pipe in his mouth and rests a single artfully painted hand on the cold cell of the thick stone windowsill. He gnaws at the end of the pipe but does not inhale and says nothing.

Theo swallows hard, his eyes raising to his silent mentor. Do they know what happened? Lila said the relationship between a charge and guardian is supposed to be private but does Veddie know? And how much does he know? Should he confess and get it over with? Or will his confession just condemn him and give him no chance to make amends? He *is* sorry, truly sorry now that he's back on the Reserve and can see more clearly the magnitude of what he's done. He's not the same person. Like when Azrael attacked him, he feels infected, altered. Angel planted a seed in him. It's hidden beneath the surface now but he fears it will soon burst forth. And he doesn't know how he'll contain it once it breaks free. This feeling. This yearning. Despite his regret, he can still feel the urgent wantonness in the background, a clammy dampness stuck between his hips.

"Tell me what happened," Veddie says, still gazing out the window, jaw tightly clenched around the aromatic pipe. "You've been gone for almost a week. If that other guardian hadn't seen you..."

"He saw me?"

"Was it an accident, Theodore? Or did you deliberately disobey?"

Theo feels his chest constrict. What can he say? What should he say? He can't even remember the reason he entered the pool in the first place. It seemed so logical before he left but now there is no justification for his defiance.

"The rumor is you that you entered by accident. That you tripped and fell in the pool. Is that how it happened, Theodore?"

Theo feels a dark rush of relief. He's asking questions. He doesn't know. Maybe he can still save himself. Maybe a partial admission will be good enough. Maybe if he is truthful about his initial offence then Veddie won't be so probing about the transgressions that followed. "It was on purpose," he admits, lowering his head in shame. "I jumped on purpose."

Veddie's eyes narrow, his gaze still focused outside the window. He clamps his teeth around the pipe and says, "Tell me exactly how it happened."

Theo tells him the story right from the beginning. He explains his impatience with the pace of learning, the disrespect from Ryder, the feeling he was being left behind, and the night the students broke into the Field. He recants descention, the stealing and the poverty, the school and the suicide attempt. He reveals all, except for just one part of the story, the biggest part of all. Hoping what he's confessed is enough, he looks fearfully up at his mentor.

Veddie remains silent after the story is done, his expression unchanged by Theo's emotional exhibition. "And that is exactly what happened?"

Theo's heart jumps a bit. Of course there is more, there is so much more, but looking at the fearful outline of his mentor against the harsh morning sun, he knows he could never tell that part of the story in any way that would make sense to the old guardian. There are some things that he is going to have to keep hidden from Veddie, permanently.

Veddie taps his pipe out on the sill, sets it aside, and turns towards Theo. "Why didn't you attempt to ascend? Why didn't you contact another guardian earlier? We looked for you for days before discovering you in the Field."

"I tried everything to escape. There was no way out. She was completely isolated. She didn't even have running water. I thought I'd never get out."

"We had to perform emergency extraction, Theodore, do you know how risky that is?"

Theo lowers his head again. No, he doesn't but he's heard enough whisperings amongst the nurses to know the act is uncommon and dangerous.

Veddie turns back to the window and drums his fingers. He seems agitated but only from the wrist down. He takes a deep breath and then speaks in a low and ominous voice, his focus back out the window. "There is a line by us unseen that crosses every path; the hidden boundary between God's patience and his wrath."

Theo's eyes shoot up, a hot flush coming to his face. "What do you...what...?"

Veddie continues to stare out the window. "Continue to tell this story to the students, even to some of the teachers if you like. I *want* you to tell them this. And believe it yourself, Theodore, if it makes you feel better. You are new here, inexperienced and reckless just like all the recent recruits." Suddenly his voice grows colder. "There is a reason for the pace here. There is a reason for what we do. How could you do this?"

"But I thought..."

"No you didn't think. You didn't think at all. You jumped in that pool against my direct orders and now that level seven is under your care..."

"Level seven?" Theo exclaims.

"Under your care. Do you understand what that means? Do you understand the responsibility of having her life in your hands? Do you realize that she is now bound to you? You are her only hope. You, who are completely unprepared for the task."

Theo feels a sweat break down his back. "But, I..."

"No! Not another word. You could at least have the decency to tell me the truth! Know this, Theodore Duncan, you can go through every hell down there, every torture, every sickness known to man, but there is only one reason an angel turns black."

Theo becomes very still. He swears he even hears his heart stop beating.

Veddie shoves his pipe in his pocket. "You are suspended until further notice. I am resigning as your mentor. You can apply for another but don't expect any responses. Younger angels may not know the reason you have fallen but the elders and senior staff will all know the truth. It is a sick, sick thing you have done to that girl. That level seven is yours now but you will not be able to help her. She should have been taken by a seven guardian and cared for properly. Now she will invade that school as fate has decreed, destroy hundreds of lives, and no one can stop her because you had to prove you were better than everyone else. I hope you are happy with yourself."

Theo is left in solitude for the remainder of the day where he sleeps in fitful bursts, plagued with dreams of death and damnation. He wakes often, sometimes to dry heave and then fall unconscious again. A greasy sweat grips his body and everything about him feels tainted. He tosses and he turns, begging for unconsciousness but it rarely comes. At times, he sees himself in the mirror that hangs across the room. He is unrecognizable, even to himself. He looks older, angrier, a dark slash of uncombed hair across his furrowed brow. A shadow of stubble grows on his chin and rising from his back are two mangy midnight wings, shabbier, more disorderly, with bits of feathers missing. Frustrated, exhausted, he puts his hands over his eyes and just weeps and weeps.

It's night the next time he wakes and he's not alone. Sitting in the armchair in the furthest corner of the room is a man with a candle. The candle is the only light in the room. Theo cannot see past it, only the hand that holds it, a gnarled olive club that can only belong to David, the deformed angel he met on the rooftop.

David mouth breathes in the corner, the candle light wavering with his unsteady breath. Suddenly he rises and sets fire to the torch near the window. The full disfigured man comes into view. Even more horrible in dim light, Theo stares without reservation at his twisted fingers, his thick lower lip, his bent down nose and greasy strands of long straggly hair. His robes are stained and dirty around the hems. His eyes seem sickly, almost red in the candle light.

"So you did it." He smiles a gummy grin. His tongue flits across his swollen lips like a man starving for a drink.

Theo pulls back in his bed, drawing his legs against his chest. "Did what?" he replies defensively. Are they talking about it on the Reserve? Does everyone know already?

David nods and runs his fingers across the back of his neck with a deeply exhaled breath. He turns his veined eyes skyward and whispers with a butter toothed smile, "That which no one speaks of."

Theo drops his eyes, feeling like he might become physically ill. Veddie must have shouted his violation from every roof top after he left.

"I remember my first time," David says and seats himself on the side of the bed near the window. "Mmm, she was a waitress, overworked, underpaid and so very, very unhappy. I was in the diner watching her, so pretty, so very pretty. They were having a birthday party at the restaurant. I tripped on a balloon. Fucking balloons get me every time."

Theo huffs out a laugh despite himself and then pulls his defenses back up. Is this what he is now? Is David what he will become? Now he understands what Ryder was trying to say to him about fallen angels. What he failed to mention is that fallen angels are not only lost but have committed the ultimate sin against their charges.

David rises to his feet, humming out his words while running his hands along his thighs. "I fell against her and she was soft. But you know already, my young one. You started so much earlier than me. If only I had known sooner, there were so many more that I could've tampered with."

"I'm not like you," Theo whispers but David keeps on talking like no one else is in the room with him.

"She had these big luscious breasts. You know the kind you just want to cram your face into. Oh, I had seen those lovely tits drenched in the shower and peeking out from the bedcovers. And I thought about her back on the Reserve. Imagined her covered in whipped cream and me licking her completely clean. But I didn't know I could. Not until the day I tripped on the balloon. You know that moment, Theodore? You've had that moment too."

Theo shudders. His moment was not so trivial. He kissed Angel in an act of desperation while she was trying to kill herself. It's not the same thing.

"And every day after that moment, I began to think about the possibilities. I tried again but it only seemed to work when she was almost asleep or on her last nerve. Oh, she was such a prude, but that all changed when I put my tongue inside her."

"Stop it! Get out!" Theo cries, sitting up and shaking his fists at the deformed angel.

"Oh, I tried to obey at first, to follow the rules of these androids. They have no feelings. They have no desires. But you and me, Theodore, we are not dead from the neck down. Oh no, we are very much alive." David hunches forward and presses his hands together between his thighs. "It was so easy," he moans. "I just put it inside her. She didn't even know what happened. The first time was in the storage room of the diner. She had a fight with her boss. She went in the back room. She was throwing stuff around. I pinned her in the corner and just climbed right in."

Theo puts his hands over his ears but can't get free from the words.

"She left that room with her skirt up over her head. That's how the adventure began. I had one taste and I knew I had to have more."

"It wasn't like that!" Theo cries. "Leave me alone! You're disgusting!"

"You might want to stop but you won't be able to. She's yours now. They can't tell you when to jump and they can't stop you from seeing her either. That is the downfall of free will and all. It's the sweetest treat in all the world. An absolute compulsion. You'll go back but there are consequences." David releases his hands from his thighs and holds them out into the light. Chuckling, he says, "Of course this is decades of disobedience. I have, in my days, been shades of gray, but she always pulls me back into the Black. Once you've tasted Eden's sweet fruit, there's no going back. But keep a sharp eye, Theodore Duncan, fallen angels have a way of disappearing around here. We're moved to the lower side of town and one day…poof…we're gone." Taking his candle,

David signs the Stations of the Cross with a dark wink and then disappears back into the shadows with a few final words. "You are now an outcast in Heaven, my young friend."

Theo falls into a kind of delirium after that. He rolls about his bed, mumbling and moaning, refusing food and drink. When he dreams, he dreams only of sex, wakes up with painful erections and is forced to grit his teeth while they quietly deflate. David's words are haunting him. He knows the secret hunger. He's hiding it but it is still there.

But days and days of sleep and solitude help the rawness fade, the emotions wilt to memories. He sees glimmers of his old self returning, a broken self but the one who used to believe in higher good, in morals, in the straight and narrow. His wild passions simmer and slowly, ever so slowly, his head begins to clear. What happened down there? It seems like a nightmare fantasy now, like watching himself act in someone else's body. That wasn't him; it couldn't be. He is not David, won't become him and is determined to change his ways. But abandoned by Veddie and god knows what else is awaiting him outside the tower, he remains sanctioned away, terrified of the Reserve, of what people know, of what they are saying. *There is only one reason an angel turns black*, Veddie said. Now he wears his shame like a scarlet letter. Only the elders and senior members will know, but he will know too. His appearance is a manifestation of his sin, a darkness forever hanging over him.

Almost a week goes by and Theo remains in bed, attended too, never spoken to, fed, washed, walked around and talked over. He feels artificial, like a ghost, like he's already banished. He never goes outside the room, only observes the quiet meadow and misty hill from the gothic window. A meadow usually milling with students studying or visiting which is now strangely empty. He goes through fits of fears think he's actually been banished, that this place is just a fabrication of the Reserve and the gates of Hell are burning right outside his bedroom door. Where do the people go who fail their judgment? Is it purgatory? Or just an exclusion from paradise?

They are simply set adrift to fend for themselves for the end of time.

One morning, before breakfast, he wakes in a stiff coffin, snaps out his limbs, releasing the grips of a quiet, calm coma. He hears dew melting off the casement and dripping down on the stone sill below. Just the quietest drip, drip, drip. He can't open his eyes, he's fossilized, more tired than he's ever been in his life. That's when she comes back to him. A quiet whisper of a voice just behind his ears.

I guess I could've been someone. I could've found a man like him. It wasn't fair what happened to me. Those filthy men go on and I have to reassemble the remains of me. Of what's left of me. They tainted who I was. Now I'm hard and mean and scared. So scared.

Theo rolls onto his back with a heavy groan and forces his crusty eyes open. Above him, the thatched cone ceiling rises up to a single point, hazy light streaming through the cracks. His chest gets tight, painfully closing off his breath. Free from his own desires, he now really sees what he's done to her, what he's done to himself. The violation of her trust, of the trust his mentor placed in him. He entered the most intimate places of Angel's life and soiled them. He deserves to be banished. He doesn't deserve a second chance.

I am an emotional affair, a quick truck honk, a slap on the ass, a drunken confession. I am never a rapid heartbeat, a gift-wrapped box, a bended knee, a dim lit candle. I am nothing to no one. Stupid desperate. Lonely loser. I hide my pain. Why can't they see? That all my love was taken from me.

He is shelter in an endless rain. A bended knee, a dim lit candle. But I can only see of the world what I see in myself. And I was planted early. With thicket seeds and overgrown weeds. It's tangled in here. So I hold to every single touch, every word he speaks, every look he gives. The smallest gestures mean so much to me. To imagine all those feelings he must have for me. The things he must restrain and hide. It's the only way that I can survive.

Theo covers his eyes and begins to sob. How could he do it? How could he do that to her? He wants to think he's better than David, but intentions aside, he raped her. He had sex with her without her permission, no matter how much he wants to believe different. And with her, a girl who has been used and abused her entire life. It makes him sick to think of how he stood in the doorway of her bedroom and goaded her to go on. Do the church, he whispered with venom dripping from his lips. And he knew what would come after. He planned it. It didn't just happen. He saw it coming; he wanted it to come.

I hate me. I'm so unsightly that I deserve solitary confinement. I'm disgusted by my perversions. My lies and pathetic fantasies. I don't think I'll ever find love. I'm broke apart. I'm damaged goods. And I don't know how to break this cycle. Ambrose means everything to me. His clarity. His honesty. He's not trying to force his will all over me. He would've been my first love, my only love. This is the man I should've had. Suddenly I see my future so clearly without all the lies and games. I wanted to help people when I was a kid. Now I just want them all to go to hell. It isn't fair. I need his love more than she does.

I have no more hope, for you, for love
The cell of the dreamer
When dreaming ends
For all I searched
All I hoped
Nothing changes
The whisper is fading
The hand dropping beneath the surface
He is my last dream
My last fantasy
My last hope
My last joy
The only one
I can't sleep
I can't wake
I can't cry
I can't fuck
Adrift, I am capable of anything.

Adrift, I am capable of anything, Theo thinks, lowering his hands from his face. How noble he once thought he was, how pure and incapable of faults, but the truth was he had never really been tested. He lived in his perfect little world, with modest struggles and no strife, everything he wanted delivered neatly to his open palms. This was his first real test of his morals and he failed in every possible way. He feels alone now, isolated, imagining the stares and whispers behind his back. Feels what it must feel like to be her.

He spends the day in mourning, refusing to eat, refusing everything. He wants punishment. He wants someone to cut open his veins and make him pay a blood sacrifice. Cut him so he can die, little deaths, every day. Release the pain and make it real. God, how much her words mean to him now, how much he understands the rage, the self-hatred, even her longing to end everything. Just to let it all go. To move forward seems an impossible journey towards an unreachable destination.

The next morning, he hears something. An old sound that he used to know. The tolls of the church tower calling all to mass. That sweet rhythmic ringing drawing the flock back to their shepherd. Theo is flooded with emotion, with the feelings he used to have when he was alive, the euphoria of gazing up at a crucified Christ, of the sacrifice given to him and of forgiveness and a new beginning. He never understood the story of the brother who went away and came back to open arms, not like he understands it now. Voices come across the meadow, hymns of praise and Theo sits up. He has to find them; he has to go to the church.

He emerges from the tower like a hibernating bear, squinting through outstretched fingers at the unsolicited sun. Dreadfully black, he can hide from no one as he lumbers past the first year dorm, his old birth. Inside the brilliant dome, fresh beds circle the exterior with stacks of gilded books on their neatly folded covers. Sunlight streams through tinted glass, leaving strewn flowers across the stone floor. He sees his bed near the back, now taken by another. He turns away, full of doubt. He turns away and startles a student entering the building.

"Sorry," the boy whispers hurrying past him, his eyes deliberately down.

The bells ring again, calling him. He turns towards the sound and climbs the street of steps up to the temple district, past the river promenade and on to where the voices rise like mountains against a prairie landscape. Church, he's forgotten this, the rejoicing, the hope, a belief in something bigger than himself, something beyond the petty needs and concerns of man. No school shootings, no slashed wrists, no suicides, no beautiful monsters.

He finds the main temple, climbs the wide open steps to the carved statues of saints and archangels. Michael guards the door like Fuseli's shipmaster, a naked soldier with embattled serpent in one hand and rippling robes gripped in the other. Warrior angels in battle: Michael, Gabriel, Uriel and Raphael. Theo stares up at them. That's what this is. War. And it isn't clean, it isn't pure or perfect. In defiance, the archangel still stands, against all odds. And so should he.

Theo's focus goes beyond those open doors to the people gathered under the wooden cross, in the overturned deck of the arc, hands up to Heaven. He enters, the only fallen angel in the room, and stands in the aisle leading up to the altar. His heart fills with sorrow. He is overcome with shame. How lonely it's been with Angel in her purgatory. He's forgotten what it means to be loved, to feel wanted, to be accepted. Overcome, he proceeds up the aisle, his eyes fixed on the window above the altar where light streams in, calling him forward. Slowly voices begin to drop as the dark angel passes by their pews, as they see the raggedy black feathers dropped in his wake, his skin bronzed like a roadside crewman. But then the voices return as he passes, stronger, more fortified. He feels their hope, their forgiveness. Come back to us, they sing. There is a place for you here. You are loved. You belong here. This is your place and we will forgive you.

As he nears the altar, the priest turns with forgiveness in his eyes. Tears drop down Theo's cheeks as offering is made only for him. He takes his communion under a hundred rejoicing voices, while images of Angel's White Book sear across his mind, of her preacher's meaty offering, of naked altar boys slaked in blood wine. He shudders and closes his eyes. Like a traffic accident seen and never forgotten, the images will always be there, her church where acceptance involves Angel servicing the lord on her knees. There is no love for her. Just the act of it. Used and abused, beaten and forlorn, she'll pull out a gun at the school prom and kill every person in sight before killing herself. His only chance, and hers, is to come back to his church and prepare for battle. Her battle is ugly and so it will be won in the same regard. He takes the bread and the wine and he is renewed. The congregation gathers around him, they pray around him and on this day he is reborn to a real religion, not just to the word but to the meaning behind it. He will survive. And so will she.

Chapter 13☙

That night, Theo sits on a bench under the stars, exhausted and emotionally drained. He leans forward, arms around his waist, craning his neck towards the star filled sky. As much as he ponders it, he just can't understand how he became so lost so fast. He has been forgiven, by the masses at least, but he still doesn't know where to go from here. He has no mentor, no place to stay. Homeless in Heaven, who would've ever thought? He has never felt so alone in his life.

"*Theo,*" a voice comes and then a hand on his shoulder. He turns and sees his old nemesis: Daniel Ryder. "Come with me."

Theo follows like a scolded child behind an angry parent. He doesn't know where they're going. He doesn't know what to expect from the Lights and Ascensions Professor. Their relationship has been one of provocation and slight. Theo keenly remembers their last argument and the way Ryder shoved him against the wall. He was surprised and angered by the sudden attack. In some ways it started the slide that led to all of this. Theo looks up at the thin professor, his eyes digging hard into his back. But as much as he tries, he can't blame Ryder for what happened below. What happened there was entirely his own fault.

He's led down the higher streets, past windows shining with happy people, past parks with grazing animals and flowers that stay open even after the sun goes down. They cross the main street between the Victory arch and the old forum to the lower side of town. Here, they enter into a more convoluted area of the city. Streets end in unsightly dead ends, houses sit in unsymmetrical patterns, and the gardens and rest areas are barely maintained. Theo glances back to the place he just came. From here, the city looms above them, the cathedral's top barely visible. And the face of the opposing mountain stands foreboding, the tree line just a few hundred feet away. They walk until the sidewalk ends. Then they go down a set of cement stairs to an underground door with metal plates and thick wooden planks. With growing trepidation, he fears he's being led to a prison. This has been a ruse to get him out of town and lock him away.

But the door is open and inside reveals a small office cluttered with jars and skulls and shells. A desk is straight across from them with a shelf of books, hand-made pottery, pallets of dried paint, and crusty brushes behind it. To the right is a cast iron stove with two worn armchairs seated to either side of it. To the left side is an old saggy couch with more books and clutter. The roof is low with solid wooden beams running across it. It's dusty and full of spider webs and poorly lit.

"Please sit," Ryder says indicating to the side area with the two chairs and a pot belly stove.

"Is this your office?" Theo asks, looking around fearfully.

"We are not all situated as high and mighty as Veddie is, nor do we all want to be."

Theo frowns at the slight. "What do you mean?"

"I mean," Ryder stands at a side table, preparing two cups of tea, "I was a peculiar sort of child in life and I'm a peculiar sort of guardian in the afterlife. You see, not everyone is struggling to reach the top. Some choose to stay at level three, or level one, or to stay behind and teach. Why I've been here twenty years now and only reached level four. I have no desire to go further." He looks over, running his thumb across his short beard and sharp chin. He's nerdish by Earth standards but not as repulsive as Theo once believed.

"But what's going to happen to me?" Theo asks, perching himself nervously in the opposing chair. It's pilled and musty, likely occupied by many of Ryder's students.

"Veddie would have you banished, of course, if he had the power to do so. He would shout and wave his fists around until no guardian dare even look in your direction."

Theo's eyes rise nervously. "And what would you do?"

"I would see you resume your studies."

"But what about my punishment?"

"Oh, you are already being punishment. Are you not?"

Theo lowers his head in shame. "Yes."

"Then that is enough." Ryder offers a cup of tea to Theo and then sits down. Theo looks over at him, really seeing him for the first time. He has warm hazel eyes and a heavy bang of thick black hair scooped across his brow. He's not particularly radiant, at least not in comparison to the glimmering crowd he used to run with, but has a luminosity all the same. His lean body is overshadowed by the breath of his huge wingspan. He has strong hands, too big for his body.

Ryder leans back in his chair and brings his tea to his chest while he continues with his speech. "What I said earlier, about aspirations, yours are very large, are they not? You wished to go to the top. To be a guardian so bright that one can barely rest their eyes upon them."

"Of course," he says, like it should be every guardian's ambition.

"And you believed, because of your religious background in life, that you were ready to take on that difficult charge."

Theo lowers his head again. "I did."

"And Veddie has revealed to you that she is a level seven?"

Theo nods.

"There is a reason she has not been matched up yet," Ryder says, sipping his tea. "Even a seven guardian would have trouble with that charge. Murder and suicide, those are not easy problems to solve."

Theo stares down at his cup, at the tiny reflection of himself inside the scented water. "Does everyone know what I did?" He cringes and adds quieter, "Why I turned black?"

"Most of the elders, teachers, or anyone who has been here long enough will know the reason, certainly some of the students may figure it out in time. To be fair, they ought to be upfront about it in your first year classes. But they don't speak about it at all. Those who figure it out for themselves are ...well, likely in your condition already."

"Does it happen a lot?" Theo asks, his voice barely audible.

"Not, it does not." Ryder replies sternly.

Theo cringes, turning a sharp shade of red. "Then how can ever I show my face again?"

"You don't know why you did it, do you?"

Theo lifts his head to stare into the compassionate eyes of the Ascensions teacher. There's no accusation behind those eyes, no disgust, not even the slightest whiff of judgment. Ryder sets his cup down and reaches for a skull on the floor near the chair. "I like to scavenge when I'm down below, maybe bring back a souvenir or two. She was in the science lab at the University of British Columbia. Such a perfectly shaped head, don't you think?"

"You can take things with you?"

"Well, as you know, not everything is the way they claim it is down there. We may have more abilities on earth than just intellect and will."

Again, Theo suffers a terrible blush. He couldn't be more disgusted with himself. And to now find himself confiding in Ryder, the one teacher he respected the least, it's a hard pill to swallow. And yet he is grateful for anyone who might reach out to him now that he's become what he is.

"You see," Ryder explains to the skull, "it's all about the Light. If you had jumped with the beginners, as you should have, you would have learned what we already know. Light isn't just *light*, just illumination representing the span of a person's aura. Light *is* the aura, *is* the spirit. Why is it that being in some people's presence makes you feel good or bad? Because you are standing in their aura, or lack thereof. To be in a person's aura is to experience their spirit. Tell me, Theodore, what was the girl like? Tell me what Angel's Light was like?"

Theo swallows hard. "What do you mean?"

"Well, was it happy? Was it sad? What was she like to be around?"

Theo sets his cup aside and folds his hands in his lap. He's tried so hard to block her out, to forget since his return. He doesn't want to remember. "I don't know. It was scary. She was sick. She was desperate, alone, lonely, lost. She hated herself so much."

"So her feelings, in simple terms, how would you describe them?"

"Lonely. Afraid. Unworthy. Lost."

"Okay." Ryder nods and sets the skull aside. "And how do you feel right now? Lonely? Afraid? Unworthy and lost?"

Theo's head begins to pound. "I guess."

"You see, when you entered her Light, you entered her spirit, and thusly became a part of it. Not having the proper education and experience, you did not know how to differentiate your own emotions from hers. You became a victim of her feelings. Her fears became your fears. Her needs became your needs. Her desire became yours as well. In essence, you became what she is and lost who you were. Who were you before you jumped? And what are your feelings now? How many of those feelings do you think are hers and not your own?"

Theo sits up straight for the first time since he entered the office. "You mean what I'm feeling, what I felt, it's her emotions?"

"Are you suicidal, Theodore? Have you ever been? But you are thinking it now, contemplating it, and yet these are not your thoughts. This is the responsibility of becoming a guardian, the management of your charge's Light, not only management but influencing it as well. You can change her Light with your own aura. But you haven't learned how to do that yet. So she changed your aura with hers. You were desperately outmatched. A level seven is a powerful spirit. You had no chance against her, not without the proper experience and education."

Theo sits back with a heavy exhaled sigh. While Ryder gets up and gathers his tea paraphernalia, Theo thinks back and re-experiences everything. Angel was afraid, so he became afraid. Angel was angry, so he became angry. She was passionate, so he became her copy. He was mirroring her emotions the whole time. Even dreamed of murdering the ones that were hurting her, like she is planning to do. And he became her lover, everything that she needed him to be. He was completely under her control.

"Do you understand now?" Ryder asks.

"I...a bit. I think I do."

"And so will the elders, despite Veddie's endless threats and complaints. You went into that pool with the noblest intentions but were unprepared for what was waiting for you. Don't think *that* hasn't happened before. Plenty of impatient students have decided to jump against orders. The only difference is what pool you decided to jump into. There is still hope, Theodore. There is always hope. Here." Ryder retrieves some books and papers and places them in Theo's lap. "These are your new classes."

Theo stares down at the stack. "But, I have no mentor."

Ryder gives him a little nod. "You do now."

Theo experiences a rush of conflicting emotion, abandoned by the one he respected and rescued by the one he didn't. "But Veddie..."

"Veddie will be furious but Veddie only sees the finish line. I am someone who understands the in-between."

Theo sits down on the sofa in Ryder's office while his new mentor rushes off to prepare his schedule. What Ryder told him about the Light freed him in some regards. It makes sense now where it didn't before. He just wasn't the kind of person to fall victim to his passions like that. But Angel is. Ryder told him that with repentance and hard work, his own color will restore and he'll become bright again. Guardians have fallen and recovered to become brilliant shining examples. It gives him hope he thought forever lost.

He thumbs through his text books and his new itinerary. It's a heavy load, twice the courses he took before. His work in level one will continue but he'll be taking courses with advanced guardians as well. Classes like *Suicide Prevention, Unstable Light, Emergency Escapes,* and *Dying with a Charge*. There's a red textbook simply marked *Sin & Temptation* that Theo doesn't even dare open.

Feeling anxious and impatient, he gets up and paces around the dim underground office. It's a far cry from Veddie's luxurious setting. Most of the things in Ryder's office look like they've been passed through numerous hands before settling here.

He passes by the desk. In size, it's no different than the one in Veddie's office, but in appearance they couldn't be more diverse. Veddie's desk was shining burgundy and accented in bronze and gold. The surface was bare except the few projects he was working on. Behind him was a glorious view of the cathedral's rising peaks. Ryder's desk is strewn with a dozen different projects. He has stacks of scratch books with formulas and verses all over them. And some sort of wooden project that looks like a science model he did in high school. Behind his desk, roots are pushing through the shelves. One huge branch runs diagonally like an artery from ceiling to floor.

He walks back to the couch, feeling tired again. As he does, he passes by a mirror. He stops to see himself. He looks haggard, used up and way older than his mid-twenties. Gone are his bright, optimistic eyes. What stares at him are cloudy, dim and lined with red veins. His bright golden hair is a dull charcoal. His skin looks scorched and his nose and lips seem bigger than before. And his wings, they are the most shocking of all. Huge black shadows loom over his shoulders. They've changed from dove to raven. It's hard to accept that this is what he's become.

He thinks about David again. Though he is a far cry from the disfigured guardian he first met on the rooftop, he sees signs of how the slide begins. Obviously, David has continued with his depraved activities but Theo has every intention of turning back. He has a second chance and he's going to take it.

Ryder returns later that day. Theo managed a fitful nap on the couch but his dreams were plagued with nightmares about Angel and all her demons, about Veddie's angry face looming over him, and about the gates of Hell swinging open. He thinks it will be a long time before he sleeps normally again.

"Everything has been arranged," Ryder says, dumping more papers across his desk. "You'll have a bed back in your old dorm and classes will begin in the morning."

"What did Veddie say?" Theo asks nervously.

Ryder gives him a queer look. "Is that important?"

Well, he is an elder, Theo thinks, but keeps his mouth shut. He doesn't want to challenge Ryder. After all, he is the only one that has reached out to him when Veddie threatened that no one else would.

"We will have some private sessions as well. Considering what you're up against, I think you could use some extra tutoring. Does that sound all right?"

Theo nods. More than all right. More than he ever expected when he laid sick in his bed. Banishment was his best hope then.

"Good, then let's get you back to your room."

They leave the dark office and step out into bright, shiny day. As soon as they are outside, Theo's mood instantly drops. He felt safe in Ryder's dark office but now that he's outside and completely exposed, he realizes people will see him, they will judge him, they will know.

They go up towards the main road. On the lower side of the city, the streets are mainly deserted but as they get nearer to the road, Theo can see the walkway is very busy. How can he just stroll out looking like this? Other than David, he has seen no other guardian in his condition. Those that don't understand will ask questions. They will want to know. Those who do understand, well, he can't even think about that.

"Are you all right?" Ryder asks, glancing back.

Theo quickly nods though he feels like he is going to pass out.

They enter the main street. People begin to stare. Sometimes it's just students who come upon him unsuspecting. They gasp and then excuse themselves. But the older ones look long and hard. Those are the looks Theo finds most unbearable. Ryder walks beside him completely unfazed by the commotion they're causing. He can't imagine Veddie would stand next to him like this.

They leave the main street and start up the street of steps. Every step they take seems to bring him lower. He can't do this. He can't just resume his studies after what he's been through. He can't bare the looks and the questions that will follow. He tries to imagine himself back in the classroom, the weird dark angel lurking in the back row. He tries to imagine himself in the dorm sleeping amongst the innocent first years whose biggest worries are exams and essays. He can't do it. He can't.

Ryder looks back when he sees Theo has stopped. "What's wrong?"

He's scared to admit he's not ready. Ryder has given him a second chance. He may never get another one. He knows what's expected of him. Study and study harder. But he simply can't do it.

Ryder returns down a few steps until he is one stair higher than Theo. With the step between them, they are now eye to eye.

Theo opens his mouth but he can't make anything come out. He feels sick, like he might pass out. Now he wishes he never left the tower, that he was still hiding his face from the world.

"All right," Ryder says. "Follow me."

Theo stares up at the words carved into the lintel over the door. *House of Ryder*. The last time he was here he scoffed at every misgiving. He was embarrassed to even be seen here. He was so concerned about his standing and his company. Now he's just grateful to be off the street.

"Leave your shoes by the door," Ryder says as they enter the main room. He slips his off and then glances back at Theo. Theo obeys, though his brain mildly protests the thought of treating such a disorganized house with any sort of reverence. He removes his shoes and walks in past the broken, spurting fountain.

"I will make you a room up. You can stay as long as you wish. Your studies can wait but you will have to get back to classes eventually. All right?"

"Yes," Theo says, relieved.

"Then follow me." Ryder takes him to the left, away from the hallway where he first met the peculiar professor. On this side of the house is a large kitchen with an island splitting the room in two and a breakfast nook inside an octagon sun room. A hallway heads to the back. The hall has several closed doorways on the left side and open archways on the right facing the disordered courtyard. Ryder leads him to the last room with a simple bed and a desk inside. It is no larger than a prison cell but Theo is grateful to have it.

"Thank you," he says sitting down on the bed, intent on staying there for the rest of the day.

Ryder leans on the doorframe. "This is the private section of the house. You won't be disturbed here but I hope that you will come to the other side soon and join with the rest of my students."

"I will try," Theo says.

Theo curls up in his little bed, faces the wall and sleeps for hours. Like Ryder said, his students occupy the other side of the house most of the day long. He can hear their voices mixed in with Ryder's and the constant sound of laughter. He has no desire to join them after his brief stint into the world today. He's worse off than he first thought. He has been damaged and that will take time to repair.

While he is in bed, he can get a sense of Angel nearby. She seems much further away when she is thinking instead of writing. Writing is still clearer, more immediate. With writing, he gets actual words in his head, he can hear her voice. But her thoughts come through more as feelings and images. The rest he has to piece together. So while he hides in his room, he gets a sense that Ambrose has done something to please her. He was nearby, maybe even touched her again. That's the impression he gets, that burning hand on her back. So for now, her demons are at bay, chewing at the walls of her match stick house until another catastrophe breaks the structure down. Her emotions seem level, she is neither high nor low. He is glad for that. He could handle neither right now.

Only after the sun goes down and he hears the last student finally pass out the front doors, does Theo rise from bed. He gets up, feeling nauseated and dizzy, and walks across the hall to the dark courtyard. He sits down by the empty fountain and stares up at the sky. Not long after he sits down, Ryder comes to stand under the main archway.

"Did you rest?"

Theo nods though Ryder likely can't see him do it.

"Do you want to talk about anything?" Ryder asks, entering the courtyard.

He does, but how can he? What can he possibly say to express what he's feeling right now? How can he talk to someone about the sins he's committed? How can anyone understand?

Ryder sits down next to him, staring up at the sky as well. "I know it seems overwhelming but it will pass. Your worries are mostly in your head. You have been forgiven and welcomed back by the majority of the community. It may not feel like it right now but you have. And once you start to prove yourself, the elders will come around too."

Theo shakes his head, remembering the looks he received today. There's no way the elders will ever forget. And his chances of becoming a warrior angel are likely over.

"Think of it like a sunburn, Theo. As it heals, the color will fade away. It happens so gradually that you may not even notice it until you are bright again. But it will happen. You just have to take that first step. And with each step you take, it will get easier."

"How many fallen angels have you brought back?" Theo asks, his voice hoarse from not speaking or drinking all day. He shuffles his fingers in his lap, his focus moving inwards again.

"How many have *I* brought back?" Ryder sighs and falls silent. "Honestly, you will be my first."

Theo's head drops more. "But what about David? Who is responsible for him? Does he have a mentor anymore?"

"What you need to understand about David is that he does not want to be saved. He is unremorseful about what he's done and continues his behavior to this day. He has rejected any and all offers of help. As you probably suspect, he is kept out of sight as best the elders can manage."

"In the drainage vaults?"

"Sometimes in the vaults. But keep in mind, we guardians cannot use force against each other. We can act only on intellect. David can be contained but not controlled. Is this what you're worried about? Because you are not David."

"Aren't I?" Theo asks darkly.

Ryder sits silently for a while and then says, "Remember your moods will help or hinder your charge. The sooner you get better, the sooner she will too. There is no sense beating yourself up over what has already happened. From this point on, all you can do is move forward."

Theo thinks about what Ryder said throughout the night. Maybe he's right. The sooner he gets back in his studies, the sooner he'll begin to heal. He wants desperately to cast off this shadow that's come over him, both physically and mentally. And Angel needs him. He has to get his head back together so he can help her heal too.

He wakes up early the next morning. Pushes the covers back and sits over the side of the bed. Already, he can hear students in the atrium waiting to walk with Ryder to his first class. It seems the House of Ryder is never empty for long. Veddie's house was so cold and quiet. Only *his* students were welcome through the front doors. Theo never saw lower level scholars spending time in Veddie's atrium. And even though Ryder has brought him in under the kindest of circumstances, Theo feels a pang of regret at losing his old mentor and his standing in the Reserve. He was on a path to greatness and now he doesn't know where he's headed. Even if he fully recovers, he knows he'll never achieve the glory he would've under Veddie's guidance. Ryder is just a level four. He has no desire to move forward. So maybe that's as far as he'll get too.

He waits in his cell-like room until he hears all the voices fade away. Only then does he venture down the hall and into the well-stocked kitchen. Ryder's home is not meager in any regard, once again, just in comparison to Veddie's grandeur does it seems small and plain. He makes himself a cup of tea, having to clean a cup from the sink first because there is no clean pottery anywhere in the kitchen. He goes to stand in the small breakfast nook in the north-east corner of the house. It is surrounded on three sides by arched windows with deep sills packed full of herbs and flowers. Like the rest of the house, the plants are weedy and unkempt but a few growths have survived Ryder's neglect. He stands by the partially shrouded windows staring out at the sandy street. There is no doubt in

Theo's mind now that there are divisions within the Reserve, the higher the level, the higher your ranking, and even the higher your house. Ryder's home is street level, or just a step above it. Veddie's rose two stories above the main walkway, it was a glorious, looming colossus. He's not only fallen physically but in status as well. Veddie dropped him as if he was contagious. It seems if he was inexperienced and under the influence of Angel's Light when he committed the ultimate sin, that he should be given a second chance.

He sighs, turning away from the window and returning the cup to its companions in the sink. He can't be ungrateful for Ryder's help. He just wishes he'd made better decision before it came to this. He has set himself back so far now.

Ambitions fading, he spends the morning in the courtyard cleaning out the gardens. He pulls the weeds from the walkway and then cuts back the growth from the beds surrounding it. Buried in the undergrowth he finds the statue of a faun and a cherub. Even a bench. Turning his attention to the beds, he pulls out tremendous piles of weeds and dead brush until the pattern of the courtyard begins to emerge. He works long into the afternoon before he clears the remaining thickets. The sun beating down on his back, he rises and looks around himself, pleased. There are five or six enormous piles of debris sitting along the octagon path but the rest of the garden is clear. It fills him with a sense of pride that he put in a hard day's work. It may be just weeding but it's the first productive thing he's done in weeks.

Leaving the garden, he continues down the hall on the public side of the house. Ryder has been gone all day long and wherever he is, so are his students. It's welcome relief to have some peace. This house is always so crowded.

He opens the first door on the right and enters a small shower room. One of the windows is open to the garden, the window not visible before because of the gardens overgrowth. So he showers while examining his work. His mind is quiet for once, not rushing around in anticipation of everything that needs accomplishing. It's something he's never really experience before. Stillness. He never wanted to. He had so much to do and the clock was always ticking. Now that he's dead, he re-evaluates the pace of his life. There is no clock, other than the one he sets for himself. And the one on Angel's life. And Angel, for now, is stable. Perhaps both of them need a rest after the week they went through together.

After the shower, he returns to bed intent on reading a few of his textbooks. He falls asleep instead and doesn't wake up until Ryder rouses him. It's night now. All he can see of his new mentor is the lantern in his hand. There's a rumble of voices nearby.

"What's wrong?" Theo says struggling to sit up. He was sleeping like he was in a coma, like he'd swallowed a whole bottle of sleeping pills.

"Nothing, nothing," Ryder says. "I was just checking on you."

"Oh," Theo says, dropping his heavy head back to the pillow. "I fell asleep."

"I see that. I'm taking some students down to watch the meteor shower. Would you like to come?"

"No," Theo says groggily, wanting only to close his eyes and submerge himself in unconsciousness again.

"I think you should come. It will be dark. No one will see you."

"No thanks," Theo repeats. "I'm too tired."

"All right," Ryder says, moving towards the door. He takes the lantern with him and soon the rest of the students leave the building as well.

Chapter 14ೞ

Theo sleeps through the rest of the night and then muddles around Ryder's house for the next few days. He finishes the garden project and then cleans up the kitchen. He repairs the fountain in the atrium and begins work on the fountain in the courtyard as well. He stays out of public eye and away from his classes. His school books remain on his desk.

Ryder is gone most of the time. Theo rarely sees him and therefore gets the house mostly to himself. For now, he is content to hide away. But on one particular morning, he wakes up to the sound of bells tolling. It's Sunday. A week has passed since he first crawled out of the tower and walked into mass. He sits up, dizzy from sleeping so many hours in a row. He stumbles down the hall and finds Ryder sitting in the breakfast nook with two plates of food at the table. Theo sits down at the unoccupied one and begins to eat.

Ryder stares over at him. "It's been a week now."

Theo nods, gulping down food like he still needs to eat.

"I think you should return to class tomorrow."

Theo sits up, setting his fork aside. The house is quiet, no sounds of voices or laughter for the first time in a week. "Where is everybody?"

"My house is closed on Sunday."

"Really? Why?"

"Because I need rest too, Theo."

Theo nods, picking his fork back up and shoveling food into his mouth. "Do I have to go back so soon?"

"You have to go back sometime. The longer you wait, the harder it will be."

Theo sighs. "I know."

Ryder rises with his plate and takes it to the sink, leaving it there for someone else to clean. "Let's go out to the courtyard."

Theo follows Ryder to the garden, abandoning his breakfast with much regret. Ever since he tended the garden three days ago, it has already begun to respond with new flower growth. Grateful plants can now spread and breathe, unencumbered by the thorny overgrowth. Ryder thanked him for the work when he first saw it but courtyard maintenance doesn't seem to be his highest priority. Regardless, Theo feels content to be out there. He feels like he has some ownership in the house now.

"The students have been asking about you. Many are excited that you've joined my house. They are, of course, unaware of the circumstances surrounding your defection. And that's likely the way it will stay. Your only real concern are the older angels. They will be judgmental at first but you are going to have to ignore that."

Theo, of course, pictures Veddie. He'll never forget the look on his face when he came to the tower. He knew all along what Theo had done and his disgust was justified. Had it been another student and not himself, Theo would have reacted the same way. How could anyone commit such a heinous act? And yet, talking to Ryder, he receives only sympathy, even hope that there might be a second chance for him.

"Your new schedule includes higher level classes, but you don't have to join those until you feel ready. Understand that this is your journey and it will proceed at the pace you decide. At least that's the way it works in my house. But you need to get out and rejoin the first years."

Theo wakes up the next morning in a state of anxiety. Ryder will accept no refusal this morning. He has to go back to class. Still, he waits until the house empties before he rises. He showers, taking extra time to work up his nerves, dresses and leaves the house for the first time in a week. He's nervous and agitated as he creeps along the streets. Though the majority of guardians are now in classrooms or in the Field, he just can't shake the feeling of being watched. He's a lumbering giant now, twisted wings, inky feathers, swollen fingers. He feels clumsy, menacing, a deformed giant plodding around in his misshapen body. He can only judge what reactions will be by what his own would've been. And he would have been less than understanding. The trip is agony. Even though he takes every back road and side route available, encounters are inevitable. Reactions range from surprise to curiosity, shock and even fear. No one condemns him the way he's anticipating they will. Not yet. Still, he's terrified he'll run into Veddie or any of the elders. At least among the first years, he feels some relief. They don't know the truth and probably won't for a very long time.

He turns the corner to Ryder's classroom. The tall brick wall around the stage hides his ingress, the same brick wall Ryder shoved him up against the day before he descended. He used to think he had it rough then. He used to think his life was unfair and unjust. He didn't even know the meaning of the words. Not like he does now.

Theo takes a deep breath and enters the classroom. He looks up to a sea of eyes staring down at him. They are full of questions. He wants to run. He wants to flee. But then Ryder calls to him. "Take a seat, Mr. Duncan."

Theo does as ordered. He takes a seat as far off to one side as space will allow. He hugs the wall, quickly opening his notebook and setting his pen overtop of it. He can feel eyes digging into his back. There's no place to hide. Behind him, a wall of black feathers scream out his guilt. If they only knew, they wouldn't even sit in the same room with him.

"Today we'll talk about ascension," Ryder looks around the room seriously. "And the Field."

Theo cringes, snapping the tip of his pencil off against the page.

"Let me be perfectly clear with all of you. If you are under the impression that I am condoning late night outings to the Field, you have been grossly misinformed. Yes, I did it when I was your level. And, yes, I did get away with it but the Field is much more dangerous than you are aware of. So let me break protocol and clear up any delusions you might have."

Theo cranes his head downwards, sure every eye in the place is on him. Why is Ryder doing this? Doesn't he understand how desperately he's trying to blend in? This conversation will surely single him out, put every focus on him. It will bring more questions and more prying eyes.

"The Field is a portal to earthly souls who need assistance. Each soul is contained in its own pool of water and that is how we gain access to them. These pools are temporary housings for lost souls. Once a charge has been cured, then that pool is taken by another soul. Be assured, there are far more souls than guardians, and many people will never get the support they need.

"If you have seen it, and I'm sure many of you have already, then you know that the paths between the soul pools are quite narrow. You may think yourself sure footed, but it's not the pathways that are the only danger in the Field, it's the sensation surrounding them. In sensing the sorrow in a pool, you may be compelled to reach out and touch the water. And just a touch is all it takes to descend. And if you descend into a vacant pool, that charge is yours, no matter what the level.

"It is one thing to descend, to graze your hand along the water of a soul pool in the controlled solitude of the Field. Ascension is another matter entirely. Now this may be beyond what first levels should be taught but, due to recent events, I believe the more information you have, the better. Consider this your advanced education."

Theo stares down at his broken pencil as the rest of the students open their books and get ready to write. If only he had heard this lesson earlier. It would've changed everything.

"Down below, opportunities to ascend come infrequently and with little notice. Not every charge lives next to a lake. Most likely you are going to have to ascend via the bathroom or the kitchen. However," Ryder says, turning to face the class who is now gripped with nervous interest, "just because you want to ascend, it doesn't mean that you can. Once you have a charge you will understand that there is an emotional bond formed between the two of you. Even when you are on the Reserve, you will still hear their thoughts in your head and feel their emotions in your heart. You will know when something is wrong and when they need help. And you can't ascend when your charge is in crisis."

Theo raises his head for the first time since he entered the classroom. You can't ascend when your charge is in crisis? That's the first time he's ever heard that. And it explains why he was unable to leave, even through conventional portals like the water in the pail. Angel was always in crises, from the minute he descended until the minute Veddie extracted him out.

"Now, as you all know, Theodore Duncan had the misfortune of falling into a soul pool. He is now responsible for a level seven charge."

Theo cringes as the eyes return to him. It is obvious by the whispers and gasps that the level of his charge was unknown to them until now. He just figured the whole Reserve was buzzing about him. He supposes it's pretty arrogant to assume his fall from grace is front and center on every mind here.

"Not yet educated on the subject, he attempted to ascend many times with no success. What were your portals, Theo?"

Theo purses his lips and glares at Ryder. Why is he calling him out? He must know that he doesn't want attention right now.

"Portals," Ryder repeats, moving center stage to address Theo in his dark, shady corner. "How did you try to escape?"

"Um..." Theo clears his throat, feeling like he might pass out. "I, uh, tried to ascent from a pail."

"A pail of water?"

"Yes."

"And what else? What other portals were available?"

Theo takes a deep shaky breath. "I...I don't remember."

"What about the bathroom?"

"She had no water," Theo replies weakly. "There was nothing I could ascend in other than the pail."

"And how did it happen? Tell the class how it happened."

Theo burns bright red, fuming. "She was carrying the pail. The water was moving and I couldn't get near it. She set it down and only when it was still, could I try and leave."

"And did you ascend?

"No. Nothing happened."

Ryder returns to the board. "Be very clear that what goes on in the Field is a serious affair. Lives are at stake there. I know you are curious, as we all were when we first came here, but you will all go there in time. Even after locating a water source Theodore was unable to ascend. Why?" Ryder writes the word *crisis* on the board. The students are in rapt attention now, mouths dry and eyes wide open.

"Mr. Duncan could not leave because his charge was still in crisis. And you cannot return until that crisis has been resolved. Sometimes you'll be down for days, months, or even years. Your charge's crisis could be a death in the family or an accident. Or your charge's crisis could be ongoing like a disease. A crisis involves an emotional collapse. Once you bring your charge's aura back up to a stable level, only then can you ascend."

Theo frowns staring down at his page. But that's not true. He started to ascend when Angel was in the bathroom and Romeo was trying to pound the door down. He fell into the toilet and started to ascend. And she was certainly not out of crises in that moment.

As if to answer his question, Ryder turns from the chalkboard and says, "There is one exception. If your charge is about to die, a portal will open up. You will have an opportunity to leave before their Light goes out. Now, some chose to stay until their charge has passed away and then they will have to be rescued from the dark. Staying is risky but you do have that choice. It is a decision you will have to make in that moment."

Theo folds his hands in his lap, shaking. What Ryder said has blown the roof off of him. Angel was going to kill herself in that bathtub. That's why he began to ascend. A portal opened up because she was going to die, her Light was about to go out. So he did save her that night. He stayed and somehow, someway, his presence kept her alive. The realization brings tears to his eyes. He lowers his head and watches as the tears drop to form blue circles on the page. The Light from that lonely little pool in the corner of the Field would've just faded from sight if he hadn't been there. So he did do something right. He did save her.

"In advanced classes you will learn that there are more ways to ascend than just water. It's actually reflection that brings you back, not so much water itself. You may access a portal through mirrors or shiny objects. Anything that might throw an image back at you. Even though you will not see your image in that reflection." Ryder looks across the group and seems to notice the growing anxiety levels. "But that is precisely why we have our first jump in the dog park. Plenty of space. Lots of water to ascend from. And we go as a group. We will be able to see each other and your mentors will be there as well. You won't be attempting any emergency exits for a long time. But let this be a warning to you if your curiosity starts to get the best of you. The Field is not a place for fun."

After class, Theo remains in his seat until the rest of the students have filtered away. Ryder gathers his things, comes down the stage steps, and makes his way over to him.

"Are you all right?" he asks.

Theo nods. Although distressed about his first foray out into the world, something has changed inside him. The knowledge that he saved Angel, a level seven charge that even seven guardians would have trouble with, makes his suffering less painful. And coming back to the classroom wasn't as bad as he first thought. Although the students were curious about his appearance, no one confronted him about it or asked him any questions. It's possible that no one will ask about what happened unless he offers to tell.

"Do you want me to walk you back to the house?" Ryder offers.

"No. I'm okay." Theo pushes up from his desk. He is okay. He feels revived and motivated to keep moving forward. He is Angel's guardian and he saved her life. He has made a real difference and that's all that really matters. The details in between can be dealt with along the way. "I'm going to Animal Auras. I'm going back to class."

Theo attends classes for the rest of the day. All of the first level students are blissfully unaware of his condition and, surprisingly, a lot of the teachers as well. In Animal Auras, Lila throws her arms around him in a weepy embrace praising him for his bravery. She tells the students that Theo has been through a terrible trauma and yet he is back in classes already, ready to resume his duties. What a hero he is! And amongst the first years, that's the impression he's getting. They gaze up at him in admiration. Word that he's now a seven guardian has spread quickly throughout the Reserve. *He's even higher than Veddie*, he heard a student whisper with awe. They seem to think that the reason he has turned black is because of distress. That he tripped into a soul pool of a level seven and suffered some traumatic experience that altered his appearance. They have only sympathy and respect for him. While relieved he has escaped judgment, at least from the first years, he feels undeserving of the labels he's receiving. He supposes criticism will come soon enough in his advanced level classes.

The next morning, Theo takes his tea into the courtyard to enjoy it in the morning sun. Mornings are always spring, afternoons summer, evenings fall, and nights are cool and winterish, sometimes even a light frost or snow settles in while they sleep. He sits down on his newly uncovered garden bench and enjoys a hot drink. He takes note of all the flowers that have popped up since the courtyard cleanout began. Even after ten days or so, the garden is really coming to life, bursting with all sorts of new foliage. Though it is small and of little consequence in comparison to some of courtyards amongst the Reserve, Theo has found a quiet beauty in it he didn't expect.

While sitting out in the spring sunrise, he hears the shower come on. Ryder showers excessively, sometimes four or five times a day. And he never sleeps, as far as Theo has seen. He doesn't even have a bedroom in the house. Sometimes Theo has caught him napping in the lounge but never because he is tired. Theo still cannot escape sleep. Every night, his head rockets to the pillow like it's full of concrete and he sleeps ten hours straight or more. He drags his ass out of bed in the morning as if he'd fallen asleep only an hour before. Maybe the need to sleep fades the longer he's here. But so far, he hasn't been able to break the habit.

Sighing, his eyes drift to the shower window and he realizes from where he's seated, he can actually see Ryder showering inside. His mentor faces the window oblivious of his audience, his head back and his arms over his body. Theo looks away as quickly as he can but he's already seen everything. Seems Ryder's hands and wings aren't the only thing oversized on him. Theo cringes and tries to shake the image from his head but it's burned in his brain, like the blood in the bathtub. Not the sight he was hoping to enjoy with his cup of morning tea.

That afternoon, between lunch and gospels, Theo is sneaking across the main boulevard when bumps into Eric. He's still careful to avoid the main thoroughfares but he has to cross the street between the Victory arch and the forum in order to get back to Ryder's house. And that crossing leads to inevitable encounters.

"I haven't seen you around lately," Eric stammers going all red in the face. He looks Theo up and then down, tightening his hands around his school books.

Theo cringes at Eric's obvious discomfort. It seems he's had to reintroduce his new self to almost everyone lately. "I've been staying with Ryder," he replies quietly.

"Oh, with Daniel Ryder?" Eric asks, confused. "But Justine's there all the time. She didn't see…"

"I haven't been out of my room much," Theo admits, now throttling his own books. Truth is, he hides in his room until he hears the voices dissipate. Only then does he venture out into the house.

Again Eric cringes, looking horribly distressed. "I'm sorry, I shouldn't have asked you to go. It was a stupid idea. This is all my fault."

Theo frowns. "What do you mean?"

"The Field," the boy continues practically in tears. "You wouldn't have went if we didn't tempt you. Everyone from that night blames themselves but it was my idea to go. It's my fault."

The revelation surprises him. It never occurred to him that Eric would blame himself for what happened. Noticing a class is letting out down the road, Theo quickly indicates that they walk towards the forum. The stone courtyard is deserted except for a few afternoon stragglers.

They sit down on the stone ledge when they get to the sunny port. Theo glances over at the boy, so innocent and so white. This was what he used to be only a month ago. Eric's biggest battle is that he feels like he betrayed a friend. Theo committed the most heinous crime possible. What would Eric think if he knew the truth?

Theo takes a deep breath. "There's something that you need to know."

The boy glances warily at him.

"I jumped into that pool on purpose," he says. "It wasn't an accident. I didn't fall in."

"What?" The expression on Eric's face changes from guilt to disbelief.

"I didn't want to wait for my first assignment. I wanted to get to the higher levels quicker. I figured if I jumped in a pool then I could get started with a charge right away. I had no idea I was jumping in a seven pool."

"Really?" Eric gasps, shocked. "On purpose?"

"So if you're blaming yourself for this, don't. I did this to myself."

Eric's face breaks into a smile and then he quickly pulls it back in. "But what happened to you down there? Was it terrible?"

It's the first direct question he's faced since returning to classes. Even though he was anticipating an interrogation at every crossroad, he's still unprepared when the query finally comes his way. "I shouldn't have disobeyed. I wasn't prepared for what was down there. Certainly not for a level seven. She was more than I could handle."

Eric now looks at him without reservation. For the first time since he transformed, Theo allows the examination. Eric is only curious; he does not fully understand why he has fallen. "Will you always be this way?" he asks.

"Ryder says I'll change back. He says it's like sun burn and it will fade over time."

"I can't believe you jumped in on purpose. Veddie must have been furious. Is that why you're hiding out at Ryder's?"

Theo sighs, staring out past him to the ocean port. "No, Veddie dropped me as soon as I got back."

"What? Why?"

Theo shrugs, though the answer is written all over him.

"But then who is your mentor now?"

"Ryder."

"Oh, so that's why you're staying there."

"For a while anyway."

"I can't believe Veddie would do that. I mean, he seems so..." Eric pauses unable to find a word to describe the imposing, unforgiving zealot that is Veddie, elder guardian and vindictive mentor. "I mean, I didn't even know you could change mentors."

"You can apply out if you want."

Eric nods, his focus fading out to the bay as well. "Does anyone else know you jumped on purpose?"

"Just Veddie and Ryder. So if you…"

"Don't worry about it. Your secret is safe with me." Eric rises, dusting himself off. "I should get to class. Thanks, Theo. Hope your sunburn doesn't last too long."

Theo smiles and watches the boy leave. Then he sits back and watches the sea birds pecking for scraps along the shoreline. He's late for Angeology but somehow classroom deadlines are not the imposition he once believed they were. Veddie would have him marching strictly to the schedule of the Reserve. Ryder lets him move at his own pace. So this afternoon, he decides to stay in the forum for a while to think. It's quiet and peaceful. Angel is alone somewhere enjoying the same solitude as he is. Strange, how linked he is to her now. How much of her emotion is his and vice versa. He supposes it will be a long time before he will be able to separate the two.

Suddenly a shadow falls over him. Theo looks up to see what's blocking his sunlight worried Azrael has found him again. Instead he finds four hulking boys blocking out his sun. Veddie's students and his former cohorts.

"Theodore Duncan," one says, his eyes glimmering with disdain. He seems to hold his chin higher, a wry smile across his thin lips. "We've been wondering where you've been hiding yourself."

Theo stares up at them. He knows the boys as Owen, Harlett, Everett, and Silas, four of Veddie's chosen eleven. He was to be the twelfth disciple. How much do they know? Would Veddie tell them the truth? And if Veddie told them, would they tell others?

"Oh, have you met Samuel?" Owen, the blondest of the bunch says, bringing forward a fresh faced boy with a beard and hairstyle making him look much like the fabled son of god. The boy does not regard him the same way as the rest of Veddie's crew does. He seems very uncomfortable with this introduction.

"Samuel has been assigned the empty room in our dorm. You know the nice one with the view of the cathedral? That's the one that you were supposed to get." Owen gloats, though the young Samuel seems oblivious to his intent. The four have come here to let him know the new order. Theo is out. Samuel is in.

"He's been up to the temple precinct already," Everett boasts. "Special invitation by Veddie."

Samuel starts to extend his hand out to introduce himself but the hand is quickly deflected by the others. He is pushed to the back of the crowd and forgotten.

Theo stares up at them, hot blood racing through his veins. They have come here to humiliate him, to challenge him, maybe even under Veddie's request. Orders to kick him while he is down. There are four of them and only one of him. For the first time, he feels a surge of anger towards Veddie. There has been no forgiveness, no understanding. His mentor deserted him as fast as he could and now has come back to rub his face in it. It seems unnecessarily cruel.

Owen runs a hand through his sun kissed blond hair. "Must be hard to be here without a mentor. Where do you live? What do you do? I suppose they've put you on the other side of town now? I guess you can still work in maintenance or as a clerk or something."

Theo feels a quiet wave of rebellion rise in him. The same one that made him look up during the orientation ceremony when Eric told him to look down. The same one that coaxed him to break into the Field. It has got him in nothing but trouble but once risen, it is hard to put down. He wants to provoke Veddie and return some of his cruel treatment. And he knows only one way to do that.

"I *have* a mentor," he states, his eyes now firmly locked on the boys.

They stutter and gasp, tittering amongst themselves like disturbed hens.

"Really," Everett, the indistinguishable one, challenges. "Then why are you here in the forum in the middle of the day? Why aren't you in classes like everyone else?"

"Because my mentor lets me do as I please. I have no vows of poverty or obedience. Not to mention with a level seven charge, I have to be ready to descend at any time." Theo is pleased as the group is taken back. No matter what they throw at him, he is a seven guardian. In that way, he will always be superior to them.

"Who is your mentor?" they shout, gob smacked and knocked for six.

"He's..." Theo pauses. He knows what the boys' reaction will be but he will tell them because it will send Veddie into a rage. "...Ryder. Daniel Ryder is my mentor."

They all laugh in unison, some so hard they double over in pain. Theo gets an urge to rush into the crowd and start thumping heads together. There may be more of them but he's meaner now, more dangerous. His dark exterior has a matching interior.

"Oh Ryder!" they exclaim. "Of course. He'll take *anything* in."

"I've never even taken a class from *him*. Veddie pulled me out as soon as he found out who was teaching it."

"He's only a level four, you know? And he's been here, what?"

"Decades?"

"Decades," they all chime back.

"Sure Ryder will be just fine if you lower your ambitions."

Theo looks up as the insults suddenly stop. It's not like he hasn't thought those very words himself, though it seems Veddie has a lot to do with that. So far he has seen little to support such condemnation. Veddie is prejudiced against Ryder and will turn every student he has against him if he has the chance. But then he notices how the boys have fallen strangely silent, staring fearfully over his head.

"What?" Then he feels something familiar behind him. All the boys' gazes have dropped to the ground and they begin walking slowly backwards. He knows what it is instantly. Azrael. She is standing behind him. Her hands come on his shoulders and she places her chin against his cheek. Veddie's students all quiver and recoil, their hands stuffed in their pockets, their eyes firmly fixed elsewhere. Azrael bares her teeth and hisses. Theo cringes, jerking away, and the boys go running.

"Theodore Duncan," Azrael whispers and suddenly he is being dragged away. He hangs like a stitched doll as she pulls him over the wall and down the bank behind the forum. He comes to rest with his legs in the ocean and his back along the incline of the shore. He cannot move. She crouches down, once again, presenting all she has. Theo stares ahead in abstraction at the sweet and sensual folds once unknown to him. Now he knows what is beyond. Now he understands what she is offering.

Her knees slam into the water as she drops down and suddenly her lips are next to his ear. Her breath is like hot lava. He can feel the ringlets of her hair exploring his neck and curling around his ears. He breaks out in a fierce sweat, his arms and legs now alien limbs on his torso.

"This one smells different now," she whispers into his ear, taking his robes and pulling him up against her chest. Theo's head falls back and his mouth drops open. He stares backwards at the bank rising to the towering balusters, through the little groves and patches of brush growing on the rocky hillside up to the endlessly blue sky.

"I like my boys intact. This one has been tampered with." She smells him like an animal would, smells his mouth, his hands and then crouches down to smell his pelvis. Theo takes in a sharp breath as her lava lips come too close to his cock.

"Broken," she whispers. She suddenly grabs his robes and rips them open, leaving his body completely exposed. He's all pulled in, terrified and bare. She puts a hand on his chest and rubs it back and forth roughly. The skin becomes hot and begins to burn. Between his legs, his organ begins to expand, begins to respond. He still stares up at the sky, his neck broken back, his body atrophied.

"Please stop," he whispers, his toes pointing straight up. The water from the bay seems boiling hot now. The ground melting to chocolate mud beneath his back.

She crawls up until her face is over his. She straddles his chest and sets her hot wetness on his thighs. His cock points up into her stomach like a clock at midnight. Her eyes focus on him, black vortexes of separating circles hypnotizing him.

"Azrael!"

Azrael backs off as a voice bellows from above. Theo's head plummets back to the shore, his body collapsing into the earth like a sack of skin without bones. He sees Ryder rushing down the bank. Azrael backs up into the water until she is submerged to her thighs. She is not afraid, more playful, smiling her cruel smile, her hands wringing in anticipation.

"Daniel," she whispers, her hands reaching for him. "We fought so hard to get you."

"And you did," he replies coming to a restless stop in front of her. "In the end, death always gets what she wants."

"Yes we do," she says with a wicked smile.

Theo stares listlessly as the two begin to whisper back and forth. He seems to be scolding her, *her*, the angel of death. And she seems to like it. She wets her lips and touches him constantly, her hips swaying towards his. She shakes her wild hair out and lifts her skirt a little. Somehow, someway, Ryder seems to win the argument. Eventually she bares her teeth at him and then turns away.

"Are you all right?" Ryder asks, folding Theo's robes back over his twisted body.

Theo only shudders out a breath, his hair caked in mud. It feels like she broke bones, broke him.

"She is persistent, I know. Come on." Ryder helps Theo stand, then pulls his arm over his shoulder helping him walk up to the bank.

Chapter 15ೞ

Theo wakes up to the sound of voices. He's back in his bed. Memories of what brought him there come back much quicker than he'd like. Azrael, again. At least she dragged him down to a deserted location before she attacked him. Saved him another public humiliation. He sits up and sees Ryder and another angel in the courtyard. Their backs are to him but he recognizes the other one as Ridwan. The guardian to the gates of Heaven.

"Are you sure?" Ridwan says. He is just as Theo remembers, gleaming, glorious. He towers over Ryder, looking twice as big in person.

Ryder, as usual, seems undisturbed by the magnitude of his company. "He is not ready yet."

Theo swings his legs soundlessly off the bed and sets them on the floor, listening intently. Are they talking about him?

"You will not hold him back if he changes his mind?"

"Of course not," Ryder says, glancing back. He returns to his conversation making no indication that he's noticed Theo is awake. "I do not make his decisions. He is free to do as he wishes."

"The elders are concerned. This is not the path he was intended to travel."

"But it is the one he travels now. I only have his best welfare in mind."

"I understand." Ridwan shakes Ryder's hand and then turns. Seeing Theo, he nods, like he used to do, and then continues down the hall and out of the house. Theo looks to Ryder intensely. He doesn't like other people planning his future without him.

"Lie back down," Ryder says, coming into the room. He sits down beside Theo and sets a hand on his shoulder. It seems more of a controlling gesture than a comforting one. "How do you feel?"

"What was that about?" Theo whispers, surprised to hear how hoarse his voice is.

"Ridwan thought you might be vying for a trip beyond the cathedral gates."

Theo experienced a nervous shock. Are they giving up on him so soon? Ryder said he was forgiven, that he was getting a second chance. Has his second encounter with Azrael impaired that?

"I told him you weren't ready."

"Why would he think I wanted to go?" Theo asks nervously.

"Ridwan can sense if a guardian is unsettled. He just came to enquire. And of course, Azrael is bringing a lot of attention in your direction as well."

Theo exhales, dropping back into bed. He wishes he'd never caught Azrael's attention in the first place. He should've just listened to Eric and kept his eyes down. "Why won't she leave me alone?" he asks quietly.

Ryder sighs, crossing the room and leaning against the desk. On top are Theo's notes and books, many of them now crusted in mud. "Death prays on the vulnerable. On the needy, the sick, the weak. Unfortunately, you fell under her radar early. Once you are stronger, she will have less power over you."

"I couldn't even move," Theo admits. "How were you able to stop her?"

Ryder smirks. "Well, me and Azrael are old friends."

Theo groans, rubbing his hands over his face. He's sure there's a story behind that but he's just too tired to ask. Instead he turns towards the wall and pulls the covers over his head until Ryder leaves the room.

That night, Theo sits in the courtyard quietly studying as Ryder's worshipers gather in the house. It's been another crazy day and he's just glad it's over. He is such an abomination now. He stands out in every situation. There's no place for him to be overlooked except in the shadows of Ryder's house. And even here it's becoming harder and harder to hide away. Even though his room is in a private part of the house, word that he's now one of Ryder's students has spread quickly through the group. And many are eager to meet him.

Not long after the gathering begins, he sees Eric down the hall peering hesitantly into his room.

"I'm out here," Theo calls, stifling a sigh.

"Oh," Eric says, swiveling around to see Theo seated in the fading light of the courtyard. "We were looking for you."

"We?" Theo asks, biting down on his lip.

Eric points back the way he came. "I have a few friends who'd like to meet you. Can I bring them in?"

Theo sighs, closing his book. At least it's almost dark, his altered figure less obtrusive in the shadow of night.

A few students come around the corner carrying lanterns. Theo sits up straighter as a beautiful redhead appears. She is the most stunning girl he has ever seen. She has strawberry curls of bouncy hair, glimmering green eyes, and the softest, sweetest aura around her. She glances demurely at him and then quickly back down.

"You remember Grace?" Eric says, pointing to the heavier girl. "And you know Justine?"

"Yes, hi," Theo says.

"And Michael is there." Eric points to the boy and then he finally focuses on the redhead. "And this is Evangeline."

Evangeline, Theo whispers in his brain. She is stunningly beautiful. Not just in appearance but in her very essence. She moves gracefully, her movements small and delicate. She smells like a fragrant breeze as she passes by him and seats herself on one of the benches. Her eyes are the most brilliant green he has ever seen. She is absolutely perfect in every way. He is completely mesmerized by her.

The crowd forms a small group around him. They talk casually about their studies, about their teachers and classes. Then the conversation inevitably sways in his direction.

"What was it like?" Eric asks. "Descent, I mean, what was it like?"

Theo clears his throat. First jump is approaching for the newbie angels. Now they're coming to him looking for the inside scoop. He supposes he can't blame them. He is probably the only one they feel comfortable asking these kind of questions to. None of them know any higher level guardians yet. "It was disorienting, at first. Like falling out of an airplane. For a few seconds, I even thought I might die. Except, I didn't. I just landed beside her in the car."

"Your charge is a girl?" Michael asks. "Is it true she's a level seven?"

Michael receives an elbow in the ribs from Eric.

"That's fine," Theo says. "Ask whatever you want." Because nothing can be as bad as the truth he's hiding, he thinks. "She is a level seven."

"How did you get out then?" the girl called Grace asks. "I hear Veddie preformed an emergency extraction."

"I ran into someone else's guardian. He told Veddie where I was. If he hadn't, I'd probably still be stuck down there."

"Were you scared?" Evangeline asks, speaking for the first time. Her voice is tranquil and melodic as a song bird.

Theo nods, not ashamed to admit it. "It was scary. I was very scared."

"So...are you a fallen angel?" Justine asks, going a bit red in the face.

Theo nods. "I guess you can call me that."

"But you can come back, right?" Eric pipes in, recalling what Theo told him earlier.

Theo catches Evangeline's eyes. God, she is beautiful. "I can. I will heal in time. I will look like I used to." Look, being the opportune word, because he will never be the man he was before he descended.

Down in the gathering room, they hear a rowdy song break out. They all look back towards the hallway, eager to return.

"Go," Theo says. "I'm okay here."

"You should come join us," Eric offers, rising.

"That's okay," Theo says. "I have some reading to do."

Eric, Michael, Justine, and Grace all get up and leave, but one remains behind. Evangeline. Theo looks at her. She is perfect. Everything he would've sought out when he was still alive. Or even after death, before Angel happened to him. It would be hard to have a normal relationship after what he's been through. And because of his muddled feelings for his charge.

Evangeline gazes at him with soft eyes. "So you fell in the pool?"

He hates that she pities him instead of loathes him. He could correct her but there's no point in being honest. There is so much he still has to lie about. He fidgets with the edge of his book not sure how to respond. He feels so out of place in their world now. He is an outcast, an outsider. He can't even remember what the concerns of a young angel might be.

"That must have been awful." Her cheeks are dusty rose, her lips small and pink. But it's her aura that strikes him the most. Inside it, he's brought silent by reverence for such a pure and beautiful Light. He feels clean inside it, hopeful, new. He wonders what his Light feels like to her. Sickly, he supposes, dark, tainted.

"Sometimes." Theo blushes, feeling like he's completely exposed. He used to be famous. Now he's just infamous.

"Do you want to go for a walk?" she suggests.

He hesitates at the offer but somehow can't find it in himself to refuse any request this girl makes of him.

They walk under a quiet velvety night and away from the ruckus of the house of Ryder. Here, far over earth's polluted atmosphere, the stars are closer, clearer. They sparkle with a spectrum of light that is not visible to the living.

"Do you ever wonder where we are? I mean, where the Reserve is?" Theo asks, uneasy around the girl. He's not sure how to even strike up a normal conversation anymore.

"Heaven?" she asks, in a soft and flowery voice.

"Yes, I mean, where is this place? Where are we physically?"

"I don't know. I guess I just accept that we're here and don't ask why."

He falls silent and they don't speak for full five minutes. He feels like a monster next to her, clumsy, ugly, unworthy of her company. It's hard to get used to this new notion of himself.

"The forum is nice at night," Evangeline comments when they enter the lantern lit courtyard.

"Yes," he says, his mind nervously recalling Azrael's assault this morning. Is she still here? Is she still waiting for him? He doesn't like to be in this place anymore. They sit down on the steps a respectable distance from each other. Down by the bay, there's a group gathered around a large bonfire.

"I don't usually go to the fire," she say, tucking her arms around her body. She's so pure, so innocent, so frail. He feels like he has to be so careful, like the slightest misstep could break her to pieces.

"How come?"

She smiles and blushes. "I hate the smell of it. I hate the smell of wood smoke. My parents died in a house fire." She takes a deep breath, her eyes still brilliant. "They live just down there," she says with a smile, pointing back towards the Reserve.

"Your parents are here?"

"Yes, they were waiting when I got here. They both became guardians."

That makes him think about his parents. And it's one of the few times he's done it since he got here. What happened after he left? What's happening to them now? They seem so far away, like some distant memory, like they never existed. It's strange that he never grieved their loss and still rarely thinks of them now.

"So, your whole family is here?"

"Not my sister," she says, falling silent in a way that makes him hold his tongue. Her gaze focuses on the moon rising over the forum. The courtyard is paved in stone with soft green moss marking the breaks between the rocks. Pillars circle the exterior and softly glowing lanterns hang on each one. Butterflies and hummingbirds remain out even at night.

"Do you ever get used to this?" he says, mostly thinking out loud.

"It's paradise, already. I can hardly imagine what Heaven will be like if the Reserve is this wonderful."

Theo feels a touch nauseated. Though it is a beautiful place, his experience at the Reserve has been less than wonderful. And he's not so certain anymore that his seat in Heaven is secured. "Do you ever think you'll go?"

"I don't know. My family is here. I think, when we leave, we'll all leave together. And I like being a guardian."

"What level are you?"

"Four."

"Who's your charge?"

She folds her hands across her lap. Her nails are perfectly formed with white crescents at the end of each finger. If he had to guess, he'd say she's seventeen, but age means so little up here.

"My level three was a boy. He was sick with cancer and went into remission. It was one of the most amazing experiences of my life. I was so happy when I left him, and so sad too. Right now, I'm helping an autistic girl. It's been very difficult. No one understands her. She's not in the place she needs to be."

Theo feels the deep sorrow in her voice, the attachment to the girl, and the love for all her charges. This is the relationship a guardian is supposed to have with their charge. A red hot flash of Angel spears through his head. Of him on top of her. Of him inside of her. Sickness follows. What would Evangeline think of him if she knew the truth?

Evangeline clears her throat. "Your charge is a level seven. It must be very difficult. She must be in terrible pain."

Theo nods, disgusted with himself. "I don't know how to help her."

"But Veddie must be helping you. He is a great mentor."

Theo chuckles, turning his eyes up to the moon. He sure is.

"We're having a study session in the library tomorrow. Maybe you would like to come?"

Theo cringes. "I don't really want to go out looking like this."

"Like what?" Evangeline smiles the sweetest smile. "Please come. I'd like you to be there."

Theo craters under another woman's charms. Seems they have more power over him than he ever imagined. "All right."

The next day, Theo sits himself in front of the library's three-story gothic windows, joining a small group preparing for their first year exams. He'll take the exams as well, though much of the material is as common to him as learning to walk. He learned his lessons in ways he will never forget. First Jump will follow shortly after exams. He'll be jumping at the same time, though to his charge and not in the dog park with the others. He can't even think about going back down right now. He's terrified of his return.

He opens his book in the crimson light cast across the hard wood table. Angel isn't the only girl on his mind this morning, the girl across the table has taken up some space as well. He glances up at Evangeline as she focuses on her notes. She is so much like he used to be but without the arrogance and conceit. If only he had found some balance earlier. His journey would've been a very different one.

Slowly more students trickle in and the study group grows around him. Eric and Grace sit on each side of him and Justine sits across the table. Some new faces join in and they start to throw around questions, quizzing each other. Theo only answers when requested or when the other students are stumped for solutions. Evangeline is quiet too, only responding when questions are directed at her. In the light of day, she seems sweeter, lovelier than she did the night before. Maybe this was what Ryder was talking about. That he needed to get out of the house and start socializing.

Thinking of Ryder, Theo sees him a few tables away gathered with some of the more unusual teachers. He seems to have their rapt attention as he holds up a small vial and shakes it at them while talking. Theo remembers the insults Veddie's students slung at his new mentor in the forum. They seem to be the only ones who share this opinion. He's heard nothing but praise from everyone else.

A loud bang draws his attention away. The front doors have been thrown open and standing in the portal is an angry visage of the all-powerful Veddie. He is swathed in white robes and religious bindings boasting his many, many academic accomplishments. His tattooed hands are rolled into angry fists. Theo's breath catches when he sees him. This is what he's been dreading and yet he invited it by challenging Veddie's students yesterday. In the moment he wanted to piss Veddie off. Now it seems like an unwise decision.

"What is he doing here?" Veddie roars thrusting a ringed finger in Theo's direction. He's not looking at Theo though, he's looking at Ryder. The Ascensions teacher rises from his chair while everyone else in the library remains seated. It is now completely silent. Veddie's eyes turn and lock in Theo's direction. Seated alone, Theo stares as Veddie charges across the floor like Zeus himself. But before Veddie can arrive, the slight and peculiar Ryder steps into his path.

"Excuse me?" Veddie says, sounding more surprised than offended.

"Can I help you with something?" Ryder stands strong, calm as midnight waters.

"What is *he* doing in here?!" Veddie roars, his finger still pointing accusingly in Theo's direction. "He is banished."

"You said he was banished. As I recall, the council did not support your decision."

Veddie skirts to the left and to the right, each time finding Ryder, nearly half his size, in between him and his ultimate goal. Theo can only stare in absolute amazement. Just like the confrontation with Azrael, Ryder is like a deer in the path of a freight train and yet he shows no fear at all.

"He cannot wander here aimlessly. *That* is against the rules. He must have a mentor to continue his studies. I will not have him attending classes under his own regulation," Veddie shouts.

Theo's eyes widen when he realizes that Veddie doesn't even know that Ryder is his mentor. That's not why he's here. He's angry just because Theo is out in public, attending study sessions and going to classes.

"Then you will be pleased to learn that he has a new mentor," Ryder replies smartly.

"He has...what?" Veddie sputters and then slowly, ever so slowly, his eyes go down to the nerdish Ascension teacher. Tones dripping in sarcasm, he says, "You, of course."

"Of course, me," Ryder returns.

Veddie backs down a bit and a wry smile spreads across his lips, much like his students in the forum did when they discovered the same information. "I should've known. I mean, who else but you would take him in?"

Theo glances around at the stares gathering in his direction. He sees questions on those faces, a lot of questions. Why does Veddie want Theo banished? Wasn't Theo one of his students? Why is Ryder in the middle of this? Theo has his own questions as well. Why does Veddie hate Ryder so much? What is this personal vendetta about?

"Have it your way, Ryder. You two are a perfect match. He is as undisciplined as you are." Veddie tosses a few angry glares back at Theo before storming from the library, but he leaves all the same. The standoff was shocking and the fact that Ryder won even more so.

Work goes on. Classes continue. Theo falls back into a new rhythm, this one at a more reasonable pace than the last. He regains his position at the top of the class, even begins to fade to a lighter grey. He stays in Ryder's house for the time being even though he is probably ready to be on his own. Azrael leaves him alone. And he does not see Veddie or any of his students after the confrontation in the library. The shock of his new appearance has faded now, so he goes out more, goes to study groups and to the library. He even goes down to the campfire and meets with Evangeline. She is lovely and refreshing and helps to keep his spirits up when they are down. Angel seems to settle for a while too. Their lives reach a tremulous level of normalcy.

His studies continue in preparation of his next jump. Unlike the first years, he is not just getting his feet wet, he is preparing for his next battle. He meets Ryder every second night for extra sessions. And though Veddie is more knowledgeable, Ryder actually shares that knowledge, which makes him ten time more valuable than Veddie ever was.

Theo can ask him anything and answers are delivered without protest. He understands so much more about what he faces than he did before. He meets with elder teachers as well. He learns what he wished he had earlier: how to separate his own Light from his charges. How to find a distinction between them. How to keep it apart from his own. Though, as he already knows, that is a task that is easier said than done. He also finds out that charges are not randomly set. There are reasons charges and guardians are matched up together. A guardians strengths should correspond with a charge's weaknesses. Seeing himself aligned with Angel, he knows that they would have never been put together. He is inexperienced sexually. He has never even met a suicidal person before her. He doesn't know poverty. While he used to consider himself privileged because of the life he lived down below, he has begun to understand that his lack of suffering before death has actually set him behind the rest of the students. He does not know pain. He does not know struggles. He glided through his life from birth to death with minimal effort. All the wealth and education in the world would not give him an experienced soul. That he is going to have to work on above. And as he has learned already, it is much harder to work on the self above. He still has a lot of struggles ahead of him.

One night, Theo makes his way across town for his nightly session with Ryder. The fall sun is setting as he travels to the office where no weather permeates. Inside the cave-like fortress, Theo finds a note indicating Ryder will be along shortly. Make yourself comfortable. Theo sets his books aside and snoops through the shelves of wood boxes and locked compartments containing Ryder's obsession with earthly oddities. He has jars of snake skeletons and a Rubik's cube with no colors and clocks with no arms. On his desk, his tinker toy contraption grows in size and width every day. Just a cube with squares and triangles and octagons, like a virus multiplying, a cancerous protein spreading. Also on the desk are quills and parchment, notes in languages he's never seen before, scientific equations he couldn't even begin to understand, and maps of places he's never heard of.

Feeling restless, Theo turns back to the couch. Not the usual spot by the fire where he and Ryder sit, but the couch in the dark corner across the room. He sits down and sets his books on his lap. Tonight's lesson, a book bound in crimson silk and leather, is Sin & Temptation. He feels dirty just looking at it. He's overwhelmed by an impression that the book is not just a general overview of deviant behavior but a novel of his escapades detailed with pictures and descriptions of everything he did down below. The trepidation gnaws at him until he snaps the book open and sees scripture and notations from the bible. No Theodore Duncan mentioned anywhere.

He sighs, closing the book as the front door opens. Ryder walks in, removes his coat and hangs it on the stand beside him. He turns to close the door and exclaims, "Oh, I didn't see you there!"

"I..." Theo begins to stand but realizes Ryder isn't talking to him. Justine, Eric's friend, is following his mentor in.

"Justine?" Ryder says, closing the door with a soft click behind her.

Theo clears his throat, intending to make himself known but something in the way that the two face each other renders him silent. Nothing palpable, just a change in the air that corrals his tongue back inwards.

"I have a meeting shortly," Ryder says, tucking a curl of his overgrown hair behind his ear and returning his gaze to the girl. She's fidgety. He seems to notice. "Is there something bothering you?"

Justine stares down at her mentor's feet and says nothing. She closes her eyes, exhaling deeply, her hands shaking. Ryder moves a little closer and takes her by the wrists. Softly, he says, "Hey, you can talk to me about anything. You know that."

"I do," she says, welling up and turning her head away. "I'm just...scared."

"About first jump? It's okay. I'll be there. I won't let you get lost."

"No. I mean, yes. I mean..."

"Justine, sit down. I'll get us some tea. How does that sound?"

Justine seems to relax a bit. "Okay."

Ryder goes to a side table and removes a pot that's been simmering on the wood stove. He fills two cups with steamy water and then spoons in an assortment of leaves and herbs. Theo quietly remains at the couch, keeping his presence unknown. He's curious to uncover some of the dissonance that surrounds his new mentor.

So Ryder prepares the tea, his back to the girl. While he does, Justine stands beside the chair by the fire. Watching Ryder, she unbuttons her jacket and lets it slide off her shoulders. It falls to the floor with a soft thump. She's completely naked underneath. She stands, waiting for her mentor to turn and make his decision. All Theo can do is sit and stare, not at her nudity, or even her body, but at the boldness of the offer she is making to him. She's just a girl, her request outrageous. And yet, Theo is as curious as she is about what Ryder's response will be.

"It's a bit hot," he says, turning with cup and saucer in hand. He jolts to a stop when he sees her. The cup rattles briefly in his hand but doesn't spill. "Justine?"

"Daniel, please," she whispers softly, her hands going nervously down her exposed body.

Ryder turns inward for a moment, at a loss for words, thinking. Then he sets the tea back beside the other cup. He walks around the chair towards her and Justine's resolve falters. She sinks back in the chair behind her, lifting a corner of her jacket in a feeble attempt to cover herself.

"I'm sorry," she whispers and starts to cry.

"It's okay," he says softly, kneeling down in front of her and helping her put her jacket back on.

"You don't like me," Justine whispers. "I'm so stupid."

"No, no," Ryder insists, closing the front buttons, his fingers fumbling with hers. Her legs poke out beneath the jacket, knees pressed against his chest as he dresses her. "It's nothing like that, Justine."

His reply only makes her cry more. He comforts her softly with a gentleness that Theo knows would make Veddie scoff. His old mentor had no concerns about the mental stumbles of his students.

"I'm so stupid," Justine says, hiding her face in her hands.

"Not stupid, not stupid, Justine. Just mistaken. We all make mistakes. It will be okay."

"But I thought…I was thinking that…Daniel, I love you."

"Justine." Ryder sits back on his knees while the girl weeps into her hands.

"Why not? You're alone and I'm alone. I don't care how old you are. I want to…be with you. You're special. I care about you. Don't you see?"

He remains on his knees, hands clasped in his lap. His heavy bang falls across his eyes and covers his reaction from Theo's sneaky perch. Ryder doesn't answer right away. He's quiet for just a little too long. Theo frowns, frozen in place. Is he considering this? What's going on here?

"Because I'm your mentor," Ryder finally replies. "I am here to guide you in your studies. There are other students here that can…"

"I don't care. Daniel, please." Justine rises suddenly. In a last act of desperation, she throws her jacket off her shoulder revealing taut spring breasts and rosy buds between. When he doesn't respond, she lunges, comes at him full force and attempts to disrobe him. She puts her hands on his chest, tries to pull him in and kiss him. Ryder rises to defend her advances, smoothly, never harshly, taking her hands down and turning his mouth away. In the end, she stands defeated, hands over her face, crying.

"We will have to talk about this another time, Justine," Ryder says, his collar torn open, his robes jumbled and untied. "I have an appointment coming in shortly. You should go straight away to confession." He turns to get the door and she wraps her arms around his waist from behind like a child trying to keep a parent from leaving. Her hands slither up over his chest like a python.

She whispers, heatedly, "But I have nothing to confess."

Ryder just closes his eyes with a hard shuddered sigh. "I'm sorry, Justine. I can't help you with this."

Justine's hands drop to her sides. She seems to accept her defeat. Her face grows sad as she whispers, "Are you going to get rid of me?"

Ryder stares for a moment at the faded girl with weeping eyes, her frock drape loosely around her newly blooming body. In a shadowy voice, he whispers, "I would never do that."

Justine's breath rises with her eyes. Ryder reaches a hand forward. He cups her chin and gently strokes his thumb along her cheek. His unusually large hands seem to dwarf her tiny face.

"Justine," he breathes and then his face drops just an inch closer. He nips, mouth ajar and then lowers and touches his lips to hers. Maybe he meant it as a comforting kiss, maybe he didn't, but Justine crumbles beneath him as he lovingly gratifies her burning request. She whimpers as her teacher, her mentor, places a kiss after kiss on her ravenous virgin lips. She gets dim, her hands in uneasy surrender between their flustered chests. Ryder's arm slips around her waist. He pulls her roughly in and she screeches in astonishment. He crushes her petite body against his, takes his big hand aggressively behind her neck and devours her youthful mouth. Justine gasps in little shrieks, eyes up and half open, her robe tumbling down over her shoulder.

Ryder pulls back with a sudden inhalation, seems to remember himself but still doesn't let her go. He presses his forehead to hers. Tears are running down his cheeks. He says, "I shouldn't have done that, Justine. I apologize."

Justine can't even speak. She reaches a trembling hand to his shoulder to stabilize herself. The silhouette of her hard pointed breast is traced from the fire beyond them. She swallows hard, struggling to look up at him. His arm around her waist is the only thing holding her up right now. She wets her lips with a quick pink flicker.

"We'll talk about this later, okay?" he says in a deep, musky voice.

Justine emits a sort of high pitched tremor, clears her throat and whispers. "Okay, Daniel."

Ryder escorts her out and then closes the door after she leaves. He leans against the door with a heavy sigh, rubbing fiercely at the back of his neck. He pushes away, takes one step towards his desk and that's when he sees Theo seated in the dark corner. He stops, his expression changing from surprise to resentment and then to acceptance.

"What are you doing?" Theo cries angrily, rising from the couch. "That girl is barely sixteen and your student!"

"I don't think this is any of your business." Ryder passes a sly eye over Theo and continues back to the wood stove to deal with his forgotten tea.

Theo takes a few steps towards him. "You didn't answer my question."

Ryder sets the kettle aside, water steaming out the open spout, and looks back at him. A darkness passes over Ryder's face, a loss of control revealing something leashed inside, something he needs to hide. "I think you should leave."

Theo throws down his most judgmental glare. "You are not the man I thought you were."

Ryder turns to face him. "And who did you think I was? The almighty and unflappable Veddie? The next Lord and Jesus Christ of the Reserve? Don't forget, you are a fallen angel, Theodore Duncan, if you have any dreams of returning to that sort of standing, you need to forget it. You have made your decision. You are with me now. Like it or just leave."

Theo wants to leave. He wants to just march out and never look back but something else is gnawing at him. Something that's been drifting up near the surface but hasn't been close enough to see clearly. Now it is all coming into focus. He stares down Ryder, standing almost a head taller than his mentor, at his sunken and woeful eyes, his thin physique, his oversized hands and wings.

"You're a fallen angel, aren't you?" he whispers.

Ryder's eyes lift slowly and the look on his face only confirms Theo's fears. Theo takes a step back and then another. He can't believe it's true. Ryder committed the ultimate sin. He put his hands on his charge. More than his hands. And this is the man who intends to bring him back from the Black? A man who lied and concealed his true identity, pretended to be better than him when in fact they were exactly the same. No, not the same. Not the same at all.

Chapter 16 ଓଃ

Theo's wanders most of the night trying to process what he's just learned. Ryder concealed the fact that he was a fallen angel. How many more secrets is he likely to uncover due to Ryder's lack of disclosure? Is this a man he really wants mentoring him? He's extremely confused and troubled by the revelation. No wonder Veddie hates him so much. And no wonder Veddie was so mad when he found out Ryder was his mentor. Who would want a former fallen angel mentoring his students? Theo's mind is swimming. He can't believe what he saw tonight and what he learned. Ryder sins are not just in the past but continue today. He is toying with having an inappropriate relationship with Justine, with one of his students. It makes Theo feel less respect towards his latest mentor but how can he judge? He is no saint either. In one respect, Ryder should be the perfect mentor, a fallen angel now come back to the light. Except for the slightly enlarged hands and wings, there is little to indicate he'd ever been marked as a sinner. In other regards, it makes Theo worry. Ryder gave in to that girl, a sixteen year old girl, and ended it with no definite conclusion. It disturbs him. It rouses him too. He thinks of Angel. He remembers that passion. That appeal. The euphoria of denying only to eventually give in. There was a moment at the door when Ryder crossed the line with Justine. Theo knows that thrill, of taking what shouldn't be taken, of giving into something that must be denied. But then his mind tumbles back into despair at being linked with such a mentor. Fallen guardian and his fallen student. Where is he to go from here?

He eventually returns to the House of Ryder simply because he has no place left to go. It seems inevitable that he must transfer out as soon as possible. And yet he's scared to leave. This has been his hiding place for a very long time.

He finds his bed and falls into it. The house is quiet, no sign of Ryder. He turns and he tosses. Studies on sin and temptation postponed until further notice. His whole life postponed until further notice. He thinks desperately of other mentors he could apply to, someone with better standing. Could he do this by himself? He has a charge and she can't be taken away so he is a part of the Reserve whether he is in classes or not. Is he to become a rogue angel among god's holy disciples? Is he to become like David, adrift and left to his own devices?

Angel is awake too. He can feel that her mind is at unrest. It's likely a result of his own unrest. He should be in better control of himself; he has more to think of than just his own sanity now. Angel's mind drifts this way and that. He gathers concepts rather than exact thoughts. Ambrose and sex and then money and bills. Payments are still looming. She still has no money. She hasn't stole since the grocery store but she will have to steal soon. And then Ambrose again. He's paid her a lot of attention lately. It has her plenty worked up. There are so many things she wants to do to him. For him to do to her.

In her darkness, a thought is rising, like a hot seed sprouting in a moist box. She's imagining a game. A computer game. Where she is the character and the man at the computer is the controller. It peaks her interest. And now she can think of nothing else.

Theo squeezes his eyes shut, his head spinning. Not this. Not now. He can't take another bout of her literary frivolities after everything that's happened today. He's barely back on his feet and stumbling the entire way. But as much as he pleads and begs, Angel reaches for the White Book.

He turns me on and I come alive. I hum into existence in a room bright with no lights. In a room with just three walls and the third one is him. Just him and his dark eyes looming in.

Theo settles stiffly back, breathing slow and easy. Why didn't he stay in Ryder's office? They could be fighting it out right now instead him all alone with her. All alone with her bountiful fantasies. He can't run. Everywhere he goes, she will follow along. Michael may handle the serpent but Theo's demon is inside.

Words appear in a text box.
USER NAME:
He leans back and I see his face. He's dark, beefy, his chest thick, his arms sculpted like tree trunks.
USER NAME: AMBROSE

Theo sighs. She's nothing if not consistent, determined to ride this fantasy until the bitter end. How much she wants it and yet the feelings behind the passion are so complicated and bleak. He feels himself being drawn in again. They are linked but she is so much more powerful than he is. He doesn't have the experience to control her the way she controls him.

He looks at me. Hard at me. His eyes move in and fill the whole screen. I stand there, gelatin skin, my hands on my hips, two girlish pony tails at each side of my head dressed in the smallest school girl outfit imaginable.

I see other things on the screen between us. A menu board of options, entrees presenting me, pictures of accessories he may use along the way, a camera, hands, toys and more. A bar labeled excitement. I can't wait to see what that's meant for. Serve me on a silver platter, Ambrose. Dish me up and savor my every flavor.

Theo shifts uncomfortably. Her damned words are so clear, so descriptive, so palatable. She is a deep well of imagination tapped into the dirtiest reservoir. Oh, the irony of this happening right after he scolded Ryder for his foray into passion. Now he is faced with the very same dilemma. Be strong, be resolute, or give in to temptation. Fall back into the abyss of sexual gratification.

I'm standing and facing the screen, my hands on my hips, unable to do anything but stare. My controls lay at his fingertips. I can't look down or around, only forwards, only at him. Wait for him. Only him.
MENU
OPTIONS
CAMERA
A camera appears in front of me. He maneuvers it and takes a picture. A still frame of me appears on his hard drive and that makes him smile. It makes me smile too though my face doesn't show it. I am his, under his direct control, can't even wink without his guarantee. So use me, Ambrose. I'm waiting.

Ambrose returns to the menu bar.
POSITIONS
Now I see thumbnails of generic girls in different accessible poses. Ambrose thumbs his pointer down the options. He makes a selection. A table comes up beneath me. I sit, open my legs and straddle a cold corner, lean back on my elbows and push my breasts towards him.
"What would you like me to do?" I hear myself say.
My short skirt rides up. I can feel the corner of the table forcing my hot thighs open, the gust of cold air rushing in to fill the gap. Ambrose looks down. Changes the angle and then looks closer.
OPTIONS
UNDRESS
A drop down list entails everything I'm wearing: school girl top, pleated skirt, red-rimmed bra, bikini briefs, and all. He clicks on the option marked:
BIKINI BRIEFS
My underwear disappears. I gasp as my ass suddenly contacts the cold table. My knees react and try to close, but my programming holds them open. I must do as commanded. He is my controller.

Theo sits up and rubs his hands over his face. Now he remembers why he did it, that sensation when he stood at the door of her bedroom and asked her to write the church. That swollen, unfastened, and senseless hunger he'd risk anything to gratify. Breathing deep, he turns so his feet are over the side of the bed and sits up, trying to clear his head. At least she is there and he is here. At least he can't touch her.

The camera appears between my legs. Ambrose adjusts it closer, skimming between my thighs until the lens is beneath the hem of my skirt. A flash illuminates the inside of my skirt. A screenshot appears between us of my swollen, wet recesses, so hungry, so hungry. Again, the skirt lights up and lightning shivers down my thighs. The cold lens grazes my skin, a hot bulb flashes and I shudder out a tight breath. I see points on the excitement meter. The game is just beginning.
SAVE TO HARD DRIVE?
Yes.
SAVE TO HARD DRIVE?
Yes.
Yes.
Yes.

I gasp and roll my head back. At least I feel like I do because I can't move. I can't move unless he moves me. Move me, Ambrose, move me.

Theo rolls back to bed and pulls the covers up over his head. His resolve is weakening. He thinks about Ryder, his disappointment when he saw his mentor give in. Now he wants to give in too. Wants to sneak his hands down and release it all. He can see it so clearly. He'll lift his knees so the blankets tent, so he can hide all activities beneath. No one will ever know. He didn't change color when he touched himself, just the night he touched her. Maybe touching himself doesn't count. So maybe he can do it now and it won't show.

OPTIONS
REMOVE
SCHOOLGIRL TOP, RED-RIMMED BRA

Suddenly my breasts break free, rip free like a shirt torn from my chest and they settle in little ripples, hard nipples automatic, up and out pleading for his waiting mouth. Except we are apart and his tongue can't reach me. But there are other things. Tools in the program to assist with frustration. Choose a tool, Ambrose. Use a tool on me.

OPTIONS
TOYS
ICE CUBE

An ice cube appears in front of my right breast. Disembodied, it jiggles as my rosy pink point pushes out painfully towards it. My hands remain behind me on the desk, unable to move, unable to release. My excitement bar reaches fifteen percent. Red rising. Red Rising. My legs are shafted open, thighs trembling from the strained position, open and unable to move. Wet and unable to come. I see something I didn't see before. A little button beside the excitement bar. It has a picture of an explosion. Explosion! Explosion!

A breath shudders from Theo's lips, his eyes open and focused on the ceiling. His god is gone now. Ryder, Justine, paradise, everything. All that remains is the outrage between his hips. He rests his hands on his chest, robes wrapped tightly around him, blankets up to his neck. Then slowly, he draws his knees up knowing it is the gateway to all that will follow next.

He uses the mouse to move the ice forward. The frigid rock contacts my tip. I shriek at the sudden and cold contact.

JIGGLE, he clicks, JIGGLE.

Twitching on its own regard, it services the right side and then the left and then down and down, right knee, left knee, and then up and up. Inside my thigh, inside my skirt and then contact. Explosion. I screech out with pleasure though my avatar reveals nothing. The shock of the slippery rock sends shockwaves through my body. God, the pleasure of being confined and controlled. My levels rise. My knees quiver and shiver for release.

Theo closes his eyes as his fingers reach beneath his robe. Up and down his rib cage falls and he scrambles to resist. But all he can think of is her, the feeling of those doughy breasts pushed up beneath him, of her hips bucking, of her slick wetness and how fervent she was inside, how she enveloped him in a taut slithery sheath and rung all his worries away. God, how he wants it now. In wild abandon, his mind goes to fanatical places. He imagines finding Evangeline, surprising her in her bed, lifting up her skirts and surprising her someplace else. Imagines her shock and surprise, her struggle beneath him as he pins her hands behind her head, breaks her open to the first man for sampling.

Mouth dry and jaw clenched, his eyes jittery and rigid in his head, he can't contain it any longer. She's done it to him again.

OPTIONS

PARTNERS

He checks through my mates, not just men but men in ready positions, ready to perform, ready to release me.

MISSIONARY, TABLE

I drop back to the table, my arms stretched up and over my head. A man appears between my legs, smooth, hairless, his eyes unfocused and straight forward. He takes my knees in his hands and lifts my legs open to either side of him. Buck naked, his fully engorged cock is pointed straight at its target. He is programmed, like me, a tool like the ice cube. His orders are to give. Mine are to receive.

Theo curses as his hand moves down. Quietly beneath the covers, he grips himself and begins to stroke. Stars go off behind his eyes. He gazes up but sees nothing on the outside. Now this is rapture. Now he remembers.

My excitement levels are rising. I come down all over. Wet and ready and gasping for air, my hands bound by tight-fisted geeks hunched over computers, he begins the sequence. He double-clicks the man alive, his eyes blinking like a clock. Tick Tock. The hips move forward until the brimming missile encounters my inflamed universe. The head pushes in, sinks like a shipwreck taking in water to the bottom of the ocean. I shudder and arch, the ice on my nipple. Wiggle. Wiggle. Explosion and I come down all over my trespasser, make his invasion easier.

SAVE TO HARD DRIVE?
NEW LEVELS UNLOCKED.
WOULD YOU LIKE TO UPGRADE?
DO YOU WANT TO SEE MORE?
YES.
YES.
YES.

Theo beats down in rhythm now, thumping his fist hard against his shank, working up and over and then down again, enclosed entirely in the fantasy, not just her words but the feeling the words cause and what she's doing in reaction. And they are doing it together even though they are so far apart. He opens his legs, throws his free hand up over his head like an eager bull rider. Beneath him the bed squeaks quietly in rhythm. He wants the blankets off now. He wants more risk. He wants to get caught. He imagines Ryder walking in and the shock of being discovered. He imagines himself running naked in the forum, spread eagle on the stage in the empty auditorium, humping on the library tables, on the park benches, in the Field, poised over Angel's pool and letting his glory shower down all over. Maybe he should go in, jump now, go to her and finish this properly. How much color is he willing to surrender for one little encounter?

Fuck me. Fuck me. Your machine makes me quiver. Hip axles swivel. The head formed just right, width in tight numbers, temperature equal. He cracks me like a whip. Cluck. Cluck. I'm wet all over. Plunging to deepest depths, dredging up the deep. I am an ocean, tides rising, the shores spilling over. Dig a hole in me, plant me over, plant me under, grow the deep. Fuck me. Fuck me. Less than shiver, more than render. Double c-plus program an incisive hard collision. Fuck me. Bind me. Seize me. Dig in. Dig fierce. Dig low.

Dig hard. Make me weep. Make me shiver. Fuck me till I rupture. Till I tither. Till I fluster. Oh god, make me over, make me under, make me hover.

Theo sucks a breath in through his teeth and throws back the covers. No exposure is enough now. He rises from bed and stumbles out into the courtyard. He crosses the path in hot-blooded fever with a full erection directing his way. He lies down on the bench, under the moonlight and continues his voyage. She's riding herself hard and he matches her every stride. Smack. Smack. Cluck. Cluck. He stares up at the moon, shoving his hips into the sky. Punches holes in the thin clouds with his eager vessel. He rocks his palm until a thready explosion bursts silently up into the moon filled courtyard. Rises up like a geyser and sprinkles down all over himself in glimmering little sparkles. He falls back to the bench, hands thrown recklessly over his head and stares down at his machine throbbing against his abdomen. Release, finally release. Finished, mind soft and free, he falls down beside her. For this night there is nothing but heat pulsing and the deepest sleep shared between them. For this night there is nothing but them.

Park your car right next to mine
Slide your hand across the door
Breach the lock and crawl inside
Finger the wheel, the dash, the seat
Smell my air, god, breathe it in
Still in stillness suffering so

Light comes in, horrible light of morning. Theo wakes and finds the sun above him. He groans, rubbing his hands across his chest. Where is he? What is going on?

Keep everything I've written down
The scraps of paper, the torn up notes
Study the circles, the swoops, the curves
The gliding connections, the open loops
The deep indentations, the frustrated extensions
So suffer feel it suffer still

Her voice is there beside him, sweetly calling to him. Aching for him. Sex and salvation clung her chest and she is whispering to him. He opens his thighs and lets the sun beat down on his insides.

Search for me with ink and pen
Secrets in an upright quill
Direct me deep inside the pages
Make me lay down next to you
Write my hands all over you
Suffer so and suffer still

Hands come up under him. Theo moans as he's lifted up into the air. A firm chest holds him close. He tilts his head towards it and he sets his tongue on the salty skin. Then he is placed down again. He reaches for his rescuer, his hips rocking urgently. A hand presses him back to the bed. He grabs the hand and forces it down. The fingers resist. They pull away. He finds them again and pushes them down again, forces them to make contact with his throbbing machine. He shutters out a breath through trembling teeth as foreign fingers graze his steaming flesh.

Think of me at night and dream
Of tangled hands and bleeding steam
Reach a hand down in the bed
Softly moan and arch your head
Be overcome beyond control
Wake up soon, wake up alone

Theo wakes up in a fright hours later, wakes up encased in his own sweat with a thin sheet draped across his throbbing body. He takes a few shallow breaths staring up at the cold grey ceiling. His memories of this morning are sharp and urgent. He can't get away from it no matter how hard he tries. Angel wrote to him and he gave in again. But that isn't the part that upsets him the most. He left his room; he went out in the courtyard. He touched himself outside hoping to get caught. And he was caught. He laid out there in the morning sun until someone found him and brought him back to his bed. That person could only be Ryder.

His face burns with shame as he recalls what he did after. He licked Ryder's chest and then forced his hands down to his cock. In the moment it was just anyone that was near and could give him pleasure. He's horrified at what he did, disgusted, and he can't even imagine what Ryder must think of him now. He's surprised he's not laying out in the street right now. Veddie would've had had him shot.

He pulls the covers over his head and turns towards the wall. Beneath the blankets, he is naked, a wall of famished flesh that never needed servicing before. Now it's hungry all the time, a thing apart from himself and beyond his control, something that has to be frequently fed. He's sick with his passion, his lust and his desires. It is always there simmering along the edges of his consciousness, threatening to boil over at every robust thought that passes through his mind.

Students are in the house again. He can hear their happy, carefree banter nearby. That used to be him. He used to be happy. He used to play by the rules. He has no choice but to leave now. Ryder will ask him to go anyway. He will returns to the dorms. He'll try to get along as best as he can. His only hope is that Ryder won't drop him as his student. Who would take him in now? A dirty fallen angel who can't keep his hands off himself.

He waits until he hears Ryder's students leave. Then he gets up, gathers his few meager belongings and continues down the hall. He glances at the courtyard as he passes, at that bench where he pleasured himself last night. If only he'd kept it in his room. What possessed him to go outside? And Ryder? His face burns to think of how he pawed all over him while being carried back to his bed. Maybe if his mentor had been female he would've felt slightly better, but he doubts it.

Head down, he goes straight for his shoes and begins to slip them on. They seem reluctantly to let him leave, the straps of his sandals getting caught around his toes. He swears, dropping his books and leaning down to untangle the mess. That's when he realizes he's not alone.

"Going to class?" he hears Ryder's voice.

He rises slowly to see his mentor seated in the breakfast nook with two plates on the table. Theo quickly drops his eyes and continues to fuss with his shoes. Ryder should be teaching his first class now. What is he still doing here?

"I'm returning to the dorm," Theo states quickly. Shoes on, he grabs his books and turns toward the door.

"There is no bed for you there," Ryder calls after him. "It was reassigned when you came to stay here. I could not hold an empty bed when so many new recruits are coming in."

Theo stops on the front porch, staring out at the sandy street. The front of Ryder's house faces the back of another. There are no windows to indicate who lives there.

"If you'd like to move back to the dorm, I'll put in an application for you. But until then, I don't think it's a good idea for you to leave. Not in the condition you are in."

Theo grits his teeth, on the verge of tears. He feels so trapped and so hopeless to change his situation. What is he supposed to do now? Go out and sleep in some alley until a bed can be found for him? Ryder is his mentor, at least he used to be. He can't avoid him forever and yet the thought of facing him after what happened makes him want to be sick.

"Come back in the house, Theo. We have a lot to discuss."

Theo experiences a hot blush and considers fleeing out into the Reserve with no particular destination or purpose. He just wants to run. And perhaps run screaming until he is so tired he drops. And maybe doesn't get up again.

"I don't want to discuss anything," he says to the back of the neighbor's house. He walks a few steps ahead but then suddenly deflates, sitting down on the few paltry stairs leading up to the house of Ryder. It's not long after that he hears footsteps behind him.

Ryder comes out to lean on a pillar, bringing his arms across his chest. He stares out at the same brick wall baking under the morning sun. "I was by no means misinformed when I fell. I was well into my education, already a level three. Oh and did I mention I was Veddie's student at the time? Well I'm sure that answers a few of your questions, anyway. My charge was young and beautiful and I was sexually inexperienced. I knew the sin I was committing when I did it. And when I fell, I fell hard. I spend months on the Reserve, mentor-less. With no guidance, I went down again and again. It seemed like I had no control over myself whatsoever. When I had finally recovered enough to reapply, I went through several crusty old mentors that had no compassion for the affliction that I suffered. And it was an affliction. A driving, senseless addiction. I had to go back to level one and start all over again. Though I have been here for a very long time, I have chosen not to progress past level four. Because of my weakness for the flesh, I quit guardianship and became a teacher. It was the best decision I made here. Yes, I should've told you, but I was afraid if I did, you'd run away."

Theo sits silently absorbing Ryder's words. Once again, there is no judgment, no disgust or disapproval. Of course Ryder would understand. He has been through the same thing. Even more so because he was Veddie's student too. It explains a lot. Not just the strained relationship between Veddie and Ryder. But why Veddie chose to drop him so fast after his first offence.

"You should stay. Whatever happens here will not get exposed to the others. You are vulnerable right now. It will be safer if you stay here."

"But what about my vows?" Theo whispers weakly, his belongings tucked under his arm like a runaway child.

"Vows?" Ryder asks.

"I have broken my vow of chastity. Multiple times."

Ryder chuckles. "Oh yes, I forgot about that."

Theo glances back at him.

"Vow of chastity, poverty, and what was the third one? Oh yes, obedience. I believe the last one is Veddie's favorite."

Theo lowers his head, annoyed by Ryder's careless reaction to something he regards so seriously. "It's not funny."

"Well, if Veddie is living under a vow of poverty, then I'm the archangel of conformity. These rules, these vows, they are not from the council or even the elders. These are Veddie's rules. No other students here are forced to be chaste."

"Really?"

"Sexuality is not banned here," Ryder says, shaking his head. "Certainly it is not shouted from the rooftops; they would prefer students concentrate on their studies, but there is no rule forbidding sexual activity. You are being entirely too hard on yourself." Passing him on the steps, he says, "Come walk with me."

They walk away from the city and down to an old path. They pass over a small meandering river. The banks are full of blooming flowers. And the prairie to either side of them is thick with multicolored grasses and wild horses grazing. From here, they can see from the flood banks all the way to the forum. At the end of the path, where the rolling prairie meets the rugged mountain hillside, is a glass building. It stands two stories high with a large peaked roof. The windows are steamed over and parts of the exterior are nearly obscured by tall vines and brush. As they near it, Theo realizes it's a greenhouse, though a very large and extravagant one. Ryder takes him in one of many entrances. It's misty and hot inside, the smell heavy and fragrant. Long rows of potted plants are set up on tables, some grow all the way up to the ceiling. There are fresh fruit trees, berry bushes, and pepper plants all bursting with their plunder. Water flows down a central aisle and feeds a fountain in the middle.

"What is this?" Theo asks.

"It's a community greenhouse. People still like to eat, even though they don't have to."

"Can I eat the fruit?" he asks eying juicy, fresh delights dangling from every branch he passes.

"You can eat anything you like."

Theo pulls off a peach while Ryder takes him down the windy, overflowing aisles to the stone pond in the center. The pool is a wide twenty foot circle, edged in stone and brimming with tropical fish. It's here they finally sit down.

Theo sighs heavily and stares down at the floor. He is so ashamed of what happened last night. And there's little Ryder can say to rid him of that. In other respects, he feels better. At least it's only Veddie's rules he broke. Though perhaps they are just as frightening as the Reserve rules.

"Are you going to be all right?" Ryder asks.

Theo takes a bite from his peach. "I guess."

"Do you want me to process the bed assignment?"

Theo stares forward imagining what would've happened if he'd lost control of himself in the dorms. It would have been no private matter then. Word would've gotten out fast. Straight to Veddie and the elders. And though he is not comfortable staying with Ryder anymore, he doesn't see any other option. He shakes his head indicating no.

Ryder strokes at his trim beard staring up into the pillars of light entering the greenhouse from above. Encased in sunshine, he looks more like an angel than Theo has ever seen before. In some regards, he is oddly beautiful. And there is no trace of the darkness that he must have suffered from. It gives Theo hope that he can regain some of his former composure. Though by the look of Ryder's hands, there will be some things that never change.

Ryder says, "I was just a boy when I came here. Much younger than you. Believe it or not, Veddie has actually mellowed since I knew him. Strict, obstinate man. Back then, he was ten times as fierce and even more unforgiving. I didn't like him right from the beginning. His world is straight up and down and mine is full of corners. I still don't understand how we got paired together.

"Still, he was my mentor and I tried to obey him. But I struggled to remain under those iron fists of his. Follow all his strict vows. I wasn't a boy forever. Soon I grew up. I wanted change. I wanted love. Religion hates women, Theo, surely you can see that."

Theo glances at him, surprised by the statement.

"The bible was written by a bunch of staunch old men who decided man is god and ruler over all things and women is temptress, prostitute and deceiver. She is the serpent taking men from their goals, their high and lofty goals. Tempting man with the forbidden fruit; the thing we want the most but are not supposed to have. She causes the fall of mankind and casts mankind out of Eden. Sex isn't the sin. Woman is the sin."

Theo is taken aback by the slander. And yet he quickly realizes that is exactly how he felt about women when he was alive. About relationships. About sex. That women were dirty, that they distracted him from his ultimate goal. He thought they were his own personal feelings, not something that might have been planted by the church.

"I can't say I share this understanding. I love women. I love sex. I love, love. And when it came time that I started thinking about a relationship, you can imagine what Veddie's reply was."

Theo snorts, smiling. Oh, he can imagine, all right.

"I guess I went through a sort of rebellion after that, and that rebellion went a little too far. When I came back a fallen angel, he never forgave me. He dropped me immediately, didn't even want to hear my story, and never wanted to associate with me again. To him, I was dead. To this day we still share a sort of thorny relationship. I regained my position here, even surpassed my former standing. Sure his office is in the top floor of the acropolis and mine is under a hill…"

Theo chuckles.

"…but we have each chosen the path we wanted. I am happy here and he is…well, he is what he is. I will never respect him. Though I must say, I was surprised to see that he dropped you as fast as he did."

"Why? He dropped you."

"Yes, but I was just an assignment. We've been waiting for you for a long time."

Again, Theo is taken aback. He stares at his absurd and lusty little mentor perched in a backdrop of peaches and roses. "What do you mean?"

"I mean, your mentorship was assigned through contest. Many applied. Of course, Veddie won. The elders are fair but they still favor him and considered him the best choice for you. It was thought that you would go very, very far here." Ryder seems to chuckle, his gaze unfocused. "An amusement that you ended up with me."

Theo takes in some air, looking out past the flowers and steamy glass windows to the quiet meadows beyond them, trying to understand what Ryder has just told him.

"Well, it is what it is, Theo. You can choose to accept their condemnation or you can rise up in defiance against it. Your path was rigidly planned before, now it can be whatever you want."

Theo lowers himself off the ledge of the pool, sits on the floor and leans back against the stone. He cannot be so cavalier about his fall. It upsets him that was chosen, that they were waiting for him. If he only hadn't jumped in that damned pool. That one little decision has cost him more than he'll ever know. It's hard to accept Ryder's silver lining. He wanted a path; he wanted to be chosen. He doesn't want to squat under a hill gazing up towards glory, he wants to be the one overtop looking down on all the others.

"What am I going to do about Angel?" he says thinking about her and how their futures are linked together now.

Ryder is silent for a while before he says, "Understand this, I loved my charge and I thought she loved me. But she never even knew I existed. No matter how real it seems, I was never there. When you fell, you thought you lost your robes but you were wearing them when you returned. You see, they were there the whole time. Your nudity was in your head and it's the same with her. Angel doesn't know you. She doesn't care about you. She never will. Realizing that fact will help you let go of her and make the right decisions when those moments are upon you."

Theo sighs, examining the specimens wedged beneath his fingertips. He thinks about what Ryder said. He was clothed the whole time. All the anxieties he suffered were in his imagination. And who is Angel picturing when they are together? Ambrose, not him, not Theodore Duncan. It's a hard truth to hear, even harder to accept.

"And the longer you hold on to this, the longer you'll be isolated. I couldn't have my charge. And for the longest time, I clung to her. I have had no one for a very long time. There's vast competition in an acropolis full of broad shoulder Adonis's and I'm just one queer science instructor conducting experiments under a hill. And if some beautiful young student should throw their affections my way, I might sway. I might. I can't make any promises to you. Nor should I. That is not what our relationship is about. If you are coming back from the Black and looking for a mentor, then I am the perfect match for you. I can show you the way."

Theo sits silently and lets it all sink in. He has to accept that he is starting from scratch again, not just as a student in the Reserve, but as a man as well. Some part of him submits to Ryder in this moment, though a little bit still clings to the former glory of Veddie and his old life here. For now, this is what his life will be.

He goes to bed weary that night and is serenaded by the sound of Angel's sobs. Sometimes she just can't hold it in. So much stands against her. She's had a bad day. He has too. But now he hears what Ryder said. She doesn't know you exist, no matter how real it seems. It disheartens him. Makes him feel all alone. That the affair was for nothing. He is nothing to her. Just an unfocused dream. Last night, he was on fire. Now there's not even a smolder left, not even a spark. He feels completely empty. Spent.

Angel cries for hours. In the wee hours, she finds a pen and begins to write:

There were so many people around today. I wanted him alone. To share moments and secrets. My mind was contesting as the minutes tick-tocked away. I was plotting, scheming. How could I get him to myself? He was right across the table from me and we barely spoke a word. They've been moving staff around. His shifts are different from mine now. I barely see him anymore. I've become unreasonable with my feelings for him. I'd hoped distance would tidy up my head, but since he's been gone, absence has made my heart a stalker.

I left the table just before quitting time. I planned go to the women's bathroom and wait for him. I'd come back to find him at the table. I'd act surprised to see him there. I knew it was stupid, it was hopeless, even shifty. I hid in the bathroom stall with my head in my hands begging myself to go home. What was I doing anyway? He is married. Wasted energy. Go home. Let him go. This is so ridiculous. And I know it. And that's the worst part of it.

Still, I waited. And when the time was right, I made my move. I don't care about later, or reality, just how it makes me feel right now. How an inviting smile and a kindly word will reheat my heart for days and days. I am an addict and he is my fix. I'd do anything for it, for just one more high. I am so desperately alone. I need him. Just a few minutes and then I'll be all right. I am addicted. He is my addiction. My addiction. My addiction.

I left the locker room, my heart sprinting. It was a few minutes past the hour. I hoped I didn't wait too long. Maybe I missed him. But as I came around the corner, I saw him using the copier. I love that copier. It always brings us together.

"Have a good night," he called as I neared and continued with his project.

"You too," I said as if I didn't spend every waking hour pining for just the smallest affections from him, as if just the tiniest acknowledgement didn't ignite my passions for days and days. My feet kept marching past him as my brain lagged behind. I couldn't wait for him at the table now. It would look like I was waiting for him. But I hadn't had my moment yet! I needed an excuse to stay behind, to catch him before he left, to give him a reason to stop at my station for a while.

Out of ideas, I left for the parking lot. I was thinking, thinking! My truck was right next to his car. It was leaking fluids all over the parking lot. This was an everyday thing, certainly not a catastrophe, but then I realized, it could be. It could be a catastrophe. A broken down truck. A lady in distress. I knew he'd stop and help me. He was that kind of man. It was sickly contrived, a red truck trap. Deceiving him for a few minutes of his time? It was madness but I was as resolved to stay as I was frantic to go.

I waited a while in nervous anxiety and then began my foolish game. I popped the hood of my truck. The wind was furious at me and slammed it back down. Go home, it said, no good will come from this. I refused to listen, even to the wind itself. I knew Ambrose would help me. I lifted the hood and it blew down again. I couldn't make it stand up on its own. I had to get underneath and hold it up against the angry wind. Ambrose exited the building. I continued to struggle with the hood and pretended I didn't see him coming. That was the greatest lie of all. And from the greatest of liars. Oh, if only they knew the games women play, the deception, the desperation. If only they knew. Help me, Ambrose, help me. Want me. Love me. I wanted to cry. I wanted to put a gun to my head. I loathed myself in moments like these and yet I forged ahead. Just one smile to keep me going, just for a few more days and then I'd be all right. I was pathetic. Pathetic and he had to know it.

He came as expected and leaned against my truck. "Having some trouble?"

"My truck is broken," I said, a regurgitated bile lie tasty in my mouth. He stopped to play just for a while. Fiddled in my engine and I got my few moments. A few jokes. A smile. He went home to his wife. I went home alone.

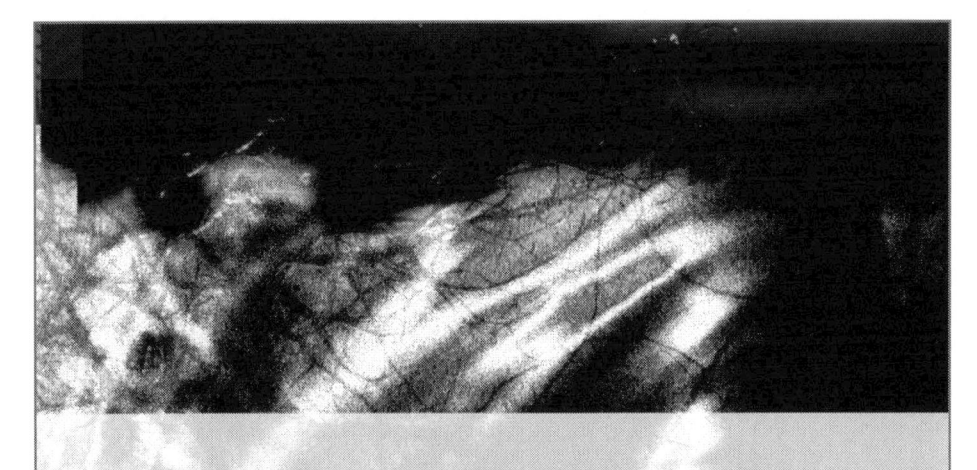

SECOND JUMP

Chapter 17☙

Theo rises long before dawn and watches the sun creep across the floor of his cell-like quarters. His room is so quiet, barren, and impersonal. Just a bed draped in a plain white sheet and a desk with a few books on it. He rises, rubbing his face. It was almost dawn when he went to bed; he hardly slept at all. His studies have been a welcome distraction but there is nothing to divert him this morning. Second jump has arrived. He can't deny it or avoid it any longer. He has to jump to pass his level. Angel is not in crisis; he does not need to go to her at all. Nor does he want to. After what happened last time he went down to her, he's terrified of his return. He's full of anxiety as he dresses, his chest tight, his breath constricted, his legs throbbing and aching. He cannot think about anything but what's waiting on earth for him. He's resentful over the first year's anxiety. If only they knew how easy it's going to be to jump with their mentors at their sides. If he'd only waited and did things in the order they should have been done. Now he's apart from the rest of them, in a place that no one can relate to except for the angels lurking in the shadows, and Ryder of course, one of the few that managed to return to the light.

Dawn is moving ever closer as he leaves his room and finds the house of Ryder deserted. No breakfast in the nook waiting for him, no students chattering from the gathering room, no one here at all. It makes him worry more. Where is everyone? Did he sleep in? He takes a few hard breaths, wrestling with the knot in his chest. So many things could go wrong today. If he falls again, he's finished.

He makes his way to Ryder's office as the dew begins to drip, glimmering from every leaf tip and roof edge as the moisture loosens and dribbles. Even the wind holds its breath and there's no sight of the creatures that usually graze the walkway at this hour. As he reaches Ryder's office, he notices shoots of lilies leaning at the base of the door. And something else. A couple sets of fresh footsteps sweating in the early dew. One big and one small.

Poised to knock, he drops his fist. How long did Ryder resist the girl? A day? A few hours? Curiosity, or perhaps the demand for anything to distract him in his state of rowdy anxiety, has him seeking out the only window accessible to the office under the hill. It's a moldy, sprouted thing, arched with four crossbars and etched in vines and god knows what other sorts of experiments seeded on the sill that Ryder has been concocting. Theo clears a small patch from the glass and peaks inside. A fire burns low in the wood stove and a few tea cups are abandoned by the side chairs. Otherwise the room is empty.

Peeping again, he thinks, pushing himself away. He's almost disappointed to find nothing there. Maybe Ryder's sins make his own more acceptable.

Returning to town, he can see clear across the meadow to the forum teaming over with students. Everyone is gathering this morning to make the pilgrimage from the forum to the Field. He thought, at first, that he would go down on his own. But he hadn't counted on his level of anxiety this morning.

Theo joins the nervous twitter of students gathered in the forum. Here and there, mentors rise above the rest, standing on pedestals calling in and organizing their flock. Theo passes from one crowd to the next, from Lila's gathering of earthy imps, to Veddie's drove of muscular contenders and then on to Ryder's crop of mismatched surplus.

"Stay together and keep your hands linked when we jump," Ryder calls over the roar. "That will ensure we all land together. If you do become lost, stay where you are until I find you. Don't go off on your own. And avoid people's Light for now. Stay in the animal auras. Today we are just going to get a feel for it. There is nothing to be worried about."

Theo glances in Veddie's direction. His group of hulking he-men tower above the rest, all male, all white, their books a little cleaner, their garments little finer. It's obvious with all the students gathered, who the best of the best is, and whose group he was meant to be in. He was chosen. Guardians fought to have him join their flock. Theo's gaze returns to Ryder's crew. The only thing common in this group is their mentor. Sadly, Theo still relates to Veddie's ideal, deep in his heart he wants to march through the town at the head of the pack with the brightest and the best. He still wants to be one of them, still longs for what should've been.

The procession to the Field begins. Students file through town much like a graduation ceremony. From windows, guardians wave, wish good luck, and toss flowers to the street. Theo falls further and further back in the convoy until he is at the rear, the last one to leave town. How hard people fight to get ahead of the pack. Ironically, Theo sees that there's another way to break away. Just fall behind. And that's what he does, falls further and further behind until the mob is over the next hill and then the next. It occurs to him that he doesn't have to jump at all. He could just leave, go on to cathedral and forget all this. Ridwan was seeking him out. That must mean he can still get in to Heaven. But could he go on without making amends for what he's done? Could he leave Angel to struggle on her own?

The gates of the Field are now visible over the hill, the cratered meadow filling with students. Theo enters last, passes by group after group of mentors and students all asking for and receiving last minute advice. He travels alone, feels more alone than he ever has in his life. He remembers the path to Angel's pool because he'll never forget it. Even though there are so many turns and bridges and ponds of lost souls, he finds his way right to hers. How much he longs for a comforting word. Good luck. Or I'll see you in a while. Or be careful out there. Ryder is nowhere near. Here and there, groups are jumping, linking hands and shrieking with excitement as souls leave bodies, as groups go stiff and stony while their spirits move on. Soon there is nothing but silence, the field full of inert bodies, not real bodies, just shelters for nomadic healers.

Theo looks down at Angel, feels his heart pinch as her image, once fading, comes back to him as strongly as before. Of her dancing in the pool. Of her beautiful body in the dark. If only he had known what was waiting for him down there. If only someone had made him understand. He never would have done this. He would never be where he is now.

Down, down, down, with the wind rushing and the cool air whistling past his ears, less like falling more like diving, cool, neat, his body like a spike launching downwards, his arms clamped down at his sides, his dive purposeful. He can't open his eyes but sees the light passing through the lids, feels invigorating rush of earth's moist air, feels the wind whip wildly past his ears. The Reserve falls further and further behind until he lands very softly next to her, this time with grace, this time intentionally. He opens his eyes. He's in a department store and Angel is pushing a cart around.

He releases a sigh, relieved that he's made it down okay. Now all he has to do is transport back up. Angel does not need him and he does not want to be here either. The sooner he gets back, the better. He glances at her, her thoughts elusive when she's not writing. She picks up a few things. Nothing of importance. He follows her up to the checkout and she pays for it all in cash. He glances at the wad of bills in her hand. Is she stealing again? He didn't get a sense of it above but it's just feelings and not actions that come through. If she steals without guilt then there would be no emotion for him to pick up on.

They go back to her meager home. Theo follows her through the overgrown yard to the now familiar creak of the front steps. Inside, the house remains as it was when he left. She's cleaned up the debris from the break in, the broken glass, the busted furniture, broken TV and table. There's really nothing left in the core of the house anymore. A piece of wood covers one of the windows in the living room and the room is very dark and depressing. The kitchen is cluttered and forgotten but there has been some reprisal in her bedroom. There's a new mattress, new blankets and sheets. Angel's eyes pass over it as she enters and Theo knows it's Bea's doing. Her parents stopped by. Her dad fixed the door and they called the police. Romeo was given a warning. The reprimand has changed nothing. However, there's a new development making the house more secure. Nestled in the center of those blankets is the dog from the alley. The big black Rottweiler rolls onto his back when he sees her, expecting affection, which she delivers.

"Hey, Theodore," she says and sets her shopping bags beside the bed.

His heart does a little leap. She named her dog after him? Ryder said that she wasn't aware of him but why would she pick that name? Is it possible he crossed the bridge between their worlds? That she remembers? It makes him excited but he quickly reels his emotions back in. It doesn't matter. That's not what he's here for. He cannot get his own emotions involved again. He needs to get to the bathroom, or to a bucket, and get back to his studies before his mind gets muddled again.

There's a knock at the door. Angel tosses her items in the closet and comes out of the room straightening her hair. Theo glances back at the bathroom as it's swallowed in the Dark.

"Are you ready to go?" Bea calls from outside.

"Just about," Angel replies, reaching the front door. She opens it and Bea is standing there. And behind her, something Theo didn't see before: Bea's guardian. Theo locks eyes with the stern old man. It's no one he knows but by the severe look on the guardian's face, this man knows him and is not too happy that they'll be spending an evening together.

Bea drive towards an unknown location with two silent guardians pressed shoulder to shoulder in the back seat of her mother's mini-van. Bea didn't have a guardian before. Theo wonders what changed in her life to bring the guardian in. He doesn't ask the man even though they are close enough to waltz. Crisscrossed in their charge's Light, Theo stares out one window and Bea's guardian out the other. A thought occurs to Theo as he watches the cars pass by on the highway. Maybe Bea doesn't need protection at all, maybe this guardian is here to keep an eye on him. Ryder wouldn't authorize it but Veddie certainly would. Anger washes over him at the realization. They're spying on him. They don't trust him to make the right decisions.

They park in a crowded parking lot and the two girls walk towards a chain link fence. As they get closer, Theo sees a line of people buying tickets and entering a kiosk. And in line are all sorts of ghouls and wizards, ghosts and cheerleaders. It's Halloween. The realization brings Theo to a standstill. He died driving home from a Halloween party last year. It hardly feels like a month and yet his body has been buried for a full year. He's probably a skeleton now. His friend from the accident has graduated by now and he can't imagine what his parents are doing. It seems wrong that they'll have to celebrate the anniversary of his death on this kind of holiday. Are his parents still together? Sometimes death can pull people apart. Suddenly he longs to know where they are and if they're still okay. Would Ryder tell him? He makes a mental note to ask when he gets back.

Inside the carnival, the girls link arms and peruse the crowd. At least Angel has Bea, at least she has someone, even if their relationship appears to only scratch the surface. They never seem to talk about anything serious but they're here for each other and that's important too. The girls are laughing and enjoying themselves but Bea's guardian retains the same leathery expression he had when Theo first saw him.

"Ooh, a psychic," Bea exclaims, pointing to a closed off tent with a cheap painted sign leaned against it. "Do you want to go in?"

Angel makes a cringy face and shrugs. "I guess. If you want to."

They wait in line but Angel seems upset. She's worried that the psychic is real and will see what her actual future is. Her plans for the prom remain unchanged. She's still preparing to aim above Bea's head. But she isn't planning on missing her own. It seems the mission is set in stone, no matter what her mood might be. It occurs to him that by saving her, he might be ending a whole bunch of other lives in the process. Is that a decision he's going to have to make? A choice between her life and the people she's planning to murder?

By the time they reach the entrance to the tent, Angel is extremely agitated. She doesn't want to know her future and she doesn't want anyone else to know it either. Both Bea and her guardian seem completely unaware. Bea thinks this is bogus fun. Bea's guardian looks like he's waiting in line to get a prostate exam. Bogus fun, for him, this is not.

They enter the tent and inside sits the most average looking woman imaginable. She looks like she's preparing to do their taxes not read their future. In front of her there's a card table with a stack of domino looking tiles face down on the surface. She looks all business and that only makes Angel more nervous.

"Come in, sit down," she tells them and points to her donations box. "Twenty dollars a reading."

Angel pauses behind her chair. "I'm broke. I'll wait outside."

"Don't worry," Bea waves her off. "I'll get yours too." She stuffs two twenties in the box and promptly sits down, patting the chair next to her. Angel sighs heavily and submits. The psychic takes a long look at Bea, a long look at Angel, and then her eyes raise up to Theo.

Theo steps back, startled, as the psychic appears to greet him. She doesn't notice the crusty old guardian standing behind Bea, just him. And she isn't just looking at some vague focal point behind Angel, she's looking directly in his eyes. The acknowledgement makes him extremely nervous.

"All right," the psychic says, her focus returning to Bea. She turns over a few tiles. "So...new love?"

"Yes," Bea exclaims excitedly. "We just met."

The psychic looks at the next tile and frowns. "He is no good for you."

"What? But...I like him."

"No good!" she says more forcefully. "There are plenty of fish in the sea and this one is just a toad."

Angel covers a laugh and Bea gives her a sharp look. "That is not funny!"

Angel straightens up but doesn't look any less amused. "Sorry."

259

The rather plain-Jane psychic shrugs and returns her attention to her tiles. "I cannot tell you what to do. I only suggest."

"Well, suggest this," Bea says, sticking out her tongue.

"Hmm," is the psychic's only reply as she turns over another tile. "There is a business in the family. You should concentrate your energies on this. There is much success to be found here."

"That sushi hole?" Bea exclaims, looking like she might be sick. "Fish makes me vomit."

"It would be very lucrative for you to get involved in the family business and not waste your time on this toad."

"Hey," Bea cries, pushing her chair back as if to leave.

"As I said, I only suggest."

"Yeah, funny, read her future instead," Bea says, screeching her chair back a few more steps and folding her arms over her chest.

The psychic turns to Angel. Angel's heart begins to pound. Bea has become silent. The crusty guardian frowns.

The psychic takes a tile and turns it over. Her hand stutters just slightly. She glances up at Angel and then at Theo but doesn't say anything. Angel swallows hard, unnerved by the silent reaction. Theo strains to see the importance of the symbol on the tile, but it is just a symbol, meaningless. The psychic seems to struggle with a response and then goes onto the next tile without an explanation.

"Ah," she says as the second tile brings better news. "New love as well. And this one bodes well for you."

"What? She gets true love and I get a toad?" Bea cries.

"Hush!" the psychic cries, slashing her hand in the space between her and Bea. "Your future is over."

Bea frowns sourly and refolds her arms over her chest.

The psychic sets her dark eyes on Angel, glancing occasionally at the shadow that lurks behind her. "It has already begun. The wheels are in motion. The connection inevitable."

Angel stares at the psychic, feeling nervous and anxious. She's picturing Ambrose and that he won't be married for much longer. That they'll be together some day. That all her dreams will finally come true. Behind her, Theo just drops his head. This guy, again.

"There have been problems in the past. A denial of your true nature." The psychic glances up at Theo with hard, dark eyes, "You must let go of this, of the person you believed you once were. This one, this love, is lost as well. You must be patient for he needs to find his way. And when he does." She raises her eyebrows. "Sex."

Angel gasps, covering her mouth and then she and Bea burst into giggles.

"You and he share a special bond. You and he will share things that no others have before. In some ways, you already have."

Bea gasps. "Are you saying she's going to get laid before me? But she doesn't even have a boyfriend."

Angel just shrinks, glowing bright red, her mind is racing with thoughts of her married co-worker. It's finally going to come true. She can't wait to see him. She has to tell him how she feels. It will change everything for her. Love will change everything.

Theo clears his throat as the psychic looks up at him again. "You have a very important decision coming up. Choose carefully. Your decision may decide your future even before it begins. You understand?"

Angel swallows hard and nods but Theo isn't sure that message was for her.

The girls get up to exit the tent but the psychic grabs Angel's arm and pulls her back in. Quickly, she whispers, "Things have been done to you, child, but those things are over. Do you understand? Over. You do yourself no justice by living in the past. The time to move forward is now. Open yourself up to this new love. He is already here, you just have to let him in."

Angel returns home, her head spinning. "I'm going home to see the toad," Bea grumbles, taking her crabby guardian with her. Now alone, Theo turns to his charge. The reading from the psychic was disturbing. That woman seemed to know he was there and what he had done with Angel. And she seemed to be encouraging him to continue.

Angel seems disturbed too. She goes straight to her bedroom closet, shutting Theo out. He sits outside with his back to the door. She's thinking about Ambrose, about all the acts of carnality she's going to perform on him once they are together, disregarding anything the psychic said to indicate otherwise. It's new hope, hope that she'll finally be with the one she loves the most. Theo thumps his head against the door, so tired of this fantasy that will never come true. He tries to pray, tries to close her out, but her mind is inside him now. He sees her as she touches herself behind the closed door. See her hands, his hands and all the fantasies that follow.

For the first time since he's known her, Angel wakes up optimistic. She slept the entire night dreaming of her one true love, her knight in a rusty red car coming to rescue her from all this poverty and despair. She imagines all the scenarios that cause the breakup of his marriage. And how he comes to her afterwards looking to mend his broken heart. They fall in love. They leave this horrible place. They live happily ever after.

She gets up early, plays with her dog, and then goes off to school. The day is sunny, her mind is sunny, at least for now it is. Theo supposes he should be happy but he's worried about where this is leading. If she decides to confess her feelings for Ambrose, it will only lead to trouble. And what happens if Ambrose gives in to her? Is he prepared to be her guardian as she enters the arms of another man? He has to. That's why he's here. To save her, to heal her Light, and then let her go. One day, she won't need him and will never even know that he existed. He'll go back to the Reserve and then what? Just start with another charge and forget her? He's slipping again, he can feel it, becoming the dark part of her instead of aiding in her recovery. But when he's inside, it's so hard to keep himself straight. Her emotions are stronger than hers, clearer, and she is not afraid to express them. He needs to ascend the first chance he gets.

Angel finds her way to first class. She takes her seat quietly. All around her students are talking and texting, leaning across rows to share photos and newly discovered apps. Angel opens her coil notebook and sketches Ambrose's name, thinking about writing him a letter to tell him how she feels. She wants to get this started as soon as possible. Her Light is big, bringing in the whole room, the chalkboard, the teacher, and everyone around her. As she fantasizes, Theo sees Bea enter arm in arm with her new beau, the Toad. He's an average looking everything, a cross between Indian and Asian, with a short crop of dark black hair. They talk briefly and then split apart and Bea comes giggling down the aisle. She slams into the chair behind Angel and grabs her roughly by the shoulder.

"Oh my god, what?" Angel exclaims, jolted from her reverie. She turns to see her friend all aglow.

"I did it," she whispers, leaning forward.

"Did what?"

"You know...*it*."

Angel frowns. "You mean?"

"Uh-huh. Last night after the carnival."

Angel's Light moves in. The news makes her feel threatened, alone, confused. One of the things they had in common was that she and Bea were both virgins. And now she is the only one left. To the side, Theo cringes and rubs the back of his neck. Technically, she's not a virgin at all. Or was his intrusion imagined, just like his nudity during the last visit?

"What was it like?" Angel asks hesitantly.

Bea shrugs. "I don't know what all the hype is about. It was over before I even knew it. But then, afterwards, we stayed in the basement until almost three o'clock just making out. That was really hot. Look, see there? That's him over there."

Angel glances over her shoulder and then back at Bea. "You really like him?"

She snorts. "Toad, my ass. That psychic had no idea what she was talking about."

Class begins and Angel turns back to her notebook and sees the name of her future lover. Doubt begins to seep in. Why is she putting so much stock on some Halloween clairvoyant?

Maybe the psychic didn't know what she was talking about at all. All of Bea's future seems wrong. How can she even think of confessing her feelings to Ambrose? What if Ambrose rejects her?

Angel continues to slide during the day. It's the little things. She overhears a group of girls say *I hate her* as she passes. Hate. The word is so strong, so absolute. There's no room for interpretation. It makes her feel worthless, alone, empty. Classes go by and her thoughts continue to spiral. Her mind is on her family, the one who always threatened to leave her behind and then finally did. Her father is a painful black spot on her soul, a sickness, a wound that refuses to heal even though the source of the infection has long since vacated. He had to be in control of everything but he was completely out of control in his own life. Then there was the boy, just some kid crossing the street on his way to school and her father came careening around the corner in a couple thousand pounds of drunken metal. He pulverized the boy. He was so drunk that he didn't even notice the collision. There were drag marks and blood that went on for blocks and blocks as her father continued to drive around with the boy hinged beneath his car. They found him passed out behind the wheel and what was left of the boy beneath the car. It was all over the news for weeks and weeks. How much her mother cried. How can this be happening to your father, she would wail. He's such a good man. She never really wept for the boy though. It was always about how the incident affected her husband, about what was going to happen to her family. Her father seemed changed though. He cried in the courtroom, talked about his own father and the abuse he endured, about the struggles in his life and how sorry he was. Even Angel believed he was changed. He served a year in jail with lengthy community service following. His easy sentence enraged the town. There were protesters the day he was let out of prison. And it continued outside their house for the longest time. That was the other house, the one before this one, when life was only a little bit bad. He was so full of penance in the beginning. He told Angel he loved her, sober, for the first time. He was going to make changes. This time it was going to be different. All the alcohol was thrown away. He joined alcoholics anonymous. But it was only a few months before Angel got the first indication trouble was beginning again. She found a tiny bottle wedged behind the bookshelf. Then her father began to take trips for work and would come back from them completely unraveled, claiming he was tired and not hung over. Then the resentment began to appear, that bitterness that usually followed an emotional breakdown when her father began to feel that his weakness was being exploited by the ones he loved, that his vulnerability was not being responded to in just the right manner. Her mother never helped the situation. She simply supported her husband no matter what he did, whether that was seeking help or falling to pieces. Things spiraled down quickly. Her father lost his job and then they lost the house. He moved them to this shack outside of town and that was only the beginning of the descent.

Angel leaves school with her Light severed in half. A happy life seems impossible in a place so far from the sun. She stands with a sigh, staring out at the emptying parking lot. All the students are rushing home to their suppers, to sisters and brothers, to a warm bed and glowing television screens. When was the last time she spoke to someone? First class with Bea? Since then her tongue has started to root in her mouth.

As if answering her silent request, a truck pulls up next to her, shiny black with girl shaped mud flaps. The passenger door is kicked open. "Going my way, little lady?"

Angel sighs and then to Theo's shock, gets inside.

Theo has to scramble to get in after her, into the gaudy black innards of Romeo's rolling playboy mansion. With no space between Angel and the door, Theo is forced to hop over and straddle the stick shift. He stares over at Angel in complete shock. What is she doing? He can't get any clear indication from her thoughts. She seems cloudy and thick, encased in fog.

"So," Romeo says, his fist securely on the stick shift between Theo's legs. "Your place or mine?"

Angel sighs and stares out the tinted side window. They're so high off the ground, they can see clear over all the vehicles on the road. The truck is such a spectacle, just screaming out Romeo's insecurities but no one in this town will ever see that. Even Angel doubts herself against so many opposing opinions. Maybe that's why she got in the truck. Just to see if there's anything human about him. But just sitting beside him makes her sick. Now all she wants to do is get away. "Maybe you should just drop me off across town."

"Okay, okay," he says, readjusting the brim of his baseball hat and shoving a dirty boot down on the gas pedal. "Honestly, sometimes you're such a bitch."

"Thanks," Angel says blinking back a few tears.

"I mean, I didn't have to give you a ride at all."

"Then why did you offer?" she retorts.

"Don't know. Must be losing my fucking mind."

"Yeah, that goes double for me."

They remain in silence for almost two minutes. Theo sits tensely between them. She's so vulnerable right now; it's the perfect time for Romeo to attack. He can't let that happen but what can he do to stop it? He was actually able to injure Romeo the last time he was here but he can't go around attacking people during his jumps. That is not how a proper guardian should behave.

Romeo removes his hat and sweeps back his stiff hair which has been recently shaved short as a pig's ass. "Aww, come on. You're not going to be mad at me now? Come one, little Angel, I know you like me. Admit it. You gotta little crush on me. Hmmm?"

Angel continues to stare out the window, feeling so alone and so lost. "Why are you so mean to me?" she whispers.

"What?" he exclaims hoarsely and then someone cuts him off in traffic. "Motherfucker!" he shouts, accelerating, putting his grate right up the driver's bumper. He revs the engine aggressively, slamming his hand on the horn and shoving his middle finger out the front window. Angel just shakes her head and turns away more.

"Fucking prick!" Romeo continues as the driver turns out of his path. "What were you saying?"

"Nothing. Just let me out here."

"Nah, I'll take you home."

"I don't need a ride home."

"Then why did you fucking get inside?" he shouts.

"Because..." Angel pauses and begins to cry.

Theo drops his head forward and rubs his hands over his face. If Romeo so much as lays a hand on her, he'll bring every Rottie in town down on this kid.

Romeo groans, agitated, and continues to drive. "So what do you want me to do? Huh? You make it impossible for anyone to like you. You act so fucking weird that no one wants to be seen with you. You never fucking talk or go to parties or comb your hair or anything. You look like shit, so what do you expect?"

"Just let me out," Angel whispers.

"Fine." He jerks the wheel to the side and the truck slams to an unruly stop with one tire up on the sidewalk. He leans over her, shoving the door open. "Get out, bitch."

Angel just turns and slides out of the seat. As she does, Romeo jerks the truck forward causing her to trip and stumble onto the sidewalk. He huffs out a laugh and tears away from the curb with an aggressive screech. Angel sits for a few minutes, unable to move. She could get up, walk home, pick up the pieces, but why? Why go on? What's the point? She considers lying in the road until someone drives her over and puts an end to all this nonsense. She considers opening her mouth and screaming until she runs out of breath. Then she sees it in her head. The school, the shooting, the blood, Romeo finally getting what he deserves. It's not much of a future, but it gets her feet moving again.

Angel drops to her bed, the only furniture left in the house, so depressed she even skips work. The pain over missed opportunities with Ambrose brings her even lower. Her dark thoughts get darker. Her stomach is tight and empty. Her body sore and aching. She makes soup from a dried powder cube and then turns on some music. She sits inside her closet and drinks the stale water. She's just so tired of trying and failing, of hoping and not succeeding, of the constant, constant struggle. How much more of this can she take? When is it going to end?

The lights flicker. At first Theo thinks it's her Light. He panics, jolting upwards, thinking she's dying. But then the CD skips and the overhead bulb goes dim and then, like a dimmer switch winding down, everything hums to a silent stop.

"Fuck," she whispers as the power company finally delivers on its threats. She's been cut off. She stays where she is and continues to sip her soup in complete darkness thinking about all the adjustments that will have to be made to compensate for another lost privilege. She can't heat water. She can't wash anything, including herself. She can't cook food, if she had any. She'll have to get candles to see at night. But most importantly, no more music. No more dancing. No more escapes. No more fantasy. How many months left until prom?

That night, Angel goes out to the porch. It's dark, the sky clear and open. She sits down on the swinging bench in front of the boarded window and stares out at the city. Lights blaze from the window of every house, from porch fronts, from garage doors, from TV's and computers. But in the Angel household, it is completely dark. The hum of technology gone, the furnace cold, the music silenced, she hears nothing but the wind passing through the overgrown grass. She releases a deep sigh of resignation. In a way there's relief. No more power means no more threats. There is nothing more they can do. At least the numbers will stop adding up. It's one less thing to worry about. She might as well disconnect the gas while she's at it. The furnace won't run without power. And there's nothing for the water heater to heat, if she were ever to get the plumbing going again, that is.

She walks out to edge of the porch, places her hands on the worn wooden railing and stares up at the boundless sky. It's a perfect night, quiet, warm, not a cloud in sight. She can't remember the last time she laid out under the stars. She used to do it all the time when her family still lived in the house. This used to be her escape. She thought things would be better if they left, but nothing changed when they did. Partially because they left with no warning. She just came home from school one day and they'd taken her sister and left. At first she thought they'd gone out of town, and when the days grew longer, maybe they'd gone on a trip or vacation. Months and months went by before she finally accepted they were gone for good. It hurt her more than she imagined. She hated them, she despised them, and yet their rejection wounded her.

They travel through the grass together, passing between abandoned vehicles and rusty barrels. The grass sits chest high in places, in full seed, like they're in a farmer's field instead in a back yard. Angel lies down in the deep thicket and stares up at the sky. She imagines that she's lying in the reeds by a river outside her cottage nestled in the foothills of the mountains. There are no neighbors for miles around, just her and her house and glorious nature. She imagines waking up in the morning and staring out the kitchen window at the frosty blue mountains, going out in the afternoon to sit by the rushing river. She imagines her dog running free, no fences, no boundaries. In the afternoons she hikes by the river. In the evening, a hearty home cooked meal. But even in her fantasies, she is alone. There is no one waking up beside her, no one exploring the river with her, and no one sharing her hearty supper. She can't imagine a world where anyone would love and accept her.

The next day, which Theo gets the impression that it's Saturday, Bea shows up in her mother's minivan. The two rattle around the house for a few hours trying to teach the dog tricks like *speak* and *kill Romeo* and then head out for some event which neither of them speak about. The event is planned and neither discuss it, therefore Theo remains in the dark.

"They should be gone by now," Bea says as she turns the mini-van out of town.

"Better be," Angel replies.

Theo sits nervously behind them amongst discarded chopsticks, cases of empty Sake and Bea's expressionless guardian. Where are they going? What are they up to? He doesn't like this one bit.

They drive away from the city for a while, then turn down a dirt road. They continue for several miles before entering an old churchyard. It's completely dark, a two-story country church house looming amongst the windswept trees and beyond it, a small cemetery.

"Ready?" Bea says.

"You bet," Angel replies.

They go to an unlatched window and shove it open like they've done it a dozen times before. As they hoist themselves inside, Theo and his compadre wait their turns side by side. The old man is staunchly unpleasant and Theo is now convinced that the Reserve sent this guardian for him and not for Bea. He's a leathery mothball, of no use to a vibrant girl like Bea. And Bea seems pretty happy, no need for a guardian at all.

They enter into the church through the window. It is a single worship-room with a kitchen in the back. Two sections of worn wooden pews separate a single red carpet heading up towards a semi-circular alter with raised pulpit and faded mural of a cross backlit by a sunrise. The stain glass is painted on, bibles old and wrinkled, and piano with chipped ivory.

While Bea and Angel disappear into the back area, Theo walks around feeling nostalgic, touching the hymnals. He's always had a thing for old churches. His church at home was a modern, grand affair, all glass and steel. A beautiful building but he loved a traditional one room steeple church. Back to basics. Less grandeur and more god. And he hasn't had much of a feel for god lately. In fact he's spent less time focused on religion since living outside the gates of Heaven than he ever did on earth. It scares him how much it seems to be slipping away. He's done nothing but worry about his own affairs since he arrived.

Hearing giggling in the back area, Theo decides he better go investigate. Peeking around the corner, he sees that the girls are raiding a fridge packed full of food for an event that must be coming up soon. They tear through cellophane like hungry bears, picking off all the sandwich meats, the good cheeses and dark chicken meat before grabbing a few dessert trays and return to the front of the church. Theo is relieved that hunger is their only crime for the night. He returns to the church and sits himself down on the front pew. After a while, Angel comes and sits down right beside him. He looks over at her becoming more certain every day that she knows he's here. And so grows his attachment to her. There's something about her, something apart from everyone else, an intimate knowledge shared between them that will never be equaled no matter how much he may try with anyone above. There is experience between them. They've done time together. He knows her inner-most thoughts and her darkest places. Knows those hands on him, what she can do to his body.

Bea fingers through the alter goods with little respect for their significance, pretends to wet her nipples with holy water and then climbs the raised pulpit, throwing a mighty fist in the air. Then she pulls on the preachers sash and shuffles a few papers, clearing her throat stiffly. Behind her, standing a few steps below, just the top of her elderly guardian's head is visible. And even the top of his head looks angry.

"Mistress know yourself...down on your knees," Bea calls from the altar, bringing all eyes, living and dead, on her. "And thank heaven, fasting, for a good man's love. For I must tell you, friendly in your ear, sell when you can. You are not for all markets."

Angel snorts and laughs. "What is that?"

"Shakespeare," Bea grins.

Angel nods and gives a thumbs up in approval.

Bea makes obscene motions with a candle and continues. "As it is said, in the book of Reproof, woman shall not lay with man unless there is a holy band around thine finger, and neither shall man lay with man, or woman with woman, or man with man while woman is watching, and certainly not when one woman is holding a camera for motion picture capture. Cast down ye unholy penis whether flaccid or erect. And then cast it up. And then down again. Anoint it in your eternal blessing, oh lord, give it strength and perseverance against the most frigid and dried up chasms."

Theo can't help but chuckle. Angel is laughing too. He looks over at her, really looks at her, at the shape and contour of her face, the curve of her lips, soft curls of uncombed hair, and the thick lashes around her deep, hardened eyes. He feels smaller than her, less alive, less than. She's just so real, so connected with everything inside her, even if it is dark and painful. He wishes he could be so bold, just cast off all his inhibitions and be raw and real like her.

"Play something," Bea says, abandoning the pulpit.

"Agh, come on," Angel groans, "It's been way too long."

"Come on. I wish I had your talent."

"So what? Who makes money playing the piano?"

"I don't know: Elton John? Mozart? Axl Rose?"

"Fine." Angel takes a seat at the piano and asks, her voice oozing with sarcasm, "Sonata or Concerto?"

"Fuck you, I want the theme from Battlestar Galactic."

"Does it sound like this?" Angel balls her hands into fists and pounds them simultaneously on the keys.

"Fuck you! Fuck you!" Bea cries over the ruckus. She wanders off and rummages through the church library, scoffing at the titles and tossing them over her shoulder. "Why *do* bad things happen to good people?"

Angel touches a single key with little rhythm or melody. Ding. Ding. Ding. And then, slap, slap as library books hit the floor across the room. Theo looks between the two when Angel's finger suddenly launch an assault on the keyboard. They rage up and down in scales of flats and sharps. Then without warning scales turns to song. She rips through the notes in utter abandon as she hunches forward like a mad scientist concocting his greatest experiment. The music is complicated, layered and raging with emotion. Just like her pen, everything comes from her fingers. Theo's whole world slows; he sits utterly mesmerized, his breath taken away. Angel turns on a discord, reaches a quiet crescendo. Her Light comes up behind him and then the Dark engulfs him, swallows him whole. He remains where he is, letting the Darkness consume him, floating, burning, igniting his every pore. Then, with a thunderous wrath, she assaults the keys with furious ire. Her Light explodes out, lashes him back in the pew, pinning him to the place where he sits, forcing him to become a part of her. He closes his eyes and succumbs, goes all the places she intends him to go and is now so willing to follow. She is all emotion, powerful, radiant; the most beautiful spirit he's ever encountered. With increasingly shortened breath, he tilts his head back and releases a sigh, lets her back inside him, gives her the power again. She is Light in absolute defiance of hopelessness. Once again, he is in complete surrender.

They drive home, Theo in the back seat with Angel while Bea's old man remains up front. "Hey, I'm not your fucking taxi driver," Bea says. Angel just groans, two seats behind Bea with her hand rubbing the inside of Theo's leg. Theo closes his eyes and rolls his head back. Every so often, the old man looks back with a disapproving scowl on his face.

"Kay, see you tomorrow," Bea says as Angel drifts from the mini-van leaving the door wide open. It's raining as they walk back to the house in the tall, dark grass. He can already tell by the way his environment is interacting with him, that he's a part of this world again. His feet are wet from the puddles. He can feel the soft mud squeezing between his toes. His robe has become heavy from dragging through the wet grass. He keeps a few steps ahead of her, walking stiffly for the front door. To the house. To the bathroom. Then water or mirror and he is back at the Reserve. There is no crisis keeping him here now. He should be able to ascend with no problems. And he must ascend before something happens.

But before he can get there, Angel comes up against his back. She snakes her arms around his chest and brings him to a stop.

"I can't," he whispers, unclasping her hands from his front like a sticky seatbelt. "If I do, I'll never see you again."

"I won't tell," she whispers hotly in his ear.

"It doesn't matter. They will know."

"I don't care. I want you."

Theo closes his eyes and takes a few deep breaths. It's time to leave. He has to go. This is the point where he ruined himself before. He doesn't ever want to feel like he did when he came back from his first jump. His head is clear enough to remember that.

"Angel, I'm sorry," he says, stepping ahead her, breaking her hold on him. "I want you but I have to go."

Angel launches forward and takes him again. Reaching from behind, she loosens his belt and pulls his robe back off his shoulders. Theo makes a grab for it but as he does, his loses his balance. He crashes forward on his knees and she comes down behind him. He takes in a deep breath as her hands plunge between his hips from behind.

"Angel, don't," he whispers as her tongue grazes the back of his ear. Her strong hands stroke him. Down on his knees, he looks down at the puddle he's fallen into, its surface boiling from the thundering rain. Water pours off his lips, off his nose, off his engorged cock. With every bit of strength he has, he lifts a hand and slams it down on the surface of the water.

Chapter 18ଔ

Theo crashes unceremoniously to the side of Angel's pool, screaming all the way up. He falls back to the ground and Veddie is there standing over him with an unlit cigar.

"Managed to behave yourself? I'm sure that won't last too long," he snorts with an angry scowl and saunters away. Theo rolls his head back to the ground, gasping. He barely escaped. Barely. Luckily, this time, he was merely the recipient and not the offender. He swallows hard, staring up at the same sky he was staring up at on earth. It was torture to leave in that moment. And he is still on fire.

He rises on his elbows and sees that all the first years are long gone, their jump probably lasting only an hour or two. How long was he gone? Was Veddie watching him the whole time? He sits up and buries his face in his hands. Angel is on the floor of her closet now, her eyes closed, her knees open. She is begging for his swift return. He glances at her steaming life pool and then runs as fast as he can. He bursts out of the front gates of the Field and then up towards the Victory arch of the Reserve. He has no idea where he's going. Can he outrun an orgasm? It's very late; the streets deserted when he enters town. Still not sure where he's going, he runs past the library, past faculty housing and then he sees the bathhouse. He turns sharply and bolts inside, finally slowing to a stop. But Angel isn't stopping. Her pleasure is just beginning and he swears to god she's picturing him as she does it. Hunched over, his hands on his knees, he tries to catch his breath. He's alone. Just the silent hiss of steam from the hot spring and two rows of stone showers open to him on either side. With no thought to the contrary, he rushes into the nearest shower stall and pulls the curtain closed. He rests against the wall, letting his body and his robes get soaked under the eternal shower. The steamy prickles of water seem only to agitate him more, the weight of his wet robe clinging to his body and increasing his excitement. He can still see her there, writhing in the confines of her dirty closet, her hands going everywhere his hands should be. He can feel the movement of her tongue in her mouth, feel the tension in her fingers as they travel, feel the mounting pressure as everything begins to swell. "Fuck," he grumbles, shrugging his robe off his shoulders and letting them fall to the shower floor with a hard, wet splat. He leans forward, bracing one arm against the wall, the showerhead beating down his neck and back. He closes his eyes and reaches his stiff fingers down. His wings expand to fill every corner of the shower, his knees weak and trembling. He keeps thinking of running back to the Field, wet and naked, and diving down to her. It would be so easy. His fingers clenched and raging, his loins aching, he thrusts his hips into his hand. In doing so, he swings his free arm recklessly out to the side and pulls the shower curtain down. He stops, gasps in a breath, completely exposed to the entire shower room. And then a dirty thought enters his mind. Continue. No one is here. Continue. It passes through him like a virus, and staring out in to the public shower, he begins to move his hips again. He thrusts and swears and rolls his head back imagining someone standing outside the shower watching him. As Angel finishes, so does he. Gasping, finally at peace, he collapses back against the wall still holding his swollen cock. He releases a tense sigh, glances to the side, and sees Evangeline standing across the bathhouse. She's staring with wide eyes, her face pale and her mouth open. Her eyes raise to his and then she runs.

"Shit! Shit!" Theo shouts, his pleasure suddenly gone. He picks up his wet robes and struggles into them as he rushes after her. His biggest fear is that she's going to tell someone what she just saw, and somehow an elder will find out, and then somehow Veddie will know what's really going on with him. That the debauchery with his charge ended but has continued on a personal level. And then they'll put restrictions on him, maybe pull out of class, maybe even take him away from Angel. The only reason he's still here is because they think he's reforming. He has to stop Evangeline.

He rushes out after her, calling her name, his body wet and swollen. His robes are so heavy he cannot keep them closed as he pursues her. "Wait!" he cries. "Evangeline, I can explain." Explain what, he's not sure. He shouldn't have done that. What was he doing openly masturbating in a public shower? Why couldn't he have been more careful? This is exactly what Ryder warned him about.

Evangeline drops her books and turns down a short alley, her golden strawberry curls bouncing over her shoulders. She kicks her robes high to expose her thin, firm calves, the divots behind her tender knees. Dark thoughts pass through Theo's mind. Now he's not sure why he's chasing her. There is a dead end ahead. Theo feels his heart rate increase at the sight of it. She has nowhere to run now. She will have to turn and face him. And who knows what will happen after that.

"No, please," Evangeline cries when she comes to the end of the alley. She turns fearfully as Theo eagerly walks her back against the wall.

"I can explain," he says darkly. She's lovely when frightened. He can see a sheen of sweat on her quickly rising breasts. Her eyes are wild and excited. Gone is her modest façade, replaced with a more animated truth.

"Please, don't," she whispers, turning her head to the side and squeezing her eyes shut.

"I'm not doing anything," he hums, moving closer. He reaches a hand to touch her trembling face. He's never been so excited in his life. Then he's taken from behind by an unbelievable force. Arms encircle his chest and a firm body comes up against his back. Theo thrashes like a fish on a hook as he's forced away from the frightened girl. He's spun and turned against the wall to see his attacker. Ryder. Theo pushes back and his hips bump against his mentor's hips. A shock of excitement goes through him. He gasps, his chest quickly rising and falling, his robes peeping open down his chest and over his thighs. Just a thin, wet tie is the only thing covering his front

"What are you doing?" Ryder shouts, thumping him against the wall.

Theo rolls his head back, running his tongue across his lips. Though he orgasmed in the shower, the run has made him stiff. He's pursing a thrilling finale and willing to get there by any means possible. Ryder pins his arms back against the wall. His shouts in his face, his chest forward, his hips too close. Theo stares back at him defiantly. He has no pity for the girl he just terrorized. All he cares about is the relentless pleasure pulsing through his veins. He wants to fight. He wants to fuck. He wants anyone, *anyone*, to surrender to his command, to his control. And maybe, somewhere in the dark recesses of his mind, he wants to be controlled as well.

Theo sits on the sagging couch in Ryder's office waiting for his punishment. He's shaking now, shivering from his wet robes as well as his remorseful heart. The fury of passion is gone and now only cold hard reality remains. He was trying to catch Evangeline, to explain himself but somewhere along the way his intentions changed. And in that moment, there was only the chase, the anticipation of capture, and what followed afterwards. He is disgusted with himself, truly repulsed by what a monster he is becoming.

The door opens and Ryder walks inside, alone, no firing squad accompanying him. At least not yet. Theo remains seated on the couch, his hands folded in his lap, his tongue in his pocket.

"Evangeline is safe with her family. She is very upset." Ryder tosses him a clean robe and then crosses his arms over his chest. "Change. You're soaking wet."

Theo rises, glancing at Ryder as he unties his belt. He looks at him again, expecting him to turn away but he doesn't.

"Go ahead," Ryder says sternly. "I've already seen it all."

Theo unties the belt uneasily. He wants to turn away but feels like if he does, somehow Ryder has won. He drops his robes to the floor and stands naked under the eyes of another man. Ryder looks down at his wet body covered in pine needles and alley dust, red and raw from tonight's exertions. Then his eyes slowly rise to meet Theo's. That's when Theo feels his resolve falter. How does he even dare to challenge Ryder in a moment like this? Ryder is all he has left.

"What's going to happen now?" he whispers, pulling on the dry robe and sinking back to the couch.

"That depends on Evangeline. I'm afraid if she desires it, you will be thrown off the Reserve. There's nothing I can do this time." Ryder becomes angry, picking up the wet robe and tossing it over a chair. "What were you thinking? Were you going to rape her?"

"Rape her?" he whispers, the words polluting his mouth. "No, of course not."

"Because, that's what it looked like when I came around the corner."

Theo lowers his head and folds his hands in his lap. Gone is the burning spectacle that gave rise to all this commotion. He thought escaping Angel was the right thing to do. Now it seems there is no safe place to run.

Ryder sighs and props himself against his desk, his arms folded loosely over his chest. "Just tell me what happened."

Theo leans forward, burying his head in his hands. "I can't. You won't understand."

"Try me," Ryder returns coolly.

"Damnit!" Theo shouts, dropping his hands. "I just can't control myself around her."

"Evangeline?"

"No, around Angel." Theo thumps back on the couch staring up at the wooden beams that span the breadth of the hill. Roots and grasses grow down beneath the planks giving the place a musty, earthy smell like a root cellar. "She has all these dirty fantasies and she likes to write them down. And she's so...descriptive! Fuck," he cries, surprising himself with the profanity. "I would never even dream of stuff like this. And when it gets in my head, I can't get it out."

"And is that what happened tonight?"

"No," he sighs. "She touched me. She had her hands all over me."

Ryder returns the sigh, pushing off the desk to pace. "I told you she doesn't know you're there."

"Really? Because she talks to me."

"Maybe that's what it seems like in the moment, trust me I know, but she doesn't see you. It's all in your imagination."

Theo rises, along with his anger. "She undressed me!" he shouts, pointing a finger at his boorish professor. "She talked to me. She begged me to stay. She looks right at me. She even named her dog after me."

Ryder looks unimpressed until the last statement. "Her dog?"

"Yes, yes, her dog. She named her dog Theo. And when she's in the mood, she sees me. She asks me to touch her. We have conversations. She answers my questions." Theo shakes his head and begins his own pacing. "She took off my clothes and fondled me. I didn't do anything. I escaped. I ascended. But when I came back there was still this…feeling. I can't think straight when it's there. I ran to the showers, but Evangeline saw me. I was chasing her so I could explain. But then…" He sighs, turning his back to his mentor. "I don't know who I am anymore. I don't know what I'm doing."

Ryder seems to back down a bit. "All right. I'll go talk to Evangeline. Maybe, if she has it in her heart to forgive you, she won't have you banished." He walks up to a doorway tucked behind his desk. It's so small and narrow that Theo assumed it was a closet. "Come on," he says, opening the creaky old door. Theo follows his mentor inside. Beyond the old door is a laboratory lined with tables, beakers and goblets. The walls are roughly carved out, with more roots penetrating the interior, some even halfway down the walls. Torches burn dimly and even a few oddly colored plants bloom in the darkness. Theo remembers the first day he met Ryder and how he said he dabbled in the Chemical Arts. Is that what this is? The laboratory for his Chemical Arts?

Ryder indicates towards a bed at the back of the room. It's in a nook inset in the wall with some worn blankets and pillows tossed carelessly around it. Is this where Ryder sleeps? In this little nest?

"I want you to stay here and stay out of sight until I figure out what to do. Meanwhile, this will calm your…nerves." He opens a chest and sorts through the containers until he finds what he's looking for. He sets the vial on the table and then a small glass. "Take just a sip when you feel any sexual urges coming on you. I'll be back as soon as I can."

Ryder closes the door to the laboratory and Theo is alone. He takes the vial, smells its contents and then pushes it away disgusted. Instead he sits down in the nook and then curls up in it. It smells so strongly of Ryder it's as if his mentor is spooning him from behind. He tries to sleep but the gurgles of bubbling experiments and the putrid smell of sweat and laboratory keep him awake. Finally, exhausted, he takes a drink of the liquid. It does as described. It calms his mind and puts him to sleep.

He hides out for a day or two, lurks in the shadows like a good fallen angel, waiting for the fallout from Evangeline. Every so often he peeks out from the laboratory door but the office remains empty. Ryder doesn't return. But neither do elders armed with pitchforks and flaming torches. Restless, he explores the laboratory while he waits. Liquid drips between test tubes, sifting multi-colored fluids into slowly filling beakers. There's an aquarium with fluorescent worms inside it. And strange plants growing along the walls. Cacti with no color, white with red thorny extensions. And another plant that looks like an overturned octopus. It grows from a pot hung upside down from the ceiling. In the chest where Ryder got him his treatment, he finds hundreds of bottles inside all marked with names like *Contemplation* and *Reason* and *Liberation*. On one of the tables, he spots a notebook marked *Deliverance* with complicated equations inside it. It has a recipe list that reads like a witches brew with powdered hooves and salted tears. Many of the ingredients are crossed out and then written again. Seems he is experimenting with this one.

That night, he sits in his dark nook and thinks about the events that transpired today. He doesn't know what happened to him in that that alley. Evangeline was terrified and that only fed his hunger more. It makes him sick to think about her fleeing into the corner because she needed protection from him. From him. And yet when the feeling was upon him, he could do nothing to stop it. Not nothing. He didn't want to stop it. He wanted to run naked through town chasing down every girl he encountered. His dick has become a shiny new toy, something he wants everyone in town to experience.

Ryder returns later. He comes in gravely, brings up a chair and sits down facing the bed. Theo rests with his knees up against his chest, hugging his legs. He glances over warily.

"You are lucky Evangeline has a very forgiving spirit."

Theo hears the news but there's no relief to follow. He does not deserve forgiveness, even though he desires it.

"I explained the situation as best I could. As much as she could bare to hear, anyway. She has asked that you stay away from her, but that is her only request."

Theo lowers his head to his knees with a heavy sigh. She was such a sweet, innocent soul. How could he have done something like that to her? What, in his mind, in that moment, made the attack justified?

"I want to be punished," he whispers.

"If you want." Ryder replies halfheartedly. "If it makes you feel better. If you want to be alone or put in solitary…"

"No," Theo says, raising his eyes. "Not to make me feel better, because I deserve it. Because I have it coming."

"All right," Ryder says, though it is obvious he is not taking the request seriously. "What would you like your punishment to be?"

Theo glares at him, tired of his passive and elusive nature. How can Ryder be so strong one minute and then flimsy the next? Sometimes he thinks his mentor is as fucked up as he is. "When Angel gets mad, she cuts herself. She says the blood makes the pain real. It helps the demons out."

"Is that what you want?" Ryder says with a lift of his eyebrows. "To have someone inflict some sort of physical punishment on you?"

Theo focuses back on the wall past Ryder's ear. "Yes."

Ryder exhales heavily. "The council won't agree to it. That sort of barbaric…"

"The council doesn't need to know about it. This is between you and me." Theo returns his eyes to his hands. It really is what he wants. He wants pain. He wants bruises. He wants something that will remind him, physically, what's at stake the next time he's tempted to let his cock lead the way.

Ryder stares blankly at him, stunned by the request. "Well I won't do it. If that's your request."

"Yes, you will," Theo says, his eyes now locked with the man seated across from him. "I want you to hurt me."

Ryder pushes his chair back, rising. He begins to pace in his usual fashion. "Don't ask me to do that. I won't. That's not who I am."

"I don't care who you are," Theo counters roughly.

Ryder's comes to a stop and stares at Theo. "If this situation is disagreeable for you then I suggest you apply to another mentor. But I warn you, you will find few that will stand behind you like I have."

Theo sighs, his resolve faltering. A beating? What on earth is he thinking? Ryder would never do something like that. And why would he want Ryder to do it anyway? "Maybe it's not Angel's emotions affecting me. Maybe I'm affecting her. Maybe this is who I am."

"No," Ryder counters quickly. "It isn't."

"Then who am I? Because I don't know anymore."

Ryder rubs the back of his neck, turning his head around stiffly. "We are going to have to step things up. I want you in advanced classes immediately. And you and I are going to work extensively on what is going on with you. I want full disclosure from this point on, do you understand? If she touches you, I want to know about it. I've never heard of a charge interacting with their guardian the way you say she has. This is more advanced than I've ever heard. And I think I want you in the BOL section."

"BOL?"

"The Book of Life. I want you to read your book. I'll approach the council on it immediately. Perhaps if you see yourself with some perspective, it might answer some of your questions."

"Okay," Theo says.

Theo returns to Ryder's house and back to his normal life. Classes begin again and his course load is twice what it was before. He moves into suicide prevention and emergency exits. He sits among the dog-eared guardians, level six and seven; his, the only fresh face among them. Quite ironically, his darkness has begun to fade. His wings have begun to molt from dark grey to a smoky white. His skin has lifted to a lighter hue. Even his hair has streaks of blonde in it. Ironic, because he feels worse than ever. He is beset by demons and at constant conflict with this new darkness inside him. Among his many private lessons, Ryder has explained that his budding sexuality would have been better served when he was alive. Dead, the emotions are too raw, too real. Especially due to the situation he finds himself in. It can be hard for a boy, a virgin, coming here and expected to deal with so many diversions. He's seen guardians of rapists, child molesters, and sexual deviants go down the same ugly path, craving things that are not normally in their pallet. Angel is no criminal but she is troubled. Ryder applies to the council but is denied access to the Book of Life section due to Theo's shaky standing in the Reserve. They said they will reconsider the request when Theo is off probation. Veddie is behind this, Ryder fumes after the refusal. He is watching you all the time now. I think he may know about Evangeline. You must be careful. You must stick to your path.

As requested, as soon as Angel reaches for the White Book, Theo seeks Ryder out. Ryder gives him some weird concoction from his laboratory that knocks him out for a few hours and then he is fine again. He doesn't go down to see her. For now, she doesn't need him. And he is grateful for that.

Theo finds himself in the library one quiet afternoon. He has an assignment that requires research and has no choice but to spend a few hours in public. He sets himself in a nice dark corner and goes about his tasks as quickly as possible. As far as his first year friends are concerned, he is simply overloaded with work and cannot meet with them anymore. Apparently Evangeline has told none of the students about the attack. And that's how he's become to think of it: the attack. Not a mistake or a misunderstanding, he attacked her. Ryder never gave him the beating he deserved but he's still getting one emotionally.

From the shadow of his little cubicle, he can see a small study group gathered around his popular mentor. Amongst the group, he recognizes Eric and a few of the other youths he used to hang out with. Evangeline is not with them. He feels like he is to blame for her absence. She is probably in hiding just as much as he is. He cringes even to remember the incident. He is trying to forget it and move on but knowing that she is suffering makes that hard to do.

Nearby, he sees Veddie at another table with some elders. Veddie's men are gathered over a scroll and it has their full attention. Theo realizes that most of the elders are male and thinks back to what Ryder said earlier: religion hates women. None of Veddie's students are female. Are things really so black and white here?

His eyes return to his new mentor. He wishes Ryder were a bit more conventional, that he didn't have such strange relationships with his students. He supposes he's included in that group too. Sleeping in his mentor's house, taking drugs to control his inappropriate sexual urges, and hiding from the elders.

Theo compares the two men, thinking about the fact that Ryder was Veddie's student. He would never have suspected if Ryder hadn't told him. He wonders how they got paired up together. They do not seem a proper match. But then, maybe Ryder was different when he first arrived. God knows, Theo has changed since the car crash that brought him here. And Ryder is a fallen angel as well, though there is no indication of that anymore. No one would ever know that he was once like David. However, it seems there are many ways to fall that won't leave a discernable mark. All sorts of deviations can take place above and below without notice.

Justine enters in the library. Theo glances her way as she stalls in the doorway. He hasn't seen her since Ryder kissed her in the office. But then he hasn't been out around the Reserve much either. How far have things progressed? Has Ryder continued with this relationship or done the responsible thing? Regardless, Justine seems angry. She marches to the table where Ryder is sitting. She seems to accuse him of something, pointing her finger at him but Theo cannot hear what they are saying from where he is sitting. Ryder rises from his seat and indicates to Justine that they are going to move away from the crowd. Justine appears to refuse and then says very loudly: *Daniel, I love you*, causing the whole table to turn. Meanwhile, Veddie is drifting further and further from his group, keenly interested in what's happening the next table over. And it's not just Veddie, librarians, teachers and students are beginning to stray from their projects to look in Ryder's direction.

Ryder takes Justine by the elbow. He does not look pleased. Justine refuses to leave, frees herself, and then holds Ryder's hand to her chest in an intimate way that makes the whole library sit up. Veddie is on his feet now.

"Unbelievable," Theo hears Veddie mutter and he returns to his group for their own heated discussion. Ryder pulls Justine towards the back of the library. Except for the beehive buzzing at Veddie's table and a few raised eyebrows in Ryder's study group, normal activities resume. Theo gets up as discretely as possible and follows in the direction that Ryder and the girl left. The old library is a maze of shelves, books and tables. The roof lowers when he enters the area beneath the Book of Life section. From here on, the journey becomes more cavernous. The shelves are dusty, books placed and not moved for years. Spiders left to their devices. He keeps walking until he hears arguing. Slowing, he peers between the shelves until he sees teacher and student standing in a clearing beside a small wooden table. Ryder seems genuinely angry. He still has Justine's arm clenched in his hand and is talking fiercely into her face. Justine seems combative and no less forceful in her responses.

"You can't act like this," Ryder shouts. "I told you before."

Theo peaks through a few dusty volumes. This is none of his business and yet he followed without hesitation. And now listens intently to the heated conversation between the teacher and his student.

"Then I'll change mentors," Justine says, running her hands through her hair. "I don't care. I'll do whatever I have to do so that we are together."

"I'm sorry Justine, I made a mistake," he says.

Justine yanks her arm free, turning away from him. Her anger seems forced because from Theo's perspective, she looks like she's about to cry. She's just a girl, body barely blooming. It reminds him of Angel and her hopeless cries for Ambrose. Why do women go after men they can't have? Of course Ryder, as well as Ambrose, are baiting these woman, making them believe they might have a chance.

"Justine, I'm sorry, I should've been stronger. I shouldn't have kissed you in the first place."

Tears finally break down Justine's face but her back remains resolved. She waits a few moments to speak and then says, "Then why did you?"

"Why?" Ryder says, and the frustration is evident in his voice. "Because you won't relent, Justine. You came to my office and took off your clothes."

Justine goes red. "But you kissed me!"

"I did. I know that. But you are making it awfully hard for me to resist."

Theo watches her reaction and knows what she is thinking because he has spent so much time in a wanton girls head. The accusation is also a compliment. Because, in her mind, he has just called her irresistible. He is also saying that if she keeps offering, then he might relent. Her tears dry up and her body loosens a bit. The next words out of her mouth surprise to both Theo and Ryder.

"Well if I'm so bad, then you should punish me." She takes a few steps and then bends down over the nearest table offering her backside to her mentor. "Punish me, Daniel," she whispers. "I want you to punish me."

Theo tightens his grip around the shelf he's peering through. It's the same request that he made of Ryder not so long ago, though his intentions were much different. He still can't understand why he asked Ryder to do it. Why would he want Ryder to hurt him?

Ryder rubs his hands over his face and looks down at the girl bent over the table. "Don't be ridiculous, Justine. Stand up."

Justine lowers her head, her backside still lifted over the table. The drape of her robes do little to hide the rounded mounds beneath. "I've been having dirty thoughts about you. I've been imagining what it would like if we were together. I've been wanting it. I've been so very bad. Punish me, Daniel, make me sorry for thinking all these sinful thoughts."

Ryder exhales through his teeth glancing around as if he's planning his escape route. "I told you before, I won't punish you."

"I've never asked you to punish me before," she says.

Theo ducks down a few shelves, his heart racing. Ryder isn't talking to Justine anymore. But this is not the same situation at all. He wanted to be hurt, beaten. Justine wants sexual release. His head begins to swim and his face flushes hot. He should leave right now. This is none of his business. And yet the exits are clearly marked and he doesn't take any of them. Instead he crouches down low and stares at the floor, his ears tingling for every word.

"Do you think it is funny to torture me? To offer me what I cannot have?"

"I don't care. I want you. And you can want me too."

"You know that I cannot have this kind of relationship with you."

"You can do whatever you want. Whatever you want. Punish me, Daniel."

"Stop it! I will not discipline a student."

It becomes strangely quiet. After hearing nothing for almost a minute, Theo peaks through the books again. From his low vantage point, he can see that Justine has pulled her robes up over her waist. Her legs are open and she wears nothing beneath. A dark crescent moon splits her silky behind, which is still mounted over the table ready for Ryder's strenuous hands. Ryder has turned away but he does not leave. Theo's eyes dart to those exposed mounds twitching for reparation. Then to his mentor's stiff body as he stands nearby. Theo braces one hand against the rough carpeting and the other hand to steady himself against the dusty shelf. He feels something twitch to life. Something that is more terrifying than anything he's experienced before.

Ryder takes a book from the shelf. He turns the red gilded, leather-bound volume over in his hands, his brow furrowed. He dusts off the cover, thinking, thinking. Theo's wets his lips, his cramped muscles crying out for air. His eyes burn between the shelves in eager anticipation.

Ryder looks back to the table where Justine still lies with her robes bunched up under her arms. He swiftly approaches her quivering buttocks. "So you want me to punish you?"

Theo swallows hard, thinking only one thing. Punish her. Punish her. He wants to see it. He wants to watch.

"Yes," Justine whispers, gripping her hands around the sides of the table.

Ryder lowers the book until it is level with her ass. Then he lightly thumps the volume against the soft swells. Justine gasps, her legs kicking out.

"Keep quiet," he says sternly. He thumps her backside with twice the force as before. "If you won't behave yourself then you give me no choice. I will punish you. I will make you behave."

Theo drops to his knees, his legs giving out. He is hot and wet with nervous anticipation. He rubs his fingers over his mouth, watching as Ryder paces behind the girl.

"You are impossible." Ryder continues, sending the volume across her backside. "You tempt me. You torture me. And then leave me to my own devices."

Justine cries out, clutching the edge of the table. Ryder thumps her again and again, sending her whole body jolting forward. She stiffens and shakes with each blow delivered. Her robes begin to fall and Ryder grabs them with a quick tight fist, pulling them up to the small of her back. He hits her harder with quick, sharp smacks, leaving harsh red marks across her ass. Justine's legs strain open, toes pointed straight down, her calves tight and trembling.

Theo takes a sharp breath. His mouth goes tight and dry as his hand drops to his lap. Through the thick gauze of his robe, his fingers graze the head of his cock which has just immerged to play. Horrible, confusing things are happening in his mind, things he does not dare to acknowledge. He stares desperately up at Ryder, at his swift controlled hand, at the muscles flexing beyond it. And at Justine presenting and begging for an ingress that he will not provide. He can see her growing wetness, her fingers clenching and unclenching the table's edge, the muscles at the back of her thighs straining for relief. Feeling sick, feeling dizzy, he reaches down inside his robes to get a better handle on his own problems.

Ryder holds the volume between his hands, watching the girl squirm. Justine is pleading for him to continue but he only walks around the table tapping the volume and observing. "You said you wanted this. So keep quiet and take your punishment."

Theo's eyes roll back in his head and he grips his bottom lip in his teeth. Yes, punish her. Punish her. He looks down at his hot pulsating head rocking between the slit of his robe, the veiny shaft stiff in his hard gripped hand. Like Justine, it is begging for more than his fingers can provide. He pumps it in tight, quiet breaths and looks back through the shelf.

Ryder slaps a hand on Justine's back and she squeals in surprise. He walks another circle around her, his eyes traveling deliberately along her trembling body. Theo peers in, his eyes two dicey slits, the blood pumping fiercely through his veins making it hard for him to keep his focus. He watches as Ryder brings the book down on Justine's ass and she shrieks, her knees moving inward. "No open," he says, kicking her legs apart. Theo gasps, grabbing himself harder. He pulls relentlessly at his shaft, watching the drama unfold. He's going to come right here, in the catacombs under the Book of Life section, and he doesn't even care. He's going to come watching Ryder and the girl. He can feel orgasm crawling up his hips like a slowly rising thermometer.

"I think they went back here."

It's Veddie's voice and it causes an immediate reaction. Justine runs off in one direction and Ryder in another. Theo launches to his feet and crashes into an escaping Ryder. A befuddled look comes on Ryder's face. "Theo? What the...come on!" He grabs Theo by the hand and pulls him roughly forward. Theo just stumbles behind him, his head a hundred paces behind. They run around a corner to a dead end. And then Ryder pulls him into a nearby closet and closes the door after them. They wedge together in tight confines, both gasping to keep quiet while Veddie investigates the crime scene.

"He was right back here," Veddie says, coming very near to the closet. "I'm telling you I heard someone here."

"I see no sign of anyone," another voice replies. "Are you sure?"

"Open your eyes. He is corrupting his students. He has to be stopped."

Theo holds his breath; Ryder's chest pressed tight against his back. There are mop handles and buckets tangled at their feet, dirty smocks swinging over their faces, and cans of old paint stacked precariously up the walls. One false step and they'll both tumble out into Veddie's waiting hands.

"Are you following me?" Ryder whispers angrily, wrapping his large hand around Theo's throat. He tightens the fingers in a quick, sharp warning.

Theo exhales a quivering breath, trying to shake himself free. It's too cramped in here. Too tight. He needs some space between his back and Ryder's front. And his erection is still jutting forward like a barbarian's sword. It is aching, just aching to be touched. Satisfaction, he thinks madly, by any means necessary.

"Did you hear what that girl said to him?" Veddie continues. "We should meet with the council immediately. There should be an investigation"

"I don't know," the reluctant accomplice continues. "Students have crushes. There is nothing we can do about that."

"Why is it every time I turn around, you're watching me?" Ryder breathes heavily across Theo's ear. "What is it that you want from me?"

Theo arches his hips away from his mentor but there's no room for relief. Veddie is still outside the door, grumbling. If he moves too far forward, the door will open. And if the door opens, there'll be no explaining this.

"My private life is not your concern, Duncan," Ryder whispers, that huge hand still tight around his neck. "Unless you'd like to make it your concern."

Theo wrenches his head roughly to the side. "If you kept it private, it wouldn't be my concern."

"If you quit following me, it would be private."

Ryder loses his grip and Theo suddenly tips forward. Quickly, Ryder snakes one hand across his chest and pulls him back before he tumbles out of the closet and reveals them both. Theo jerks violently, disturbingly aware of the smell of his mentor's sweat, sweat like in that bed in the laboratory, on that musty couch in his office, and in every corner of Ryder's house. He has to get out of here. He has to get free. What's happening here is not okay. It's not right. Tears break down his cheek. He pushes away harder and Ryder drops his hand from Theo's chest to his waist. Theo gasps at the suddenly transference. Ryder's hand is just inches above a burning hellfire. He struggles against the hand and feels the sweet stiffness intensify. Burning, swelling, agonizing tightness and suddenly he is on the other side of temptation. That place where nothing else matters.

"Tell me what you want from me," Ryder whispers, his lips grazing Theo's ear, the hard prickles of his beard against Theo's cheek. "Tell me."

"Shit," Theo whispers. He clamps his hand over Ryder's and pushes it down. Unlike the night in the courtyard, this time the hand does not resist. Sinuous, foreign fingers come down over his straining, aching flesh. Theo reaches up for the bar above his head. Bare hangers jingle as he struggles to keep his balance. His head rolls back over Ryder's shoulder. A light detonates behind his eyes, from velvet darkness to the sun's surface blindness as an exquisite intruder invades his dark shadows. He succumbs to the madness, to pleasure and denial, to this world in the closet where suddenly none of the rules apply.

Chapter 19∞

Theo lifts his head with a painful gasp. His head is burning, spinning, ten miles thick. He releases a long shuddered sigh, his eyes focusing forward. He's in the library, seated at his cubicle. A book falls off his table with a sharp slap. Everyone looks over. It hits him all at once: the shock, the shame, the horror. What did he just do? Across the room, Ryder glances up at him. Theo experiences a hot, angry flush. He quickly picks up the fallen book and dives behind his cubicle. But as he does, he sees his stuff on the desk, exactly as it was before he followed Ryder under the Book of Life section. And his neck hurts like it's been at an unnatural angle for a very long time. How did he get back here? He glances up at Ryder again, short of breath. Ryder sits, looking exactly as he did before the incident happened. Theo ducks down again, looking at the crumpled pages of his textbook. He touches his cheek to find wrinkles that match. Was he sleeping? Did he fall asleep? Was this all a dream? Chest constricted, he searches for signs, for memories of how he and Ryder managed to escape that closet and return so casually to the library after such an encounter. He is certain that if his mentor just manhandled him, the last thing he'd do would sit down in the library and act so nonchalantly as to not arouse the suspicion of anyone in the room *and* fall asleep. What happened under the Book of Life section cannot be real. The closet cannot be real. It cannot.

Theo retreats into the forest below the misty hill. Under cover of the trees, he checks his body for signs of disturbance. He doesn't know what he expects to find. Manly finger dents across his chest? A long black hair lodged in his robes? There is nothing abnormal, no aches or pains, no scratches or burns.

Frustrated, he sits by the quiet stream and buries his face in his hands. He has to get away from Ryder. Things are only getting worse under his mentorship. Everything is spinning out of control. The closet dream, if that's what it was, makes him nauseous. He tries to ignore it but the memory is foremost in his conscious and demanding constant attention. Where is this pursuit of sexual gratification going to end? Rape and buggery? His body swells at the memories of chasing Evangeline down the alley, of being crammed in that quiet, forbidden closet. Disgusted, he moves into the stream, sits in the frigid water until he's sure he'll never have an erection again.

A twig breaks. Theo jumps, turns, and sees David. He emerges through the twisted trees like he is one of them, all full of knots and holes, braided limbs and hair like dried leaves. His oversized hands speak volumes where they did not before. Now that Theo knows what he really is, he never wants to be near him again.

"Troubled, my young friend?" David asks. He crosses the stream, not even bothering to lift his soiled robes from the water. Soot travels downstream towards Theo's legs. He crawls out of the water, revolted by David's grubby trail. He is like a disease, a sickness, and Theo is worried that even being near him may result in further infection.

"You look distressed," David says with a pleasant smile. "Would you like to tell me all the lurid details? I am eager to hear more of what is going on around the Reserve these days."

"What do you want?" Theo grumbles irritably, pushing up to his feet. He squeezes his wet robes out and reties his sopping sandals. Can't he get a moment to himself in this place? All he wants is some peace and quiet so he can clear his mind and get his head back together.

"The real question is, what do you want?" David croons, tucking his stringy hair behind his ears. "What desires are burning inside that lusty heart of yours?"

Theo narrows his eyes at the dirty angel and then turns back into the woods. If David won't leave, then he will.

"I was down to the library," David calls with a smile. "It has become a very interesting place as of recent."

Theo stalls, feeling like he's just stepped into quicksand. Except it is not the mud that threatens to consume him but his own guilty conscience. What does David mean by that? Was he there? Did he see what happened between him and Ryder? But the closet wasn't real. It's not real! Can David see into his thoughts? Into his dreams? But why would he even dream something like that? Why would something like that ever come into his head? Is it part of the darkness, his sickness, or did it come from somewhere else?

"You might need this." David says, breaking Theo's anxious reverie. He tosses something in the stream between them. Rippling beneath the surface, Theo sees a key. He doesn't pick it up or ask what it's for, just continues to stand, staring across the river at David. "If only I had gotten started as early as you. Think of all the things I could've done."

"I am not like you!" Theo shouts, his outburst disproportionate to the accusation. "You're disgusting! You're sick! Stay away from me!"

Calmly, David crosses the stream again, releasing another snake of sludge down the river. He stops as he's passing Theo. "Oh and say hello to my old mentor."

Theo's eyes narrow. "Your old mentor?"

David just smiles a mouth full of crooked butter teeth.

"Your old mentor?" Theo asks, getting more uneasy. He cannot mean what Theo thinks he means. "Who is your old mentor?"

David smiles, turning away. "I see you have started behaving yourself again. Such a shame. Such a pity. When there is all this...flesh for the taking."

"Who was your mentor?" Theo shouts.

"It seems my dear Daniel has an appetite for flesh as well. But he was always smarter than me, craftier. He keeps his activities behind closed doors and beyond the prying eyes of the council. People like you and me? Well, we just can't hold it in, can we? We have to bring it out for the whole world to see."

Theo turns back, wanting to run, wanting to scream. He can't believe what he just heard. He can't even process it. His eyes fall on the key glittering beneath the surface of the shallow river. What is it for? Why did David give it to him? He snatches it out of the water and stares as it as the stream meanders around his ankles. Unlike David, he leaves no sludgy residue behind. Resolve rolls in around him like a thick, warm fog. He's done crying and lamenting. It's time to take some action against what has happened to him here on the Reserve. It's time he starts taking control of his own life, get free of Ryder and even Veddie. He's tired of being the victim of his own whims and passions. It's time he goes off on his own.

Theo stands in line at the administration office fingering the key in his pocket. This is where Veddie first brought him to sign up for courses. It's swarming with shocked students, all glassy eyed, waiting for the next phase of their lives to begin. Or deaths. Because that's what the Reserve has been for him so far. The end of everything he used to be. And the birth of things that would've seemed unimaginable before. He is a wreck. And David's revelation has done little to resolve that. It seems like he can't trust anyone here anymore. Veddie lied about his education. Ryder lied about who he is. And David is just a liar. He will have to become his own guide from this point on.

When his turn comes, Theo approaches the woman behind the desk. He knows the first thing he has to do to get himself free of Ryder, get himself out of that house. Of course it means an increased risk of exposure but he's just going to have to be more careful now. "I'd like a new bed assignment," he tells the woman seated behind the table.

The woman looks up sourly. She seems decidedly unpleasant. "Ask your mentor."

Theo taps his fingers on the table. "I can't. He's...unavailable. He asked me to come here and do it myself."

Theo woman straightens a thick stack of papers and sets it aside reluctantly. "Fine then. Where you like a bed?"

"In the first year dorms," he says.

She runs her finger down a list. "All the beds are full. I can put you on a waiting list. What is your name?"

Theo clears his throat. "Theodore Duncan."

She looks up at him in a way that makes him extremely nervous. Like she knows who he *really* is. Why he fell. Why Veddie dropped him. What he and Ryder did in that closet. He cringes. But that was only a dream. Not real. Not real.

"Duncan," she repeats, going down the list again. "You already have a bed in that dorm."

"No, I don't." Theo says, getting annoyed now. "It was reassigned."

"Reassigned?" the woman exclaims. "That is the same bed that was assigned to you when you first arrived. It has not been assigned to anyone else."

"But..." Theo falls silent. Ryder said his bed was reassigned. Why would he lie about something like that? And he swore he saw another student's books on that bed the other day. What the fuck is going on here?

His head is spinning but he still needs to find out what the key is for. He takes it and thumps it down on the desk. It could be for the Book of Life section but he has no idea. If it's for something prohibited, he could get in trouble for bringing it out. But he has to know. "I don't want to lose this. Is there somewhere safe to keep it?"

"Excuse me?" the old hag replies.

"You heard me," he says, raising his voice, his patience gone. "Where is everyone keeping their keys?"

Her face twists up into a witches scowl. "If you are unable to keep track of it yourself then leave it in the main library. The librarian stores Life keys there."

Life key, that's all he needs to know. Theo snatches the key up and gives her the rudest look he can manage. With this, he can get answers to everything. Thank you, David.

The library is fairly busy when he arrives. He looks down at the key in his hand, suddenly having doubts. The spiral staircase to the Book of Life section is in the center of the library. He'll be seen by everyone as he ascends those stairs. And if the key doesn't open the door, then there might be questions as to what he is doing up there.

Before he can contemplate the risks involved, he finds himself crossing the library floor. If he's learned anything from Angel, it's to commit his crimes with confidence. Be bold. They're looking for the suspicious ones, the shifty eyed ones lurking in the corners not the ones striding out in the open. So he climbs up the stairs, each step echoing loudly through the main room, and sets his key inside the lock. He turns it and the bolt falls open.

He closes the door behind him and enters into the church-like stillness of the Book of Life section. It's eerie and silent like a graveyard. The windows are all covered and sunlight sifts through the dark curtains in long stabbing beams. The carpet beneath his feet is thick and lush and he walks as soundlessly as if his feet were not on the ground at all. The shelves around him are old, made of wood, and some are very dusty. Books sit reverently in their places, each volume a little different than the others, different shapes, sizes, widths and colors. On the bindings are single names. Anthony Johnston. Marvin Smith. Some books are the size of encyclopedias while others are thin as a children's novels. The books appear to be in alphabetical order, so he goes searches for the D's. He finds not just one Theodore Duncan but dozens of volumes under his name. Even so, he recognizes his own volume right away. Clean. Orderly. Refined. It's a tall book with a crisp, clean binding, gold accents, and silk pages. The cover is silver-blue with his name printed neatly across the front. He remembers it tucked beneath Veddie's arm when he arrived for judgment. Walking through those water filled vaults seems like centuries ago. Suddenly he longs for his old mentor, for the order and prestige he was promised on first arrival. Ryder's teachings are leading to nothing but trouble. Standing here, staring at his Life book, he decides that he has make an appeal to Veddie. If he explains what has happened, certainly Veddie would give him a second chance. He can't go on like this. He cannot continue this journey with Ryder.

He slides the book from its place amongst the many Duncan's. None are relations to him, as far as he knows. In fact, the Duncan's stretch up and down the whole aisle. He supposes there are uncles and grandparents here amongst the volumes. Maybe when he has more time and more motivation, he might look up some of his ancestors. But he needs to find Angel next. He turns to begin his search but realizes that he doesn't even know her last name. "Shit," he grumbles, looking down row after row of volumes.

With no last name, he doesn't know where to begin. He walks randomly around, hoping he might stumble upon it by accident. But after almost twenty minutes, he gets nervous about the time. He has to read through his book before someone catches him. He needs to get his head back together, to touch base with the man he used to be before he came here. Angel's book, no doubt, will have to be given to him now that he is her guardian. He will have access to hers long before he will get access to his own.

He finds a table in a corner by an arched glass window. The window is frosted over giving him light but privacy as well. He walks towards it but then something catches his eye. He stops by the thick, violet hardback marked Daniel J. Ryder. He stares at it wryly and then pulls it off the shelf as well. Might as well find get some truth about his mentor while he's at it.

He sits down in the nook and opens his book. The first page has only his name written in elegant script. He flips to the next page. Theodore Duncan, born to Andy and Dianna Duncan. Weighing in at six pounds, seven ounces. He turns the page. He needs to get to the important stuff, the days and months before his death. He skims through the early years. His first words. The day he took his first step. His favorite toy. He glances up at Ryder's obscenely colorful book perched on the table in front of him looking like the interior of a gypsy cabana, then back down at his own neat and fresh narrative. He's angry and wants to read Ryder's but he has to get through his own volume first. He continues. The day his elementary school burned down. The day he met his first best friend. Good boy so far. Nothing surprising or unexpected. Seems like he always had a sense of right and wrong. Good and bad. He glances up at Ryder's book again. He's so angry at him for lying about David and his bed reassignment. But he was angry before that, disturbed over the closet dream. It happened right below here, right under the Book of Life section. He gets an urge to go investigate. To go check that closet and see if it's real. But what if it is? He's not sure he can deal with that right now. No, he has to read his book while he has the chance. He has to calm down and get himself focused. He reads on.

He goes to school. He goes to church. He says his prayers. He listens to his parents. Hard working boy. An acceptable amount of friends. What he notices though, even at a young age, is that he has no particular attachment to anything or anyone around him. No real emotions. He's a bit robotic. A bit dead inside. That is surprising to him; he never considered himself cold when he was alive.

He glances at Ryder's book again. That book is just gnawing at him; it's cover as subtle as police sirens in the dead of night. Exhaling angrily, he slides it over. He'll just have a quick peak and then focus on his own book. He opens to the first page. Daniel Jeremy Ryder. The title is handwritten in decorative script. He turns to the opening page. Daniel Ryder, born to Gerry Ryder and Natasha Clark. Moved a lot. Parents were separated before he was born. His mother was a nurse. His father owned a car repair shop. He and his dad rebuilt classic cars together. He visited his mother on weekends. He went to school in a town called River's End. He was a quiet boy, small for his age, and not too popular. He never really fit in at school. He never met his father's expectations.

Late in his teens, things start unraveling. He had a crush on a girl that went unrequited. He was targeted by school bullies. So far a pretty average existence. But then Theo comes to something labeled *The Match*. The event is highlighted in his book like it is something important. A turning point. Ryder is in his late teens. He's being forced to play team sports or get expelled. He has signed up for wrestling. He hates wrestling. But it seems that he doesn't hate his wrestling partner so much.

Theo frowns, pushing back from the book. He stares at the stained glass window, his mouth gone dry. Tentatively, he returns to the story, nervous about where this is going. It's the day of the match. He fights the boy, his wrestling partner, someone he knows well. There is a moment during the match where he knows what the problem has been the whole time. He has found the missing piece to the puzzle and with it everything makes sense.

Theo closes the book shut and pushes it away. Feeling sick, he shoves it a bit more until it falls off the other side of the table. His own queries about Ryder are suddenly answered. Ryder's keen interest in him. Ryder bending backwards to help him. Ryder taking him into his house. Ryder wanting all the explicit details of his sexual struggles. Theo folds his arms over his chest, rocking back in his chair, irritated. This is what it's all been about. Ryder is interested in much more than his education. Theo rises from his chair, no longer able to sit. With growing horror, he remembers how he touched himself in the courtyard. How Ryder caught him there. And how he forced his mentor's hands on his body. Ryder probably thinks he wants him.

Theo paces in front of the table. Maybe he's making too much of this. What about Ryder and Justine? If Ryder is gay, why is he kissing girls? But Ryder grabbed him in the closet. No, he scolds himself, the closet wasn't real. He dreamed that. But why would he dream Ryder was gay? Why would he even think that? Did he subconsciously suspect? He flinches at how he so utterly exposed himself to this man, let all his vulnerabilities be trusted into his hands. Ryder didn't have his best interests in mind. Ryder was just interested. He coerced Theo into his house where they could be alone. And then he made him all confused.

Calm down, he thinks, calm down. After all, Ryder has made no moves against him. It is him divulging in front of his mentor. Letting it all hang out. Thinking he might actually be sick, he remembers how Ryder made him disrobe in front of him, how he looked at his body while he was naked. And then, with a terrified jolt, he remembers asking his mentor to discipline him. And even worse, how he touched himself when he watched Ryder discipline Justine. But that was a dream. *A dream*. It was not real. It did not happen. Theo looks down at Ryder's book on the floor. He can't even go near it. Ryder tricked him. He tricked him. He lied about being fallen.

He lied about David. And now he's lying about his sexuality. Ryder has been lying the entire time.

I wake up in dirt. There is garbage beneath my feet and the sound of cars rushing by. The grumbling of angry lives filter through thin brick walls and I look up. It's dark and it's cold. I hear strange echoes and see a light in the distance. As my eyes begin to adjust, I see pasty windows rising on both sides of me and a sliver of sky visible above. I'm in an alley.

Theo slams the door to Ryder's office open. It's late. Ryder's there. Spread out across his sofa drinking wine, looking satisfied as a freshly fed feline. He tips his glass to Theo, his other arm thrown lazily over the end of the sofa. "What's on your mind, Theodore Duncan?"

Theo thrusts the door closed. Dust drops from every seam in the roof as he does. He gets a whiff of the place, a whiff of Ryder's musky sweat and his anger skyrockets.

He's been pacing outside the office for hours fighting with himself whether to confront his mentor or just go home. He wants to put an end to this unhealthy relationship between them. This is a man who succumbs to his every passion and Theo is trying to control his.

"So are you going to tell me the truth this time?" he demands, his body like a missile on the verge of departure. He can barely look in his mentor's direction. He's afraid if he does, he'll blast off into oblivion.

"I'm sure I don't know what you mean," Ryder replies, taking a sip from his drink. He slides his long, uncombed bang to the side of his face with a pinkie finger.

Theo's eyes dart from his mentor's face to the exposed flesh of his chest. He's assaulted by a torrent of seedy musings, of waking dreams and horrible reality, of the dark disturbances of his soul. His imaginings have no boundaries anymore, they go wherever they please, darting this way and that with no regards to his own reservations. He blames Ryder for that. Ryder is the cause of this. Ryder is corrupting him.

Clutching my purse, I move quickly towards the sounds of cars, of people and safety. I don't know how I got to this alley but I have to get away. A man appears at the mouth of the alley blocking my path. A hat hides his face from me. He looks like a detective. He wears a trench coat. I see thigh-high mud boots and nothing else. I stop. I back a few steps away. He advances.

Ryder says something, but Theo can't hear him. Angel is writing hotly in his ear. She's uprooting all his dark woodsy places.

"I saw David," Theo shouts like it's loud in the room.

"Okay," Ryder says, sitting up straighter. "Where have you been? You missed our session today. Do you want to tell me what's going on?"

Theo turns a hard eye on his mentor. He has only one question but is terrified to hear the answer. He only feels safe inside his angry accusations.

"How many have you lost?" he cries.

Ryder squints at Theo as if he's the one who's been drinking. He sinks back in the couch like a lion lounging at the mouth of his den, his legs open, his robe unfastened to mid chest, the knotted tie barely keeping everything inside. Theo's eyes drop to that exposed skin again, to that flat hairless chest, creamy like warm yogurt, to the dark slit in his robe between his legs. He shudders, turns away, feeling sick.

"Theo, it's late. I've had a long day. If you'd like to..."

"No!" Theo shouts and the volume of his cry is enough to rouse his mentor from his lolling state. "We are going to talk about this now! Now! I'm so sick of all this...bullshit! How many have you lost, *Daniel*? Just tell me that. How many of your students turned out like me? Or David?"

"David?" Ryder sets his drink aside. "What did David say now?"

Theo focuses on the experiments sprouting on the windowsill past Ryder's ear. His head is spinning. Angel is spinning his head around. He keeps thinking about that dream, the closet, the Church, Angel's alter boys, the shower and Evangeline. There's pressure building that no amount of rage will release.

"He said you were his mentor!"

Ryder sighs, looking tired. He lifts his arm behind his head, widening the yawn in his robe. Theo focuses away but his mind won't. Everything is sex now. Everything.

"Did he give you the key?" Ryder asks.

"The key?" Theo shouts.

"To the Book of Life section? Did he give you the key?"

Theo turns back to his mentor and stares at him incredulously. "You knew?"

"It was my key. I gave it to him."

"Why?" Theo cries.

"Because the council wouldn't allow me to give it to you. I had to find another way. I figured if David gave it to you, then they couldn't link it to me."

Theo grits his teeth. Did Ryder want him to stumble across his book? To see who his mentor really was? A secret message between teacher and student? And now Theo has come just as requested to answer Ryder's calling. Ryder is filthier than he ever imagined.

"Why didn't you tell me he was your student? Don't you think that was slightly important?"

Ryder sighs, running a hand back through his hair. "Do you believe everything you hear, Theo? Must you come rushing to me all fire and brimstone every time you think something is slightly out of place? You are exhausting me."

"You're my mentor. I think I have a right to know how many failed experiments you've gone through before you got to me. This is my life you're dealing with. My life!" Theo cranes his head back trying to block out Angel's imaginings. She is hot to trot and he wants to play too. Only when they were together did the world seem right. He's sick of the Reserve, of Ryder and Veddie, of all the rules and regulations. He just wants to break out, throw off the shackles of civilized society and follow his shadow into absolute depravity.

"Well, I hate to disappoint you but David craves chaos. He is suffering and wants to make everyone else suffer as well." Ryder picks up his drink and begins to sip again. "Did you get into the Life section?"

"Oh you know that I did," Theo challenges, folding his arms tightly over his chest. His blood is pumping so fast he thinks he might pass out. He's so humiliated by his own naivety and so hurt by Ryder's continued betrayals. He feels like he's hit a point of no return. That he's crossing a line that can never be uncrossed.

I turn to leave, to find another avenue of escape, and face a second accomplice. This one is shirtless with a mask over his eyes and nose, with dark gloves up to his elbows and a kilt that only covers the back. I am surrounded.

I turn to run but the one in mud boots grabs my elbows from behind. He forces my arms behind my back while the masked one opens his belt to reveal a thick stiff cock turned slightly to the left. He's lean and he's muscled, looking hungry as a starving dog. Blinds from a nearby window cover him in zebra stripes, his eyes, his mouth, his shoulders, his hips, lines of light and dark, lines of a man divided. I struggle and plea but the masked one holds firm. He's shown me his and now he must see mine. He reaches forward and pulls my shirt up over my head. The one behind forces my legs open. The masked one looks hungrily down, grazes a nipple with his hard plastic glove. The gloves are wet, they leave something sticky that adheres to my skin and I can't help but react.

"I'm so sick of your shit. Why can't you just answer my fucking questions? How are you any better than David? He preys on them down below and you prey on them up above." Theo tightens his arms around his chest, ready to explode. His head is hot and overloaded. His fuse is short and it's lit.

Ryder sets his drink aside and rises. He ties his loose robe and Theo sees that huge anchor meant for a ship of much bigger proportions. He winces and grips his teeth together, his tongue pressed hard against the clenched bones.

"What are you talking about?" Ryder takes a step towards him but Theo steps back. "Why are you acting like this?"

"I know about the bed," Theo blurts.

"The bed?"

"In the dorms. You never gave it away."

Ryder stalls, staring at him incredulously. "Your bed? What do you mean? "

"In the dorms! In the dorms! You said it was reassigned but it wasn't! Why are you lying to me?!" He glares hard at his mentor. Feels like he is too close even though he stands half a room away.

"I was trying to protect you," Ryder says, his face darkening. "Can you imagine what would've happened if you returned to the dorms, acted there like you did in my courtyard?"

Theo sucks in a horrified breath. He doesn't like how Ryder worded that. Did it in *my* courtyard. Is that what he wants? Does he want him to come play in *his courtyard?* So angry and so pent up, Theo finally shouts, "I read your book!"

"What?" Ryder looks down. He's troubled now. He understands what Theo is accusing him of. "I sent you in there to read your own book. I sent you in there because I saw that you were struggling and I hoped that some perspective would help you out."

"Oh, is that why?" Theo replies insolently. "Because it seems like you wanted me to know something else."

Anger finally crosses his mentor's face. His eyes flash up to meet Theo's. "Did you like it? Did it get you off? What was your favorite part? How did you like the ending?"

"I didn't read the ending. Just enough. Just enough." He stares hard into Ryder's hazel eyes. His temper is in threads now. Blood is throbbing through his head, through his cock. This is a very dangerous game he's playing.

He reaches down, slips his rubber fingers around the waist of my skirt. I push and I shove but I can't get my hands or my legs free. The one behind moves closer. I feel his hand on the back of my neck, the brim of his hat in my hair.

The masked one kneels down, first one knee then the next and takes my skirt down one agonizing inch at a time. Down over my hips, down until a crinkle of hair is visible. He licks the hair, laps at it, making it wet and glimmer in the dim alley light. He pulls my skirt down further, hips, knees and then to my feet. He looks up as his tongue goes in. I can feel the rims of thigh high boots pressed against my ass from behind. A cock waiting behind me as I glitter in front.

"Is that what this has been all about? Is that what you want from me?" Theo accuses, feeling as though he's about to lose his mind.

Ryder chuckles, mimicking the way Veddie used to laugh at him. "What exactly is it that you think you know?"

"That you're gay!" Theo says with disgust. He watches as Ryder's jaw tightens and his hands form fists at his sides. He looks up at Theo with so much fury in his eyes that Theo back a few steps away, a few steps closer to the pot belly stove.

"Name for me one time, *one time,* that I acted inappropriately with you. I am the one who stopped you in the courtyard. I am the one who stopped you in the alley. I am the one who took you in when no other mentor would even look at you. I have stood up for you, defended you, supported you..."

"But why?" Theo returns angrily. "Why are you doing it?"

"Why? Maybe you should ask that question yourself. You are the one who can't control himself. You are the one exposing yourself to me. You are the one touching himself in the corner of my house."

Theo goes bright red. The closet flashes through his head. Of what he did while watching Justine's punishment. Of being jammed in close quarters with his mentor's hands on his body. It was so real. So real.

"Get away from me," Theo whispers. "Don't come near me." He turns for the door but Ryder steps in the way. Theo thumps him in the chest, knocking him back and then retreats between the two chairs by the fire. Blood is charging past his ears as he crouches down by the stove. The fire is crackling hot, snapping and popping, a warm glow emanating from its glass window.

The masked one brings his fingers back up. He slips his plastic thumb between my hips and then puts it inside. I arch back against my rubber captor. One thumb and then two, and then the fingers and all the rest, he pushes them up like an eager miner, searching for a shower of gold. I gasp, arching, screaming, lift up on my toes and howl up at the thin alley sky.

Theo gasps out his breath. Angel's story has made him stiff as nails. He needs release and Ryder is the only one here. He starts to panic. Ryder says everything is his fault. It seems like it is. It seems like he's been the one asking for it. But he doesn't want it. He doesn't want anything from Ryder.

"Just calm down," Ryder says, setting a hand on Theo's shoulder.

"Stay away from me!" Theo screams and explodes from his corner by the fire. But he trips and falls back against the burning hot stove, scalding his palms. Ryder catches him at the chairs where they used to sit and drink tea so politely. Theo spins around throws Ryder against his desk. He means to run out the front door but in his confusion, he enters the laboratory instead.

Panicked, he enters the backroom, pulling down bubbling experiments and books full of research, his hands burning from the fire. Ryder catches him and forces him to the ground. Theo lands on his back and stares helplessly up at the roots dangling from above. At the heavy wood crossbeams spanning the dark little cave. At the raven haired man who now kneels over him.

Suddenly the man behind me becomes impatient. He takes me by the throat and pushes me forward. The masked one rises and catches me against his chest. They begin to take turns. Each entry forcing me against the chest of the other. One enters and then the next, one from behind and one from the front, their frothy cocks crashing and lunging against each other, fighting for occupancy. I am lathered in the sweat of two men I do not know. Suddenly the decision seems unilateral, they will both have me at once or none at all. Carefully placing themselves front to back, two swollen heads perch themselves at the mouth of my tiny orifice. They push in and I'm filled to explosion, inch by inch they progress together, crammed together, the two titans' battle for dominance.

Theo cries out as Ryder thumps down on his thighs, his stiff rod encased in his mentor's warm robes, the swollen head pressed up against Ryder's stomach. Then panic follows. He bucks his hips and throws his mentor off. He rolls up to his knees and faces Ryder who is also on his knees. His hands are blazing from the stove, the skin beginning to peel. But there is only one place where the pain is unbearable.

"Is this what you want? Is this what you want?" Theo cries, throwing his robes back and exposing his throbbing monster to his mentor. Again, there's a rush of pleasure. It's show and tell time. Look what I have. Look how big it is. His eyes rise recklessly to his mentor. And the look on his face is unreadable. He is a stone. Unmoved by the gesture. Theo experiences a shock when he realized he's being rejected.

"Go ahead," he goads, holding his rod out and shaking it. "I know you want to."

"You have no idea what I want," Ryder replies calmly, coldly.

Furiously, Theo grabs Ryder and pulls him forward. Ryder slides on his knees across the wet floor crashing up against Theo's body. Theo takes him by the back of the neck and slams his lips into his mentor's so hard that their teeth ring. Then he reaches for Ryder's cock. That's when his mentor punches him in the face.

Chapter 20 ∞

The next time Theo wakes, it's morning. Dim light filters in through the greasy windows of Ryder's underground office. For a few minutes, he's not sure how he got here or why he's sleeping on the dilapidated couch in the corner. Then he feels a pain on his face. He touches his cheek and the swollen lump brings a rush of horrid memories from the night before. What he did last night, he cannot excuse it or explain it. Nor does he want to think about it, not ever again.

He rises from the couch painfully slow. The office is thankfully empty. No sign of Ryder in the main area or in the laboratory. But just a glance into the back room sends his mind reeling. He sees broken test tubes and books scattered across the floor. He also remembers himself on his knees exposing himself to his mentor. Not just exposing this time but asking Ryder to join him. With a sick remorse, he thinks of how angry he was when he was rejected and then how he reacted after. Long live the almighty erection, he thinks bitterly. Praise be to the orgasm and anything and anyone that brings him to that conclusion.

He passes by the mirror and sees himself a few shades lighter than the last time he looked. His wings are dusty white now. Gone is the roadside tan, replaced by his natural creamy complexion. He turns his burned palms up to the mirror. Though remarkably healed, it's still an ardent reminder of the line he crossed last night. His transgressions know no bounds now. It seems there is nothing he won't do for sexual gratification.

He leaves the office, not sure where he is going. He walks aimlessly through the lower parts of the city as the sun lifts over the horizon. Long shadows leave dark corners down narrow streets and alleyways. A good place for a fallen angel to hide his dirty secrets. And he has so many to hide now. He takes a deep breath, stopping in the middle of the road and staring up at the sky. Maybe it's time to leave. Would Ridwan still let him pass? He is helping no one in the state he's in now. And he's afraid what will happen if he stays any longer. How long before he becomes David? How long before he is living in the forest and descending to earth merely to satisfy his own sexual cravings? Even worse, having his thirst quenched while he is above. Sins below affect his physical transformation but the ones he's committing above are tearing him apart morally.

He lowers his gaze from the sky and experiences a shock when he sees Ryder walking down the street. The rising sun casts a brilliant light around him, his dark hair glinting, his oversized wings making him appear more like a demon than an angel. He is too far to read the expression on his face.

Theo is unable to move, unable to breathe. He stares at Ryder and Ryder stares back at him. Those things he has been trying to avoid are now dancing gleefully around his head. Last night, everything seemed possible. Man or woman, he didn't care who touched him. He just wanted to be touched. But that's not true and he knows it. He didn't want to be touched by just anyone. He wanted to be touched by Ryder.

He descends later that day, needing to get away from the Reserve for a while. Angel is at work. Unlike him, she looks pretty satisfied with how things went the night before. She wrote herself off and then had the best orgasm of her life. Oh, he knows how happy she was. Half the reason he ended up in that office was because of her hot words in his head. He was so angry after he read Ryder's book and so pent up from the exertions of the last few days. If only he'd just gone off by himself and waited until the morning to confront Ryder. Then none of this would've happened.

Angel hums as she puts her things in her locker. She's thinking about the psychic and about Ambrose. She's dreaming about all the scenarios that will bring them together. The divorce and how she will comfort him in his hour of need.

Or maybe he will just cheat on his wife with her. A wild and secret affair carried on behind closed doors. It's the last one that gets her the most excited. To have a taste of something forbidden.

Forbidden, he thinks, as he follows her back to the meeting room. He supposes, a few days ago, he might have thought a married affair forbidden too. But he has since learned that there are cravings that are much more illicit. He wanted something last night that has never touched his pallet before. And even now, he cannot clear his head of it. Even though he so desperately wants to.

"Hey Angel!" cries the loud girl as they come into the meeting room. "Come over here and congratulate Ambrose. He's got great news."

Over and above a group of jeering employees, Angel catches a glimpse of her dark haired hero. He's red faced and smiling.

"Congratulations," they all keep saying. "Great news!"

Angel peers over their shoulders trying to catch a glimpse of him. Then she hears, "We'll have to bring in some cigars."

Angel backs away, her heart going dark and cold. Is he having a baby with his wife? Are they pregnant?

"Do you know what it is? What do you want, a girl or a boy?" another person asks.

Angel turns away from the ruckus, her whole body vibrating. Time slows like a clock stuck in molasses. Like the day Romeo dumped her on the sidewalk, she is unable to move for what seems like hours. She's telling her body to quietly exit the building but in her mind it's Hiroshima. She can't form clear thoughts, it's all emotional, raging, raging. A tear breaks loose and Angel quickly walks out the door. Keeping her eyes fixed firmly on the pavement in front of her, she walks briskly towards her truck. All she's thinking is truck, drive, home. She gets in the truck. She turns the key over. The truck only sputters. "Come on, you motherfucker! Come on!" She turns it over again. It doesn't dare disobey. She puts it in gear and drives out of the parking lot. The Light pulls in around them and Theo is genuinely scared. There's no words in her mind, it's just hot red burning wildfire. He swears he can hear her knuckles cracking around the steering wheel. She's driving faster and faster, her red rimmed eyes focused straight ahead.

Theo looks over at her. Wind is racing past the unsealed windows so loud he can barely hear his own voice. Smoke begins to emit from the vents. And then he hears the sound of a train.

"Angel, no!" he shouts, trying to grab the wheel. He couldn't see it before but the image is clear in her mind now. There's a train crossing the tracks. She's going to hit it at full speed. She imagines the truck being ripped in half, her body rolling out into the field. She breathes her last few breaths and then there is finally relief. Ambrose will hear about it. Maybe he'll be upset, though is probably too happy about his new baby to care. At least she won't die alone in her house and lie there for weeks on end. At least she'll die somewhere people will find her and people will know. But it all ends today. Right here. Right now.

"Stop it! Angel, stop it!" Theo cries, shoving her and then kicking at her. "Don't kill yourself over some stupid fucking boy. He just a kid! He's is not worth this. Angel! He's not even worth you."

Angel begins to cry but she is not slowing down. The train is louder now. It's a horn wailing, warning her to slow down. Angel can't wait to hit it, to feel the impact, to feel every bone in her body break to pieces.

"Angel, don't! Please! Angel I need you. Angel, I love you. Don't leave me like this." Theo shouts.

Angel's grip on the wheel loosens, then she presses her foot on the brakes. The truck slows to a stop. Even as they idle, he can feel the ground shake from the train.

"I love you," he says softly. "Don't leave me."

Theo sits in the library with his head on the table. People are staring and he doesn't care. Somehow it has all come undone. And he can't hide his pain anymore. He stopped Angel today but she will kill herself eventually. That, he is sure of. And yet, somehow, it all still comes back to him. Her death is his failure. His worries are about his insecurities. He's lost himself. He doesn't know who he is anymore. Maybe he never did. Maybe he was just following the rules and reaping the rewards that come with doing what you're told. But now there are no rules to follow and he is completely lost without them.

Veddie is nearby. Theo caught him looking his way in smug satisfaction. He supposes his old mentor has been vindicated by his failures. There is no compassion over a student who has lost his way. No patience for someone who needs to slow down and reassess. No understanding for circumstances that might have caused him to take a few wrong turns. Only Veddie's obvious pleasure in seeing someone he detests, fail. All along, Theo has been longing to return to him and plead for another chance. But he has rarely contemplated whether Veddie was worth the effort.

He returns his head to his desk, feeling so lost and alone. He hears Ryder's voice nearby. He is quietly talking to a student who has called him in concern over Theo. To hear that voice that has led him so astray so many times only intensifies his anxiety. Ryder is the last person he wants to see right now.

"Let's go upstairs and talk," Ryder says quietly, approaching the desk and touching his shoulder.

Theo jerks at the contact and slowly raises his head. Inches from his face is that face again. It sends a kaleidoscope of emotions through him too complex to sort out. He rises because he doesn't know what else to do. He leaves his books in a nice clean stack and follows Ryder to the stairs up to the Book of Life section. They climb the spiral staircase situated in the center of the room. Their footsteps echo off the metal, breaking the tombstone stillness. Theo just grips the cold railing and takes each step one at a time. It feels very difficult, like he's been climbing for days and days.

But before they can reach the top, Veddie appears at the base of the steps. "You can't take him up there," he growls, thumping his foot on the bottom step. The stomp vibrates up the staircase sending a violent wave of agitation through Theo.

Ryder turns, for once towering over his rival. "He can come if he's with me."

"He's on probation. He's not allowed up there. Do you want me to speak the council about this?"

The council, the council. Veddie's like a kid tattling to his parents. And for the first time since he's arrived, Theo stops feeling worthy of the punishment and starts to resent it. Veddie said it himself, Theo is not his student anymore, so why is he always getting involved in his affairs? Why doesn't he just get out of his life and concentrate on his own students?

"We're going upstairs. If you would like to document this for the next council meeting, go right ahead. I imagine your list of complaints is getting pretty lengthy by now." Ryder turns and continues climbing

More venomously, Veddie whispers, "I swear to god, Ryder, I'll see you finished here one way or another. You'll be bunked in the vaults with all your other failed experiments. You don't fool me with your color. I know who you really are. And I will make sure everyone finds out the truth."

"Are you finished?" Theo shouts, turning. His skin is prickling, his patience thin as a wet tissue.

"Excuse me?" Veddie recoils, looking more than a little shocked.

Theo turns and thunders down the staircase until he's nose to nose with his former mentor. "Back...the fuck...off." He points a finger in Veddie's chest with every word he says.

Veddie stares in stunned disbelief. He steps back and for once in his life is rendered speechless. Theo continues to glower at him until Veddie finally relents and returns to his table. Furiously, Theo turns and stomps up the stairway as loudly as he can manage. Let them all look. He's so sick of hiding. Stare, everyone, stare. Witness the dysfunctional freak show that is Theodore Duncan.

Theo follows Ryder to a secluded nook in the back of the Life section. A table is framed by a stained glass window beneath the recess of a stone gothic arch. A dark velvet curtain drawn is open to each side of the window. Two chairs wait for occupants. A few books have been left there, not Life books, but reference and gospel.

Theo sinks down in a chair and rests his head against the window. He stares out but can only see bits and pieces of the Reserve through chips in the stained glass. The sun casts colored light across his face and body.

Ryder sits down across from him, his big hands folded in the scattered light across the table.

Theo swallows hard, his heart now beating rapidly. His head still dropped against the window, he says, "I'm not...I'm not..."

"I know that," Ryder returns.

Theo falls silent, blood rushing to his face. He has so much to say that he can't even speak a word. Ryder also falls into an uncommon silence. The two men sit like stalemated chess pieces in the quiet recesses of the Life section.

"I'm so sick of all this sin," Theo finally says, a tear falling from his eye.

"Sin?" Ryder counters. "What sin are you talking about?"

Theo's eye slides towards Ryder and a dark look comes over his mentor's face.

"Oh, I'm not angry at you, Theo," he says, "but at the people who programmed you, people like Veddie, people who think there is only one clean path to salvation. Even so, you are your own man now and are still clinging to their lies."

Theo sighs and turns his gaze back to the painted window. "This is not who I am. This is not me."

"Theo, for once in your damned life just feel something because you want to feel it. Stop living your life according to someone else's ideals. These things don't just *happen*. What transpired in the laboratory doesn't just happen."

Theo swallows hard, his hands twisting together in his lap. He cannot even bring himself to look in Ryder's direction. "It was a mistake. I shouldn't have come to the office but you keep lying to me."

"I am not lying to you." Ryder sighs, his eyes also going to the stained glass window. The picture depicted is a dove with a branch in its beak. "I'd like to say I understand, that I was once like you, but I never was. I always challenged the rules. I never believed just because I was told. I've never held myself to any specific ideals, other than the ones that I personally endorsed. You are right, I have been interested in you since the minute I first saw you."

Theo's eyes dart in Ryder's direction then look quickly away. Even though he suspected, hearing the truth is more disturbing that he imagined. He feels violated, deceived, and humiliated.

"It's true. I noticed you when Veddie forced his way to the front of the line during admissions. He would've made you just like him. A shining little example of himself. I suppose I did no different. I had my own agenda with you as well."

The admission angers Theo, makes him feel used and sick. Everyone here had plans for him. No one cared what he wanted. He lifts his head off the window to finally face his mentor. "You mean…like one of your conquests?"

"My conquests? You mean Justine?" Ryder exclaims. "Contrary to what you might believe, I have never slept with her. Yes, I shouldn't have kissed her. I should've been stronger. But we can't all be as perfect you. You are a very selfish boy. Born spoiled and died just the same. Have you thought about Evangeline and what you have done to that pure spirit? Or what you have done to that girl down below? No, you have only one main concern. And that is yourself." Ryder rises, preparing to leave. "Return to your studies and I'll return to my teachings. I suggest you do not leave my home but I am foolish to believe you will be swayed in your stubbornness. I suppose we are the same in that way."

"I'll never be like you." Theo says harshly, angry at having his future destroyed by the ambitions of other men. "This was always about her. You just got in the way."

Ryder pauses as he leaves but does not look back. Message received.

Theo moves back into the dorms that night, removing his few belongings from Ryder's house without a word to the owner. He tries to go back to class but everything seems so pointless now. Though Ryder will still teach him, Theo will not go near him. And with no mentor, he can accomplish nothing on the Reserve. Angel, it seems, has given up as well. She has quit her job after the news of the pregnancy. And without hope for Ambrose, she has little to stabilize her. Her fantasies have turn ugly, even violent. She imagines kidnapping Ambrose, tying him down and molesting him while he begs her to let him go. And somehow, somewhere in her troubled, twisted mind, there is still a love story at the end. Somehow, he comes to see that her attack is a display of love. Somehow they still live happily ever after.

Save the Date has returned with a vengeance. She's working out the details, thinking more specifically about the ones that will live and the ones that will not. She roams through the school looking for good locations. She finds a vantage point in the gym and watches students play volleyball. She imagines what they will look like when they are scattered dead on the floor. Romeo won't be first. She wants him to understand what's happening. She wants him to see all his friends die. She wants him to suffer before she ends his life. She has also decided she won't kill herself in the gym. She doesn't want the town to have the satisfaction of such a clean ending. She wants them to think that she's escaped and got away with it. She wants them to have no answers as to why it happened. She'll give her dog to the Yu's and then she'll burn down the house just before the prom. The fire will keep the police busy while the dance floor fills with blood. Then she will run out into the forest, into the mountains, and kill herself out there. That is how the story of Angel will end.

Theo finds a message on his dorm bed later that week. He's on academic suspension and imagines he can thank Veddie for that. He shouldn't have challenged him in the library, after all he is an elder. Not to mention he's missed too many days to even count and hasn't written an essay or been to an exam or study group in weeks. With no place to go, and nothing to do, he finds himself wandering the Reserve with no particular destination. He finally ends up on a rooftop overlooking the meadow that surrounds the gates of Heaven, that gleaming golden cathedral under the guard of Ridwan. Even with a clear view of it, he can see no way to access the area. The closest he can get is this rooftop. And it's a hundred foot fall to the ground before the cathedral. Would he die if he jumped?

He got burned by the stove. Oh, the irony of killing himself just outside the gates of paradise.

He lies back and stares up at the still sky. What he wouldn't do for a good thunderstorm, a nice erratic wind dislocating shingles and knocking over planters. Maybe a lightning bolt setting the Field on fire. Anything to send elders and guardians rushing around in a panic. Something other than this constant state of eternal bliss. The monotony of perfection is driving him mad.

He stretches his arms behind his head. Only here, close to the gates of Heaven, does Angel's voice seem quieter. He could descend but what's the point? She only calls him down for one thing. And if he goes down, he will just give her what she wants. Maybe he should just fall back into it. Be a victim to his every desire, just like David. And David seems pretty happy. You never see him on a rooftop contemplating suicide.

"I've been looking for you."

Theo closes his eyes as he hears Ryder's voice behind him. He cannot deal with this. Not now. He's been avoiding his old mentor like he has contagious skin lesions. And the longer he stays away, the more dreadful the anxiety over their first encounter becomes. The things that happened their last days together were unforgivable. Theo has pushed them completely out of his head and refuses to deal with them entirely.

"I've lifted Veddie's suspension," he hears Ryder say. "He's not happy about it, but he'll rue the day he tries to suspend one of *my* students."

Theo sits up, keeping his gaze steadily on the cathedral in front of him. His back is stiff and tight to his old mentor. He's so tense right now, he swears if Ryder even touches him, he'll erupt like an un-pinned grenade.

"You can't avoid me forever." Ryder says, his voice indicating he has not moved from the location he first spoke in. He is calm and still, his tone neither friendly nor hostile.

"Oh, I think I can," Theo returns quickly, hoping to curtail this topic of conversation before it begins. A horrific vision of himself flinging his robes open on the laboratory floor flashes across his mind. Of him waggling his cock out in offering to his mentor. He closes his eyes and exhales heavily until the image goes away.

"So you're giving up then? Going with Ridwan?"

"I didn't say that," Theo counters darkly. Not giving up. Just going away. Away from you. His heart jumps when he hears Ryder moving closer. He tenses, anticipating contact, but his mentor comes to stand at the edge of the building and goes no closer. From the corner of his eye, he can see Ryder is staring out at the cathedral and not focused on him.

"It was wrong of me to put you between Veddie and myself. This is not your fight."

"He's an asshole. Fuck him." Theo spits the slander out towards the holy cathedral. He's actually relieved to hear himself say the words out loud. He's not proving himself to anyone anymore. They can all go fuck themselves.

The bells start to ring, calling the masses to church. Is it Sunday? He has no sense of time anymore. He steals a glance at Ryder surrounded in curious light, his powerful wings overshadowing his fragile body. I'm not like you, he thinks as loudly as he can, I'm not gay. *Gay.* The word sits in his mind, foreign and unpleasant, like something that doesn't belong there and will hopefully go away soon. He's not gay. He's not. But then what is he? Their last few days together were shocking and frightening. He *was* aroused when those things happened, the laboratory, Justine's punishment, and the closet, but it was just excitement for excitement's sake. Angel was the one arousing him; Ryder got in the way. Either way, the entire incident disturbs him greatly. The Reserve has been one hard education for him, life lesson after life lesson and all learned in slips and stumbles. He understands Angels yearning to die now. How easy it would be to just let go, to give up, to walk away from everything. He just wants life to stop moving. He keeps thinking about all the things Ryder said in the library, about him being spoiled and selfish. He knows it's true but he's so tired of the constant internal struggles. He knows he's not really being himself, but who is he really? When he was alive, there seemed to be little change between his public and private persona. He never let himself just be himself, even when alone. He always acted as if someone was watching him. Always assumed someone was because he was the great Theodore Duncan. Of course he had an audience.

"I better go." Ryder turns from the edge of the roof. Theo raises his eyes to the clouds, refusing to even meet his gaze once. "You better come to class. I didn't lift that suspension for nothing. And you can't hide forever. If it's me you despise, then do it to prove Veddie wrong. And to save Angel. You don't have to like me one bit, but I'm all you've got right now."

Theo lets out a long breath after he leaves. A tear of sweat breaks down the side of his face. In a way, there's relief that the first encounter is over. And Ryder's demeanor with him has not changed. He is not flinging himself all over him in hopes of pursuing some sort of illicit affair. No, Ryder is, as usual, unfazed by everything that happened. Even the slight Theo last left him with appears to be forgotten. Maybe it is time he goes back to class. And maybe it's time he starts to honestly confront himself over what's been going on lately.

Chapter 21 ☙

Theo shows up for Ascension class the next day. It feels like a hundred years since he first thumped his self-righteous ass down in the front row and sneered up at Ryder. He was just a boy then, a child even. Sheltered, inexperienced, and in complete denial of who he really was. He had no real emotions, no real passions. How he despised Ryder at first sight. Thought him a feeble fumbling fool, emotional, and therefore inferior. He can't deny that Ryder exhibits a strength that Veddie could never match. He supports his students no matter what the cost to himself might be. And although Theo is very uncomfortable around him now, he is grateful to still have a mentor. To have a second, third, or even fourth chance.

Ryder turns from his chalk board and acknowledges his arrival with a pause in his gaze as his eyes scan the crowd. Theo can only stare helplessly back, feeling wave after wave of uncertainty and confusion. Who is Theodore Duncan, really? If he is so straight, then why did he expose himself to Ryder so many times? After all, it was him and not Ryder that instigated every incident between them. He regrets not finishing his own book when he was in the Life section and thinks he will have to remedy that as soon as he can. He used to think he was destined for greater things, that he was chosen. He was a superior being, given wealth and advantage because he deserved it. But that's not the way things happen at all. It was chance. Just like Angel's misfortune is chance too. Had she lived in a different town with different parents, she would be a whole different person. And now that he's been moved into a different town with different people, the same thing has happened to him. For the first time in his life, he feels a hot tempered defiance rise up in him. Like it's bad for him and he'll do it anyway and damn all the consequences. Something's changed in him, something fundamental. Maybe it's the stress of the last few months, his conflicts with Ryder, or Angel's adventures that have driven him crazy, but he feels like he's broken the shackles his upbringing, his church, his parents, and even society have placed on him. He finally feels like he's becoming a real person, his true self. No matter how terrifying that true self might be.

Theo sits on a rooftop watching the warrior angels make their way towards the stage for orientation. It is not the same experience from so far above but he doesn't dare go any closer less Azrael get a whiff of him. The mighty procession that was so awe inspiring from the front row is little more than a country parade from three stories up. He wants very badly to go down and join the others, to experience the excitement he felt the first time he saw it, the thrill when he realized that he was going to become one of them. He had mighty high hopes back then. Now he's just hoping to get through the day without shaming himself in one way or another.

He stares down at Veddie perched so proudly among the warriors. Feelings of resentment have continued to develop for his old mentor. Over the last few days, he has begun to see what a cruel and uncaring man Veddie really is. It seems he's more concerned about how his flock looks than about the actual flock. He is rigid and vindictive and hardly worth the time Theo had invested in him. Unfortunately, it seems that the only way to get to the top here is through Veddie. Theo hasn't just come to question his old mentor but the entire system as well. It seems pretty easy for someone to get lost between the cracks. And not a lot of concern if they do.

He sighs, staring down at the crowd. A few people are staring up at him. Then one points. Theo shrinks back still feeling like he's the ogre he once was when Veddie first extracted him. But he isn't. He looks as normal as the rest of them, so why are people staring at him? Can they see his guilty conscious? Do they know what his real sins are?

Another student looks up. And then another. Theo pushes back from the ledge and is surrounded in hot syrupy light.

Electricity is buzzing around his ears. The first thing he thinks is the Dark. He's being swallowed by the Dark. But that's impossible. There is no Dark in Heaven, only on earth. More people are turning and staring. More people are pointing. A sun rises behind his back. His whole body begins to burn and he breaks out in a heavy sweat. Everyone is turning back to stare at him now, even the warriors on the stage have risen from their seats to look.

Theo's knees crumble beneath him. He lands hard on the stone rooftop. A glorious aura surrounds him. He lowers his head and sees his shadow stretched out across the crowd below, backlit by the most blinding light. His blood turns to gold. His heart into a feather. His body into air. He looks carefully to the side and sees a foot beside him in a winged sandal. It is so bright that he can only look for a second and when he looks away, his eyes are full of blotches. Down below, he can hear people shouting the same word. Gabriel.

Theo glances again at the foot. It shimmers as if there are two images switching back and forth, like he is opening one eye and then the next and continuing to do so in rapid succession. The creature is both solid and spirit. The power so great, so exhilarating that Theo struggles just to keep consciousness. All of his worries are blasted away, all his petty concerns, his passions, his fears, gone. Everything seems so small and insignificant in the presence of what must be the archangel Gabriel.

"Rise, child," the spirit speaks. Theo hears the words both with his ears and inside his head. The words seem to come from all around, from above and below and yet they are not broadcast for all to hear, only for him.

He struggles to his feet and continues to stare out towards the crowd. He is shaking now. His legs trembling and threatening to collapse. There are two shadows across that crowd now. His shadow which appears antlike in comparison to the winged being towering beside him. There is something swooping around them, orbiting, moving too fast for Theo to see. He gets the impression that they are birds but he doesn't really know, just feels the wind whisper as they graze around his body.

"We would like this delivered to Ridwan," the spirit of Gabriel speaks. His voice is deep and lovely and soothing. He gestures his hand towards the street and the people below fall to their knees.

Theo looks down as a scroll is offered to him. He stares at the parchment sealed in gold and enclosed in a milky white hand. The skin is almost transparent and there are no blood or bones beneath. In front of him is a wall of golden amour and wings of clouds. He slowly lifts his eyes to the green eyed guardian of love and beauty. His hair is fair with a touch of auburn and his appearance so lovely that he could be either man or woman. Theo falls to his knees again, unable to remain standing in such a presence.

"It is urgent," the spirit says and Theo jerks as the angel leans down and transfers the scroll to his hands.

"Yes, I will," Theo replies though is not sure he actually says the words out loud. "Thank you. I will. Thank you."

"And Theodore Duncan?" the voice continues.

Theo closes his eyes feeling another swoon coming on. He cannot retain his composure for much longer. This Light is too powerful, too honest, too magnificent. He feels his own spirit breaking down and fusing with the archangels. His feels his own spirit becoming inert in the presence of a much more dominant one. If the archangel stays much longer, he will lose himself completely.

"Your journey is just beginning. This is a time for the strong." Gabriel says, stepping back and disappearing into his own Light.

Theo carries the scroll like a ring bearer. He holds it proudly in front of him as he slowly walks up the same aisle the warriors did, enjoys the same awe and admiration as the ones who just came before him. And he knows that what Gabriel said is true. He is not finished here. His dreams are not over. He will still sit amongst the heroes of the council. He will become the warrior he envisioned he would be. Veddie and his council be damned. He is completely renewed after being in the presence of Gabriel's Light. It has brought him back to life. And something else too. He feels liberated from all the fears that have been holding him back. He's not afraid to face who he really is anymore. In fact his worries about himself seem petty after being next to such an incredible spirit.

He stops at the bottom of the stairs leading up to the stage. Every eye is on him now, but there is not a word spoken. "I bring this for Ridwan," he whispers but feels like he is shouting in the deathly silence. He lifts the scroll to see the elders seated at the table. Veddie is holding back a look of disgust. Azrael is pursing her lips at him. The twins from judgment whisper back and forth to each other.

Ridwan rises. Theo drops his eyes but keeps the scroll outstretched in front of him. The scroll is made of parchment and thin as air but he can barely lift it, the contents so important and so grave. As Ridwan descends the stairs, Theo can see his own aura causing a shadow behind the guardian of paradise. He knows it is not his aura but the residue of the experience of being in Gabriel's Light. But for a moment, he experiences his future self. Like Angel's true being that is so beautiful and true, he sees that he also has a potential that has not been fully tapped yet. That he is destined for great things, just not the things he had originally planned for.

"Thank you, child," Ridwan says and takes the scroll from his shaking hands. Then Theo turns from the elders and slowly leaves the assembly.

Theo sits in a café slowly sipping mint tea. It has been a few days since the incident at orientation but he is completely revived. And more. He feels like the cobwebs have been cleared from his eyes. He sees Veddie for the tyrant he really is and for the first time since he got here, truly breaks the ties that bind him to his old mentor. He has no desires to return to the house of Veddie. And Ryder? Being admired by another man is not the fear he once believed it to be. In fact, his overreaction in the library seems silly now. Maybe something happened in the closet and maybe something didn't, and it's not the end of the world if it did. He will simply process the emotions as they come along. Theodore Duncan is no longer fossilized in stone, he has become a part of the evolutionary process.

What Gabriel gave him was a gift and, by the sounds of it, not something that is given out every day. The gift of the experience of his Light, of his presence, of his truth, and it has helped Theo focus back on the important things. He has no doubt that he will save Angel. No doubt he will regain his standing. No doubt that he will rise to the highest order of guardianship. He feels an excitement he hasn't felt since he first arrived here.

"*Crazy about that Theodore,*" Theo hears behind him. He glances behind but a large plant blocks his view of the people at the next table. And obviously their view of him as well.

"I know," the other voice says. "Meeting the archangel. Wow."

"That must have been incredible. I've been here ten years and that's the first time I've even seen one."

"And he was standing right next to him."

"Who is Theo's mentor, do you know?"

"I think it's Veddie."

"No, something happened. Veddie isn't his mentor anymore."

"Oh yeah, isn't it Ryder now?"

"I don't know. Maybe."

Theo returns to his tea. He drinks and listens to the conversation, curious to hear what talk around the Reserve is saying about him, Ryder, and Veddie. For him it has been such a circus that he imagines it has been the talk of the whole town. But to others, it is likely regarded as a simple mentor switch and nothing more.

"Things have sure changed around here. It's not like it used to be. There's so much conflict."

"Well, there is a war down below."

"Yes, but there's always a war down there. Now there is fighting up here too."

"That's true. Like Veddie and Ryder. They're always at each other's throat."

Theo quietly sets his cup down and leans back in his chair. He squints through the plant, trying to see if he's knows the gossiping angels but the foliage is just too full and rich.

"Well," the voice becomes quieter, "I think it's because he's...gay."

Theo's eyebrows raise. Was he the only one who didn't know? No, of course not. Justine has been pursuing Ryder so she must have no idea as well. Again, he ponders the encounter between Ryder in the girl. If he is gay then why is he fooling around with that girl?

"Gay?" the other voice says. "I believe he's bisexual. Do you think Veddie would target him because of that?"

Bisexual? Is that what Ryder is? Bisexual? Theo contemplates the word for a while. For some reason, it sits better with him than the word gay did. And it answers his question about why Ryder has pursued both men and women. He doesn't know what that means for him. And that's okay for now.

"He might. Veddie is set in the old ways."

"And Ryder is a bit..."

"Unconventional?" the voice offers.

Chairs squeak as the gossip turns juicier. "Were you there at the library that day?"

Theo sits up. The library? What about the library?

"When that girl said she loved him? What was her name?"

"Justine, I think. She caused quite a stir. He looked pretty angry when he dragged her under the Life section."

Theo looks across the boulevard to the looming order of the main library, its pillars gleaming white, its brilliant stained glass windows, its wide walkway of marble steps, and somewhere deep inside, beneath the Life section, tucked in the disordered labyrinth of forgotten narratives, is the closet. He stares, unsettled, at the unassuming edifice of stone and brick. Maybe it's time to find out the truth. He needs to go to the library and retrace the steps of the dream and see if what happened in that closet, if it even exists, is real. It's time to find out the truth. It makes no sense to run from it anymore.

Theo enters the library. Despite his new found confidence, he feels himself shudder as he sees the table where Justine and Ryder fought. And then further back to where the roof lowers and the shelves become more squat and mazelike.

Somewhere, back there, Justine was disciplined. And somewhere, back there, he got into a closet with his mentor. Maybe he fell asleep after Justine confronted Ryder. Maybe the fight is real but the closet was the dream. Because it's one thing to expose himself to Ryder while under Angel's influence and quite another when he is aroused because of something he seen his mentor do. Straightening himself out, he walks beneath the Book of Life section and into the labyrinth. If it was a dream, then he has never actually been in this section of the library. And yet things seem disturbingly familiar. It seems that he is following a path and it doesn't take long until he finds the clearing with the table and a red book resting on top of it. It looks like the book Ryder spanked Justine with.

Feeling more wary, he abandons the table and heads in the direction he and Ryder fled when Veddie broke up the party. He turns down a couple quick corners and there at the end of a row is a closet. He stares down that long corridor, a large lump forming in his throat. It's a closet but is it *the* closet?

He folds his arms over his chest staring down the closet door. Is he ready to know this? Maybe he should just go back. Return to his studies. Stop with this nonsense. Even if it did happen, even if he and Ryder did end up in that closet, does that change anything? It doesn't necessarily mean that he is gay as well, just that he has no sense of his sexual boundaries anymore. Like Ryder said, guardians of child molesters and rapist can crave things that aren't normally on their pallet. This is no different. Is it? Theo drops his hands to his side and takes a deep breath. Just go look. Just look in the closet and see if anything is familiar.

He marches down the aisle tucked between two dusty shelves of outdated periodicals and flings the door open. Yes, it's a broom closet. Yes, it has many of the items that were in the dream: a rod with empty hangers, paint cans on the floor, artist's smocks and more. And yes, it looks like it's been kicked around a bit. But that doesn't prove anything.

"*I'm not sure,*" comes a voice from behind him. Theo jumps and sees a shadow of someone in the next aisle. Without thinking, he steps in the closet and swiftly closes the door behind him. His breath slightly elevated, he strains to hear the voice again. It's tight in here. If two men were inside, they would be pressed firmly together. Right up together. Back to back or front to back. Or front to front. The image makes him twitch. A vein of stimulation begins to branch from his gut. Broom handles are pressed against his side. A smock grazes his shoulder. His feet are restrained between pails and paint cans. He reaches his hand up to the bar across the top of the closet. A few coat hangers jingle in response, just like they when Ryder grabbed him. No, he forced Ryder's hands on him. He runs his fingers across the back of his neck, then down the front of his robe, opening it a little as he goes. He moves his hand inside and runs a nail across a stiff nipple, feels another part of him getting stiff as well. His fingers drop to the tie on his robe. He looks down but can only see the barest trace of an outline in the restricted light of the closet. His other hand tightens on the bar above him. Hangers jingle playfully. He takes another deep breath and then unties the robe. It falls open and a cool wisp of air rushes into the slit. Wetting his lips with his tongue, he lightly rakes his fingers across his hard stomach. He remembers more now. They argued in here. Ryder made accusations that Theo was harassing him. They were tight together and Theo's cock was like a tower in front of him, a monument to sexual repression and denial. It was a siren in the dark calling his mentor to arms. Ryder's hand fell to his chest. It was tight and hot and clenched against his body. Yes, Ryder did want him. How could he have not seen it before? And yet, every encounter they've had was instigated by himself. He went looking for trouble and found it every time. Theo lowers his hand to his bellybutton, to his pelvis, to his hips. He arches silently as he grazes the thick muscle in between. The pleasure is undeniable. Radiant. Incredible. He struggles against balance, gripping the bar above him as tightly as he grips the one below. The hard, swollen head of his cock bumps against the door and he imagines what it would be like to have that hard head bump with another. With another specific person. Who would be willing to. Right now. The idea sets off bombs in his head, breaks down barriers erected since childhood. What if pleasure if just pleasure? What if love is just love? What if there were no boundaries? What if he could do anything he wanted? What if he could do *anyone* he wanted?

Theo opens the door to Ryder's office. He steps inside and closes it behind him. He leans against the door and unties his robe, letting it fall open to either side of him. He rolls his head back, staring up at the heavy beams on the ceiling crisscrossed with determined roots. He reaches up and touches one, pulls it loose so it hangs down like a dirty icicle. He runs his hand along its length, slick from the humidity of the dank underground office. His hand comes away wet and muddy. He runs his palm down his chest leaving streaks of mud across his skin, camouflage for a lusty soldier. He scans the office with half set eyes. Everything looks dirty to him. The way the chairs by the fire are positioned. The side by side indents on Ryder's couch. The way the bottles touch each other on the shelves. Everything seems to be a message to him. But where is the proprietor of all these covert insinuations?

His eyes fall on the mirror on the opposite wall. From where he leans against the door, he can see his whole reflection, see his naked body spread across the chocolate wood, see the smears of muddy fingerprints across his chest, see the slight lift of his swollen cock. He remembers how he first saw himself in this mirror after the fall. How he could barely stand his own reflection. Now he languishes over his image, soaks up his sex without reservation. Lets himself become aroused for arousal's sake.

His eyes drift to the laboratory door standing slightly ajar. He pushes off the door and saunters in for a look. The room is steamy, pungent, and gurgling. Theo passes between the tables of fiery burners and gurgling beakers to the chest against the far wall where hundreds of vessels sit labeled and ready for consumption. Here is where he used to come to regain control. Take a potion to knock himself out for a few hours when Angel was aroused. Now he wants his sexuality to be awakened. He wants to experience it. To explore it. He's not afraid of what's looming in the dark corners anymore.

He turns from the shelf and sees Ryder's notebook spread open on the shiny silver lab table. He fingers through pages of equations and formulas. He stops when he comes to the page marked Deliverance. And in subtext beneath the title: sexual freedom and spiritual release. Instead of binomials, emotions factor into the equations. Theo tries to read more but he can't get that subtext out of his head. Sexual freedom and spiritual release. He notices, nearby, a beaker bubbling marked Deliverance. He touches the thin neck of the beaker and recoils from the heat. Seems the formula has just been finished. But has it been tested?

Theo returns to the House of Ryder in time for a nightly study session. He hasn't been back since he packed his things and fled. He was so angry and so afraid when he left. Now he willingly returns, running towards those things he was trying to escape from before. The house is full, the gathering room and kitchen spilling over with students. They are all different levels of education and experience but brought together under the influence of one man: Daniel Ryder. Theo's eyes travel over his mentor brazenly. His hair seems longer, messier, falling thickly past his shoulders. And his hands. Theo suppresses a smile as he sees them. Those hands say so much about the owner now.

Ryder is talking to a couple students in the kitchen. Justine is there, hovering eagerly nearby. Her eyes lingering on him longer than the rest. It seems her discipline has done little to alleviate her affections. Theo imagines it has only aggravated them.

"Someone vandalized my laboratory," Ryder says to the others. "It was a terrible mess when I went in this afternoon. Has anyone been in my office lately?"

"Why would someone do that?" Justine exclaims, tilting her head and curling a finger deep in her hair. "That's awful. Are you okay?"

Theo smiles. Things became a bit…unhinged after he drank Deliverance. He hardly remembers what followed. Just that he woke up extremely satisfied. And took off in search of his mentor.

Ryder's eyes lock on him as he passes by. They seems more guarded now, more reserved. They are not the same eyes that so graciously invited him into his house, who forgave his every misdeed on the journey in between, who vandalized the laboratory along with him not so long ago. Ryder seems damaged today, frazzled. And Theo thinks he is likely to blame for that. He made it clear in the Book of Life section that he wanted nothing to do with him. That he hated who Ryder was and didn't care if they ever saw each other again. And though Ryder has welcomed him back as a student and has been polite to him, they have had little personal contact since then.

"Are you going to join us for study session today?" Justine asks her mentor eagerly.

Theo runs his fingertip across his lips and continues down the hall. He feels Ryder's eyes on his back as he leaves and is not opposed to it as he once was. He turns into the courtyard he so carefully tended during his stay. Already all his hard work is getting grown over, thorny bits absorbing the newly budding flowers. He sees the shower through the vine covered window, remembering the day he spied on Ryder. He didn't mean to but it happened all the same. And for some reason, it kept happening. Was he unconsciously willing it to happen? Why is it such a horrible sin to experience both sexes? It doesn't seem worth all the hype. Don't people have bigger things to worry about? War, famine, disease? His, is a religion that oppresses, that judges, that bullies. A religion that will only recognize men as priests. Straight men. If god is supposed to be the embodiment of love, then why are his followers so judgmental?

He shakes his head and continues out the other side of the courtyard. This leads to the public side of the house, a place he's rarely spent time in. Here is it louder, full of students, the rooms frenzied and noisy. Theo passes by the shower with a sly look inside. He is horny. Unbelievable so. Deliverance is still charging through his veins. And he loves the way it feels. He passes by Ryder's library. He remembers sitting inside waiting for their first meeting. There was a bird loose in the room. He was Veddie's little disciple then. Oh, if only his old mentor could see how wonderfully he's gone astray.

He opens the only closed door in the hallway. There, he experiences a shock of surprise as he sees that same bare white leg stretched out on an exam table that he did his first day here. But instead of slamming the door closed, he slips inside and shuts the door behind him. What he finds is a sculpture, in fact a room full of them with tools and shavings spread all over the floor. They must be Ryder's creations and are magnificently formed. But the one on the table catches his attention the most. It is of a naked man lounging back lazily in a chair, his legs lolling open. There is no question as to what the sculpture signifies. Theo passes around it, musing over the thing, letting his eyes wander and explore. Behind him, he hears the door open.

"What are you doing in here?" Ryder says. "Study group is down the hall."

Theo glances back at Ryder. He's not sure if it's Deliverance or his own sexual awakening but doesn't see the face of a man anymore, not in the sense of man being his opposite and completely void of possibilities. What he sees now are possibilities and undeniable opportunities.

"Just admiring your handiwork," he replies, returning his attention to the artwork. "These are yours, aren't they?"

Ryder approaches the table where the sculpture reclines. One hand of the sculpture dangles inside the thigh. The other is draped lazily over the arm of the chair he's sculpted into. The eyes are closed, the head tilted back, the mouth slightly ajar.

"This room is private," Ryder says, giving him a strange look. "You should not be in here."

"It's in the public side of the house," Theo retorts, resting his hand on the youth's knee. The stone is smooth and hard beneath his palm.

"Well, this is room is off limits." Ryder eyes him distrustfully. He probably thinks Theo is looking for trouble. And he is. But not in the way Ryder supposes.

"Then I guess we won't be interrupted." Theo traces his finger up the stone thigh a little. He thinks about Ryder's body in the shower. How he moved when he thought no one was watching. How he looked when he was wet. Suddenly he wants to know what that wet skin feels like up against his.

Ryder frowns, his eyes darting from Theo's face down to the hand slowly moving up the sculptures thigh. "What's wrong with you?" Then a look of worry crosses his face. "Have you been down to see Angel?"

Theo's gaze travels up the muscular curve of the youth's thigh to the stony down between the legs, then to the docile, yet ample organ resting beneath. He remembers how aroused he was the night he ended up in the courtyard. How he laid out on the bench completely naked and just gave himself to the night. And then afterwards, Ryder found him. He remembers the excitement to have another man's hands on his body. He's toying with experiencing that sensation again.

"Have you seen Angel?" Ryder repeats with more urgency. "I told you..."

"No, I haven't seen her," Theo replies, continuing his slow exploration up the sculptures thigh. "I haven't seen her at all."

Ryder glances back as someone taps on the closed door. They tap again and then footsteps slowly fade away. He turns back to face Theo, suddenly putting it all together. "You were the one who destroyed my laboratory."

Theo raises his eyebrows with a wry smile. "Was I?"

Ryder pauses, looking more concerned now. "Did you take something?"

"Just a little spiritual release."

Ryder's face darkens and his eyes drop. He seems to be mentally tallying up his formulas and then comes up with a gasp. "You drank Deliverance? That is not a completed formula."

"Feels completed to me."

"Well, it's not. And you have no right to be sampling my formulas without permission. They are dangerous." Ryder pauses, staring up at Theo's lusty eyes. "This can't keep happening."

"What can't?" Theo asks eagerly, letting his hand fall from the statue. He stands and faces his mentor, the table and stone block between them.

"You can't keep coming to me in this state and then blaming me for what happens when you do."

Theo drops his eyes. He supposes it's the truth. Angels wet his appetite and somehow he always ends up sniffing around Ryder looking for bones. But isn't this what Ryder wanted? He admitted himself that he was attracted to Theo so why is he so resistant now? Again, his arrogance prevails. Now that he is interested, he expects Ryder to succumb instantly, to let him explore his every curiosity without question.

"Do you really object so much?" He looks across the open knees of the sculpture to the thin, athletic frame of his Ascensions professor. He knows there is nothing beneath those robes. Most angels wear wraps or briefs to protect against unexpected drafts, or just for decorum's sake, but Ryder lets it all hang out. A practice Theo has recently subscribed to.

"I did not say I objected," Ryder counters, staring hard across the sultry sculpture. "I only suggest that you do not know what you are asking me. Or are ready to face the consequences if I submit to your request."

The idea that Ryder is even considering submitting to his request sends him into a tizzy. He braces his hands on the table and leans forward. "I don't believe I've made a request."

"Then why don't you make one?" Ryder returns the challenge, raising his arms and folding them over his chest. His wings curl over him like a vulture perched on his shoulders.

Theo straightens and walks around the table. He comes to stand a few feet from his mentor. He runs his fingers down the hem of his neckline letting Ryder know that what he is offering is himself. His blood races through his veins as Ryder's eyes drop down to where he's fingering the belt of his robe, toying with opening it up again to give Ryder another look. It appears to amuse his mentor at first but then he becomes frustrated and angry.

"I'm tired of playing these games with you. Crow all you want but you are still Veddie's disciple and would leave me for him in a heartbeat, given the chance. You have no sense of what you are and simply become the mirror of whoever you are near." Ryder turns and stomps towards the door. But as he's reaching for the door handle, he pauses and looks back. "You rejected who I am. You rejected me. That was your choice. You can't just come running to me when that girl gets you in a knot. Then run away crying when I give you what you ask for. I meant what I said before. You are self-centered and need to start thinking how your actions affect others."

"I am. That's what I'm doing." Theo unfolds the ties around his robes. He releases the soft loops and bends and lets the white robe softly fall open. His heart is beating out of his chest as he presents himself a second time to his mentor. Maybe Ryder is right. Maybe Ryder's Light has overpowered his. Or maybe this is Deliverance charging through his veins. But if he doesn't act now, then the urge will remain unexplored. This feeling will die and he will not have the encounter he seeks. And in this moment, he is hungry for a new experience.

Ryder keeps his eyes level with Theo's, ignoring the staff of flesh offered below. "If you are confused about your sexuality, there are plenty of men who would be eager to help you work out your dilemma."

"I don't want other men," Theo returns, taking a step closer. "I want you."

Ryder's eyes drop down a bit. If there's one thing Theo knows, it's that his mentor is a victim of his own persuasions. Tempt him enough and he will give in.

"Daniel? Daniel?" Comes a voice from outside the door. It's Justine looking for him again. "The study group is ready. Are you all done in there?"

Theo turns a hard gaze on Ryder. "Are we?"

Ryder allows his eyes to drift down Theo's body a little. The tiniest smile seems to cross his lips. "No," he says slowly, moving towards the door. "We have not even begun."

Chapter 22☙

For the first time since he died and entered the Reserve, Theo goes the whole night without sleep. He sits under the stars and greets the morning as if he had rested the whole night through. If Deliverance has vacated his system, there is no indication. He feels no differently than he did yesterday. The urge to cross over is still there. Maybe even stronger than before. He was terrified at the thought of being gay, but somehow the word *bisexual* has a nice ring to it. He could have a bit of both worlds and not be pigeonholed into either genre. Explore a little of everything sexuality has to offer.

He retrieves his books from the dorm, where he has been living since he and Ryder parted ways, and heads out for his first class. It is far too early and no one will be there yet. Maybe he just wants to sit in the auditorium alone. Maybe get freaky in front row center. Then sit there all period with the knowledge of what he did in his head.

But his early morning perversions are sidetracked when Theo rounds a corner and runs into Ryder and a group of his students already on their way to class. The two men pause in the street, facing each other, the tension heavy between them.

"Good morning, Theo," Ryder says evenly. "On your way to the auditorium?"

"I am," Theo replies in the same tone, clasping his books in front of his hips. "Is that where you are going?"

"Later, I am." Ryder clears his throat, surrounded by students staring up at him with star struck eyes. "And how are you feeling today? Are you still suffering from those side effects from that…medicine you took?"

"I am," Theo says, gripping his books a bit tighter. "Terribly so."

"And how bad is your discomfort level?" Ryder sweeps his hair behind his ear with his hand and glances down at those books. "How uncomfortable are you?"

Theo restrains a smile. "It is unbearable. If I don't get something to relieve the pain soon, I don't know what I'll do."

The students look eagerly between Theo and Ryder, then one asks clueless, "Side effects?"

Ryder turns his head towards his students but his eyes stay locked with Theo's. "Theo is my new lab assistant. He is helping me with my work."

"Ooh," the students cry eagerly, mostly girls. "Do you need other volunteers? We could help too."

Ryder runs a thumb across his lower lip, his tongue slithering beneath parted teeth. "Thank you, but no. Theo has been asking for this position for a while."

"I have, haven't I?" Theo narrows his light eyes at his professor. "Anyway, when should I stop by? The sooner we get started with this, the better. Shall I come by your office? Or would you prefer we do it in your home?"

Ryder's eyebrows raise. His voice is slightly challenging when he replies, "The laboratory will be fine. I'll have everything at my fingertips there."

"When do you want me to come by?" Theo asks.

"Come by anytime," Ryder says with that same edge in his voice. "I am ready for you at any time."

A horde of students come to worship service that afternoon at a small chapel just outside the park. Services are ongoing throughout the day in the many chapels situated around the Reserve. Students may participate at their convenience. And when the professors are free, they come in and do the sermons. Today the visiting professor is Veddie. Theo just happened to pass by and see today's headliner. Feeling saucy, he decided to go in and see what sort of fire and brimstone message his old mentor was giving out today. Inside, most of the room is packed with Veddie's followers. Theo leans against the wall, facing the church pews. It is standing room only by the time he arrives.

Veddie is at the podium delivering his message with a heated resolve. He actually reminds Theo a little of Hitler the way he raises his fists and barks out his furious direction. Ryder was wrong about one thing: Theo does not have any desire to return to his old mentor. In fact he wonders how he could have ever strived to be like Veddie at all. If not for his fall, he would still be in that crowd, swallowing every word from Veddie's mouth like a spoon fed baby.

He scans the crowd, seeing a few of the students that taunted him in the forum. They stare brightly up towards their mentor, their eyes alight, their chests puffed out. Then, amongst the fair haired and pallid faced devotees, he sees Ryder. Theo's eyebrows raise when he notices the crank in amongst the clique. He supposes his mentor is here for the same reason he stopped by, to see what the old man is grumbling about now. Theo studies his side profile, trying to understand what it is about this man that has transformed his beliefs. Why, in just a few weeks, an immorality has become an adventure. His pursuit of Ryder has his full attention now, the way his cock did when he first discovered he had one. Except with Ryder, there are no repercussions. Physically anyway. He can dally around with Ryder all he likes because it will leave no discernable clues on his physical body. And apparently that's all that matters up here. That things appear okay on the outside. At least, that's the impression he's getting.

Veddie's tangent continues, his voice echoing harshly over every corner of the room. Ryder's attention begins to drift. His gaze travels across the arc shaped roof, to the pilasters and glazed windows above Theo's head, then his eyes fall on the man himself. He raises his eyebrows and Theo shrugs in response. A slight smile crosses Ryder's lips as his attention returns forward.

A scream fills the room. Theo looks around unsure what is happening. It is a loud wailing noise and is actually coming from outside the building. People rise and shuffle around, looking worried. Veddie begins to frantically gather up his books. Other teachers and guardians start shoving their way towards the aisles. The alarm sounds again, an air raid siren, and this time students begin to panic. They start filling the aisles and shoving their way towards the door. Theo also starts pushing his way out, thinking the building must be on fire or something. The pace is sluggish though, people moving down the aisles like a leisurely mud slide. And it gets worse the closer they get to the single exit where all three aisles converge at the end. The siren sounds again. Theo strains to see past the painted windows, to see what's happening outside. What is going on? Are they under attack? Just then, he's taken by the arm and pulled from the crowd. Before he knows what's going on, he's standing in a side corridor. Ryder is the one who pulled him there.

"What's happening?" he exclaims.

"Come on." Ryder turns down the hallway. They are in the administration section of the church, in a hallway with small offices bordering it. At the end of the hall is an exit to the outdoors that obviously no one else has remembered in the growing panic.

"What is it? What's going on?" Theo cries.

"It's a disaster," Ryder explains without turning back. "Something's happened down below, a fire, or an earthquake, or a flood. Or it could be an attack, like a bomb or mass shooting. The siren is to warn us of an influx of dead." He stops at the end of the hall to face Theo, breathing hard. "There could be thousands on their way."

Theo's first thought is Angel. But no, if there were trouble, he would feel it. And she has been relatively steady for weeks now. "What should I do?" he asks.

"Nothing, just get off the streets. Classes will be cancelled. We need time to process all the new arrivals. It will be chaotic for a while."

The siren sounds again. Theo looks up, shocked and excited by the disruption. It's what he's been waiting for. Something to upset this idyllic, ordered paradise. He looks at Ryder who stares out towards the panicked students. His eyes are bright and excited, a slight sheen resting across his neck and collarbone. At the end of the hall, students stream past the exit, all frantically focused towards the back doors, unaware of an idle exit to the side of them. Stomps and shouts and slapped hands and dropped notebooks echo down the hall towards them. They can hear their gasped breath and erratic heartbeats. They can smell their panicked sweat.

Theo gaze focuses back to Ryder who stands just a foot in front of him, his body heaving, his chest quickly rising and falling. Ryder's attention also pulls back to the boy in front of him. They stare for a few seconds, both breathless. Theo can see that his mentor's eyes are still guarded, that he does not trust Theo's intentions. He thinks this is a game for him. Another adventure in his endless quest for sexual thrills. Maybe he's right because Theo isn't certain why he's in such hot pursuit of his mentor, just that it's in his head now and won't go away until he does something about it.

He reaches a hand for Ryder but Ryder pulls back. "Don't," he whispers, his eyes dropping.

"I thought you wanted this," Theo returns, his hand still reaching forward. He touches the soft hem of Ryder's robe and then gently brushes his thumb against the exposed skin of his chest underneath. It's hot and moist and he can feel Ryder's rapid heartbeat beneath the surface.

Ryder's hand comes up to clasp Theo's wrist. He holds it there but does not push it away. "Do you think I want this, Theo?"

The siren wails again. Feet are crashing past the end of the hallway. Shouts are shaking the windows. The whole chapel trembles under the panic and confusion of escaping angels. Except for these two at the end of the quiet hallway. They have stopped running altogether.

Theo leans slightly forward and this time Ryder does not pull back. He brings his mouth very close to his mentor's waiting for his heterosexuality to kick in. "I think you want me," Theo whispers, wetting his lips.

Ryder huffs out a laugh against Theo's mouth.

"And I think I want you too," Theo says and Ryder stops laughing. The tight fist around his wrist loosens and Theo slips his hand beneath the hem of Ryder's robe. He can feel the curve of Ryder's collar bone and the firm muscle beneath. He moves a step closer. That's when a door slams nearby. They look to the side and see Veddie standing in the hall, his gaze unfocused. But then he turns towards them. They jolt apart but not nearly fast enough. Veddie stops. He stares. His mouth begins to drop open. He looks like he doesn't quite comprehend what he just witnessed. Both Theo and Ryder continue to move apart but it is too late. Veddie's not sure what he saw but he will figure it out soon enough.

Now they are running. Running like two kids who have just stolen their first candy from a department store. Like they did it and they got away with it and are now fleeing to enjoy the spoils of their crime. And they've done none of the above. They didn't do it or get away with it. Veddie saw them together. Maybe they weren't in the throes of passion but Veddie could tell something was up. Once he puts the pieces together, this will only lead to more trouble.

People are everywhere, some rushing with a purpose, but most just fleeing without the facts. The siren is still howling. The streets are packed with confusion. The two men pound through the streets, legs and arms pumping, neither knowing where they are going. Ryder pauses, looks around and ducks into an open doorway of a house. He pulls Theo inside just enough to be out of sight and then turns to him.

"He saw," Theo whispers. "I think he saw us."

Ryder runs an oversized hand over his own face, a thin sheen of sweat now covering his skin. "I think he did."

Theo stands a head higher than Ryder, looking down at him, his chest heaving, his heart racing. There is an excitement in the air from the fear and chaos that is only intensifying their own emotions. And now that Theo's admitted what he wants, he can think of nothing but. Of all the forbidden fruits he's decided to sample on the Reserve, this is, by far, the most rousing.

Ryder looks up at him, reaches a hand to trace the line of his chin. Theo's skin sizzles as the tips of Ryder's fingers graze his electric skin. His blood has been replaced by high octane fuel. His breath is a whirlwind. Outside the door, the sounds of screams continue to race by, sirens wail, and feet thump furiously against the pavement. The dead are coming, someone cries, the dead are coming!

"What has changed?" Ryder whispers. "What is different now?"

Theo rolls his head back. "I don't know. Nothing. Maybe nothing. Maybe it was always here. Maybe I just didn't want to see it."

Ryder raises his eyebrows and a little smile crosses his lips. Theo sees those lips and he suddenly wants them, wants to taste them, wants to see what they feel like beneath his own. He leans down swiftly before he can reconsider the craving. He has been thinking entirely too much lately. Now it's time to do something about it.

"Is someone there?" A voice comes unexpectedly from the next room. They break apart like teenage lovers and flee from the building. They enter back into the stream of people heading up the street. Though they want to run, they can barely move with the crowds around them. Theo allows himself to be pushed up against the backside of his mentor, allows the entire length of his body to come up against another mans. Only a thin cotton robe separates their naked bodies. His cock has become hard against the swells of Ryder's ass. His chest is wedged between Ryder's stiff wings. Ryder moves abruptly ahead of him, allowing himself to be jolted and swayed by the crowd. They are pressed in from all sides, bodies brushing and bumping, unbeknownst that in amidst the chaos, passion is budding.

Theo sneaks a hand beneath Ryder's wing and around to his chest. Beneath the sweat soaked robe, beneath the perspiring skin, he can feel a heart raging beneath. He struggles to get his fingers inside the slit of the robe, then simply pulls it open and off Ryder's shoulder. Even though they are surrounded by people, no one is even looking at them. They all straining forward, racing down the narrow street like panicked bulls. There's no sense to the stampede, no reason, other than to provide a cover for two men exploring each other in full public view.

The siren slowly wails again and then a booming voice fills the air. *The following people are to report to the observatory immediately.* A long list of names is announced and continues to go on and on as they run. Ryder's name is among them.

"I have to go to the observatory," Ryder shouts back over his shoulder. The crowd enters into a covered portion of the road. Theo recognizes it as the one he first passed beneath when he arrived at the Reserve, the one lined with scripture. The normally peaceful underpass is now packed with people, the sounds of their shouts echoing painfully off the carved walls. And it's dark with so many people inside. So dark you can barely see your hands in front of your face.

Someone steps sharply on the back of Theo's foot. As he recoils, he gets an anonymous elbow in the face. He's pushed forward again, and when he rejoins his tandem scurry with Ryder, he finds that his mentor has turned around to face him. At least he hopes it is his mentor because it is too dark to see. His body crushes up against a hard muscled chest, against rigid back stepping thighs. In the dark, he finds the mouth he's been seeking, and in the slow ingress of fear, their lips are pushed together. Theo devours his mentor, running his hands over his body, touching and squeezing and tasting as quickly as he can.

"How long will it take?" Theo gasps against Ryder's mouth. "When will you be back?"

"I don't know. I don't know." Ryder says, pulling Theo against his chest. They embrace furiously as the line of light indicating the end of the covered tunnel begins to approach their secret rendezvous. It moves over the heads of the panicked parade. Over hands thrust up into the air. Over broken wing tips and gasped open mouths. When it reaches their covert encounter, they find that they cannot break apart. Ryder attempts to reconcile his disheveled robes but has to remain facing Theo as the crowd continues. They walk, chest to chest, thigh to thigh, two eager bodies glancing hotly against each other.

Theo just stares at him, at *him*, this man, this teacher, this mentor who has somehow managed to turn his entire life around. Where, before, he resented being uprooted, now he is eager to be planted in new gardens.

"Where can I find you? Will you be at home?" Theo asks hotly, walking Ryder backwards towards the street of steps. Where those two streets connect, he can see that the swarm is

345

breaking apart. Elders and mentors are bleeding up the steps, while other are breaking off into the lower part of the city, towards the refuge of their homes.

"I don't know. I really don't know," Ryder replies, staring helplessly up into Theo's eyes. So much is happening down below, so much skin friction, glancing grazes, secret offerings and promises that will have to be kept another time. From the neck up, they are simply two men talking closely but from the neck down they are breaking every rule.

They come to the street of steps and Ryder is pulled one way and Theo another. Theo falls back reluctantly as Ryder is swept away. Hot and throbbing, he just stands and stares, unwilling to accept that he must wait days even weeks for this adventure to continue. Painfully aroused, he turns towards the lower side of town. He has no choice. He will just have let this simmer until Ryder is available.

Around dusk, the first of the dead begin to arrive. It begins as a trickle of lanterns coming down the misty hill, down through the forest and through the Victory arch. They come up the street of steps then disappear into the network of alleys and pathways that head towards the catacombs of judgment. Theo sits on the roof with other guardians watching the new arrivals. It is said that thousands are coming. Though no one is certain what disaster led them here.

"Hey," Eric says from behind him. "Have I missed anything?"

"It's just starting," Theo says, making room for him on the crowded rooftop.

"Do you know what happened? I heard it was a flood or something. Like a tsunami. Just wiped out an entire town."

"I don't know. There hasn't been an official announcement yet." Theo focuses down where the newly dead are being transported down the street below his feet. Most of them are Asian so rumors of tsunami may be true. It could be an earthquake as well. "Did you give up your bed?" he asks. First years that have been here longer than a month have been asked to give up their beds in the dorm to make way for all the new arrivals.

"Of course. I don't need to sleep anyway," Eric says, swinging his feet over the ledge. Theo stares down at the people being led by lanterns on the street below. Though there must have been injuries, like with his own car accident, everyone has arrived in tact. Physically, anyway.

Theo huffs out a laugh. "Last night was my first night without sleep. I think, if I had a bed, I could sleep for ten hours straight."

"Really? I stopped sleeping a couple weeks after I got here," Eric replies.

"I wish," Theo groans. No matter how hard he tries, he just can't break any of his old earthly habits yet.

The stream of lanterns leading from the misty hill begins to thicken. They come through the night like a snake on fire. Below them, the wails and cries become louder as the crowd gets denser. There are so many of them. How will the Reserve handle such an influx? Theo thinks of how much personal attention he needed upon first arrival. And the mentors here are already overloaded with students. Selfishly, he also realizes it could be a long time before he sees Ryder again too. It will be a while before any issues between them get any resolution.

"Wonder if there's anyone I know," Eric muses. "I'd really like to see my parents again."

Theo is once again struck by how rarely he's thought of his parents. What if they die? What if they become guardians on the Reserve? What would they think of him now? He is a far cry from the obedient, god fearing child they buried last Halloween. He thinks they would be horrified to see what he's become.

A woman looks up from below and locks eyes with Theo. It is just a quick moment but Theo is struck by the shock of death fresh on her face. He knows what it's like to be living one minute and dead the next. He took one breath driving his car and the next on the misty hill. It was that fast. And if it was a disaster that killed all these people, they may have come here the same way he did. It will take a long time for them to accept that their lives are over.

Though he offered his help, as most of the students did, they were told simply to stay out of the way. To go down to the forest, or to the library, or descend for a while until things settle down. After the dead are processed, then there may be ways to help, but for now, it is judgment and processing will be the focus of the guardians. How many of them will stay on the Reserve? How many will be turned back and taken away? Theo still hasn't seen where Malik takes the unworthy. Cold fingers of fear grip his heart. What if they find out he's unworthy? Veddie talks of banishment but what does that really mean? And if Heaven has been such a visceral experience, he can only imagine what Hell would be.

The next few days are exactly as Ryder described. It is crowded chaos as the new recruits start spilling out onto the streets. It's hard to take a step without bumping into a bewildered character. To ensure a seat at orientation, one must arrive hours before it begins. And most are just turned away. The dorms are filled to capacity and many sleep two to a bed or on the floor. The streams of souls entering the cathedral continues day and night. As well as the ones led out of town by Malik. Sunday service has been moved out to the forum. Classes are still out of session.

Theo jumps, as many other do, just to get some space. Though jumping into Angel's Light is hardly space at all. She is chronically depressed now. Ambrose is gone and there is nothing for her to look forward to anymore. She dreams of him constantly, desperately trying to think up situations where they'll cross paths again. She even thought of instigating a small get-together to say goodbye to the people from work as a cover to see him again. But in the end, she doesn't think she deserved a small get-together. Her attendance at school is rare. She only goes to get handouts from the cafeteria, use the showers, and show up to enough classes to keep her from getting expelled. Save the Date is set in stone. She knows where she'll hide and who she will take down first. It is now only a matter of counting down the days until prom.

Theo spends a few days with her and it brings her mood up a little. She takes walks with her dog. The old beast is very protective of her and she hasn't had an incident with Romeo since he arrived. She dreams her dark dreams, plays with herself, schemes, and spends time with Beatrice Yu. Life is as it's always been for her. A constant struggle. A downward spiral. And she intends to strike before she reaches the bottom. There doesn't seem to be anything Theo can do to change her mind. He has not given up hope. He will fight until her last day. Prayers and meditation have never worked with her. It seems the only way he can get to her is physically. So he touches her and whispers in her ear and is careful not to let her touch him too much. Now that he has a potential outlet above, he finds he can control himself better down below.

He returns to the Reserve after a few days. Things have settled down a bit. Classes are starting again. And though thousands were brought in, only hundreds were chosen as guardians, or decided to stay on as guardians if they were chosen. Still, it's crowded. The forest or meadow is the only place for some quiet contemplation, and likely that contemplation will come with some disruption. With no place to put his stuff, Theo left his schoolbooks on a bench beside the street before he descended. They are still sitting there, undisturbed, when he returns. He picks them up and walks aimlessly through the city. He could go see Ryder but he will be overloaded with students. Maybe tonight, after the kids have gone to bed, then he'll sneak through one of Ryder's windows and see if he's available. Just the thought makes his cock twitch. He can't wait to start this up again.

He turns down an unfamiliar avenue and ends up on the water road that leads to judgment. He hasn't been back here since he was deemed worthy, though he has idly searched for the location. It seems things are hidden in full view on the Reserve. Like the entrance to the vaults or to the cathedral. Though they appear to be out in the open, he could never find them if he tried. And discovering the water street was purely by accident.

He steps down into the rushing water that pours out of the mouths of statues. At the end of the street he can see that great yawning chasm that leads down to judgment; he can hear water dashing down into its depths. Distracted, he doesn't notice Veddie until he steps down onto the street and right into his path. Theo gasps in surprise, then quickly sedates himself. His old mentor comes to an unruly stop, glaring down at him, disgusted. He's forgotten about what Veddie saw in the church hallway. Even a dinosaur like him would put the pieces together eventually.

"Move from my path," Veddie demands, though there is ample room on the street for twenty or so people to stand side by side.

Theo looks up at him coldly. This is the first time Veddie has acknowledged his presence for weeks. Feeling saucy, he replies, "You move."

Veddie's eyes light up, his dander rising. "I do not move for you."

"Then I guess you are stuck here." Theo retorts, studying his old mentor, judging him like never before. The anger lines on his face seem prominent now, cutting deeply between his brow and at the corners of his mouth. Theo supposes they were always there but he used to see them as a result of his intense nature and not from a hateful spirit. He still wears his silver rings like brass knuckles across each hand. Has he ever punched someone with those? He's sure Veddie is thinking about it now. And his hair is much greasier than Theo remembers, slicked tightly back in controlled waves. The tattoos on his bulging forearms are of virgin and son, with crosses on the backs of his hands and scripture from the Old Testament along the sides. Religion is Veddie's entire world. There is nothing else for him; he is completely black and white.

Veddie continues to stand his ground, glowering hatefully down at Theo. "I cannot believe I ever accepted you as a student."

The insult cuts a little, though it shouldn't matter anymore. Acceptance is still so primal in him. He finds it hard to be hated, even by the likes of Veddie. Wanting to return the wound, he replies, "Ryder has been an excellent mentor."

Veddie's eyes narrow. He gets hot in the face. "You have indeed fallen."

Theo raises his eyebrows, trying to appear more nonchalant than he feels. "So what if I am? How is it your business anymore?"

Veddie suddenly grabs him by the scruff and shoves him back against a pillar. Theo struggles against the grip, his collar choking him, his feet barely touching the ground. He wonders if Veddie can kill him. Physically, he outweighs him but is it possible to kill someone in Heaven?

"You will see soon enough," Veddie growls. "You'll be sorry you ever crossed paths with me."

Even in the scuffle, it occurs to Theo that Veddie probably can't do anything. If he suspects Theo is dallying around with Ryder or that he is gay or bisexual, so what? If the council didn't banish him for sleeping with his charge, how could they banish him for this? On the surface he appears as white and orderly as everyone else. And he and Ryder are both consenting adults. Veddie may not like it, but what can he actually do?

"I'm not sorry one bit," Theo returns hotly. "Ryder has taught me more in the last year then you could teach me in a lifetime."

Veddie angrily thumps Theo against the pillar.

"Oh I like him," Theo says. Veddie's grip loosens and Theo drops from his hands. He dashes to the side, shouting, "I like him *a lot*. And there's not a damned thing you can do about it, is there? Is there?"

Veddie swipes at him but Theo runs back the way he came. Veddie points a ringed finger as he sprints away. "You misjudge my power here boy. I get what I want and you will be sorry. Mark my words."

Veddie keeps a watchful eye in the days that follow. Often, Theo finds him standing on the road to Ryder's house or outside the first year's dorm. He is a constant presence now, always watching, waiting, hoping to catch Theo in some immoral act. But even if Theo wanted to start something, he can't get near Ryder. Day and night, his mentor is on the move. He only sees him in passing or from a distance as he is rushing around inside a crowd of anxious students.

Excitement on the Reserve has started to settle as the students from the disaster enter classes and start accepting their new reality. The first years who gave up their beds have to be placed in different locations. Some have bedded down in their mentor's houses or have been taken into other guardian's homes. A new dorm is being built on the lower side of town. Theo, so far, is still homeless. Though he would certainly enjoy bedding down in his mentor's home, he just can't risk it while Veddie is watching so closely. And even if Veddie wasn't there, Ryder's house is full. He has a student sleeping on every sleep-able surface. Ascensions class is now filled to capacity. Worship services are standing room only. Though it is crowded and often inconvenient, it is good news for the souls in the Field. More students means more guardians and more help for ailing spirits. Disasters are not misfortunes up above; they bring an influx of angels for the ones still left below. Sometimes it is thought that disasters are brought about just to bring in more recruits. And disasters often happen in poorer areas because the souls are less tainted there. Rich people forget that it took a community of people to get them where they are, poor people still need to rely on each other's charity for survival. A spirit in need is a humble spirit and therefore more qualified for guardianship.

Sitting on the rooftop that overlooks the cathedral, Theo ponders his own qualifications for guardianship. In finding out how ill-equipped Eric and his friends were when they became students, he was outraged that he stood on equal grounds with them. But he has learned during his stay that there is a very big difference between acting religious and being religious. He has simply been acting. Now he is not sure what he is anymore. He cannot deny that there is something after death because he is living it, but what is beyond those cathedral gates? And who? If there is indeed a single essence running the entire show.

He watches as another soul is escorted across the flower filled meadow to the cathedral gates. The building itself is built entirely of gold and when the sun strikes it in just the right manner, it is blinding. The archway where souls enter through stands open day and night and glows brightly from within. Ridwan stands like an action figure before that lustrous portal, greeting people as they approach and guiding them into their permanent retirement. He briefly wonders if his worthy judgment could be revoked. Could he do something above that would change his final resting place? Sometimes he thinks he pushes his luck too far. He has challenged elders, broken vows, indulged in all sorts of deviant behavior and is planning for more licentiousness in the near future. He knows the bible says that it is a sin for man to lie with man. Well, to be clear, it never states it was a sin, it merely said that man shall not lay with man. And those words did not come from any god or spirit affiliate with said specter, those words were laid down by a human being. The same way the Catholic Church made suicide a sin in order to deter martyrdom. Killing yourself was never a sin in the bible. It didn't happen until the fifteenth century. So what is the word of god and what is the word of man? Theo doesn't really know anymore.

Hearing the noon bell ring, Theo sighs and rises from the ledge that has become his temporary den. He descends the ladder to the street and heads towards his next class. Since it's noon, he is already late but he is not concerned. He has taken what Ryder said about learning at his own pace to heart. He is on his own schedule now and moving at a speed he is comfortable with.

Walking down the main street, which is mostly deserted because classes are in session, he spots Ryder approaching surrounding by a group of students. Pots left simmering on the back burner start boiling again. He has been eager for weeks but forced to keep his desires in check. He has barely seen Ryder except in sanctioned locations. There has been little to no conversation between them. And as Ryder approaches, he knows that will not change today. Ryder is overwhelmed by new recruits. A girl is pulling on his sleeve.

Another is shouting something over his shoulder. He drops a book and then trips over it. The group comes to a halt as someone behind him retrieves the lost item. Ryder glances at Theo and nods. Theo returns the gesture. But just as he's passing by, Ryder slips his hand around Theo's bicep and brings him to a halt.

"We are having a study group this afternoon. Will you come?"

Theo pauses, his bicep flexed beneath his mentor's fierce grip. Ryder's thumb moves against the muscle causing shivers to run up Theo's back.

"Where are you having it?" Theo replies evenly, though his dander is plenty up.

"At the library. Sort of a meet and greet for my old students and my new. Will you come?"

"I certainly will," Theo replies with a smile.

Chapter 23∞

Theo showers before the study session. He puts on fresh robes. And nothing else. His whole body is tingling as he leaves for the library. Of course, they will be surrounded by people, no chance for any devious behavior, but the library has such dirty connotations for him. Even in a public place, he knows almost anything can happen.

In the library, he finds the usual study group gathered around his mentor. Eric, Justine, more girls and their friends. There are new faces too, most of them Japanese. It was announced a short time ago that the disaster was an earthquake. It was not altogether unexpected as populations living on fault lines are prone to seismic activity but the magnitude of the shift was a surprise to people above and below. Most of the deaths occurred in the collapse of an overcrowded school. Though many adults arrived, the majority of the new students are teenagers.

Theo sits down at one of the tables reserved for Ryder's students. He nods as the haunted eyes of the latest arrivals glide over him. He knows what they are going through: the confusion, disorientation, the denial. He still has trouble accepting his own death. The Reserve feels like bible camp. And once the summer is over, he'll be heading back to his regular home.

A ruckus fills the air. Theo glances across the library to where Veddie and his students are gathered. They exchange boisterously at their table, their clatter drowning out everyone else in the room. He notices that none of the new arrivals, being short, dark haired, and Asian, were invited to join Veddie's group. His remains an elite, white, and male dominated society. Theo briefly lock eyes with his old mentor.

Veddie has not forgotten the incident on the water road. The glare returned is acidic and laced with needles. He supposes Veddie's quest to have him banished has failed once again and now all the old man has left is dirty looks. Veddie's good opinion used to mean the world to him. A dirty look would've destroyed him a few months ago. Now it is more of an irritation and, again, makes him wonder why his old mentor won't just let him be.

"So new people meet my old people," Ryder begins, standing at the head of the table. "I know there are still a lot of questions. Feel free to ask me or one of my students during this session. We are here to make this transition as easy as possible." He glances at Veddie's table as the boys all shout out at once. For such a small group, they make a lot of noise. "I could use a few volunteers to help me out."

Theo lifts his hand without hesitation. Justine's hand is also waving wildly in the air. As well as a few others.

"Thank you," Ryder says. "Volunteers, please come forward."

Theo pushes out of his seat. He approaches the dark haired professor and stands directly across from him. They exchange a look before the others arrive and Theo knows there will be trouble in the library today. Ryder didn't invite him here because he needed more volunteers.

"Okay," Ryder says to his helpers. "We're just going to go around the tables and help out where needed. I'm not sure if you've noticed but we do not speak the same language. However, we all understand each other. That is the way the world first broke apart, not only in language but religion as well. We were split apart at the beginning and now we bring all the pieces back together again after death. When it comes to religion, no one is right. But no one is wrong either. We are all pieces of a giant truth.

"So, focus on the new arrivals. They have been through a terrible trauma. You remember what it was like when you first came here. It can very confusing in the beginning, so be helpful and considerate. Talk if they need to but don't force conversations. Some people just need the quiet."

The volunteers split up and begin walking back to the tables. "Theo, stay back," Ryder calls as he is about to leave.

Theo turns to face Ryder. Now that the others are gone, the space between them seems very small. "Walk with me," Ryder says and the two begin to circle the tables. Across the room, Veddie's eyes are hotly on them. "He's been watching a lot. I'm not sure why," Ryder comments.

"We had a little…discussion the other day," Theo muses. "It didn't end well."

"Oh, so that's what's going on." Ryder chuckles. One of the new students gestures to him for help. He leans down and talks with the girl. While he does, Theo stands behind him, his eyes locked with Veddie. He restrains the urge to make thrusting gestures at Ryder's ass. It would probably launch Veddie into outer space. Probably a good place for him. He'd get along well with all those cold, inert bodies drifting around.

"Yes," Ryder says, rising. "Come to my office anytime if you have questions." The two continue to troll around the tables, their shoulders brushing as they walk. The silence between them is very heavy. There is so much to be said but hard to express with so many people around.

"I can meet you tonight," Ryder says, directing Theo from the crowd. They stand beneath a towering stained glass window, bathed in its radiant light. "Can you meet me after sundown?"

"Yes," Theo says, experiencing a jolt of excitement. And fear. He wants this to happen but is nervous about the encounter as well. He keeps anticipating his return to heterosexuality, that the switch he turned on will suddenly turn off, but it hasn't happened yet.

"Come to the forum. There's a little cove across the lake. We will have to swim to get there." Ryder's eyes flicker towards Veddie's table. The old man is burning holes into them with his eyes. Has he finally made the connection? Or would a crusty, old mind like his simply refuse to connect those gleeful, gay dots? Or even acknowledge the existence of an alternative lifestyle? For Veddie, even mainstream sex is unacceptable. Abstinence is the only option. It seems the uptight and intolerant will keep making the rules and free spirits will keep breaking them behind closed doors.

"Okay." Theo smiles a bit, blushing and looking down at his feet. "But I don't really know what I'm doing." His heart is pounding pretty hard. It's really going to happen now. There's a time and a place, all he needs to do is show up. And then…well, he can hardly think of it. The very idea sets his skin on fire.

"Well, neither do I," Ryder says, raising his eyebrows.

Theo looks over at him, completely shocked. "You mean…you haven't?"

"I thought you read my book?"

"I skimmed it," Theo admits, embarrassed to remember how he reacted afterwards. He was so disgusted. He was so outraged. He just picked out the details he could use against Ryder and threw the rest of his Life book aside.

"I was barely out of the closet when I died. I never slept with anyone on earth. I died just like you, a virgin." Ryder drops his eyes, blushing a bit himself. The light from the stained glass window paints his hair, his skin, giving him an ethereal glow all over.

"But here?" Theo asks, confused. "You never did anything here?"

"Well, the closets are pretty full on the Reserve," Ryder says. "And I spent a good portion of my time up here fallen. To be certain, you are the first man I have ever pursued."

Theo's head spins a bit by the admission. Not just that Ryder is as inexperienced as he is, but that his mentor chose him to be his first. The idea that they are both novices fumbling around in the dark sends his temperature soaring.

"So, I am to be your first?" Theo whispers, leaning a little closer. The idea makes him feel bolder, braver, like he is the one in control now. He's not sure why; he is just as green as Ryder is.

"As you are to be mine," Ryder returns with a sly smile.

The two men turn from the window and experience a shock when they see Justine standing right beside them. She is close enough to hear everything they've said. Neither of them heard her approach nor know how much of their conversation she has overheard.

Tuesday, you roused me, you were eager on my doorstep. You mounted the stairwell. Spent the night under my breath. In the morning, you lingered. All over me. All through me. I tossed for an hour, maybe two, imagining that if we could, oh how we would. And how it would be so, so good. Some people say we leave our bodies in dreams. Well, last night, our souls sought each other out, we reunited unconsciously. I frolicked so hard with you that I woke up in residue. Reminders of you and our midnight encounter. Spirits delivered what bodies denied. I was so drunk in my bed thinking of you. You're so far from me now. I have no way to reach you. I don't know where you are. But on Tuesday, I never felt closer to you.

Angel is stirring as Theo circles the tables. And this time, he is the one causing her arousal, stimulating her senses, bringing her pen to life. It has always been trouble for him when she writes him off around Ryder. He has been running away from this very thing for long time. Today he welcomes it. Embraces it. A few tables away, Ryder moves like a ghost amongst the students, his mind far from his duties. Tonight, they come together. And what happens when they get to the cove will be decided when they get there. All Theo knows is that the few times they've crossed paths, it has been a rowdy adventure and he is itchy with anticipation.

I know it's time to go but neither of us are leaving. There is something uncommon in the distance between us. A certain energy concerning us when we're all alone. It is distinctive. It is complicated.

I glance over and he's staring at me. A firm, lengthy look and I'm forced to turn my eyes away. Maybe it's not the wives and the girlfriends keeping them at bay. Maybe it's me. Maybe I don't want them to come. Maybe I pick them because they can't come.

Ryder's bumps a chair and drops his papers all over the floor. Theo stares at him hard, remembering how he used to hate his clumsiness. As Ryder crouches down to retrieve his things, Theo rounds the table to assist. Glancing at Veddie, he raises his eyebrows and then goes down on his knees, disappearing from sight.

"Can I help you with this?" He says, crouching down.

"You are trouble today," Ryder glances at him and lowers his eyes with a smile, picking up his strewn papers. "But then I think you always were."

"Perhaps I was. It took me a long time to accept that." Theo smiles, his hand grazing Ryder's as they reach for the same page.

"Accept what?"

"Who I really am," Theo returns as the last page is retrieved.

The two men rise from the sea of students simultaneously. Veddie is on his feet now, straining to see what is going on and no amount of poking or prodding will get his attention back to his students.

Finally he sees me, really sees me. In the face of all my fantasies, my siren songs, my wretched pleas, now I am afraid. His hand touches the side of my neck. I jerk a little, surprised by how cold his fingers are. He's a little shaky. His face right next to mine. I can feel his breath against my cheek. He shifts closer, both of us breathing more rapidly.

"Jesus," he whispers near my lips, "will you kiss me?"

I push forward and fall into his fresh mouth, his sweet lips, his soft tongue. We kiss in swells, our faces pressing and releasing in gentle undulations. A trickle of sweat passes down the ripples of my spine. I lift my hand and trace his smooth earlobe. It's finally mine. I want to taste it. I want it in my mouth.

"I'm sorry," he whispers, pushing back a little. "I can't do this." Even as he says it, his thumb is sliding back and forth across my chin, his forehead still against mine. I release a few shaky breaths. He's so close. I can see nothing but his moist mouth, his glimmering teeth, and his tongue like a slippery snake gliding across them both. I know this is wrong. It will only hurt us in the end. And the last thing I ever want to do is hurt him. But that kiss! I felt that kiss everywhere. The urge is so strong. To feel him, his hands and wet skin, his body sliding in.

Theo slips around one of the wide, stout pillars beneath the Book of Life section. He is on fire. Already. He's no match against Ryder's dirty looks and Angel's filthy imagination. He's never going to make it to the cove. Behind him, he can hear the soft murmur of students, the slithery whisper of pages turning, wet quills scratching, and the creak of stairs being mounted. In front of him, the musty periodical section sits empty and untended.

He's thinking about pulling it out right here. Just a quick tug to get his head straightened out. It's risky. Anyone could walk around the pillar and see him. Anyone. He rolls his head across the back of the pillar, trying to get himself under control. But when it's on him like this, he can think of nothing but execution. A frenzied, hot tempered release that might hold him over for a few hours until he can get to the source of all this frustration. But he can't do it here. It's too risky. He can't.

"Right, I'll get it. I think there's something in the periodical section," he hears Ryder's voice. He passes by the pillar, completely unaware of what's pressed up behind it. The rush of air left in his wake sends Theo over the edge. He opens his robe and exposes himself to his mentor's back. Ryder fingers through a few volumes while Theo fingers himself. His mentor picks out a book, turns, and jolts to a sudden stop. He stands, mouth ajar, staring at the frenzied student playing with himself behind the pole.

"No, just give me a second," he calls to someone at the tables. "I'll bring it to you." He walks forward slowly and Theo explores himself without shame. He rolls his head back across the pillar, his body red and hot. Ryder's eyes are all over him but it's the anticipation of contact that has Theo's temperature rising. It's like the night in the courtyard all over again, except this time he is fully aware of what he is doing. Yes, he has been asking for this for a long time.

"Yes, I'm coming," Ryder says in a more frustrated voice. "Just wait there. I'll be there in a second. I have what you need right here." He continues to walk towards the pillar, holding the book against his chest. His eyes explore Theo's body without reservation. And the lower his gaze goes, the hotter Theo gets. There is no uncertainty now. He is taunting Ryder with it, tempting him, begging him to come in for a little taste, an appetizer before the main dish is served. And when the shadow of the pillar falls over his mentor, when it hides him from the view of the students at the table, Ryder launches forward. He covers Theo's mouth with his hand and uses his other one to take over what Theo has started. Theo arches his head back in a silent cry as an alien hand makes contact with his home planet. He lifts his hands over his head and lets Ryder control him completely. He gasps out little breaths as wave after wave of pleasure rocks his body. Ryder moves his hand from Theo's mouth and kisses him. Not like the kiss in the laboratory where two heads knocked together in confused frustration, this one is done with intention, knowledge, and sentiment. Theo grabs the back of Ryder's neck and pulls the kiss in deeper. His whole body is slaked with sweat now. His hands flutter over Ryder's body, grazing his chest, his hips, his cock.

There's a gasp nearby. The two men both look to the side, their bodies still hotly pressed together and standing there is, of course, Justine. She stares, her eyes wide and confused, her mouth parted in a silent denunciation. If she was unsure about what she heard earlier, this scene ought to clear up any confusion.

Ryder slowly lifts his hand from Theo's cock and holds a finger over his lips in a *shhhh* gesture. Then his hand returns back down. Theo jolts as his mentor brazenly begins to stroke him again right in front of the girl. Justine's eyes snap down to the floor. She remains still for a second or two and then quickly walks away.

"You dirty fucking bastard," Theo whispers as his mentor continues to pull him off. He gasps and thrusts and when the time is near, he grabs the back of Ryder's neck and pulls him in as close as space will allow. He grits his teeth against Ryder's throat, grasping a fistful of his silky hair. He joyously releases into the tight, foreign fist of his mentor and then drops his head softly back against the post.

"I'm sorry," Theo whispers, looking anything but. "I couldn't wait."

"Don't be." Ryder breathes against his mouth, running his wet hand up Theo's chest and around the back of his neck. "We should leave now."

"Leave?"

"To the cove." Ryder backs away, straightens his robe and adjusts his hair. "I'll leave first. Wait a while before you follow."

Theo remains where he is, exposed and wet, his whole body trembling. He takes a few moments to breathe, to try and compose himself, but he is out of his mind right now. Crazed. All he wants is to get out of this stodgy library and into the dark, wet recesses of the forum cove. If what just happened is a precursor to what is going to follow, he may just die from sexual satisfaction this evening.

He rounds the pillar after only a minute or two, unable to wait any longer. What he sees on the other side brings him to a slow stop. Ryder is stalled just a few feet ahead of him. Across the room, Justine is sobbing to Veddie. Uh-oh, Theo thinks, his eyes snapping to Ryder's stiff back. Another council member approaches Veddie. They speak in a tight circle, the two men glancing hotly in their direction. Justine is blubbering between them, leaving no detail of what she just witnessed unturned.

"Just wait," Ryder says without turning back. "Just wait a second."

Across the room, the grumbling continues. Theo hears words from Veddie's mouth like *outrageous* and *disgusting*. In between those words, his eyes ricochet between Theo and Ryder.

"We better leave," Ryder says, this time looking back. He's gone a bit pale.

"But what can he do?" Theo asks, his happy high fading.

"About us? I'm not sure," Ryder says quieter. "But he is going to try something." He begins to walk between the tables, heading in the general direction of the door. As he does, Veddie slowly breaks from Justine and moves to block the exit. Soon, the other council member is with him too.

"Is there another way out?" Theo asks.

"No, that is the only way." Ryder glances over as Theo steps up beside him. "But if he wanted to cause a scene, he would've done it already. He would've charged right over here and let us have it."

"So what's he doing then?" Theo asks, glancing warily at the two men blocking the door. What will locking him inside the library do? And are they really in trouble? Can Veddie really detain them for fooling around? To do that, he would have to admit that the affair between him and Ryder exists, and Theo doubts Veddie could do that.

Students maintain their quiet conversations as Theo and Ryder continue towards the barricaded door. Other than Justine sobbing at an empty table, nothing has changed. Though a few students have gone to comfort her, studies go on, everyone unaware that there is a conflict rising. Only the two men at the door and the two men walking towards it have any idea of what's really happening.

"Return to your table. You two are not leaving," Veddie says as they near him. He lifts his tattooed arms and crosses them over his inflated chest. He is so disgusted that he can't look either of them in the eye.

"You cannot keep us. We've committed no crime," Ryder says.

"Oh I think you have," Veddie snaps, his cold and hateful eyes buzzing a few inches above the Ascensions teacher's head. "The rest of the council will arrive shortly. You are both being taken into custody."

"Custody?" Ryder cries a little louder. "For what, exactly?"

"Public indecency. Threatening the virtue of others. Degradation of the human spirit. And immorality," Veddie finishes. Behind him, the brick wall of a bald council member stands with his arms tightly crossed over his chest, mimicking Veddie's cross stance.

"Immorality?" Theo exclaims. He braces himself for Veddie's gaze but it never comes. He, like the man behind him, keep their attention focused elsewhere as if even glancing in their direction may spread the virus of homosexuality. As if it is something that can be transmitted and caught. Oh, if only it could be. What Theo wouldn't do to see Veddie and the man behind him overcome by their passions for each other. Especially if it was done against their own wills. "And exactly what sort of immorality have we committed?" Theo challenges. "Tell me what crime I am being detained for or else I am walking through that door."

Veddie's eyes flicker down for a second, almost coming into contact with his, then quickly focus back on that distant point high on the horizon. "Do not challenge me, boy."

"Challenge you? I only ask to be informed about the nature of my crimes. Tell me what they are, Veddie, tell me what I have done wrong or else let me go."

"Sit down and shut your mouth!" Veddie shouts, losing control. A few students within hearing range turn back from their chairs and look up at him. If they were not in the library, if there were not so many witnesses around, Theo thinks the old man would strike him right then and there. Instead, he wrestles his temper back down and when he is calm again, he says, "You can explain your actions to the council. You two are going straight to trial."

"Bullshit!" Theo returns, but then he sees a line of angry old men coming up through the courtyard of the library. The council. He looks over at Ryder.

"You are finally going to get what you deserve," Veddie says, a satisfied smile spreading across his face. "Banishment."

Ryder pulls Theo back a few steps. They huddle up and talk in lowered voices. More people are starting to notice what's happening by the main doors.

"Can he do this?" Theo whispers. "He can't have us banished, can he?"

Ryder looks at the cluster of old men approaching the library. "I don't know. These are Veddie's men, *his* members of the council but not all of the elected members. They do not speak for the entire council. But if we don't get representation, we could get locked away before anyone finds out what Veddie has done. He could make us disappear."

Theo glances at mob mounting the library steps. There are enough of them to restrain both him and Ryder. They could get captured and locked away before anyone realizes they are gone. Theo thinks about how long it took anyone to notice when he jumped against orders. It was a week before anyone came looking for him. By then, Veddie could have them both locked in the deepest, darkest dungeon.

They retreat back into the library as, one by one, the council members enter the door. Justine rises from her chair and sobs out Ryder's name. No one is paying attention to their studies anymore. All eyes are on the commotion up front.

"Can we get out through there?" Theo says, glancing up at the Life section.

"No. But we could hide in there. It could buy us some time," Ryder replies. The men are moving towards them, slowly spreading out to cover the room like an alluvial fan.

"You have your key?" Theo whispers as they carefully retreat towards the stairs. The men are advancing slowly, trying to appear casual even though they are doing nothing of the sort.

"Yes." Ryder reaches for the handrail of the shiny black staircase to the BOL section. He takes out his key and puts his foot on the first step. Veddie is coming too, moving slowly like a cat stalking a mouse. If the council realizes what they are doing, they will pounce. So, at the same time, the two men turn and thunder up the old staircase. As the council charges for them, they fumble to get the keys in the old lock.

"Get him!" Veddie shouts and the spiral staircase is now shaking with the approaching horde. Ryder jams the key in, turns it, and the bolt slides free. They rush inside and pull the door closed. Ryder's key is still in the lock. Theo quickly reaches through the bars and breaks the old key off in the lock just as Veddie reaches the top. Theo backs away, smiling and holding the ornate handle between his fingers. Veddie fumbles to get the broken key out but it is bent and jammed inside. He slams his huge fists against the ornamental grate, screaming.

"Cowards," he shouts hatefully, shaking the bars the way he'd certainly like to be shaking their necks. "You choose the offence, then you choose the consequences that come with it."

"What offence, Veddie? What is my offence?" Theo mocks, backing away with broken key in hand. The chase is over and his dander up again. They will have to remove the door to get inside. And that will take time. Time to commit a few more atrocities right under Veddie's nose. The idea has his blood boiling.

Veddie bares his teeth and them, looking very much like the way Azrael used to. But she is not here and neither is

Ridwan, Malik or any of the other higher echelon council members. What would they say about this witch hunt Veddie has orchestrated? Would they agree with it or condemn it?

Theo passes behind Ryder who looks about as shocked as the rest of them over his uprising. As he does, he winks over his new mentor's shoulder at his old one. Then he slaps Ryder in the ass. Hard. Ryder jerks forward in surprise. Veddie shouts and thrashes against the bars like an enraged bear.

Touch it and release it
I want to see your muscles straining
Your stomach shaking, your face distorted
I want to see you sweat because of me

Theo chases Ryder into the back of the life section. They don't have much time. Already the gate is being attacked with various tools. Veddie, Theo supposes, is now being tortured by his own imagination, about his visions of what is happening in the dark recesses of the Life section between the two men he detests the most.

Ryder turns against a shelf as Theo approaches. A wall of books comes up against Ryder's back. His hair is tousled and a light sheen covers his face. Theo slows to stand directly in front of him. He lifts his fingers to the split in Ryder's robe. Beneath that split, Ryder's chest is quickly rising and falling.

"You wanted full disclosure?" Theo whispers, tracing his fingers down the soft divide. "She is writing to me now."

"What does she say?" Ryder breathes, looking up into Theo's face. His tongue grazes his lower lip, his teeth a glimmering line beneath his parted lips. A vein beats rapidly in his neck, the pulse visible through the skin.

"She says she wants to see you sweat because of me," Theo leans forward and presses his mouth to Ryder's. There have been kisses before but not one like this, not one with his full passion and knowledge behind it. This is what he wants and this time he knows it. This time he has no fear of it. Only the fear of the gate that holds them in here and the divide upright men maintain between love and religion. He backs away from the soft lips of his mentor and takes a book from the shelf behind him. A red book. He fans through the pages, every part of him standing at attention.

"You asked me to punish you once." Ryder takes the book from Theo's hand, his chestnut eyes rising to his. The dark shade of bang now clings to his wet forehead

Theo eyes the book in mentor's hands. "Would you like to do it now?"

A smile turns up the corner of Ryder's mouth. At the other end of the library, they can hear Veddie shouting to get a hammer and pick. They will knock the hinges off if the broken key cannot be extracted. It won't be long until he's inside.

Theo backs away and moves to a nearby table. Glancing at Ryder, he turns towards it and drops his robes to the ground, leaving his body exposed. Tingling all over, he leans forward and braces his hands against the surface of the polished wood. Breathing hard, he lowers his head and stares down at the hard line of his cock, eagerly awaiting his reprimand. He has been such a bad boy lately.

I want your hands
Your mouth
Your hips
Your cock
I want to hear you gasping
Pleading
I want to see you struggle
Pray

Theo arches back as the book makes first contact. He closes his eyes and releases a long breath. His ass stings from the assault. Ryder is behind him, out of view. He can only guess where he stands by the sound of the old floor creaking beneath his feet.

"You have been a tease," Ryder says, giving him just the lightest touch with the surface of the crimson book. Theo jolts all the same, jerking his hips forward at the surprise contact. "You keep showing it to me and then telling me I cannot have it. So what is your decision Mr. Duncan? Are you going to give it to me or not?"

Theo looks over as Ryder appears at his right shoulder. His eyes flicker down to observe that his mentor is naked too. And every bit as inflated as he. If not for Ryder, he would have marched along the same little beaten path never knowing the length to which pleasure could stretch. He would've taken the way a hundred feet have tread before, ate only the fruit from the acceptable trees. Now he knows the draw of an un-tread path. He knows the limits to love and pleasure. His mind has been awakened to an all-encompassing erotica and there's no going back after this.

"You can have it. Have me," Theo replies, breathless, leaning towards his mentor's mouth but then the book strikes his backside again. Theo cries out in surprise, his hips vibrating forward. The shouts by the gate fall silent as stodgy men strain to hear something to validate their fears. But Theo is only gasping now, his hands gripped around the edges of the thick table. He struggles to maintain his control but this is excitement beyond anything he's ever experienced before. It is the forbidden nature of the act added with the risk of exposure driving him wildly beyond the edge. He almost wishes the men behind the gate could see him from where they stand, could see what's going on, and what's about to happen.

The book strikes his backside with a touch more than playful force. Theo spins around and grabs the hardback which is still firmly gripped in Ryder's hand. Gasping, naked, they stand eye to eye and challenge each other, the book the only obstacle between them. That is when they hear the gate break down.

Make you stiff
Make you full
Make you wet
Make you gleam
Put your face in it
Put your cock in it
Fill me up
I want you to fill me up
I want you to
I want you
I...

They race around one shelf and then another. Behind them, they can hear the men approaching. They've found the red book and their robes on the floor. Veddie is screaming at his men. *Find them! Find them! Before anything else happens!* Oh, how they fear it, that one small act that is no one's business but the two people involved. It is not about the love or the relationship or the bond formed between the similar sexes, it is just that one small sexual act that must be stopped at all costs. That is what they are picturing as they race through the Life section. It is the deed straight men fear because they worry it will be turned on themselves. But what they forget is that sex is earned through trust and time. And straight men are so constipated and insecure that no adventurous man would want one anyway.

They come down a narrow shelf and at the end, is a closet. A closet. The closet. Without a thought, the two men tumble inside and discover with surprise and delight that the door locks from the inside and requires a key to penetrate. This tiny room is just as tight and cluttered as the one downstairs, though it is papers and periodicals not cleaning supplies that restrict this space.

"Back in the closet again?" Theo whispers as they come together in the dark. He can see nothing but the slice of light cast across their toes as they face each other at the bottom of the door.

"Story of my life," Ryder chuckles.

"Down there!" They hear Veddie shout. *"In that closet."*

Theo turns the bolt on the door. It will buy them minutes, nothing more. And he is nowhere close to being done. He presses Ryder up against the wall with his naked body, all their parts coming into contact. A fierce swell of exhilaration washes over him as that inflated rod intersects his like rival swords, like crossed weapons on a wooden shield. He doesn't want this to stop. He doesn't want this to end. He needs hours to explore this new sensation. He needs days and days on end.

Ryder grabs him by the ass and pulls him in closer. The closet door is now being pounded on by angry fists. Pressing his hips against Theo's, Ryder whispers, "You'll need to run."

"Run?" Theo gasps against his mentor's mouth. He braces a hand against the wall as one of Ryder's hands moves down. The heat between the hard line of their bodies is like molten lava. It is so intense that it threatens to melt their skins and fuse them eternally together. Angel is his victim now, succumbing to his every passion. She has run out into the yard and writhes naked in the long grass, calling to him, yearning for him. And yearning for something she can't even explain, for the union of the two men in the closet.

"Try to get to the forest. Or down to the Field. If you jump they can't get you without an emergency extraction, and Veddie will need authorization for that."

"What about you?"

"I am established here. It is harder for them to make me disappear. But you..." The door rattles just inches from their shoulders. Cracks are starting to appear at the corners of the doors. "I am sorry," he whispers, "I have not been a very good mentor to you."

Theo rolls his head back as Ryder's oversized hand finds his red line. He grabs him and pulls him tightly against his sweat soaked body, digging his fingers around the curve of his mentor's ass. Burying his head in Ryder's wet hair, he run his lips and tongue along the salty skin of his neck. He exhales a few shaky breaths as Ryder's heavy hand tightens around his molten core. Orgasm is creeping up his spine. All he needs is a few more minutes.

The door is pulled from its hinges and bare, unfiltered light explodes into their shadowy playroom. Theo is pulled one way and Ryder pulled another. Robes are quickly wrapped around their bodies. Ryder is struck on the head and Theo knocked down the ground. Their hands are bound behind their backs and the two men are led through the Life section. Ryder needs extra support, as he is woozy from the blow, but the men at his sides look repulsed to even be near him.

Veddie snorts, wipes his hand across his mouth as if he's trying to rid himself of an unpleasant smear. "I warned you, Ryder, but you didn't listen. If you insist on breaking the rules and having relationships with your students, then you can do it from the vaults."

Ryder shakes his head, regaining some of his consciousness. His arms are turned painfully behind his back at the elbows. His hands are starting to turn purple. "This isn't about a relationship with a student, it's about who I'm having the relationship with."

The other guardians force their gazes straight, standing as far away from Ryder as space will allow. All of them are repulsed, horrified, terrified. Small minds have such big fears to contend with.

"I knew it was only a matter of time," Veddie continues, sounding extremely satisfied. "All I had to do was sit back and wait."

Theo stares daggers into Veddie's back. He has not been bound as tightly as his mentor. His hands are tied at the wrists, leaving him a little space for movement. Once they clear the library, he will make his move. But before that happens, he needs to let Veddie know that he is not beaten. Not by a long shot.

"I chased him," Theo boasts, "I instigated it. It was me the whole time."

Veddie glances over his shoulder and then back to the broken metal doors lying beside the spiral staircase. The gate is now bent and twisted, hammers and chisels strewn across the doorway. "I don't care how it happened."

"You should," Theo continues. "Because I am the one who lured him into depravity. You may get me but I'll see that you never get to him."

Veddie stops as they reach the head of the staircase. His face is swollen up like a blowfish. "No one will believe you."

"Why not?" Theo returns. "I'm the fallen angel, aren't I? A victim to my own depravities? No different than David, you said it yourself. Take me to trial but I won't change my story."

"Theo, what are you doing?" Ryder calls from behind.

"You'll never get to him." Theo continues to challenge his old mentor. The men who restrain him are so loathe to be in contact, that he easily breaks away and gets into Veddie's face. Down below, students are now gathered around the staircase, looking up. Some are even reaching for the railing. Theo knows the advantage is his now. There are witnesses everywhere. There is no way Veddie can lock them away without notice. In fact, this is an opportunity to expose his old mentor for who he really is. "You are weak and small minded little man who has no control over himself. You have no power over me. You never did. Ryder is twice the man you'll ever be."

Veddie punches him right in front of the council and all the students watching from below. He hits him and hits him until his rings come away with blood. The room falls very silent as Veddie's fist finally slows. Theo's head hangs under a bruised and bloody brow. And even though he is wounded, he is surprised to find he is not hurt. Because, of course, Veddie cannot physically harm him. He can only effect the will. And Theo's will is much stronger than Veddie ever imagined.

Seeing an opportunity for escape, Theo launches to his feet and races down the stairs. Hands still bound behind his back, he reaches the library floor and slices through the students on his way to the door.

"Get him!" Veddie shouts, and this time there's something new in his voice. This time Theo hears fear.

Escape. He's never run like this before. He should be afraid but all he feels is exhilaration. He bursts out the courtyard, down the few steps leading up and then off into the street. Guardians are in hot pursuit. But he is nimble and wry, and running on pure adrenaline. He storms down the main promenade knocking down students and sending books and papers flying. He descends the street of steps like there are wings on his feet. Reaching the main road between the Victory arch and the forum, he frees his wrists and tosses the ties back over his head. He laughs as he continues, jumping over a fountain and catching his robe on hand of a statue situated in the middle of the crystal blue water. The robe tears from his body. He leaves it behind, running wild and free, naked through the street of the Reserve. He remembers his first jump, how ashamed he was of his body, how he tried to cover up even though no one could actually see him. Now he runs like a crazed nudist, body parts rippling in the wind, his thighs pumping in rhythm with his blood. He doesn't even see the reactions or hear the voices of his pursuers. All he sees is the road ahead, hears the slap of his bare feet on the marble walkway, the sound of his breath racing up and down his throat. He knows where he is going. He is not going to the forest. Angel is calling out for him, hungry for him. She wants to play too. And he is not going to leave her hanging. He feels like a wild animal set loose on the unsuspecting villagers, an animal beset by hunters, an animal with no fear that they'll ever catch him. He leaves it all behind as he reaches the city limits. He's getting faster now, crossing beneath the Victory arch with the Field visible in the valley below. I'm coming, Angel, he thinks, pursuers hot on his heels. But they won't catch him. They won't tame him. Not anymore. Ryder showed him that he is still wild and now he wants to embrace this beautiful monster he is becoming.

He rounds the open gates of the Field and splits a group of first years in two. They shriek and duck, the girls covering their eyes. One boy falls into a pool, swept away into an unassigned soul. He has no time for regrets, just keeps his feet pointed forward. Up the hill, then to the right, he sees the bench near the branch in the path. How he sat there and lamented after his first fall from grace. Now he is running gleefully towards his next descent.

He reaches the corner with the tree and takes a hard right. He passes between the hoarder and the old woman in the diapers and then dives into the pool mid-stride. His naked body stumbles for balance at the edge of the abyss while his soul soars down through the clouds. He stretches out his wings, his arms, his legs, feels the rush of air against his weightless body. He opens his mouth and laughs in the descent, feels on the brink of madness and embraces it fully. He crashes to the earth in the field behind Angel's house, crashes into her, into the mud and deep reeds of her cluttered back yard.

"I'm here," he whispers, "I'm here."

BANISHMENT

Chapter 24☙

Theo is dragged from the field. This time he is not taken quietly. He shouts belligerently at Veddie who hasn't looked back since the elders extracted him, wrestled him to the ground and took him into custody. Though he has not seen his reflection, he knows his darkness has returned. He is taken under guard through the streets of the Reserve. Classes are just coming out and he has a captive audience for most of his trip across town. He struggles the entire way, still raging on pure adrenaline from his escape and capture, and everything that happened before. The last time he had sex with Angel, he was full of regret, uninformed, and misled. Last time they pitied him, an overzealous youth who'd gotten in over his head. This time he knew what he was doing. He gave Veddie the exact excuse he needed to put him underground. There will be no testifying on Ryder's behalf. He will not be heard at all. He has no doubt about that.

They take him up the street of steps and then veer off the main road. He knows where they are going, to the place where Veddie always threatened to lock up Ryder: the vaults. The realization makes him fight harder but with so many guardians detaining him, he has little chance of escape. They bring him to where a lone man guards a long deserted alleyway. The guard unlocks the gate at the end of the alley and seems to smile when he steps aside. Theo stares at that gaping doorway, that dark yawning mouth leading into unknown, and panic begins to rise. He needs to escape before they lock that gate behind him. He's not going to have another chance once he's inside. He thrusts his feet downward and jams his heels into the ground. The men at his sides stumble at the unexpected brake. He twists from their grasp, darts between their legs and begins to run. The baffled men have barely even registered the breakout until Theo reaches the end of the alley. He chuckles and turns and then someone strikes him down.

The sound of the gate slamming echoes distantly. In his head, Theo is still running, fleeing into the labyrinth of the Reserve. But when he opens his eyes, he realizes that he's lying on his back in a stone cavern. He turns his head to the side and sees the alley, the guard, and finally, the firmly closed gate.

He sits up slowly and touches the welt on his head. He didn't see who hit him but he imagines it was probably Veddie by the ring sized ridges across his forehead. He thinks that he has never been hit so hard in his life. Well, except for the car accident that started this all. And perhaps the assault at the Book of Life gates. And even though there is no pain with this injury either, the tightness of his skin over the swelling mass is uncomfortable and his head feels like it is ringing.

He sits back slowly until his head rests against the wall of the cavern. The gate is secured with a lock and chain, a guard ensuring even the most clever will not get very far. A breeze wafts up from behind him. He looks down the cavern but can see nothing, hear nothing, not a whisper, not a voice, nothing to indicate what might be hidden in the darkness beyond. And there's a disconcerting smell floating up as well, like moldy, old bread. The cavern is vaulted on the top and lined with thin, decayed bricks. Below him, the cobblestones are cracked and missing large pieces. An old clay pipe runs down the center of the floor, partially submerged. He doesn't want to go back there. He could get lost. His head is slow and thick from the return of his darkness. He wants to stay by the gate but it is pointless. He can see no way of escaping from this door. David escapes all the time, so there has to be another way out.

Trying to remain focused on escape, he retreats into the tunnel, glancing back towards the entrance every so often to keep track of how far he's gone. The tunnel slopes gradually downward at a steady pace, never turning or branching off, just straight down. As he gets deeper, he becomes more nervous. The air is heavy with hopelessness and depression. It's like it is a physical thing weighing him down, like something he could catch if he isn't careful. He trails his hand along the rough wall as he walks, his fingers becoming thick with dust as he does. He wishes he could see something, anything to indicate where he is going.

Becoming increasingly unnerved, Theo stops. The light from the gate is just a pinprick now. It occurs to him that he could be walking himself right to the gates of Hell. Is that what this is? As hard as he strains, he can see nothing ahead of him. Where is he going? Why did he think this was going to lead somewhere? What if it just keeps going down? What if it goes nowhere?

He looks back at the tiny light, the only recognizable landmark he has. Maybe there was a turn off along the way, something he missed. How could he be walking so long and encounter nothing? He should go back, just to be sure. He turns around and begins to travel back towards the light. As he does, he carefully checks both sides of the cavern for doorways or hidden passageways. But it is the same chipped brick surface everywhere he goes. And behind him, the musty breeze seems heavier at his back.

He picks up his pace as the light gets nearer. Suddenly he needs to be back in the light. He needs something for his eyes to focus on. He keeps moving and the light becomes larger. Then, with an excited gasp, he realizes that there are no bars across the entrance. The door is open! He can run right out!

He begins to sprint now, though awkwardly with his swollen limbs and oversized wings. He feels bigger than last time he fell, more deformed. Even his hands are like thick gloves overtop his own skin. But he can't worry about that right now. Just escape. He rushes to the doorway, blinded by the bright light.

"What the fuck?" he whispers, stopping in the doorway. This is not the guarded gate he first woke up at. He is at the entrance of an underground catacomb, similar to the one he first visited with Veddie to face his judgment. Except this one is three stories high and far from glorious. Narrow walkways crisscross up the walls to span each story. And each level has a line of cell doors leading off as far as the eye can see. Theo only has to take one look to know that this is a prison. He looks back towards the dark passageway. He took no turn off, just walked straight back to the light. How is it he's arrived here?

He returns into the dark, runs madly now, sure that at the other end he will find the gate. He runs and runs but the tunnel just goes on and on. And that pinprick of light is no longer visible. Still, he knows logically that there is only one way in and, therefore, one way out. Perhaps it is night and the gate cannot be seen. He continues to run but finally slows, out of breath. He is too sluggish, a beast of a man now. He only has half the endurance he had before the fall. He rests against the wall, gasping. The only light he can see is the one he just ran from. If he ran towards it again, would he find the exit?

Seeing no other choice, he goes back towards the light, hoping that is the case. He jogs lightly, his heart strained and beating out of his chest. Even as he nears he can see that it is not the exit but the same doorway he just fled from. Should he go in? Maybe David escapes from somewhere inside. He is getting nowhere in this tunnel. Still, he feels a certain foreboding about voluntarily entering his own prison. He does not want to get trapped down below. Even if Ryder knows where he's been taken, if he is not in this prison already, how would he ever find him here? It would be better if he kept in the shadows and kept moving.

He peers inside from the doorway. It is a dank, awful place. Light dimly streams from portholes in the street three levels above. And above, angels walk over them, completely unaware of what's hidden beneath their feet. What street is the prison under? The road to the forum? Past the libraries? What a horrible thing to keep beneath the gates of paradise.

He looks up at the cells. All are closed and locked and he can see no one inside. No one walks the prison floor either. Not even guards. But he hears things. Moans. Cries. And feels the despair. Still peeking in the door, he glances up to the portholes, manholes that line the street three stories above. Unreachable. Nothing to scale or to climb.

Suddenly he is grabbed from behind. He howls as two guards take hold of him and then wrestle him to the ground. He screams echo up through the caverns, dust rising up in the dirty, slanted light. But it is a fight he quickly loses. They shackle his hands and his feet and then carry him up the catwalk towards the cells. The old structure sways and shakes as they ascend and Theo struggles more hoping it might collapse and give him an opportunity to run. But the walkway holds and soon he is dragged into a cell. They strike him, strip his shackles off, then his clothes as well and lock the door behind him. Theo lunges at the gate, grabbing for a fistful of guard but they pull away without a single word. They do not even speak to each other.

Gasping, Theo looks back at his cell. It's small, grey, with a hard wooden bed in one corner and a desk with no drawers in the other. At the back is a closet, empty, without even a hanger inside it. He turns back to the barred entrance and shakes it violently. He may be lumbering but he is also strong. He clamps his huge hands around the bars and tries to bend them outwards. Then he rams them with his shoulders. They are unmoved. And likely will not be moved without the assistance of a key. Dropping his head, he stares across the chamber to a man behind bars on the other side. He is not dark at all, but white as the angels above. He looks old and hard and stands with his face braced between the bars, unmoving.

There are no days or night in this prison, just the dim light of burning torches which barely stave off the eternal underground darkness. Being already dead, Theo does not have the needs of regular prisoners. There are no breaks for food, for bathroom, for exercise. Guards circle from time to time, nameless, faceless, and do not respond to shouts or protests. They simply check to see that all the doors are still secure and carry on. They do not even converse amongst each other. It is shockingly quiet most of the time except for Theo's heavy breathing and busy hands. He is in the grips of the fall now and he has no need or want to control it. His mind goes everywhere and anywhere it pleases. For a while he hides his activities in the corner of the closet, the only place in the cell that provides him any privacy. But soon he begins to venture out, becomes more bold, more daring. He lies on the bed in full view of his cell door and thumps his hips against his fist. Then he goes to the desk, opens his legs to the cell door and plays vigorously. Soon he begins to hope that someone will catch him, the way Ryder did when he ventured out into the courtyard of his house. But this time his fantasies are much dirtier, much darker. Shameful. Sinful. Even dangerous.

It goes on for days. For weeks. Until his palms are raw and his thighs blistered. Growing more sick and more brash every day, he now does it when the guards pass by, goading them to stop for a while, to watch or even join in. If one even glances his way, his excitement increases tenfold. He dreams of restrictive devices, tight little sleeves, anything he could slide himself inside of. He crawls around in his cell trying to fashion pipes and tubes out of bed springs and mud. Then shoves himself inside until the contraptions break into pieces. God, he wants to fuck. What he wouldn't do if he were let out of his cell.

He gets up one morning. Or evening. He really doesn't know which. Hearing the guards making their rounds, he seats himself atop his desk and opens his legs towards the door. He begins rubbing his raw flesh, sweat forming on his brow, his anticipation growing as he hears the footsteps grow closer. He is filthy. His chest smeared with mud, his feet so dark it looks like he's wearing black socks. His hair is thick and matted and his wings crusted with sludge. His cell reeks of lust, the walls, the floor, the bed, all marked with his sex. He is not focused on those things though, only on how he can get his next orgasm. What new twist will aid in his amusement. And then those few happy seconds of tension and release. He must do it twenty times a day. Thirty. He doesn't even know. He doesn't even care.

The steps come closer. Theo smudges his fingers up and down his shaft, pointing it out towards the cell doors. He imagines capturing one of them and buggering them. Or maybe both of them. First one and then the next. Or maybe he'll poke one while the other one does him. He sees a shadow approach his gate and that thin orgasmic lightning bolt rumbles up his penis. He pushes his hips forward, opening his legs wider. He can't wait for them to see. He wants everyone to see. He wishes he were on stage surrounded by thousands. All of them waiting in eager anticipation.

But as the owner catches up to his shadow, Theo's hand stops stroking. Standing at the cell doors is Veddie. Theo pulls back, closing his legs and turning to the side. He drops his head, folding his hands in his lap. Veddie looks over the cell, looks over Theo then turns back to the guard. "Just as I expected," he grumbles coldly. "Just as I always expected."

"What do you want us to do with him, sir?" one of the guards asks. "No one wants to check on him anymore."

"Don't do anything. Leave him rot."

Theo closes his eyes as his former mentor strolls away. Suddenly the veil is lifted. Suddenly he can see himself as other must see. The condition of his body. The shambles of his sickening room. Of his sickening life. He is repulsed by himself. By letting himself fall so far with no restraint. He is heavier and darker than he's ever been in his life.

Depression follows. A long, dark, endless tunnel of hurt and pain that makes even the thought of rising out of bed impossible. Like the lust that overtook him, he does little to restrain his feelings of hopelessness and regret. His fantasies turn to suicide but he is so overcome by listlessness that he would never complete the task. He curls in his bed day after night after day, shivering and naked. Some days, he does not move at all. Does not even open his eyes. Just remains in the darkness behind his eyelids, a prison inside himself. He can form no clear thoughts in his mind, fantasies begin and then fade with no conclusion. Some days, he thinks that he should get up, should try and find escape, but he never finds the strength to execute his plans. And soon he stops caring all together. Stops trying. Stops hoping. And eventually stops dreaming too. He will become like the guardian who stands with his face eternally pressed between his prison bars. The guardian across the prison from him who, even though his darkness has long faded, remains forgotten in this place by whoever put him there. Was it Veddie? Or are there others hiding their failed projects down below? This seems to big an operation for just one man to orchestrate. Whatever it is, Theo has stopped contemplating why he is here or how he will get out. He has stopped contemplating everything.

One day, he is jarred from his bed by a loud clack. He turns his head with a groan and sees that his cell door is open. Open. He tries to remember why he wanted the door open but it is unclear now. He rolls back towards the wall and tries to fall asleep but that open door keeps nagging at him. Open is important, but why? He can't remember why.

"Come now," a voice booms through the quiet cell. Theo gasps and turns towards the voice. Looming over his bed is the disfigured outline of David. The hulking beast tosses a robe at him. "Can't let them win so easily, can we?"

Theo stares up at him in utter confusion.

"Get up," David says. "Or do you intend to die down here like the rest of the vermin?"

Theo sits up slowly, feeling like he's had an overdosed of sedatives. His head is a thick cloud, his eyelids so heavy he can barely open them. He slides his stiff legs over the side of the bed. He is streaked with mud from ankle to hip. He has abrasions and sores around his pubic area. His hands are chapped with blisters. He can't remember the last time he ate or drank or spoke.

Shuddering, he pulls the robe over his shoulders and leans forward on his knees. He cannot even get his fingers through his hair. There is a sandy grit across his forehead and the bridge of his nose. His body aches like he's been tumbling down the side of a mountain since he arrived.

Door. Open. Door. Open. It keeps repeating in his head until he slowly rises and plods towards freedom, not even sure why he is going there. He steps out onto the flimsy walkway, feeling it sway beneath his feet, or maybe he is the one who is swaying and the walkway is standing still. Only a thin bar keeps him from toppling three stories down. He grips the bar and looks over the edge, a rush of blood going to his head. Feeling faint, he presses back against the wall, spotting that white angel standing at his cell door. He stares blankly forward, not even blinking.

Trying to remain focused, he moves toward the stairway. He proceeds down the catwalk feeling as if his arms and legs are filled with concrete. Peering above him, he can see light and dust drifting down from the storm drains. A whole city of sinners hidden beneath the feet of divinity. Secrets the elders don't want the others to know. People thrown away and forgotten, left for dead. If only they could die. He's shocked by the magnitude of it. Of how far the elders will go to maintain their perfect world.

He continues across the ground floor of the prison. He can hear quiet murmurs from above. Silt raining from the ceiling settles in his matted hair. David is ahead, turning down that same corridor he first entered through. Theo forces himself to move faster, worried he may be left behind. They continue down the dark hall and then come to an intersection. There were certainly no intersections when Theo came down this hall. They go right and enter a large, underground cavern. It is dark and musty, with a few tendrils of light escaping through cracks in the earth. The rays cast light over an old fountain. Theo goes to stand on its edge. It's broken and dried up and at the center is a Cherub lifting a fish towards the Heavens. But the cherub is missing its head and the fish is laced in cobwebs.

Confused, he turns around and David is nowhere to be found. He rushes towards the hallway and bumps into him standing quietly in the dark.

"Lost, my young friend?" he says. "This is not the way out."

"So, where is it?" Theo asks dully, pins and needles forming in his arms and legs. He is suddenly very thirsty and wishes the old fountain were working.

"Where it's always been," David returns coyly, his voice deep and very loud in the empty cavern. He cranes his head up towards the fissures in the ceiling, cracking his thick neck as he does.

Theo frowns at the oversized, deformed angel. "So, where is the exit?"

"It is nearby," David says with a sway and a smile.

Theo's eyes go dark. He feels the sharp edge of agitation returning. "So why don't you let me out?"

"I did let you out," David chuckles. "Why, we are out right now. Free. On our own command."

"Yes, but I need to get above," Theo insists, pointing up to those cracks in the ceiling. "Where is the way out?"

"In time. You are not ready to leave yet." David just smiles, looking down at Theo with red-rimmed, yellow-centered eyes. It seems David freed him just to make a point. He holds the keys to their cells. He knows the way out. And he will only gain freedom when David decides to let him go.

Chapter 25ଔ

Beset by exhaustion, Theo curls up in a corner of the cavern and naps furtively. It is very dark in the room and unlikely he would be found even if someone made a pointed search. Knowing that, he still sleeps restlessly. David said the exit was nearby. So he will search as soon as his strength has returned. But right now he is so overcome by fatigue that he could not stand if he wanted to.

He sleeps for hours, maybe days, until his head begins to clear a bit. Unlike the last time this happened, he now knows the stages of the fall. The lust. The depression. The loss of self. Though he is still victim to the symptoms, he is not as confused as he was the last time. He knows that the affliction will fade and soon he will feel like his normal self. Likely it will take longer than before as he is more troubled than the last time. And his physical body is much more deformed. He can only imagine what he looks like now.

Days go by, more days with the tiniest shafts of light spindling down through the walls to indicate the rising and setting sun. He sleeps when those spindles go away and searches for the way out when they are back. He continues to hide in the fountain room, though it is darker than his actual cell. His cell. He shudders to remember it and the things that happened in there. He wishes he could bathe, could wash away the memories from his stint into madness.

More troubling, he cannot hear Angel and worries something has happened to her during his fall. He has no sense of her emotions. He cannot hear her writing. Ryder said that they can't take her away from him but they are indeed separated now. Perhaps it is his own darkness that is causing the rupture between them. Or perhaps she is already dead.

Save the Date completed and Angel processed and rejected from the Reserve. Taken back the way she came to some unknown Hell he is likely also bound for.

He shouldn't have slept with her again. But he descended right into her open arms. Right into her open legs. And in the state he was in, there was no turning back. He might have been able to hide in her Light had he not succumbed to temptation again. If he hadn't been so blatantly unaware when that ringed hand came out of the sun for the second time.

He worries about Ryder too. Veddie threatened to send both of them to the vaults so he could be down here too, trapped in one of those hopeless cells. He wants to go back and search for him but is terrified of being caught. Sure, David could free him again, but he could also choose not to. It seems he is going to spend his entire tour through the Reserve under another man's control.

Sometime later, he wakes to find David standing near his sleeping corner. He is his usual saucy self, somehow retaining his perverted brilliance despite his fall. "Still no luck?" he croons, stretching his arms out so he appears crucified beneath the cracks of light.

Theo sits up slowly, rubbing his sore neck.

"I have something to show you," David continues. "I think it may interest you."

The tiniest glimmer of hope enters his body. The way out? It might be. He rises from the floor like a ninety year old man, his legs and back cramped and tight. "All right, let's go."

Theo follows behind David, shaking the cobwebs from his brain. They enter the hallway that he's been avoiding for weeks. The hallway that should lead directly to the outside gates, to that long alley with the guard standing outside it. Somehow that exit has disappeared.

David turns and begins to walk towards the prison and then stops about mid-way up the hall and pushes on a section of the wall. To Theo's surprise, the hallway turns, like a train changing tracks. Now the pinprick of light that leads to the left, to the prison, appears on the right. That is how they did it.

Once he got far enough in, they turned this section of hallway like a revolving door and no matter how long he searched, he would not find the way out. Theo lunges towards the light but David catches his arm.

"That is not the way," he says and pushes the secret door again. The intersection turns again and now there is no light at all.

"We are not the only secrets they hide down here," David says as they continue in total darkness. Following the sound of David's feet, Theo pats his way along dusty stone wall until he sees another light in the distance. His heart leaps at the sight of it. The way out. Finally. But as they get closer, Theo realizes that they are not approaching an exit but a room lit by torches.

"I thought you were taking me out," he says angrily as they enter an octagon room, a door set in each plane. The room seems to be of some importance. The floor is a mosaic mirroring the geometric shape of the room. The doors in each plane of the octagon are finely crafted.

"Once you see this, you may decide to stay below." David takes out a ring of keys and stands in the middle of the room. Words are written above each portal but Theo does not recognize the language.

"I seriously doubt that," Theo says, looking around. He doesn't like this room. It's heavy and oppressive. It feels like they shouldn't be in here, like this is a forbidden place.

"Do you?" David grins. "Are you sure about that?"

"Yes!" Theo shouts back at him. "Stop playing games with me."

David cracks the fingers of his left hand and then his right, snaps each one in such a slow manner that it could drive Theo mad. "I come here when I'm in the mood for a good jest. Religion is a finely crafted art, you know? Designed rather than created."

Theo exhales, angry that David has misled him. It seems he will not be getting out any time soon.

"Go ahead. Choose a door. You will not be disappointed."

Theo snatches a torch off the wall. Fine, he will play David's games. But only in the hopes that it will earn his trust.

He points the door nearest to him. David titters and indicates he open it. Inside, there is a storage room with books inside.

"Storage," Theo says, pulling the door back closed.

"Not just storage. You must look harder than that if you want to see the truth."

Theo rolls his eyes with another frustrated sigh. He reopens the door and enters. The room is filled with dusty book shelves. In the center, is a table with several scrolls and sheets of parchment laid out on it. The table is streaked with ink marks, chips and stains. Around the exterior of the table, the floor is intensely scratched, as if chairs have been frequently dragged around it.

"The Gnostics," David calls from the octagonal room where he still standing in the middle like the center spoke that turns the wheel. "Amongst other titles you might have missed along the way. You see, they let us read only what they wanted us to read. But there were more texts before the interference."

Theo skims over the table seeing the gospels of Thomas, Mary, Truth, Phillip, and Judas. He's dimly aware of their existence. Hoaxes, he was told, scrolls dug up in the eighteenth century or something. Nothing he had any particular interest in at the time nor is does he find the revelation very engaging right now.

"Jesus was married, of course. Just like his mother, that blessed, little virgin. There is no such thing as immaculate conception. They just wanted to separate sex from religion. Because it's so dirty," David finishes with a smile.

Theo circles the room, illuminating the many titles in all sorts of different languages. Perhaps if he was in a different situation, he might be interested in exploring the room more but right now his main concern is still escape.

"That is only the beginning, of course. The bible was edited down to what *they* believed religion should be. But it is not the whole of it. The truth would put an end to the church's domination. As all things, they saw an opportunity for power and they became corrupt. Men are such insecure little creatures, don't you think?" David chuckles.

He supposes it could be true. After what he's been through lately, he's not as devout as he once was. Had this been shown to him a few years ago, he would've burned the room to the ground. Now it sort of makes sense. There may be religion but it had to be filtered through man first. Like that game when you sit in a room and pass a phrase from one person to the next and by the time it reaches its conclusion, it is almost unrecognizable.

He exits the room, shutting the door behind him. He'll mention it to Ryder once he's free. Perhaps he already knows. That wouldn't surprise him either.

"Chose another one," David offers like a girl showcasing sports cars. "I think you will like what you see."

Theo sighs and goes to another door. He really doesn't care about all this right now. His only hope is that one of these doors leads to the outside. So perhaps his reward for playing David's games will be freedom after all. He enters another storage room full of dusty books. Except these books are not gospels but from the Life section of the library.

"Why are these down here?" he asks moving closer, brushing away names now concealing in dust. Is this where they store the books of the ones who are rejected? The ones who fail judgment and are taken away by Malik?

"They are our books, of course," David calls from outside the room. "And other failures that have been neatly swept beneath the carpet. Part of the way they make us disappear. Things go wrong and they conceal our very existence. They hide our Life books. One must keep the gates of Heaven neat and tidy."

One book in particular catches his eyes. It is new and obviously recently placed. He goes to it and finds own Life book. Across the cover are the words: Theodore Duncan. It hits him hard. They intend him to remain down here until no one from above remembers him anymore, to stay until he ceases to function like that guardian with his head against the bars. He picks up the book and dusts off the cover, his dander up now. The hidden gospels were mildly interesting but this room has him very upset. There are lots of books here, lots of names and guardians that the Reserve has disappeared. But where are they now? All hidden in these vaults? Because David is the only fallen angel he has ever seen above.

He stomps towards the door but on his way out, he sees something else, something that shakes him to his very core. Angel's book is down here too. He takes the book, furious, his blurry mind now firing at full capacity. It's one thing to banish him, but why is Angel being swept to the side as well? Has he damned her by mere association? Or, even worse, is she dead already? He returns outside to where David still remains in the center of the room swinging that key ring full of secrets on the end of his finger. It is obvious from the look on his face that he's enjoying himself.

Theo tucks the two Life books under his arm and goes to the next door. Only six doors left. He is now more determined than ever to get to the surface. No books behind door number three but mannequins and old statues heaped together in a room. There are so many that he cannot even step inside. He glances back at David who is smiling and pointing eagerly at the room. He looks back inside, unsure what the significance of stored lawn art might be. But then he notices that all the figures stand in the roughly same poses with their hands at their sides, their eyes closed and heads tilted slightly down. He opens his mouth to speak and then pauses as something flashes into his mind. The way the guardians look when they descend into soul pools. They stand with their hands at their sides, their eyes closed and their heads tilted slightly down.

"Oh my god," he whispers, stepping back from the room. "These are guardians?"

"Were," David says, rather amused with himself. "Lost in the Dark."

Theo stands for a second, trying to process what he's seeing. "So their souls became lost helping a charge and..."

"They gave up the search. Their bodies were tossed in here. Certainly we cannot have so many soulless shells lurking around the Reserve. It might frighten off new recruits."

Theo looks back into the room, horrified. It's not just that they're dumped here but the unceremonious way they are tossed together, like old rakes in a garden shed. Some are upside down, arms and legs tangled together. What disturbs him most is that some are chipped. Some are even broken. The search for them not only forgotten but abandoned. And somewhere, down on earth, all of these guardians are lost outside their charge's Light. He remembers what the Dark was like, horrifying even for just a few seconds. He can't imagine being eternally trapped in that living hell. This is supposed to be Heaven. How can something like this be happening?

He closes the door slowly, trying to process what he's just seen. It's outrageous, criminal, and now he needs to escape, not only for his own freedom, but to expose what going on down here.

The next rooms are not as engaging. They contain banned religious and erotic art, goddess materials, records of crimes the church and its followers have committed, and any paintings or sculptures that made use of the swastika before that symbol was inherited and defiled by the Nazi's. Nothing engages him the way the second and third door did. It seems this octagonal room is the hub of all the Reserve's dirty secrets.

He looks at the final door. David is jittering with excitement. The keys jingle in his hands as he shakes. Theo opens the door and inside is a short hallway and a ladder leading up to a manhole cover. The way out. He lurches forward but David catches his shoulder.

"Do you plan to give us all away?"

Theo pauses glancing up at the brilliant rays of light penetrating the manhole and hears the rush of busy feet above. He can't leave now. Everyone will see. And though this room and the prison desperately need to be uncovered, he must act carefully. He must get some powerful people on his side before he dares expose what Veddie and his council have been up to.

"It is best to keep our activities under the cover of darkness," David advises, guiding him away from the ladder.

"Why is it here?" Theo asks, indicating to the last door which David has now closed. "Wouldn't people start asking questions if they uncovered a locked door in a room under a drainage cover?"

"Many of the elders do not want to travel through the vaults to get here. So, this entrance was built for easy access."

David explains. "And as far as you young ones are concerned, you are too busy gazing upwards to notice what is going on right below their feet."

Theo reluctantly steps back from the door though he is extremely eager to leave this place. "Then I will wait here until nightfall."

Theo remains in the octagon room, worried that if he leaves he may never find the secret door again. David said that guardians rarely come into the room during the day, simply because they will be spotted descending through the manhole. As far as they know, none of the prisoners have discovered the secret turn in the hallway. And even if they did, one would also need keys to escape. But somehow David has acquired both. Even with David's assurances, Theo jumps at every creak and shuffle, thinking that the door will swing open and Veddie will be behind it. Also making him nervous is that room full of empty shells. Guardians carried off the field and tossed into a storage room, hidden away from the Reserve like the rest of the fallen angels. These angels committed no crimes, except doing their duties and having the misfortune of stepping outside the Light. How many of them are there? Wandering around in the dark abyss, hoping and praying that rescue is coming? He will never forget the hopelessness of being lost just a few days and he wasn't even lost in the Dark. Perhaps that is what hell is. Perhaps that is where the people who are rejected go. Not into some flaming pit but dropped back down into earth's blackness. To be forever forgotten.

He checks the door to see if it's dark yet. Light still pierces through the holes in the manhole cover. He tries to remember where he saw drainage vents while walking around but his eyes were rarely cast down to the street. This place was so magical on first arrival. In some ways, he wishes he could regain that innocence, to have his old self and his belief system back. But to do that would require ignorance of all the atrocities he's discovered along the way.

Shaking his head, he returns to the musty room full of forgotten Life books and sits down at the table in the center. He places his and Angel's books down in front of him. He looks down at the covers, both as different as the owners. He opens Angel's book first. He runs his hand over her name written on the very first page. It's written in scrawling script, muddy with thick lines. The first thing he does is flip to the end, and much to his relief, he finds that the narrative continues. He doesn't know why he can't hear her but she is alive and okay. He goes back to the beginning. Angel, born to Karen and Sean. She is the second of four children, her sister is the middle child and the youngest, twins, were stillborn. Her parents were on the poor side of average, both coming from challenging backgrounds. Things were okay at first. They played at family for a while. Had meals around the table. Birthdays and Christmas parties. Every year they had these reunions and all the extended family would get together. There would be kids and bonfires and food on the grill. That's when the drinking started, through family communion.

Angel was never popular in school, not even before her father's crimes. She kept mostly to herself lacking the social skills to make bonds with others. When she was young, she stayed close to teachers, and remained unnoticed by the other students. But in her teens, her family transferred to the town she lives in now. They moved away from the family and the reunions. The only thing that remained from the early days was the drinking. They became isolated, her mother miscarried, and the family started to fall apart.

Theo is surprised to learn that her father's hit and run was not the first time he had gotten behind the wheel drunk. In fact, he drove drunk probably two or three times a week, sometimes picking up Angel from school while completely intoxicated. He would drive her home and she would cling to the far side of the vehicle praying that no one would get in their way. He was stopped by the cops three times with minor penalties. And each time he was caught, it would stop the drinking for a while. But eventually it would always start up again.

Their lives revolved around her father's behavior. Everything had to be adjusted to Sean's moods and manners. He hated noise. The smallest sound would send him into a rage. A chair leg dragging across the floor. The bathroom door closing too loudly. Even the girls talking quietly in their room could bring on a tantrum. He would storm into the room screaming at them to shut the fuck up, just for talking. As a result the house became silent as a tomb. There was no music allowed. The television could be on only if the sound was on the lowest possible setting. Just one notch above mute. And this was only one of his many anxieties. The family spent all their time and energy trying to figure out ways to keep him calm and under control. It consumed their lives. Angel was the only one who couldn't seem to accept the insanity of the situation. She was the only one who dared challenge their status quo.

Things were bad but they weren't unbearable. Angel met Beatrice Yu in seventh grade. Bea was ostracized for being Asian, for being too short, for her stiff black hair which the kids called greasy, and for the unidentifiable things she brought in her lunch. Their friendship seemed to form out of necessity but continued due to compatibility. The union boosted Angel's spirits. Made her think things might be okay. At least there was one other person in the world who was similar to her.

Then the boy came into their lives. The boy Sean ran over after a particularly good bender. He stumbled out of the bar and spent a full ten minutes trying to insert his key into someone else's truck. His head drooped forward sleepily as he finally realized his mistake. The only time life was bearable was when Sean was drunk. For the father and the family. Sean would pass out in the living room and be unconscious for hours and no amount of slamming doors or screeching chairs would rouse him. And the vice-grip he held on the family would release for a while.

Sean found his truck and turned the engine over. He accelerated against the concrete divider in front of him before realizing it was there and then put the truck into reverse. Reaching behind the seat, he pulled out another beer from his emergency stash and wrestled the cap off with his teeth. He took a swig and then tucked it between his legs.

It was late, thankfully, dark, and the streets are mostly deserted. Every time a vehicle met him, he would squint his eyes against the blinding light until tears broke down his cheeks. He drove straight through red lights, not even seeing them there, kept crossing over the middle line and then overcorrecting and almost hitting cars parked on the other side of the road.

He didn't even see the boy. His beer tipped and slopped all over his lap. Cursing, he snatched up the beer, his focus down. There was a thud. Nothing significant. Just a thud. He looked up groggily then went back to the business of his tragically wasted road beer. Perfectly good drink gone to waste. He was furious.

What follows is already well known to Theo. It has made Angel the outcast that she is today. It's hard to read. He can't imagine what it was like to live. Angel never had a chance. She was cursed from the day she was born. Cursed with her family. Abandoned by the guardians. Her book is small and tattered compared to his grand narrative. It is wrinkled with neglect, edged in dust and more the size of a child's diary. And most disturbing is how many pages remain, maybe twenty or so left to fill. Not many left. Her end is already decided. Angel said once that suicide is her destiny. Perhaps she was right. Because this book does not have enough pages for her to change her mind and live a long and fulfilling life.

He closes the book and sets it aside. He goes out and checks the manhole again. Still daylight. He returns to the storage room and slides his own book in front of him. He started the narrative in the library then got sidetracked by Ryder's book. And then got sidetracked by the man himself. He had few concerns about himself when he opened his book back then. He was pretty certain he knew everything about himself that needed knowing. Now he is more nervous about the contents that lay before him.

Theodore Duncan. He had goals not dreams. There were things he was going to do, he knew he was going to achieve but he was never passionate achieving those successes. As a teenager, he was popular. He went to a nice school, got excellent grades, and was pretty normal. But Theo notices something he was oblivious to before: the women. Girls watching him, trying to approach him. Friends of his friends who held secret crushes for him. And how his cold heart passed over them. Like they didn't even exist. In fact, he had no women friends at all. While his buddies were masturbating wildly in every corner of their houses, he was reading theology books and meticulously studying for exams. And he definitely thought he was superior to everyone else. In his memories, he saw himself as humble because that's what a good religious boy would've been, but it's pretty obvious that he regarded himself very highly in comparison to other people. A chosen one. Not unlike the chosen son. Someone who has come to save this broken world, round up all the lost sheep and lead them into salvation. What did he think he was, the messiah? It wasn't all his fault; he can see that now. He was being coached by his parents, his community, and his church. He was set into religion like an arranged marriage. Baptized before he could speak. Communion before he could think. Bible school as a kid, choir and bible studies and religious concerts as a teen, and university training as a young adult. He sat there all bright-eyed and bushy-tailed soaking up his orders like a sponge. From the very beginning, he believed absolutely. Why wouldn't he? It's the way it always had been. And he had no reason to question of any of it.

He reads on, becoming more disheartened as he goes. He thought he was a role model to others, that everyone looked up to him. But a lot of his friends mocked his uptight behavior. Lots of people called him Mr. Roboto behind his back. He didn't really do anything important when he was alive, just prepared for some missionary quest overseas where he was going to save the unworthy savages. Something he was keen to mention every chance he got. Look what I'm doing. Correction, what I'm *going* to do. When the time is right. When opportunity presents itself. But there were opportunities all around him that he chose to ignore. He walked right past people in need in his school, every day. People just like Angel. What a self-righteous, self-centered fool he was. His education and his religion were both excuses to serve his own fragile ego. He wasn't really religious, he was just following a credo. He liked the way religion sat on his shoulders. From his high vantage point, he could look down on the others, all the underachievers, the fallen masses. Perhaps the most shocking of all was to see how his parent so blindly signed him up for a belief system that they themselves knew virtually nothing about. Had voodoo been the norm, then he'd be poking pins into a paper doll instead of signing the Stations of the Cross. They went to church and said the words, attended meetings and put money in the pot. They were securing a place in Heaven but there was no fundamental belief system behind it. Of course, he studied and read and knew his religion inside and out but he never thought to question the study materials themselves. He thinks of all those edited books of the bible in the next room over condensed by man to serve his own means. He would've died for this religion. But what is his religion really?

People were trampled by his arrogance, people he didn't even see. A girl in his Chemistry class sat behind him every day. She was so fond of him and it took her forever to approach him. He was on his way to a lecture series when she stepped in his way. He was curt and impatient with her. She was an obstacle blocking his path and nothing more. She was devastated by the rejection but he never noticed. He never noticed anything. He's shocked to see that his behavior hurt his mother too. He was cold and withdrawn with her, setting her aside like all the other women in his life. His own mother. Why didn't he ever see that?

He comes to his dismal end. To his untimely death. It was Halloween night. His bad friend, Buddy, used to hate to drive with him. He used to complain about the horsepower wasted when Theo was behind the wheel of one of his father's luxurious vehicles. Man, if I had this ride, I'd leave some rubber on the road, he used to complain. This night was no different than any others. He was driving Buddy home. He stopped at a light. It turned green. He pulled cautiously forward. Then they were t-boned by a dump truck. It split the car in half, ripping the front seat from the back. The cab, with Theo and Buddy still inside it, spun through the intersection and wrapped around a pole. Theo's hand remained on the wheel but the rest of his body was torn asunder. Buddy was on the better side of the wreck, he was rescued by strangers before the car went up in flames.

Theo turns the page and stares at the empty pages that follow. He thumbs through the blank sheets, hundreds of them uncompleted. Unlike Angel, it seems he was meant to live a much longer life. His was cut short before his time. Maybe there were things that he could've done along the way to prevent what happened. Whatever it is, his book will remain unfinished.

Chapter 26ଙ

Theo checks the manhole again and this time no light shines through. His heart begins to pound. Escape, finally. How long has he been below? He has no idea. It could be weeks or even months. Time travels so different on the Reserve. He gathers his books and cautiously lifts the manhole cover. The street is deserted. He sets his books up on the street first, then climbs out after, carefully returning the vent cover back in place. He's surprised to see he's on the main road between the forum and the Victory arch. Hard to believe this glorious boulevard is hiding such a nasty secret underneath. He notes the location of the manhole before sprinting off into the nearest alley. He's on Heaven's most wanted list now. If any of the elders were to spot him, then the chase would be on. And he's not sure he could outrun them this time. During his last chase, he was completely healed, his body and joints back in their proper proportion. Now his knees are thick and his feet are like clubs. The span of his wings seems twice as wide, cumbersome and very heavy. He cannot allow himself to be seen, not by anyone.

His first destination is the house of Ryder. If Ryder is not there, then he will hide until someone he can trust arrives. Maybe one of his students. Find out if Veddie was able to make Ryder disappear too. It would not be so easy to put his popular mentor down. Hundreds of students would be out searching the streets for him. But he has no doubt Veddie will try. And if there's a way to have gotten Ryder locked up in the vaults, then Theo will have to go back down and find him. He really hopes that is not the case.

At the House of Ryder, he peers in the windows for the usual crowd of students. There is no one inside. Not that unusual for this time of night. He enters the quiet house and searches all the rooms but finds them empty. Reaching the courtyard, he pauses to stare up at the starry sky. It seems like years since he's seen it. Or breathed the cool, clean evening air. He closes his eyes and fills his lungs. He's never been so happy to be free in his life. To just walk outside. Or shower.

Shower. He knows there is urgency afoot but twice as urgent is the need to clean his filthy body. He exits the courtyard and takes the first right into the large shower room. Inside, water sprinkles eternally down in dozens of little spouts mounted on the ceiling. It is as if the room is raining. He drops what remains of his clothes and stretches out his arms, tilting his head back. Mud flows off him in rivers, black snakes of sin and decay slithering towards the drain and disappearing. He opens his mouth and lets the water run down his throat. He turns his head and lets it fill his ears. He brings out the soap, rubbing it through his hair, now matted into a helmet. Then he washes down his body. And then rinses and then does it all over again. Maybe three or four times before the emotional grime has washed away as well as the physical.

From there, he pads naked down the hallway and puts on one of Ryder's robes. It carries that musky scent that used to repulse him when he first arrived here, but now he breathes it in eagerly. He's forgotten about all the trouble they were about to get into before Veddie interfered. Once everything has settled down, he hopes to get that started again.

Still under the cover of darkness, he leaves the house and heads down towards Ryder's office. The streets are deserted for now. He speculates about where the guardians go at night. None of them seem to have the need for sleep like he does and yet they are not roaming the streets. Is there a reason why everyone goes in at night? Is it because that's when the fallen angels come out to play?

He sees a light in the window of Ryder's office and is flushed with relief. He knocks softly on the door and enters. It's empty. Just a lantern left unattended on the windowsill, its fuel burned almost completely away. He glances out towards the greenhouse. It's the last place he's going to check before dawn. Then he'll need to find some cover during the day and decide what he is going to do. He takes the path to the hothouse, enjoying the feeling of the warm grass beneath his bare feet. The moon is out and seated high in the dark sky, casting a long shadow out in front of him. He thinks about his future here and if he still has one. He cannot return to classes or become a guardian. Or sit on the council with Ridwan and Malik. He is doomed to run with the likes of David, trying to stay one step ahead of Veddie and his angry councilors. He still regrets his loss of status here. And yet what he's learned down in the vaults makes him wonder whether he wants to be a part of this system at all anymore. Veddie, he can understand, but how could the council be condoning what's going on below? And how many more know about it and say nothing?

He enters into the musty heat of the greenhouse and breathes in the deliciously fragrant scents of petunias, thyme, ivy, and rose. The aisles are lit by tea lights that twist and play in the breezes from the ventilation fans. Plants spill down into the aisles. Potato vines. Sweet peas. Pumpkins. The leaves that weave across the floor create a soft mat for his feet to walk on. He breaks off a piece of chocolate mint leaf as he passes by and places it in his mouth. He is hungry, ravished now that something savory has touched his tongue. His stomach growls angrily and he plucks a cucumber off a nearby plant, brushes off the spikes with his fingers, and devours it in two bites. Then takes a sweet pepper and breaks it in half, shoving it quickly into his mouth. Then some plump strawberries. Only then does his stomach quiet a little.

He turns down the main aisle and comes to the bubbling fish pond at the center of the greenhouse. He sits down on the brick ledge and listens to the fish quietly nipping at the surface for a treat. Water, not once in his life had he ever been thankful for it, not like he is now. Weeks or months, or however long he was down below, he didn't drink a drop, never felt a splash of it against his face, had no way to clean himself off. Theo hoists his legs over the ledge and drops his feet into the pond. They sink down an inch in slimy debris before settling to the bottom. He can feel the gunk ease between his toes and a rush of fish encircle his legs. They kiss at his calves looking for food. Feeling saucy, Theo shrugs off his robes and walks to the center of the pond naked. He realizes now that no matter how the guardians try to control him, his mind will always be free from this point on. There is nothing they can do to stop that.

He turns in little circles watching the fish follow his trail, his wings extending slightly out. He makes another revolution, and when he comes around, Ryder is standing there.

"Theo?" Ryder whispers incredulously.

Theo pauses, his hands outstretched. He can say nothing in reply. Just stares as his heart begins to pound. His mentor looks older, more haggard but retains his shiny white façade. Veddie did not banish him as hoped. But it looks like he has had an effect on him regardless.

"Shit," Ryder says, stepping into the water. He splashes across the divide and pulls Theo tightly against him. "I have been looking for you for so long."

Theo returns the embrace, surprised at how hungry he is for human contact. He clings to his mentor's body so tightly he can barely breathe. "How long have I been gone?"

"It's been a month," Ryder says against his ear. "Where were you?"

"In the vaults. In the prison in the vaults."

Ryder pushes him back to have a better look at him. "Are you all right? How did you escape?"

"I'm okay," Theo says with a smile. "Are you? What happened after I left? Did they banish you too?"

"Oh Veddie tried," Ryder says, tightening his hands on Theo's shoulders. "But Justine recanted her story. Said she was making up our affair to get back at me for rejecting her."

"Justine? Really?" Theo replies, surprised she would make that sort of sacrifice for the two of them.

"And by the time I got done with that, you were gone." Ryder shakes his head looking at him. Then he pulls him in and embraces him again. "I looked but I couldn't find you. They've changed the vaults since I was last there. They have so many tricks and traps. I searched and searched but I couldn't find my way to the prison."

Theo exhales a heavy sigh. It's so good to be outside, to be talking to someone, to be somewhere beautiful. "So, am I officially banished?"

"Officially?" Ryder says over his shoulder. "No, but if the others see that you've fallen again…well, they won't be so forgiving the second time around. You will need to stay out of sight until you are healed."

"I can do that," he sighs. It's better news than he hoped for. A couple months of hiding and he could be back in circulation again. Back to his studies. And back to Angel. Thinking of her, he says, "I can't hear Angel anymore."

Ryder steps back from him, looking concerned. "You can't hear her?"

"No, and I can't feel her either." He swallows hard. "I've got her book so I know she hasn't died, but why can't I hear her anymore?"

"I'm not sure." Ryder takes Theo's hand and takes him to the edge of the water. "I will look into it in the morning but, for now, we need to get you hidden somewhere."

Theo picks up his robe as he steps from the pool but does not put it on. Instead he flings it over his shoulder and continues to walk naked. His new body is not pleasant to look at, but Ryder doesn't seem offended by his appearance. He supposes he has seen himself in the same way many times before.

"Where should I go?" Theo asks, picking a few more cucumbers before they leave the greenhouse.

"Back to my house for now. Does anyone know you're above?"

"Just David. He showed me the way out."

"David," Ryder says with a long sigh.

"There's things you need to see, things I need to show you down in the vaults. I know another way in. You need to see what is happening down there. They're hiding stuff that…"

"In the morning." Ryder quiets him, reaching for his hand and taking him out into the frosty morning. "First, let's get you back home."

Theo sits at the breakfast nook. Sun is streaming through the lattice throwing brilliant white stripes across the small round table. Weedy, dry plants spill over the windowsills. Outside the air is still and cool, another spring morning on the rise.

He looks over where Ryder is preparing breakfast in the cluttered kitchen. He's not sure what his role on the Reserve will be now but he is happy with who he is becoming. He feels like he finally being his true self. At least with Ryder, he is. It's going to take a long time to repair the damage he did with Angel. His only mistake during the events leading up to his imprisonment was jumping down to Angel in such a passionate fury. He had to know what was going to happen. Now he is heavy and deformed and an outcast once again.

Ryder brings breakfast to the table and sets it down. It's Sunday, so the house is quiet and there is little fear of intrusion. Veddie and his thugs will be at mass. Today, there will be some peace and quiet to help him settle his nerves and decide what to do next.

"Looks good," Theo says, fumbling to get the tiny fork in his big fingers. Now that food is in front of him, he's famished. He's only ate a few pieces of fruit since he was banished over a month ago.

"Hungry?" Ryder asks sitting down across from him, looking amused.

"Starving," Theo says, shoveling in a mouthful of food. The eggs ignite against his tongue like tiny sparklers. He grabs a piece of bacon and shoves that in too.

"You never did get over it," Ryder comments, filling Theo's cup with tea and then his own.

"Over what?" Theo grabs a piece of toast and quickly butters it.

"Your need to eat or sleep. It's odd, that's all. You shouldn't have those urges after a few months. It just earthly habit and not hunger that compels people to keep eating and sleeping on a regular basis." Ryder slices his egg and neatly places a piece in his mouth. He slowly savors it, handing his food in a much more hospitable way than his companion. "Are those Life books?" he asks indicating to the two books on the table.

"Yes, mine and hers. I found them in..." He pauses, too impatient to finish his sentence. He inserts an entire boiled egg in his mouth. "...down below. Glad I did because it's the only way I can find out what's going on with her." He opens Angel's book as he eats and turns to the last written page. Script appears from the hand of an unseen writer. He's not sure why their bond has been broken, but at least he has the book, this can tell him what is going on with her, though not in the detail he could take in with direct emotional contact.

He scans the last few paragraphs. There is something wrong with Bea. Romeo and company pulled some sort of nasty prank on her. It seems they paid a boy to date her and dared him to take her virginity. Theo pauses, thinking back to that brownish boy Bea was dating when he was down below. That was all a prank?

"Is she all right?" Ryder asks, sipping at his tea.

"Yes," he says, irritated. Fucking Romeo again. What he wouldn't do if he could get his hands around that kid's throat. He imagines how it would feel if he broke every bone in Romeo's neck, snapped them like chicken bones. The image sends a flush of excitement through him.

"Not many left," Ryder comments.

"What's that?" Theo says, pulled out his disturbing revere.

"Pages, I mean," Ryder says, indicating to Angel's book.

"I know," Theo says with a hard swallow. "It doesn't seem fair. There's nothing I can do. Her end is already decided."

"You're right, it isn't fair."

"I have so many pages left over," Theo comments, returning to his breakfast. "It makes me wonder if I could've changed something before I died. If I made different decisions, then I could've finished off my life." He closes Angel's book with a soft thud.

"You have what?" Ryder asks, setting his cup down.

"You know, empty pages? Because my life was cut short before my time?" Theo says, looking thoughtfully into his mentor's eyes as they narrow, his face darkening.

"Empty pages? Can I see that?"

Theo glances at his exquisite book and is a bit hesitant to let someone else see how uninspiring the contents actually are. "I guess," he says, sliding it over. He supposes, of anyone in the world, he has the least to hide from Ryder.

Ryder opens the book and goes straight to the back. He fans through the glossy white pages, bereft of its story. He frowns deeply, his eyes flickering as if he can read some sort of invisible script written there.

"What's wrong?" Theo asks.

Ryder glances up. "I don't exactly know. But this," he points to the blank pages, "this isn't right."

Ryder leaves after breakfast and Theo retreats to his old room, reading Angel's book as it writes. She is at the Yu's house now. Bea is refusing to come out of her room. Her parent's have closed the restaurant and are talking to the police. The police don't think it's a police matter. Just some prank between kids. The Yu's think a bunch of boys harassing their daughter is no joke. They are shouting in Korean in the front room while Angel is tapping on Bea's locked door. Once again, when someone is in need, all of her own problems take a back seat. She comes to the rescue as quickly as she can. In her core she is the kindest, most caring person, but she will never see herself that way. Theo remembers the old guardian that accompanied them to the Halloween carnival. At the time, Theo was convinced that the old man had been placed there to spy on him. Once again, he was a victim of his own arrogance. That guardian was there for Bea. But how a callous old man could help a firecracker like Bea is beyond him. Seems they could match her up with someone more appropriate.

He sits back on the bed as the bells signifying the end of mass begin to toll. He wonders what happened after he left. Was there any fallout after the incident in the library? Justine saw them together but how many people did she tell? And did Veddie get any flack for beating him? He attacked him in a room full of students and everyone saw. He touches his face but if there were bruises, they healed long ago. It seems only right Veddie would be reprimanded. But this is Veddie. And apparently if you get high enough on the Reserve, you can get away with murder.

He stares down at Angel's book as the script pauses. He's disturbed that he can't hear her, that he can't even feel her emotions. And he's worried Veddie did something to sever that connection. But he doesn't dare go to the Field and get caught by an elder. For now he has to rely on Ryder who has gone out to do a little investigating on his behalf. He is going to check on Angel's pool and make sure nothing has been tampered with. And he is also going to enquire about Theo's book. He seems upset about all those empty pages and Theo doesn't know why.

He lies back on his old bed, absolutely exhausted. He didn't sleep much last night and has been napping in a stone corner three stories under the Reserve for weeks now. He relishes the feel of soft sheets and a supple pillow. He closes his eyes for just a few minutes and is asleep for the rest of the day.

"Wake up! Wake up!"

Theo squints his tired eyes open, feeling like he has been asleep for minutes instead of hours. His head is pounding. He tries to sit up but is too dizzy to rise. "What's happening?" he groans against the velvety folds of his pillow, his eyelids drooping again.

Ryder is holding a lantern over him. It's dark out now, the soft glow the only light in the room. "Get up! There isn't much time."

"Time for what?" Theo grumbles, running his hands over his face. He feels like he's been drugged. Ryder pulls him up to sitting but he slumps forward, unable to hold his own head up.

"What's wrong with you?" Ryder says setting the lantern aside.

"I don't know," Theo moans. "I'm just so tired."

"We have to go. Right now."

Groggily, Theo stumbles from bed and pulls on his robe. "Where are we going?"

"Just come with me. Hurry. Before Veddie finds out I know."

"Know what?" Theo takes a few unsteady steps into the hall and then leans against the wall for support. Ryder is already at the front of the house buckling his shoes. He helps Theo into his own shoes and then takes his hand and leads him out onto the street.

"Are you all right?" he asks as he pulls Theo along.

"I don't know," Theo says, shaking his head. "I just can't wake up. I'm so tired."

"The fall will do that to you. Come on, we don't have any time to waste."

"Where are we going?" Theo asks, struggling to keep up. "Is this about…"

"Shhh," Ryder says and pushes him behind a hedge. Down the road, he sees a few guardians approaching with lanterns in their hands. Ryder puts his light out and gets down lower.

"What's going on?" Theo whispers, finally feeling his balance return. His head clears a bit too. It was morning when he dozed off and now he can see another morning approaching on the horizon. Has he been asleep for twenty-four hours? No wonder he's so groggy.

"Just wait," Ryder says, his focus on those guardians. "I'll tell you when we get there."

"Get where?"

"Just wait."

Theo holds his tongue impatiently as the guardians near. The guardians are escorting a young woman into the Reserve. She must be a new arrival from the misty hill. But something is wrong with her. Theo squints between the bushes to see that she has blood on her clothes. And when she gets closer, he can see it comes from cuts on her wrists. A suicide. He gasps, his eyes darting up to her face, but the girl is not Angel. But one day it will be her. One day they will take her through the Victory arch covered in blood. And not all that blood will be her own. What will be her judgment then? Will they consider the bullying, the poverty, her family history? Or just send her straight to Malik? The sight of the young girl shakes him. She's Asian, like Beatrice Yu. Then with a few missed heartbeats, he realizes she *is* Beatrice Yu.

"Shit!" Theo says, bolting from behind the bush.

"Theo!" Ryder cries, making a grab for his arm as he passes.

Theo crashes out onto the street in front of the trio. The two guardians come to an abrupt halt, pushing Bea back as if she must be protected from him. One of the men drops his lantern on the street. It cracks and breaks, the puddle of fuel igniting into flames.

"Bea? Bea?" Theo says, grabbing for her. "What happened? What did you do? Did you do this to yourself?"

"Theo, stop!" Ryder shouts, coming onto the road. The guardians are backing away from Theo, looking very afraid. Ryder tugs at his arm, but Theo is a hulk of a creature now. Not even Veddie could physically overpower him. He wrenches his arm away and continues to call out Bea's name. Slowly, from between the shoulders of the men, she looks up at him. Her sadness turns to fright. She turns away and begins to cry, holding her bloody hands over her face.

"We have to go now!" Ryder says and this time Theo allows himself to be dragged away. He didn't mean to hurt her or to scare her, but Angel! What will happen when she finds out Bea is dead? Does she know it already?

"I have to go back," he says, turning to find Ryder in his path. "I have to get to Angel's book."

"I'm sorry, Theo, I really am, but this can't wait." Ryder pushes him forward. Theo resists and a fight breaks out. They brawl for a few minutes on the street of steps until someone comes out of their house and calls for help. That's when they both begin to run. They race up the street of steps and take the main road past the library. And though Theo urgently wants to get back to Ryder's house, back to Angel's book, he also knows he cannot be caught out on the streets like this. The sun is coming closer to the horizon. Long fingers of light are beginning to stretch across the sky. If Veddie gets word he's out, then the hunt will be on. So he follows Ryder as he crosses the river and heads up into the mountainside. There are only a few buildings tucked in the trees, mostly observatories and archives not open to the public. They run up the steep, narrow trail towards a white dome. It is semicircular and made up of hundreds of rectangular planes. Theo assumed it housed a telescope but notices now that there is no opening in the top. It is a completely sealed dome.

"I knew something was wrong when I saw your empty pages," Ryder says, slowing, out of breath. "But it took me a while to figure it out."

Theo just gasps and slows as well. He doesn't care about his book. Just what's going to happened to Angel when she finds out about Bea. It will devastate her. Bea's suicide might rocket her right to the end of her pages. He doesn't have much time. He needs to get to her pool and descend as quickly as possible, even if it means getting caught again.

"I always thought it was odd the way Azrael went after you," Ryder says, walking now, though quickly. He takes out a large key ring and begins to search through it, walking up the twisted path to the big, white dome. "I mean, she likes to bully new arrivals but I've never seen her so preoccupied with one person. I should've known when you told me about Angel though. I should've known something was wrong when you said she could respond to you. I mean the dead can't talk to the living. You exist on two different planes. But I didn't put it all together. Not until you told me about your book."

"What about my book?" Theo asks, looking back impatiently. He needs to get to the Field now. Whatever this is, it can wait. It is not as important as getting to Angel.

Ryder trips over a root and quickly rights his footing. "Those pages are your life. No more pages, no more life. You have only an allotted amount of time given to you. Like you said, there is nothing you can do to change that. Once you've died, your book is over. The pages are complete, full to the end. Your book is done." Ryder takes in a deep breath. "You said you died in an accident?"

"I was hit by dump truck."

"But did you die? Did you actually die?"

Theo rolls his eyes, groaning. "Well, I'm here, aren't I?"

"Are you?" Ryder says, stopping at the doorway to the dome. "I think you aren't supposed to be here, not for a very long time. The only thing that makes sense is that you are in a coma. Brain dead but your body is still alive. It's the only way you can be both up here and down there at the same time."

Theo stares up at his mentor who stands a few steps above him. "A coma? What do you mean?"

"You can't be extracted from the earth while alive. That's impossible. But dead, as you saw, you can be pulled out. Veddie did it when you were first stranded with Angel and again before you were imprisoned. And even that is a risky and rare maneuver. I don't think you were meant to die in that accident. I think you were supposed to recover and go on to finish your life. That is the only reason you would have so many unfinished pages left in your Life book. But Veddie took you early. He stole you from your life so you could join his elite minions. Like I've said, we've been waiting for you for a long time. Once Veddie won the contest for your soul, I guess he couldn't wait any longer. He saw an opportunity to take you out and he seized it. Then he covered it up. That's why he's been after you so ardently since you joined me. If anyone found out what he did, he'd be finished here. I've never heard of anything like this ever being done. I mean, if it's true...Theo, I think you are still alive."

Theo stares, trying to understand. Alive. Alive? He can't process what Ryder is telling him. It's just too much for his fallen mind to take in.

Ryder finds the key he is looking for and turns towards the lock. "If you were in an accident and emotionally damaged, then you would've needed a guardian. I'm betting you probably have a pool out in the Field. And if that's so, you might be able to go back."

Theo stands as Ryder snaps the bolt to massive white door open. Alive? Could it be? Somewhere, in some hospital, his body sustained by fluids and machines, his parents holding out hope against hope that one day their son will regain consciousness. And somehow, though he remembers little of them, he thinks his mother would never give up. For some reason, the impression remains strongly in his mind that she would do anything to keep him alive. And if he is alive, if he is in the Field, then maybe he can go back. And with a jolt of excitement, he realizes he could find Angel too. Not just hover around in her aura but talk to her, touch her, become a part of her life. He could drive right into that town, punch Romeo in the teeth, and take Angel away from that horrid place. The idea fills him with such a thrill but then he thinks about Ryder and this mess left behind with Veddie. How can he leave Ryder at a time like this?

"But what about Veddie? If he finds out that you know, then he'll come after you."

"Let's just find out if it's true. And if it is, then we get the right people involved to get you back where you belong," Ryder says opening the door to the dome.

Theo enters the observatory which is no observatory at all. The room is cool and dark, illuminated from all sides by a soft blue light. It is perfectly circular, the floor like glass and the walls mirroring the outside shape of the dome. In the center of the room is a large sphere hovering a few feet above the ground. There is nothing else in the concrete tomb. Just a yawning silence that seems to consume every sound. He opens his mouth to speak but his voice disappears before it even reaches his own ears.

Behind him, Ryder pushes the door closed. Though the door is a heavy steel monster, it makes no sound when it shuts. And neither do Ryder's feet as he crosses the floor towards the large orbiting sphere. He touches the globe and the earth appears on its surface, all the oceans and continents at his fingertips.

"Where did you live?" Ryder asks and Theo hears his voice inside his own head. Though his lips move, no sound escapes. The silence around him remains completely undisturbed.

Theo comes a bit closer, staring up at the earth orbiting in the middle of the room. "I don't know," he replies with no words, not surprised that he can't recall the city he came from. He wishes he had his Life book right now. And Angel's. He desperately wants to know what is happening with her.

The globe turns beneath Ryder's fingers though he does nothing to start the spinning. "We'll have to do a manual search then."

Theo looks up as an image appears on the outer wall, projected from a thin stream of light projecting out from the dome. Then another. And another. Until Theodore Duncan's from all over the world cover the walls of the room.

"So many?" he whispers, staring out in awe.

"Just the ones that are in the Field," Ryder clarifies. "I assure you there are many more Theodore Duncan's than the ones you see here."

"So what happens if I have a pool?" he asks, turning in a circle.

"You jump in. Reunite your body with your soul. I think it's that easy." Ryder turns away from the sphere. "Let's just find out if you're here."

Theo approaches the outer walls. Under each *Theodore Duncan* is a brief description of the person claiming his name. Age. Sex. Location. Level of need. And each is accompanied by a small picture like on a driver's license. He searches through old men, little boys, and a transvestite. What if his parents gave up hope and let his body die? It's been over a year, why would they still believe he could come back after so long? He skims through picture after picture, recognizing none of the faces.

"Here you are," Ryder says from across the room. "I found you."

Theo turns, his heart pounding. Ryder points to a picture and frowns back at him. Then his face breaks out into a smile. "You? Really?"

Theo comes to stand beside his mentor. He stares at his life in summary form. He looks so young. So blonde. So wide eyed and innocent. This is the body waiting for him down below, but the man inside is so greatly altered. What would it be like to go back? To get a second chance at life? He scans down the statistics alongside his photo. His name. His age. Where he lives. His level. Ryder's level, he thinks ironically. Maybe they would've crossed paths even if Veddie hadn't interfered. Male. Straight. He smiles a bit at the last one. Guess it hasn't been updated recently. And lastly, and what makes his blood race, his plot number in the Field. He is in the Field. He is still alive.

Chapter 27 ∞

"I can't believe it," Theo says as they leave the observatory. And he really can't. Not just that he's alive but that Veddie had the balls to pull him out of his life and thought he would get away with it. "What do we do now?"

Ryder locks up the observatory and the two men return towards the river. "We need to get you back to my house, right away before Veddie or the others find out. And, honestly, I doubt the council members who are supporting him have any idea you are a stolen soul. No one would stand for that. That crime is Veddie's and Veddie's alone."

"Home," Theo whispers, trying to imagine himself back on earth, back at his parent's house, back in school. The idea is a bit unsettling. He wishes he had more time to think about it. "Will I remember any of this?"

"It's hard to say. You might rationalize it as a dream. Or you might not remember it at all. I suppose it depends on how open-minded you were when you were alive."

Oh great, he thinks, that's encouraging. He doesn't want to forget this experience. And with a bit of panic, he realizes, he could forget Angel too. "Do I have to go? Do I get a choice?"

Ryder stops and turns back to him. "Why would you say that?"

"It just...what about Angel? I mean I have weeks before she tears that school apart. I can't just leave her."

"Yes, but time goes much faster up here. You've been here over a year but it doesn't feel like it, does it? That's because it's probably been only a few months since your accident. Essentially, you'll be traveling back in time. How much time, I can't really say. Since no one has ever been sent back to their body that I know of. But if you remember her, you will have time to find her."

Theo swallows hard, feeling his chest tighten. "What about you? What about the Reserve? I don't want to forget all this. I don't want to forget who I am now."

Ryder sighs, thumbing through the key ring. "I'm not sure that can be prevented."

Theo drops his eyes, suddenly feeling very hopeless. He thought he was gaining his freedom but he's actually about to lose everything. "I don't know if I want to go then."

"Theo," Ryder says, reaching for his hand. "You are still alive. You can't stay here."

Theo looks at his hand embraced in another man's hand. Down below, this will be an abomination to him. This will be a sin. He doesn't want to go back to that tight ass, small minded, little zealot he used to be. He feels like he's finally come into himself. He lifts his eyes to his mentor's face. "Will you still be here when I get back?" he asks.

"I will. And for me, there'll be little time passed until your return. But for you...well, you will be an old man when you come back. You may not even remember me."

Theo pulls Ryder close and hugs him. He stares over his shoulder at the glorious golden city realizing that this is probably the last time he's going to see it for a very long time. And even though the journey has been full of strife, he will miss everything about it.

"Don't give up hope," Ryder says over his shoulder, rubbing his hand along Theo's back. "You don't really know what will happen when you return. You could remember everything. You could find Angel and save her. Anything is possible now."

"I guess," Theo says as they break apart. He lowers his head and quickly wipes away a few tears.

"And if you ever come up in the Field, for anything, I'll be your guardian."

Theo smiles at that. "Really?"

"Of course."

"I thought charges were assigned?"

"Well I'm sure I can find a way around that." He makes a tripping motion. "You know how clumsy I am."

Theo accepts the promise, though he knows it could be a futile one. Who knows what will happen to Ryder after he leaves. This whole place is ready to explode, and most of it is his fault. He feels tremendous guilt at leaving Ryder right now.

"Come on," Ryder says with a pat to the shoulder. "Let's get you back to your body."

They have no choice but to travel the main streets. There's only one way to get back to the lower side of the city. They go past the library, the faculty offices, classrooms, all quiet at this time of the morning. They reach the street of steps without meeting a single person. Both men have moved from a jog to a sprint. They need to get somewhere safe and fast. They will need people on their side before Veddie finds out what they know. But they only get half way down the street of steps before they are ambushed by the council. Men step out on the street, blocking their exit. And more appear behind. Last to arrive is Veddie. He looks extremely pleased with himself.

"He is not allowed out on the streets," Veddie growls, looking distastefully at Theo. "He has been banished."

"Only by you," Ryder says, trying to sidestep him.

A smug look crosses Veddie's face. "And how, exactly, do you intent to bring *that* back into polite society? We all know what he did with that girl. It's a crime that should be punishable by death."

Ryder and Theo exchange a look. Veddie is only after them because Theo escaped. He does not know that they found out the real truth. It gives them time. All they need to do is get past Veddie and his men.

"Then take us to the council," Ryder counters, offering his wrists forward. Then more darkly, he adds, "Take us to the full council. We wish to speak with all the members."

"You have already spoken to the council and have been handed down your punishment. *You* may have escaped your reprimand but I will see that *he* rots in the dungeons forever." Veddie snatches up the wrists Ryder offers and then Veddie's men move in. They easily overwhelm Ryder but Theo is more unmanageable. He takes the first council member who approaches him down with a single thump to the chest. The second one he simply clamps his huge hand down on his face and shoves him back off his feet. He goes through the third and the fourth in much the same manner but his eyes are locked on Veddie. The other men are merely obstacles on his way to his true goal. He wants the kingpin, the headmaster who orchestrated his untimely death, the one who snatched him from his hospital bed and left his earthly body to die, the one who thought he'd found another drone to round out his perfect army. But his death never took. He can see that now. Part of him was still alive. He had to eat and drink and sleep like any normal living person. He was always in conflict. He never adjusted the way the others did. His death never felt real and now he knows why.

The closer he gets to Veddie, the more furious he becomes. As far as he's concerned, what Veddie did was murder. He killed him. Or he would've have if Ryder hadn't discovered the truth. Eventually his body would've died on earth and no one on the Reserve would've been the wiser. He crashes through the last council member and is surprised to see that he can stand eye to eye with Veddie. Not only is he bigger, he is taller as well, a hulk of man, twice the size he used to be.

"I know what you did!" Theo spits the words into Veddie's face while shoving an oversized finger into the middle of his chest. He shouldn't say it but is full of fury right now. And physically unstoppable if he chooses to be.

"Theo," Ryder whispers harshly, still being restrained by the last council members standing.

Theo doesn't heed the warning. He knows Veddie's ignorance is their advantage but he is just too angry to stop himself right now. "You stole me! You took me before I was dead! I know everything!" Theo shouts and the smug look on Veddie's face slowly drops away. "You can lock me away in the deepest, darkest hole you've got here, but I'll get out. And I'll see that you pay for this."

Theo watches with great satisfaction as all the color drains from Veddie's face. He can see that his old mentor had no idea they were on to him. In that moment of weakness, Theo sees an opportunity for escape. He launches forward but then something catches him from behind. There's a whistling sound and then a crack and then everything becomes silent.

When Theo wakes up, he is on the boulevard between the Victory gates and the forum. He is on his knees beside Ryder and they are both bound and gagged. The back of his head throbs from the unseen blow that must have knocked him out. Behind him, recovering from their wounds, are Veddie and his council. In front of him, backlit by the rising sun, are the remainder of the council members. Malik is there, looking more fierce than Theo's ever seen him. With him today are his crows but also a black wolf sways and growls on his left side. He hold a long crooked staff, his bruised fist clenched around the knotted wood. Azrael is there and no less frightening than her companion. Her serpent hair twists and lifts around her head. She is so angry that her light glows red. She stares at the two of them with her circling eyes, her head bobbing back and forth like a seized second hand clock. Along with them, he sees the twins from judgment and further back, hidden in the blinding light of the sun, the Holy Spirit. Ridwan stands to the side as well as other upper echelon members that he can't recall. Looks like the gangs all here, he thinks, staring up at them, but whose side are they on? His or Veddie's?

Veddie strides past the two bound men and gives a quick bow to the line of champions. "I have captured the fugitives," he says respectfully, gesturing back to Ryder and Theo. "They have injured many of our members during the foray."

Theo's eyes light up and he begins to struggle. Veddie intends to mislead Malik and the others and since both he and Ryder are gagged, they do not have an opportunity to explain their side. He tries to wrestle his arms free, which are both bound behind his back at the wrists, but tumbles forward in the dust as he does. He has to get his hands free and get his gag out. He has to explain to them what really happened. Because, as far as they're concerned, Theo is just a deviant, fallen angel and Ryder his partner in crime.

"Stay still," Veddie shouts, pulling Theo back up to his knees. "Show the proper respect in front your superiors."

Theo comes to an unsteady stop, a cloud of dust sifting down from his hair. He looks over at the Ryder and Ryder shakes his head, no. Stop fighting. Theo frowns at him and shakes his head as well. Doesn't Ryder understand how serious this is? How much trouble they are in if Veddie is allowed to narrate this story?

Malik and Azrael exchange a stern look, then the angel of death and the angel who guards Hell turn their gazes to the men facing them. "We know of your crimes," Malik growls, his voice rumbling the ground. "Now will begin a course of action to right the wrongs that have been done here. Kneel down."

Theo glances up at Hell's guardian, unsure of what to do. He is already kneeling. But the look on Malik's face makes him lower his head further, until face is against the street.

Azrael steps angrily forward. From Theo's vantage point, he can only see her bare feet as they thump across the stone street. But then they veer to the side to where Veddie is standing. Theo turns his head cautiously to the side to see Azrael standing in front of Veddie with her hand on his shoulder. "Malik told you to kneel," she whispers venomously and her snake like fingers tighten on Veddie's shoulder. Theo sits back on his knees, watching in shock as Veddie buckles down to the ground. "Kneel!" she screams at the rest of them, her voice shrill like a banshee. The rest of the council tumble to their knees. While Malik watches, his powerful arms crossed over his huge chest, Azrael slithers between the cowering men until she is satisfied that they are sufficiently frightened, then moves to Theo and Ryder. She sniffs at Theo and he keeps his eyes locked at her feet. "We knew there were something wrong with this one right from the beginning. He does not smell dead." She smiles, revealing a mouth full of sharpened teeth and moves on to Ryder. She slips her fingers under his gag and releases it from his mouth.

"Mister Ryder," she hums, her voice turning sweet and seductive. "We like him bound and tied."

Ryder huffs out a laugh. "You read the book, then?"

"Of course we did," she says with a smile. "We would not refuse any request you make."

Ryder returns the smile. "Then everyone knows?"

"We do." She rises and turns and now more warrior angels are coming down the street. They come to stand in a line in front of the kneeling men. Azrael walks back to join them.

Unable to speak, as Azrael chose to leave him gagged, Theo can only enquire at Ryder with his eyes.

Ryder chuckles, his hands still bound behind his back. "Don't look so surprise. As soon as I suspected, I spoke with Azrael. I figured she, of anyone, would understand what the blank pages meant. We still weren't certain at that point, so she took your book and I went to find you."

Theo thrusts his chin at Ryder, eyes wide and eyebrows lifted. He has so much to say right now but can't get a single word out.

"Sorry, I should've told you. I knew Veddie would be waiting but I had no idea you'd go after him like that."

Theo wants to argue more but movement in the sky distracts him. He looks up to see four angels on winged horseback circling like vultures above them. They are the archangels: Michael, Gabriel, Rafael and Uriel. They come down to an unsettled stop behind Azrael, Malik and the other warriors. Their horses buck and shake their heads, rising up on their feet then settling back down. The animals have hair like Azrael, like the creatures are underwater, and their eyes are spinning pearls. Atop them, the spirits who control them are no less magnificent. Theo only stood in Gabriel's shadow and was almost completely overcome. Now they are all here and their combined Light rivals the rising sun behind them. Theo can hardly stand to look upon it and yet he cannot bare to look away. It is such a magnificent display of ancient power, powers that were here at the beginning of time and will be here until the very end.

"Veddie," Malik calls. "Dynamic authority, elder guardian and warrior angel. You who patrols the forces of darkness, govern the rise and fall of nations and is responsible for all religion, are charged with a crime most unmentionable. The theft of a living soul. The theft of the soul of Theodore Duncan."

Beside him, Veddie is cowering in fear. The all-powerful Veddie finally brought to his knees. Even though his behavior has finally been exposed, it is not a moment that Theo can enjoy. The red pinpricks of Malik's eyes aren't even focused on him and Theo is shaking. He experiences a moment of regret and remorse. Sure, Veddie deserved to be punished, but will they send him to Hell? Or kill him right here? That is not what he wanted. He wouldn't want Malik's anger focused on anyone.

"Do you have an explanation for your actions, Veddie of the Powers?"

Veddie stares down at the ground, his hands clasped in his lap, his whole body shaking. What can he possibly say to satiate this holy council? There is such a display of force as to bring Satan himself to regretful tears. Seeing them here, Theo can only imagine the battles that took place at the beginning of time, the powers that fought to take control of this world. And in this moment, his faith is reaffirmed, not to the church or to a religion mapped out by rigid Christian men, but to a balance of light and dark, to an authority trying to keep this planet on its feet, to a flawed divinity scratching its way through history much like its subjects are. He is certain of one thing, facing this row of ascended deities, we are not alone on this planet. Not at all.

As Veddie's silence lingers, Malik decides to continue, "You, Veddie of the Powers, are charged with the sins of greed, pride, and deceit. You have misled this council and acted against the laws of the guardians. The first offenses may be forgivable but the last is inexcusable. For the theft of a living soul from its body, you are banished from the Reserve. Dishonorably discharged. You will be stripped of your status and removed from this holy city in shame and disgrace."

For once in his life, Veddie does not object. Not only is he led away in silence, so are all his council members, certainly to be dealt with in the same manner.

Once Veddie and his men are gone, Azrael steps forward to speak. Because of the force of all the Light behind her, she is only a shimmering shadow leaving painful blotches in Theo's eyes when he glances up at her.

"You do not belong in this world," she says, gesturing for him to rise. "You have come to us too early. The crimes you have committed here are on Veddie's conscious and not your own. Rise, child."

Theo struggles against his restraints and they fall away as if his ropes were made of tissue paper. Removing his gag, he rises on unsteady legs, a twisted, dark visage amongst this heavenly brigade. He lumbers forward, feeling his deformities more than ever. Do they know everything? Everything? Because if they do, Veddie might not be the only one under judgment here. He comes only as close as he dares. Azrael may be on his side now, but she still terrifies him to death.

More angels come forward to stand with Azrael. Ridwan in his golden armor. And the twins who Theo can never recall their names. Between their identical hands, they hold his Life book. Theo experiences a moment of embarrassment over having so many glorious guardians reading his sad little story. What is it that made him so important to them? That they would have a contest for his soul? What he read between that ornate hardcover left him less than thrilled. Perhaps it was what he was meant to be after the accident. Maybe that car crash would've set his priorities straight.

"It is time for you to return home," Ridwan says. Behind him, the archangels have begun to stir. Theo feels a tightening of his body and then cries out as his skin begins to crack. He covers his face and feels it falling off in bits and pieces. "Be still," Ridwan's voice breaks in. Somehow, the words alone calm him down. Theo closes his eyes as his twisted, sinful shell breaks away revealing his true self beneath. He is then reborn to the glorious bright spirit he was always meant to be.

He rises, his Light now equaling the men he faces. His head is so clear. His heart so big. He sees now that, one day, this will be his destiny. He will be amongst the warriors. He will stand on that council. He will fight the good fight again, but this time with real faith and religion guiding his way.

"Return his Life book to the library," Ridwan tells the twins. They nod and turn back to the city. "And Daniel Ryder, stand as well."

Theo glances back, having completely forgotten that his mentor was still here. Ryder rises unsteadily, his hands still bound behind his back. His face is white washed against extreme light, like someone is shining a powerful spotlight in his direction. He squints against the auras he faces, his eyes starting to tear up.

"You will take the boy home," Ridwan says. "Return him to his earthly body."

When the commotion is over, when the archangels have ascended and the holy council gone back to their duties, two men stand alone on the street. Theo is so bright now that he casts a shadow behind Ryder.

"So this is the real you," Ryder says, a smile playing with the corners of his mouth.

"I guess so." Theo returns the grin, looking down at his brilliant hands, turning them over and then back again. He moves forward and removes the ties around Ryder's hands. Ryder shakes his arms out and rubs his wrists.

Out on the street, windows begin to lift and doors creak open. A spring morning is rising once again and angels are venturing out. Seems like this showdown was not unexpected. Seems like guardians were warned off the streets this morning. Even now, they trickle out carefully, shielding their eyes against Theo's blinding Light.

"Should we go?" Ryder says, indicating toward the Victory arch. They have their orders. Take Theo to the Field and return him to his pool. There is no time for good-byes, to pack his things, or even take one last walk around the Reserve. He is trespassing on holy ground long before his time.

"What will you do now?" Theo asks nervously as they turn towards the Victory arch. It's hard to believe he's going out to the Field and never coming back. At least not for a very long time. This place has become his home. He has a lot to fear in returning down below.

"I don't know, Theo, I really don't. Things are going to change, that's for sure."

Theo looks over at Ryder, his adversary, his mentor, turned lover in the end. So much has changed since he came here. What if he forgets everything when he descends? What if he simply wakes from his coma and thinks this is all a dream? He will have lost so much and won't even know it.

They pass beneath the soaring pillars of the Victory archway and on into the meadow. It is deserted this morning, except for a few souls being led down from the misty hill. He has done one thing that no other soul has ever done. He will come down that hill twice. And who will he be the second time? How much will have altered since his last stay here? He doesn't want things to change again.

Feeling more unnerved the closer they get to the Field, Theo keeps talking. "What do you think they'll do to Veddie? What is banishment, anyway?"

"I don't know. Maybe I don't want to."

"I didn't know they'd go after him like that," Theo says, remembering how terrifying it was when the guardians confronted his old mentor.

"It seems like they've been on to him for a while," Ryder says. "They suspected foul play but didn't have proof until you were stolen. It's a big deal to banish an elder. I have never seen it done before."

They fall into silence, the heaviness of the moment finally settling in. Theo is going back to his body and Ryder is returning to help put the Reserve back together. It will be a long time before they see each other again. Waking up this morning, Theo had no idea the turn his life was about to take. He reaches for his mentor's hand as they enter the gates of the Field. His body is out here, somewhere, adrift in one of these pools. The only difference being that his pool has no soul in it.

"I'll make sure Angel gets a good guardian," Ryder says, tightening his grip on Theo's hand. "I'll make sure she's taken care of."

"Make sure it's a girl," Theo jokes, though is struggling with a large lump in his throat.

Ryder chuckles dryly. "I will try."

They cross the Field in silence, only share what they are feeling between the fingers of their linked hands. There are a few guardians at attention, down below doing their sacred duty. They will not know what happened up on the Reserve until they get back. What a shock it will be to find Veddie gone. Not just gone but banished. Theo still feels pangs of guilt over that. Surely Veddie did a lot of good here before he became corrupt. But it was not his decision to see the old man go. He hopes there will be some way for Veddie to heal, wherever he is going. He hopes it is not an eternity of pain and torture he faces.

They reach his pool much sooner than Theo would like. Heart pounding, he looks down into it. Unlike the other pools, there is no emotion surrounding this one. Because his soul is right here. Is this what it's like to be brain dead, he wonders? To have a soul passed on and a body still alive? It's so strange to see his reflection beneath the surface, to see the image that was chosen to represent his strife. He is in a hospital bed. He is full of feeding tubes. He's pale and thin, his normally trim blonde hair grown nearly to his chin. His face looks grey and cold. He looks dead. He can't imagine what would motivate his family to keep a body like that alive. But he's glad they did. He is getting a second chance at life. And a chance, though a slim one, to find Angel and save her.

"Are you ready?" Ryder asks, tightening his grip on Theo's fingers.

Theo cringes at the words. He looks over at Ryder and then embraces him tightly. "I'm scared to go back," he whispers.

"I know but it will be all right," Ryder returns, holding the boy as tightly as he can. "What you've done here is important. You've changed the course of the Reserve. And you're not even supposed to be here yet. Imagine what you will do when you return."

Theo chuckles and closes his eyes, trying to soak up every detail of the embrace before he leaves. He feels the soft curl of Ryder's hair against his cheek. The quick rise of a hard chest against his own. Another man's breath hot against his neck. He doesn't want to leave this behind. He doesn't want to leave his mentor behind. He's so worried about the uptight body he might return to below. But he is changed. His soul is changed. So it should be changed down below too, shouldn't it?

"I'm going to miss you," Ryder says, easing him back a little. He stares hard into Theo's face. They exchange a soft kiss and then Ryder says, "You be careful down there."

Theo exhales a laugh against his mentor's mouth. "You be careful up here."

Ryder smiles and then pushes him a little. Theo jolts, trying to regain his balance, his feet right at the edge of the pool. Then his eyes return to Ryder and he remembers that, this time, he is supposed to fall in. He takes a deep breath and then nods to the man that holds him. Ryder gives him one last squeeze and then lets Theo's body fall. Theo tumbles backwards, his heavenly body accompanying his soul instead of standing sentinel outside. He crashes into the water and his body drops beneath the surface. The pool ripples violently then slowly calms. Ryder covers his mouth, staring as the water goes blank and still, as Theodore Duncan vanishes from the Field.

REBIRTH

Chapter 28☙

All around him it is warm and quiet. He sleeps the deepest sleep with no worries or concerns. There is no life above or below, there is no self at all, just a womb like embrace of unconsciousness rocking him gently from side to side. He slumbers in perfect stillness until the birth of his new life begins. Then he is broken from his peaceful nap and begins the shocking journey back to the surface. It's pain that greets him first. A tight stiffness that slowly seeps in. His joints begin to twist and bind, his bones begin to bend and break. A hot sting starts in his chest and expands outwards. He feels pressure on his body, something pressing down against him, something holding him down with a heaviness he hasn't experienced in a while. In his mind, a slow pulse of awareness comes to life, a beat of urgency telling him to hurry, to remember.

He opens his eyes but only sees light so brilliant and blinding that he has to close them again. He takes a breath and his lungs are heavy and wet. In the distance he can hear footsteps shuffling by. People talking in low voices. A steady beeping. His finger moves. It send a shock of tingles up his arm, making him aware that he has an arm. He taps his finger on something cold and hard and hears a *ting, ting* sound in the distance. Is that the sound of his finger tapping? It sounds so far away.

The next time he wakes, it's night. That slow beeping continues. He opens his eyes and this time the brilliant light is gone. Above him are symmetrical ceiling tiles, each with dozens of little holes in them. He imagines himself as a worm passing in and out of those holes until every one has been penetrated.

There are things in his face that shouldn't be there, things in his nose, down his throat. He wants to pull them out but he can only move that one finger. His eyes travel across that worm hole ceiling. He takes a few heavy breaths. He has no sense of who is he is or where he is. Only the feeling that he has been gone for a very long time. From his restrained position, he surveys the room in which he lies. He is surrounded by machines. There is a window to the right of him and only darkness beyond. He looks away from it, remembering that he is afraid of the darkness and that he must not let the darkness touch him. On the left side of him is a door that goes out to a dimly lit hall. There is no one walking by. At the foot of his bed is a painting of an angel. Theo's eyes focus on that painting. He knows angels. He knows angels. The statement drops into his memory banks but there is no meaning behind it. There's only a moment of urgency and that fades as well.

He sleeps again and the next time he wakes, it's morning. Sunlight streams in through the window beside him. The hallway is bustling with activity. With a shock, he realizes he's peeing but the bed is not getting wet beneath him. He tries to stop it but the stream just flows and flows. He remembers water flowing down a street, water rolling down a dark stairway. There was an endless reservoir of water. He taps his finger on the bed rail. Ting. Ting. Outside the door, a man comes to a stop. He's a younger man dressed in jeans and an oversized tee-shirt. He has a scar on his face and most of his hair is gone.

"You have got to be fucking kidding me," the man says when he see Theo. "Dianna! Dianna! You better get your ass down here right quick."

From further away, Theo hears a woman neatly reply, "Buddy Johnson, how many times do I have to tell you to watch your language?"

Buddy. Theo's eyes go to the man, a young man around his age. If he had hair, it would be red. And if he were closer, Theo would see the freckles on his face. Both these things he knows, but he does not know who the man in the doorway is.

"Oh, you're going to thank me in a minute," Buddy replies, a huge smile on his face. He looks over at Theo and begins to laugh.

"I am in serious doubt of that," Dianna Duncan says, rounding the corner. She comes to a sudden stop when she sees Theo. And Theo sees her and remembers mother: harsh, strict, careful, adoring, dedicated, loving, mother.

"Oh my lord!" she cries, dropping her coffee at Buddy's feet. "Theodore!" She launches forward and smothers him with kisses. Her tears drop onto his face. She grips his hand and kisses it but he does not feel the touch, though he sees the hand moving in hers. "Oh, I knew it," she cries, "I knew you'd come back to us. They told me to give up. They told me there was no hope. But I knew. Buddy!" she calls back in a shrill voice that Theo knows is uncharacteristic for her. His mother is quiet. His mother is demure. His mother doesn't cause a scene. "Go get his father, immediately."

"Where is he?" Buddy asks. He nods and winks at Theo as if they are sharing an inside joke. But Theo does not know what that inside joke is.

"In the cafeteria. Hurry." She turns her attention back to Theo. Though her tears are running, her makeup is not. She squeezes his pale, emaciated hand in her strong tanned one. On her fingers are rings filled with diamonds and gold. A silver chain glimmers around her wrist. Emeralds and diamonds are in her ears. Her hair is perfectly in place. He's remembering everything about her, how she keeps the house so clean, how she doesn't even know how to boil an egg, how she likes to sit front row center, just like him. He remembers something else too, how coldly he used to regard her, how he withheld his affections from her, how he said he loved her but never really felt it. But that is not a memory from his life. That is from somewhere else.

Theo stares up at the doctor surrounded by his mother, his father, and the guy named Buddy. There is a nurse in the room as well. They are all looking down at him excitedly. The doctor checks his vitals and shakes his head. "He is a very lucky young man," the doctor says. "I did not think he'd be coming back to us."

"It's a miracle," his mother whispers, tightening her grip on her husband's hand.

Theo glances over at his mother, a tall svelte woman with carefully sculpted sandy blond hair. Her skin is smooth and tanned. Her appearance in perfect order. Beside her, is his father Andy. He is a striking blonde, tall, physically fit and adorned in the same expensively cut clothing that his mother wears. They were wild with emotion when they first came in the room, hugging him and sobbing, but now they are their calm, reserved selves again. His memories of Buddy have not returned. He knows his mother is his mother and his father is his father, but doesn't have any specific memories around the redhead with no hair.

"We won't know the extent of his injuries until Theodore is moving around more," the doctor explains. "I never believed he would come out of the coma, so everything from this point on is a gift as far as I'm concerned."

"Thank the lord," his mother whispers, looking skyward with gleaming eyes.

"We never gave up on you," his father says, sounding extremely pleased.

"We'd like to have him moved to a private room," his mother says. "And have my physical therapist brought back in."

The doctor indicates he'd like his parents to move out into the hall. His mother asks Buddy to stay inside while they continue to talk. Buddy moves to stand beside the bed. He shoves his hands into his pockets and Theo gets a flash of someone looking like Michael Jackson. Then Michael the archangel. Then a line of men with wings and brilliant light, then a crash and a fire and metal twisting and people screaming.

"Crazy, hey?" Buddy says, looking down at him. "We really didn't think you'd ever wake up. You remember much?"

Theo stares up at him densely. He can see, now that he's closer up, that Buddy's hair was burned off as well as his eyebrows.

"Do you remember anything?" Buddy asks, his voice growing more concerned.

Theo looks to his parents out in the hall and then back to the redhead. He can't speak because of the tube down his throat so he shakes his head for no. He does remember some things but there is no head shake for *a little*.

"Do you know who I am?" Buddy asks.

Again, he shakes his head no.

Buddy's eyebrows raise, at least the place where they used to be does. "You don't remember me? Your best friend? Your partner in crime? Thanks a lot, old pal."

For some reason, a tickle of laughter raises in his throat, but it only comes out as a cough. And when he coughs, the tube in his throat catches and he begins to choke. The nurse rushes back in and pulls the tube abruptly out. It tears from his raw throat leaving a burning sensation behind. He gags a few times then settles his head back down. Now everyone is back at the room staring at him.

"You okay, son?" the doctor says, pouring him a drink of water.

He nods, taking a long, cool drink. He closes his eyes as he does, remembering the street filled with water. Water rushing past his ankles. Water in fountains. Water in courtyards. And angels. He has special knowledge about angels. He settles back on his pillow and closes his eyes. He intends to rest for just a second but when he wakes up, it's night again and everyone is gone. He swallows, his mouth dry and realizes that he can move his arms. He lifts his right hand and runs his fingers across his dry lips. The other hand seems dull and unresponsive. He reaches with his good hand to the table beside the bed, his shoulder filling up with tingles. He tries to lift a glass of water off the table but it's too heavy for him to hold. He tries again and it falls off the table and breaks. He thumps back against his pillow as a woman comes in.

"You're awake?" she exclaims, coming to his bedside. "I can't believe it."

He nods, looking up at the girl. She is in a pink dress with long dark hair flowing around her face. He knows a girl with long dark hair. A girl that dances. His heart jump-starts and his heart monitor jolts to life. The woman glances over at it. "Are you okay?"

Theo stares up at her with enquiring eyes. She says, "Oh I'm sorry, my name is Sasha. I was just getting in to work. I haven't put my uniform on yet."

"Do you dance?" he whispers, his throat raw and sore. It feels like he hasn't spoken in a very long time.

"Dance?" she exclaims. "No, not me. I'm way too uncoordinated."

"But I remember you," Theo says, staring at her so hard.

"Well, I have been your nurse for these past few months," she says laughing. "That could be why you remember me. Are you okay? I should punch in and then I'll come back and clean up this broken glass."

"I'm okay," he says, his eyes following her out. That is not why he remembers her though. The girl that dances with the flowing dark hair is vivid in his mind. She is more of an emotional impression than a picture in his head. And he keeps thinking of water. Maybe it's because he's so thirsty.

He stares up the ceiling after the nurse leaves, taking another journey through the wormhole. He has been here before, in a bed, in recovery. But not here, somewhere in between here and there. Someone was looking over him, but in a different way than this. And the place was hilly and green and surrounded by cool mountains. But how did he get here? Why is he in the hospital? He has the impression that he voluntarily entered this place, that he walked in. Is he here for a surgery? Perhaps to remove his deformity. His good hand stutters up to his face. He runs his fingers across the skin and finds it smooth and without flaws. But as his fingers go down his neck, he finds the skin wrinkled and scarred. Like a burn. Was there a fire? He thinks there was but that was years ago. So much has happened since then. There have been so many changes.

The nurse with the flowing hair returns to clean up the glass he broke, except now she is in uniform and her hair is tightly bound behind her head. This time she causes no emotional reaction from him. He has no memories of this girl as his nurse.

"Would you like another drink?" she asks when she is done.

"Yes," he replies, his voice still weak.

She brings him a glass and he drinks and then rests back with a sigh.

"The doctor will be in to check on you this morning," she says, setting the glass aside. "How do you feel?"

He searches his data banks for a word to explain his present state. "I don't know," he finally says. "Strange, I guess."

She takes out her pen, clicks it and touches a point on his arm. "Can you feel this?"

He nods, staring up at her, trying to get that dancing girl back in his head.

She touches the other arm. "What about this?"

"Yes," he says.

"And this?"

He looks down because he feels nothing and thinks she must be pulling a prank on him. He sees the pen against the back of his other hand. That unresponsive hand. It looks much whiter than his other one. He shakes his head, no.

"Okay, well, that's not too surprising considering that one was reattached."

Reattached? He gets the impression of his hand driving a car by itself, like a horror movie hand taking off from its master and driving away.

The nurse lifts the blanket up to his knees and then presses the pen into his leg. "Feel that?"

He nods.

"Oh that's great," she exclaims. "And the other one?"

He nods as the pen presses into his skin.

The nurses pulls the blanket back down and returns the pen to her breast pocket. "Well, we should wait for the doctor, but it doesn't look like you're paralyzed. I'm betting you'll walk again."

He looks up at her with that same blank expression he's had since returning here. Returning. That's right, he's returning from somewhere. He's been on a long journey and now he's come back. But where is he coming back from?

"Do you remember what happened?"

"No," he says, staring up at her for an explanation.

"Do you know who you are?" she asks.

He shrugs. "Not really."

"And your parents? Do you remember them?"

"A little."

The nurse looks around guiltily and then reaches in the dresser beside him. She pulls out a newspaper. "I don't know if I should show you this. It might upset you. But your mother insisted on keeping this at your bedside since the accident. She said one day you'd be sitting up in bed and reading it. Well, I had my doubts, so here." She hands the paper to him and lifts the bed so he is slightly reclined.

Theo's eyes jitter across the headline. *Two boys seriously injured in yesterday's accident.* He looks down at the picture of a dump truck surrounded by ambulances and police. A fire crew is dousing a twisted pile of metal wrapped around a telephone pole. The story below reads: *Theodore Duncan and Buddy Johnson were seriously injured in a two car collision that occurred at 12:30am at the corner of 39th ave and 65st. Their two door vehicle was side-swiped by a city dump truck that failed to stop for a red light. As a result, the vehicle Duncan and Johnson were driving in was torn in half. Johnson was taken to the hospital with serious injuries. The jaws of life were needed to free Duncan, who is in the county hospital undergoing surgery for life threatening injuries. Duncan received third degree burns while being trapped inside the burning vehicle. Charges are pending against the driver of the city dump truck.*

Theo lowers the paper to his chest, holding it there. He stares across the room at a painting of an angel. Michael Jackson, that's what Buddy was dressed as, a half white, half black Michael Jackson. And he was dressed as the devil. And apparently that was very funny to Buddy. But that was so long ago. Over a year ago. Has he been here for a whole year?

"How long have I been in here?" he asks, still staring at the painting.

"I guess it's been four months now."

Only four months? But he knows it's been longer than that.

"Did it help you remember?"

"A bit," he says, looking over at her, handing the newspaper back. "But things are very jumbled."

"Well," she says with a wry smile. "You were pretty jumbled. Anyway, the doctor will go over more of this with you and what you're going to need to do to get out of here." She pulls a curtain between his bed and the other bed in the room. "You're getting a roommate today. I don't imagine your mother will be too happy about that."

He chuckles. Somehow he knows that's the truth.

"There was a terrible tour bus accident this morning. The bus went right down the ravine. This place will be filling up today with recovery patients." She gives him a wink and a smile. "I'll try to pair you up with someone nice."

His mother comes to visit shortly after the doctor stops by. She is all bright-eyed and bushy-tailed as she enters the room with a large shopping bag in her hand.

"Theodore!" she exclaims when she sees him sitting up. He's actually just propped up by the bed but she is no less thrilled. A few more of his tubes have been removed. The doctor recommended he try eating on his own today. However, the catheter will stay in until he is more mobile. The doc was happy with his initial muscle responses. "You are in remarkably good shape for a man who's been in a coma for four months," he said after testing Theo's legs. He went on to explain that his hand was severed during the accident and though it was reattached, it is not healing as it should be. He said that his memory loss is not unusual and would most likely be temporary and told him he received third degree burns to the right side of his body while being trapped inside the burning vehicle. He did most of his healing while he was in the coma. Every time the doctor says the word coma, though, Theo finds himself getting upset. No, he wasn't in a coma. It was something else. He asked if he could have a mirror before the doctor left. He took it and stared into a reflection he did not recognize. He was too thin. Too blond. And he looked so young. In his mind, he is so different. He is big and powerful and, for some reason, brunette.

"Your father will be by later," Dianna says, setting her shopping bag on the chair beside the bed. She gives him a quick squeeze, commenting that he has gotten way too thin and that she will have to get him home and on a proper diet as soon as possible. She grumbles about the hospital food and about the fact that they are bringing another person in the room and that the hospital bedclothes he's wearing are so unflattering. "I bought you a nice sweater. It'll look much nicer on you." She sets the sweater across his lap.

Theo lifts it up, his arms still tingling every time he moves them. He has no strength at all. He tries to tug the store tag off but his fingers are too weak and he gives up. "It's pretty expensive," he comments. The sweater retails for a couple hundred dollars. "You couldn't find something cheaper?"

His mother looks at him like he's stark raving mad. "What on earth are you talking about?"

"Nothing. Thank you." He rests his arms on the sweater, trying not to look at his pale hand. It's five shades lighter than the rest of his arm and has a nice Frankenstein stitch around the wrist.

"I'm preparing a lawsuit for that," his mother says, indicating distastefully to the hand. "I don't know what sort of…butcher they have for a surgeon here but that is unacceptable."

Theo frowns up at his mother who claims she is going to sue the people who saved his life. "Don't," he says. "It's fine. I'll make due."

"No son of mine is making due. They turned you into a…a…monster," she fans a hand beneath her chin.

Monster, Theo thinks, getting a rush of blood to his face. A beautiful monster. Dancing in red. Scars on her wrist like the scars on his. Then the image fades away as well as his blush. "I don't want you to sue them," Theo says, raising his eyes to his mother. "Don't sue anyone over this."

Dianna briefly meets his eyes, then clucks her tongue. "Goodness sakes, Theodore, what sort of drugs do they have you on? You don't even sound like your normal self. I'm sure once you are feeling better, you'll agree with me whole heartedly. After all, we will need plastic surgery to deal that scar. And maybe some sort of dye for your skin so that the color is more normal." Dianna continues to unload her shopping bag. She sets some scented candles on the nightstand. And a framed picture of Jesus, which gets his dander up for some reason. Then she sets a bible in his lap. King James version with an elaborate leather cover with his name embossed on the lower right hand corner. He flips it open and lets the delicate gold-edged pages fan across his fingers. He knows that this is his favorite bible, of which he has many, but he is uncomfortable having it near him. He wraps it in the sweater and sets it aside. His mother finishes by placing some slippers at his bedside, some herbal teas in his top dresser drawer, and then a handmade quilt over his thin sheet cover.

"We'll be moving you home as soon as possible," his mother says, seating herself delicately in the chair beside the bed. "And hiring a private physiotherapist. This place is so..." She looks around, displeased. "Well, we are just so thankful that God has given you back to us."

Theo stares at her blankly, holding his tongue. He's not sure why, but every time she says something religious, he feels the need to protest. But isn't he religious too?

"Oh look, here comes your friend," his mother exclaims. "Good, Buddy, you come in and keep Theodore company while I give his father a call."

Buddy enters the room with a huge paper cup in his hand. "See, I drink coffee now. Like an addict. Look what you've turned me into."

"You didn't drink coffee before?" Theo asks, his eyes raising to the scar across Buddy's face. He got that in the accident. And his hair, unlike Theo's, has not grown back. Buddy's red hair has been replaced by scar tissue. His skin is wrapped around his head like a turban.

Buddy snorts, plopping down in the seat. "I wasn't much into non-alcoholic beverages."

Theo passes Buddy the stuff his mother left on his lap and indicates he wants it left on the bed side table. "Think I do remember that."

Buddy sets the items aside and glances back as the nurse enters the room. She waves at Theo, then disappears behind the curtain, preparing the other side of the room for his new roommate. *She's hot*, Buddy mouths silently. Then quietly adds, "Picking up the ladies even while you're dead."

Theo rolls his eyes. "Not so much anymore," he says, indicating to his bad hand.

"Well at least you still got one hand," Buddy says making stroking gestures into his lap.

Theo chuckles, thinking that he wouldn't have laughed at that joke before. He would've found it crass and low brow. But how could one coma change him so much?

They both look over as another man is brought in the room. The curtain blocks their view but they can see shadows through the curtain. He's moved from a gurney onto the freshly made bed. And then the nurse begins to attach tubes to him, the same sort of tubes that Theo had pulled out today. The heartbeat monitor sets a steady beep in the room, falling into line with his own.

"Who's that?" Buddy asks quietly.

"Some sort of tour bus accident?" Theo says, unsure.

"Oh, that tour bus?" Buddy says. "Complete mayhem. You should've seen it. Bodies all down the hillside. What a fucking mess." He falls silent as another frantic man enters the room. The man rushes beside the bed and begins to pester the nurse with frantic questions. *How is he doing? They wouldn't let me see him in emergency. Only family was allowed in. It's a crime what they define family as. Is he going to be okay? I can't get straight answers from anyone.*

The nurse calms the visitor with easy reassurances. He's doing much better now. He has regained consciousness though is heavily drugged right now. He isn't very responsive. You can sit beside him but he won't be talking for a while.

The man thanks her then pulls a chair next to the bed. Then he softly kisses the unconscious man on the lips and tells him everything will be okay.

Buddy turns with his jaw hanging open. *Gross,* he mouths silently and then puts his finger down his throat and pretends to gag. He covers his mouth, restraining a laugh. "Your mom is going to have a cow," he whispers.

Chapter 29☙

Theo sits silently after Buddy leaves, staring at the two men behind the divider. He is disturbed but not the way Buddy was. This has something to do with him but he has no idea why. He wishes he had something from home, something to help anchor him to the real world. Did he keep a journal? Somehow, he thinks not. A journal would require introspection. And he was a brick wall before the accident. But how will he sort through this fog and find out what's nagging at him? He feels so lost right now.

He takes the bible from the night stand and stares down at its elaborate cover. He knows this bible was treated with reverence. It was a gift from his parents for his confirmation. He carried it along with his school books in university. And though his other bibles are dog eared and have underlined passages, this one is clear and crisp as the day he received it. He opens it up again, cautiously, almost warily. He fans through the pages and then his eyes fall on a random line. *Praise ye him, all his angels; praise ye him, all his hosts.* He frowns at the passage; this one has meaning, has weight to it. It's not just words but something he's seen carved on a statue or on a wall. Something he saw after the accident. Praise ye him, all his angels. Angels?

He looks up as someone else enters the room. "Hello Jesse," a woman says to the man seated on the other side of the curtain. "How is he doing?"

"He seems better. The nurse was very encouraging." Jesse rises from his chair. He offers it to the woman.

Theo watches the shadows pass by each other, the woman now sitting in the chair and Jesse is now standing at the foot of the bed.

"It's so nice of you to stop by," she says. "I still can't understand what he was doing on that tour bus in the middle of a work day. Has he said anything?"

"No not yet," the shadow named Jesse says. "The nurse says he's heavily sedated."

"Well it's not important. Not now. I'm just glad he's alive."

"I am too," Jesse says in a quieter voice. He says goodbye to the woman and leaves the room. It's silent again. Theo's attention returns back to his bible. He marks the page where that passage is and then begins to flip again. Another passage jumps out at him. *For he will give his angels charge of you to guard you in all ways.* He dog ears that page as well. Angels. Angels. What is it about angels that keeps catching his attention? Were they watching over him while he was in the coma? But he wasn't in a coma; it was something else. It feels like years, not months have passed since he and Buddy left that Halloween party. He flips through the bible again and stops at one of the many illustrations inserted randomly through the book. This one is of an angel standing on a rock with his rod raised high in the air. Below him is a man cowering in shame. And behind the angel is a light that descends from Heaven and intersects with the end of the staff. The angel is haloed in light, his wings transparent, his face luminous. Theo stares at it for a long time as a short circuit in his brain attempts to reconnect things that he needs to remember.

The rest of the day is filled with visits from his father and mother, with the nurse and the doctor, so that by the time visiting hours are over, he is glad to be alone. Also plagued by visitors is the man who shares the room with him. Though it obvious to Theo that the man named Jesse is also his lover, the woman, possibly his wife, remains unaware of the fact. And from what Theo can piece together from the conversations he's heard, the man in the bed told the woman he was going to work, then went out on a tour with his lover instead. He doesn't feel the way Buddy does about the two men in love. He thinks that it should bother him if he recalls the man he used to be before the accident, but that part of him has changed as well.

That night he turns on the TV and listens to it quietly while the other man sleeps in the room. He flips mindlessly through the channels not sure if he even wants to watch anything. Unable to find anything of interest, he settles on the news. He watches the weather and a story about a missing boy. Then the head newscaster returns looking very serious, saying they have more details about their top story. There's an aerial shot of a school with police all around it and kids running out with their hands over their heads. Underneath it reads: school shooting; ten students dead. Theo sits upright, staring at the screen. School shooting? It makes his blood stall in his veins. Is that his school? Is that why he's so concerned? But he doesn't go to high school anymore. He's in university. He leans forward as the newscaster continues. "Details are still sketchy at this point but ten youths have been confirmed dead and dozens more wounded in today's Columbine style shooting. Most of the victims are between the ages of sixteen and eighteen. The shooter has also been confirmed dead among the deceased. The identity of the victims and the shooter have not been released at this time."

Theo stares up, mouth agape, as bodies beneath blankets are rolled into ambulances, shots of frantic kids waving out broken windows and kids running away covered in blood. Parents are shouting into the cameras. Kids are crying. And cops are frowning.

"Isn't that awful?" his nurse, Sasha says, as she enters the room with his supper.

"Do they know who did it?" Theo asks, his mouth suddenly very dry. This shooting has upset him more than he can understand. He can hardly breathe looking at the images of those kids being wheeled away under bloody covers.

"Not yet. It just happened this morning." She rolls a table in front of him and sets down a plate. "Ready to try some solid food?"

He was hungry before the newscast but now he just feels sick. He looks down at the plastic divided tray filled with powdered potatoes, ground up meat, and runny pudding. Even if he was hungry, he's not sure he'd want to eat this food anyway.

"Here, I'll turn it off," Sasha says, seeing that he's upset.

"No," he says sharply, then eases back on his harsh tone. After all, he's not angry with her. And he made a vow to treat women better, didn't he? He seems to remember that. "I just want to find out what happened."

"We all do," she says, looking up at the screen with a sigh. "I mean what kind of monster could do something like that?"

Theo jolts with the thought: a beautiful monster, that's who. A beautiful monster would do this. And it would be a justified retribution. He gets an image of blood dripping down the side of a bath tub. And red poetry written on a wall. And the shooting taking place in the gym, during a dance. Did the newscaster say that?

"Are you okay?" Sasha asks. She leans down and offers him a spoon of mashed potatoes. His first impulse is to push her and the food away. He feels so sick right now.

"Yes," he answers pleasantly, allowing her to spoon-feed him, though his arms work just fine. "I'm just having trouble remembering things, that's all."

"Still?" she asks, looking surprised. "But I thought you got your memories back?"

"I do remember some things, like my mom and dad but there are events around the accident I just don't understand. I'm remembering things but I can't place where I know them from."

The worry seems to leave her face and she offers him another spoon of mashed potatoes. "You suffered a major trauma. Some people remember afterwards and some people will never recall."

Theo stares up at her thinking he's heard those words not so long ago. And it wasn't a woman give that advice to him, it was a man. Not a man, but a boy. The name, Eric, pops into his head. But he doesn't know anyone by that name.

Later that night, the man in the other bed wakes up. He cries out and then becomes silent. Theo can hear his heart monitor racing and the man breathing heavily.

"You all right?" Theo asks, looking over at the dark sheet hanging between them.

"Where am I?" comes a thin, raspy voice.

"In the hospital."

"Why am I here?"

"There was an accident. You were on a tour bus and it crashed."

There's a long silence. "Oh yes, I remember. How long have I been asleep?"

"Most of the day."

There's another long silence. "Has anyone come to visit me?"

Somehow he knows this fear, the fear of being discovered, of being found out. And the deliciousness of a forbidden affair. "They've both been here."

The man clears his throat and then coughs. "My wife and...and..."

"Your friend," Theo says evenly.

"Shit," he hears the man whisper.

"Don't worry," Theo says, though it's really none of his business. "She doesn't suspect anything."

More silence and then his voice returns sounding even less reassured than before. "How do you know?"

Theo sighs. "There's not much to do in here but listen to other people's affairs." He didn't mean to use the word *affair* in that manner but he leaves it all the same. "I'm Theo, by the way."

The man finds the call buttons and rings for the nurse. "I'm Daniel."

Theo's head jerks towards the man behind the curtain. Daniel? The name ripples through him like an electrical charge. The first thing he thinks is, did he follow me here? But then he thinks, did who follow him here? And follow him from where? Daniel. Oh, he knows that name and intimately. It arouses him, it disturbs him, it makes him shake all over. Suddenly he needs to see the man on the other side of the curtain. He sits up and attempts to turn off the bed but his legs follow limply behind. He knows if he sets them on the floor then they will just collapse under him. Frantic to see the face of Daniel, Theo pushes himself off the bed anyway and receives the expected results. The nurse Daniel called for himself runs to help Theo instead. As she does, she swings the curtain aside and Theo sees his roommate. He is a black man, bald, with his arm and leg in a cast. He is not the Daniel Theo knows.

Theo lays in bed long into the night, staring blankly into the darkness. He was so certain he knew the man across the room from him that he risked breaking his own legs to confirm that fact. It's not the man, he realizes now, but the name that plagues him. Like the school shooting. It'll be ten years until morning before he can turn on the TV and see the more about the shooter. He is certain the identity of the shooter will open up his mental block. But somehow, he knows, that information could destroy him as well. He needs his laptop, badly. If there were only some way to contact Buddy or his parents. He feels so helpless and that is a feeling he knows he's undergone frequently during the last four months. Why is the man he used to be before the accident such a mystery to him?

Unable to sleep, he reaches across the bedside table for a pen. Then he takes out his bible, the one he was so careful never to make a mark in. He sets his pen against the inside cover. Pen on paper is a familiar sight for him, comforting and disturbing. He sits for a while staring at the gilded page, so clean and so white, then writes the word *coma*. He stares at it and then crosses it out. Then he writes the word *Daniel*. That word sits better. Underneath Daniel, he writes *Angels*. That also seems right so he continues to write. He brainstorms a list: shooting, reservation, masturbation, suicide, murder, and sex. He stares at this troubling catalogue defacing the inside of his bible. Some of the words seem wrong. Mostly reservation and murder. The others seem to fit though. He continues with the words: paradise, field, fucking, naked, school, library, light, dark. Again some of the words don't sit right yet but he knows that they all belong together. More words come to him now: dog, cafeteria, hallway, money, dirty, water, bathtub, Romeo. That last one hits him hard. Romeo. He hates that name. In fact just looking at it sends him into a rage.

He sits back with the list in his lap. Words are coming and so fast he can't even write them down. Naked, naked, sex, judgment, book, life, books, life books, life books, library, sex, running, running, naked running, angels, angels running, angels shooting, killing, murder, revenge, retribution, dancing, dancing, running, fucking, running, sin, sex, and salvation. He closes his eyes feeling something stirring beneath his mother's hand-made quilt. For a few seconds his cock begins to lift and swell, then pain from the catheter jolts him back to reality. He opens his eyes and exhales deeply. What the hell is going on with him?

As soon as the hospital begins to stir the next morning, Theo turns on the television. The news is on. A woman is being interviewed. A banner beneath her face indicates that her son was one of the boys killed in yesterday's shooting. Over and over again, she says, "What kind of monster would do this?"

Theo knows. He knows. He opens up his bible and writes Beautiful Monster at the top of the list. A beautiful monster, he thinks, that's who. And as the mothers and fathers cry out *why, why*, Theo knows the answer. It is so clear in his head. Because they deserved it. The words seem cruel and uncaring in the face of so much grief, but he just can't shake the feeling. People don't just shoot up schools for no reason. No, someone has given her a reason. Her? He looks up at the screen, his heart thundering in his chest. Did they say the shooter was a girl? Why would he think that then? As far as he knows, no girl has ever shot up a school. He closes his bible with a frustrated thump. He needs his laptop. He needs to find out who this shooter is.

"Oh my baby," Dianna Duncan says as she swings around the corner. "You look wonderful today." She kisses him on the forehead and sets a tray beside the bed. "Breakfast! I don't want you eating this hospital food. All carbs and proteins, no proper vegetables. Eat."

Theo glances at the tray of assorted veggies. He is hungry. Starving, actually. It seems like that is a familiar feeling as well.

His mother grimaces at the television and then turns it off. "Don't need to see that at this hour," she comments, then smiles as she sees his bible in his lap. "Catching up on your scripture?"

Theo sets the book on the far side of the bed from her. "Something like that." God forbid she sees what he's written on the inside cover. As Buddy predicted, she would indeed give birth to a cow.

His mother sets a bag on the bed beside his feet. Inside are his school books, and, glory of glories, his laptop. "Thought you'd like to do some catching up while you're in here. You've missed a whole semester but if things go well, then we will have you back by the time winter semester returns."

It occurs to him that he has no idea what month it is, or what day either.

His mother clicks her acrylic nails on the bed railing as the nurse enters the room and tends to the bed where his neighbor lies. She is obviously irritated with the intrusion.

"He was in a tour bus that crashed," Theo comments softly.

"Well, it is certainly is getting crowded in here," his mother replies in clipped tones.

They fall silent while the nurse tends to the man. Theo can see his mother's lips twist unhappily. Dianna Duncan likes her privacy. Walls, good solid fences, tightly closed curtains. Mama doesn't like to share. And her son having to split his hospital room with another person is eating her up. He can see she's about to say something when Jesse enters the room. Of course his mother has no idea that the two men are together.

"*Oh I'm sorry,*" Jesse says, carrying a big bouquet of flowers with him. "*I thought you'd be alone.*"

"That's all right, Jesse," the nurse replies and then adds in lowered tones. "*There is no one else visiting him this morning.*"

The two men chuckle and then thank her. The nurse checks behind the curtain at Theo. "Oh, Mrs. Duncan, I didn't know you were here. I'll come back later."

His mother nods curtly, not bothering to ease the woman's worries over her intrusion.

"*She knows?*" they hear one of the men say after she leaves.

Dianna Duncan frowns, looking very disturbed. "I will have you moved as soon as possible. I am certain we can get a health worker to come to our home if needed."

"Mom, it's all right. I don't mind."

"It is much too…crowded in here," Dianna whispers with a glance towards the flimsy divider separating the room. "How am I supposed to have a proper visit in this…tent city? At least you should have a room to yourself so you can recover properly"

Jesse chuckles. *"As long as your nurse is the only one that figures it out. What did you say about the tour bus?"*

"I haven't said anything," Daniel replies. *"But I'll think of an excuse."*

Theo hears something across the room, like a hand sliding over skin. His eyes snap up to his mother but she is still looking at the curtain as if she's trying to figure out how she can wheel her son out of here, heart monitor and all, without anyone noticing. The sliding skin sound continues and Theo hears the slightest moan from one of them. He grips his bible and glances at his mother. She doesn't appear to have a clue about what's going on behind that curtain.

"Uh, mom," Theo says, trying to get her attention back his way.

"Oh yes," his mother says, rolling a table over with the food she brought spread across it. "Eat. You look like a skeleton."

The nurse leans back in the room and raps on the wall a couple of times. *"I was wrong,"* she says to the two men behind the curtain. *"She's on her way."*

There's some shuffling on the other side of the room and Theo can only imagine what they were doing over there. In fact, it's not just an imagining, he knows exactly how what it feels like to have a man's hands on his body. He reaches for a carrot, grateful that the tray has been placed so conveniently over his lap.

"Stay," Daniel whispers. *"You're just visiting."*

"I'm a terrible liar, you know that," Jesse says, gathering up his things.

"Leave the flowers then. She knows you're my best friend."

"Yeah, I sure am."

There's a sound. The unmistakable sound of two lips exchanged a kiss. Dianna Duncan's mouth drops open and her hand clamps down on the bed rail. Her rings clink loudly against the metal railing and all the blood drains from her face.

"Tell your wife I say hello," Jesse calls back wickedly as he leaves.

Daniel chuckles. *"I'll make sure and do that."*

Dianna turns and there's hot lava bubbling up in her eyes. For her, what just happened behind the curtain is a moral sin. It offends everything she believes in. It is an affront to her very religion. Man shall not lay with another man. So it is written in the bible. The same bible her own son scratched a filthy list in last night. And marriage bonds are sacred. It is a union only severed by death. She won't stand for this. Dianna Duncan will not rest until she sets things right.

A few seconds later, Daniel's wife enters the room. *"Was Jesse here? I think I just missed him."*

"Yes," Daniel replies lightly. *"He was here but had to get to work."*

Dianna seems to make a decision and then takes a step towards the curtain. His mother is not the kind to sit idly by when there's something she can interfere with.

Theo grabs her by the arm. "Don't you dare."

Again, his mother looks back at him like he just beamed down to his planet. "What are you talking about?"

"That is none of your business," he whispers, surprised he has the strength to hold her at bay.

"I am not going to let him get away with that," she returns, exclaiming just a loud and clear as she pleases. Behind the curtain, husband and wife have become silent. "They should be arrested. It's sick. It's disgusting. At least have the decency to keep it behind closed doors where decent people can't see it."

Needing a quick resolution, Theo says, "You stop it right now or I won't let you come visit me anymore."

Dianna Duncan pulls back with a shock. Theo does not have the strength to hold on to her arm as she pulls away. "Theo! Why would you say something like that?"

"I mean it," he says darkly. "Let it go."

She glances at the curtain and then back at her son. "What has gotten into you? Honestly, Theodore, I hardly know you anymore."

"Just sit down and have breakfast with me, all right?" he says softer. "I don't want a big fight right now. I'm tired."

Dianna glances at the curtain again but then reluctantly submits. This isn't over, Theo is sure of it, but she surrenders for now, returning to the chair beside his bed. She watches her son uneasily as he eats his breakfast.

After both women have left the room, Theo hears the man behind the curtain say, "Thanks for that."

"Sorry, my mom is kind of religious," Theo says, pushing his bedside table away. His mother was visibly shaken when she left. He feels bad about the threat but, for some reason, it's important that the affair on the other side of the room continue.

"Those are the ones that generally give us trouble," Daniel replies. "You know, the ones overflowing with god's love?"

Theo chuckles at the joke and then falls silent. "I used to be just like her."

"Really?" the man says, his voice softening. "What changed you?"

"It was a man…named…Daniel," he says slowly, surprised to hear the words from mouth. Yes, his name was Daniel too. He was a teacher? He swipes at a memory but it is passing by too quickly to catch. What did he mean by that? What is he saying?

The man on the other side of the curtain looks at him and says, "I assume your mother doesn't know."

Theo is still wrestling with what he just said. Daniel? Is he saying he had an affair with a man named Daniel? Is he saying he's gay? That word does not sit right with him. He sighs, looking through the curtain at his roommate. "You could fill an ocean with the stuff my mother doesn't know about me."

The man laughs. "Were you in the tour bus accident too?"

"No," Theo says, resting his head back against the hard hospital bed. "I was hit by a dump truck four months ago. I just woke up from a coma."

"A dump truck?" Daniel says. "Oh wait, are you that Duncan boy?"

"Yes, that's me," he replies, surprised the man knows who he is.

"I actually thought you died in that accident," he says. "Can't believe you survived that. Your car was ripped right in half. And burned up too."

"I know. It's a…" He pauses about to say *a miracle* but was it? Somehow he thinks there were a lot of logical events that led up to his recovery and return. But he can't remember any of them.

"Well thanks anyway," Daniel says from behind the curtain. "Appreciate it."

"No problem." Theo says, picking up his bible. He opens it and looks at the name he wrote near the top of the list. Daniel. But the fleeting memory is gone. He moves his pen to the bottom of the page and writes *gay*. It doesn't look right. But it's doesn't look wrong either. So he leaves it for now.

Theo takes his laptop and searches for information on the shooting. He checks out all the major media sites and watches uploaded videos from networks and private phones, anything to give him more information on the shooter. He has no interest in the victims or the families or the death toll, just the person who put this whole production in motion. He eventually finds out that the killer was a boy from the school, not a girl. He was an isolated, ostracized kid who spent most of his days in his basement playing war games. He was not from a poor family or even from a bad neighborhood. His parents couldn't be more average. Though Theo receives some of the answers he was looking for, he comes away unsatisfied. This is not the person he was expecting to find. But who then? And who is Daniel? He taps the name into an internet search just to see what comes up but the results don't trigger anything. He finds the song Daniel from Elton John. And reviews from the latest Daniel Day Lewis movie. But not the Daniel that triggered the memory. He tries the most hated of hated names: Romeo, but comes up with the predictable Shakespearian results. His Romeo is not a romantic. His Romeo is not worth the paper it would take to put his name in print. His Romeo deserves to be shot up in a school. The thought send his brain spinning. He is so close to uncovering the mystery between his old self and the new but he just can't make the connections. What happened to him after the accident? He can tell by his parents and Buddy's reactions that he is not acting as they expect him too. They are baffled by his behavior and shocked by the things he is saying. But he is only acting in a way that has become natural to him.

He looks through his old school books and notebooks searching for clues about himself. There is nothing personal in anything he owns. His name is written neatly in the top right hand corner of every text book. Otherwise there isn't even a mark inside them, not even a notation or underlined phrase. His notebooks record his teacher's lectures word for word, he does not record any interpretations of his own. There's nothing in the margins. No girl's names with little hearts around them, no doodles of houses or flowers or cubes or boobs or cocks. Looking through his notes, he can't even tell which classes he likes or dislikes. They are all recorded with the same ironclad attention to detail. He was going to be a missionary? A humanitarian? He had no emotion at all, as far as he could tell.

And religion. Somehow, he feels like he has inside information on that subject and everything he learned from church and school is inaccurate. The bible, once sacred to him, has become an exaggeration of possible historical facts. After all, the authors of these books are just men interpreting what they believe to be true. It does not mean it is the actual truth. It seems pretty logical but he never even bothered to question the information before his coma. One thing is for sure, he can't go back to university, not under his current major. In fact, he doesn't want to go back at all. At least not right now. That's going to be a hard one to explain to his mother.

Sasha returns in the afternoon and removes a few more tubes, including the catheter. "Stepping up to bed pans," she jokes as she covers him back up. "How do your legs feel?"

"Like rubber."

"Well, we should get you in a wheelchair. We can go outside for a walk and get the blood flowing. It's so beautiful out."

"That would be nice," he says.

So he's wheeled outside for a walk, gets some sun, some fresh air, then is brought back in for a shower. He suffers a great big hard-on in the shower with his nurse and apologizes profusely.

"Oh it happens all the time," Sasha says without a hint of concern. "At least you're not like the old guys. Those buggers are so proud of themselves when it happens."

After the shower he's fed and put back to bed. The shower has left him disturbed but it's not because of Sasha. It seems he had another shower where his erection was also an unwelcome intruder. But where was that? He seems to think it was at work, but he doesn't work. He's never had a job in his life.

Exhausted from all these half revelations, Theo puts out the light and goes to sleep. But late that night, he's awoken by a voice.

"How did you get in here?"

Theo opens his eyes but doesn't move.

"I snuck in with the evening shift," Jesse whispers. *"Is he asleep?"*

"Who? You mean the Duncan kid? I'm not sure."

Theo hears footsteps approaching and closes his eyes. Thank god the heart monitor is not connected or it would give him away. He breathes deep and long and keeps himself perfectly still.

"He's asleep."

Theo's eyes pop open as he hears something slide off and hit the floor. Then the bed next to him creaks.

"I just couldn't stay away," Jesse whispers. *"And your wife never leaves. When are you getting out of here?"*

"Not soon enough," Daniel replies.

Hands begin to slide, skin on skin and then there is only the sound of breathing next door. One moans and then the other, and the bed beneath them creaks in soft rhythm. Theo's eyes close and his mouth opens as his own hands go down between his legs. Finally free of the catheter, he fingers his hard shaft, feeling trembles of excitement spread up from his hips. On the other side of the curtain, the breathing increases, skin sounds turn wet, he hears slick sliding and mouths moaning and then Jesse breathes out his partner's name. Daniel, Theo whispers into his pillow, quietly tugging away. Blood pumps hotly through his veins and his body swells with heat and excitement. Daniel, oh Daniel, he hears behind the curtain. They are grunting now and the soft creaks of the mattress have become rigid cranks of the bed springs. Theo slips back the covers and lets his cock out to breathe. The cool air comes in around him like an intruder's breath and he begins to work it more aggressively. Daniel, he thinks, punching his sweaty fist. Daniel, against the pillar. Shhh, he says to Justine and...oh, Theo pushes harder into his hand. Test tubes breaking and on the floor. His mentor, Daniel is his mentor. Theo pushes in time with the men next door, his bed springs now matching pace with theirs. His cock ripples through his tightly clenched fingers, rupturing through the fabric of space and time. Piercing the virginity of his lost memories. Daniel in the kitchen. Daniel on the floor. No, her father's in the bathtub, itching no more. She cuts herself so she can die. She falls in the forest so nobody hears. God, he whispers as his hard, shiny head crashes through his fingers, as it punctures through the dark, through the air, as he pokes holes in the clouds, in the courtyard, in his mentor's house. He pushes harder, his weak fingers shaking against the force, as he plunges himself into the soft folds of the Angel, of his charge. Smack, smack, cluck, cluck, tick tock. He thrusts his hips one final time and spews out like a fireworks on New Year's eve. His cry of exclamation hidden beneath the finishing cries of the couple beside him. He lowers his hips to the bed, his trembling fingers weak from the workout. He tumbles down through memory after memory. Angel, Daniel, Veddie, and then the supporting characters: Evangeline, Justine, Eric,

Romeo, and Beatrice Yu. Oh my god, he's back. He made it back to earth. And he remembers everything.

Chapter 30∞

Theo wakes up the next morning to a brand new life. To his real self. There is nothing between him and the Reserve now, or Daniel, or Angel. All his memories have come back to him. And with them, the memories of his true self as well. He sits up in bed staring out the hospital window at the sun rising over the dew covered cars in the parking lot. Not only is he alive again and given a second chance at life, he also has a second chance at saving Angel. No, she is not the shooter from the news but where is she on her timeline? And how much time does he have until her end begins? Ryder said there would be a jump back when he returned but Theo did not think it would be such a big jump. When he left the Reserve, he had been with Angel for over a year. But now only months have passed. Bea hasn't committed suicide yet; she may not have even met the boy who led her to that act. And while Save the Date is still on for prom, it is only February and prom isn't until June. He has plenty of time to get to them both. He's thrilled at the thought of physically entering her story, to meet her, and hopefully become a part of her life.

Using a variety of search engines, Theo begins his search for Angel. Though his Reserve memories are strong and true, he cannot recall Angel with equal clarity. It was like trying to recollect his life after he had died. He knew all the characters but could not remember the details. He was there. He knows that. He knows her. But he can't remember specific names, like her town or her school. He knows her town was small and located in a farming community. It has one high school and a sushi restaurant owned by the Yu family. He wishes he knew the name of the restaurant, that would narrow his search down dramatically. He searches the Yu name but it is not an uncommon last name and he comes up with too many results to sift through. He knows the daughter's name is Beatrice, but only the parent's names would be found in a phonebook or rental agreement. He searches through a few social media sites but comes up with nothing. He focuses on the restaurant but it seems every small town has an Asian restaurant in it. The list he comes up with is miles long. It could take him weeks, even months, to search through them all. Feeling discouraged, he simply enters the name Angel. Results return with religious iconography, names of songs, bands and movies, and famous celebrities. He sighs, leaning back in his bed with a growing headache. How is he ever going to find her?

He opens up a map and lets his mouse hover the planet for a while. She could be anywhere. He tries to remember landmarks, the school team name, any street signs he saw along the way, but nothing stands out. He has nothing relevant to enter into the search engine. With growing terror, he realizes that he may not find her until she is a news story like that kid from the school shooting. He can't let that happen but how can find one girl among billions of people?

Frustrated, he opens up a new window and enters the words *private detective* into the search engine. He goes through a number of websites until he finds someone local he thinks is competent. He sends off an email with a brief explanation of his problem. No specifics, simply that he is searching for someone and has few details go on. How much he reveals to this investigator will depend on how badly the search goes.

"Wow, you look amazing," Sasha says when she comes in to check on him. "You must be feeling lots better."

"Much better," he says. And he does feel better despite his setback with the search this morning. He is his old self again. Not the man before the accident but the man molded on the Reserve. He is so happy that he recovered everything. Angel isn't lost and neither is Daniel.

"Your physiotherapist will be starting with you today," she says, setting his breakfast in front of him. "He wouldn't normally start so early but the doctor is impressed by your muscle memory. He says it's like you've been running in your dreams."

Theo chuckles at that. Yes, he has. And mostly in the nude. He looks up at the nurse and she blushes. It occurs to him that the girl has a crush on him. In the old days, he wouldn't have cared much either way. If he's not interested in her, then why is it his problem? It's the same attitude his mother has. Who cares if the hospital is overcrowded, it's only her son that matters. She's only concerned with things that concern her. He doesn't want to be that way anymore. Now he has much more empathy for the people around him. And maybe it's because he's been through more and he can understand people better than when he was a sheltered kid in his parent's home. He had money so he didn't have to care, get involved, or even be nice.

"How long do you think before I'm out of here?" he asks, digging eagerly into his breakfast. It's good to eat again, to feel hungry and then satisfied afterwards. Everything is more real here, more tangible, easier to deal with.

"Oh, I don't know. I bet you'll be walking and back to normal in a couple months."

"A couple months?" he exclaims. "That long?"

"Well you have been in a coma for a long time. And the trauma from the accident is severe. You are lucky to be walking at all. Or alive."

"Months," he whispers, thinking of Angel and her troubles. Does he have that kind of time? Prom is in June. He's going to have to work hard to get to her in time. He looks at the girl with the long dark hair standing at his bedside. She's been his nurse since the day he woke up. He can't even remember her missing a day. He also notices that she is awfully thin, her hemlines frayed, and that her shoes are very tattered.

"How long do you have to go to school to be a nurse?" he asks, shoveling a forkful of rubbery eggs into his mouth.

"Oh a long time," she says, sounding exhausted. "It's crazy long."

"It must be expensive. I mean student loans and stuff."

She smiles but Theo can see a burden behind her eyes. "Very. I mean you can get scholarships if you're smart enough, but I had to do it the old fashioned way. Loans and more loans."

Theo looks down at his breakfast, his heart racing a bit. He doesn't have to wait for Angel to start helping people. It's just like university. He thought he was preparing to save the universe through his education while ignoring people in need all around him. But it doesn't have to be that way. He has unlimited money. Trusts, accounts, savings, gold bonds; money his parents never even look at, don't even care about. All that money for just one family. It seems obscene to think that he never gave any of it to anyone. He vows that he is going to change that behavior right now. He can't help them all, of course he can't, but he can pick and choose the people he crosses paths with. Deserving people who could use a leg up. People who a few thousand dollars could make a huge difference in their lives. He has millions. Millions. It never mattered to him before, not the way it does now.

When Theo returns to his computer, he finds a reply from the private investigator. His name is Jackie. He would like to meet with him and get more information. A deposit is required. He's had too many people stiff him when the outcome wasn't what they wanted. He tells Theo a criminal check will be done beforehand to ensure that he is not stalking someone or violating a restraining order while seeking this person out. If everything checks out, then he will be happy to help him find Angel. Theo emails a reply, letting Jackie know more about his situation. He is in the hospital recovering from a car accident and cannot meet right away. He authorizes Jackie to do any sort of criminal and background check on him required and asks that he come to the hospital for a meeting. He says he will pay any amount of money to find this girl and time is of the essence. He sends off the message feeling much more satisfied that the search for Angel is underway.

Afterwards, Theo does a little research on his nurse, Sasha. He discovers that the average nursing student leaves the classroom with thirty thousand dollars in student loans. He's surprised at the cost. He goes online and looks at his own accounts. Numbers in the six figures across all the board. A big line of zeros following every account. Those numbers never meant anything to him before. He has no limitations, can go anywhere and do anything he wanted. So now he's going to send a few of those zeros his nurse's way. And he's not going to stop there. He's going to leave a trail of zeros all the way back to Angel.

Two months have passed by the time he's able to leave the hospital. It's now the middle of April. He's worked hard to get back on his feet but the damage from the accident was extensive. The best he's done so far is to walk with the aid of a crutch but mostly he uses a wheelchair to get around. The doctor says that his progress is incredible and the fact that he's leaving the hospital two months after waking from a coma can attest to that. However Angel's time is running out. He has just six weeks until the prom and who knows how much time until Beatrice Yu commits suicide. If he can get to Angel quickly, he might be able to save her best friend too. Jackie has been employed as his private investigator since their first visit but the search has not gone as well as he hoped. With only the names Beatrice Yu, Angel, and Romeo to go on, there have been few leads up until this point. Jackie is now focusing primarily on the restaurant and is investigating small towns in search of the Yu's. He says he should have something in the next week or so. Until then, all Theo can do is get stronger, heal, and prepare for the battle ahead.

On the day he leaves the hospital, he packs up his few belongings and then leaves a card on the table for Sasha. Inside is a certified check for one hundred thousand dollars. It's a tremendous gift but he barely feels it financially. Emotionally too, he supposes, as he cannot fully appreciate what kind of freedom this financial boost could give her. But this isn't about him. That is the one thing he just couldn't grasp in his former life. Charity had to involve some sort of personal payoff for him to be interested. Now he gives, knowing he will likely never even see the reaction on the girl's face or the changes in her life that will follow. Now, it is good enough just to give and not receive.

He rides home in the back seat of his mother's new Lexus. His father is at the wheel. The two chortle away in front while Theo looks out the window at the houses as they pass through town. He's driven this old road a hundred times or more and has never really looked at the people who live here. Now he sees past the tattered walls on the run down street and imagines the people inside, people just like Angel. His parents scoff at the lower-end neighborhoods with their cluttered yards and rusty vehicles. Why can't they just clean themselves up? Why can't they get a better vehicle? And a better house? These people are just lazy. A burden to society. But the truth is, they are just poor. They don't have time to clean up their yards. They don't have the money for unrusty vehicles. They are living in the best house they can afford.

The further they drive, the wider the streets become, the yards get bigger, the houses taller, and then they enter the exclusive, gated community where he and his family reside. At the end of the street, a mansion rises bigger than all the rest. It is obvious who the king of this neighborhood is. Not just the neighborhood but the town too. They are the wealthiest people he knows. The fountain in the front yard cost one hundred thousand dollars. The same amount of money he left for his nurse this morning. Money for something that displays water in their lives. Money that can change the course of a life for others.

Where he used to be comfortable surrounded by opulence, it seems to weigh on him the closer he gets to the house. It just seems like too much grandeur, too much status. Just too much everything. As they enter the gate, Theo looks across the immaculately trimmed lawn to the oversized double doors of the mansion. His mother was very specific about those doors. She wanted to make an impression on anyone who entered her property. And she spent a fortune on them, for doors they never even enter or exit through. They use the entrance to the house from inside the garage. He can hardly even look at those doors now without thinking about what just one could do for Angel. It's such a waste.

Dianna sighs as they park in the garage and the overhead doors close without a sound. "It's so nice to be home."

Theo sighs but it's not for the same reason. Home has become a stranger to him, a place that causes him conflict instead of comfort. And there is trouble on the horizon. He's quitting university. He's running off to find Angel. His parents aren't going to be happy for long. He doesn't want to hurt them but he is on a mission now. He cannot hide in this shell any longer.

"Maybe we should put an elevator in," his mother says as they exit the car. "I mean I've always wanted one and now that Theodore is home, he'll need one to get upstairs."

"We don't need an elevator," Theo groans as his father sets his wheelchair beside the car door. "I'm only using the chair temporarily. And I'm already walking with a crutch."

His mother sighs. "Andy? Don't you think it makes sense?"

His father looks over at her as Theo struggles into the chair. "My father would roll over in his grave. You know that he doesn't want me..."

"...tampering with the house," his mother finishes with a roll of her eyes. "I know. I know."

"I don't need an elevator," Theo says again, but he can see the idea is firmly planted in his mother's head. She's already deciding where it will go, what it will look like, and which designer she can call to get it started.

Andy rolls Theo into the large kitchen, one of many that occupy the house. "Why don't you and I go car shopping today, Theodore? I know you can't drive yet but you'll need a new one to go to school in the fall."

He's going to have to tell them about school soon. Not today though. Even if he was going back, the campus is just across the river. It would be so much faster to cross the bridge on foot instead of getting in his car and driving all the way downtown. And yet he never walked before. It was a pain. He didn't want to carry his books. He didn't want to show up at school with his hair messed up. He liked to show off his cars. "Can we do it another day? I think I'd like to just stay home for a while."

"Of course! As soon as you're feeling better," his father responds cheerily. "You just get yourself settled in."

"It's so good to have you home," his mother sings from the kitchen. "Shall I get the kitchen staff to whip us up some tea?"

"Yes please," Andy says, sounding very pleased. "I think we would all enjoy that."

Theo sits in his chair in front of his bedroom mirror. A thin, sullen stranger stares back at him. He had gotten used to himself as this dark, brooding guardian and now he is so pale and skinny and blond. His hair is almost to his shoulders and is the same golden color of his fathers. Gone is the athletic build he had before the accident. He is skinny and wiry, every vein in his body so prominent that it practically sits on the outside. And his skin. He unbuttons his shirt and carefully lowers it off his shoulders. He has burn scars on his right side from the base of his neck down to his hip. The scar wraps around his side like an unwelcome hug and feels tight and stiff compared to the rest of his skin. There are minor burns down his right leg as well. And then there's the severed hand. That thing that his mother can't even bare to look at. She has spoken at length about prosthetics and cosmetic surgery. He has been resistant to change anything, not until he saw himself in front of the mirror today. What will Angel think of him? He is not the handsome man that he used to be. What if she thinks he's ugly? What if she doesn't want anything to do with him?

He gives his reflection a cross look before he rolls his wheelchair to his bedroom window which overlooks the Olympic sized swimming pool in the back yard. He should start there. Start swimming and get fit. And his hair? He decides he has to dye it black, an homage to the fallen angel he used to be. The idea seems to sooth his nerves and it gives him other ideas as well. He wants a tattoo. He wants different clothes. He needs a change on the outside to reflect the change on the inside. It's time to let everyone know that Theodore Duncan is not the same man he used to be.

"Honey, I'm home," Buddy says entering the Theo's room. He sees the owner of said space and comes to a dead stop. "What the fuck?"

Theo grins from his bed, his computer on his lap. His hair is now raven black, messy and cut in a punk style. His mother was so excited when she dropped him off at her favorite salon. She was less thrilled when she returned to pick him up.

"Shit," Buddy says, sitting down at the nearby desk with another coffee in hand. "You know Halloween is over, right?"

Theo gives him the finger and Buddy bursts out laughing. "So I guess when you were in the hospital they removed that giant stick up your ass."

"That appears to be the case," Theo says, deadpan. He watches as Buddy nurses his hot beverage. He supposes if caffeine is his only vice from his near death experience, he can't complain. He really knows nothing personal about his friend and his friend certainly knows nothing about him. He is just a hang-out buddy, someone to call for a casual movie or a dinner out. But before he died, he really did consider Buddy his closest confidant. Now he misses that closeness he had on the Reserve. His friendships were so intense, so involved. He cried, he screamed, he fucked. Now, back on earth, things are so level and so quiet. He's so restless he feels like he's going to jump out of his skin.

"Let's get out of here," he says, pushing off the bed.

"Go where?"

"I don't care. Let's go downtown." Theo shrugs on an old jacket. He hates all his clothes. Everything is so neat, so polite, so agreeable. He takes his crutch and swings it under his arm. Time to get his transformation started.

Theo sits in the passenger seat of Buddy's beat-up car. No heated seats or navigation systems here, it doesn't even have proper seat belts and the windows only roll half way down. The back seat is full of garbage, mostly empty fast food bags, and the exterior looks like it hasn't been washed in years. He used to be mortified to be seen in this clunker, but now it doesn't bother him at all.

"So are you getting a new car?" Buddy asks.

"Yeah something with roll bars," Theo comments.

Buddy snorts. "No convertibles, then?"

"I was thinking more of a used vehicle."

"A used car?" Buddy exclaims. "Your mom's not going to like that."

"Well, I'm buying it, not her." He falls silent, realizing the irony of critiquing his parents since every cent in his account comes from them.

"Gawd," Buddy groans. "You get a brain transplant in the hospital too?"

Theo looks over at him. Though they haven't spoken about the accident, they share one thing in common: their burns. Though Buddy's burns are less severe, they are more prominently displayed. Theo keeps his marks tucked away. His wrinkled shriveled skin hides beneath several layers of clean cut dress shirts.

"I mean you went to sleep Ned Flanders and woke up Marilyn Manson. What's the deal with that?"

Theo shrugs, feeling no need to explain himself. If he's causing this much fuss with a hair change, he can't wait to see the reaction when he quits school, gets a tattoo, admits he's bisexual. Oh, there is loads of fun coming.

"So what kind of car are you looking for?" Buddy chuckles and then points out the window and laughs. "Here's one for you."

Theo looks to the side and sees a Thunderbird parked outside a trailer in a dingy used car parking lot. It's a classic car, charcoal black, but what makes this bird a spectacle are the murals along the sides. It is covered in tombstones and crosses, painted with demons and creatures. It has big chrome teeth along the front and shiny eyes for wheels. As soon as Theo sees it, he wants it. He can see his new self behind the wheel causing a scandal everywhere he goes. Most importantly, he can see Angel seated beside him loving every minute of it. "Let's go look," he says.

"No fucking way," Buddy says, driving past the lot. "That car has been for sale forever. And do you know why?"

"Course I don't," he replies, glancing back as the car disappears from sight.

"Because the guy's son killed himself in it."

Theo's mouth drops open. "Seriously?"

"Seriously. Gassed himself right in the driver's seat. The old man has been trying to get rid of it for years. Fucking suicide car."

Theo returns to face forward but there is an awful gnawing in his chest. He has to have that car. It's urgent now that he owns it, that the suicide car becomes his own. "Come on, let's go back."

"You have really lost your mind," Buddy says, pulling a U-turn at the next intersection.

Buddy parks behind the Thunderbird and revs the engine. "If you drive home in that, you'll put your mother in the psych ward."

"I'm just looking," Theo says, opening Buddy's screechy car door. He swings crutch out and lands awkwardly on it. There's something about this car. Just looking at it makes his heart race. It's so absurd, obscene, obnoxious, something that he wouldn't be caught dead in before he died. Now it's calling to him. Death car. Suicide car. On the window, a small sign says: *for sale*. And it looks like it's been there for a very long time.

"That thing is deranged," Buddy calls out his car window. "It'll never pass an inspection. It will cost more in repairs than it would to buy new."

Theo cups his hands over the tinted windows. Inside, he can see a dated '70's dash complete with 8-track cassette deck and large clock-like odometers. The seats, to his shock and delight, are fashioned like tombstones. *Here lies...*is printed across the place he'd rest his head while driving. And the stick shift is a skull. He exhales a deep breath, fogging up his view. He steps back and surveys the artwork on the side. What he first thought of as loud and gaudy is actually quite intricate and complicated. There is a delicate mist that runs along the length of the car with a faded cemetery disappearing into the rear quarter panel. Crosses replace modern day tombstones and are set on erratic angles down the hillside. In the mist are glimpses of tortured eyes and faces.

He runs his hand along the length of the car as he walks around to the front. The grim reaper crawls across the hood as anxious souls flee from its scythe. It looks like a monster. Like a beautiful monster. This car must be his. It is part of his transformation. It will be part of him. He turns to the trailer which acts as an office at the center of the lot but the sign on the door says it's closed for the day.

"Come to your senses?" Buddy asks as he returns to the passenger seat.

"No, they're closed," he says, sounding disappointed.

"You were really going to buy that? Somebody died in there. It's disgusting."

"People kill themselves every day," he says, falling silent, thinking of Angel.

"True, but it doesn't mean you have to buy their cars."

Chapter 31ଔ

Theo stands in front of the mirror the next morning staring at his naked reflection in the mirror. When he turns to the left he looks pretty normal, albeit lanky and awfully pale. When he turns to the right, he's all twisted and deformed. He's starting to get used to it though, even feels some attachment to these scars. After all, they are battle scars, like wrinkles earned from a hard but happy life. It would be a shame to get rid of them, to get the plastic surgery his mother is so enthusiastically planning for. He turns to the front and runs his fingers across his chin, looking at his face. His eyebrows look funny. He should go back to the salon and have them dyed the same color as his hair. He loves his hair now. It's the same color as Ryder's. He drops his hand to his chest. What muscle remains is tightly fastened with thin stretched skin. Not an ounce of fat remains on his body. His belly button is a taut, winking eye. He allows his hand to travel down lower, watching in the mirror as his fingers pass over his cock.

Knock. Knock. "Breakfast is ready," Andy Duncan calls through his bedroom door.

Theo's hand quickly drops away. "I'll be right down." He's got to move out of this house. But what's the point of getting a place until he finds Angel? He will have to contact the investigator today and see if there are any breaks in the case.

He turns away from the mirror and empties a few bags out on the bed. After they went to the car lot, Buddy took him downtown for some shopping. Theo picked up new clothes and he bought Buddy a few things as well. They went for lunch, which Theo paid for, then they passed by a place called Gothic Medical. Theo was drawn by the dark displays before he even knew what the store was about. Buddy protested, asking Theo if he knew what The Gimp was and what happens to good boys in bad places like this. Theo just ignored him and entered into the mysterious wonderland. Gothic Medical specializes in custom medical supplies. Wheelchairs that looked like side cars for Harley Davidson's. Leather arms slings. Pimped out crutches. Tattoo dressings for casts. Everything the injured wild man could want. Theo picked up a brace and a walking stick. The walking stick looks like something you might see Dracula strolling around with. And the brace has an upturned hand that holds your own when you lean on it, making it look like one is locking fingers with the dead. He also picked up some fingerless gloves for his reattached hand, though the man at the counter had mentioned several times how *freaking cool* it looked and that he wished he had one just like it.

Theo puts the ensemble together. He puts some charcoal cargos on, a tight, stenciled tee, and a worn leather jacket. He slips on a pair of fingerless gloves and clunky motorcycle boots. He goes back to the mirror and is pleased by the transformation. He doesn't just look different, he looks a bit frightening. Like he did when he was fallen. And the clothes add some weight and definition to his body. He loves it.

His parent's reaction is far from love. When he comes down the stairs leaning on his Dracula cane and dressed like one of the Ramones, his father spits up a bit of his scrambled eggs. He wipes his mouth with a napkin and says, "Going to a costume party, son?"

His mother turns and gasps out a little squeak. "Theodore Duncan! You are not going to church like that."

Theo plops down at the table. "I'm going to town today," he says, picking up a fork with his good hand. Time to get the car. Time to finish the transformation.

"Not going to church?" His mother sets down her fork and then her knife, then presses her hand on Theo's forehead. She looks over at Andy. "Call the doctor. I think those pain pills are causing a reaction."

Theo jerks his head free from his mother's hand. "I'm fine. I don't need a doctor."

"I'll make an appointment right away," his mother says, snapping her fingers and pointing to one of the staff members. "Bring me my phone."

"I am fine!" Theo says, thumping his fist on the table.

"Well you don't look it," Dianna says, returning delicately to her high backed chair and punching a few numbers into the phone.

"He says he's fine." Andy lifts his paper and returns to his stories.

"Andy!" Dianna cries. "I will not have him showing up at church dressed like some sort of hooligan."

"You prefer I show up in the nude?" Theo counters.

Andy snorts and Dianna sends a glare across the table. "This is not funny."

"Besides I'm going to town today. Buddy is picking me up. We've already made plans."

"Oh no he's not," Dianna counters. "You are coming to church with us and that's final. Everyone is expecting you to be there. What will they think if I show up without my son?" She gets up and leaves the table as the doctor answers the phone. They can hear her exclaiming about side effects down the hallway as she walks away.

"You're upsetting your mother," Andy says into his paper. "She has a big to-do for you planned after church today. You should go."

"I'm busy today. I have plans."

Andy lowers his paper, frowning. "On a Sunday?"

"It can't wait." He pauses as his mother shouts *dressed like a serial killer* into the phone. The words echo down the hall and into the main dining room.

His father shrugs. "Well, you are acting peculiar. Are you really feeling okay?"

"I feel fine," he sighs, the excitement of this morning's makeover now drained out of him. Is every step he takes going to cause a fight with his mother? What happens when he quits school? When she realizes he's never going back to church? When he runs away to find Angel? He can't leave his mother behind like a wounded bird but he can't stay here and play these games anymore. He's changed. She's just going to have to accept that.

"All right," Andy says. "I'll talk to her."

Dianna returns to the table and sits down with a satisfied thump. "I've got him an appointment first thing in the morning. The doctor thinks it might be a hormonal imbalance."

Theo frowns and is about to speak when his father steps in. "Well, we'll see what he says in the morning. In the meantime, Theodore has made plans for today. He did not realize it was Sunday. So let him go play with his friends. And we can do the church thing next week when he is feeling better."

Dianna's mouth twists into an unhappy frown. She looks over at Theo and then her face softens. "All right," she says, likely agreeing because she doesn't want to be seen in church with her son dressed like an undertaker.

Theo looks up as an old man steps outside the dirty trailer at the center of the car lot. He looks a bit like a Willy Nelson who's been run over a few times and left for dead. He's covered in tattoos, including the lower part of his chin. One of his eyes is glazed over with a cataract. He wears a bandana over his long, thinning hair.

With Buddy reluctantly in tow, Theo approaches the man. He used to be scared of places in this state of disorder, people too. He wouldn't even go into a building if the façade wasn't pleasing to his eye. And he only associated with people who looked proper to him. He imagines what he's been missing because he made judgments on face value. The people and experiences he passed up on because everything had to look a certain way. He would've missed Angel if he still held these same ideals.

They follow the man as he enters an office with a high counter near the door and an old sofa and coffee machine against the far wall. Rusty license plates line the wall behind the couch and are from all over space and time. The trailer has seen better days with its stained cork tiles bowing down from the ceiling and yellowed linoleum swelling up from the floor.

The walls are wood paneling and are cluttered with car memorabilia and family photos.

Theo's eyes pass over some of the pictures as he approaches the counter. It looks as if the man's life is full of people, people on motorcycles, people gathered around camp fires, people at tattoo parlors. Many of the photos are of the owner and a younger man that could be his son. But these photos are very old, because the man in the photo, which must be the man behind the counter, is young in the pictures and hardly resembles himself. He is dressed more conservatively, with no visible tattoos at all.

"Ooh, coffee," Buddy says, launching himself towards the bubbling machine.

"Are you looking for a car, son?" the man asks in a haggard voice. He opens an ancient coiled book with lists of checks and balances. There is no computer anywhere in sight.

Theo looks over at him. His face is well worn from the sun. He has big strong hands that seem to dwarf the small pen in his fingers. His hair is dark, graying, and braided to each side of his neck. There is something oddly familiar about him but Theo is certain he never crossed paths with anyone like this in his former life.

"The car, the Thunderbird, I was..." Theo pauses as the man flinches. Visibly flinches. He knows there is a price in the window but it seems there's more to this sale than meets the eye. "Is it for sale?"

The man nods tightly but doesn't look up at him. There is definitely something wrong. The car may be for sale but this man does not want to sell it. Theo's eyes go up again to scan the pictures behind the man's head. Maybe that is where this familiar feeling is coming from. This man looks so completely transformed from the person he used to be. He seemed, at one time, to be following all the rules in his neatly pressed suit and short trimmed hair, posing so serenely with this obedient child at his side. But now he is completely broken out of his shell. So much more expressive than the man he used to be.

"I'd like to buy it," Theo says, bracing for the man's reaction.

Buddy spits out a bit of his coffee and grumbles something over by the sofa.

"Yes, it's for sale," the man says, still looking down at his book. He slowly and reluctantly turns the old notebook to a page that has seen plenty of miles. It reminds Theo of Angel's journal, of Save the Date and all the suffering and pain that went into those pages. He feels funny about the sale, not right, even though he desperately wants the car. He supposes he could just have another one made up like it, and spare the man the pain he is obviously suffering by having to part with it.

"Is it...special?" Theo asks, trying to gauge what the problem is.

The man now looks up with terrible pain in his eyes. "It was my son's car."

Theo glances to the photos behind him, to the picture of the man and his boy. "Is that your son?"

"It was," he says wearily.

Theo glances back at Buddy who sits on the couch drumming his fingers impatiently. "Hey, I'm going to be a while," he calls. "Why don't you go out there and pick out something for yourself?"

"Huh?" Buddy says, looking up at him densely.

"Looks like some nice classic cars out there. Go get one. It's on me."

Buddy's eyebrows slowly raise from a frown to delighted surprise. He dances over to where Theo stands and hugs him vigorously from behind. "Have I mentioned lately that I love you?"

"Just go," Theo says, rolling his eyes.

Buddy prances out into the lot and then Theo is alone with the man. "I'm Theodore," he says, offering his hand.

The man shakes his hand. "Gerry."

"Listen, if you don't want to sell it..."

"No," Gerry sighs heavily. "I mean yes. I want to sell it. I mean I need to sell it. I don't have a choice. I need the money."

Money, again, forcing people to do things they don't want to do. He decides then and there he won't take the car. He'll get something else from the lot and give it a custom paint job.

Even though the car outside is just calling to him for some reason, he will not hurt this man to get it.

"It was your son's car?" he asks, already knowing part of the story. Buddy said the owner's son killed himself in it. It seemed like crazy fun when he looked at it yesterday. But today he witnesses the painful truth. Someone died in that car. Someone who just didn't have the strength to go on anymore. And this man, his father, was left behind to pick up the pieces. And that is fun for no one.

"Yes," Gerry says, stepping back so Theo can see the photos better. He smiles at the pictures of his son as he remembers. "It was a dream of his to build that car. We worked on it for years. He designed the mural."

"It's amazing," Theo says. "And did he paint it as well?"

Gerry sinks back on an old stool near the streaky window. He stares out at the Thunderbird parked right next to the trailer. "He died before we could finish it." Gerry is silent for some time before he says, "He took his own life."

Theo drops his gaze, staring down at his hands. "I'm sorry."

Gerry continues, his voice edged in grief. "He never said anything. He never even left a note. One day he was here and the next day he was gone. He was so young. Not even out of school yet. He didn't even know who he was yet. I don't know if he was being bullied at school. I don't have any idea why it happened. It was such a long time ago, but it seems like only yesterday. I miss him every day. Now he is gone and his mother is gone and no one in the family wants to keep the car. I have to sell it. But I can't just sell it to anyone. I hope you can understand that."

"Of course," Theo says. "It doesn't have to be that one. I can buy a different one." Theo eyes the elaborate tattoos along Gerry's arm. "Did you design those yourself?"

Gerry lights up at the topic change. "Yes, it's all custom work."

"Where did you get it done?" Suddenly he wants a tattoo, or ten, or twelve. Wasn't that going to be part of his transformation?

"The shop behind the laundromat. My brother runs it. Best work in town."

"Do you have his card? I'd like to get some work done." Theo takes the card offered to him and shoves it in his pocket. He's getting an idea, something to cover his entire back, something with Angel on it, something with beautiful monster. "Could you design mine? I'll pay."

For this sale, Gerry seems much more eager. He flips to an empty page in his notebook and writes Theodore at the top of it. Theo leans over the counter explaining his ideas while Gerry, obviously talented, begins to sketch out an outline. In his rough sketch, he has a girl crucified on a cross, with wings on her back and Beautiful Monster written across the top. Then he begins to fill the background with cross work and a cemetery.

Gerry turns the page to face Theo. "That'll be the basic idea, but I'll need some more time to work out the details."

Theo stares at the image, his heart pounding in anticipation. Somehow he's captured it, even a likeness of Angel only from his quick description. "Fantastic. It's exactly what I want."

"I can set you up an appointment. For a tattoo this size it will take considerable time and a fair amount of money."

Theo shrugs. "Set it up. How much do you want for the design?"

Gerry seems to shrink back from the offer, uncomfortable when money is brought into the equation. "Don't worry about it. Free of charge."

Theo shakes his head. "This is great work. I want to pay you for it."

Again, Gerry cringes. Theo knows that he needs the money very badly and yet he refuses. Theo takes out his check book and writes down a number with a bunch of zeros after it. But this won't be the only money Gerry will be getting from him. He folds the check and sets it on the counter. "If you don't cash it, I'll just drop the cash off. So take it. I have tons of money."

Gerry takes the check and folds it in his pocket without looking at the amount. "I'll set up the appointment."

Theo nods. "And I'll take whatever car my friend picks out today. But I also want something for myself." He goes to the door and pulls the tattoo card from his pocket. Across the top it says: Nathanial Ryder. He grinds to a halt as he sees the name. Ryder? He takes a few shallow breaths looking out at the gaudy Thunderbird. In Ryder's Life book, he said something about working on cars with his father. Theo looks back at Gerry who's busy working on the tattoo sketch. Is this Ryder's father? But that would mean Daniel Ryder is the boy who killed himself in the car. Theo remembers Ryder commenting wryly on his Life Book. *How did you like the ending*, he scoffed. But Theo never read the ending. He just knew that Ryder died as a boy. He turns the card over in his trembling fingers. It can't be true.

"What was your son's name, by the way?" he calls back, trying to sound casual, though his voice comes out rather high-pitched and tremulous.

Gerry looks over at him and Theo see it now, sees all the resemblances he should've seen before, sees the reason why this man was so familiar to him. "His name was Daniel."

Theo closes his eyes and stumbles down the trailer steps. His heart is thundering through his chest. Daniel Ryder. He stops in front of the car. The car where his mentor took his own life. How come Ryder never tell him how he died? And how could he sum up such a tragic conclusion with the words: how did you like the ending? He knew what Theo was going through with Angel's suicide attempts and yet never said anything about his own. He runs his fingers gently along the hood of the car, feeling an electrical charge run up his arm. It seems like fate has led him here. It's as if he was guided to this place. And now he knows that he must have this car. He must have Daniel Ryder back in his life again.

Unable to sleep, Theo wanders into the back yard late that night. Though situated in town, the mansion takes up nearly five acres of land, all of it neatly sculptured and manicured. In the center is the pool with the hot tub offset to the side. An area of patio stone has been built to the right with a group of fine wicker chairs, a table, and an umbrella. Gardens are off to the left and to the back. They are all carefully situated to be viewed from the windows in the house.

He lies down on a dark part of the lawn. The city lights block out the view of the stars. Only the strongest planets manage to pinch their light through the pollution and the glare. It's not the sky he used to watch from Angel's yard. From her home, thousands of suns and planets and galaxies were visible. Where is she now? Where is she on her timeline? The search for her is taking too long. Jackie has found nothing. It's such a great big world and Angel is just one small girl. But he managed to stumble across Ryder's father. And he wasn't even looking for him. So it gives him hope that a meeting between him and Angel is still possible.

He sighs, opening his shirt a little and running his fingers along the burn down his chest. His body is so foreign to him now. There's a whole new landscape that needs to be explored. And his skin is so sensitive and reactive. He can't seem to keep his hands off himself. But then he hears the door creak open.

"Theodore! Are you all right?" his mother cries, rushing towards him.

Theo closes his eyes with a sigh, folding his hands across his stomach. "I'm fine."

"Oh my goodness, when I saw you laying there, well, I was about to have a heart attack. Did you fall down? Are you all right?"

Theo looks up when she nears. "No. I'm just resting."

His mother stands over him, towering like a pastel giant in a frilly housecoat and fuzzy slippers. Though she's obviously concerned, he can see she pulled the rollers from her hair before coming outside. God forbid the neighbors see her undone. Even during an emergency.

"Well, there are some perfectly good chairs right here. Why don't you come up and sit on one?" She slides a chair forward and indicates that he join her. Because chairs are for sitting on and grass is for looking at, and not the other way around.

"No thanks. I'm fine here," he says, a little annoyed his party of one was cut short.

"Theodore Duncan," his mother sighs. "I can't have you lying here in the middle of the lawn like this. What would the neighbors think?"

"They can't even see us."

"Yes they can." Dianna indicates towards a corner of the yard where a distant window hides behind a large oak tree. Does she think someone is sitting behind it with a binoculars trying to get a peek at them at three in the morning?

"I'm comfortable where I am."

"It's dirty down there. Come sit up on a chair." Dianna seats herself down in a chair as if showing him how it's done.

"It's not dirty," he counters. "It's just grass."

"It's full of worms and dirt," she says distastefully. "Why don't we go inside? I can make us some tea. Your father tells me that you've been looking for a car. Why don't we go down to the dealership after we go to the doctor tomorrow?"

Oh yes, the doctor. He forgot about that. He's going to get a treatment to cure him of his new hairstyle and clothes. To make him sit up straight and go to church like a good boy should. To return to the front row center Theodore Duncan he used to be before the Halloween crash. Little does his mother know that this is a permanent alteration. "I just want to be alone," he grumbles. "Why can't I get a few minutes to myself anymore?"

His mother whimpers a bit and then looks like she's going to cry. Theo instantly regrets being so harsh with her. He gets up and sits in one of the patio chairs. "I'm tired, that's all. I didn't mean to be rude."

Dianna dabs a tear from her eye. "I just missed you so much."

"I'm here now. I'm home," he replies, trying to sedate his mother.

"But you are so…different now. I don't understand why everything has changed so much," she says, getting herself back under control.

"Mom, I was in a coma for four months. That changes a person."

"But you dress so horrible and you won't go to church. And your hair." She touches a charcoal strand. "Your beautiful blond hair. I don't understand what has happened?"

"A lot," he sighs. He sees now that can't tell his mother the truth. It would kill her to know what his future plans are. Better to let her believe that he's returning to school in the fall. That he's going back to church. That he doesn't have fantasies about both women and men. She is his mother and he loves her and he knows that she probably visited him daily during his coma and hassled the staff at the hospital for four months straight. For him, it has been a year of change, but for her, he is still the sweet, obedient boy who was torn so unexpectedly from her life all those months ago. Wanting to ease her pain a little, he says, "I had a...sort of a...near death experience."

"What?" she says, leaning in closer.

"I think I was dead for a while. My body just didn't know it. I went somewhere else when I was unconscious. Mom, I saw angels."

"You what?" she exclaims, a look of awe coming over her face. "Angels?"

"Yes," he says, knowing this is one of the few things he can share with his mother, one of the few experiences he had on the Reserve that she will accept and understand. "I spent time up there in that place after death. I saw the gates of Heaven."

"Oh my goodness!" his mother exclaims. "Why didn't you tell me this?"

"Because..." He pauses. Because there's so much he has to leave out. However, he also realizes, there a things he can share with his mother that would make her very happy. Even if it isn't the whole truth.

"Oh Theodore!" his mother exclaims, embracing him. "You should've just told me in the first place. Of course you would be changed after an experience like that. Of course."

"It took a while to get it straight in my head, but mom?" He pushes his mother back and looks her straight in the eye. "Relax, okay? I've changed but I'm okay. I just have some things I need to work out and I need some space to do that. Can you do that? Can you relax?"

She smiles wryly. "I think you know that I can't."

He chuckles a bit. "Well, how about you don't call the doctor every time I show up in a new outfit?"

She rolls her eyes. "All right. All right. Should we go in for that tea now?"

"That would be nice," he says, rising and putting his arm around his mother as they go back into the house.

Chapter 32ଔ

Buddy drops Theo off at the tattoo parlor Friday afternoon. "Good luck with that," he chuckles as he drives away, gulping down a large cup of Joe.

Theo stares up at the musty laundromat with flickering neon sign that says *open twenty four hours*. Inside are a few people folding their laundry amongst rumbling industrial sized dryers. Through the large glass windows, he can see to the back of the room where a tattoo shop is tucked away. He experiences some anxiety. Is he really going to do this? He's never considered putting a permanent mark on his body, let alone in a place like this. But this is a Ryder doing the work. An uncle of the boy he knows all too well. He has to go forward.

He enters the laundromat and passes through the washing machines and detergent dispensers to the back of the building. There, a small door takes him into a waiting room that is painted with graffiti. One other man waits in the room. He's rough looking, his head tucked inside a motorcycle magazine. There is no front desk.

He spies a sign on the wall. It says *buzz for service* and there's a button beside it. He pushes the button and waits outside the closed door. From where he stands he can hear the sound of ink machines and music playing. It's hot and humid from the industrial dryers.

The door opens and a girl covered in tattoos leans into the waiting room. "You need help?" she asks, her eyes going over him disinterestedly.

"Um, I'm here for Nathaniel Ryder."

"Oh right," she says, and he sees that she has a huge ball through her tongue, not to mention the barbell hanging from her nose and through her lower lip. "Come inside. He's ready for you."

Theo follows the girl down a long hall. He's surprised and relieved to see it's clean like a dentist's office. There are a rooms down each side of the hall and each is decorated to the style of the tattooist inside. He's led into the last room on the left. Ryder's room.

"Gerry left this. If you don't like it, Ryder will make any changes you want."

Theo turns to comment but she shuts the door and she's gone. Ryder. It makes him smile to hear the name said out loud again. He picks up the envelope left by Gerry and looks around the room. This space is not as brash as the others. Along one wall are the same family photos he saw in Gerry's trailer. There's a tattoo chair in the middle of the room, leaned back like a torture device. Beside the chair is a steel tray full of tools and paint. On the desk is a bouquet of black roses.

Theo sits awkwardly on the oddly position tattoo chair and opens the envelope with Gerry's finished artwork. His mouth drops open when he sees it. The sketch begun in the trailer hardly resembles the masterpiece finished here. It is obvious much time and effort was put into every detail. Beautiful Monster is printed at the top but is so stylized that you have to search to see what it says. Angel is more detailed retaining her long dark hair and flowing red dress. She bears the wings of an archangel and behind her are demons and dark creatures, all lurking as if to pounce forwards and capture her. With that, are interwoven vines and gnarled branches, even flowers and rose blooms. It reminds him so much of artwork on the Thunderbird.

Then the door opens and Theo's breath is taken away for a second time. Entering the room is an older and wilder version of his former mentor. Nathaniel has side burns and messy black hair that is longer in front and shorter in back. His tattoos go from his elbow to wrist but nowhere else on his body that Theo can see. And the eyes. As soon as Theo looks at him, he gets uncomfortable. They are the same eyes that used to taunt him on the Reserve.

"You're Theodore?" the elder Ryder asks. Unlike Gerry, the similarities between Nathaniel and his heavenly relation would not be missed if Theo happened to meet him on a street corner. The resemblances are uncanny, though this Ryder has stubble instead of a beard and his nails are painted black and he has hoops in his ears. They look roughly the same age, even though they would be uncle and nephew. Theo supposes that is because of the time difference between the earth and the Reserve. Heavenly Ryder has lived three lifetimes in comparison to his earthly counterpart.

"Have you had a look at the sketch?" Nathaniel closes the door. "If there are any changes you would like to make…"

"No, it's perfect," Theo says, gripping the paper firmly in his hand. "This is what I want exactly."

"Okay, then take off your shirt and lay down." Nathaniel begins to organize his tray of torture instruments.

Staring at him, Theo slowly unbuttons his shirt and then tosses it on the chair beside him. Feeling saucy, he crawls on the dentist's chair and stretches out on his stomach. The chair is cool and tacky against his moist skin. He takes a few deep breaths as Nathaniel swings his tray around.

"Oh," he says, coming to a stop. "Gerry didn't tell me you were burned."

"Is that a problem?" Theo asks, glancing sideways at Nathaniel's knee, his thigh and then up a little further.

"No, but it will be harder to ink," he says, examining the skin on his back with fingers encased in cool plastic gloves.

Theo tenses as the latex slides across the sensitive burned area. How much harder, he thinks, his cock turning into a lump of coal beneath him.

"It will hurt like a son of a bitch and the image will be a little distorted because of the uneven skin. Do you still want to go on?"

Hell, yeah I do. "Yes, please," he says, breathing a little harder, gripping his hands around the sides of the leather bed.

"Okay. I'll start with the outline first and do as much as you can endure in one sitting. Then you will need a while to heal before I can start again. This is your first tattoo?"

"Yes," Theo says and can hear his own heartbeat thumping through the bed.

"Guess you wanted to jump in head first."

Theo restrains a laugh. Yes, head first would be nice. He closes his eyes as the machine starts up and Nathaniel begins his work. The ink machine arcs across his back while Nathaniel's stomach presses in and out of his side. He can feel his tormentor's heart beating as his naked forearms slide across his back. He smells like Ryder too, that musky, underground, sensual stench that used to disturb him so much when he first arrived on the Reserve. Now he eagerly breathes it in as needles punch across his back sewing lines of ink into his skin. The pain is tolerable on his healthy side but when the needles graze across his freshly healed scars, he pulls in a gasped breath. Nathaniel stops, the machine hovering over Theo's back.

"Are you okay?" he asks.

"Yes," Theo whispers tightly.

"Can you continue?"

"Yes. Don't stop."

The needles hit him again, thrusting down through the surface of his crusty skin. Ink and blood begin to seep around his sides and pool beneath his sweating chest and stomach. The moisture beneath him becomes slippery and hot. It moistens the front of his pants. He squeezes his eyes shut as the strokes becoming more intense and painful.

"This is quite burn. Do you mind if I ask how it happened?"

"I was in a car accident," Theo mumbles, knowing he probably wants to hear more but finds himself unable to dispense with the details. The procedure is more painful than he expected.

Nathaniel pulls the needle down a particularly sensitive area of his burn. Theo's hands clamp around the edges of the bed, his nails digging in. His teeth clench as the needle bounces across the crackled skin. His eyes gets heavy and his head starts to swim. And then there's only darkness.

Theo blinks his eyes open. For a second he thinks he's back on the Reserve with Daniel Ryder hovering over his bed. Instead, his eyes focus and he sees an earthly copy looking down on him from above.

"You passed out," Nathaniel says. He wets a towel and dabs Theo's forehead. "Are you on any medication?"

"Pain pills," he says, sitting up groggily. He looks down and sees his chest streaked with ink and blood.

"There will be blood," he explains. "Especially with your injuries. I'm surprised you got as far as you did. Here." He gives Theo a juice box, like the ones he used to drink as a boy in school. Theo sips on the straw, gazing up at the mature Ryder. "It's to bring your blood sugar up. You'd surprised how much a tattoo can take out of you."

Theo continues to drink, clutching the towel to his lap, his chest quickly rising and falling. He wants Nathaniel. He wants to fuck. But this isn't the time, or the place, or the person. "When can we get started again?" he asks eagerly.

"Not for a while, your body needs to rest." Nathaniel checks his book, just a coil notebook, no computer, just like Gerry. "Come back in a week. We'll do it every Friday until it's done." He looks back at Theo, dark hair, dark eyes, his body so much like the one he knew so well on the Reserve. "Feeling better?"

Theo's cheeks are now flushed and hot. "A little."

"I'll wrap your back for tonight. Take it off in the morning though, the tattoo needs to breathe. Keep it out of water for at least four days. Only showers. Don't soak it. Next week we'll finish the outline and start the shade work. Make sure you eat a big meal before you come. And take some of your pain pills. It will help."

Theo nods, sucking his juice box dry. He sets it aside and stares up at Nathaniel.

"There's a bathroom down the hall where you can clean up. Do you feel well enough to walk?"

"I might need help," he says, seizing an opportunity to get closer to this Ryder. But as he eases off the table, he is surprised how dizzy he actually is. Nathaniel swoops in to help him stand, lifting him against his side, an arm slung carefully against his back. Theo clings to him like a girl in a romance novel until the spinning stops.

"Sorry," he whispers as his balance returns.

"Don't be," Nathaniel says as he walks him out in the hall. "It happens all the time."

Not like this, Theo thinks, leaning hard against the muscled frame of Nathaniel Ryder. It is a body foreign to him and yet one he knows so well already. He thought his infatuation with the same sex was limited to just one man. He can see now that it might include the extended family as well.

"There are mirrors inside, so you can have a look at what was done today," Nathaniel stops at the door the bathroom. "Do you need me to come in with you?"

Theo's eyes shoot up to his captor. For a second, he think he sees something there, something in return. Perhaps the uncle and the nephew have more in common than they know. But it could be his own imagination too, his own wishful thinking that he could reignite the passion he had up there, down here.

"Thanks, I'll be okay." He leans on the doorway and watches as the modern day Ryder saunters away. Then he rushes into the bathroom and locks the door. Inside, the walls are covered with posted advertisements for local bands and clubs as well as spray painted with graffiti. There is a toilet and urinal and a floating sink. One blacked out window stands high in the corner. And then there's the mirrors. Theo turns and sees himself standing against the color strewn door, shirtless, his chest streaked in ink and blood. His hair is wet and slicked to his head. He walks closer to the mirrors and turns his back. The mirrors are set at angles so he can see the front and back of himself at the same time. The mirrors are streaked with the finger marks of previous admirers. He turns and sees angry welts of artwork across his back. Like whip marks. And that's how he feels, like he's been whipped. He admires his chest and the ribbons of ink traveling down his skin. The ink and blood continue down and follow the curves of his hips into the front of his pants. Unbuttoning his jeans, he slides them down to his knees, a tired but heavy erection falling out into view. His underwear is full of ink. His cock has ribbons of black around it. He lifts his hands above his head and looks in the mirror. His back is throbbing painfully, especially on the burned side.

"Are you all right in there?" comes a knock at the door.

Theo looks back where a shadow appears beneath the crack in the door. Just a panel of hard wood between him and his tormenter. "What's that?" he says, sliding his hands down the ink and blood on his chest.

"I asked if you were all right. Do you need any help?"

I need some help, he thinks. Come in and I'll show you how you can help me.

"Theo?" The doorknob turns a little one way then the other. But the door is locked. Does Nathaniel have a key?

Theo's hands dive down. He works his member furiously, rolling his head back on painfully sore shoulders. "Just a minute," he gasps. The thought of the elder Ryder bursting through the door and catching him brings him to an abrupt end. His nerves pinch and twist as early orgasm rains down on him. His whole body releases and hums with euphoria. He rolls his head back, releasing a sigh. "Just one more minute."

"Okay, I'll be in my room if you need me," Nathaniel says and his footsteps fade away.

Spent, Theo pulls his pants back up and uses the towel provided to clean the ink and blood from his chest. Shirtless, he leaves the bathroom feeling wild and virile, his new toy purring to sleep in his pants. He struts past the rooms full of half-naked men and woman all at the mercy of their tattooist. Though he is half the man he used to be, muscle wise, he feels ten times the man he used to be on the inside. There is no shame over who he is anymore, or over his body, or over sex and sexuality. Life is about pleasure now, adventures, and new experiences.

"How does it look?" Nathaniel asks him as he enters the room.

Theo turns his back so the new Ryder can see. "Looks great already."

"Well, let's make another appointment then."

Theo picks up his shirt but does not put it on as Nathaniel scratches his name in his coil notebook. God, he hopes this tattoo takes forever. Friday is now his favorite day of the week. Nathaniel bandages his back and Theo leaves the room shirtless. And leaves a hundred dollar bill in Nathaniel Ryder's tip jar as he goes.

Theo gently dabs the wounds around the tattoo, looking over his shoulder in the bathroom mirror. He's gone for three sessions now, though none as exciting as the first. Angel is nearly done and he can get a sense of what the landscape behind her will look like. Beautiful Monster is starting to take shape and will be magnificent when finished. Now that it's started, he can't wait to get it done.

He sets the bloody towel aside and carefully pulls a loose tee-shirt over his torso. Nathaniel thinks that this Friday may be his last appointment. He is excited to have the tattoo done but is sad that his time with the Ryder's will soon be ending. He still has to buy a car or two from Gerry but after that he will have no more excuses to go and visit the family.

He goes downstairs, not really sure what to do with himself. He was always busy, before death and after. This is one of the first times he has ever been idle. It seems so strange not to have a purpose or direction. He feels like he's just waiting around for his next project to begin. And he is. Angel is still heavy on his mind. He doesn't have much time before prom. And Bea has even less. Yet, still, the leads he has given his investigation have gone nowhere. He wishes he could remember more. Specific names and locations would help immensely. But he has nothing but first names and vague descriptions to offer. Beneath the surface is always a hot thread of anxiety. Where is she in her time line? Will that time line change now that he isn't her guardian? Will he ever be in her life? Because he would have to exist simultaneously to both be alive right now and be Angel's guardian leading up to prom. He doesn't know if that's possible.

He sits down at the table by the living room window and stares out at the crystal waters of the pool. He has so much and she has so little. If he could only find her, then he could do something to change that. He sighs, sitting back in his chair and thumping through a few pristine magazines that have never been opened. That's when he hears his dad talking on the phone.

"Well, if the insurance agent is done with it, then I want it taken to the junk yard." There's a pause. "No, nothing inside. We can replace anything lost. Yes, exactly. All right. All right. Then I'll see you in the morning."

Theo gets up and finds his father in the kitchen. "What was that about?"

"Nothing," Andy says. "Just what's left of the car wreck. They're going to get rid of it tomorrow."

"The car is still around?" he asks, shocked.

"It's in a garage downtown. It took a while for the insurance agency to look it over." His father reaches in his pants pocket and then his jacket. "Have you seen my keys around?"

The wreck. Theo had no idea it was still around. It fills him with curiosity and dread. "Is it all right if I go see it?"

His father pauses. "Um, I don't think that's a good idea, son. It was an awful mess. And damaged so badly from the fire that it's basically unrecognizable."

"I'd still like to see it." Though he's not sure that's true. He does want to see it, feels compelled to visit the wreck that changed his life before it's hauled off and destroyed, but is also nervous about revisiting the moment it all ended. After all, for him, he was simply whisked away to a misty hill. In reality, his body was ripped apart and hauled to the hospital where teams of surgeons tried to stitch all his pieces back together.

"You can go if you want." His father sighs and pats him on the shoulder as he passes. Then he stops and turns suddenly. "Son, you're bleeding."

"I'm what?" Theo looks back at his father.

"On your back." Andy frantically grabs him by the collar and attempts to look down his shirt.

Theo wrenches away when he realizes where the blood is from. "Don't."

"I'm calling the doctor," Andy says, now fumbling around his pocket searching for his phone, which is still sitting on the table after the call he just made.

Theo grabs his dad by the arm. "It's a tattoo. That's why I'm bleeding. I don't need a doctor."

"A tattoo?" His father gasps. "Are you serious?"

"Yes, I got it started a few weeks ago."

"A tattoo?" Andy repeats, incredulous. "But...why is it bleeding? They're not supposed to bleed are they? A tattoo?"

Theo sighs, releasing his father's arm. "Sometimes they do. It's part of the healing process. So, can I go see the wreck before it's gone?"

Andy also sighs. "I guess, if you want to. But don't tell your mother I let you go. And don't tell her about the tattoo."

Theo pushes the key in the lock and opens the door to the dark warehouse. He reaches around the side of the door for the light switch and flicks it on. At first nothing happens. Just a soft hum fills the air. He waits at the open door anxiously and then, one by one, the fluorescent lights ignite. And heaped in the middle of the empty storage space is a piece of mangled metal. Theo loses his breath as soon as he sees it. From where he stands it doesn't even resemble a vehicle; it doesn't even have a particular color to it anymore. Was it silver or black? He can't even remember.

He shuts the door behind him and slowly enters the room. Getting closer, he can see that it's actually in two pieces, though he cannot tell which is the front part of the car and which is the back. He circles around it at a great distance seeing a wheel and a door handle. Metal is folded like the vent of an accordion. Pieces of broken glass are sprinkled around the wreck. He can see the places where the car must have been cut to get him free. It's unbelievable that he could survive it, let alone be walking around it right now.

He swears, moving closer. The car stands so silently now, all alone in this immaculate showroom like a piece of fine art but at one time it was screaming, and he was screaming, and his bones were breaking, and his blood was flowing. He couldn't get out. His legs were trapped and people were outside pounding the windows. He takes a deep breath and peaks into a porthole that used to be a window. He sees part of a seat that has burned black as charcoal. Dried blood is everywhere. The stick shift is bent in half. How did he ever get out of this alive? It is a miracle, though he has frequently claimed it not to be. There isn't even room for a human being to fit inside the space where the driver's seat used to be. Not even one who's been bent and broken. Folded between the seat and the metal, he sees the pitch fork that was part of his devil's costume. He reaches in and tries to pull it free but it's melted into the seat.

He pushes back, shaken and nauseas. Perhaps his father was right. He should've left it well enough alone. But then something comes to his head, something right out of the clear blue sky. Ramirez. Romeo's last name was Ramirez. He takes out his phone and quickly calls the private investigator. He shouts the name excitedly in the phone knowing it could be what they need to break the case. Romeo will help him find Angel. And then he'll destroy Ramirez and make all of Angel's dreams come true. Oh, it's about to happen. He just knows it. Feeling revived, he leaves the warehouse without another look at the wreck.

Chapter 33ଓ

The next morning, his mother shows up for breakfast looking very distressed. She's gone all pale and is pacing anxiously.

"What is it, Dianna?" Andy asks, rising from his chair.

"There's some sort of *person* standing outside the front door," she whispers, pointing a well-manicured finger at the rarely used entranceway doors.

"Person?" Andy asks, moving towards her.

"Well, *person,* you know. Some sort of person who does not belong here." Her painted mouth turns down in a worried frown and the two go the front window together and peak between the curtains.

"Well, he certainly does look out of place," Andy mumbles, carefully observing through the slit in the fabric.

"Out of place?" Dianna exclaims, pulling back from the window. "He looks like some sort of convict or something. We should call for help."

Concerned a Jehovah Witness or Girl Guide is about to get taking down by Duncan security officers, Theo joins them at the window and is shocked to see Nathaniel Ryder at the front doors of their house.

"How did he get past the gate?" his mother frets. "Do you think he broke in?"

"Well the gate beside the flower garden doesn't lock." Andy says, nose pressed to the glass. "Anyone can get in there."

"It doesn't lock?" his mother exclaims. "Why do we have all this security if any sort of street person can just wander into our yard?"

"I'll call for help," Andy says.

Sighing, Theo pushes the window open and leans outside. "Hey," he calls, pointing back towards the garage, "I'll meet you at the side door." He turns and sees both his parent's eyes focused intently on him.

"You know this *man*?" his mother whispers, pointing towards the window.

"He's just a friend. Someone I met in town."

"A friend?" His father's eyebrows lifted high on his forehead. "What sort of friend is he?"

Theo leaves the room without further explanation but knows this conversation is far from over. He goes out the garage door and meets the elder Ryder out the side entrance. While Nathaniel looks pretty normal in the tattoo shop, he definitely looks out of place amongst his mother's peonies and cupid statues.

"I shouldn't have come without calling but I didn't know your number. And, well, everyone knows where the Duncan's live," Nathaniel says.

"It's not a problem." Theo extends his hand and enjoys Ryder's firm grip, his palm stiff and dry. The back of his hands are inked all the way down to his fingertips.

"How is your back doing?" he asks, breaking the handshake and crossing his arms over his chest. Theo restrains a smile. His nephew used to stand the very same way.

"It bled a bit at first, but it's better now." Out of the corner of his eye, Theo notices the front curtains winking open and closed like a flirtatious school girl. Hoping for a little more privacy, he says, "Let's walk around back."

The two men walk around the corner of the house. Oh, Theo is sure that the spying won't end there. His parents will just move to the back window and pretend to be busy with the plants on the sill. Theo looks over at Nathaniel and those dark Ryder eyes look back at him. It's so hard to remember that they are not his mentor's eyes. And that his Ryder is gone and he won't see him again until the day he dies.

Nathanial sighs, his arms still wrapped tightly around his chest. "Look I shouldn't be saying this, but I talked to Gerry yesterday and he says that you were interested in buying the Tombstone Thunderbird."

"Tombstone Thunderbird?" Theo asks.

Nathaniel rolls his eyes and smiles. "Well, that's what the family has always called it. And the name has sort of stuck."

Theo snorts. Tombstone Thunderbird. It's perfect. "Yes, I did but Gerry seemed upset when I asked about it so I didn't push him."

"But you still want it?"

"Of course, I would love have it."

They enter the back yard through an arched iron gate and pass between gardens just beginning to bud with flowers. "That's a big pool," Nathaniel exclaims, looking pretty astounded by everything in the back yard, not just the lake in the middle of it. "I mean I knew your family was rich, but…" He falls silent.

Theo is embarrassed he brought him back here, like he was doing it to show off and he wasn't. He just wanted some privacy. "It's my grandfather's money. We just inherited it. And he had a lot of it."

"I see that." Nathaniel sighs and then sits down in one of the garden chairs. He looks up at Theo. "I want you to buy that car."

Theo's eyebrows raise. "But…"

"You know what happened in it, right?"

"I've heard rumors," Theo says, sitting down too. He wishes he actually read Ryder's book. He was so angry that day and couldn't wait to sling it out with his mentor. He had no idea how complicated Ryder's story actually was.

"Well, Gerry's son, his name was Daniel, he killed himself in that car. It was really unexpected and no one knows why he did it. He didn't shoot himself or anything like that. He hooked the gas pipe to the window. He died from inhaling the fumes. Gerry found him like that in the garage."

Theo looks at his hands trying to picture the vibrant and determined Ryder that he knows today taking his life. He just can't piece it together. Ryder seems unstoppable in death. How could he be so different in life?

"Him and Gerry didn't get along so well. I mean Daniel was so...different. But the one thing they had in common was that Thunderbird. And when Daniel died, Gerry just kept working on it. Year after year, he put all his money into it. Eventually his ex-wife couldn't deal with the debt anymore and quit speaking to him. That's when Gerry moved out onto the lot."

"He lives there?" Theo exclaims. "In that trailer?"

"Yes, in that junkyard, just him and that damned car. He's finally willing to sell it but he's trying to get someone in the family to take it. We don't want him to have that car anymore. We don't even want it in the family. And we have to get him off that lot. He won't leave the lot as long as the Thunderbird is there."

Theo sits back heavily, staring out at the pool as the sun casts diamonds across the surface of the water. He can't imagine someone living on that lot, living amongst those wrecks and calling that trailer home. He wishes he could go there and tell Gerry that his son is okay. He's better than okay. But how could anyone believe such a story?

"He'd kill me if he knew I was here," Nathaniel muses, his voice softening. "This might sound a little weird, but what are your intentions with this car? Why do you want a car that someone killed themselves in?"

Big question. And he's got some big answers but he can't tell the living Ryder the truth. It would sound completely absurd. He thinks carefully before answering. "I know a girl who's going to kill herself," he says, raising his eyes to the soft hazel gaze of Nathaniel Ryder. "I want to save her in that car."

A smile turns up the corner of Nathaniel's mouth. "That's the best answer I've ever heard." He extends his hand and Theo shakes it again. "Push him. Tell him what you told me if you have to. Do what you have to do to get that car away from him. We will take care of Gerry once the Thunderbird is gone."

Later that day, Theo returns to the used car lot. This time on foot because he's determined to leave the lot in the Thunderbird. And this time it's not just because of Daniel that he's pursuing it. He want to set Ryder's father free as well. Because Daniel isn't suffering, not in the least, and his father shouldn't be either.

He enters the chain link fence and his eyes fix on the monstrosity parked next to the trailer. His heart races a bit when he sees it. It's not just a car but a piece of the past. A coffin for Ryder and a black hole for his father. Theo approaches it like he's in an old west movie facing down a villain. It seems bigger today, bulkier, more garish and dangerous than he ever remembered. As he nears it, he runs his hand along the hood. Ryder breathed his last breath inside this car. He ascended and was greeted on the hill by Veddie. Fresh off a suicide attempt, he was escorted down the streets of the Reserve and judged worthy by the twins in the underwater cistern. He was taken under Veddie's wing as a student and that is where the real adventure began. Death is so much more than anyone here can understand. It is simply a doorway to another existence.

Theo enters the trailer where Gerry sits inside, head focused down on the numbers in his book. He didn't give the trailer much attention the first time he came in here. It was simply a dirty, old office in some dirty, old lot. But now that he knows Gerry lives here, he regards it with more scrutiny. It isn't just dirty but derelict. The roof sags in and the walls are yellowed with water stains. He notices a door near the back which must lead to Gerry's living area. It doesn't even have a door knob on it, just a big round hole where one should be. He can't imagine that the space behind that door is much of an improvement over this one. This place, like the car, is an embodiment of Gerry's grief. His own personal prison. Which he has placed himself inside of to punish himself for his son's death.

"How's your tattoo going?" Gerry asks, setting his pen aside. He is dressed in the same clothes he was the last time Theo saw him, his hair in the same thin braids as well.

"Good. Should be done my next session. It's pretty painful though."

"Yes, Nathanial mentioned you were burned."

"It was a car accident."

"Oh, so you're *that* Theodore Duncan."

Theo nods, getting a little tired that his name will always be associated with his parent's money and that accident. "Listen," he says, leaning on the dirty countertop. Time to make his move. He's been planning the best way to separate Gerry from the Thunderbird, to give the old man some financial freedom and not make it look like he's some rich kid's charity case. He sees only one way to do that. "I want all the cars on the lot."

"Okay," Gerry says, not hearing Theo right. He turns to a page marked *sales* and picks up his pen. "Which one do you want?"

"No, I want *all* of them."

"All of them?" Gerry exclaims, looking up. "But…"

"I want the lot," Theo says, carefully dolling out the story he concocted on the way here. "I'm going to start rebuilding cars with that friend I brought here the other day. This is a good location. And the cars are already here."

Gerry's eyes narrow a bit. "Did Nathaniel tell you to…"

"No," Theo quickly interjects but can tell Gerry is not convinced. "It's something I've been thinking of doing for a while. We're going to hire at-risk youth," he says, his new lie gaining momentum. "We are going to teach them to rebuild cars and they keep the cars they rebuild. Sort of like Habitat for Humanity but with automobiles. Anyway, it's just in its infancy right now. First, I need the cars." It's actually not a bad idea. Buddy loves cars. Theo wonders if he'd actually be interested in taking on the project if he decided to try and do it.

Gerry folds his leathery hands over his ink stained book filled to the brim with unpaid debts. This is the only life this man knows. And he looks reluctant to let it go even with such an easy way out. Nathaniel said to push him or Gerry will die in this lot. Seeing him now, in this nest of poverty and filth, Theo knows that is the truth. So he throws down his last stipulation, knowing this is the demand that could end the deal.

"I have one condition," Theo says, carefully. "I want the Thunderbird as well."

Gerry looks up, his eyes wide. They begin to water and he quickly turns around. "I can't give that car away," he says, his voice weak and shaky.

Theo draws his arms around himself, looking at Gerry surrounded by his son's photos. The memory that Gerry is holding onto is his son's death and not his life. Though he had Daniel until he was a teenager, it's the suicide that he relives over and over again. Theo doesn't know how he can break this man from that car or from that moment.

"You're not giving it away; you're giving it to me." Theo urges softly. "It's not for the project. I want the car for myself."

"I'm not giving it to anyone," Gerry returns tightly. He wipes a smudge from one of Daniel's photos but it only leaves a bigger smudge behind. He wipes it again, but the stain spreads across his son's face. He tries to lift it off its hanger but the picture falls and breaks. And then Gerry breaks too. He slides down to his knees and struggles to hold the sobs inside. But the pain he holds inside is too great to contain.

Theo comes around the counter and kneels down as Gerry sobs and picks the photo up from shards of broken glass. The photo is faded, in black and white, but the boy beside the man is unmistakably Ryder. How can he make Gerry understand that his son is all right? That he doesn't need to punish himself for something he could not control? The emotions are so raw that it would take a lifetime of therapy to remedy Gerry's feelings of guilt and regret.

Gerry lowers his head to hide his tears but one drop lands on the picture and spreads across the surface. "Get out," he whispers as his dead son's face begins to distort beneath the tear. "Get out of here and never come back."

"Please Gerry," Theo says and is surprised to find tears springing to his own eyes. He takes the photo from Gerry's trembling hand and looks down at the picture of Daniel affectionately. "I know your son. I know him."

Gerry releases an angry wail and then turns on Theo. A fight breaks out and Theo tries to wrestle the father down amongst the broken glass behind the counter. "Sick of you kids and your fucking jokes!" Gerry screams at him. "This is not funny! What happened in that car is not a joke! My son is not a joke!"

"No, he's not," Theo says tightly, still struggling to keep the old man still. He's old but he's tough and determined to escape from his grasp. Theo knows he has lost him now. He will not get Gerry from this lot. He will stay here and die with the Thunderbird. So he has nothing to lose by telling him the truth. He has to try and make Gerry understand or all is lost.

"You kids come here and you…" Gerry sobs and then jerks violently. "My son died in that car. He killed himself. And everyone thinks it's a joke."

"It's not a joke," Theo says, sweat now tricking down his back. He feels like he's trying to hug an angry bear. All Gerry wants to do is get away from him. "I am not joking. I know your son. I know Daniel."

"Fuck you!" Gerry shouts. "I'll call in the family! We will make you pay for this!"

"I died in that car accident. I wasn't in a coma for four months; I was dead. And I know it sounds crazy and I know you won't believe me but I went somewhere. I went…" Theo sighs, struggling to make the story sound reasonable. "I ascended. I went into the light. And I saw your son when I was there."

"You don't even know him," Gerry cries. "You shut your fucking mouth."

"No, I do know him." Theo struggles to keep the man still but his arms are starting to quiver and he doesn't know how much longer he can hold on. "I know Daniel. I met him there. And he is okay. He wouldn't want you to live like this. He wouldn't want you to remember him like this."

Gerry slumps forward and Theo cannot hold him any longer. He sits back against the counter as they both gasp to catch their breath. How can he make Gerry understand? There has to be a way to break through. Then he gets an idea. He has knowledge of very personal information about Daniel Ryder. Something his own father may not have told anyone. If Gerry even knew.

"I know your son was gay," he says quietly, bracing for the reaction.

Gerry's back straightens. He's silent for a long time before he says, "Who told you that?"

"No one did. I know it because Daniel told me himself."

"You don't know that," Gerry says softly. "You're just making up stories."

"He is still living...up there. He's a teacher now." That gets a reaction from Gerry, but Theo doesn't know why, so he keeps on babbling hoping he'll hit on something meaningful. "He's a bit of a scientist too, inventing these strange creations. He collects things, all these oddities he finds on his travels. And, god, is he ever loved. His students love him. He is the most popular teacher there. He trains people to become guardian angels. Oh, I know that sounds crazy but he trained me. He taught me how to be a man. And he saved me too. I am a better person for knowing him."

Gerry slumps against the side of his counter and begins to sob uncontrollably.

"I don't know why he killed himself. I don't think he knows why either. It just doesn't seem like something he'd do. But he doesn't dwell on that moment at all. He doesn't even think of it. He has moved on with his life and he would hate to see you here like this. Holding on to this. I don't need that car. If it's all you have of him, then keep it. But give me the lot. And leave this place. You don't have to live like this anymore. I am giving you an opportunity to start over."

Gerry remains where he is, sobbing. He has completely shut down. Theo looks down at the shards of broken glass scattered around his feet. He can't leave him like this. He's worried if he does, Gerry will kill himself. He reaches up to the counter and takes the phone off the hook. Then he dials Nathaniel's number.

Buddy drops Theo off for his tattoo appointment that Friday. He hasn't heard a word from the Ryder family since the incident in the trailer. Nathaniel came after he called. Then more relatives were called in and Theo was asked to leave. Theo has been plagued with guilt ever since. All he wanted to do was reassure Gerry that his son was okay but he just couldn't convince him that the stories were real. And in the end all he did was make things worse. He's not even sure he should be here right now, or that he has any standing left with the Ryders at all.

As he nears the building, he is surprised to see the Tombstone Thunderbird parked outside the laundry. It's the first time he's seen it anywhere but in the car lot. He approaches it slowly expecting the car to be full of angry Ryders armed with clubs and knives, but it's empty. Perhaps the mob is waiting inside for him. He opens the door to the laundromat. It's strangely deserted today which only adds to his unease. When he gets to the waiting room for the tattoo parlor, it's also empty. Nervously, he knocks on the door.

"Oh, hello, Theo," the girl with the barbells in her face says as she answers the door. She takes him down the hall with an affectionate hand on his back. "Nathan is waiting for you. Do you need anything before you go in?"

"Um, no." he says, confused by her friendly reaction. She's been cold to him since the day they met. He can't imagine what has changed.

He rounds the corner and finds Nathaniel inside. The room is completely dark except for a single spotlight hanging over the tattoo bed. Nathaniel looks up. He is dressed casually in jeans and a button up shirt which is mostly buttoned down. Theo stops when he sees him, still nervous about Gerry and why that car is parked out front.

"Thanks, Darla," Nathaniel says to the girl behind him. "I don't want anyone in here until I'm done, all right?"

"Do not disturb. Got it." She nudges Theo playfully in the room and closes the door behind him. Theo stands rigidly a few steps inside the entranceway, staring at the elder Ryder. Something is off. He's still waiting to be pounced by Ryders. Maybe that's why the girl was so happy. She knows a beating is on its way.

Ryder pats the tattoo bed. "Come now. Don't be afraid."

Theo enters the room and sits down carefully on the bed. Nathaniel is also acting strangely. Too friendly. And where is Gerry? If the car is here, then the man must be also.

"Take off your shirt," Nathaniel says. He turns and snaps on his black gloves.

Despite his anxiety, Theo feels his cock twitch. He's been flirtatious with the elder Ryder in the past few appointments and he hasn't protested much. Trembling a little, he removes his shirt and sets it aside.

"The bottom half as well," Nathan says, his voice completely straight.

Theo swallows hard, staring up into those smoky Ryder eyes. He can't get a fix on Nathanial's intentions. His face is a brick wall. He reaches down to his button fly and the elder Ryder's eyes drop to watch as he slips his pants down to the floor and steps out of them. He would be thrilled if not for the car out front.

"All of it." Nathaniel indicates to his underwear, his eyes unmoved.

Theo shudders, his knees going a bit weak. If it's an ambush waiting for him, then he is walking right into it. But somehow he just cannot say no to a Ryder so he drops his drawers and stands naked in front of this man, this stranger he only knows through family association. Oh, if only his former self could see him now. That restricted, constipated little fool who couldn't have even comprehended an encounter as complex as this one. Even his new, wild self is having trouble wrapping its head around what's happening right now.

"Lie down," Nathaniel says, taking some time to look him up and then down. Theo tentatively lifts himself up to the tattoo chair. He lies back slowly, the cool leather sending shock waves through his naked skin. He grips his hands around the thick foam mattress. The single spotlight is just above his hips, heating and highlighting the sensitive area.

"You change your mind?" Nathaniel says, coming to stand over him with a tattoo gun in his black gloved hand.

"W-what?" Theo whispers, his whole body jittering.

"You getting a tattoo on your front?" he asks. He fires up the gun and the five stabbing spines buzz to life.

"Oh." Theo blushes, turning over slowly. He exhales as he comes down on his front and the leathery folds of the chair embrace his naked skin. His heart is racing and he can hardly breathe. Nathaniel sits down on a stool beside the bed. He is no longer wearing a shirt. Theo jolts as Ryder's hands come down on his back.

"Relax," he whispers.

Theo exhales and closes his eyes. Whatever is going on here, revenge for upsetting Gerry does not seem to be the objective. No, Nathaniel seems to have his mind on something else entirely. Theo exhales as the needles press into the soft skin of his lower back and begin their journey upwards. His director works slow and methodical, pressing shades of red, blue, and yellow permanently between the layers of his skin, separating his pores and working the ink gently in.

"You should be careful what you do in the bathroom," Nathaniel comments, his voice deep and deliberate. "There's video surveillance in there."

Theo's eyes widen, his lusty fantasy disrupted.

"Everyone watched you." Nathaniel pulls his stool up closer. Theo jolts as Ryder's knees contact his naked side, those wiry, muscled legs opened to him. He's all crammed up underneath, a sweaty sheen between him and the plastic bed.

Theo cringes, remembering what he did in the bathroom after his first session. His face burns as thinks of the girl with the barbells. Is that why she was suddenly so friendly to him?

"So, who is your beautiful monster?" Nathaniel rises and moves to the sink. He rinses his hands and gets a jar from the cupboard above him. Theo closes his eyes trying to get his head back together. The combination of low blood sugar, anxiety over being taped and watched, and excitement over why Nathaniel is inking him naked is making his head spin. Is it possible that the uncle shares some of the nephew's inclinations? Is it possible that there is only one Ryder wanting to jump him in his vulnerable state?

The tattoo tray slides back into view. Theo turns his head towards his captor and is shocked to find Nathaniel naked, just hot hard skin going down beneath his line of view. Ryder sits back down on the stool, opening his legs again. And, oh yes, all the Ryder's are extremely gifted. The needle carves into his skin again. Theo gasps against the ungiving leather of the tattoo chair. God, how he wishes this sofa had fingers, had folds, had little crevasses he could sink inside of. He is so hard right now and everything is jammed up underneath him. He fantasizes about rolling onto his back, about offering to the uncle what the nephew already experienced, and of the wild sexual encounter that would follow. Could he really do it twice in one lifetime? Fall for two separate Ryders?

"Your beautiful monster?" Nathaniel repeats when the silence has gone on too long.

"She's...uh," Theo gasps. "She's the girl...the suicide girl I told you about before."

Nathaniel opens his legs a little more. "And you're going to save her?"

"I am," he whispers, staring down those open thighs like he once did with Azrael.

"In the Thunderbird?"

"I had hoped so," Theo breathes, his voice barely audible. He's so hot and so sticky, his back stinging from the tracks left by the painted needles. A drip of sweat slips down his forehead and lands on the bed in front of him. Then another. He stares down at the little spots wanting to lap them up with his tongue, lap up Nathaniel as well.

"This is a serious commitment, a tattoo like this. What if you can't save her?"

"I will," Theo says it as surely as he believes it. He will find her. He will save her. There is simply no other option.

Nathaniel rolls his stool back and tosses an ink soaked rag into a basket near the sink. Then picks up a new one from the counter. He turns, and Theo sees that full, virile body stretched out in front of him. Nathaniel brings a bottle of water back with him. Drinks it over his back. A drip of water lands on Theo's hip. It slowly slides down his body, around the curve of his thigh, and down past his throbbing cock.

"Gerry is giving you the car," Nathaniel says, sitting back down.

Theo's head jolts up.

Nathaniel presses his head back down to the bed. "Stay still."

"He's giving me the car?"

"He won't take money for it." The machine starts up again. Theo arches slightly as the needle moves into his burned skin.

"But he will take money for the lot." There's a long pause and then Nathaniel says, "There were only two people who knew Daniel was gay. Only Gerry and I ever knew and neither of us told anyone. That's how he knew you were telling the truth."

"So he believes me?"

"We all do," Nathaniel says. "Because you are too young to have ever known Daniel. And you knew things that Gerry knew. About his collecting stuff. And how he wanted to be a teacher. Stuff that no one else could know but him."

Theo exhales, feeling tremendous relief spread through his body. "So Gerry is going to move out of the lot?"

"He has left it already. And if you are serious, then the family is prepared to sell you everything."

"I am serious." Theo's head begins to buzz. He feels the world sliding back and forth like he is in a gently swaying hammock. He didn't eat before he came. Nathaniel told him to eat. Now he is dizzy and exhausted and feels his consciousness slipping again.

Theo wakes up with the rising sun. He sees a long shadow of tangerine across the shiny metal tray near the bed. His eyes move to the divots where the buttons pierce the leather bed looking like soul pools spread across the Field. His whole body is numb and murmuring and mumbling. A hot sheet of pain sears across his back.

"I told you to eat," Nathaniel says. A juice box appears in front of his face, as well as the naked body of Nathaniel Ryder. Theo pushes back with a painful gasp and sucks hungrily on the straw. The sweet, cold liquid rushes down the back of his throat. "I hope you don't mind, but I kept working while you were passed out. The tattoo is finished."

"Finished?" Theo says weakly. He drinks the juice box dry, feeling a rush of adrenaline race through his body.

"Yes. All done."

The pain and numbness in his back makes his head spin. He feels dirty; he is dirty, his front creased from the plastic bed and smeared in ink and blood. Nathaniel hands him a towel and clicks off the spotlight. The room is now only lit by the sunlight cresting through the narrow slatted windows of the dark gloomy room. Theo wipes down his front, staring up at Nathaniel who stands in front of him completely nude. He is beautiful with that same lean muscled build Daniel had. But wilder and more unpredictable than his nephew. And a little more frightening too.

"Do you want to see it?" Nathaniel asks.

Theo's eyes go up. "See what?"

"The tattoo?"

Theo exhales a laugh. Of course, the tattoo, because everything else is being presented to him like a Sunday buffet.

Outside the door, someone knocks. "Are you finished yet?" the girl with the rings in her face asks.

"Not quite yet," Nathaniel says to Theo. He stares at him hard for a few seconds then says. "Try and stand up."

Theo rises on shaky legs.

"There's a mirror against the wall." Nathaniel points. Theo walks unsteadily towards his reflection. Elder Ryder walks behind him. When they reach the mirror, Nathaniel puts his hands on Theo's shoulders and looks at him through his reflection. "You ready?"

"Yes," Theo whispers.

Nathaniel turns him around to face him. Theo's heart rate rises as two strong, male bodies face off against each other. He is hard and so is the man who stands in front of him. Theo exhales, his chest moving slowly in and out. He wants to respond but this Ryder sets the controls. He is not a victim of his whimsies like his nephew was. He lifts his hand to Theo's chin and turns his face to the side. "Look."

It takes Theo a second or two before he realizes Nathaniel means *look in the mirror*. Theo turns his eyes back and sees his Beautiful Monster in all her glory. She is brilliant, she is animated, she is alive. And around the crucified girl are the demons who hunt for her heart and the cemetery that wants her body and the angels that are trying to save her soul. "Oh my god," he whispers. "It's perfect."

Ryder slowly turns him around again so he faces the mirror with his captor behind him. He can feel Nathaniel's swollen cock against his back. Then his hand comes around the front. Something cold shocks his skin. He gasps and sees Nathaniel is holding a key against his chest. Theo takes the key into his hand, his fingers touching Nathaniel's as he does.

"For the car," Nathaniel whispers in his ear then he slaps him hard in the ass. "Be good to her."

Theo shrieks at the unexpected contact, then turns and watches as Ryder saunters away. No, there will not be another notch on his bedpost from the Ryder family tree. This, like the car, may have been a thank-you for helping out Gerry. But it is clear, as Nathaniel pulls on his pants and begins to set his tools in the sink, that Theo will leave with his tattoo completed and his appetite unsatisfied.

Theo pulls his car into the parking lot outside the private investigators office. He turns the engine off and sits in the quiet for a minute. It is all coming together now, Ryder, the tattoo, the car. And now a lead. A solid lead. The investigator called him while he was driving home. Said he needed him to come down to the office right away. Theo knows in his heart that he's found her, that his next adventure is about to begin.

He straightens himself up and exits the car. Oh, the car is spectacle all right, more than he even imagined. People point and they stare. Adults roll their eyes. Kids clap in delight. Teenagers give him a sly smile. He can't wait to really get it out on the road, get it into Angel's town. He can't wait to get her in it and get their new life started.

He opens the office door and steps inside. The investigator, who Theo only knows as Jackie, waves him in.

"Did you find her?" Theo asks eagerly but is met with a guarded look. His hot high shatters. "What did you find?" he asks, more panicked. "Is she okay?"

Jackie passes a clipping from a newspaper. It's an obituary. Theo's hands shudder and he drops it to the floor. He scrambles down, picking it up. Oh god, please no. Please don't let this have Angel's name on it. Please. He fumbles to open the clipping and holds it with shaking fingers. It reads:

Beatrice Yu tragically lost her life on Tuesday, April 5th. She will be forever missed by her loving parents. Services will be held on April the 11th in St. Josephs Cathedral. All mourners are welcome to attend.

"Shit!" Theo cries, crumpling the note in his hand. "Shit. Shit. Shit."

THE RESCUE

Chapter 34☙

There's an acuteness in grief. Everything seems to have a sharper edge. With the worries of everyday life dulled away, the real pain can make its debut. Beatrice Yu is dead. For Angel, even weeks after it's over, the words still don't sit well in her head. Now there is a sickness in her heart that has no cure. No medicine or treatments can ease the pain she is suffering. It's thick and it weighs her limbs down, making even the most mundane task insurmountable. Pointless, really. Cleaning the house, paying the bills, eating, sleeping, none of it seems important anymore. She just wants to lie face down on the road and let the vehicles run over her. And she's sure that they would, over and over again without bothering to stop. After all, she is the daughter of the man who dragged a boy under his truck for sixteen blocks. A deserving end for someone like her who comes from someone like him.

Angel looks up, shielding her eyes from the painfully bright sun. It seems like it's been sunny every day since Bea died, as if her death has had no consequence on either the natural or unnatural word. Angel was removed from class and told about Bea by the police. With no one else to care for or support her, she fell into the cop's unsympathetic arms. Since then she has been consumed by grief, besieged by fits of crying and painful hyperventilation. She hid in her house for days and days just holding her dog and crying until her eyes were too swollen to shed another tear. A legion of emotions assaulted her at once. Denial, remorse, regret and then anger. And now there is only one emotion left. Now it's just anger.

Romeo was questioned by the police over the incidents leading up to Bea's suicide. Then they questioned the boy hired to court Bea. But in the end it was ruled a suicide. It was her choice to take her own life and everyone was tapped on the knuckles and sent on their merry little way. Probably didn't hurt that the cops are related to Romeo's family. Bea's funeral was deserted. No one from the school came. It was only Angel and a crowd of Asian relatives. Since then, she has been unable to face the Yu's. The guilt keeps her away because there is only one person other than Romeo who shoulders the blame for Bea's death. And that's her. She was so wrapped up in her own stupid problems that she didn't notice Bea was drowning too.

There's no morality in the world anymore. No one cares. No one is required to be accountable for their actions. This world no longer fears god or nature; it's a plague of apathy that threatens the fall of man now. Greed and excess are to be uplifted and admired. The needs of the one are thrust above the needs of the many. The weak are left to be pulled apart by the wolves. And that's what Angel feels like. Pulled apart by predators. Held together by bits and pieces and it will take one last glancing blow before she crumbles to dust.

She readjusts her backpack, the load of her disassembled shotgun shifting across her painfully sore back. She can't wait any longer. She took all her journals to the burn pit last night and lit them on fire. She left a note for the Yu's on her counter asking them to take her dog. And then she loaded everything she would need for her last day at school. Unlike Save the Date, she has no good plan for how this day will go down. But somehow, someway, everything will end today.

And she longs to die. There is no point for her existence anymore, except to be the object of suffering and pain. She has spent her life struggling for the smallest things that are handed to most people on a silver platter. She can't even turn on the taps for a glass of water. The house is cold and dark. Every major utility is either shut off or in arrears. But home is nothing compared to what she has suffered at school. She has struggled since the day she was born. Every moment since her horrible birth has been leading up to this one final moment. Death is so close now. It paces her side by side. She recalls a line from a Dickenson poem:

Since I could not stop for Death,

He kindly stopped for me.
The carriage held but just Ourselves
And Immortality.

Angel experiences the slightest dab of warmth in her cold and broken heart. She imagines Death on his shadowy carriage, fierce horses flailing and bucking, shrouded in the blackest mist. He'll be waiting outside the school for her. He'll raise his bony hand and call her forward with the come hither of a single finger beckoning. She'll know his face because they are old companions. He'll know her because she is finally answering his call. He'll have her carriage waiting out front and anyone who crosses her path on the way to Romeo will come along for the ride. Death will whisk her away and she'll never return to this place again. She's not worried about hell. She's been in it for eighteen years already.

Angel enters through the front doors, glancing up at the shiny school emblem overhead. This high school will become one of the many driven into infamy by a discarded student tossed to the side by the popular masses. When the survivors are interviewed, they won't mention the years of intimidation and abuse she suffered at the hands of her bullies. No, they will send off glowing accounts of Romeo and his followers. Everybody loves the dead. Seems dying washes away all your sins. Not hers though. She'll live on in infamy, finally breaking from the shadow of her father's disgrace. A once nameless exile, she will be cast in into the hallowed halls of high school justice. No one will care about her side of the story, except she was *that* girl whose father ran over *that* boy. Will anyone come to her funeral? Will she even have one? Or will she be plunked in the ground unceremoniously next to the only Asian girl that dared to be different in this stupid, simple country town?

Thoughts of Bea makes her head spin once again so she focuses on the task at hand. Find Romeo. Hopefully he's standing in a crowd of his friends. She hasn't seen any of them since Bea's suicide. She imagines they are sniggering over the results of their jest, having a real good laugh over how well their prank turned out.

Inside the school, she finds her lock on upside down. She opens the combination backwards and gazes into the empty locker, her empty life. When she is gone, they will just move someone else in like she was never here. They will happily forget her. And she is only too happy to be gone. This life has been too long already.

She carefully sets her bag inside. The gun is in a few pieces but it won't take long to put back together. It was her father's gun. Left leaning in a closet when they abandoned her, as if offering her a solution to all her problems. If things get too bad, you always have this way out. Won't he be surprised when he sees what she's done? Then he can live in the aftermath of someone else's crimes for a while. See how it feels when she had to live inside his.

A hand comes down on the locker beside her. It jolts her out of her unhappy reverie. She turns to find Romeo there, one hand braced against the lockers, the other on his hip.

"Well, look who's back." He grins, a toothpick twitching between his teeth.

Angel's eyes jolt back into her locker, staring at that loaded bag, her heart beating out of her chest. Has he actually come to gloat about what he did to Bea? Maybe she should've come in shooting and not given him a chance to say anything. She can't bring the gun out now. He could disarm her before she even got started.

"Thought you were gone for good," he says, his voice pleasant.

Angel glances at that blustery, sun drenched, farm face concealed beneath the shadow of his tilted baseball cap. His eyes are squinty and shit brown. His nose is cracked from too much sun. And his front teeth don't match up quite right. She shudders at the sight of him. He is the ugliest person she's ever laid eyes on.

Romeo wiggles that toothpick around his mismatched teeth with his fat snake-like tongue. "You know, little girl, I..."

That's when a man rushes past them. Fast. Romeo is knocked right off his feet. He crashes onto to his back and his boots swinging comically up into the air. "Hey, watch where you're fucking going!" Romeo shouts, pushing up to his seat.

The man, with dark hair and black clothes, looks back darkly and says, "I was."

Romeo stumbles to his feet, his cap now on the floor between them.

"Nice hat," the man says, a smirk on his face. "You get that at the thrift store or something?"

Angel's eyes rush over the man. He is stranger, not from here, leaning heavily on a gothic looking cane. His clothes are wild and eccentric. And his eyes. They are so light against his dark exterior that they seem to glow. She shudders, pressing back against her locker, feeling her legs go weak.

Romeo swipes up his hat and slaps it against his leg. Angel has never seen him so flustered in her life. She's surprised he doesn't just attack the stranger but another look at the man shows that he is quite a bit taller than Romeo. And there's something disturbing about him. He seems a bit unstable and dangerous.

Romeo stabs a finger the man's direction. "You're about to get your fucking ass kicked, buddy." He says it but doesn't take a step closer.

"So do it," the man replies, standing his ground. "I'm standing right here. What are you waiting for?"

Angel exhales a breath, her eyes glazing over. No one has ever stood up to Romeo, not even teachers that he's harassed. This is the first time she's ever seen someone confront him. And it's amazingly exciting.

"Is there a problem?" a teacher asks, stepping out of his classroom.

"This kid is harassing me," the man says, pointing his cane at Romeo. "He's got a real attitude problem."

"What the fu... *he* knocked me down," Romeo cries, sounding like a little kid tattling in the playground.

"Enough! Ramirez, back to class," the teacher says, not interested in Romeo's side of the argument.

Romeo points back to his bully who is walking backwards and chuckling.

"Now, Romeo!" the teacher shouts and suddenly everyone is joining in on Pick on Romeo Day. "You too, Angel, enough horsing around."

Angel doesn't even glance at the teacher. Her eyes remain fixed on the stranger as he backs away. He smiles at her and then disappears around the corner. Angel turns back to her locker. She's trembling from the encounter, from the shock of the sudden blow that sent Romeo reeling. Then to him, the stranger, and those eyes, those haunting eyes. *Watch where you're fucking going,* Romeo said. *I was,* replied the stranger. I was. I was.

"Angel!" the teacher scolds again. "To class."

Angel gasps, unaware that the teacher was still standing there. She glances back to the hall where the man, perhaps just a dream, disappeared. Who is he? And will she ever see him again?

Angel sits in the basement of the library, the bag with her gun in it on the cubicle in front of her. This morning, her decision was absolute. It all was going to end today. Now she's not so sure. She hunches forward in her little space, shaking. She can't focus on the killing. She can't focus on anything but those few minutes in the hall. But how can she go home without doing what she came here to do? She feels queasy at the thought of returning to her empty home, to the burn pit in the back yard where all her lovely journals are in ashes. And to that sad little letter pleading with the Yu's to take care of her dog. It was supposed to be all over today and yet she can't find the motivation to do it. Not while the dark stranger could be somewhere in the school. She doesn't want this to go down while he is in the building.

Ambitions lost, her mind drifts to the man. She struggles to recall every small detail of the meeting but it happened so fast, so unexpectedly. He had dark hair and his clothes were unusual. He seemed to be injured, at least he was leaning on a cane. But not some old man cane, it was shiny black with a polished silver head. Is he a student? Someone who has just transferred here? Someone who's going to be around for a while? The idea fills her with excitement but then another thought occurs to her. What if he was just a delivery man? Someone passing through that she'll never see again. Like a comet tracing a quick streak across the dark sky of her life.

She replays the encounter over and over until she's sick with the visual. The man, what he said to Romeo, the way he acknowledged her before he left the hall. She goes over it so many times that the details become smudged. What does it all mean? Probably nothing. Probably nothing at all. She hates that he's here, that he almost saw her in her darkest hour. And that thought drops her mood more. She's pathetic. How could this tiny, little encounter have such a huge impact on her? He probably didn't even see her. And if he did, why would he care at all? She flips back and forth between dreaming and fretting, between hoping and fussing until exhaustion takes over. Days end, she takes her backpack and walks right out the front doors, instead of her usual escape out the side cafeteria door.

Outside, the crowds are gathering in the parking lot. The sun continues its unbearable shining. Romeo's stands with his girls by his monstrous four by four. Parked where Death was supposed to be, carriage and all. He should've been carried out in a body bag, instead he is strutting in front of his stupid girls not knowing that today was the last day of his life.

Angel forges forward, glancing at the bike stand where her only means of transportation still sits unusable. She can't afford to fix it and is too tired and depressed to bother. Wanting to avoid Romeo, she diverts off the main sidewalk to teacher's parking lot where faculty is trickling out towards their economy cars. It's there she sees the man again. Her heart flips at the sight of him, a stanch intense pain pinching her chest. It's almost panic. There he is. Not a student or delivery man but a staff member, parked in the staff parking lot, leaving at the end of the day with staff personnel. A permanent fixture? God, she hopes so.

She slows her pace but continues to walk, trying not to be too obvious in her examination. Her dreams of love are long dead. Her romantic heart died with Ambrose but her very soul expired the minute Bea took her life. She didn't know the depth to which sorrow and pain could take her until then. Since then, the pursuit of love has seemed frivolous and unappealing. And yet here he it is. And she is surprised to feel her heart beating again.

She eyes the dark stranger, disturbed by the arresting vibration she experiences when she sees him. It's an urgency to become noticed, to get acquainted, to be discovered. Her feelings are immediate, irrational, frenzied, jumbled up in her head and all trying to get out the same small egress at the same time. All kicking and screaming for first dibs. Anxiety wants him, no yearning does, no lust wants him, lust wants him. Still, she maintains a facade of calm, watches him as he charges across the parking lot in the same hurried fashion he traveled through the hall. She takes notes, memorizing details as quickly as she can. She has crazy thoughts of rushing up to him and throwing herself at his feet, begging him to take her with him. His black hair gleams in the afternoon sun, and suddenly the grassy fields are full of sparkling dew, and every vehicle in the parking lot is a glistening treasure, the leaves applauding his very existence like clapping hands. The sun outlines his dark form and Angel feels like she could be melting. He is the most beautiful man she's ever seen. She ignites in a full blush, nearly walks into a tree and students laugh and point in her direction. She barely hears it, just pushes around the tree and continues on. The man stomps among the cars and minivans then drops down and disappears. She hears a car door slam and then the most awful roar brings half the quad's attention towards the teacher's parking lot. A car backs out, a gruesome thing with an amplified muffler that would neuter the balls off Romeo's trailer hitch. The car skids in her direction, a demon on wheels, chromed teeth and mirrored windows, the body covered in ghouls and graveyard crosses. Angel just stands, mouth agape as he races past her, his eyes focused forward, ringed fingers on the leather clad wheel, the side profile of his face now tattooed in her mind. As he nears Romeo's crowd, he guns the engine and clips a puddle of water near the group. A wave of mud splashes over the trio. Romeo and his girls come away screaming and soaked. The man takes the corner with loud screeching wheels and leaves a trail of black smoke as he disappears down the street. Angel ducks behind another tree, holding on to it just to keep from passing out. Death did come to the school today, just not the way she anticipated.

Theo paces past the window of his second floor apartment suite. The trip here was madness. He drove for days and days with no sleep and little food. Gnawing at the back of his mind was constant regret over taking the car instead of a plane. He didn't think when he left. He just left. He got to town a few days ago, an unremarkable bit of real estate situated picturesquely between corn husks and cow pies. It's smaller than he imagined, more intimidating when experienced through Angel's eyes. He stopped at the first 'for rent' sign he seen for a small one bedroom loft above a saddle repair shop. Fully furnished, he simply threw his belongings in the door, paid two month's rent up front, and went out in search of Angel's house.

But finding her has been more challenging than he anticipated. He searched for landmarks, tried to retrace trips they'd taken home from school, but his memory from his guardian days is flawed. Unable to find her house, he decided to go to the school. That is the one place he knew he'd find her. He applied for a job and made sure they knew how much money he had and implied he may give some to the school to ensure he'd get himself inside. They took him in to cover a maternity leave.

He had such high hopes coming in to town. Find Angel, rescue her, whisk her away to a wonderful new life. It was going to be so much easier than when he was a guardian. But as a guardian, he was always with her, he always knew where she was and what she was doing. Now he doesn't have any sense of her. He could be in this town for weeks and never see her. Not to mention, life is more complicated than he expected. And his emotions are harder to control. Coming into the school today, he saw Romeo and lost his mind. He introduced himself to Romeo the best way he knew how. He didn't even see Angel until he turned around. He was so shocked, so surprised that he just grinned at her and left. Although relieved to finally find her, it infuriates him that the first impression he left her with was him being a bully. The very thing she hates about Romeo. His vengeance against Romeo was supposed to be more subtle, more complicated, a footnote to the main story. But when he saw Romeo, he was so blinded with anger that he missed the reason he came here in the first place.

After the fight with Romeo, he took a few moments to compose himself and returned to the hall but Angel was already gone. He went to the science lab hallway and then searched all her usual haunts but he couldn't find her anywhere. After school, he waited outside the cafeteria doors but she never showed. He left the school angry. Time is running out and he wasted his first chance with Angel fighting with her enemy.

After school, he searched all over town looking for her place but there was nothing familiar anywhere. Returning home in frustration, he passed by a Korean restaurant with cracked windows and an 'out of business' sign posted half-hazard across the door. He slowed his car to a stop in the middle of the empty street. One light burned quietly in the apartment above the store. He's angry that he spent so much time fooling around at home. He might've had a chance to save Bea too.

He turns from the small apartment window and sits down on the bed. His phone is ringing. It's his mother again. He sighs, staring down at the number. His parents are in a panic over his sudden departure. He feels bad leaving them so soon after his recovery but he needs to focus on Angel now.

In the old days, an encounter like today would have had Angel singing for days and days. She would've laid in bed with her journals and her sketchbook dreaming up all sorts of scenarios that might bring her and the dark stranger together. She would've sketched out his face, would've traced his lips imagining what it would be like to kiss them, would've perfected the hands and imagined them all over her. And it would've made her genuinely happy for a while. It used to be that the fantasies were enough. But her happy high fades as she reaches the gate around her house. She sees that place, that horrible cell she has been trapped in for so long, her dog's face fogging up the bay window, and her mood instantly drops.

She comes in the house and sinks to her knees. She shouldn't have let the stranger distract her and yet there he was, and apparently part of the school in some regard. Some derelict janitor or something, she supposes, no teacher would get away with what he did in the parking lot. She wants to feel joy over the introduction of the curious, new man but she knows that hope is a dead end street. There is no reason to try anymore. Nothing will ever change. She is trapped. She is cursed. The only way out is at the end of a shotgun.

She lies down in the entranceway not even bothering to close the door. From here she can see up past the cheap cupboards with their missing and askew handles, to the letter leaned against the broken toaster asking the Yu's to take care of her dog. She made a decided effort to clean off a section of counter so that it could be easily found. She assumed that the Yu's would be the only ones to check her house after the incident, but what if the cops came instead? They may not bother to honor the wishes of some Columbine kid. She wraps her arms around her dog and kisses his head, apologizing for leaving him alone. He wriggles and rolls on the floor thinking they are playing some super fun game. She tells him she loves him and she will try to make things better for him. He's just happy that she's here. He doesn't care about the rest. In the end, Angel closes the door and tries to get some sleep. Hopes that tomorrow will be a better day.

Angel walks to school under sheets of freshly pouring rain. She has mixed emotions today. In the tiniest corner of her mind, a seedling keeps breaking above the surface, no matter how hard she tries to push it down. What if he...what if she...but don't even think it. Don't even dream it. Even if he was interested, even if he wasn't married or probably snatched up by the most smoking hot girlfriend, even if by some wild, crazy twist of inconceivable fate he actually noticed her and was interested in someone as boring and pathetic and dirty as her, so what? Even if he actually likes her, she could never let him close to her, never explain state of her house or the cuts on her arms. She could never make him understand the chaos that has become her life. No matter what, it is over. It's too late. Even if. Even so.

She enters the school from her usual side entrance and crosses the empty cafeteria. The lunch room sits almost six feet lower than the walkway. It's enclosed with a railing and there are only a couple exit points. It occurs to her that if she did it here, they'd all be penned in like pigs for the slaughter. There would be no place to run. She could assemble her gun in the bathroom down the hall. It's just a short walk to infamy after that. In a way it's easier with Bea gone. There's no one left to aim above. Except him. Except that damned stranger.

She retreats to the library for the morning, finds her favorite downstairs cubicle, pulls the chair deep in the confines of the pressboard walls and rests her head on the hard desk. The windows in the basement are small, rectangular and street level. Feet rush by, voices exclaiming, laughter echoing. They always seem so happy out there, in the crowds, with their friends. She has no friends now, thanks to Romeo. She can't let herself get distracted. She can't forget what he did. She has to make him pay.

She closes her eyes to rest but only sees the stranger, or at least the twisted illustration her mind has molded him into. Sort of a dark gothic superhero on his cemetery stallion. Who is he? And where did he come from? And most importantly, why is he staying in a shit-hole town like this? Why would anyone stay here if they didn't have to?

She tenses as she hears the laughter of two women she really doesn't want to see right now. Stacey, and her equally stupid companion, Mary-Anne. Both good friends to Romeo and have dated him at different times. Dating Romeo. How low can a girl sink?

"You, sir, are in trouble," Mary-Anne giggles.

"What are you talking about?" growls a male voice. The man's voice is very near to where she hides in her cubicle. She's shocked to find out that she was not alone down here and equally concerned that she was unaware of that fact. Nervously, she peaks through a missing knot in the cubicle wall. And there he is, standing just a few feet from her, the stranger. Angel's eyes go hungrily over him. He's wearing a laminated identification card categorizing him as a member of the school staff. He's a librarian.

Mary-Anne's hand flutters up to her over inflated chest bursting from a spaghetti-strap tank top. She has three little hearts pasted to her left breast as if the sheer size and lack of coverage didn't bring enough attention to the overcooked muffin tops already. "My goodness," she says to Stacey. "This one is a beast."

"Like a wild animal," Stacey exclaims, brushing a few locks of her long, loopy hair over her shoulder. She's squeezed into a strapless dress that doesn't go far enough down or come far enough up. "We saw you in the parking lot yesterday."

"That's great," he says and turns away from the girls, focusing on a rack of returns.

Angel watches eagerly from her hiding spot as he begins to sort through the books. Her eyes go through his messy hair, longer in front and very unkempt. She notices from the opening in this shirt that his chest is tightly muscled, as well as his forearms. She tries to see the name on his staff card but it swings back and forth around his neck making reading impossible. One of his hands looks fake. And he leans heavily on his right side as if injured in some way. She notices his cane leaned against a nearby library table. It's the same one she saw when he knocked Romeo down in the hall.

Stacey clears her throat, recharging the smile across her plastic face. "What we mean to say is that we saw you in the parking lot yesterday but you obviously didn't see us."

The man raises his eyebrows and he turns to them. Two brilliant smiles shine back at him as he does. "Yeah, I didn't notice you at all," he says flatly and then returns to his books.

"Well, we didn't think so," Stacey giggles nervously, running her painted nails across the hem of her dress. "Because you, mister, splashed us with that crazy, nasty car of yours."

"It sure is sexy," Mary-Anne says, eyeing the man's behind as he leans down to place a book in a shelf. "Maybe we can go for a ride in it sometime?"

Angel rolls her eyes and moves away from the knothole. This, she doesn't need to see, or even cares to hear, but she is trapped here for the moment and must endure this pathetic mating ritual.

"My daddy owns the mall," she hears Stacey pipe in. "And the most the stores in town. We can show you all the hot spots."

"We have the best bar for miles," Mary-Anne brags proudly. "And there's a country jamboree every summer that you just can't miss. If you want to be someone here, you have to be seen with our crowd."

Angel drops her head down to the desk and closes her eyes. She's surprised that those two nimrods have taken an interest in someone as unusual as him. But if they have, then she really doesn't have a chance. Stacey and Mary-Anne have everything, at least everything that satisfies a red blooded man's checklist, which appears to consist of tits and ass and insane stupidity. No guy has ever refused an offer from those two. Angel smiles a little though, thinking how Romeo might react to his girls chasing the man. She's betting he's not too fond of the new librarian.

"That's okay," he says dully. "I've seen enough of this town already."

The girls sputter and wheeze out shocked gasps. They exclaim to each other how droll he is and, my goodness, where did he come from? They've never seen anyone like him before. Boy, he sure has a nice cane. Can they touch it? Can they? Oh my god, Stacey's having a party this weekend. Does he want to come? They could introduce him to everyone who's everyone.

"Oh that would be great," the man grumbles. "And who are all these people that I just have to meet?"

"Well, Romeo," they exclaim excitedly. "You can't really be in here without knowing him."

"Romeo. Ramirez," he says, breaking the name into two distinct, disgusted sentences. "Yeah, I know who that shit is. He isn't worth the time it took to conceive him. And I imagine that probably happened in the back of some fucking pickup truck."

Angel rises with a gasp. She jumps back into the knot hole and sees the two girls staring up at the man with pale faces.

"W-what?" Mary-Anne stutters.

"You actually hang out with him? I can't believe that," he says and he's intimidating when angry. His voice has such a command to it. And what he's saying about Romeo! She can hardly believe her ears.

"I mean, I know you school girls are worried about your reputations and all," he continues. "So it surprises me to hear that you want to associate with someone like him."

"With Romeo?" Stacey says, blushing, back peddling. "I mean...we know him."

"Yeah, we know him. I mean it's a small town, everyone knows him," Mary-Anne adds, her eyes flickering nervously up at the angry librarian.

"I mean, if I throw a party, then everyone hears. I mean, everyone wants to come. And I can't always keep it exclusive," Stacey finishes. How quickly they turn on one of their own. Angel is amazed.

"So will Romeo be at this party?" he demands.

"Well, I...I..." Stacey stutters.

"Because I can't be seen at that party with Romeo," he says. "Only stupid girls hang out with idiots like him. Are you girl's stupid?"

"No," they exclaim densely. "We get straight A's."

"By taking tests?" he counters.

Angels covers her mouth to hold in a laugh. He's mocking the girls but they don't seem to understand that. She looks up at the man with stars in her eyes. She has half a mind to step from her hiding place and introduce herself, even with Stacey and Mary-Anne in the same room. He's incredibly exciting but he also makes her nervous. What if talks to her the way he's talking to the girls? What if he's that sharp with everyone? He could just be a mean person.

"I'll tell you what," he says, picking up his cane in his right hand and his books awkwardly in the pale left hand. "You tell Romeo not to come and I'll be there for sure."

The girls slowly reanimate. They giggle and clap and tell him they will make the arrangements. Angel's eyes return to the cubicle as her heart falls. He's going to their party? But she thought he was making fun of them? At least it sure seemed that way. The girls shimmy their short skirts and vast implants back up the stairs to the main floor. When the man is alone again, he mutters two very important words. As if.

Chapter 35☙

Theo thumps himself down at the end of the science lab hall, the place where he used to meet with Angel when he was dead. He's been here a lot hoping for an accidental encounter but he can't find her. His worry is turning to frustration, even panic. He's only seen her once since he got here. What if he doesn't get to her in time? What if she's lying dead somewhere, dying, thinking no one cares? He saw her locker yawning wide open today, completely empty and it sent him into a frenzy. He was so frustrated above when he could do nothing to help her, but results from below have been much the same.

He sits down on the bench situated by the viewless window. His dead hand has taken a turn for the worse. He may have to amputate it but vanity holds him to the dying appendage. He suppose it doesn't matter anymore, blending in hasn't been his biggest strength since his return. He's worried that this image, this thing he's become, will frighten Angel. The fact that Angel's two biggest adversaries are hitting on him doesn't boost his confidence much. Then today, someone stole his cane during lunch. He left his other one at his parent's house so he will have to get a crutch from the local drug store. He doesn't like crutches. They make him look him disabled. He suppose he is now, but he just doesn't want to look it. He wants to make the best impression when he and Angel finally meet.

He removes his jacket and sets his hand on his knee. He carefully unfolds the bandage around his wrist revealing Frankenstein scars circling the wrist bone. He struggles to get out a new bandage. Everything seems to be working against him today. He tries to wrap the new bandage around but each time he begins a revolution, the binding comes loose and falls away. He tries a second and third time, his frustration growing. His worries over Angel and anger over Romeo all seem to come to blows right here with this bandage. He turns it again and it slips to the floor. He grabs at it and swears at it. It's then that he notices Angel standing down the hall.

Angel slips out the side door of the cafeteria and is horrified to see Romeo's truck idling there. Plumes of diesel fumes fill the loading dock with noxious smoke. The back gate is down, revealing a black bed liner and chrome tool box inside. From inside the cab, she can hear music blaring.

"Fucking what?" She hears Romeo say and Angel steps back into the shadow of the door jam. She takes a deep breath and tries to blend as much as possible.

"We thought we'd just do something Sunday instead," she hears Stacey say. "A small get-together."

"That's retarded. We party every Saturday night. Why the fuck would we get together Sunday?"

"Because, um, Stacey's dad needs the place," Mary-Anne stutters.

Angel peaks around the corner and sees the three standing at the rear of the truck. The girls are trying to ditch him so they can party with the new librarian. Angels wonders how the stranger knows Romeo. And why he hates him so much. Everyone in this town idolizes the little shit. Everyone but the angry librarian.

"So tell your dad to fuck off. Saturday is our night to party." Romeo brings something out of his jacket and sets it on the tail gate. It's the stranger's cane.

"Where did you get that?" Stacey asks, reaching for it.

"I stole it from the gimp," he brags, snatching it back up.

"The gimp?" the girls exclaim. "You mean the new librarian?"

"Cripple-brarian, is more like it." He laughs and tries to break the cane in half but it won't snap. He smashes it on the tail gate but nothing happens. So he throws it in the back of his truck with a heavy clunk. "Come on. I got to pick up some stuff." He walks up the loading dock to the cafeteria and pushes up the overhead door. The three disappear inside.

Angel stands in the doorway a few seconds after the voices have left. She wants that cane. But she will have to climb in the back of Romeo's truck to get it. And if those three are standing by the doors, then they will come after her. She remains still for a few seconds longer then launches forward. Her heart pounds as she approaches the truck. She has always avoided it; this is the first time she's ever intentionally gone near it. She steps up on the back tire, leans over the box and reaches inside.

"Hey!" she hears Romeo shout. "What are you doing to my truck?"

Angel grabs the cane and drops back to the ground. And for some inexplicable reason, she gives him the finger before she sprints away. Romeo screams out in anger and tries to pursue her but Angel has wings on her feet today. She races away, giddy with excitement. She doesn't know why she flipped him off. She knew it would make him angry but she just couldn't stop herself. Maybe it's knowing the librarian shares her opinion that made her act out. Whatever it is, she now has the man's cane. She stares down at it as she slows to a walk. It's so long and sleek, with a stylized silver head at the tip. Maybe she should take it home. She can't imagine what it would be like to touch herself with something he owns. The idea is enticingly dirty and reawakens something that has been dead inside her for a long time. Her thoughts have been consumed by death since Bea died, both her own death and the ones that will die along with her. This is the first time she's had a passionate thought for months.

She walks down the science lab hall, turning the stick over in her hands. She's halfway down the hall before she realizes someone is there. She stops dead in her tracks, bringing the cane to her chest.

Theo falls silent, the bandages clenched in his fist. His curses are still echoing down the hall. Nice, Duncan, nice.

Angel swallows hard and her feet start walking towards him. She has a reason to approach him. I found your cane. No, that sounds stupid. I found your...stick? How about I want your stick? She blushes and drops her eyes, getting closer. The angry librarian is sitting in her favorite spot staring at her. She's so scared but she can't stop her ingress. She has to meet him. She just has to. All her normal inhibitions don't seem to apply.

Theo stares at her, distressed that she saw the fit he threw. He had so many scenarios that involved their first meeting. Him throwing a tantrum and swearing at a bandage was not one of them. Her steps slow as she nears. He glances up again and, god, there she is. Angel, in real life. He can hear her breathe. He can smell her. And he could touch her, if she decides to let him.

"I think this is yours," she says, her voice so thin and light. She offers it to him and he lifts his beautiful light eyes up to hers. She is stricken on impact. Completely lost.

Theo takes the cane as equally dumbstruck as her. "Thank you."

"Romeo stole it," she says, feeling so very, very self-conscious.

"Yeah, we don't get along too well," he replies.

"I've noticed."

He looks up at her, surprised. "How...did you..."

"Um," she quickly breaks in. "The hallway where...I was, uh, there when you ran into him."

"Oh yes."

"Did you...hit him on purpose?" Angel asks, breaking out in a nervous sweat.

Theo shrugs and smiles. "Possibly."

Angel smiles back at him and feels herself relax a little. He isn't talking to her in the harsh tones he addressed Stacey and Mary-Anne in. In fact, he seems very nice. She glances down at his hand which sits so awkwardly in his lap. "What happened to your hand?"

"It fell off," he replies. Really? Fell off? That's his best explanation?

She smiles again. "Fell off?"

He grins. He's so nervous. He can't believe it. I mean, he knows her. Biblically. They have been through so much together and yet this is like a first meeting for him. "I mean, in a car accident."

"Well, maybe you shouldn't drive so fast."

Theo frowns. Why would she say that? How does she know what kind of driver he is?

Angel seems to catch herself and explains with a blush, "I mean, I saw you in that...car in the parking lot."

"Oh," he says. Crap, she was there when he splashed Romeo? Did she see him bullying again?

"It's a nice car," she says. Nice car? Nice conversation, Angel. Talk much? "I mean, it's different. I've never seen anything like it."

"It's a friend's car. And, well, he was pretty different too."

"Was?"

"He's not here anymore," Theo says awkwardly. He can't seem to get his words out right. He sounds like such an idiot.

"What happened to him? Was he in the car when you..."

"No, I was driving someone else. I mean, it was a different accident."

"Dangerous driver." She smiles shyly.

He returns the shy smile, a warmth exploding from his chest and spreading out all over his body. "That guy actually walked away from the accident."

"What about the other guy? Is he...did he die?"

"Um..." How much should he tell her? Should he just jump right in? He wants tell her everything but she looks so fragile and broken. He could scare her by telling her the truth. "He was a friend, a good friend. He, um, he killed himself in that car."

Angel lowers her gaze with a rush of blinked back tears. She takes a deep breath, trying to reign in her emotions back in. Her heart pounds so fast that she's sure he can see it beating out of her chest. Say something, Angel, don't just stand here. He's going to think you're crazy. You are crazy, you know that?

Theo's angry when he sees he's upset her. Why did he say that? Of course it would upset her. "I'm Theodore Duncan, by the way," he says, trying to bring the conversation back on track.

Theodore Duncan, the names resounds like she's heard it a million times before. It comes with the familiarity a celebrity's name would. "Um…Angel," she says to the floor, feeling raw and exposed, wanting to run yet never wanting to leave his side again. "You're the new librarian?"

He tilts his head, surprised again. "How did you know that?"

"I mean, I was…in there, in the library and I saw you and I figured you worked there or something," she fumbles, all a blush. This is the third time she's admitted to knowing something she shouldn't about him. He must think she's a stalker.

She's been in the library? He gave Romeo's girls a nice thrashing there but he thought he was alone. Was she there again? He has got to reign in his personal vendetta. He doesn't want Angel to see him acting this way.

A silence lulls and Angel gets nervous. She feels like she's imposing now, wasting his time. "I should, um…" She points back down the hall.

"Listen, can you help me with this?" Theo says quickly, lifting the bandage, trying to find an excuse to make her stay a bit longer. "I can't get it on." He stares up at her. She won't refuse someone in need. He knows that about her.

Angel raises her eyes enough to see that he's asking her to wrap his wrist. He's asking for her help. She takes a deep breath, coaching herself to remain calm, be cool.

Theo watches her as she takes the place across from him. They have sat here many times before but she doesn't know that yet. He studies her face as she unravels the tensor bandage, her hair in perfect waves across her perfect eyes, her perfect mouth. His feelings are raging. He's like a rodeo bull tied at the gates. Frothing and clanging at the social barriers he must endure to get closer to her. Hold back, Theodore, keep it in control. She's okay. She's alive. You've got here in time, so don't frighten her away.

Angel's stares down at the hand oddly attached with a line of angry looking stitches across his wrist. She takes the bandage and carefully wraps it around the wounded area. There is something about him, something so familiar but she can't quite place what it is. She's having trouble controlling her emotions around him. She feels like she's going to explode. That all the wounds she's so carefully sewn up are going to come apart and spill her very guts and soul across the science lab hallway.

Theo watches her little hands moving carefully around his own. The 'D' of Dead she carved on one of her arms arcs out from her sleeve. I was there, he thinks, I was there when you did that. We have been together for so long already. Remember me, Angel, remember who I am. She glances up as if answering his query but her eyes are deep, dark wells. The pain in her so acute and unmistakable. Why hasn't anyone reached out and helped her? Is it because of the stigma surrounding her father? Or because there is such a wave of negativity around her that no one dares get near?

"Does it hurt?" Angel whispers, her eyes dropping down to the bandaged area.

"It doesn't," he says, feeling like the pauses between their conversations are centuries long. He's so busy processing, scheming, sensing, reacting. She's here, she's finally here and he could never have predicted how strongly he'd feel. He's on fire, no steaming, because the fire has already begun months earlier. He has been forced to throw water on it until they were back together again.

"It looks like it hurts," she hears herself say, though doesn't remember forming the statement in her mind. She fastens the bandage and pulls back from him feeling very unstable. He doesn't pull away when she's done. He leans forward and looks up at her with eyes that see straight through her. Such beautiful eyes. So sharp and so piercing that she cannot stay in contact with them for long.

"It doesn't," he says. "Not anymore."

The bell rings and Angel glances up at the clock. Lunch is over. No one killed in the cafeteria today. Again. She blushes at the thought. She can't do while this man, Theodore Duncan, is here. She can never let him see who she really is. "I should go," she says rising. Classes are resuming. She can hear the sound of angry feet approaching. This is always her time to run. Either get into a classroom or out of the way until the hallway is clear again. But Theo rises with her and stands to face her as the hallway fills with people. And it is the only time Angel has ever felt safe in a crowd.

"Maybe I'll see you in the library sometime?" he says. He doesn't want to go. He wants to throw her over his shoulder and run off into the mountains with her like a caveman. He's found her and he doesn't want to lose her again. He makes himself a silent promise that he will follow her home tonight. That he will find her house and he will keep watch. From this point on she will never be alone again.

"Okay," Angel says, also reluctant to leave. To her, he is a bright shining star who has appeared during one long and endless night. He leans on his cane, thanks her again, and then turns and hobbles into the crowd. She watches until she can't see him anymore and then sits back down on the bench.

Angel leaves the school that day feeling strangely optimistic. Meeting the angry librarian was thrilling. And though she knows she should be upset about Bea and Romeo and the rest of the shit in her life, all she can think about is him. She leaves through the side doors today, more eager than usual because it takes her out through the staff parking lot. Parked amongst the grey and silver sedans, she sees his car at rest. The car was exciting before, shocking, but now it calls to her in different ways. Theo's friend committed suicide in that car. Like her friend committed suicide. And like Angel's always meant to do herself. It really is Death's car. But the grim reaper has come in a much different form than she expected. And he makes her want to do anything but die.

She wants to wait for him but is scared to make such a bold move. She doesn't want him to know how interested she is, how desperate, how pathetic. If he knew who she really was, he would run away screaming. And she wants this fantasy more than any she's had before. Maybe because it's her last fantasy. Maybe that's why he resounds so strongly in her head. Because either this one works or everything ends at prom. She's surprised to hear the ultimatum in her head, that she is even considering him as an option over her revenge for this school and what its bullies have done to her.

She sighs and turns down the main road leading out of the school, a two lane drive with a row of trees down the center lane. She has no one to socialize with after the final bell, so she takes the walk in solitude. She shifts her bag on her shoulder, really missing her bike. The walk home has become long and arduous and she is so tired. She jolts as she hears that car fire up. It's him. He's in his car now. She glances back but the trees block her view. Shortly, he will drive right past her. If she had the nerve, she would turn and playfully thumb a ride. But she won't because there is nothing playful left inside her. And they don't know each other. They've only talked one time. He could refuse her. And she thinks that would kill her right now.

She grips her backpack tighter as she hears the car round the corner. He's not speeding like yesterday but the car roars none the less. Death's car. She smiles as she thinks of it and tries to imagine what it would be like to ride inside with him. And wonders where his going now, what he does after school, and where he lives in town.

"Hey, Angel, want a ride home?" she hears as the car slows to a stop beside her.

She sucks in a breath. It was one thing to meet him in the hall, but to see him in this car, in his natural habitat, is ten times the thrill. The window is rolled down and he is leaned over the seat looking up at her. The way he bends over causes his shirt to yawn open. Her eyes go eagerly over his chest, then stop with a shock at the burn going up the side of his neck. Is he burned? She never noticed that before.

"Um," she says, dumbfounded by the offer. The interior looks like the inside of a coffin. The seats are tombstones. And the lovely smell he gave off in the hall is so much stronger in the car. She reaches for the door handle and her hand stutters. She can't let him drive her home. He can't ever see her home. Or ever know what a monster she really is. Her hand retracts and it's so physically painful to reject the offer.

"I, um...she says. "It's okay. Nice day for a walk."

"You sure?" he says and how badly she wants to say yes. Yes to everything. But she can't. And she thinks this is the most she has ever hated herself.

"I'm okay," she says with a weak smile, though tears are welling up in her eyes.

"All right. Rain check, then?"

She nods but can't say another word. He drives away. Tears come then and she quickly wipes them away. On her arms she can feel the scars of Dead and Loser throbbing, mocking her. Why did she do that to herself? She could never explain why she cut those words into her arms. She never considered there would anyone she had to explain it to. She picks up her pace now eager to get out of here. But another car pulls up beside her. Actually a truck, low rider and bright pink. Along the side it says: *Spoiled Rotten*.

"Oh. My. God," Stacey says, leaning over the passenger's seat. Angel gets another chesty eyeful but not as enjoyable as the last one. In the passenger seat is the ever-faithful Mary-Anne.

"Are you trying to pick the librarian up? As if," Stacey grins.

"As if," Mary-Anne repeats.

"Honey, everyone knows who you are. And *what* you are." Stacey smirks, pointing a sparkly pink nail at Angel's crotch. "At what they could catch."

"Eww," Mary-Anne says, twisting her mouth up into a grimace. "Gross."

Angel continues to walk, but the girls pace her with the low rider.

"Why don't you just leave already? Get lost?" Stacey says. "No one wants you here anyway."

"Not me, that's for sure," Mary-Anne grins.

"If I looked like you, I'd never show my face in public."

"I'd burn my face right off," Mary-Anne says and the two snicker away.

Angel continues to walk, keeping her eyes forward. Her face is burning with humiliation.

"You stay away from my man!" Stacey shouts and revs the engine.

"Bitch," Mary-Anne says to her friend. "He's mine and you know it."

"You wish."

"You wish." The two cackle with laughter and the truck speeds away. They run the stop sign at the end of the street without even looking to see if anyone is coming. A driver screeches to a halt and honks. The girls just wave their arms out the windows and wail with laughter.

Angel focuses on the sidewalk as she continues off school grounds. She knows those are two are idiots but it still hurts to hear slanders like that. They're wrong about one thing though. Neither of them will ever have Theodore Duncan. For some reason, he has a grudge against Romeo and his entire crew.

She's almost at the end of the street when another truck pulls up beside her. "You have go to be fucking kidding me," she whispers, not even bothering to look Romeo's way. The truck stops, jumps forward a few feet, and then stops again.

"Hey!" he shouts, revving the engine. "Look at me!"

Angel just waves him off and keeps walking. She's almost at the stop sign, then she can cross the street and jump the meridian to the dead end road. Romeo can't follow her there. At least not in a vehicle.

"Don't think I didn't see what you did. You stole something out of my truck and I want it back."

"It wasn't yours to begin with," Angel says, turning and shooting a glare in his direction.

"Yeah, well I heard you've been swiping shit down at the gas plant, you little pick pocket. And all over fucking town. So I guess I'll just talk to my uncle at the cop shop about that. And why you're taking stuff out of my truck."

Angel sighs, her happy high simmering down lower. She's so sick of Romeo and his fucking truck. She's so sick of hearing him brag about the rims and the paint job and the sound system. And how he cries and wails every time he gets the tiniest rock chip or scratch. She'd love to set the whole thing on fire.

"Are you listening to me? Cunt?" he shouts as they reach the stop sign together.

Angel stops at the crosswalk and looks over at him. He's pathetic and she doesn't know why she didn't see it before. "Fuck you," she says.

"Excuse me?" Romeo shouts, jerking his wheel wildly to the left as he attempts to lean out the passenger window.

Angel turns and points a finger at him. "You heard me. Fuck you! Fuck you, asshole!" Then she runs across the street and jumps the meridian. She turns as she runs and laughs and makes sure he sees it. Inside the truck, Romeo explodes. He jerks the truck towards the meridian as if he's going to ram it. Then he reconsiders. That would leave an awful lot of scratches on his baby. Instead he skids to the right, leaving rubber and diesel smoke all over the intersection. Angel continues to run but can't help smiling. Even laughing. Oh she'll pay for that later. But she doesn't care. Just knowing Theodore Duncan hates him makes her want to fight back too. And she never considered that she ought to look at the integrity of the people insulting her before accepting their condemnation.

That night Angel sits out on the deck and stares at the bright city lights thinking about Theodore Duncan while her dog pants noisily at her side. She never made the connection between his name and her dog's name until she came home and said it out loud. Is that why it's so familiar? Because her dog has the same name? She's upset about the missed ride with him today but decides that if he asks again, she will accept. She doesn't have to bring him out here. She could have him drop her at any house in town and pretend it's her own. He doesn't need to know that this place is part of her life. She wished she'd thought of it earlier. The day would've ended much differently than it did. Though she's not sorry she told Romeo off. It was one of the most liberating moments of her life.

She stares up at the stars, the sky suddenly full of possibilities. So many points of light, so many galaxies where other life could exist. The vastness of space makes her life seem so small in comparison, as well as her problems. She hasn't thought about the stack of bills waiting on her counter. Gas goes out on Tuesday. Threats from the insurance company go on and on. She has tax bills she can't pay, mortgage backed up, and a fridge yawning painfully open.

This place is hell. Ever since the break in, she can hardly stand to be inside it. Yet it is the only place she has. The only place she belongs. Here with all this garbage. She sighs and imagines running away with Theo and starting a life with him, in some place that has nothing to do with this house or this town. She pictures herself running away from here, no more pain, no more bullies, no more death. The weight of it all has made it hard to conceive of a place where someone like him could care about someone like her. It just doesn't seem possible. And yet today, in the science hall, he seemed so accepting of her. Her looked at her so kindly and seemed interested in everything she said. He didn't talk that way to Stacey and Mary-Anne. He replays their first encounter in the hall knowing that the collision with Romeo was on purpose. It seems all the sweeter now that she has that knowledge. She knows it's impossible for them to be together, but tonight she just doesn't care. She just wants to bask in the moments they spent together and look forward to more encounters tomorrow.

Theo sits in his dark car just across the street from Angel's house. There are no lights here, his obscenely loud car hidden away in full view. He followed her home as planned, keeping back just far enough that she couldn't see him but so he could see her. Once he was on the street leading out of town, he knew the way. He had walked it a hundred times and from the right starting point, it was simple. He's intensely relieved to have the house in his sights now, to know where it is and where she is as well.

She's sitting on the porch with her dog, hidden behind the weeds and the abandoned cars. Sometimes she's so still, he can't even tell she's there. Until she packs up and leaves with him, he'll be here every night. He's not sure when or how he'll reveal himself. After today's encounter, he knows he'll need to take it slower than originally planned. His story is so fantastic, so unbelievable. Telling her the truth will be too much. She has a right to her secrets. She would be horrified if she found out that he knew all of them.

He stares up at the stars through his tinted windshield, remembers the night in the grass when they stared up at them together. They've experienced so much between them. Maybe she will remember in time. After all, this was a guardianship that had never happened before. His soul was above while his body was below. He came back from death and remembered her, so maybe with the right stimuli, she will remember him too.

Chapter 36ଛ

Angel descends the front steps to the worn path between the high weeds of her front yard. She looks towards the clump of houses marking the city limits. Somehow they seems less sinister knowing that Theodore Duncan is in one of them. Her mind is filled with him as she crosses the yard and she fails to notice a duffle bag tossed carelessly in her yard. She trips over it and skins the knee of her only good jeans. She looks back, cursing. Behind her, is a bright backpack with its mouth dangling open. People dump garbage in her yard all the time. It's a bit of a joke with the kids at school. But this bag looks fairly new. She opens it up. The first thing she finds is a wallet. In the wallet, nearly seven hundred dollars in paper money and a debit card that some moron has pasted his pin number on the back of. "What the hell?" she whispers, shaking the rest of the contents onto the ground. A stash, a glorious stash, falls at her feet. She paws through the find. There are cans of soup and spaghetti and chili, a pair of shoes and flip flops, both in her size. There's a summer dress, a new pair of jeans and a nice shirt. She tucks everything back in the bag, looks around to see if anyone is watching, then takes it back in the house. There, she opens a can of chili and splits it with the dog. Then she takes the wallet, empties everything out of it except the cash and the debit card and puts it in her own backpack. She kicks off her ragged shoes and tries on the shoes from the bag. They both fit and look expensive. She puts on the flip flops and tries on the jeans. They're a bit big but still nicer than anything she's ever owned. The shirt fits perfectly.

She leaves in kind of a drunken stupor. Instead of going straight to school, she turns down towards the shopping district. Normally, this is a trip full of anxiety. If she's heading towards a store, then she's contemplating stealing something. But now she has cash and some forgetful loon's card. She should make some purchases on it right away before the owner realizes it's gone. She turns into the south common shopping center. There, she enters a clothing store and walks among the racks of shirts and pants. Normally she buys food when she gets money, but today her mind is on Theo. She wants him to notice her. She wants some nice new things to impress him with.

"Can I help you look for something?" A lady appears beside her.

"Um, I'm just browsing," Angel says.

"Oh yes," she exclaims rubbing the tips of her overly manicured nails together. "We have some lovely new things in. What size are you?"

Size? Angel snorts. Is starving a size? "I don't know?"

"Well, you are very small. Maybe a two or a three?" The woman points her towards the petite section. "Anything in here should fit just fine." She turns to leave and then stops. "Oh, sorry, but you have to leave the backpack at the front. Store policy."

Angel passes it to the woman without a thought. Normally they would have a right to suspect her but not today. Today she has cash and who knows how much more in the debit card. Yes it's still stealing but not in any way this woman will find out about.

As she browses through the store, though, she starts to feel anxious. She should be using this money for food or bills, not on an outfit to impress the new librarian. It's such a waste of money but she wants him to notice her today.

She takes a few outfits into the change room and places them on the bench. That's when she remembers she's still carrying the shotgun in her back pack. And that back pack is at the front counter right now. It sends a jolt through her heart. She completely forgot about it. She even walked through the detectors at the front of the store. Why didn't they go off? Will they go off when she leaves? If the woman goes through the bag, then the police will be called. Will Theo hear about it?

She leans against the wall of the cubicle as her unsightly reflection stares back through the mirror. What the fuck is she doing? Clothes shopping? Meanwhile Bea is cold in her grave and Romeo is walking around town free as a fucking bird. Was her friendship so insignificant that one pretty face has her turning her back on her responsibilities? Romeo must be made accountable for what he did.

"How is everything going? Would you like something in a different size?" the woman asks.

Angel scowls at her reflection. "Sorry, guess I'm not in the mood to shop."

Angel arrives at school parking lot after lunch. She escaped the retail store without incident and without purchase as well. And now she is back here, missing her chance to bloody up the cafeteria again. The longer she waits, it seems, the more unwilling she is to go through with it. She's beginning to wonder if she really has the nerve to kill someone. She can't even kill herself.

Working her way between the deserted vehicles, she jolts as she sees Theo walking ahead. He is stomping through the parking lot in a way that is becoming familiar to her. She stares at him, her head swimming, her dark thoughts fading. She wants to call out to him but resorts to following instead, hoping he might turn and notice her. He storms down an aisle of cars, then goes right and then left. He is in the student parking lot, not the staff, and seems to be headed in a specific direction. He disappears behind a van and Angel hears a long, painful screech. She stops, even ducks down. What is he doing?

The next time she looks up, he's gone. Angel waits only a few seconds before retracing his steps. She finds the van and walks around to the other side it. Parked behind it, is Romeo's truck. And along the side panel of the garish black monster is a long and angry scratch, unmistakable keyed. She whispers out a breath, tracing her finger along the deep gouge that penetrates all the way down to the metal. It's scratched from the rear lights to the driver's door. Romeo is going to lose his mind when he sees it.

Angel moves quickly away from the truck but her mind is spinning. Theo doesn't just dislike Romeo, he hates him. Passionately. She wonders what happened between them to cause him so much disgust. For so long, it has been only her against the local bully. She's never even seen him pick on anyone but her. So, in many ways, she took the responsibility for her own bullying. Like she had it coming. Like she deserved it. But did she? And who is Romeo to pass down judgment on her? What makes him so qualified? He's just some rich, spoiled farmer's kid who has been left to his own devices. What will happen to Romeo out in the real world? Adults take action against bullying the way kids never could. They can call the police, file charges. Hell, they can punch back. School is the only place where bullying is really allowed to flourish. Romeo doesn't know it, but his short reign of power is about to come to an end. And maybe that doesn't even need to involve her. Maybe the end of high school will solve that problem for her.

Theo pulls a chair up to the table. He is in the cafeteria with a few newly hired staff members gathered for a brief orientation. They are mostly women, mostly middle aged, and all dressed in a very neat and reserved fashion. There is one other male at the table and he is wearing a suit and bow tie. Theo stands starkly out amongst the others in his punk attire.

The head librarian rises. Theo has had the pleasure of learning what a strict and unpleasant woman she already is. She hovers where he works constantly making little remarks about dress code and shift start times. He needs to be at the library precisely five minutes before shift begins. And the color she prefers her employees to wear are neutrals and grays. And swearing amongst students is strictly forbidden. But try as she might, she will never get him to care about his library conduct. He is not making a career out of this.

"My name is Sandra," the head librarian states. She has a seriously short cut of mousy brown hair and always dresses in the same floor length skirts and knee length sweaters. "These are your admissions packages." She hands thick brown envelopes to each person at the table. "These will give you a rundown of school rules and regulations, proper attire…" She seems to look particularly at Theo when she says that one. "…as well as a school map and phone numbers to all the staff and administration."

While the others open their packages and riffle through its contents, Theo keeps his hands folded over the sealed envelope, his thoughts on how he can coerce Angel into another conversation today.

"If you would all open your packages and follow along," the head librarian says, glancing Theo.

Theo looks up at her, returning her stern stare. He used to love these kinds of ordered people. Now he finds himself irritated by anything that reminds him of his old self. He'd like to break this tight-assed woman out of her controlled, routine lifestyle and show her how much of the world she is actually missing by living under so many regulations.

"Mr. Duncan?"

Theo raises his eyebrows at her, his hands still folded on the envelope.

"Sorry," the lady seated beside him says softly. "Perhaps he is not able to…" She gently slides the envelope from beneath his hands and opens it assuming that because of his injured hand, he is unable to do it himself. She quickly snaps the brown package open and sets the materials in front of him.

Theo's eyes drift as the head librarian drones on. Then he sees Angel coming around the walkway that surrounds the cafeteria. Her head is down and she does not notice him. He hates that he doesn't know what she's thinking. Yesterday, he offered her a ride. He had the whole afternoon planned. They'd talk in the car and then he'd take her out for lunch. Maybe go for a walk after. But she said no. He was devastated by the rejection, thinking that he has become too weird for her liking. It took him a while to realize that he offered her a ride *home*, when he should've just offered her a ride. Of course she wouldn't want him to see her home. At least that's what he hopes is the problem. Because if she doesn't like him, he doesn't know what he can do to change that.

He watches her as she walks around the cafeteria, never once looking up at him. Does she still love Ambrose? He knows she quit but her feelings for him didn't end with the job. And he returned to his body after Bea killed herself, so he doesn't know what happened during those weeks in between. He never considered that he might come here and fail. He never considered that she might not be interested in him. His feelings for her are so strong that he can't judge her reactions properly. It makes him very scared to think that she may not like who he is or what he's become since the accident. Once again, his arrogance takes center stage. No matter what happens, he still thinks he's special, he still thinks he stands out among the rest. He supposes he does but not for the reasons he's hoped.

Angel, look at me, he thinks, staring at her so hard. Let me in. I am here for you. I came here for you. Her head seems to tilt in his direction but then she focuses forward and finally disappears from the room.

Angel passes by the glass doors of the library several times, her heart racing. He's in there, somewhere, amongst the worn books and dusty librarians. All she has to do is go inside. But she can't get herself to do it, in the same way she couldn't get herself to look at him in the cafeteria this morning even though she knew he was there. She so scared of what's happening now. Suddenly she sees what she wants and it's so much more than Ambrose ever was. Ambrose was a crush, an infatuation, nothing compared to the way this man makes her feel. But that's irrational, she hardly knows him, she's overreacting. She can't have him so it's stupid to even worry about it.

The doors swing open and she sees him standing inside. Her heart leaps at the sight of him but then she sees he's not alone. Standing in front of him is a girl. Not Stacey or Mary-Anne or any of the girls she knows. But she is pretty and she is smiling up at him. Before the double doors swing close, she sees the girl touch him on the shoulder.

Angel turns and knocks someone over. She doesn't even stop to see who she's assaulted. She flees down the hall and then into the basement where the choir practices. There she hides in an abandoned practice room. A girlfriend, of course he has girlfriend. She was stupid to think otherwise. He was only being friendly to her. She rolls up her sleeves and traces the path that the razor once did. It doesn't matter anyway because she's dirty and worthless and used up and empty. What could she ever offer him? She can't imagine what she must look like to him. The shack rat in her torn sneakers and stolen clothes. It isn't fair. Her whole life isn't fair. She could survived before him but now that she knows he exists in the world, she can't.

She closes her eyes and rests her head against the wall, knees drawn against her chest. She can see it so clearly in the quagmire of her mind, in a thick mudslide of emotions, as she puts the gun to her ear, pulls the trigger, and out the side of her head comes confetti. A celebration of brains gleefully escaping like colorful strands of shredded paper, finally free from the prison of her mind, free to split apart and go their own directions, not to live forced together in place so small and so divided. And then it will all be over. Would Theo mourn her death? Would he even care? She hopes her soul doesn't linger. She hopes she dies and there is nothing in the afterlife. She just wants to sink into the quiet darkness. Just drop into the cool, quiet earth and never be seen again.

She leaves through the emergency exit in the basement ten minutes before the final bells toll. The alarm has been broken for years so she has no worry about setting it off. From here, she can cut around the back of the student parking lot and be gone before anyone even steps out of the classroom.

She looks up at the shining glass windows of the library as she passes by, her heart full of sorrow. She didn't talk to him today; she hardly seen him at all. It's so painful to know he is in there and she is out here and that's the way it's going to stay. She rounds the corner to the parking lot and there's a crowd gathered around Romeo's truck. She stops, completely exposed on the hillside and then ducks beneath the shadowy branches of a spruce tree. She crouched down by the trunk, wondering why there are so many people out before school is over.

"I'm calling the cops!" she hears Romeo roar and then he traces a line along the side of his truck. "This is fucking vandalism."

She forgot all about this morning's keying. Romeo has just discovered it. And he's making such a scene. His girls are cooing and coddling while he paces the length of his truck. Then he turns and punches it so hard that Angel jumps. Though he hasn't reached his full potential yet, Romeo is on his way to becoming very dangerous. Right now he's just a school yard bully but what is in his future? Home invader? Serial killer? Hit man? She thinks the last one would suit him quite well.

Down in the teacher's parking lot, she hears the Thunderbird roar to life. Everyone in the parking lot looks over as the metal monster slowly takes the turn out towards the road. Romeo, above all the others, seems to have a keen interest in the new librarian. He suspects but doesn't have proof that Theo vandalized his truck. Angel can't help but smile, even after the day she's had. If she lives long enough to see Romeo's last year in high school filled with humiliation, it will make all the years prior worth it.

Theo sits in the Thunderbird across the dirt road from Angel's house. He's been here since dusk but has seen no sign that Angel is inside. In fact he hasn't seen her since she walked through the cafeteria this morning. If she came to the library, she hid herself well. Even if she did come, she might have been spooked off by all the girls suddenly so eager to expand their education. Seems like since he started in the library, attendance among girls fifteen to eighteen has skyrocketed. He's surprised by his popularity considering his appearance now. He would've thought the burns, the hand, and the cane would turn women off. Apparently they see him as wild and dangerous. He really doesn't care how the majority of the female population view him, he's only concerned with just one.

Too worried to sit any longer, Theo pushes out of the car and sneaks across the road towards her house. The only thing that could give his approach away are the lights from the city.

But the grass in Angel's yard is so high, he thinks he can get pretty close without notice.

He opens the gate with a painful screech. Then something shifts on the porch. Theo freezes. Has she been sitting out there the whole time? If she's seen him, then he'll have a lot of explaining to do. He's not supposed to know where she lives yet. And certainly shouldn't be sneaking in her yard in the middle of the night.

The shape on the porch rises, then hunches down, then charges toward him. "What the fuck?" he whispers. He stands for a few seconds before he realizes it's the dog coming towards him at an alarming speed. Dog Theo may have known him when he was dead but he doesn't seem to care for him alive. Theo hobbles back towards his car but he can't move fast enough. The dog leaps on him from the back and pushes him to the ground. Theo crashes to his stomach and then rolls to his back defending himself against happy licks and slobbers.

"Okay, okay," he whispers, sitting up. "Good boy."

The dog sits back on his haunches and wiggles his ass back and forth. "Where's Angel?" Theo says, pushing up to his feet. "Is she home, boy? Let's go look." He returns the way he came, this time with a hundred pound accomplice. The dog huffs on his ankles as he makes his way down the narrow path. The house is completely dark. But with no power, that doesn't mean she's not home. He's almost at the front steps when his phone rings. Theo yanks it out of his pocket but cannot find the volume switch. Instead, he ducks behind a barrel and opens the line. Gasping, he sits with the phone in his lap while the dog snuffles at his ear.

"Hello? Hello?" his mother calls. "Is that you dear?"

Theo picks it up with a quiet swear. "Mom," he whispers.

"Theodore? Where are you? Why are you whispering?"

"I'm at the...library," he replies quickly. He jerks his head as the dog sends a wet tongue across his cheek. "Stop that."

"Excuse me?"

"I wasn't talking to you."

"Are you there with someone? Theodore, who is there with you? Your father and I are very worried. You missed your appointment with the plastic surgeon yesterday."

"I'm not getting surgery," he says quickly, glancing back towards the dark windows of the house.

"Well, I will reschedule your appointment for next week. But you must be back here by Sunday at the latest. We are having a brunch at the church and everyone will be there to meet you."

Everyone but him, he thinks but doesn't say because he really doesn't have the time to get into a huge argument with his mother right now.

"Who is that?" his mother says. "Who is breathing into the phone?"

Theo pulls away from the dog again. Dog Theo drops down to the grass and rolls vigorously on his back.

"Good lord, Theodore, your voice is so raspy. I will make an appointment for the doctor tomorrow. I will need you to come back tomorrow."

"Mom," he says with sigh. "I'm not coming back tomorrow."

"All right, Tuesday then."

"I don't know when I'll be back."

"Theodore Duncan, I want to know where you are and what you are doing. Your father and I are worried sick."

"Mom, I am fine. I am okay. And I really have to go."

"Is it drugs?"

Theo mouths the word *what?* silently into the phone. "Drugs, mom? Really?"

"Well, there was that strange person who showed up at the door and now Buddy tells me you've been down to the tattoo parlor? Please tell me you did not deface your body with some sort of boat anchor or sailor girl."

Boat anchor or sailor girl? It's been a long time since his mom has been near a tattoo shop.

"And I was watching this talk show yesterday about how people get addicted to pain killers after surgery. Is that what this is? Are you in some sort of homeless place shooting it up?"

"For god's sake," Theo says, losing his patience. "Mom I have to go. I will call you later." He hangs up the phone and then finds the mute button just before it rings again. He puts in in his pocket, but his pocket continues to glow as he crawls from his hiding spot. Dog Theo jumps eagerly to his feet and follows along. That's when Angel steps from the front door and calls for the dog. Theo stares up at her dark form as both he and the dog crouch in the grass on all fours. Angel sits down on the creaky porch step and the dog trots up beside her and sits down. The two sit quietly together while Theo tries to maintain the awkward position in the grass below the stairs. With his bad leg and bad hand, he can't hold himself in this crouch for long. Thankfully, she gets up a few minutes later and goes inside the dark house. Theo rises to his feet, staring up at the shack she calls home. This is taking too long. He is going days without seeing her or talking to her. He needs to establish a connection with her right now. He decides then and there that if he doesn't make some headway with her tomorrow, then he will have to approach her and tell her his story. He doesn't want to do it that way but he may not have a choice.

The next morning, Theo parks his car up the street and out of sight from Angel's house. And when she leaves for school, he turns on the engine and follows her. He stays back as far as he can but if she turns around, she will see him. He doesn't exactly blend in amongst the blocky, grey SUV's that have exploded in popularity with the rise of the beige nation. Anonymity is the new norm. Blend in, don't stand out. Be what everyone else is. Have what everyone else has. Look how everyone else looks. And he stands out in stark contrast, even in this hillbilly town where the thrill of conformity has been slow to catch on. But he has to take that risk. He can't go another day without seeing her. Every day missed is a day closer to Save the Date. He hadn't counted on Bea being dead when he got here. He had hoped he would get to her in time. But now that she's killed herself, Angel is at much higher a risk than before. She has no guardian now, unless Ryder has found someone to replace him.

But Angel doesn't turn. She walks straight to the school, her head down most of the way. She's ten minutes late when she gets to the parking lot. She's the only one there but then Romeo's truck drives up. He parks it, gets out and leans against the side with his arms crossed over his chest. He doesn't say anything, just stands there and watches her as she takes a large circle around him to avoid his path. And after she enters the school, he gets his books and struts away.

Theo glares at the dark haired teen as he disappears inside the school. Romeo stopped just so he could intimidate her, just for the fun of it. Then went on with his day without another thought. It occurs to Theo that if he got rid of Romeo, it would buy him some time with Angel. After all, that kid is the focus of Save the Date. Of course he can't murder someone, even though the idea sounds quite appealing right now. But there are other ways to ruin people.

He takes out his phone and calls Jackie. Asks him to look up a kid named Romeo Ramirez. Find out who his family is. Find out if he's ever been convicted of any crimes. It's urgent, he tells his investigator, I need the information as soon as possible. He doesn't tell him that he wants to use it to ruin Romeo. Jackie would never go for that sort of ruse. Satisfied, he slips his phone back in his pocket, staring at Romeo's beloved truck. He's fixed the scratch across the side and has added a new detail. Across the tinted black window in bold white lettering are the words: *no fat chicks*. Theo gets an idea, in fact several. The first involves a can of black spray paint and some selective editing, but the second and more satisfying scheme will involve a few phone calls, a tow truck, and a wrecking yard crusher.

Chapter 37ೞ

Angel attends a few morning classes, mostly because if she doesn't go to class soon then she will get expelled. And she can't leave the school with so much unfinished business. Both Theo and Romeo are nagging at her today. One she desperately wants to see and one she hopes to never see again, unless it's at end of a gun barrel. Sometimes she gets so angry that she's only a clean razor swipe away from ending it all. And then the next day she is fine, hopeful even, that something positive could come from the new librarian.

She sighs, staring up at the blackboard where the teacher scratches out mathematical formulas, knowing this information will never be applicable in her life. She has some pretty serious decisions to make in the next few weeks and fractions and binomials will have no part in it. She imagines the prom again, the dresses covered in blood, cheerleaders screaming, band guitars stumbling to a stop as they begin to understand what's happening. But then another fantasy crosses her mind. Theo asking her to go, taking her as his date, entering the gym at his side and all the girls are so jealous. Both fantasies are so fantastic, so absurd. But, in her mind, the first one seems more plausible than the second. More realistic. More reachable.

Angel looks up as the bell tolls for lunch. An entire class gone by and she didn't write down a single thing. She picks up her books and waits until most of the students are gone before she leaves. Then she quickly exits the room, takes a short cut down to the cafeteria, which is just filling up with students, then escapes out the side door. But as she steps outside, she hears a fierce rumbling. Romeo must be at the loading docks again. She peaks around the corner but

Romeo's truck isn't there, instead idles the Tombstone Thunderbird.

"Oh, hey," Theo says, stepping from the docks. This is no coincidence. He's been waiting here, knowing that she frequently chooses the side exit to the main doors. And, thankfully, today she did.

"Hi," Angel replies, smiling shyly back at him. She wasn't prepared to see him though has thought of nothing but since their last encounter in the science hall. Her heart pounds at the sight of him. He is stunningly gorgeous and dangerously exciting and she can hardly believe he is still wasting his time here at this redneck school.

"Haven't seen you at the library lately," Theo comments casually, coming around the side of the car to where she stands. It's a bit of a trap he's laid here. He has practically blocked her exit from the cafeteria with his car so that she would be forced to stop and talk with him. He has to make a connection with her. He has to make her understand that his being here is no accident. He is here for her.

"I was in class." Sure she went to class. Today. But has otherwise been lurking around the library in regretful sorrow wanting to go inside but still so disturbed by the girl she saw him with. Who was that girl? She wasn't someone that Angel knew from school. That gives her a little comfort. If he was dating Stacey or someone like her, she thinks she'd just shoot up the school right now.

"You want to have some lunch?" Theo asks, and sees her glance nervously back at the cafeteria. He doesn't have to be her guardian to know what she's thinking. Crowds and bullies and the chaos of the school canteen. Quickly, he adds, "I packed way too much today. I was going to go eat on the lawn." He points to the little park out behind the school where a few students are perched against trees or stretched out on the grass. It's the first warm sunny spring day. The first one with hints of summer in it.

"Okay," she says nervously. She's scared but she is not passing up another opportunity to spend time with him. Girlfriend or not.

They sit down under an old tree, the sun laced through its high branches. The grass beneath them is freshly trimmed. Birds are chirping nearby. Theo sets down his backpack and places the food between them. After confirming Angel was in her first class, Theo went to the grocery store and picked up a bunch of food. Every part of their casual meeting was orchestrated after that. A red truck trap, Angel might call it, but now she is here and he has the whole lunch hour to sway her in his direction.

Angel sits down, eyeing wonderful spread of food almost as tantalizing as its owner. It's not just that you don't have enough food when your poor, but you never eat anything of variety. Just the same low grade cans of cheap discount slop. She's been eating lately thanks to the fool who dropped the knapsack in her yard, but is scared to spend too much. The cash was great, she paid off a few bills, went to the grocery store, put gas in her truck. But the debit card is trickier. She doesn't know the limit on it and knows it could be cancelled at any time. If she was going to use it, she should've used it right away.

Even though she had breakfast this morning, Angel finds herself starving again. There are meats and cheeses with French bread and mountain water, fruit and veggies and chocolate for desert. She starts with the sliced cheese while Theo thumps his backpack into a pillow and stretches out on the grass beside her. She used to envy the students getting hot food in the cafeteria, but now they're eating swill in comparison to this feast. She eats ravenously. She doesn't want to look like a pig but she just can't stop herself. This is stuff she can only afford to steal. But this time she can eat with no guilt whatsoever. This food is legally acquired.

Theo rolls his head across his pillow to look at her, his eyes starkly blue against the green foliage. She smiles nervously in response, both hands full of food. He looks like her forest god. What it would be like to make love with Theodore Duncan? As his gaze turns up to the sky, she quickly looks over the rest of him. He is in a white shirt that fits him loosely, with a few buttons opened down his chest and the sleeves turned up his arms. His white hand, the dead hand as she's come to regard it, rests motionless against his chest while his good hand fiddles with the grass at his side. His legs are long and lean and clad in expensive denim. His feet in big clunky boots. Beside his legs, nearly buried in the grass, is his Dracula cane, the one Romeo tried to steal. He has a nice strong side profile, a perfect model of a man. Yet it's what he's done to deface the standard edition that appeals to her the most. He could be one of *them*, one of the herd plodding blindly through the sanctioned channels of life, but he has chosen to defy that standard. He has the looks and yet he chooses to protest, to be conspicuous, to be bizarre. That is incredibly thrilling to her.

Theo feels a buzzing in his pocket and lifts his head. He glances at Angel and smiles, pulling his phone out. It's his mother again. He sets the phone down beside him and lowers his head back down.

"Is it important?" Angel asks quietly, nibbling now, her appetite finally satiated.

"My mom," he says with a sigh. "She is persistent."

His mother. She can't imagine what kind of woman raised him. Or what it would be like to live in a house with him. Or to be by him all the time. "What are your parents like?"

Theo snorts out a laugh, rising up on his elbows. But when he sees her and thinks about her family, he regrets his reaction. His parents are saints compared to hers. He softens his tone. "I mean, they're okay. A bit religious but I really don't really have any reason to complain."

"Religious?" she asks, surprised.

"Oh yes. Couple of real holy rollers."

"Really?" she asks, genuinely surprised by the information. She's so curious about him, even about the most basic details of his family life. "Do you have any brothers or sisters?"

"No, just me." He looks over at her again. Should he ask her about her family? He doesn't want to appear disinterested but he already knows everything about her. In a normal situation, he would enquire but it seems deceitful to pretend he doesn't know. Not to mention, she won't want to answer anything about that horrible family of hers. It will only make her uncomfortable. "I'm an only child. We live up in the city. My dad's a real a social butterfly. Mom has all her religious events. They're both really busy with their lives. Me too, I guess, with university and all."

"University?" Angel runs her fingers through her hair feeling all warm and fuzzy. She loves learning stuff about him. Everything is such a surprise.

Theo chuckles. "Yes, I was a religion major."

"Religion?" Angel exclaims. "So you're religious too?"

"Well, not so much anymore. I mean, there is definitely something out there, I just think that organized religion has it all wrong. I used to really believe in it though. I saw myself going overseas and converting the uncultured masses."

Angel smiles, though her stomach turns at the thought of him going overseas, of going to a place so completely unreachable to her. "So what are your plans now?"

"Honestly? I don't really know *what* I'm doing anymore."

She looks over at him and his eyes are on her, intense like when Romeo stared at her in the parking lot this morning but with very different reasons. She blushes a bit, focusing her attention down into the thick blades of grass around her legs. But when she looks up, he's still looking at her. And the way he stares at her makes her dizzy. She tries to calm herself down because this is all for naught. He has a girlfriend. She saw that girl in the library touch him. And he didn't react like he did with Stacey or Mary-Anne. Or did he? Because the door closed before she saw his reaction.

"Here," Theo says, feeling like he's losing her again. She just goes so far into her own head and he knows the damage she does when she's in there. He fishes his wallet out of his pants pocket and takes out his license. "This is what I looked like before the accident."

Angel takes the identification card and she cannot believe the man in the photo is the same man sitting in front of her. He is so blond, clean cut, and preppy looking. He looks so unlike himself that she quickly scans the name at the top of the card to see if it's him. While she has it, she also takes a quick tally of his age and the address on the card and any other pertinent information she can take with her.

Theo lifts his hands behind his head watching her as she muses over his driver's license. Oh it is a spectacle to him too, but he supposes it would be the other way around if his former self saw his future self. What does Angel see? Does she prefer his clean cut version from before the accident? Or the oddity he is now?

"What happened?" she asks hesitantly. "I mean to change you so much?"

Theo leans up on one elbow, the burned skin pulling tight beneath his side. "A lot. I was in a coma for four months. I was clinically dead. Brain dead. Then, one day, I came back."

"From the car accident?"

"Yes. A dump truck ran a red light. My car got tore right in half." He makes a chopping motion over his wrist. "And my hand too. They tried to reattach it but it isn't taking too well. They tell me I was trapped inside when the fire started. My hair was all burned off. And my side as well."

Angel's eyes go down to the opening in his shirt. It yawns open like it did the day he offered her the ride. She can see inside to where the burns begin.

"Do you want to see it?"

Her eyes shoot up to his, guiltily. Did he see her looking? She was looking right down his shirt. She didn't even think about it when she was doing it.

"It's all right. I'm not embarrassed to show it."

Angel blushes deeply and drops her eyes to her hands. Yes, she does. She wants to see the burn. And him with his shirt off. But there is no way she could ever say yes. She's too tongue tied to say anything. But then Theo sits up and unbuttons his shirt. He works clumsily due to his lame hand, unhurried like a strip tease, releasing each clasp with careful consideration. He opens the shirt and exhales, like clothing is a burden to him, and turns his side so she can see the burn. Angel swallows hard, her eyes going hungrily over his charred skin. He's thick across the chest, his stomach taught, his chest lightly haired. His stomach scoops down below his ribcage where more muscles dive down into his dark jeans. Her eyes go down over his hips, eyeing that pleasant swell between his legs and then jolt back up. When her eyes rise to his face, he's giving that same intense look as before. Her heart pounds and her sweat begins to run. Other picnicking students are looking over at him too. She quickly secures her eyes back down to her hands. But not before she notices the edges of a large tattoo coming around his side from the back.

"Do you have a tattoo?" she whispers weakly, needing to change the topic and quickly.

Theo swiftly closes the shirt. The tattoo. Because it's on his back, he often forgets it's there. And in hindsight, it probably wasn't the wisest thing to do because spread between his shoulder blades is Angel's darkest secret. Beautiful Monster. He could never explain why he has her words across his back. He looks up and sees her receding back into her head again. She probably took his reaction as a rejection.

"It's not finished," he says. "It's a bit of a mess right now. I don't want anyone to see it."

"What's it of?" she asks, feeling like he might be lying to her. It drops her mood a bit but she struggles to bring it back up. She has to enjoy this. She doesn't know when she will have an opportunity like this again.

Theo thinks quickly. He finally answers with, "I guess you'll just have to wait and see when it's done." It's a good answer. It breaks the tension. He shouldn't have taken his shirt off in the first place. What was he thinking?

"Bet your mom loved that," Angel says, releasing her hands which she has just realized are in tight fists.

"Oh she hasn't even seen it. She thinks it's a boat anchor or a sailor girl."

Angel chuckles, feeling the last of her tension drain out of her. She's fascinated by his transformation from good to bad. That he was so firmly settled into one mold then completely broke into a new one. It gives her hope that she could do the same.

The bell tolls indicating lunch is over. Theo sits up. He looks over and sees Angel gathering her things. He has to go back to work and she has to go back to class. He hates all these rules he has to follow now that he's back below. He was hoping this lunch would last all afternoon. He's still not certain if she likes him or not, she is so guarded in her affections. It will take many more meetings like this one before he has any sense of how she feels. He wants to do something concrete before she leaves, something to indicated that, for him, this was more than just a casual meeting and to secure another date in the future. But can he do that without scaring her away?

Angel feels his eyes on her again as she gathers her things. She pretends not to notice but she's getting more and more nervous. Then he says her name and leans over and brushes her hand with his own. She looks up with a gasp and he is so close and his eyes are so intense.

"Angel, I think you are beautiful," he says to her. "Do you want to do something after school?"

Angels drops her eyes quickly and her face grows very hot. The words entered her like a bolt of lightning, so powerful and illuminating. She can't even process the compliment or the request made after. She nods quickly, not trusting herself to speak.

"Yes?" he asks.

"Yes," she whispers, then rises and rushes off without another look back.

Theo slides books back into their rightful place under the watchful eye of the head librarian. Oh, she hates him all right but she doesn't have any reason to fire him. Not yet. He sighs and takes shelter behind a particularly large block of calculus textbooks. Day's end is an eternity away. He made a play for Angel, a pretty big one as far as he's concerned, and she said yes. He was scared shitless when he asked her. She could've said no and where would he be then? Everything leading up to this moment would all have been for naught.

His quiet reverie is broken by laughter. A bunch of girls enter the library and sit down at the table on the other side of the shelf he's stocking. Present are Stacey, Mary-Anne and a bunch of other girls he'll crouch behind this math shelf for the rest of the afternoon just to avoid.

The conversation exchanged between the girls at the table ranges from music videos to shoe stores, from the new nail salon in town to the boys they'd like to date. Stacey appears to be the leader amongst them, with Mary-Anne the less popular sidekick. It's likely that if Stacey says it's cool, the other girls will follow along, no matter what the topic is. Their conversation now sways to people they think are losers. They laugh at the boy with the broken glasses and pose theories as to how he became such a bore. They giggle and try to pair him up with geek girls from the science lab and howl with laughter as each one is suggested. Eventually the head librarian comes to the table and tells them to quiet down. After she leaves, their conversation sways to the head librarian and whether she's ever been laid, and then they start pairing her up with gross faculty members they know. Then their conversations turns to him. Where is the other librarian, they ask coyly, their sharp tongues dripping with lust. Has anyone seen him today? He's so dreamy. Theo drums his fingers, staring through the shelves at the girls sporting more paint than professional circus clowns. I heard his hand was cut off in a bar fight, one says. I heard he lost it in a motorcycle accident, another says. Stacey brags that he's coming to the party this Saturday. The girls titter around the table. I had to get rid of Romeo to get him there, Stacey says. He really hates Romeo. You think maybe they'll fight? Ooh, I'd love to see that.

The girls fall silent as Angel passes by the library window. They all look and stare, the air around them burning with excitement.

"Oh. My. God," Stacey says, "Did you see what she was wearing?"

"She's had those same pants on all week," Mary-Anne exclaims, giggling.

"Gross. And her hair? Does she even comb it?"

"Why bother? No one looks at her anyway."

The girls cover their mouths and giggle with laughter, then start to pair her up with other losers in the school. Theo glares through the book shelves at the stupid, insensitive girls. Then he sees the head librarian leaving for lunch. It's just the opportunity that he's looking for. He pushes back from the math section and stomps towards the table.

"She's got a thing for the sexy librarian," Stacey whispers hotly across the table.

"No!" another girl exclaims. "How do you know?"

"I saw her sketching a picture of him in class."

Theo pauses, just about to round the corner to where the girls are. Angel is sketching him? She only sketches men for one reason. That means she *is* interested. He's thrilled but then the girl's voices remind him of his present mission.

"Pathetic, right? As if *she* would ever have a chance with *him*." Stacey turns her nails towards her face and examines them carefully. "You think we should play a prank on her?"

"What kind of prank?"

Stacey eyes each nail thoughtfully. "Well, we could write a letter to her and pretend it's from him. You know, like how Romeo did to Bea."

The table falls very silent. It seems like Stacey has gone too far but then the girls slowly warm up to the idea. They whisper and chatter until they are all shrieking with laughter. Theo has had enough. He comes around the corner of the shelf.

"Oh!" Stacey exclaims. "What a lovely surprise. Girls, this is Theodore Duncan."

Theo stops between the chairs of the powdered princesses. He faces Stacey from across the table. What he really wants to do is pop the blond ditz right in the mouth, leave a nice pile of bleached teeth on the table in front of her. But that could lead to his firing and he needs this school to get close to Angel. Besides, there are other ways to hurt girls like Stacey.

"Hi, Theo," Stacey says with her biggest brightest smile. "All set for the party on Saturday?"

"Party?" he asks, pretending as if he has forgotten.

The smile stutters on Stacey's face, then quickly returns. "You know, silly, the party on Saturday night? All the best girls are coming."

A bevy of perfectly lined lips smile up at him, but Theo's gaze remains on the headmaster. "Oh that's right, Janet," he replies. "I forgot all about it."

Stacey's mouth drops open. "I'm Stacey!"

"Stacey?" he asks confused. "I thought your name was Janet."

Stacey laughs nervously. "Now, you're just being silly. Everyone knows who I am."

"Sorry, Janet."

"Stacey!"

"Right," he says darkly, leaning his good hand on the table. "You girls are talking a bit loud. The library is for studying, not gossiping. If you don't have anything better to do than gossip about what other people are doing, then I suggest you leave."

The girls look up at him, surprised by his harsh tone. Mary-Anne opens up her text book and flips mindlessly through a few of the pages. But not Stacey. That thin plastic smile remains fastened to her face. "Speaking of gossip, you are not going to believe what girl has a crush on you," she announces.

"Oh yes, tell him," Mary-Anne says, suddenly reanimated. "Wait until he hears,"

Theo leans a little closer to Stacey and she pulls back a bit, though the smile on her face does not budge. "Who says I like girls?" he whispers.

The girls gasp and screech. Scandalous, they say! He is such a tease. He is nothing but trouble. They shriek and cluck their tongues and click their nails across the table top, dazzled by his shocking statement.

"I told you to be quiet!" he shouts and the whole table falls silent. A few students at neighboring tables look over. Theo focuses back on Stacey whose omni-smile is starting to waver a bit. "So tell me, who has a crush on me?"

Her voice is much quieter when she says, "This gross girl from school. She lives in this dump outside of town. You don't know her. Or would even want to."

"Oh, Angel?" he says and then it's his turn to smile. And he smiles as brilliantly and eagerly as he can manage. "Yeah, we just had lunch together today. She's a wonderful girl."

Stacey frowns as she tries to comprehend what he's saying. Now all her girls are wedged deep in their textbooks pretending like they never knew her.

"Will she be at the party?" he asks, his eyes never breaking from Stacey's.

Stacey gasps. "Of course not. That's ridiculous. Why would we ever invite *her* to a party?"

"Because she's so interesting? Sexy? Pretty? How about because *I* want to see her there?" Theo counters and no amount of rouge can put the color back in Stacey's face.

"Pretty? Sexy?" she exclaims and now she's starting to lose her cool. "Well, I guess you're new in town and you don't know about her family or what they've done. You know that they…"

"Shut up." Theo snaps and Stacey's eyes finally fall away. "I am sorry that your queer little mind has taken some sort of sordid interest in me because those feelings are certainly not returned. You see, there are consequences to your actions. You may not be able to see that from this ignorant little town you squat in, but in the big picture, you pay for the shitty way you treat people. And you and your little friend Romeo are in for some big time karma."

"Excuse me?" Stacey exclaims hotly. "How dare you…"

"You know what I hate *Janet*, do you?"

Stacey purses her lips into a thin line. Around her, the girls continue their intense studying. One girl excuses herself and leaves the table. Even Mary-Anne shuffles her chair a bit further away from her friend.

"I hate people who bully just because they can. Just because they get a little higher in their tiny corner of the world and decide they can hold themselves over others. You know what I hate, *Janet*? Fucking bullies, that's what I hate!" He spits the last few words so harshly that a few spatters land on her face. She gasps and swipes them away, disgusted. He isn't done though. "You think you're something else, don't you? You think you're so special? You think you can go around this school treating people however you please, well here's a prime opportunity to unleash your supremacy. Why don't you tell me this juicy gossip you and your girls are so excited about? Because your lives are so small and meaningless that this is all you have to do to fill your spare time? Focus on what other people are doing? I guess that's because you all are doing nothing with your own lives."

"Now wait a minute," Stacey protests. More girls get up and leave the table. Now everyone in the library is staring over at the pale faced girls.

"No, you shut up. For once in your life, you shut your fucking mouth and listen to someone else. Don't ever come around me again. Don't ever come around Angel again. I swear to god if I see you looking sideways at *anyone* in this school, I'll ruin you in ways you can't even imagine. Everyone has something they want to keep hidden. I'll make sure your secrets are spilled across the biggest billboard in town. I'll give you a little taste of what it's like to be on the outside. To be treated like you treat others."

Stacey, now pale as a ghost, blinks a few times and then bursts into tears and runs out of the library. Theo turns, panting like a caged animal just released from its captor. He is exhausted and excited from his outburst. Once he started, he just couldn't stop himself. The thrill of finally being able to defend Angel was too much to resist. He stood helplessly by for so long while she was attacked again and again. He takes a deep, satisfying breath and notices how silent it has become. He looks around. Everyone is staring at him. Every single person in the library. And most of them look pretty pleased with what he just did.

Theo turns when he hears his name shouted in the hall. Romeo is approaching with a sobbing Stacey clinging to his arm. And he looks like he's ready for a fight.

"You're finished here, Duncan, finished!" he shouts. He shakes off Stacey's arm when he's a few feet away and launches forward, thumping Theo in the chest with both hands.

Theo stumbles back a few steps but regains his balance quickly. He moves forward until they are only a foot or two apart. "Really? Tell me how you are going to do that. Because I'd really like to know how a little shit like *you* plans to finish *me*."

"He was so mean," Stacey sobs behind him. "He said I was ugly."

"You are ugly!" Theo shouts over Romeo's shoulder. Romeo raises a fist up to hit him and this time Theo catches the blow. He knocks Romeo's fist aside and returns the favor. He has a lot of height over Romeo and weight too even though he has lost a lot of his bulk since the accident. Romeo reels back from the punch, nearly knocking Stacey to the ground. He gets his feet under him but looks more wary about a physical confrontation now that he sees how strong his opponent is.

"You're not going to win against me in a fight, Ramirez," Theo says, feeling much more confident now. This is the first physical fight he has ever been in. Ever. And yet he feels like an old pro. "So make your threats and I'll make mine and we'll see who the successor is."

"Fuck you," Romeo shouts. Theo can see that he's trying to come up with a clever counter response but the hamster wheels in his head are moving much too slowly.

A couple of students come around the corner. They're chatting away until they see Romeo and Theo. One looks at the other and they both begin to chuckle. "Switching teams, Romeo?" they laugh.

"What?" Romeo shouts. "What are you fucking talking about?"

"Nice sticker on your truck," the other one says. "I mean, I always suspected, but your kind isn't usually so bold." Both men burst out laughing and then walk away.

Romeo turns his hateful eyes on Theo. His cheeks have gone bright red but his fists aren't so quick to fly this time. "What the fuck did you do to my truck, faggot?"

"Takes one to know one," Theo returns cheerfully. "Hear you country boys like it up the ass."

Romeo ignites at the accusation and when he can't think of a comeback, he slams his fist into his open palm. "You wait. We're gonna get you after school, Duncan. It's one thing to insult my girls, but I ain't gonna stand for anyone messing with my truck."

"Hey," Stacey protests, realizing where she stands on his priority list.

"Shut up, bitch." Romeo cries. "I'm in the middle of something. Can't you see that? So, shut up."

Stacey recoils, her eyes filling with tears.

"Did she tell you not to come to the party Saturday?" Theo asks and Stacey's eyes widen. She backs away a few steps and looks around like she's making an escape plan.

"What?" Romeo cries.

"Oh yeah, guess she chased you away so I could go instead. Right, Stacey? Are we still on for Saturday? Because there still is a party Saturday. They told you not to come so they could invite me. Did she tell you there wasn't one?"

Stacey drops her eyes when both men look back at her. She fiddles with her purse for a few seconds then digs out her phone and holds it to her ear. "I have to take this," she whispers, walking away, well aware that the phone never rang before she answered it.

"It doesn't take much to get them to turn on you, Romeo. I told her not to invite you and she didn't."

Romeo's balled up fists begin to sway at his sides. He really doesn't have the mental fortitude to match wits with anyone. All he can do is yell and punch. But he can't hit Theo and win. Not on his own. At least he is a quick learner in that regard.

"Why don't you go online and see who I am and what I have so you can understand what I can do to you. I've got enough money to buy this town twice over. I'll can ruin your family if I want to. I can get your house repossessed. I can get your farm shut down. I'll see you begging on the street for money. I'll black list you in every college in the country. I'll make your name so dirty that no one will even want to speak it. Watch me, Romeo. Watch what I can do to you."

"Try it, fucker. I ain't scared of you," Romeo cries, but he looks worried now. His little tyrant mind is spinning, trying to understand everything Theo is saying. But before he can wrap his head around it, Theo continues.

"And contrary to what you might believe, you *can* be charged for bullying someone to death. I think I'll get some lawyers involved on behalf of the Yu's. Time for you to pay for what you did to their daughter."

"The Yu's?" he asks and is genuinely confused. He bullied a girl to death and doesn't even know her last name. Unbelievable.

"Bring your boys after school, Romeo. Bring them all. Wait for me in the parking lot because I'm going to wipe your name right off the face of the earth. But know if you touch me, I will sue your ass from here to Jupiter. You'll spend the rest of your natural life working shit jobs to pay my dues."

"Then I'll fucking kill you," Romeo says, then turns and storms away. "I'm going to fucking kill you, Duncan!"

Chapter 38 ☙

The final bells toll. And for Angel it has felt like weeks since she met Theodore Duncan for lunch. Since he said those words: Angel, I think you are beautiful. And then the second phrase, equally shocking as the first: do you want to do something after school? Those two sentences have played over and over in her head like a skipping record ever since she heard them. At first, all she felt was sheer elation. She walked the halls for almost forty minutes not even sure where she was going. It was the highest of highs. Theodore Duncan wants her. But then the doubts crept in. She has so much to hide from him. She can't even wear a tee-shirt around him or he'll see how she cut herself. And what if he asks to see her house? What if he finds out about her father? But then cautious optimism returned. Who cares? He makes her feel so wonderful. And when she's with him, she forgets all her problems. And if she's going to kill herself anyway, then why not go out and have some fun before it happens? Why not try and enjoy what's left of her life? And maybe, in the process, she'll find a reason to keep on living.

She ran off so fast after his proposal that she didn't even make plans for where to meet. She checks the cafeteria door but no one is parked at the loading dock. So she exits the front doors with the rest of the students spilling out. The crowd makes her frantic. She is so scared to be out in the open. It leaves her vulnerable for an attack. And Romeo has been plenty riled up since Theo arrived in town. What will happen when they find out he is associating with her? Will Romeo and his gang go after Theo as well?

Skirting around the slow moving crowd, she heads towards the teacher's parking lot. It's only then that she sees he's waiting, Tombstone Thunderbird parked across the end of the walkway that leads straight from the front doors. Parked where Death's chariot was supposed to be the day he first arrived. He's leaned against the passenger side, arms crossed over his chest, staring out towards the student's parking lot. She follows his gaze and sees a crowd of people pointing at Romeo's truck. She saw the offensive message he had pasted to his back window this morning. No fat chicks. But sometime during the day, someone painted over the 'fat' part, so now it just says: *no chicks*. Angel raises her eyebrows and then a laugh creeps up her throat. She lets it bubble up over her lips, her laughter joining with the others. For once, she is not the target of a cruel attack, her bully is. And he is going to lose his mind when he sees the new message across his back window that either questions his sexuality or states, straight or not, what woman would even want to have him?

Her attention returns to Theo. His focus is on her now. She is so scared and so excited to see him waiting there, leaned against that car. That car which she is going to be inside in just a few minutes. In that car with him. Where are they going? And what are they going to do? She has no control once she gets inside death's chariot. She walks a little closer and then stops a dozen hasty feet before him. She stands and she stares and he does the same. He is a force of nature, feral, fierce, rowdy, and free. She feels helpless near him, completely under his spell. She's anxious and nervous but there's no denying her need to be with him. She's wanted this since the very first day she saw him.

Theo pushes off the car and opens the passenger door. He holds it open and waits for her. It's an invitation he can't even verbalize. I've known you forever. Come meet me again. I'll show you who we are together. Just get in the car, Angel, I'll remind you of what we used to have. Once you remember, the possibilities are endless.

Angel stares at that open door. It's so dark inside. A beam of sunlight illuminates the headstone seats. Neon lights across the floor guide her in like a plane to a landing strip. Her feet are cemented to the pavement. Her mind says yes but her body won't respond. She swallows hard staring at that open invitation. She feels like she is saying yes to so much more than a ride. She feels like this will change everything. She wants to go with him, no doubt about that, but her mind is so muddled, overloaded, ill-prepared.

Her feet start moving before she makes the decision. She supposes in moving forward, she already has. She approaches the idling beast, her anxiety growing. What does she really know about this guy? He could be another set up like what happened to Bea. The realization fills her with dread but she quickly stuffs it down. After all, Theo hates Romeo. If this was a ruse, there is no way Romeo would sacrifice his pride to humiliate her. Would he? She looks up into Theo's beautiful face. Would he?

She sinks down in the seat and takes one last look at the outside world before the door is closed after her. It just can't be a trick. Romeo would never chose someone like Theo. He wouldn't know what to look for; he couldn't even guess. Could he?

She sits quietly in the dark, the windows all tinted black. Dozens of crosses hang like stars from the ceiling. The head of the stick shift is a skull. A bead of light slithers across the back window. The seats are all custom leather, the backs inscribed like tombstones. *Here lies...*is where she rests her head. It's bitterly ironic knowing that someone actually died inside this car. The driver's door opens. Theo drops inside. He closes the door and the daylight goes out.

"You ready?" he says with an ominous smile.

Angel shudders as he suddenly pulls away from the curb. He places his good hand over the steering wheel as he awkwardly maneuvers the stick shift mostly with his bad one. They tear down the road leaving the school. Angel folds her hands tightly in her lap, staring out the window at the world rushing by. Everyone gathered around Romeo's truck now turns and looks in their direction. She can only return their gazes with big, hollow eyes. She feels so completely outside herself right now, in a place that is so disjointed and yet so very familiar. Why does Theodore Duncan call to her so strongly? She feels like he is her salvation. But she can't trust anyone. She can't care for anyone ever again.

As they turn onto the main road through town, an old lady pulls her rusty Oldsmobile clumsily in their path. Her car careens from side to side, her head barely visible above the seats. Angel feels her tension mount as the woman continues her vehicular meanderings. But Theo isn't upset at all. In fact, the incompetent driver isn't bothering him at all. He pulls back a few car lengths and cruises behind her like he's in a Sunday parade. No angry fists out the window, no swearing and tailgating. Angel settles back in her seat a little, feeling a bit more relaxed. She looks up at the crosses pinned to the soft top. Each one is unique, some are pendants, some badges, or from necklaces and earrings. It's more of a collection than a decoration. Angel traces her fingers along them.

"You're really obsessed with death," she whispers, the first words passing between them since she accepted his wordless invitation.

Theo turns his head and smiles, his bright white teeth brilliant against the black background. "Well I was dead for four months."

Angel stares up at the stars. "What do they all mean?"

"I don't know. They were here when I got the car."

"What was his name? The boy who used to have this car?"

He smiles inwardly remembering everything that passed between him and *the boy who used to have this car*. Will he ever tell her the whole truth? Would she understand? Would she want to? "His name was Daniel Ryder."

Angel's head is swimming with questions but she is scared to touch a topic like suicide, even with someone who is obviously so familiar with it. The pain of Bea's death is still so raw inside her, not to mention her own suicide looming on the horizon. But it's hard to think of Save the Date when Theo is near.

"He was seventeen when he died, just a kid," Theo says. "Just a boy."

"Were you close to him?" Angel asks quietly, again thinking of Bea.

"Very close," Theo answers, his heart warmed with thoughts of his former friend and lover.

Angel swallows hard, nervously twisting her hands in her lap. "What do you think happened to him? I mean, do you think...because he killed himself...that he is going to hell or something?"

Theo holds his place in the parade the old lady in the Oldsmobile is creating through town. Behind him drivers are swerving out to the left and right looking for opportunities to illegally pass, willing to risk their lives and the lives of others just to get home a few minutes earlier. It doesn't matter that the woman is obviously disoriented, it's every man for himself out on the roadway. "I'll think, when you die, you just work out the rest of your shit after you're dead. It doesn't go away. It doesn't get better. You still have to deal with all your issues, so it would be better to fix things before you go." Theo falls silent, feeling very satisfied with his answer. That way suicide seems less like a solution and more like an extra complication on top of an already troubled life. He desperately wants to get suicide out of her option menu.

"Do you remember what happened when you died?"

Theo glances in her direction. "It was confusing and chaotic. I didn't know I was dead. I dreamt I was alive. But I still had all the same problems."

Angel wants to know so much more but falls silent again. She's thinking about her best friend doing the very thing she's been threatening to do for years. It took guts to end her life, to go through with the act, but where is Bea now? She doesn't like the way Theo talks about death. It doesn't sound like the quiet relief she was hoping for. Is Bea suffering where she is? How could death be worse than life? It doesn't seem possible but Theo makes her doubt everything she thought she knew. She never could have predicted he would come into her life. And now they're together, in his rumbling beast of a car, driving off into the unknown. It's not the same as being in Romeo's flashy oversized pickup. Romeo is presenting; Theo is expressing. This car *is* him. He has been dead. His friend died here. He is obsessed with death. But in a way she's never considered before.

Theo turns down a side street, pulling out of the angry convoy. He struggles with his dead hand every time he needs to shift. It's something he didn't consider when he bought the car.

"Is it hard?" Angel asks, focused on his crippled hand.

Theo turns his head with a devilish gleam in his eye. He didn't even think when he did it, just assumed she would get the joke. Afterwards, he quickly looks away, regretting the insinuation. But to his surprise Angel huffs out a laugh and turns her gaze out the passenger window.

"Pervert," she retorts playfully.

Heart beating a bit faster, he replies, "Takes one to know one."

Angel stares out the window restraining a smile. *Is it hard?* As soon as he said it, her mind went straight to trash. The idea of Theodore Duncan hard is too much to absorb right now. She wants so badly for him to just drive her out of here but can't gather the nerve to ask. What does he want from her? Why are they in this car together? What is he planning to do with her? Is it really hard?

"So let me," Angel says her face igniting in a full flush. An idea has formed in her mind. An exciting and terrifying idea.

"Let you what?" Theo says, his heart picking up a bit.

"Shift," she says, going back to her initial question. Is it hard *to shift?* That's what she meant to say seeing his wrist bent at such a strange angle. She places her hand on the stick shift. Feeling wild and abandoned, she says, "Drive."

"Where?" he breathes, the car idled at a red light.

Angel points to the horizon. "I don't care. Just drive."

Theo hesitates. He looks up at the red light. Stop, it says, you are not allowed to go forward. But then Angel shifts up a gear. Theo hits the gas and the car shrieks through the red light, leaving the obedient and the law abiding behind scratching their heads.

"Go faster," Angel breathes, forcing the stick shift up another level. Theo slams his foot down on the gas. He has the direction but she controls the speed. Hands clenched around the steering wheel, he skims around a truck and into oncoming traffic. A car is coming towards him. He swerves back into his lane at the last moment, just missing the car. He hears angry honks receding in the distance. He hits the hammer harder.

"Go faster, go faster," Angel goads, both hands on the stick shift, her head down by his shoulder. He runs the next stop sign, narrowly missing a bus, and then thunders past the city limits and out onto the highway leading out of town. He stares ahead in horror at all the obstacles in their path: vehicles, cyclists, hikers, birds. All he has to do is take his foot off the gas to stop the madness. He doesn't have to do this and yet he can't stop. He rockets through traffic, passing on the right and on the left. He swerves around a box abandoned on the highway and the back wheels lose control. He swings back into oncoming traffic and clips off the side window of an approaching vehicle. Glass explodes past his window. He jerks the car onto the opposite shoulder and passes six cars on the right side. He doesn't know how fast they're going. He doesn't dare look away from the road for one second.

Angel squeezes her eyes shut, the thrill of acceleration making her nauseous. She's putting them both in danger. She shouldn't be doing this and yet it's like she's outside herself, looking in. It's like she's dreaming and knows she's dreaming so to hell with all the rules. She can't even see the road. She has no idea what's coming. She has no idea the dangers she's putting them in but she can hear the chaos they're leaving in their wake. She feels like the gun is to her head and the confetti has been set free. And Theo is the one that pulled the trigger.

Heart pounding, sweat pouring down his body, Theo passes too close to a car and clips the bumper. The Thunderbird jolts sideways, and then begins to turn backwards. He screams and closes his eyes. It's happening again. The screeching and the metal twisting, then the blood and the fire. He came back to save her and now they'll both die together. He feels only motion, tires squealing, the car spinning and then a quick, jolted stillness. Hands clenched to the wheel, he slowly opens his eyes to see that they're parked across a dirt road that heads away from the highway. The front end of the Thunderbird is in the ditch. Theo sees cars on the highway slowing to stop. They'll call the cops. They probably already have. He has to run. He jams the car in reverse and it coughs up out of the ditch. Aiming his wheels towards the dirt road, he slams on the gas and they're off again. A huge plume of dust rises up behind them making it impossible to tell if they are being followed.

Angel sits back in her seat, releasing her hold on the stick shift. She doesn't know what came over her. She's never lost control like that with someone else around. It was thrilling and terrifying at the same time. But now Theo has seen a bit of her true self and how recklessly she lives her life. And it won't be long before he starts making his escape plan.

Theo releases a shaky breath, his head dropped back against the headrest. Somehow they're alive. Somehow they survived. And the experience was gripping and electrifying. His shirt is soaked with sweat. He releases a few buttons near the top wanting to take it completely off. To get naked and run like when he fled the Reserve. Except this time she'll be running with him. He can't believe what just happened. It was like the way she controlled him when she was his charge, how he succumbed to her every emotion, fell under the power of anything that came into her mind. He feels ashamed that he put her life at risk and yet excited that she trusted him to guide her through the adventure.

After a long and tense ride, Theo turns the Thunderbird down a road leading to a place called Ghost Lake. A sign by the side of the road says: camping, swimming, boating, and a general store. There is no verbal decision made to go there. It is simply a destination, perhaps a place to hide until he is sure they are safe. No one is behind them but surely the incident has been reported. He left that highway in mayhem.

The trees open up to a modest lake and a small beachfront completely deserted. A lake store sits at the edge of the beach, the windows dark. Theo drives through the parking lot towards the gated off beach. He intends to park by the gate and then sees that it's slightly ajar. Feeling impulsive, he keeps going. Angel shrieks as he knocks the gate open with his bumper. He drives down on the sand until they're parked at the water's edge. The sun is going down. A few shore birds scatter at their arrival. Theo turns the engine off, takes out the keys and drops them in the cup holder. It was a fight to get her here, right until the very last minute, but they are here, they are alone, and finally he can begin to make her understand.

"You all right?" he asks, rolling his head across the headrest and looking at her with a heavy sigh.

"I think so," Angels whispers, staring at his mouth, his lips, his dark hair falling across his eyes.

"I'm going to see if there's a vending machine at the store. Do you want anything?"

She nods and then watches him leave. Once he's gone, she opens her window and leans out for some air. The sky is a deep blue with thin clouds stretched across it. The first stars are beginning to emerge. The wind is completely still. She can hear the sea birds chirping down the beach but there is no sound of humanity. No voices, no laughter, no engines, no televisions. It's just him and her; the whole rest of the world could shrivel up and die for all she cares.

She runs her finger along the word *Thunderbird* written in neat script across the dash. The steering wheel is leather-bound with indentations along the back for fingers. For his fingers. She touches the places where his hands just were and then glances back to see if she's still alone. She is completely obsessed with him. And yet fear holds her back. One thing she's learned for certain is that there is an ocean of secrets hidden behind most people's façade. She has to be careful not to give too much away in case this isn't what it appears to be. Because she is only holding on to her sanity by tattered threads right now.

She pops open the glove compartment and looks inside for anything that would tell her more about him. But nothing inside the compartment belongs to Theo, just to the boy who used owned the car. She finds old insurance and ownership papers, drivers test manuals, and an envelope bereft of its contents. Daniel Ryder, it says across the top with his address and phone number. She places the envelope back where she found it and then notices a strange space between the glove compartment and the dash. She pushes her finger between it and finds a book hidden in the space.

Resting her head against the tombstone seat, she opens the small book and a piece of paper falls out. She retrieves it, opens it up and finds a hand-written message. It says:

Please tell mom I'm sorry but this is the only way. I feel like such a burden on everyone. It will be so much easier when I'm gone. I'm tired of being alone, of being an outcast, of being outside. I don't fit in anywhere. No one likes me. I don't have any friends. I feel so trapped here. I have to get out before I hurt someone more than myself. I am so sorry.

Angel folds the note with a painful gasp. His suicide note, likely never found in this secret hiding place. She glances back. Theo's is still fighting with the vending machine beside the store. Angel opens the book the note fell out of and realizes it's Daniel's journal. Even without reading it, she feels the weight of the life lived and lost inside it. These words are the only thing left of him. Overwhelmed, she thrusts the book into her bag and leaves the car with the suicide note in her hands. A note likely intended for his parents and never found. His last words silenced. She's overcome by grief and worried Theo will return and find her like this. Blinking back tears, she takes Ryder's note to the water intent setting the note into the lake. But instead, she walks in. Shoes, clothes and all, she enters the icy lake, walking further and further in towards the setting sun. She reaches a sharp drop off in the water, the bottom no longer visible past this point. She takes out the note, spreads it open on the water and watches as the moisture slowly penetrates the inky words. It sinks down into oblivion. Overwhelmed, she also takes that step, drops over the ledge and down into the frigid water. It comes up over her like a fierce hug constricting her chest and pinching her eyes. She drifts down to the bottom imagining the end of the world. The apocalypse. Cars abandoned roadside, front doors yawning open and she is the only one left. All the bullies are silent. All the money is gone. All the people are dead. She can go where she pleases, do what she wants, and no one can stop her. She sees the gun to her head, but the confetti won't come out anymore. Theo has taken away Death, her only refuge, so what is there now?

"Stupid machine. I only got a few..." Theo reaches the car and sees the empty seat. "Angel?" He looks around but she's no where around. He sets the food down, panic instantly setting in, a hundred scenarios racing through his mind. Did someone from the highway follow them? Did Romeo follow them? Where is she? "Angel?" he calls as he walks a little in one direction and then another. And then he sees bubbles out in the water. "Angel!" he shouts and runs towards the lake. He rushes in, tripping, falling, his broken hand dragging in the heavy water. He reaches the ledge, dives down and finds her beneath. He bursts to the surface with her in his arms.

Angel gasps, her reverie in upheaval. She's above the surface now but doesn't know why. Theo's there, his body firm against hers. She lost track of time in Ryder's underworld. It was just her and the inky trails of his suicide note. God, Theo must think she's crazy, because it's true. She is crazy. And he will find out the truth eventually. And then he will leave her. And the longer he stays, the worse it will be when he's gone

Theo carries her back to the car and sets her shivering body against the passenger door. "What happened? Are you all right?" He tries to clear some sopping wet hair from her face but she turns away, a dark look flashing across her face. Frustrated, he rises and stares towards the last rays of sun fading over the lake. Maybe she dies either way. Maybe her Life Book will expire whether he changes her mind or not. After all, she only has a few pages left. Maybe there is nothing he can do to stop it.

"I found his note," Angel says softly.

Theo turns to face her. "What note?"

She sighs, wrapping her arms around her chest. "Daniel's suicide note."

Theo drops his head into his hands. Ryder left a suicide note in the car? How did he miss it? And how could he leave it out for her to find?

Seeing Theo upset, Angel begins to break down. "I...just wanted to set it free...in the water. I'm sorry. I'm so stupid." She pushes off the car, suddenly angry with herself. In doing so, she pushes Theo back a few steps and he stumbles to a stop just inches from her. She keeps her eyes down, focused intensely on the drips of water traveling down his chest.

"You're not stupid," he says softly, adjusting a few strands of her wet hair.

Angel shrinks from his touch even though she wants it so much. Why does she have to be like this? Why can't she just be normal?

"Do you want to leave?" he asks.

"No," she replies quickly.

Theo leans in and presses his lips to her cold, shuddering mouth. Her Light responds, a pulse of warmth pumping outwards, folding him in that familiar sensation. He backs away and looks down at her shuddering form. "I have some dry clothes. You should change."

Angel settles back against the car, shaking but not from the cold. The kiss came so quickly, so unexpectedly, but when his mouth touched hers, something exploded inside her. Something raw, something untamed, suddenly she was in that final moment of sexual release, in that euphoric place where all her tensions melted away. Except it was just one kiss, one quick and cold touch that sent her over the edge. Theodore Duncan kissed her. She can hardly believe it.

They sit in the back of the car eating food from the vending machine as the stars slowly appear in the sky. Conversation is quiet and simple. They are both exhausted and overwhelmed from the afternoons excitement. Eventually, the night grows cold and dark. Theo sees Angel shivering again and asks her to sit beside him. She doesn't respond. He asks her if he scares her. She says that isn't it at all. I just don't know what you're doing here, she says. To be with you, he replies. She sits a bit longer, tears glimmering in her eyes, and then slides closer, leaning stiffly against his shoulder. He never expected her to be so restrained around him but people are different by themselves. Few people show their true identities out in the world.

Angel settles back in her seat, shoulder to shoulder with him. It's so strange to be touched, to be talked to after so much isolation. It's harder than she thought it would be. Even now, she cannot relax against him even though he has asked her to. They sit for a long time without speaking and she worries the entire time that she is being too quiet, too strange, too introverted. Say something to him, she goads herself, say something to make him stay. Stop sitting here like a stupid, mute idiot. Talk to him.

Theo folds his hands in his lap, still cold from the unexpected swim. She's finally here with him but the walls she's built around herself are ten miles thick. He's not sure what he can do to break them down. If he says too much, she will bolt. But if says too little, he may lose her anyway.

"What's your dream, Angel?" he finally asks. "I mean, if you could have anything in the world, had all the money in the world, what would you do?"

"I don't know," Angel says, sideswiped by the unexpected question. "I've never thought about it."

"So think about it now. What would you do?"

She tries to find an answer that would appeal to him but her head is completely blank. Sure she has dreams. They involve the high school gym full of blood. But is that really what she wants now? Or is she hoping for a different future? Then it occurs to her, an answer so simple and yet so painful. She struggles whether to tell him such an honest truth. She doesn't want to but feels like she owes it to Bea.

"I want my best friend back," she whispers and a rush of tears spill down her face. She shudders out a sigh and then drops her head against his chest. Sobs come next and she just can't hold them in. Theo's arms come around her and he brings her closer to his body. She hears his steady heartbeat through his chest and it calms her some. God, she is tired. Her whole body just aches from the burden of her horrible life. What is her dream? The idea is so painfully unimaginable to a girl who can't even get three meals a day. How dare she dream? It's as pointless as shopping without money, building gardens with no flowers to plant, gassing up a car with no wheels. Her breath slows and her mind stills. When she is very near sleep, she begins to whisper mindlessly, to babble, to ramble. Her mind cracks a little, unable to hold so much pain inside. Poetry pours from her lips and she feels on the brink of madness.

"In a place where love can't seed, the darkness settles cold and deep. It closes like a comforting fiend. Empty regrets don't repair lost time, lost joy, lost faith, lost heart. Leader of the family takes us all to hell, to a land of regret and self-pity, of selfishness and pure hatred."

Theo stares straight ahead, his breath low and shallow, afraid even a single movement will shatter her spell. She is a prophet and rebel poet; an embodiment of her soul's spirit. He's tired too, exhausted. His own tears still wet on his face from Angel's only wish. To have her best friend back. To reverse the hateful acts that led to Bea's suicide And, yes, to see the bullies that led Beatrice Yu astray pay for what they did. In blood. Oh, he knows her ultimate dream.

"I don't want to die," Angel says, completely outside herself now. "I want escape, to leave, seek freedom, put my feet on mountain paths. Aim for the peaks and never come back. Sleep by the water with the spray at my back. Rock rising, plates converging, snow-capped peaks where none can travel, land untouched, unsoiled by man's thunder feet. I want to go off the grid, be accountable to no man's hand, eat what I grow, live where I build, water from the sky, heat from the fire, food from the earth. I want to go back to a time where man lived in fear of nature, not the other way around, where all I use I understand. I want to unplug, disconnect, kill the noise, cover my ears, close my eyes, hear nothing but the earth creak, in stillness just breathe, just be. Exist only because I am, not because I tweet, I text, I post, I buy, I need, I want, I go, I go, I go. I am, I am, let me be, I am. In stillness, breathe, I am, I am."

Angel finally falls asleep against his chest, but her words gut Theo, leave him empty and shaken. They keep him up for the rest of the night with tears dried to his face. She is a force of nature and he worries, if she survives this, how he can ever keep up with her? He's like a man with a bucket at the base of breaking dam. Even if he can save her, can her ever be enough for her?

Chapter 39ଛ

Angel stares out the passenger window as Theo drives her home. It's nearly dawn. She can't remember the last time she was up this late, or had anything to do that would require her to come home with the sun. It seems like days have passed since they left the high school that afternoon. She can hardly believe what has happened since then. She feels raw and exposed and even a little sick. And yet somewhere in that mess of emotion, there is excitement and hope. She wishes she hadn't burned her journals. She has so much to write and nothing to record it on. She's already forgetting details of their first meeting, about their encounter in the library, and about the picnic at the school. She wants to hold onto every memory, so afraid he will walk away at any moment.

But he hasn't left. In fact, he doesn't even seem fazed by what happened. She almost killed him on the highway with her stupid antics. She's embarrassed to remember taking that stick shift from him and forcing him to drive so fast. And she can't even explain what she was doing underwater. She doesn't really know why she did it. And then she cried in the car and babbled about a bunch of strange stuff. Everything is just hitting her so hard right now. For some reason, she can't hold her defenses up around him like she can around other people.

She exhales a deep breath, glancing over at him. It's so hard to keep herself level. This is what she wanted, dreamed of all her life. Love and companionship, someone to accept her, to spend time with, to be with. He's everything she's ever wanted, even things she didn't know she craved. He's dark and beautiful and an outcast like her, at least in some regards. He stands out starkly amongst the masses and despises the people who pick on her. He's like a god to her, seated in the Tombstone with the music rumbling all around him. She loves his weird hand and that he does nothing to conceal his oddities. Doubt is always there but she wants to give in to him, to give him everything. But how can she do that being the person that she is? He doesn't want a girlfriend who cuts herself. She is dirty and broken and can't imagine why anyone would join her team.

She glances at him again, staring at his profile against the highway lights, the crest of his uncombed hair, the strong veins of his broken hand over the wheel, his forearms tightly muscled. She remembers how his arms felt when he carried her from the water. She experiences a rush of heat to her body at the thought of the kiss shared after. Yes, he kissed her after the day they'd had, after the highway and the suicide note. Despite all the difficulties, she thinks, once the dust has settled, she will remember this as one of the greatest nights of her life.

"Sorry I have to be back so early," Theo says as the silence stretches on a bit too long. "But we can do something again if you like?"

"Okay," Angel says without a single thought to the contrary. She stares out the passenger window, biting down on a smile. Again? He wants to see her again? After today?

Theo takes the back road into town on his way to Angel's house. He can't get a sense of her mood. The night did not go as planned and yet was strangely thrilling. His heart races every time he thinks of the highway ride and her heartfelt poetry afterwards. He doesn't want to leave her at all but he has to meet the Yu's today and set up the lawyer they intend to sue Romeo with. If not for that, he probably would've just stayed out at the lake for the rest of the day.

He parks in front of Angel's house and lets the car idle noisily. The sun is just below the horizon and stabs of light are reaching up into the sky. "So I'll see you again? I have to go up to the city but I will be back later."

"Okay," Angel says with a quick glance in his direction.

"Okay," Theo says, staring at her. But then his phone rings. The lawyer is calling him already. He needs to take this.

Angel gets reluctantly out of the car and pushes the door closed, looking in the window at him. She wants to kiss him again but she is just too overwhelmed. She needs time to process. Maybe get a new journal and get some of this written down. "Thanks for the drive," she says, fumbling for the right words. "I had fun."

Theo's face breaks into a smile. He picks up his urgently ringing phone and says, "I did too."

Angel also smiles and suddenly she is giddy all over again. She backs away as he revs the engine, her heart soaring a hundred miles above her broken little body. She turns back for one last look as her dark and handsome hero pulls away from the curb. He opens his phone and she hears him laugh and say, "Romeo."

Angel takes a few unsteady steps as a cold, dark stain spreads across the center of her bright happy place. Did he just say Romeo? Is he on the phone with Romeo? She turns and stops as the dark spot begins to expand. Romeo set Bea up. Bea fell for it so hard that she killed herself when she found out it was a lie. She takes a few more sickly steps and then looks back to where his car was parked. He's gone and so is that wonderful, lush feeling of new love, that soaring happiness that chased all her worries away. Now her troubles are back tenfold. She stumbles up into the porch, her bag falling and spilling out across the porch. She drops on her knees, her Light shrinking in the presence of a common dark. A painful arrow shoots right through her stomach as she realizes Theo took her home. He drove her right up to her house. But she never told him where she lives. He's not supposed to know where she lives.

She falls on her knees as dog Theo paws and whines behind the front door. It's all fading like the quickly retreating night, the euphoria of the first kiss, their sweet embrace by the lake, and even their first chance meeting in the school hallway. It was all a set up. He was watching. He was waiting. That's how he knew how to get to her. He knew all her haunts. An unwelcome germ plants itself inside her, spreading doubt, disbelief, anger, and regret. Theo is a trick. Romeo planted him. Of course, how could she be so fucking stupid? How could she possibly believe Theo was real, that a guy like him could just wander into town, that something so beautiful could come to her so easy? She rises with a heavy breath, then starts kicking her bag across the porch. How Romeo and Theo must congratulating themselves now, plotting their next move against her. Stupid Angel thinks someone could fall in love with her. Stupid Angel falls for anything.

She opens the door and the dog rushes outside to pee. She steps inside and begins to cry, holding her stomach and falling to the ground. Fool, fucking fool, how could you believe? There is nothing for you. Nothing. You are nothing. You are nothing. Stupid. No one believes in you. You aren't worthy of love. You aren't worthy of anything. Worthless. Stupid. Foolish girl.

But he hates Romeo, she thinks with a brief flicker of hope. He hit him in the hall. They fight all the time. How could Romeo know what she wants? That she would want this? Would they go so far for just for a ruse? But Bea believed it too. She wasn't stupid. She was an honor student. They had to be clever to pull her in. They had to bring in someone she'd never seen before. And Bea was infatuated with him. Talked about him so much that it made Angel crazy. Now she wishes she could just hear her voice one more time. She can't even think of what those boys did to her, of Bea's last days on this planet. This was a game to the death and Beatrice Yu lost. How can she even doubt that Theo is the same thing?

Angel crawls to her feet, goes to the nearest wall and presses the top of her head against it. She's thinking about the gun, about laying her brains to rest on moldy brown carpet. Then they'll have their satisfaction. But what Theo said about death…but Theo is a liar. Liar, liar, fucking liar with his pants on fire. She has to make them pay for this. She shouldn't have let herself get distracted. She shouldn't have believed. Those boys deserve what's coming for them. But Theo? He was so beautiful, so perfect…god, she wanted too much to believe.

Angel punches her fist against the wall. She recoils with the pain of first contact. Not to worry, the blows will get easier as she goes along, her nerves will swell and numb and pretty soon she'll feel nothing. She curses herself and smashes her fist again, breaking skin, separating knuckles, and cracking plaster. She punches and punches until one sharp blast sends icicles of acute distress angling up her wrist. She backs off but she is far from over. Stupid Angel, stupid! She slaps the side of her face thinking about the encounter in the science hall. Of course he knew she'd be there. That's where she always goes. That's where Romeo sees her sitting. Stupid. Stupid. She punches the wall again, her teeth clenched, hot tears coming down her cheek. With a painful sob she remembers his story of Daniel Ryder. How could that be a lie too? Was the suicide note planted there for her to find? Were they all crouched in the bushes, laughing as she dropped underwater? She punches the wall again, the divots between her knuckles no longer visible. There's blood on the wall. All a trick. All a ruse. There is no coming back from this.

She sinks down to her knees, then further down to curl on the carpet, holding her throbbing hand and sobbing. Her dog returns, breath reeking from eating grass. He whines and nudges her face with a soft wet nose. He gets down on his stomach and sets his jowls on her outstretched arm, two shiny orange eyes alert with concern.

"I still love *you*," she whispers, unable to resist the absolute affection offered by a loyal pet. She offers him a hand and he rubs his face into it. "Let's run away together. Let's go to the mountains. Would you like that? I'll be a wild woman and you my loyal hound." She thinks of Theo's words from the night before, the cruelness of his asking about her dreams, making her believe only so he can destroy her. He will get his wish, she thinks angrily, he will get it tonight.

Theo returns home on the highest high. It was the craziest day and yet somehow it all worked out in the end. He can't wait to see Angel again. But all that will have to wait. He has contacted the Yu's and they are eager to begin. They will be meeting in the city today to go over the details. The local police department could be as guilty as Romeo. The cops ignored the Yu's accusations because Ramirez was a blood relative to the chief. And if that's true, this case could be much bigger than a damages suit. They could be looking at a police cover-up and neglect. And since Romeo was never properly charged or investigated, they could even take him to trial for Bea's suicide if they can get enough evidence together.

He sits back in his bed and mulls over the thought of Romeo on the stand defending his freedom. Better yet, he pictures Romeo in jail defending his manhood. He's not sure he could get a murder charge to stick. Maybe manslaughter? His lawyer says that the kids who tricked Bea actually posted online videos of their exploits. Whether they intended to bully Bea to death remains to be seen. But Theo is optimistic that either way, this is going to cause a hell of a lot of trouble for Romeo Ramirez.

He's been up to other things as well. He's contacted a real estate agent and purchased some land out near the mountains. He's going to build a house for Angel. Perhaps a bit presumptuous, but he remembers that dream she had when the power was turned off, about a cabin by the mountains and a stream through the land and her dog running out in the yard. It's not much to ask for. She just wants a quiet life and to be left alone. And he is more than willing to provide that for her. At least with house part. He is hoping her new dreams will involve him alongside her.

Feeling satisfied, Theo finds his keys and gets ready to drive up to the city. Things could not be going better.

Angel crawls into bed, her eyes swollen, her fists bleeding. She is just a single nerve now. A hot, throbbing gash. She doesn't eat or drink, just lets herself dry up and starve, too tired to wash up or even close the front door. She rests her heavy head on a bunched up pillow but can get no sleep. Save the Date isn't an option anymore. Revenge is too much of an effort, too complicated, too messy, too involved. Death is coming right now. It's just one tug of a razor away. She knows there's a pack in the medicine cabinet. Ten steps to the bathroom and it's over in a matter of minutes. Fuck what Theo told her about death earlier. Theodore Duncan is a fucking liar.

What a fool she was. How quickly she fell for his ruse. All her barriers came crashing down at the slightest offering of affection. She should have known better. Life doesn't give her chances. Life wants to see her dead. Suicide is her only option. The universe wants to see her die.

Sleep eventually comes but doesn't give her any release. She wakes up mid-afternoon with a mountain of pain parked on her head. She manages to get up and close the front door. That's when she notices her bag on the porch where she dropped it. There, peeking out from the corner of the bag, is Daniel Ryder's journal. Could a group of illiterate morons like Romeo and his buddies have enough brain power to fabricate an entire journal? So maybe the boy and his car were real. Maybe it was another kid they bullied to death. Maybe they stole his car. Maybe they didn't know about the journal or the suicide note. And if so, this journal is real.

She crawls into bed and places the journal on her lap. It's a small book, maybe the size of a toaster pastry, bound in silk and decorated in dragon emblems. It's neatly closed, neatly pressed, no dog eared pages or scratches or scrawlings like in her journals. Just tidy little entries all labeled with times and days but no months or years.

She opens the binding and goes to the last page, wanting to see his final entry. She touches the words, so carefully scripted. His writing is so precise, even artistic. The entry reads:

It's Tuesday night again. Nothing has changed this week like I had hoped it would. Sometimes I don't know why I try. Spent the night watching TV, then had a bath and went to bed. Dad wants to work on the car but I'm too tired. Maybe tomorrow will be better.

She flips backwards, letting the neat little pages pass through her fingers. She expected some grand affair at the end, an emotional entry raging with sorrow and despair. It's as if he didn't even know it was going to happen himself. She opens it to the front page. It says: *Daniel J. Ryder* and underneath his name is a drawing of a single flower. Right there, she is convinced it is an actual journal. Because this little drawing is too tender for a bunch of Neanderthals to create.

Angel sits back more comfortably assured that this is no hoax. She grips the journal clumsily with her bruised hand, her eyes so bleary she can barely read. She's eager to go on, to delve into all that is Daniel Ryder and forget everything that is Angel.

I hate gym, reads the first entry. *I know all I've talked about the last year has been my Annabelle. Beautiful, shy, little Anna hiding in the corner trying so hard not to be noticed. I never did get the nerve to talk to her. I've dreamt about her so much that it's become this huge event in my mind. Now she's more fantasy than reality and I'm afraid to take that away. I am so full of desire right now. It oozes from every pore of my body. All I want is to be with someone, to give, to share, to hold, to touch. I am phoenix desire wrapped in white plastic. A sliver of the man on the outside that I am on the inside. The boys hate me, call me a sissy and a fag. I need to get out of this small place, to get away from these small people and their small, little minds. I want to go somewhere big, where people are different, so different that I won't even be noticed. I want to go anywhere but this nowhere town. I'm tired of being ridiculed for who I am. What's so bad about being different anyways?*

Stupid, soulless Richard rules this school with his fists. And no one will stand up to him in fear of losing their face. But Richard was gone on Monday. Thank god, because Monday is wrestling and Richard likes to twist you until your bones crack. The girls always go outside to do track when the boys wrestle. Poor Anna and her bad knees being forced to jump hurdles. I don't want to wrestle; I'd rather do track. I hate being told what to do because I am a boy. The boys will stay in the gym and wrestle, the girls will go outside and run track. Boys drive trucks. Girls play with dolls. Boys are athletic. Girls are creative. Men are supposed to be machines: emotionless, sturdy, providers; brick walls of truck driving meathead muscle. I am none of these. These rules don't apply to me. Don't tell me what I am. I'll be who I want to be.

So it's Monday. The girls went outside. I felt strange as Annabelle looked back at me. Like something could've happen if we weren't stuck in this stifling place where dreams go to die. But those opportunities will never happen here. She went out to do track and I stayed inside to wrestle. We were all relieved that Richard was gone. He knocks our heads together all the time but in gym it's considered a sport. They pitted me against Nicholas instead, going by size and weight we were roughly evenly matched. My plan was to submit and lose as quickly as possible. But that didn't happen at all.

The entry ends there, the outcome of the story left dangling. Angel turns the page. There, sketched between the pages are two men's torsos twisted like classic Olympians, completely nude. Angel's eyes run over the image, the faces unfinished, the legs fading away at the knees. One man is being pushed to the floor. He has his hands over his head and his legs pinned back. The other man holds him down. Both men are erect. Angel bites her bottom lip, unwittingly aroused even in her sorrow. She's never seen anything like it, never even considered two men as a sexual fantasy. But the image of these two men together has just opened her eyes to a whole new erotica.

She turns to the next entry, dated a few days later.

Wrestling again tomorrow. I've been thinking about it all week, about what happened last week. What did happen? I don't know. I think something did happen and I don't know what that means. This small town is getting even smaller. God if they hate me now just wait until they find out what I've been thinking about lately.

Dad wants a man's man but he got me instead. I can't let him know what I've discovered. It's always been difficult between us. He's spent his whole life trying to understand me. Like there is something about me that is so out of place that it needs to be deciphered. He's never really accepted me and won't until I take on the family business, get a girl, get married. At least we have the car to work on. It's the only place that's safe for us anymore. I can't wait to drive it. We're painting it black like I hoped. Now if I can only convince him of the mural. I've sketched out what I want and he said he'd rather set his hair on fire than paint the car like that.

Angel turns the page and sees sketches for the mural that did eventually end up on the car. She knows now that the car is real. Daniel is real. And when she reads his journal, she feels like he is sitting right beside her. But Daniel's writing is so much more level than hers. He understands what's going on around him and can vocalize it so easily. He seems so much less tortured than her. So why did he kill himself?

She reads late into the afternoon as Daniel's obsession with Nicholas grows. But he also loves Anna and doesn't know how the two fit together, or how he can feel so strongly for both sexes. He's bullied by Richard daily. Picked on and persecuted because he doesn't like sports, because he'd rather be in the science lab than smoking pot out behind the lounge. He has a real love for order, for math, the arts, for mysteries about the universe that most students will never ponder in their entire life span. He talks eagerly about Calculus and calls it the *sexy math*. His only real friend is his nerdy compadre named Jules. But Jules knows nothing about what he's discovered about himself recently.

Daniel is obsessed with death but not death like she knows it. Not this release from the never-ending pain of life, but with cemeteries and the paranormal and unsolved mysteries. His obsession with the otherworld seems strongly misaligned with his need for order and answers and yet they coexist seamlessly, like his love for both men and women. He doesn't fight the inconsistencies in his life the way she does. He embraces them. His favorite haunt is the River's End Memorial cemetery just outside of the town where he lives. It has graves dating back to the 1800's. Sometimes he stays there all night when he wants his dad to think he's out with friends.

Anna sat next to me today, the next entry reads. *She is so beautiful. She was having trouble with an equation and I showed her how to do it. She said, "You're Daniel, right?" Those are the first words she's ever spoken to me.*

Me and dad went the city the other day and I went to the drug store while he picked up auto parts. I found this…magazine. I stole it because I couldn't be seen buying it. I keep it under my art box because I know dad will never mess with that stuff. But he would crucify me if he found it. He would never speak to me again if he knew what I was fantasizing about lately. He only likes me if I become what he wants me to be. He would never like me for the real me. I just don't understand why a guy like Richard is the norm and I am the variable.

I am a coward, reads an entry a few days later. *For some reason, Richard turned his sights on Anna. I don't know why. She has done nothing to him, just keeps quietly to herself. I have to think that I am the reason she has come under his sites. Because I like her, now Richard does not. She is such a pure spirit, so fragile, so sweet. I have been so afraid this would happen. She is a delicate flower and will crumble to dust under his fist.*

Today, Richard pushed her down in the hall. She had books in her arms, so she couldn't keep her balance. She fell right on her face. Richard and his buddies just laughed and laughed. And I just stood there. There were so many of them on his side and I was scared to intervene. I didn't want Richard to come after me. I didn't even help her up because all the boys were standing and watching. And she saw my inaction. She saw me just watching. I have never been so ashamed of myself. I always considered myself a hero.

Angel sighs and leans back against the wall. She wonders if anyone has ever watched her get bullied and wishes they could've stopped it? That thought has never occurred to her. Romeo is an asshole. Other people must see that too. It can't be just her. She always believed she deserved to be an outcast but Daniel never thought that. He blamed the bully right from the start. She's only recently come to realize that too.

It's my seventeenth birthday today. Had a little party with just me and Jules and my family. Mom seems weird lately. So unplugged. She stayed for the cake then disappeared for the rest of the night. After Jules left, I went to the cemetery. Told dad some friends were taking me out but, truth was, I just wanted to be alone.

I want this year to be different. This year I want to find love, get the car done, maybe even get a job in the city. I meet with the registrar of the university tomorrow. With my grades I can get accepted into any school I want. I've been going through the courses. I definitely want to take advanced Calculus, Art History, Chemistry, and Philosophy. High school has been hell, but there will be no Richards in university. From what I hear, he's working at his dad's gas station after school. If that isn't justice, I don't know what is.

Things have turned bad, the next entry reads, *I got beat up after school by Richard and his friends. They were picking on Anna and I just couldn't take it anymore. Richard hit her with rock and I told him to stop. He called me a fairy and then punched me in the face. The next day Anna wasn't at school. I thought, I hoped anyway, that she had faked an illness and was staying home for a few days. But I learned later, that she's left the school for good. Her parents pulled her out after the rock incident. They've moved away.*

Now dad has told me that he doesn't have the money to send me to university. He used my school savings to pay down some debt on his business. I can't even get a student loan because his credit is so bad and I have no one else to vouch for me. He says I'll have to work in town until I can get enough money to go. But there's only one place to work in town. The gas station.

597

I can't stay here for a few more years; I can't even stay here for another day. My father fucks up his business and I have to pay. And my Anna, poor Anna, leaving this place thinking that no one cares. She's right. No one here does. And now I'm trapped here.

It's the second last entry in the journal, the last being the quick note that he hopes things will be better in the morning. Angel's guess is that he never saw another morning.

Chapter 40ॐ

Theo doesn't get home until the next day. It was way longer than he wanted to be gone but the case against Romeo kept growing and growing. Romeo and Stacey post everything. Their videos were found all over the internet and most of them involved incidents of harassment and bullying, and there were a lot more kids than just Angel and Bea who were coming under attack. It seems the Yu's case wasn't the only one being overlooked by the local police. There is the possibility of getting more families involved, of taking this case to a whole other level. Bea's suicide was the most extreme situation but other families had to move away, sell their homes, and put their kids under psychological care. The Yu's want vengeance. They are willing to wait a little longer while the lawyer tries to contact other families. They want to sue Ramirez, Stacey, and the police department. No amount of money can replace the loss of their daughter. All they have left is to try and right the wrongs left behind.

Theo showers and makes a quick breakfast. He wishes Angel had a cell phone so he could let her know he's running late. She is in such a fragile state right now. He doesn't want to leave her alone for too long.

He glances at the phone as the head librarian calls him again. He thinks his days at school are finally over. He's not going to miss those nasty stares much. After the old croon is done leaving a voice mail, Theo goes online and checks his accounts. He sees no activity on the debit card he left in Angel's yard. He'd rather see her use the card than stealing, even though she doesn't know the card was meant for her, but she hasn't made a single purchase on it.

Theo sets down his phone, thinking about what he should do with Angel this morning. Maybe stop by and take her out for breakfast. Or, better yet, bring breakfast to her. He knows how she hates crowds. Then an alarming realization comes to him. He's not supposed to know where she lives. He drove her home yesterday morning without even asking for directions. A tremor runs through his body. Did she realize what happened? Did she catch the mistake? He is keeping so many secrets from her and without proper explanation, her mind could run wild with a blunder like that. He grabs his jacket and his keys and runs out the front door.

The dog begins to bark and Angel hears the porch step creak. Panicked, she grabs Ryder's journal and runs into the closet, closing the door behind her. Then, on second thought, she leans back out and whispers for the dog to come. If Romeo is out there, she doesn't want her dog hurt either.

The two of them huddle inside the dark closet and wait for the intruder to go away. There is a knock at the front door, then another and then she hears Theo say, "Angel? Are you here?"

Angel experiences a horrible shock. He's here in her house, in this horrible, hellish place, seeing how she lives, seeing who she really is. He's not supposed to know she's living here at all. She cringes as he calls her again. Hearing his voice, that voice she used to love, brings tears to her eyes. She was so infatuated with him. She really believed that they were fated to be together. All the time she spend thinking of him, watching him, trying so hard to let him in past her walls, it was all in vain. Fuck Theodore Duncan. She wonders how much Romeo is paying him for this. What his final payoff will be if his mission is successful?

"Angel? It's Theo? I'm coming in."

Angel grabs the dog and tries to keep him quiet. Theo comes down the hall to the bedroom. He enters in with another knock. She sees him now. He's holding a grocery bag of food. It breaks her heart to recognize all the traps he laid for her, how she slowly followed the cheese through the maze. It breaks her heart even more that she still wants to fall for them.

To pretend she doesn't know just so that she can spend a few more minutes with him. It was so exciting, so thrilling to be chosen by him. It's all she can do to contain the sobs, her dog, and the emotion boiling up in the little closet.

"Angel?" Theo says and his eyes turn towards the closet door. Angel shrinks back. Why would he look in the closet of all places? Has he been spying when she's here alone? Have they all? Are they watching her in her bed? Have they seen the things that she's done? She shudders as he takes a step forward, moving further into the shadows. Her dog is getting unruly. Angel tries to take his collar but he suddenly bursts out of the closet and runs towards Theo. Angel's face contorts in pain but she cannot leave the safety of the closet to help him. She thinks about Daniel and Anna and how he let the bullies hurt her. Can she sit here in the shadows while Theo hurts her dog?

"Oh hey, buddy," Theo says, crouching down and rubbing the dog's head. "Remember me?"

Angel's eyes pop open. She carefully peers around the closet door to see her dog affectionately bouncing up on Theo's thighs. They *have* been in the house. So much so that the dog isn't afraid of them. Her dog hates everyone. He chased the mailman right over the fence. The utility guys won't even come by her place. But now he jumps up and down like he and Theo are old friends. How long has this plan been in the works?

After Theo is gone, Angel packs a few things, takes her dog, and leaves the house. This time she knows she will not be coming back. Her home isn't safe anymore, not that it ever was. But now that she knows the boys have been inside watching her, she can't stay a minute longer.

Her backpack stuffed with everything she owns, she and the dog walk into town. She'll stop at ATM and take out as much as the debit card will allow. Then go down the farm supply store. There, idling in the parking lot, will be dozens of trucks, the owners carelessly inside drinking overpriced coffees and ordering farm supplies. She's always known that if she needed to steal a vehicle, that's where she'd go. And she's surprised the place hasn't been plundered before. Trucks worth tens of thousands of dollars are just left running with the keys in the ignition. She can't imagine having so much money to spare.

She goes to the ATM first, thinking once she has the truck then she'll want to get out of town as quickly as possible. She really doesn't know where she's going. Or what she'll do when she gets there. She has Ryder's journal in her bag, as well as the pack of razor blades. Secretly, she always knew it wouldn't be pills, poison or guns. Deep down, she always knew that it would be a good, traditional suicide. And though death isn't foremost on her mind right now, it will be once she is alone and has had time to think about what those boys have done to her. At least she didn't sleep with Theo. Bea gave that boy her virginity. It must have hurt very badly to learn it was all a trick. She tried so hard to get Bea to talk to her, but she wouldn't even let her in her room. She never saw her friend again. Except in the casket.

She withdraws six hundred dollars because that's the daily limit the card will allow. At midnight she will do it again and then leave the card behind. Someone will be missing it soon. And it's too easy to track her if she's leaving a paper trail behind. Once she has the money, she walks to the farm store. Dog Theo trots eagerly at her side, lunging at every person who passes by. Angel doesn't even bother to restrain him. Just lets him scare the living shit out of anyone who dares to get too close. She'll have to change his name now. She wonders about Theo, what his real name is, and what sort of horrible person could agree to do something as deceitful as he did.

At the farm store, trucks are lined up as expected, idling, keys in the ignition. Many are not even within view of the front window of the store. Angel pokes through a few and finds one with a cell phone and a full tank of gas. She pats the seat and the dog jumps inside. Then she puts it in reverse and drives out of the parking lot. She takes the shortest route out of town. The sun is down now, which makes her feel safer in the stolen vehicle. By the time the theft is called in, she'll be long gone. She picked an older model truck, something without GPS or any sort of police tracking system. The phone she can't keep for long either. It could be traced. She just wanted to use it for the map, get a sense of where she's going, then get rid of it.

When she's out of town, she parks at a dead end road and take out the phone. She opens the map and expands it so she can see the whole area around the town. She scans the towns, just dots on lines, and finds a road that will take her to the mountains. The mountains, of course, that's where she should go. But it would be safer to use back roads and stay off the highway, so she finds a pen and paper and draws out a route that bypasses all the major arteries. Then she tosses the phone out the window.

She heads west, trying to keep her mind off Theo and Romeo. Why didn't she just do this before? Just leave? That house is not her responsibility. Her parents are never coming back. Is that why she was holding on to it? Because she thought one day they would? She hopes that's not the reason but can't discount it. The urge to gravitate towards your biological parents is so primal, even when they don't deserve your devotion.

She glances over at her dog who's grinning with his head out the window. She pats him on the back and he barks and shakes his head out in the wind. She smiles and focuses back on the road, feeling better with every mile she puts between herself and her prison. The mountains, she can hardly imagine it. Already her original intentions are fading. Maybe she doesn't need to kill herself like she first thought. Maybe she just needs to get away. She'll have twelve hundred dollars by the morning. Maybe she could find a job at a resort. Rent a little room somewhere. Forget everyone she left behind. Even him. Even Theodore Duncan.

A sign appears in the distance. As it nears, she sees the words: River's End. River's End? Why does that sound so familiar? She takes the turn off, deciding this will be where she makes her last bank withdrawal. Off in the distance is a small gathering of lights. Another farm town full of bullies and rednecks? She wonders if all small towns are like the one she just left. These little villages boast of their friendly, welcoming communities but those kinships are only shared through like-minds, lifestyles, and religions. It's only welcoming if you're one of them.

She takes the turn into town, cruising through the dark streets like a predator. Her stolen truck glides past a deserted main street, one store, one gas station, a liquor mart, a library, then down another street which takes her past the school, River's End School. Again, it's so familiar but she can't figure out why.

She stops at the smallest bank she's ever seen with no drive-through ATM and the front doors locked. She will not getting any money here. Annoyed she wasted so much time, she takes the dirt road out of town and sees another sign coming up. River's End Memorial. That's when she remembers where she knows it. She brings the truck to an abrupt stop and takes out Ryder's journal. And there it is, in his own handwriting: River's End. This was the town he lived in. Died in too. She even passed by the school where he and his Anna were bullied.

Angel follows the signs to the cemetery. It stands alone in a field surrounded by a black iron gate with a row of trees circling it. There is no church house at the center, just tattered graves with farmer's fields bordering the outside. She turns into the gated off approach and shuts off the lights. It takes a while for her eyes to adjust. A full moon floods the cemetery with light. Angel takes the journal and gets out. She hops the fence, while dog Theo stops to pee on it, and takes herself into the yard. She drifts dreamily through the ancient tombstones, many of the names long worn away. There are unmarked crosses and places where just dents in the grounds indicate that the dead rest there. In the center is a small crypt with a sealed stone door and the words *Alis Grave Nil* printed across the lintel. A small bench is situated under a tree to the side of it. Angel sits down and sets the journal beside her, trying to imagine Daniel Ryder sitting in this very same spot. It is so peaceful and quiet and the only sound is the night breathing. In the moonlight shadows she can see statues of mother Mary and tombstones shaped like hearts, and long forgotten plastic flowers woven with spider webs. A freshly covered tombstone sits in one corner, a mound of dirt parked over it like a pregnant belly about to give birth. She imagines a hand rising out of it and shudders. She's glad she brought the dog. If the undead were to appear tonight, they'd reconsider their reincarnation when they saw him.

She sighs, watching dog Theo race around the dead in delight. Theo. The name hurts her now. She let him in so quickly. And she ignored all the warning signs. She can't imagine what motivates the mind of a bully. It must be such a dark place. Like Richard and his face pummelings. Seems every town has to have one. Poor Daniel. He'd almost gotten out of the town and then it pulled him back in. She still doesn't understand his suicide. Despite all his troubles, he seemed so sensible. Or maybe that is just what he chose to write about. Not everyone is as forthright as she is in her journals.

Leaving his journal on the bench, Angel gets up and walks amongst the graves feeling as dead inside as the ones lying below. She passes by stone after stone imagining her name in place of the others, her body gently at rest beneath the surface. How still and quiet it must be inside the earth. She still yearns for that end, for the silence of death. She reads the stones that are legible. A baby who died after two days of life. And then a man who lived almost a hundred years. A lot of the markers are crosses with no names at all. Down at the far corner, she spies a particularly gothic looking cross that catches her interest. She turns that direction as her dogs zooms past in pursuit of some exciting, new discovery. He snuffles at a tombstone, pees on it, then pounces on some plastic flowers, tearing them loose from the ground with his teeth. Angel passes him with a pat on the head then goes to the gothic cross. There are new flowers placed on the grave even though the stone looks decades old. She kneels down in front of it. Daniel J. Ryder is written across a small plaque mounted at the base of the cross.

"Daniel," she whispers, touching the letters of his name. They buried him here, in his favorite place. His father didn't even know that he'd done his son such a favor. She traces the curves of his letters, wishing she had kept the suicide note. It should be here with him. Romeo could not be involved with Daniel's death; the dates on this tombstone are too old. So how did these boys ever find out about him? Did they buy the car and stumble across his journal? Did they sit around and laugh as they read it? It seems the bullying doesn't end even after death.

Tired, completely spent, Angel lays down on Ryder's grave and stares up at the moon. If she could bring him back to life right now, she would. She would take him to the mountains with her and they could hide from the world together, seek solace in nature. Angel feels her eyes drooping. She is so exhausted. When is the last time she slept? She thinks she's been up for almost forty-eight hours now. She closes her eyes, the ground over Ryder's body so soft and warm. Maybe just a quick nap, then she needs to get back on the road.

Angel gasps, her eyes blinking open to a rising sky. The sun has just peaked over the horizon but a low blanket of cloud disperses its light. Fog sits above the grass like the earth is steaming. Angel looks up and sees a gothic cross rising above her head. The morning dew condenses on her skin like wet beads on a cold glass. She feels a hot tear break down her cheek. Her clothes are heavy and damp and yet she is not chilled. No, just the opposite. She is sweltering. On fire. And something else. Someone is with her.

Her eyes lower to see a man seated across her legs. At least she thinks it's a man because the sun surrounding him is so intense that she can only see the outline of something vaguely resembling a man. He seems larger than life, supernatural, an apparition framed against the light.

"Remain still," he says and sets a hand on her shoulder pressing her back against the grave.

Angel holds in a breath, the man's touch so tender and powerful. Tears of dew trickle down her skin. The man sets out a cup, several vials, and a large crystal bottle. Angel's eyes roll back to the sky. There's not a breath of wind. The damp earth intrudes into her back, the wriggle of its little creatures finding their way underneath her resting shell. The man's breath exhales visibly and hangs in the mist. He takes the crystal bottle, a satin cord around its neck with the brand of the archangels anointed across its label. He pulls the cork out with his teeth and pours the liquid into the chalice. As he does, steam escapes the bottle, joins the mist they now live in, in this land with no sky, only the earth and the wet.

"Drink this," he says and slips his hand behind her neck. He lifts her up and she follows like a rag doll, her arms dangling dead in the grass, her head dropped back. "Angel," he says more forcefully. "Take the glass. Drink from it."

Angel reaches forward and folds her hands around the cup. She sees his face now. A dark bang sweeps across his smoky eyes, framed in the thickest, most sultry lashes. The trim edges of his beard sparkle in the waking light. He's dressed in a white robe embellished around the hems, two medals around his neck and something glittering in the hair behind his ear. Beyond him, illuminated by the sun, feathered apparitions lift up and out, nearly twice his size. Her eyes go up to the massive appendages and then down to where that face still watches hers, his mouth slightly open, his eyes sturdy and resolved.

"Daniel?" she whispers incredulously.

He seems to smile, a secret smile shared between two secret keepers and those decidedly large fingers reaffirming their grip on the back of her neck.

"I see you've been reading my journal," he says. "How did you like the ending?"

"I didn't like it at all," she replies, her hands still trembling around the chalice.

"Tell me, has he found you?" Ryder asks, his eyes sparkling.

"Has who?"

"My Theodore."

"Theodore," she whispers, half-engaged. The fog is dense around their shoulders, the humidity unbearably thick. She swallows hard as she closes her eyes. She sleeps for what feels like the longest time and when she wakes up, he's still there holding her head in his huge hand like a newborn baby.

"Drink," he says, moving the glass towards her face.

"What is it?" she whispers, looking down at the steaming liquid.

Ryder puts his free hand beneath the chalice and lifts it to her lips. "I call it Deliverance."

Angel tips her head back and the liquid glides down her throat. She inhales deeply, arching back, all her muscles tensing. Ryder lowers her back in the grass. His knees sink into the earth as he sits back on her thighs.

"It's liberation through exorcism, consecrated blessing with a touch of river baptism." He brushes his large fingers across her wet cheek.

"Am I dead?" she breathes.

"You've been dead for a while," Ryder replies and presses his palm to her forehead. "I release you Angel, from all the things that bind you to your past. All the evils in the world that conspire to hold such a spirit in captivity. To all that would bring you down, drag you out, feed on your vulnerability and weakness. Angel, you are strong but this is a fight you cannot win alone."

Angel moans, her hands coming up and over her chest. She feels an intense pressure mounting inside her body like something is about to burst out. Her eyes in little slivers, she gazes up at the glorious face that hovers over hers. Daniel delivered, released from all his childhood anxieties. Daniel the man, the angel, his earthly body buried beneath her, his heavenly body seated above.

Ryder trails his fingers through the wet grass and lifts them over her face. Fingertips shimmering with morning dew, he traces a cross on her forehead and then draws a steaming little number in the divot between her collar bones.

"There are forces trying to bring you down. To destroy you. To end this precious spirit because it is just that. So precious. This is much bigger than you can ever imagine. Everything is together. Everything is all. Angel, if one tree falls in the forest, it does matter."

Angel stares up at him, her eyes welling over.

"There are people watching you who want to help you but their own fears hold them back. Even some of the ones that seem determined to bring you down have guilt about their actions. And Theodore…"

Angel squeezes her eyes shut but the tears still break lose.

"He is true; he is real; he has come for you. I know it seems that evil is everywhere, but there are only six of them. They go by the names of Odium, Envy, Apathy, Misery, Severence, and Sadism. It is these six evils that fight for possession over the good. Understand this: suicide is a doorway. Suicide allows these spirits access to the outside world. After you die, they escape into the world through your death. They use your death to infect others like a virus. You are a doorway, and a very powerful one at that. You die and those six gain access. That is why they fight so hard for you. But we Holies have seven. We are Love, Hope, Compassion, Temperance, Union, Grace, and Divinity. Life is our doorway. Death is theirs. The powers are waging war for your very soul."

Angel looks up as he leans over her body, bracing his hands at her shoulders. He is brilliant and bright, heat radiating off his body like he is the sun that is rising in the sky.

"Let all evils leave this mind." He moves his hand to her forehead. "Leave this body," he continues, placing his hand over her heart, leaving a burning sensation behind. Angel arches back, releasing a long heavy breath. She watches as the hand lifts, sees the steam left beneath the fingers and as they continue down further. He sets them on her pelvis just above her pubic bone and whispers much darker, "Leave this sex."

Angel launches up grabs him by the collar. She yanks his robes off his shoulder, trying to keep her balance. His chest heaves with heavy breath.

"Tampered with," he breathes, hand still low on Angel's stomach. "Too early for you to remember but the damage has been done. An early introduction can become obsession and possession. It is a battle not only for soul and for body, for the grace and sexuality."

"For sex and salvation." Angel whispers.

Ryder eyes lift to hers. "Sex and salvation. Precisely."

Angel looks down at his chest, now exposed in the filtered sunlight, at the little hairs standing at attention, at the quick rising and falling of his folded stomach, at the hard tips of his pointed nipples. She releases the fist still clenching his robe and gently brings her fingers over his heart. She turns her eyes up to his, feeling the rapid, fluttered bleating of a human heart beneath the intensely warm glow of an angel's flesh. Insect trails of sweat bleed down from his hairline, continue down his face, his neck, his chest, and then down even lower.

Ryder continues his blessing. Darkness has found a home in you. Darkness is no longer welcome. Let there be only love. Let there be only peace. Forget your dark dreams, Angel. They serve you no longer. Angel just shudders out breath after breath, her eyes tightly closed, the hand on Ryder's heart now balled up into a fist. No one person should be what you have been through, he tells her. You have paid your dues in abuse, in poverty, in depression, and in shame. I am your Light now Angel; I am your protection.

Angel trembles, taking in the hot fumes of fog, her hair in wet rivers down her back. She feels angry pieces breaking off inside. Like chunks of rust clinging to the side of a ship, drying, cracking, and breaking away. Mouth ajar, she turns her head up and feels a drop of rain hit her tongue, then another. She opens her eyes and a drop falls right inside. She stares up through the shimmering drop as if underwater and then blinks the water away. She slowly lowers her head to see him there, this angel of the Light, still surrounded by his runny sun, brilliant extensions rising from his back like giant prehistoric hands. She places her palms on his thighs and uses them as leverage to free herself from beneath him. Once free, she sits down between his knees. Her head feels light and unburdened like she's been buried for a very long time and suddenly sprung to the surface.

"You are free," he whispers. He fills the cup between them and offers it to her again. More Deliverance, spiritual ecstasy contained in crystal. Angel drinks half and then, taking the cup into her hands, she brings the rest her liberator's lips. Ryder wets his lips, eyes glimmering golden specks, his face dripping with a misty sheen. Rain falls harder now sending rivers down his nose, over the hills of his lips, burdening those thick sultry lashes. She pushes the glass to his mouth. "Drink," she whispers.

Heart contesting, Ryder takes it in his oversized hands intent on setting it aside and beginning his ascension. His work is done here. *Done here*, he thinks, his eyes lowering to the thin wet drape of her shirt following every curve of her body. He inhales and exhales sharply, can hear nothing but the succulent splashing of water filling the drenched cracks of the earth. He turns his head skyward and tries to focus on the Reserve, on his vows, on his obligations. Drink, she whispers, drink. Ryder swallows hard. Maybe he is the one who needs Deliverance. After all, why does this keep happening to him? Why do they keep falling into his path? He came here to help her, to help his beloved Theo, and here he is again, caught in a forbidden appeal with a body eagerly offering him all the places he loves to explore. There's no escape for him once it begins. And yet the glass is here and the girl is here and Ryder takes the glass and puts it to his mouth. He turns the glass up and a rush of hot liquid slides down his throat. Deliverance, exorcism, ritualistic sexual healing. It all comes over him all at once and more powerful than he ever imagined. He closes his eyes and exhales into the sky, his mouth titillated by the droplets of falling water. Angel rises on her knees and pulls his face against her chest, holding him against her breast.

Closing her eyes, she rests her cheek against the top of his head and feels his gargantuan hands enclose around her sides, thick wet fingers of her suicide angel leaving dents across her back. She brings her hands up to his hair digging them deep into the nape. She's hit by wave after wave of deja vu.

"Are you alone?" she whispers running her cheek across the top of his hair.

"No. Not anymore," he breathes into her swollen breast.

"Good, I want it to be fair."

"What fair?" He clings to her now like she just did to him, using her for support, knowing if she lets go he'll never get back up again.

"The world." Angel replies, feeling wild, feeling strong. She lifts his face away from her breast and looks down on him intensely. She runs a finger down the slippery slopes of his cheek. She finds his mouth and touches her fingertip to it. He responds with the slightest kiss on her fingers and Angel swoops down.

Ryder rises up, inhaling her with a kiss. His hand so tight around her waist that he lifts her off her knees. Already wet, they slide across each other's faces in delirious passion, rocking, shaking, neither one in control of their inevitable destination.

"I do need release," she whispers. "I do. Daniel, release me."

Ryder clears a tangle of her glorious hair from between their mouths. Shakes his own hair back and moves in. Open mouthed, he turns her head to the side. He feels her fingers around his neck, then across the plane of his collarbone, then just a sliver of nails grazing downwards.

Angel lifts her shirt, pulls the wet sticky fabric over her head and hurls it across the cemetery. Ryder sees it for a second, spinning like a Frisbee, disrupting the swirls of fog. And for a second there is clarity: Theo, his duty, the precarious state of the Reserve. He jerks forward and back as Angel roughly disrobes him. He stares out as that spinning shirt settles to the earth. He can't do this. He can't. And yet Deliverance is charging through his veins and that familiar burning is taking hold of him, that itch in need of scratching and all other priorities start falling to the wayside.

Daniel, he hears her whisper. He straightens, naked, robes now down around his knees. I love it when you call me Daniel, he hears himself say, bringing his sinfully large hands up to her face. She kisses his lips, kisses his neck, kisses his chest and goes down further. Ryder brings her back up weakly. We mustn't. We can't. She kisses his chest, his stomach and goes down further. Ryder rises with a groan, lifting Angel up in his arms. Oh, it's painful to stop but he knows the consequences of these actions too well. There are bigger things at play than his own personal satisfaction. His needs he can take care of above, and, oh, how he will once he ascends, but for now he cannot lose focus on why he came here.

"I can see why he fell for you," he whispers holding Angel in his arms, his robes down around his ankles, his body naked and slick.

Angel touches his face, his wet hair, his wet lips, her whole body aching for his touch. But then there is softness and stillness and she feels the earth come back under her back. "Go back to him," Ryder's voice whispers softly in her ear. "He has come here for you."

Chapter 41ଔ

Angel wakes up in a warm beam of sunlight. Birds are chirping overhead. A light breeze rustles the leaves. She rolls on her back and stretches, feeling like she just had the best sleep in her life. But then she looks around and realizes she's in a cemetery. She sits up, confused, her back soaked from sleeping in the wet grass. What is she doing here? It feels like she ran a marathon last night, but what happened? And how did she get here?

She looks out across the cemetery to the truck parked on the road, its windows glazed over with morning dew. That's right, she drove out here last night with her dog. Realizing she does not see him, she whistles and he comes bounding out of the woods. He showers her with grateful kisses and then plops down by her side, panting heavily. Angel rests her hand on his heaving side, taking a deep breath of fresh morning air. She feels completely at peace. She's not sure why. Something has fundamentally shifted inside her. Like someone cleared away her soiled glasses. No longer does she have to peer through the smudges and try to see the real picture. Suddenly it's all there.

She can't believe she slept so long. And the dreams. Daniel was there. She can't recall specific details but the emotions and sensations are very clear. It was as if he came back from the dead last night and set her straight. He filled her with love and hope and chased all her demons away. She lifts her hand and turns it over, looking at the bruises she inflicted yesterday. From knuckles to wrist, it is a sickly green bruise, deepening to red and then to black at the crest of each swollen knuckle. She was so convinced that Theo and Romeo were together yesterday but it seems silly today. Romeo would never sacrifice his own pride for anything, or let anyone to touch that stupid truck of his.

She rises and dusts herself off, then goes to the bench where she left her things last night. She picks up Ryder's journal. She knows now that he is somewhere safe, that he made it, and that neither bullies nor death destroyed him. And she knows that her bullies won't destroy her either. Romeo is not worth the trouble. He's cruel and he's ignorant and she can't understand why she allowed him to control her behavior for so long. Yes, her father has his own history that shadows her, but she is not her father. She didn't do anything wrong and doesn't deserve the condemnation she received from that town.

She returns to the truck, resolving to sneak it back to the farm supply store. She's not going to steal anymore. And she is not going through with Save the Date. Just the thought of killing all those kids makes her queasy. She's not a murderer. What is she thinking? And doesn't want to end her life anymore. She has a feeling things are changing for the better, that she is just on the cusp of a brand new life. It would be a terrible shame to leave it all now.

Angel backs the truck from the graveyard, glancing one last time at the lone grave in the corner. She smiles, pats her dog and begins the drive back into town.

Theo paces his tiny kitchen, cell phone in hand. It's been two days since he's seen Angel and he knows something is seriously wrong. He went by her house again. Nothing had changed since he was there the night before. The bed was in the same twisted knot. The bag of groceries was still in the fridge. But this time there was no sign of her dog. If she were just walking around town or hiding out at school, her dog would still be at home. But there is no sign of either of them.

He searched all night, then came home and slept for a few hours. As soon as he woke up, he was out on the pavement again. He searched her home and then the school but she has completely disappeared. Back in the apartment again, panic is really starting to set in. He could call the local cops but they wouldn't help. He saw how they handled Bea's death. Bunch of fucking idiots. And there's no other resources in a town this small. He has half a mind to kidnap Romeo and torture him until he talks. He supposes threatening the kid might be his best bet. He should go to the school and start knocking some heads together until someone says something.

Exhausted, he has a shower and looks in the fridge for a quick bite to eat. That's when he hears the buzzer from downstairs. His apartment is just a three room suite above the saddle shop with a long stairwell leading down to the street level door. He closes his robe and ties it as he quickly descends the stairs. And when he opens the door, Angel is standing outside.

"I didn't mean to wake you," Angel says, looking up at him.

"Angel," he exclaims, his heart racing. He can't believe she is standing here after all his worry and panic. A huge wave of relief goes over him.

"Can I come in?" she asks and sets her hand on her dog's head. "He'd like to come in too."

"Of course," Theo says and quickly moves to the side. He lets the two in and then closes the door and locks it up tight. He follows her up the stairs. There are twigs in her hair and her back is damp. Maybe she was sleeping out in the yard like she did the night the power went out. But for two days?

Angel ascends the sharp stairway to the apartment. When she gets to the top, she sees a kitchen to the right. A single set of cupboards lines one wall with a bright shiny window inset in the middle. Sun beams in from that window making the whole kitchen glow. On the wall across from her is a stove and an older model fridge. And on the wall to the right, a Formica kitchen table with three mismatched chairs around it. One door goes off to the side. It's simple, clean and obviously decorated by an older woman.

"Do you want some breakfast?" Theo asks, getting a bowl and filling it with water. He sets it on the floor for the dog to drink.

"That would be nice," Angel says.

"Just give me a second," Theo says, turning into the bedroom. He takes a few things out of his dresser and drops his robe on the bed. He can't believe she's here. He was so scared. He was so sure he'd lost her. He has to make sure they are together all the time from now on. He's not sure how he's going to do that but he'll start with breakfast.

Angel stands in the kitchen staring out the only window in the room. It looks out over the back of the store. The owner has put a small patio out there, though this apartment does not have access to it. She looks back towards the bedroom. Theo is just behind the door changing his clothes. The bedroom is simple, with a bed against one wall and a window facing the street. Another door leads off to the right, probably the bathroom.

Theo scrubs a hand through his wet hair, coming back in the kitchen. Angel stands by the window surrounded in light. He can't place it, but there is something remarkably different about her this morning. Even though she is dirty and her clothes are rumpled, she just looks brilliant. "What do you want for breakfast?" he asks lightly, like he hasn't spent the last two days searching every inch of this town in a complete panic for her.

"Anything would be nice," Angel says, looking fondly in his direction. She is so glad to see him again. It was so painful to turn against him when she thought he and Romeo were together. Unnatural to feel ill will towards him. This morning everything seems right again.

"Would you like you use the shower?" Theo offers, setting a pot on the stove. "I might be a few minutes."

"Okay." A shower. When is the last time she bathed? "Is it okay if he stays with you?"

Theo looks around. "Oh, the dog? Yup we're good."

Angel enters the bedroom, remembering something. How he pet the dog when he was in her room and said *remember me?* Something isn't right about that but she sweeps it from her mind. She isn't going to deal with it right now. Theo could know where she lives because everyone does, everyone gossips about her and her horrible house. It wouldn't be so hard to find that out. She supposes he could know the dog the same way.

She goes into the small bathroom, not much bigger than the one in her home. A few of his shaving things sit by the sink. A rusty toilet is beside the counter and the shower is by the door. She pauses as she sees herself in the mirror. She is filthy. There is a smudge of dirt on her face where she slept on the ground. And twigs in her hair! She pulls them out, angry she did not check her reflection before coming here.

She removes her clothes and turns on the shower. A glorious waterfall of clean hot water falls effortlessly from the shower head. She steps beneath and her eyes roll back in her head. She picks up the soap that he uses against his body and lathers it against hers. Mud foams and washes neatly away down the drain. Her hair is next. And once the water dampens her scalp, she feels how sandy and itchy it is. She washes it again and again until the water runs clean. She turns and lets the purifying deluge run over her sore, tired body until the hot water tank can keep up no longer. She turns off the taps with much regret and stands for a few minutes naked in the shower, naked in his home and imagines what it would be like to be naked with him.

She opens the shower door and a rush of cool air disrupts the swirls of steam. The whole bathroom is shrouded in fog. The mirror and the small window are completely obscured. Even the toilet and sink are sweating. She opens the window a little to let the steam escape, then takes a soft, clean towel and dries her body. The towel smells like him. She rubs it everywhere, getting his musky scent all over her body. Setting the towel aside, she looks down at her grubby clothes, her torn shoes, her ripped underwear. She can't bear the thought of putting those disgusting things over her brand new body. Instead, she slips out the bathroom door and puts on the robe that Theo left on the floor. It smells even more like him. She wraps the velvety cloth eagerly around herself and cinches it at the waist. She walks out the bedroom barefoot, her body still steaming from the heat.

Theo opens the fridge regretting it's so poorly stocked. He could set out such a feast for her but he only has a few eggs, bacon, orange juice and one apple. He boils the eggs and fries the bacon and cuts the apple into several slices so they can share. Then he sets the sad little table with mismatched china and fills the glasses with orange juice. Dog Theo is following his every step, so he goes through the fridge again and gives him a raw egg in his empty water dish.

He listens to the water run as bacon fries on the stove. Now that she's here and he knows she is safe, he can feel how tired he actually is. His bones ache. His head throbs. And he is dizzy from lack of food and sleep. He wonders how he can tempt her to stay here with him while he catches up on rest. After the last few days, he doesn't dare let her out of sight again. It's just way too close to prom. And he still can't get a sense of where her head is at with regards to that year end finale.

As soon as the water turns off, Theo brings the eggs and bacon to the table and dishes them out. He takes the pots to the sink. When he turns, Angel is standing in his bedroom door wearing his robe. And the way she looks takes his breath away.

"Hope this is okay," she says, indicating to his robe. "I didn't want to…"

"No, it's fine," he answers clumsily. He looks at the little breakfast he's set out. "Sorry, it isn't much."

"It looks great," she says and slides down in one of the chairs.

Theo sits down across from her and cannot stop staring at her. He just can't place what has changed in her. She looks different. Her skin seems to glow. Even her posture is relaxed, not as guarded or tense as before. But there are also signs of disruption. Her eyes are swollen and puffy from crying. And he can see terrible bruises across her hands. It looks like she may have even broken her knuckles. What happened to her? Where did she go? He's nauseous looking at those bruises. He came way too close to losing her. And he has way too many secrets. He decides he needs to start confessing before he slips up again.

"I have to tell you something," he says, tapping his fork in his plate.

Angel looks up, startled. She has already demolished her eggs and is picking apart the bacon. Theo has not even taken one bite.

He takes a deep breath. Don't screw this up, Duncan. He will have to tell her everything but it can only come a little at a time. He has to be careful with every word he speaks. "I know the Yu family."

Angel drops her eyes down to her food and she scrapes the remains of her eggs around. Theo knows Bea? But how? If Bea knew someone like Theo, she certainly would've mentioned him.

"It's hard to explain but part of the reason I came here is to get Romeo charged for what he did to the Yu's daughter. I came down as soon as I heard what happened to Bea." He swallows hard, staring at her but she won't look up at him. It's true, Bea's death is what brought him here but the real reason is much bigger than that. To tell her that would be too much to absorb right now. Telling her that would mean explaining what happened to him between his death and rebirth. And he doesn't think she's ready to handle that story yet.

Angel exhales a shaky breath, her hand tight around her fork. She's not sure why, but it disturbs her that his appearance in this town was not accidental. That he came here with a purpose. And if he knew that she and Bea were best friends, then he hid that fact from her. Why would he do that?

"I should've told you earlier. We just got the lawsuit started this weekend."

"But...the library?" Angel says to her plate, getting that sinking feeling that this is all part of some grand trick again. She asked him several times why he would come to a town like this voluntarily and he deceived her every time. Or did she ask him? Maybe she just thought it and didn't say it. She can't remember.

"It's just a cover," he says, and that is the truth. "I didn't come here to become a librarian."

Angel raises her eyes back to him uneasily. When she sees him sitting there though, it's hard to hold her resolve. After all, there's nothing wrong with him coming to town to defend Bea. In fact, it's absolutely wonderful that he is going to make

Romeo pay. And it explains a lot. His first encounter with Romeo. Watch where you're going. *I was. I was.* Then he splashed Romeo and the girls in the parking lot. And keyed Romeo's truck. And probably lots more that she's not aware of. It does seem like he came here bent on vengeance. But what else does he know? If he knows about Bea's family, does he know about her father as well?

"People like Romeo, they're a dime a dozen. Weeds. Easy to grow and hard to get rid of. They're all the same and they pop up everywhere. Flowers," he says, focusing his gaze more intently on her, "they have to struggle more to survive."

Angel drops her eyes again and feels tears coming. A huge burden lifts from her shoulder as she realizes that she doesn't have to get justice for Bea's death. Theo is doing that for her. And in a way she never considered. She just wanted blood spilled but an end like that is much too easy. Theo's way involves suffering and humiliation. With a jolt of excitement, she realizes, Theo's way could involve jail time.

"Is that okay?" he asks, unnerved by her silence. He can't get any sense of how she feels right now. Her exterior is so much calmer than her interior. "I should've told you earlier."

"No, it is," she answers quickly and feels her face flush hotly. She realizes she has to make her own confession. And perhaps risk losing him while doing so. But he is the one person in the world that she cannot hide anything from, that she does not want to. "I have to tell you something too," she whispers and sets her fork aside. "My father killed someone."

"I know," he replies, softly. "I know what he did."

Angel's eyes shoot up to his, but his expression has not changed. She shouldn't be surprised. It's probably the first gossip he heard when he came to town. "He was a drunk," she says. "And he drove drunk all the time. And he was a horrible man. He took my sister and my mother and he left me here." Angel folds her hands in her lap, her appetite completely gone. Even though everyone knows this story, she has never voluntarily told anyone. "He ran a boy over in town. He killed him. It was a terrible thing. And the judge let him off with a slap on the wrist. Everyone hates me because of it. The place that I live…my house is…" She pauses, trying to find a word for it. "…hell. It has no running water, no heat or electricity. I don't want to go back there ever again."

Theo reaches across the table and opens his hand to her. She looks at it, her hands still folded tightly in her lap. "Then don't go back," he says.

A tear breaks lose as she stares at that open palm. Is he asking her to stay with him? Is that what he's asking?

"Leave this town with me," he says, pushing harder. "We can go anywhere you want. Let's just get out of here."

Angel twists her fingers in her lap. She can barely breathe. She feels like she is going to black out. "To the mountains?"

"Yes," he says and a warm smile spreads across his face. "Let's go to the mountains."

Tears fall and Angel doesn't even try to stop them. She lifts her hand and carefully sets it in his open palm, accepting his invitation.

THE ROMANCE

Chapter 42∞

Angel wakes up in a place she doesn't know but this time there isn't any fear or confusion. She's somewhere warm and safe. No harm will come to her here. She glances towards an open door to a kitchen where she can see the corner of a stove. Food is simmering on top and cupboard doors are opening and closing. She can hear her dog's nails clacking across a linoleum floor. She closes her eyes and tries to remember how she got here but her head just swims when she does and threatens to take her back down to unconsciousness. Then she hears Theo's voice. It surrounds her like a warm sunny day. She exhales a long, happy sigh and opens her eyes to see him standing in the doorway, backlit by the rising sun. She has seen him like this before, in a doorway framed by light, watching her in her bed. He is so familiar to her. She feels less like she's meeting someone new as she is resurrecting an old acquaintance.

"Did you sleep okay?" he asks, a spatula in his hand.

Angel stares up at him with the adoration one must feel while meeting a lifelong hero. To her, he is absolute perfection. Coming to the rescue of her and to Bea's family as well. That horrible black smear on her soul where Save the Date resided is starting to fade away. She doesn't have to deal with Romeo anymore. She is leaving with Theo and hopefully never coming back.

"I did. How long was I out?"

"Sixteen hours."

She sits up in bed and sees she's still in Theo's robe. She remembers sitting down to eat with him and then taking a short nap while he made a few phone calls. She must have fallen asleep. It feels like a week has passed since then.

"Hey, Angel?"

Angel glances to the doorway where he now faces the stove. Dog Theo is snuffling around at his feet waiting for scraps to fall.

"Use the shower if you want. It'll be a bit before breakfast is ready."

"Okay." She goes into the bathroom and closes the door behind her. Inside, she finds a stack of his clothes sitting on the toilet. But when she moves them, she realizes they are not men's clothing. Amongst the pile, she finds a woman's shirt, sweater, jeans, even socks and underwear. Are these for her? Did he go out and buy her new clothes? She picks up the shirt and shakes it out. It looks like it would fit her and everything in the pile is of fine quality. Very expensive. She glances back towards the closed door. She's not sure how to feel about Theo picking out her clothes, especially her intimates, which also looks like they'd also fit. Blushing, she turns and unexpectedly sees herself in the mirror. She has a slight bruise across her forehead and her knuckles are black. But nothing compares the scars on her arms. Dead on the right and Loser on the left. She drops her eyes. Even the bruises on her fists don't speak as loudly as these words do. If only she could change what she did that night.

Theo sets out breakfast for Angel for the second day in a row. He's had a busy morning. He ran out and picked up a few things for breakfast, then he bought Angel new clothes and shoes. Then he visited a travel agency and picked up some trail maps. The woman at the travel agency recommended an old mountain resort just six hours away. He put a deposit down for the entire top floor. He's not sure if Angel would even want to go there, but he'd rather have something booked than not. The resort can be a starting point. Once she is there and safe from harm then they can go anywhere she wants. The goal is, as it's always been, to get her out of this fucking town.

When he got back to the apartment, he was surprised to find her still asleep, so he took the dog out for a walk and then got started on breakfast. He's discovering that he's not much of a cook. He watched the chef prepare food at home but has only been cooking on his own since he moved into the apartment. So he picked up a few fruit platters as well as vegetable trays to make up for his culinary inadequacies. All of that he now places on the table along with the hiking maps and travel guides.

Angel comes in the room dressed in the clothes he bought for her. She looks so rested and relaxed. When he first met her in the science hall, she was in so much pain that she was physically hunched over. She was thin, pale, and a few steps away from death. And even as the days progressed, that same frantic look remained in her eyes. But there is a different look in her eyes since she disappeared three days ago. She looks happy and content as she softly pads past him with a shy smile. Even the way she moves seems more relaxed

"This looks nice," Angel says, sitting down to a table full of food. Food comes effortlessly for the second day in a row, like the shower and water, everything is here and available for the taking. This is the life that Theodore Duncan leads, one of opportunities and excess. She still cannot understand why he is here with her, but she has decided to accept it for now and simply go along for the ride.

"Sorry, I'm not much of a cook," Theo says, taking the seat across the table from her. Angel's plate is already full of food. An herbivore, she is not. She is stockpiling food like a feral dog who doesn't know when his next meal will be coming. Theo intends to put a stop to that. She will eat as much as she wants now and whenever she wants. From now on, Angel will want for nothing.

Angel picks up a map while snapping off a piece of bacon in her mouth. She's never liked pork much. Her father would always cook it when drunk and the smell of burning bacon was like a fire alarm to everyone in the house. It meant to batten down the hatches. Daddy's drunk again and no one is safe until he passes out. But somehow, the smell of bacon is succulent when Theo's hands have prepared it. And instead of her father's burned pork chunks floating in an overheated skittle, these are light salty strips that just shatter in her mouth. She eats two more as she unfolds the map.

"They're trail maps," Theo says, like he has intimate knowledge on the subject. The only trails he and his parents ever explored while staying in the most expensive resorts in the mountains, were the ones to the souvenir shops and restaurants. But these maps intrigue him. They show trails out into the back woods that have been created by decades of hikers before. Some go hundreds of miles into the forest and encounter points of interest along the way like waterfalls, lakes, vistas and more.

Angel eagerly examines the trails, imagining her and Theo deep in some forest together. It seems too good to be real. She is not only leaving this place, but leaving it with the greatest man she has ever met. It brings up a nagging question though. This one, however, is not as taboo as some of her other queries.

"How rich is your family?" she asks, plucking a few pieces of fruit from the finely arranged tray.

Theo looks up surprised. "What's that?"

Angel blushes and focuses down on the trail map. "The girls talk about you in school. I hear all kinds of stories."

"I bet." He pauses, thinking about his answer. "I'm rich. The whole family is."

"Like Stacey's family?" she asks, disgusted to even speak the name. But Stacey is from the wealthiest family in town and therefore her only reference point. "Rich like that?"

"Stacey's rich like my mom's gardener," he retorts and Angel raises her eyebrows. "I could buy and sell this whole town."

"Why do you stay here though, in this apartment? You could go anywhere you want."

"Because it's the first thing I saw and I wasn't planning on staying in town long."

Angel's heart drops at the thought of him leaving. She hoped they would go to the mountains together but maybe she is just a charity case for him. Maybe he is just building her a boat and then setting her to sea on her own adventure. She'd still take the offer, of course. She needs to get out of this town so badly, but she was hoping they would go together.

Theo sees her reaction and starts to scramble. Something is wrong but he's not sure what. Perhaps his wealth turns her off. After all, it's the rich kids in town who picked on her all her life. "I mean I came here for the Yu's and that is going really well. And Romeo is about to get payback in dozens of ways. So I'll be in the area while the trial proceeds." He pauses. "I've been wanted to ask you something but I don't want to upset you."

Angel's heart begins to pound. Upset her? She gets that familiar sick, sinking feeling. It's a trick. A ruse. A red truck trap.

"Would you testify?" he asks quietly. "Against Romeo?"

Angel slowly raises her eyes, a huge wave of relief washing over her body. Her, in a courtroom, getting justice for Bea's death. It is even better than Save the Date, because Romeo pays and she gets to go on with her life.

"Of course I will," she answers, barely breathing. "I would love to."

"Awesome," Theo says, a smile spreading across his face. "So how about a trip first? To the mountains."

Angel's heart starts pounding again. "I've always wanted to go."

"Any mountain in particular?"

Angel smiles and then finds herself laughing. She's not sure why. The question just strikes her as funny. Like you could visit just one single mountain.

Theo smiles too, thinking that this is the first time he's seen her laugh. He takes out the brochure for the resort and sets it on the table. Angel's laughter falls silent and he's worried he's acted too presumptuously by making arrangements without asking her.

"What's this?" she asks. She opens the pamphlet and is greeted by a lovely old-world resort tucked high on a mountain ledge. It's the most beautiful place she's ever seen.

"Well, when I was picking up maps this morning, the lady recommended it. She says it's virtually deserted this time of year. And look!" He leans over, pointing to the map. "It's only six hours from here. And within walking distance of the trails." He glances up at her, a little anxious. "Do you want to go have a look at it?"

Angel's eyes slowly lift slowly to meet his. She's still not sure if this voyage is solo or not but she wants to see the mountains and be in that place she's always dreamed of. And if it turns out that he wants to stay there with her, then her dream will be ten times what she ever imagined.

Theo packs a few things for the road trip, takes another worried phone call from his mother, and then loads up the Thunderbird. It's only when he stops to fill up with gas and sees the local newspaper does he remember something he forgot to take care of. The clerk at the gas station just shakes her head when she sees the front cover of the paper. "I know the family," she comments grimly. "Who would do something like that?"

"I can't imagine," Theo says with a great big smile. He struts out to the car and tosses the newspaper onto Angel's lap.

Angel picks up the paper as Theo pulls the Thunderbird away from the gas station. On the front cover of the local rag, usually brimming over with stories of baby races or knitting club charity work, is a story that says: *School yard prank goes too far*. Angel glances at Theo who just raises his eyebrows and returns his attention to the road. Angel focuses back on the newspaper. A large photo shows the school parking lot where a mangled piece of metal is being loaded onto a flatbed truck. A big crowd is standing around it. She reads: *Yesterday, a school yard prank went too far when eighteen year old Romeo Ramirez's truck was found flattened in the high school parking lot.* Angel starts to laugh and covers her mouth. *Ramirez' King cab was reported missing the day prior where it was allegedly towed from the school parking lot without the owner's permission. It was returned one day later after it had been flattened at a local junk yard. The owner of the junk yard commented that the truck arrived at his lot with orders to demolish. He did not know the vehicle had left the lot after the procedure was finished. The tow truck driver who removed Ramirez's truck and returned the wreck has not been located. Ramirez was rightfully upset when interviewed and claimed he had been recently targeted by a faculty member from the school and had several incidents with the man involving vandalism to his vehicle. The incident is currently under investigation by the local police.*

Angel smiles, setting the paper down in her lap. She exchanges a look with Theo and then they both start to laugh.

"He probably thought yesterday was the worst day of his life but he doesn't even know what's coming yet." Theo pulls into the parking lot of the only travel agency in town. "Just one more stop," he says. "You want to come in?"

"No I'll wait here." Angel says, content to just be still.

"I'll be back," he says, leaving the car idling. Angel watches as he hobbles across the parking lot, leaning heavier on his cane than she's seen before. Worry creeps in for him and his health. After all, he was in a serious car accident, wasn't he? And in a coma for months. Should he be running around like this?

She sits back as her dog jams his head in between the front seats. He shakes a rumpled envelope between his teeth. "Theo!" she cries and then smiles. Why *did* she pick the name in the first place? It's an awful big coincidence. She never knew anyone with that name before. It just came out of thin air. She wrestles the large envelope out of the dog's mouth. The envelope is torn and so are the magazines that were housed inside. She points a finger back to the dog and tells him no. Then she sits back and inspects the damage. The envelope looks old and it isn't addressed to Theo but to Daniel Ryder. Inside are a few magazines. When she takes out the journals, her eyes widen. They feature naked men. Not just naked men but naked men together. Her eyes shoot up to the travel agency building. Theo is still inside. She starts to open one, then movement by her window catches her eye. She quickly stuffs them in her bag as Stacey and Mary-Anne pull up in their low rider. Stacey gets out and glares in the direction of the Thunderbird. Then she sees Angel sitting inside. Her mouth twists up sourly and she quickly joins Mary-Anne as they scurry towards the mall. Angel can't help but smile at the shocked look on their faces as they glance back at her sitting in the seat that all the girls want to occupy. Theo has done more for her than he could ever understand. He not only silenced her bullies but turned the tables on them as well. Soon they are going to learn what it's like to be exposed and attacked. She hopes the next time she sees them will be on opposing sides of a court room.

They head west. Angel sees acreages zoom by and another small town approaching on the horizon. She's invigorated by the sight of new places, new lives, new things to see. She likes the little farmsteads with red barns and cows out back. And the newly budding fields stretching out for miles and miles behind them. There's so much space and so few people. It's the way, she thinks, the world was meant to be. Not all crammed together like sardines in indistinguishable planned communities all trying to live the same indistinguishable sardine lives but to be sprawled out across the country side with plenty of room to live and grow. This is the life she wants. Peace and solitude.

She's so tired and every time she closes her eyes, the whole world begins to spin. She slept sixteen hours last night, she should be up for days, but she can hardly keep her eyes open. And as much as her mind protests that she must take in every moment, she eventually fades to sleep.

Theo turns down the radio and lets Angel rest. He grows more content with every mile that passes between them and the town. It's hard to believe that only a year ago he was preparing for finals, meeting his professors, and planning his winter courses. He thought he knew exactly where his life was going. This however, he could never have predicted.

Angel sleeps for hours. Theo's tempted to wake her as the mountains become visible but wants her to rest. He soon enters the foothills with long expanses of rolling prairies. The mountains are closer now, huge giants spanning the horizon. The sun has come up clear and bright and everything looks completely new. He planned this trip for her but he finds himself getting excited as well. The trips he and his parents took to the mountains were far from wilderness adventures. They saw a few sights from their car windows, took a ride up the gondola, and then went shopping. Even at home, he rarely spent time outdoors. He was always in the library or in a classroom or in his house at home. Nature was more of concept to him than reality. Sure there were beautiful places out there, but he was busy and didn't even consider driving out to the wilderness just to explore. It fills him with a sense of adventure. Nature is not like the city, there are no doorways, no street signs, no sidewalks to tell you where to go. In nature, you make your own way; you choose your own adventure.

Beside him, Angel begins to rouse. She slowly lifts her head and then her eyes open. "Did I fall asleep?" she asks, groaning. Her head swivels to the window and she gazes out at the view. "Oh wow," she whispers.

"We're pretty close now," Theo says. "Maybe an hour until we get there."

Angel settles back in her seat, edgy with excitement. How many nights, while her father raged around the house drunk or when Romeo was lurking outside her door, did she think of this place, imagine its quietness, its perfect solitude? No people, no cars, no schools, no houses, no bullies. The gentle giants spread across the horizon drizzled in freshly fallen snow. Clouds pass just below their peaks, tectonic rock that has seen the beginning of time, folded and sculpted and lifting to unimaginable heights. The air seems clearer already. It seems to fill up her lungs and cleanse out all the sickness of the city. Like the starry sky, the sheer size of the wonder in front of her makes her troubles seem so small. It takes her breath away. It fills her with a kind of exhilaration and hopefulness she didn't think was possible anymore.

"What do you think?" Theo asks, proud like he's the one who put them there for her enjoyment.

"It's amazing," Angel whispers, looking over at him. And he's amazing, but she leaves that part out. She's scared to tell him how she feels, to reveal the depths of her emotions. And every minute she spends with him, her feelings only grow stronger. She had reservations before, worries, but all that has left her since the visit to the cemetery. She's not sure why that trip changed her so much. But she is more content to be in the moment and enjoy Theo's company for as long as it lasts.

The road ahead begins to twist and climb, following the course of a raging river. Snow drifts down in places even though it is almost summer. They come around a corner and bighorn sheep are licking the salt off the highway. They remain unconcerned as Theo slowly drives by. Angel cranes her neck around to see them, her hand on Theo's shoulder. Theo glances over at the hand on his shoulder but her attention is on other things. Her Light is brilliant, warm, thick and pulsing through his body. He's beaming too, his own Light mixing with hers. He sees everything with new eyes when she's with him. He never used to be excited by anything before he died. He had become quite jaded. Angel has helped to make him appreciate everything.

Entering the parks, Theo finds a roadside turnabout and parks the car. They get out into the crisp air and take in the sights. On one side of the road is a weeping wall rising up hundreds and hundreds of feet. Water seems to leak inexplicably from the solid rock surface, running in little rivers down the stone wall. On the other side of the turnabout, the landscape tumbles down to a fiercely running river, a wall of trees and shrubs behind it. Beyond that, rises the bold and unyielding face of a triple peaked mountain. Theo looks back at Angel who is turning in a slow circle, her head craned upwards, her mouth dropped open. He remembers how desperately he wanted to help her when he was dead. It was the simplest things with the simplest solutions that he couldn't address while being a guardian. He has fought for this for so long, for this moment and now it is finally here. She is away from Romeo, from that house, and that horrid town. And off to a place that she has always dreamed of going. The adventure, for them, is just beginning.

   Angel walks down by the river for a while just to watch it flow. The river is roaring beside her, thousands of gallons of water racing by. So much water just coming endlessly from the mountains tops, rushing and looping over itself, ebbing up against the shore and crashing over river rocks. She experiences a surge of hope and excitement. It rushes over her as swiftly as the rapids in the river beside her. It's hard to believe that this place is only six hours away from shit-town. If only she had known this sort of paradise existed so close to home. She could've started walking and never come back. But if she had, she wouldn't have met Theo. She glances over at him as he comes down to the river to join her, his hair drifting around his face from the spray of the water. His skin glimmers in the moisture, his lips so perfect, his eyes as brilliant as the sky. Everything seems possible when he's at her side. She can't believe how quickly her life has changed in only a month's time.

They take the turn off to the Middlewood, the resort the travel agent recommended. The road leading up is precarious and pitted, cutting dangerously close to the cliff's edge. No guard rail guarantees their safety. Only good sense and vigilance keeps the Thunderbird on the road. Those that rely on boundaries to keep them in line will not survive in a place like this. The road switchbacks back and forth up the mountain side. A low blanket of fog descends over the road, obscuring their view. One final turn takes them into an old village dusted with a fresh skiff of snow. It seems to perch defiantly on the side of the mountain and at its peak, the Middlewood resort stands like a stoic old guardian overlooking her tenants below. Driving down main street, they see a ski shop, a café, a few bed and breakfasts, a gas station with just one pump, and a mountain equipment shop. On the next block, there is a market, a few quant gingerbread looking houses and then the curved road heading up to the resort. The road narrows now, is unpaved, and leaves only enough room for one vehicle to pass through. It closes in even further for a couple hundred meters and then opens up to a magnificent old building, a castle in the clouds. A product of a time when finer craftsmanship was required. No detail is left undone on the old giant, every window ledge, every roof peak, every veranda spindle has an artist's touch left behind on it. It is much more than either of them had expected.

Parking under the stone archway between the hotel and the parking lot, they're greeted by attendants who load their belongings onto a cart and take them inside. Overwhelmed,

Angel moves next to Theo and grabs onto his arm. Theo looks down to his side and then covers her clinging hand with his own. The air has bite to it at this altitude, uncommonly fresh, clearing out the cobwebs and the pollutions of the city. It feels like they've entered another time as they pass through the castle courtyard and strain their eyes upward at the looming structure. Stained gothic windows and crouched gargoyles gaze back down. The walkway is made with large cuts of stone and on either side of the wide wooden entranceway, there are flaming torches.

Angel clings tighter to Theo's arm. It's too much. Like leading a starving mouse into a cheese factory. She doesn't know where to look and is overwhelmed to the point of tears. She follows him into the lobby to the main desk, past the sweeping staircases lined with woven carpets, past the hand carved statues and thick wooden railings, over the polished marble and mosaic floors and under glass and crystal chandeliers. It's warm and smells like burning wood and up through a massive skylight, she can see the snow slowly drifting down. Even in her wildest dreams, she couldn't imagine a place like this.

"For Duncan," Theo says when they reach the front desk. Though they haven't actually discussed their stay here, it seems the decision was made the minute they saw the building. They simply cannot turn away. The front clerk, a rather reserved looking older man, searches his books and says, "For the top floor?"

Theo nods. It's the power and freedom money gives him that he's learned to appreciate the most since meeting Angel. He's never had trouble spending it, wherever and on whatever. A new car, a vacation, the latest technologies, he's never cared what it cost. He's gotten some perspective in the past few months about what this kind of money can do. And is more focused on how he can use his money to help others now.

"Very good." The man clacks away on the computer. "There is an avalanche warning up in the hills. If you are planning on hiking, it's recommended that guests go down to the basin. Would you like any maps of the area?"

"We've got some," Theo replies with a nudge to Angel.

Angel looks up at Theo with a sort of wild adoration. He doesn't even know how much he's doing right. So many men are putting on a show but they have no idea what it is women are looking for. Theo just has it, no preparations or performance required. And he has such a command to him. People listen to him. They scurry to obey his directions. She's so amazed by him.

They take the elevator up a few stories, its windows open to the exterior valley. With every floor they ascend, the view becomes more splendid and luxurious. The last few floors they must ascend on foot. Angel continues to follow in a sort of drunken stupor, certain she'll wake up and find herself on the floor of her old house, alone and hungry, with only her dog for companionship. And yet the dream continues. They enter the top floor and the hallway is lined end to end with a clear domed roof. At the end of the hallway, stained glass doors open out to a patio with the most breathtaking view of the valley below. They have their pick of any room, the whole top floor, including a spa reserved just for themselves. Angel is led into room after extravagant room, each with its own stone fireplace, richly decorated seating, arched windows even a grand piano in one. The beds seem ten stories high with ornately engraved headboards and dressed in fine linens and plush pillows.

Angel goes into another room while Theo checks out the patio. It's fresh and clean and with more furniture than she ever owned in her life. A dozen places to sit, comfortable places with impressive views. A breakfast nook is in one corner surrounded by windows, a tea setting awaiting their use. She's here, she knows that this is real, and yet she can't picture herself existing in this fantastic setting. This is the venue for royalty, not for her and her grungy dog. She experiences a moment of panic. How can this possibly last? He's going to find out who she really is and then he is going to leave her. Standing in front of the window, watching the snow slowly drift down, she desperately tries to blink tears from her eyes. This will end and when it does, how will she ever go back to her old life?

Chapter 43 ☙

Theo makes a few calls to the Yu's and his lawyer in the downstairs lobby. While he does, Angel wanders around in a complete daze. She passes through a dark arched hallway lit only by candelabra. The hallway glimmers in the lowlight, lined with dark gothic windows the size of double doors and the floors are paved in black glossy tile. The whole place seems to glow with warm, honey light entering into every inviting corner of the hotel. And it's almost completely deserted. Not a person in sight. Angel's post-apocalyptic utopia.

Finding an empty lobby, she sits on a wide leather chair facing a large coffee table with a bowl of fresh fruit and a few posh magazines on it. The room is huge and she feels very small inside it. She hears voices out in the hall that are making her nervous. Then a man suddenly comes in and plops down in the seat across from her. He's blond, dressed in shorts even though it's snowing outside, and a brightly colored hoody. His hair is tied up into dread knots with strings of beads woven inside. He has a piercing through his ear and his eyebrow. She glances back down the empty hall looking for a quick exit while the young man shifts around in his seat like a newborn squirrel. His head seems to bob to an invisible beat and he crosses one leg and then switches to the next, then back again. Angel tries to ignore him but his movements are so erratic that it's hard not to stare.

"Hey," he says, catching her looking at him. "You staying at the resort?"

Angel nods and then glances back down the hall. Where is Theo? She doesn't want to be alone with this guy.

"You're the ones that rented out the top floor?"

Angel nods again, her attention returning nervously to the man. Is he going to make fun of her? Tell her that she can't even afford to rent a broom closet here? She feels out of place even though the guy in the next chair looks like he bought clothes from a paint rag store.

"I'm Xavier," he says, leaning forward and offering his hand to her.

Angel looks over at the hand adorned with wooden rings and braided bracelets. She doesn't know what to do. No one ever talks to her. She's never had anyone come up and introduce himself except Theo. She reaches tentatively across the coffee table and the guy gives her a friendly shake. His hand is warm and chalky and rough with calluses.

"I work down at the ski shop." He bobs his head, a few long dreads tumbling across his shoulders. "I lodge overtop the store for the winter and then in the summers I just sleep out by the river."

"You sleep by the river?" Angel comments, surprised to hear her own voice. It's such an odd statement and she can't help but question it.

"Or wherever. Depends on who's up here. In the winter it's the skiers and in the summer it's the hikers. So a bunch of us might go up to the mountain pass and camp for a few weeks. I mean I don't work much in the summers anyway. Not too many people renting skis in July."

"So you don't have a house or anything?"

The boy snorts. "A house? What for? A house is a trip-trap; a conventional life makes you stick. Then you gotta work all the time to pay for the house. And then you're like living for the house and the car and all the shit you've collected inside it, but you're not really living, you know? You're just coming home for a few hours every night, eating, sleeping, and then going back to work. You ever hear that song: *I buy my car to drive to work; I drive to work to buy my car*? Come on people, think! Consumerisms a trap, girl. A way for the government to control the masses. To curb their ambitions and numb their minds."

In a million years it never occurred to Angel that she could do something else, that she could just leave society, take off, get some seasonal job in the mountains and spend the rest of her life exploring the wilderness. The only thing she's ever seen people do is get married, have kids, buy a big house and a big truck, spend their days working and their weekends barbequing. She didn't know other options existed. "But how do you live out in the wilderness?"

"Like people used to live. Course now we pack freeze-dried meals and water purification tablets but the rest good old Mother Nature takes care of. Some summers I climb the summit and some of them I just go down by the dried river bed and look for fossils. I don't keep them or anything because that's just more stuff to maintain, right? Less stuff, less work. Less work, less stress."

"I see," Angel says, having some sort of a break-through. She likes the idea of no stuff. No house, no school, no bills, and, best of all, no people. She could do this. This is a life that appeals to her.

"I mean winters are good too, skiing or boarding or sledding is awesome. But they're so busy! This place is like a stomped-on anthill in the winter. Everyone is scrambling to get away from the city but they have to do it during the same government sanctioned holidays. So every long weekend all the drones just end up coming out here together, waiting in lines for the ski lift instead of waiting in lines at the gas station. It's like totally crazy if you really think about it."

Angel sits back, her mind swimming but in the most wonderful way. She never knew that there were people who thought like this. She thought that she had to be in society, follow the rules, that there was no other option but to be like everyone else. But this Xavier has found another way. Why can't she?

"I'm Angel, by the way."

"Angel, that's a cool name," he says. He thumps his bare feet onto the ottoman. It looks like they haven't been washed in quite a long time. Wiggling his toes, he says, "Well, this has been fun but I gotta go find something to eat. If you guys are looking for good spots to hike, come find me. I know all the places, stuff off the beaten path."

"You live above the ski shop?" Angel asks, really truly interested in seeing this guy again.

"Well, I'm renting out a couch on top of the ski shop. My buddy lives there. We call him the Gummy Bear. He runs the shop. If you find him, he'll know where I am."

"Gummy Bear," Angel says with a laugh. Xavier rises then pauses. He's staring out the window at a woman approaching the resort. Angel looks out the window too. The woman is towing a pink suitcase behind her with a designer bag slung over her thin shoulders. But what catches their attention are the spiky high heels she's wearing while trying to traverse the icy sidewalk. She takes a careful step and then another, her pointed, angled toes slipping and sliding precariously over the icy surface.

Xavier bursts out laughing. "Unbelievable! Only people would wear something on their feet that makes it harder for them to walk. Fucking idiot morons is what we are. It's like tobacco or alcohol. If a bear ate a poison berry, he'd spit it out and stop. But people just keep shoveling those poison berries in their mouths."

Angel smiles, watching the woman stumble and slip, her shoes an obvious disability. He's right, no other creature on earth would purposely strap something to their feet that makes it harder to walk. It seems completely insane.

"I don't get it, Angel. This whole notion that we need people around us to be healthy and whole. If that were true, I'd find salvation in a shopping mall food court. People are a sickness on this planet. They are a plague. They use and abuse everything they come in contact with. Oh yeah, now there's a social consciousness, now people put their cans in a blue box and feel good about themselves, but then they flush five gallons of water down the pipes to wash away two teaspoons of piss away. They're discovering all these new ways to save the planet, but people are the ones who destroyed it in the first place. I fail to see the value of mankind. I seek my salvation in Mother Earth, in the spirits of the wild, in the creatures of this planet. They have so much more to teach us than the guy in the coffee shop line. People have lost their way, Angel. Don't buy into the lies. There's so much more out there for us to experience."

Another girl enters the room. She has orange hair and a backpack slung over her shoulders. She gives Xavier two thumbs-up as she crosses the floor, her feet planted firmly on the ground in sensible hiking boots. "Ah, now here's a girl who makes sense to me. My partner in crime. Alice in wonderland, this is the Angel of mercy," Aside he adds, "The one that rented the upstairs."

"Oh you're the one? I was expecting some stuffy old shirt in some big fucking SUV." She extends her hand, her nails ragged and short. "Nice to meet you. If you need any hiking advice, we live with the Gummy Bear."

Angel shakes her hand and feels no judgment from the girl. She isn't scowling at her clothes or making fun of her hair, in fact it doesn't look like Alice has combed her hair in quite a long time.

"Well, we gotta go. Keep in touch, Angel of mercy." Xavier and Alice link hands and stroll down the hall together.

Theo shuts off his phone and stuffs it in his pocket. He's eager to get this vacation started but he needs to keep an eye on Romeo's case as well. He rises from the chair in the small lobby he was seated in, surprised to find Angel gone. Across the room, the dog has curled up next to the fireplace and fallen asleep. He paid quite a bit extra to get the animal allowed in the resort. But he knew that where Angel goes, so does the dog. And he wanted to make sure that she was completely at ease.

He walks around with the dog in tow until he finds Angel sitting in a lobby looking uncommonly relaxed. Seeing her, the dog races into the room and drops his head in her lap. She pats his head and then looks back at Theo.

"Should we go explore?" he says and she rises with a smile. The sun is just going down and through the window, the mountain side glimmers with shop lights. "It pretty cold though. You want to stop somewhere and get a jacket?"

Angel nods and then lowers her eyes as he removes his jacket and gives it to her. "Thank you," she says quietly, overwhelmed by his affections.

They leave the dog with one of the attendants and walk down the narrow road to the main street of the village. It's still dressed up with Christmas lights even though it's summer. And with the snow gently falling down, it could be December up here while it is June everywhere else. Entering main street, they find an idyllic little hamlet hopping with life even though there are hardly any cars parked on the street. There's a pub with the front door open and a live band playing inside, and an equipment shop with a few customers inside. And then a two story motel with a series of peaked roofs over every window. They pass by a restaurant that's geared towards a fancier clientele. And then a ski shop with jackets, boots and gloves inside, as well as hiking and ski gear. They decided to stop at this shop first.

"I didn't know it would be so cold," Theo says, holding the door open for her.

"No, me neither." Angel enters the rustic shop full of snow shoes and handmade toques.

"Get anything you like," Theo offers. "I need some stuff too."

"Okay," Angel says, glancing at him as he walks away. She peruses a selection of Nordic coats, each with thick fur lined collars and cuffs. The prices are outrageously expensive so she tries not to look at the tags.

"Doing some hiking?" the shop owner calls. He's a big, burly guy with a full beard and thick curly hair.

Angel glances back at Theo, feeling like he should be the one to answer. But the stranger is talking to her. "I think so," she answers quietly.

"Those are the best jackets," he says and he has a nice deep voice, very soothing. "They come apart so you can layer up or layer down. You been here before?"

"First time," Theo calls, then weaves his way between the racks to Angel's side. "We need some gear."

The man looks down at Theo's cane. "Be rough hiking with that cane. You should go to the equipment shop. They got some great knee braces."

"Oh," Theo says, glancing down at his cane. He didn't even think about hiking with his leg. "Actually, it's a hip injury."

"Oh, then you ought to get a solid stick then, something with interchangeable points for the end and something that supports you up under the armpit. That thing will just slip and slide out on the trails."

"Thanks," Theo says, extending his hand. "I'm Theodore and this is Angel"

"Nice," the man says, shaking Theo's hand. "Everyone calls me Gummy Bear."

Angel stares up at him. Gummy Bear, of course. Xavier said he lived above the ski shop. Angel shakes his hand, staring up the big burly man who looks like he could snap a man's torso in half but would be more likely to iron the creases out of his shirts. She always blamed herself for her exclusion but now she's beginning to see that it's the people around her that caused her isolation and the town itself she should've been blaming. She's met three people since entering this town and all of them have been pleasant and friendly.

They continue to walk down the street exploring the quant town. These aren't like the shops Angel knows from back home with their huge parking lots and giant neon signs. These shops are dark and warmly lit and full of oddities and knick knacks. There's a bakery with a man rolling out dough on a bread board and a pizza shop with big fire furnace at the center where the pies are being prepared. There are two little art galleries displaying paintings of the local sights from the local artists. And a place with handmade jewelry. Everyone is walking to their destinations. Not the hurried, frantic rush of the working masses as they run from their cars to the grocery store, but the leisurely saunter of the retired vacationer free to slow down and enjoy an easier pace of life. But these people aren't retired, far from it, most of the people in the town look like they're under twenty-five.

She glances at Theo as he walks beside her, looking so handsome in his new Viking wear. She still knows so little about him, about his family or his past, and yet feels such a strong connection to him. She remembers what it was like when she thought he was mixed up with Romeo. The betrayal was just too much to bear. Even now, she cannot think of it. He simply has to be real because she won't accept any other alternative.

"Hey Angel! Darling."

Both Theo and Angel look up at the voice beckoning her from above. A few guys are leaning over the balcony drinking from steaming mugs. One of them is the Xavier.

"Nice jacket! Did you meet the Gummy Bear?" he calls down and Angel can feel Theo looking at her curiously.

"I did," she answers quietly, intimidated by all the men staring down at her, as well as the one on the street beside her.

"Ready to hit the trails, then?" Xavier asks, taking a big sip from his mug.

"Think so," Angel says, her whole body tensing. It's so hard to be in a group without preparing for an attack. Xavier has been nothing but nice and his whole philosophy about life is so appealing to her, but she can't get over the fear of being in a crowd.

"Hey, I've got something for you." Xavier disappears for a few seconds then returns and drops two books off the balcony. Angel catches one and the other one lands on the street beside her. Theo picks the other one up. "They're trail guides. I marked the best ones."

"Thank you," Angel says, fanning through the pages.

Theo looks up at the group of men smiling down at Angel. He gets a little bristly and moves his hand to the small of her back as if to claim Angel as his. The men, however, seem unconcerned and return to their own conversation as soon as they leave. Theo looks down at the book that is the end result of a conversation he had no part of. How does Angel know these men? They've just barely arrived in town. And competition wasn't something he had considered in his plan to swoop in and save her.

"I met him in the lobby," Angel offers, feeling like she needs to explain herself. "His name is Xavier."

"What were you guys talking about?" Theo asks, going a bit dry in the mouth. He can't believe how jealous he is. It comes over him in sickening waves and he can do nothing to contain it.

"Just trails and stuff," she says, finding it hard to put into words the conversation she shared with the hippy wilderness kid. "Him and his girlfriend live above the ski shop."

Theo feels his prickles settle down at the mention of a girlfriend. Jealousy, he was not expecting. He just assumed that he and Angel were meant to be together and that union would magically fall into place. It didn't occur to him that he would have to work to reestablish the connection. Or that there would be other men to contend with.

"I'm thinking maybe I can stay here from now on," Angel says, the admission making her both excited and scared. "That I'll stay here and do what Xavier does. Have nothing. Own nothing. Work part time in the winter and go off into the woods in the summers."

Theo thinks about the land he's purchasing for her and the house he's planning to build. He thought he was making her dreams come true but what if she doesn't want those things? Is there even a place for him in her life anymore? "So you don't want to live in a house?"

Angel swallows hard, tucking the books away in her bag. The doubt in his voice crushes her rising hope. What is she thinking? That Theo was going to finance her future endeavors? That he would stand idly by while she indulged her own fantasies. He has a life of his own, a family back home. Irritable, she replies, "It's not that I don't want one, I just can't afford to live in one. I'm just so tired of struggling for everything. I know you can't understand this but the money you spend on that resort would last me a year, maybe two."

"Do you not want to stay there?" Theo asks, now visibly upset.

"No, it's not that…it's…" She falls silent, angry that she threw his hospitality back in his face. She can't seem to explain this without insulting him. But how can someone like Theo understand what she's been through? "It's just a lot to get used to. And I don't want to get used to it because then I'll have to go home and there's nothing there for me. You'll leave and I'll be alone again and I'll have nothing." She moves away from him embarrassed at how emotional she's getting. She doesn't want him to know how important he really is to her. If she admits it and he leaves, she'll just dry up and blow away.

Theo pulls back his quills, annoyed he got upset with her. "Who says I'm going away?"

Angel stiffens, pulling away further. Tears come to her eyes. "Why would you stay with me?"

How can he make her understand this without spilling the whole sordid story and completely freaking her out? He's so torn about what to tell her and what to keep secret. "Angel, I know this sounds crazy but I bought you some land."

"What?" Angel says, clutching her bag tightly to her chest.

Theo shoves his hands in his pocket feeling like the gift is more pretentious than he intended. He was planning her life without even asking her. He's sorely disappointed to realize this may not go as anticipated. "Look, I've been really selfish all my life. I've never helped anyone with anything and I doubt that would've changed if I hadn't been in the accident. But it did happen and now I want to help people. I want to help you if you will let me."

Angel keeps her back to him, too stunned to reply. In one sense she is thrilled that he has actually come here to rescue her. But then she is worried that he just considers her a charity case and will leave once he believes she is settled into her new life.

"I bought land right outside the parks, maybe an hour from here. It doesn't have a house on it, but it will, if you want one. And it won't be a struggle, I promise. I'll build it as big or as small as you like. I will make it completely off the grid, solar power, thermal heat, well water. All you have to do is live in it."

"But why would you do that?" Angel says, tears now sliding down her cheeks. This can't be real. It can't be. Again, she worries that this is somehow another trick from Romeo, that him and his boys are crouched around a corner ready to spring out and attack.

"Because I care about you, Angel. I care about what happens to you. I care about where you live and that you're safe and happy."

"But why?"

Theo sighs, frustrated. This would be so much easier if she could just remember what happened between them. "Because I do. You're just going to have to accept that. And if you don't want the house…"

"No, I do, I do." Angel takes a big shaky breath. Feeling like she is about to disappear, she whispers, "I'm sorry about who I am."

The self-deprecating remark infuriates Theo. He turns her around to face him and shouts, "But you're not the way you are! You are what they made you into. Just like I used to be a product of my own environment. I would be whatever they told me to be. I would believe anything they said. But who are they? Nothing! Certainly not even a tenth of the person that you are. Don't you understand? I see through all of that. I can see who you really are. Don't tell me you're unworthy, tell me *how* you're unworthy, otherwise I won't believe it. People did bad things to you, you were picked on in school, your dad is a fucking asshole; how does that make *you* unworthy? It sounds more like the people around you were unworthy. I know you don't understand why I care about you but one day you will. And Angel, if you don't want me, then at least take the house. Because I want you to have a place where you are happy and secure."

Angel stares blankly up at him for a few seconds and then rushes into his arms. She crashes into his chest and holds on tighter than she ever held anyone. She shudders against him, her whole body shivering. "I want it. I want it," she whispers against his rapidly beating heart. Never have words meant so much to her. They rip through her, rip things apart, but only the bad things. She clings to him like a tree in a monsoon vowing that as long as he allows it, she will never, ever let go.

Chapter 44ଔ

They sit by the fireplace of a quiet lodge while snow continues to fall outside. There are only a few customers in the restaurant. They sit silently, each trying to absorb what happened earlier. Angel is completely overwhelmed. The whole day from beginning to end has been an unbelievable ride. She's never traveled so much, talked so much, or seen so many things. And the things that Theo has said to her, she can hardly even believe they are true. As for Theo, he's worried about where he stands with her, worried about this need to control her, and just plain worried. It's not like he tosses some money in her direction and all her troubles go away. She has decades of psychological abuse to sift through, issues of abandonment, feelings of worthlessness, inferiority and more. This property he bought for her was supposed to be a surprise. He wanted to lead her out there and she would leap into his arms with gratitude. Now he feels he did it out of jealousy. How dare Angel have a dream without him? He was supposed to be her every dream. He can't believe how much he's still battling with his own arrogance. And to top it off, he yelled at her. He said the nicest possible things while doing it, but he shouted them at her out of his own frustration. In the end, she ran into his arms, but he is not happy with the way it happened.

"What do you want to eat?" Theo asks, when the silence has gone longer than he can stand.

"Everything," Angel replies with a quiet smile. Maybe a forced one. He isn't sure. She excuses herself and goes to the bathroom. He watches her leave and is suddenly filled with dread. Like she's going into that bathroom and she's never coming back out. Behind him, the waitress chats to a man sitting alone at a table. "Oh are you finished the book?" she asks. "No," he replies, "I have a few pages left." A few pages left. He thinks about Angel's book and what Ryder said about once your pages are gone. Angel didn't have that many pages left. He felt like he defied the rules coming back so maybe he could defy Angel's pages as well. But he didn't really defy the rules, did he? He was stolen from a life half-finished. He had plenty of pages left and was simply returned to where he was supposed to be. Angel is supposed to die at the prom. That is under a week away. She may still die even if he takes her away.

He looks at her fearfully as she reappears from the bathroom. Can anything be done to change the rules or is her fate decided by her Life book? He feels like he's going to be sick. He supposes he could make the last week of her life as happy as possible but his selfish nature can't accept that she could leave at the end of this. It's something he hadn't considered until just now.

Angel returns to the table finding Theo looking very pale. "Are you okay?"

Theo swallows hard. He does not want ruin this for her. "I just looked at the menu," he says wearily.

"Do you want to leave?"

He does. Suddenly this place that seemed so cozy and inviting is now stiff and claustrophobic. The big chandeliers loom dangerously above Angel's head. The wooden beams that span the ceiling must be thousands of pounds. And the stiff, overly dressed waiters have poison dripping off the tip of their tongues. "Yeah, let's go," he says suddenly rising.

Angel looks up surprised.

"Let's go," he says. He offers her his hand and she takes it and they rush out of the restaurant without paying for their drinks. Angel shrieks as they flee back towards the hotel. They don't look back to see if anyone is pursuing them but in a town this small, they will be found eventually. They stop beside a small pub, gasping for breath. Inside a fiddle band plays. They can see Xavier and some of his buddies sitting around a fire.

"Let's go in here," Theo says, wanting to change what happened earlier today. He is not some petty, jealous boyfriend. He is not even her boyfriend, he supposes. And even if he was, he does not own her.

"Okay," Angel says, normally terrified of places like this full of loud music and angry strangers. But some of these strangers she knows. And Theo is at her side to protect her.

They go inside and the group waves them over. There's four of them sitting around a circular stone fire pit. Even though there is a large cone exhaust above them, the room is musky with wood smoke. The group have their hats and mitts drying on the ledge of the fire, as well as their bare feet.

"Hey, it's the Angel of mercy," Xavier says as they near. Theo glances at her as everyone greets her like they already know her. Angel only waves shyly.

"I'm Theo," he offers as if anyone in the group is interested.

"Oh yeah," Xavier says. "Top Floor Theo."

Suddenly the group becomes animated like they have intimate knowledge of the guy called Top Floor Theo. The group introduces themselves as Xavier, Alice in Wonderland, Gummy Bear and lastly, the Sleeve.

"Tell them why you're called the Sleeve," Gummy Bear shouts.

"Here, sit down." Xavier offers a few chairs to Theo and Angel.

The guy called the Sleeve, who appears to be in his twenties and wearing a Mohawk toque, laughs and says, "Yeah well I was spring skiing down Boulder mountain and got caught in some brush."

"Yeah, and he comes down the mountain and both his sleeves are torn off. Those sleeves are still up on the mountain top waving like a couple of victory flags," Xavier finished excitedly. The rest of them laugh like it's the funniest thing they have ever heard.

Angel takes a seat between Theo and Xavier. This is the largest group she's ever been in, who wasn't bullying her anyway. But none of them look at her like she is out of place. And, unlike her school, these people are all shapes and sizes; they dress completely differently and seem to have nothing in common. Instead of beers and wings, there are fruit drinks and veggie trays. And instead of bragging about their money and their trucks, they brag about mountains conquered or who has the biggest scar.

"The thing about backcountry hiking," Xavier explains, leaning towards Theo and Angel, "is that there's no shortcuts; there's no easy way to do it. You get these god damned urban mountaineers who come into town and buy up gear then spend all their time hiking from souvenir shop to souvenir shop."

"Yeah," the Bear adds, and he is a bear. His arms are like swollen sausages and his chest must be three feet thick. He looks like a burly old lumberjack but with the temperament of the Easter bunny. "Bunch of armchair tourists go out on the buses and experience nature sitting on their asses protected by glass windows. Like nature is there for their amusement. That's the problem with people these days, they think the whole purpose of their existence is to be constantly entertained."

"People are idiots, now-a-days," the Sleeve snorts. He flips off his toque and he's actually balding and is way older than he initially looked. "I mean we used to be explorers, discoverers, artists. We knew how to build things, how to grow things, how to earn our lot in life. Now people just sit in front of a box and watch other people live their lives while their own lives go to waste. It's totally ridiculous."

"Money and influence doesn't get you anywhere here," Alice says, the only girl in the group besides Angel. "A good climb tests your fortitude, cleanses your spirit, recharges your Chi. I can tell when I've been away from the trails too long. I just get heavy from the world and need to get back out there and remember what life is really about."

"Where are you two thinking of hiking?" Xavier asks.

"The guy in the resort recommended the basin?" Theo says, feeling very out of place in this group. He is the very person they have been ranting about. That's the exact kind of mountain holiday he and his parents used to take.

"Oh yeah, the basin is good," Xavier says, taking out his map as quickly as one would a wallet. He sets it out and traces his finger along the trail. "See the first part is for the city folks. Nice paved path up to the lookout point. Oh it's a great view but the real hike begins after that. You see, where it says: *Danger, do not go over the guard rail*, that's where you go over the guard rail. There's a trail down the side leading to the glacier. You got to go in the bowl to really experience it."

"And down there, you have to explore the caves." Alice says, her carrot red hair done up in two wide braids to each side of her neck. "There's a lot of warning signs but just ignore those. You can go right into the glacier. Touch ice that was formed millions of years ago. It's a real blast from the past."

"Try not to take anything though," Xavier adds seriously. "There's too many people plundering the mountains. Mementos from the mountain should be found here," he says and points to his heart.

Angel looks around at the group who is just gleaming from experience, an experience they just can't wait to share with other people. It's so hard to believe that that just a month ago she was all alone in the world and that everything was completely hopeless. Who knew so much could change in such a short time? And it's all because of the man sitting next to her. She looks over at Theo who is still an oddity even amongst this group. It's been a funny day but has ended perfectly.

"We should go up to Middlewood after this," the Sleeve says, running a hand over his peach fuzz head. "There is this fucking car in the parking lot..."

"Oh yeah!" Xavier shouts. "That death car. I seen it this afternoon. Kick ass. We should go find out who owns it."

"Yeah and see if we can get a ride," Gummy Bear adds.

Theo restrains a smile, finally having something that these guys could find admirable about him. "I'm sure that can be arranged."

Alice's eyes widen and she exclaims, "That's your car?"

Everyone looks over at him and he shrugs. "It belonged to a friend," he offers proudly.

"Kick ass," Xavier exclaims again. "You don't suppose a few trail bums could get a ride in that?"

"I think that's a possibility."

"Nice," Xavier says extending two enthusiastic thumbs up.

"How did you two meet?" Alice asks Angel. She leans forward on her knees and that's when Angel notices a very distinctive scar on her wrist. There can be no question as to how that kind of scar got there.

Angel looks up at her and then carefully around the group who are all munching on carrots and staring intently at her. "I was being bullied at school. Theo saved me."

Theo experiences a warm rush of emotion. Of course, that's exactly what he did. But to hear her say it sends him through the stratosphere.

"Oh, cool! That is awesome." Alice exclaims. "Where do you go to school?"

Angel points east. "Nowhere. Just a town back that way."

"That fucking red neck town?" Alice exclaims. "Like six hours back that way?"

Angel opens her mouth to question Alice but the group is all riled up now. They're all shouting about truck driving hillbillies and how the world has completely gone to pot. Finally, Alice silences the group. "See? I was bullied," she says and thrusts her suicide scars out for everyone to see without an ounce of shame. "I tried to off myself but I just ended up in the hospital. Stayed in general admission for three fucking weeks like I had a broken leg or something. Never once talked to a psychiatrist or psychologist, whatever the difference is between them. And this dumb shit doctor would come by every morning and throw the blankets off my feet and wake me by yanking on my toes. It was a nightmare. Until Xavier came in."

Xavier holds his neck up by an invisible noose and sticks his tongue out. "I got admitted for trying to hang myself." He looks at Alice and they both begin to laugh. "We suck at suicide." The whole group joins in the laughter except for Angel and Theo. "Anyway, I met Alice and we got the fuck out of there. And it's been sunshine and rainbows ever since."

"Sure has, baby," Alice says and leans her head on his shoulder. Then she shakes out her sleeves and sits back sipping on her fruit drink. No one in the group is disturbed by the story. They all just nod and continue with their meal like this suicide romance is completely acceptable. Angel stares at Alice and then at Xavier, so amazed by their candor. For Angel, her scars are so shameful, and they are. The words on her arm are something she never wants to share with anyone. But these two act like their attempted suicide isn't such a big deal, just a mistake they made along the way to finding themselves and each other. And there's no shame in revealing that fact. It gives her hope that Theo might also be as accepting, that she could be that honest with him and it would be okay.

Angel and Theo walk back up to Middlewood with their arms linked together. Though the day started pretty rough, it has ended well and both are very tired and ready for some sleep. Theo can barely keep his eyes open as he didn't sleep the night before. And Angel, even though she slept for last two, feels like it's been weeks since she's been to bed.

They walk silently under the stars embraced by cold mountain air. Most of the shops have closed up for the night. The Xmas light are still on and escort them back up to the resort which now glows from within. For Angel, this has been the most wonderful night of her life. She's met people she really likes and who seem to like her. And Theo, she doesn't even have the words to explain what she feels for him yet. It just too grand an emotion to put into words.

They enter the ancient hotel and pass through the quiet lobby. The elevator takes them up the first five floors, the rest they climb on their own. They groggily ascend the stairs to the top floor and find dog Theo resting peacefully in the hallway.

"We'll have to take him out hiking tomorrow," Theo comments sleepily and the dog's head pops up. He bounds over excitedly, obviously well cared for by the hotel staff.

"Bet he'd like that." Angel catches the dog in her arms and eases him back down to the floor. She rises and stares up at Theo, falling silent, unable to voice what she is feeling right now. He is simply everything to her. She doesn't know how the world existed before he came into it.

Theo also stares, feeling raw and heavy with emotion. He thinks that he could tell her everything right now and she would understand. But it's late and Angel is safe and now he has plenty of time to ease her into the truth.

The next morning, they take the drive out to the basin launching point. The morning is warm, an unexpected overnight snowfall now heavy on the trees and melting on the roadways. Their car is the only track through town. And though it is early, Xavier and his friends are already out on their patio. They wave as Theo and Angel drive by. For Angel, the whole thing remains an unbelievable dream. She rolls down the window and takes in the fresh spring air, staring out at the mountains she hopes to stand on top of one day. This is so removed from her old life that there is nothing to even ground her to her horrible past. She is well rested, well fed, and cared for. She has no bills, no concerns and no worries. And it's all thanks to the man sitting next to her.

She looks over at him absorbing every detail as if this is the last time she'll see him. Him leaving her is always a worry in her mind, but a worry that is fading. He looks like a Viking in his Nordic coat and leather gloves, albeit an unusual one. His blond roots are beginning to show. And she can see the branches of his burn scars tracing up his neck. He is such an anomaly, such an oddity, just being near him is such a thrill.

She focuses forward as they reach the turn off to the basin. It's just off main street, probably close enough to walk if they had known better. There is no one else in the parking lot and not a track in the freshly fallen snow. A few outhouses line one side and to the other side is the staging point for the hike. The air is heavy and misty and they can only see a few hundred feet in front of them.

"Are you ready?" Theo says, feeling exhilarated as well. He gets his hiking braces and steps out of the car. The air is heavy and moist. And because of the dense fog, they cannot see where the path goes

They stop at the staging point where several walking sticks are leaned against the kiosk. Used by one hiker then left behind for the next. It seems there's a camaraderie amongst hikers that has been lost on the rest of the world, a willingness to share and experience life. There's a mentality of awe and reverence that neither Theo nor Angel has seen before. Even Xavier and his friends, who are at the age where most boys are drinking and chasing girls, have been taken in by the soothing arms of Mother Nature. It seems they have found the secret to happiness that everyone else is trying to track down with wedding rings and credit cards.

Maps are posted on the kiosk showing different paths in the area. And it also gives some background information as how the trails were first formed and what the basin is. "It's a kettle lake," Angel says, tracing her finger along the trail they'll take. It's only a mile from the starting point. An easy paved path according to Xavier and company. There is no path past that point. That's where the real hike begins. Climb over the guard rail and ignore all the warning signs. "A deposit formed by passing glaciers. The lake melts off the glacier every summer and the glacier is slowly deteriorating over time. Thousands of years ago, this whole area was underneath the glacier."

"Wow," Theo says, staring up at the map. Oh he's seen glaciers, from the windows of his parent's luxury vehicles. They might even stop roadside and actually get out of the car to enjoy the view. But he's never seen one up close. "And it's only a mile. Not that far."

Angel leads the way too excited to fall into her usual place, a few steps behind. The dog is already long gone into the mist. Theo takes the rear, finding the walk more difficult than he imagined. The path climbs steadily upwards, the fog so thick and dense he can only see the rocks on either side of him. The path itself is well maintained, paved, with stones and boulders that were placed there by hand. Though the air is misty, it's still warm and heating still. Warm splats of snow drop from nearby trees. In some places it sounds like it's raining.

Angel hikes up with surprising speed, the gap between her and Theo getting wider and wider. It's only when she reaches a bridge crossing a small stream that she realizes she's left him behind. She rests against the log bridge looking eagerly up to where the path continues. The fog is lifting a bit but she still can't see their destination. All she can see are rocks fanning out from the paved path and smell the radiant cool air coming off the glacier. In the distance she hears her dog barking excitedly. His voice echoes wildly in the mist.

Theo arrives to the bridge embarrassingly out of breath. It's just like the old days when he tried to pace her as a guardian. He shouldn't be surprised she's so limber; she's walked miles and miles every day of her life. And he's really feeling the extent of his injuries out here. The high altitude and cooler temperatures are hell on his twisted joints.

"Just give me a minute," he gasps, plopping on the bench near the bridge.

Angel looks forward, her heart racing excitedly. "Where do you think we are?"

Theo takes out the map and together they investigate. "Here's the bridge," he says, realizing they've barely begun the hike. The kiosk said it was only a mile to the lookout point, but failed to mention that mile is straight up. "It's still quite a ways."

They continue. The path rises relentlessly upwards and Angel is off like an agile mountain goat. Theo lumbers behind, sweating and gasping, wishing they were there already. He gets up to a bench where Angel is sitting and waiting for him. She isn't even breathing hard. He sits beside her. The mist has risen just above their heads to reveal that the path they're walking is near the edge of a slope, one side rising steeply upwards, the other falling quickly down. And below a vast valley is beginning to be revealed. It's dotted in melting snow, red like an Arizona landscape with sparse trees and vegetation. It's the debris field of the glacier as it melted and receded. What's left in its wake are pebbles the size of shells and boulders the size of cars.

"Wow," Angel whispers, staring across the valley at the swiftly rising rock face that disappears into the clouds. She still cannot see the top of the peak. Mist rises into the air, evaporating in spiraling columns, sucking itself up into the clouds. And the clouds are just meters above them, she can almost reach her hands up and touch them.

"Ready?" Angel says, pushing up off the bench. Dog Theo suddenly makes a reappearance. He sits down, his tail wagging impatiently, then turns around and takes off down the path again.

"Go." Theo says, once again forcing himself to relinquish control. "I'll catch up. Just go. Don't wait for me."

Too excited to refuse, Angel turns and bounds up the path as excitedly as her dog just did. The mist is lifting even higher and so is the grade of the path. Now the rock eratics that dot the valley become larger, some ten or fifteen feet tall. The path cuts along the scree slope and soon, very distantly, Angel can see a blue-green pool emerging from the mist. Fog seems to birth from its waters, the concentration much higher here than anywhere else. It's surrounded by freshly fallen snow. She runs from this point, reaching the lookout point. Here, are a few more benches, another information kiosk and, of course, the guard rail. She looks back down the path but Theo is no where in sight. Ahead she can see her dog already down by the water's edge. She can't wait. She leaps over the rail and takes the goat trail down the steep decline leading to the lake. As she descends, the fog begins to lift rapidly. She gasps, turning in a circle to see the rock walls around them getting higher and higher. It seems that they'll never end, just keep going up and up. Ahead, is a crystal aqua lake at the base of a massive glacier.

"Oh my god," she whispers, running clumsily down the path towards the lake. The mist suddenly evaporates, the clouds and the fog swallowed by the rising sun. The whole valley is bathed in light. Angel stumbles to a stop seeing that she is surrounded by mountain peaks. She is nearly at the top of them and still they rise for miles and miles. And down in front of her, the clear kettle lake floats with miniature icebergs. The glacier rises behind it, seated between the crest of two mountains, its arms spread out like a crucified Christ. Back the way they came, she sees Theo, just a dot on the horizon, standing at the lookout point.

Wildly aroused, she runs until she reaches the shore of the lake. She stops at its edge, gasping for breath. The water is still and clear as glass. It is full of big chunks of ice. Across the water is the tail of the glacier that runs down from the crest of the mountain to the water's edge. There are several waterfalls pouring off of it. The sun peaks out over the edge of the mountain and hits her with warm vibrant light. She closes her eyes and tilts her head back. And then the glaciers begin to crack. The first time it happens she opens her eyes and looks skyward, the sound very much like thunder. But the second time it happens, she looks up to the hanging glacier. The sun is heating its surface and causing it to shift the same way a frozen lake would crack under a change in pressure. The sound is spectacular.

"Wow," Angel whispers staring up at the ice giant.

Theo sits down at one of the designated benches, his hip throbbing painfully. He is covered in sweat and gasping for breath. He can go no further. But even so, the sight is spectacular from where he's perched. Now that the fog is gone, he can see out over the entire valley. He is neatly situated between two mountain ranges facing the old glacier straight on. And down in the basin, is the emerald lake and Angel. She and her dog are trotting along the rocky shore towards a cave in the glacier. They trot right past the warning signs and down under the massive glacier. There are warning signs where he sits as well. Do not cross. Stay behind the barrier. Avalanche area. Glacier caves can collapse at any time. He watches with discontent as she disappears inside one of the caves. Sure he has saved her from Romeo but her death could still be coming. She could be taken down at any time and in any way. He never asked Ryder if a Life book could be bargained with. He supposes anything is possible but he needs to be prepared that her book is set. Angel may not be here a month from now. He should be happy that she will die a happy person but it doesn't make him feel any better. He had pictured them together forever. He wanted to change the fate that has already been decided for her.

He rises and goes to the railing when she does not come out as soon as he hoped. The path below the railing is too sharp for him to negotiate. He'd never make it down if something happened to her. But then Angel reappears and she and her dog come back around the lake. He experiences euphoria at her return and then great satisfaction that he has made this all possible for her. He has to be strong. And he has to be willing to let her go when the time comes. Maybe her Life Book can be renegotiated, maybe not. But he will have to make the best of every minute they have together.

Chapter 45 ☙

"Hey!" comes the greeting as Theo and Angel arrive at the pub that evening. Xavier and crew already have their places around the fire. A few other groups have gathered around the tables but don't make near the noise that the locals do. Angel takes a seat which has now become her place around the fire but Theo gets a phone call before he can sit down. "Oops, I have to take this," he says and goes back out onto the street. Angel looks back nervously at his form visible through the frosty window. She's now alone with the group. Even though this group has proven themselves to be kind and worthy people, Angel will never be comfortable in a crowd again.

"Go hiking today?" Alice asks.

Angel nods, trying to reason with her unease. Romeo is gone. Stacey is gone. No one will pick on her here. "At the basin."

"Oh nice. How far did you go?" the Bear asks. He holds a mug of tea dwarfed in his giant hands. The waitress comes. They order Kim Chi and a vegetable tray and some flax seed bread.

"Did you go down to the lake?" Xavier asks.

"Uh-huh. And into the cave," she replies. It doesn't help that there are two other groups in the room that she doesn't know. And since she is among the group by the fire, they are the center of attention.

"Sweet," Alice says. "You can climb up the mountains from there too. There's a trail to the left of the lake. Nasty scramble but you can get right up over the glacier."

"Really?" Angel asks, genuinely interested.

"Yeah, nice hike. We should go some time," Alice offers. She takes off her socks and puts her feet on the fire. She looks over at Angel, then looks at her closer. "You don't wear any makeup, do you?"

Angel lowers her head as all the attention focuses on her. No, she doesn't wear makeup. Partly because it's too expensive and partly because she doesn't know how to apply it. And it certainly isn't the first time someone has mentioned it to her. The girls at school made fun of her all the time because of it.

"That's awesome!" Alice exclaims. "You're like the first girl I've ever met who doesn't wear that shit."

Angel looks up, shocked. She was bracing herself for ridicule and received praise instead. She just never knows what to expect with this group.

"Yeah, because that stuff is all lead and chemicals," Xavier snorts. "Skin isn't a protective coating, it's an organ, it absorbs things. If you put on eye shadow, you might as well be eating it too."

"Even nail polish will get absorbed into your system," Alice adds. "Would you drink a bottle of nail polish? Or eat a stick of lipstick? Because girls are doing it all the time. Smearing that crap on their faces with no question about what's actually in these products or what they're putting onto their bodies." She rolls her eyes and sighs. "There's so few of us sensible girls left, Angel."

Angel stares at her, surprised. She never thought about it that way. And it's true. She's never seen anyone question what's in the products they're applying to their skin on a daily basis. She doesn't even know if ingredients are listed on the package. And though her lack of cosmetics was not some sort of personal stand she was making, she now feels better for it. Maybe even a bit proud.

"Was there a kid named Romeo at your school?" the Sleeve asks out of the blue.

Romeo. Just the name makes her jump. Why are they talking about Romeo? Do they know him? And then with growing momentum, her worries expand to encompass Xavier and friends involved Romeo's grand scheme to destroy her life. Could they all be a part of the prank?

663

"Oh yeah, *that* fucking kid. Did you know him? He was at that school you went to," Xavier says, his dreads all tied on top of his head in an uneven pony tail.

"Yeah, I know him," she says slowly, nervously. "I went to school with him. He's an awful person."

Show her, they start whispering, then Alice fumbles around in her bag. She brings out her phone and punches a few buttons. Then she hands the phone to Angel. There's a picture on the screen with an arrow over it. She stares down at it unsure what to do.

"It's a video," Xavier says, pressing the arrow. The screen comes to life showing a reporter outside her old school. A banner across the bottom reads: *small town bullying leads to big time consequences*. Angel's heart begins to pound. That could've been the very banner that would've appeared after Save the Date. Did someone else do it? Did someone else finally crack and take the law into their own hands?

Local police Chief, Peter Ramirez, is being investigated after he ignored allegations that his nephew's bullying led to the death of eighteen year old classmate, Beatrice Yu.

Angel sees the name and feels tears coming to her eyes. She tries to pull them back in, but she cannot.

"Hey, are you okay?" Xavier asks, putting a hand on her arm.

Angel pulls away and turns to watch the video, her back to the group. She knows she's being rude but she can't help herself. Her heart is beating out of her chest. Could it finally be happening? Could Romeo finally be paying for what he did to Bea?

Bea's parents are shown standing outside their restaurant which has been painted with racial slurs. The broadcast continues: *Yu's parents are suing the Ramirez family and the local police department. They claim that Romeo Ramirez and Stacey Reiser hired a local boy to court their daughter in a cruel prank for their own entertainment. Once the game was over, the Ramirez boy revealed the trick and the devastated Yu girl committed suicide shortly after. Complaints to the police department went uninvestigated.*

A shot of Stacey's farm is now shown and the same reporter stands at the end of the driveway. The large ornate entrance way with the Reiser name carved across the top leaves no doubt as to who's farm the reporter is standing in front of. A tiny sliver of laughter rumbles up Angel's throat but can't get past the lump that is forming there. Stacey made such a fuss over that entranceway, announcing it to everyone who would listen about team of artists they hired to design and install the artwork. Angel bets she never expected the entrance to gain infamy in this manner.

It is on this farm where Ramirez and his associates planned their malicious courtship of Beatrice Yu. An incriminating video was posted online showing Ramirez and Reiser interviewing boys they intended to hire with the purposes of humiliating the Yu girl. Money was to be exchanged when the task was completed. The Reiser farm was searched and among the items removed were several cameras and video phones.

Angel covers her mouth as her whole universe, just her and this phone, begin to shake. Though she knows others are near and that Theo is coming back in the room, she cannot hear any of them. She cannot see anything but this tiny, little video.

Since the story broke, students from local high school have come forward with their own allegations of harassment and discrimination involved with Ramirez and Reiser.

"Romeo would follow me home and try to give me money to have sex with him," a girl says. Angel doesn't know her but she is soft spoken and looks very unhappy. Her face is a bit blotchy and she wears smudged glasses. "Stacey and Mary-Anne wouldn't leave me alone. I was scared all the time. I thought they were going to kill me."

"Bullying is out of control in this town and the teachers do nothing," another student says. "Romeo tried to run me over in the parking lot. My parents went to the cops and they told us to come back with proof. Then the police chief told me to join the football team and to stop whining."

The reporter is now standing in front of the courthouse. *"Stacey Reiser refused comment as she entered the courthouse today. Because of the video she and Ramirez posted, she is now also facing charges in the death of Beatrice Yu."* Stacey is shown running up the steps covering her face, her over-inflated breasts jiggling madly as she flees. *"Romeo Ramirez had plenty to say when arriving at the courthouse today."* Romeo is shown stepping out of a brand new truck. His dad is with him and both of them start shouting obscenities at the camera. Most of it has to be covered over with smudged mouths and bleeped audio. A shot of the police chief is also shown as he enters the courthouse avoiding the cameras. A banner under his bloated, red face says the department is being investigated by an outside source.

A sob breaks from Angel's mouth. She looks up and sees several people looking at her, including the other groups in the pub. She hears someone chuckle and sees two guys seated across the room smirking and looking over at her. The Bear rises, his feet hitting the ground like two pillars of cement. The guys look over at him and their laughter fades. But the Bear isn't done yet. He takes those cement feet across the pub floor. Just before he gets there, the two men get up and run out the front doors.

Theo comes quickly over, kneeling down beside Angel's chair. "What's wrong?"

Angel just hands him the phone. She's crying and it's terrible crying and she can't stop it. Theo watches the video and then looks up at her. "Finally," he says, reaches forward. Angel embraces him and her crying turns to laughter.

"Beatrice Yu was her best friend," Theo says over Angel's shoulder at the rest of them. "That kid in the video bullied her to death."

"Oh my god," Alice says and then she's in on the embrace too. Then Xavier comes in and then the Bear until they are all one big unit clamped around Angel. Never in her life has she felt so loved. She just closes her eyes and lets it all in, lets the tears fall without shame and accepts that from this point on, she does not have to be alone anymore.

Theo closes the hotel door behind him with a soft thump. It was another exhausting day, both physically and emotionally. What happened at the pub was not part of his plan. He didn't hire a reporter to do a story on Romeo, though in hindsight it would have been a good idea. He imagines the story was picked up because of the police cover-up and then gained momentum from there. Angel was upset but those tears had a lot of joy in them too. And Xavier and his friends have suddenly become a huge support system for her. Those guys adore her and Theo is now happy she has them in her life.

Too wired to sleep, even though it is close to midnight, Theo lights a fire and sits down on the love-seat that faces the hearth. The rooms they've been staying in are across the hall from each other and have identical décor. It's not until Theo reaches for his bag does he realize that he is actually in Angel's room. They were so tired when they parted ways that they didn't even notice the switch. He'd really like to brush his teeth but Angel is probably already asleep and he doesn't want to wake her. Instead he reclines at the fire and thinks about what sort of adventures they can go on tomorrow. Thinking of trails, he reaches over the side of the couch again for his maps but instead he finds Angel's backpack there. That's right, he's not in his room. He looks down at the pack thinking that she would have a map too and notices the newspaper he picked up leaving town. The one with the story of Romeo's flattened truck. He takes it out and unrolls it, sad he did not get to see Romeo's reaction in person when he found his baby steamrolled in the parking lot. But as he unrolls the newspaper, Theo is surprised to find a magazine hidden inside. His mouth drops open when he sees it. On the cover, there are two men facing off, naked, with healthy erections. They are muscled athletes and the challenge they deliver to each other seems very clear. Across the top of the glossy spread it says: Nude Wrestling. He sits for a second, staring at it, not sure what to do. Are these Angel's magazines? But she never had a same sex fantasy when he was with her. He fans through the pages expecting that the subjects must be both male and female, same sex and mixed couples, but the entire magazine is devoted to men. He shifts uncomfortably, glancing at the closed door. He should put it away. This is none of his business. But he finds himself sitting back and going through the content more leisurely.

What he finds are still frames of men wrestling in front of a private audience. They begin the match clothed but as the battle ensues, layers are slowly torn away. The matches consist of two to four men and some even have oil thrown into the mix. The photos of these muscled, straining men reignites a passion that hasn't been lit since he left home. One that the Ryder men seem to inspire. These battles remind him of the fights he used to have with his old mentor. What it felt like to have another man take control of him and how badly he protested it in the beginning. And how that unwanted affair slowly took hold of him until he finally gave into his passions. He takes a deep, hard breath, trying to clear his head. He is so hard right now. He won't sleep until he does something about it.

Angel reaches down for her bag so she can give a few treats to her dog before going to bed when she realizes the bag isn't there. She stares down at the empty space beside the couch. She's sure that's where she last saw the bag but it isn't there. She checks by the door and then by the table and then begins to worry. Did she take it with her when they went hiking? Did she leave it out on the trail somewhere? There are things in that bag that she wouldn't want anyone to find. Especially Daniel's journal and his magazines. She paces around a bit trying to remember if she was carrying anything out on the trails. She's sure she wasn't. Then, with a bit of a shock, she thinks of the pub they visited afterwards. She was so upset over Romeo. She probably left it there.

She goes to the window and stares down at the town below her. Did someone find it? Did they look inside? She finally feels like she found people she can relate to, but what would they think of her if they saw what was in that bag? She paces back to the living room and then to the window again. The pub probably isn't open until the afternoon. She won't even be able to go down and look until then. And what if Xavier took the bag home? Why did she have to keep the magazine? She should've just left it in the car.

She goes into the bathroom and stands in front of the mirror trying to decide what to do. Then she sees a bag that isn't hers. It's a small, square sack with a razor and toothbrush and comb she doesn't recognize. She's about to reach for it when she sees a pill bottle near the sink. It's only when she reads the name on the label, does she realize she's in Theo's room and he is in hers.

Relieved that the bag isn't lost, but worried that Theo might find it, she makes her way across the hall and softly taps on the door. It's very quiet inside. He must have gone to sleep. So maybe she can just slip inside and get the bag without him noticing. She carefully turns the knob and the latch clicks open. He didn't lock it. That's good. Putting a little pressure on the door, she creaks it open a bit.

She experiences a shock as she sees Theo is sitting up on the couch just a few feet away from the door. A fire casts warm light across his front. And parked beside him on the floor near his feet, is her bag. She pulls the door lightly closed but as she does, Theo's hand goes down his chest and pauses at the button on his pants. She stops, her hand still tight around the knob.

His dead hand always gives him a shock. Although barely mobile, it still provides cool and surprising pleasure. He trails his fingers down his chest. All he can hear is the snapping of the fire, see it flicker behind his closed eyelids with the images of those men engaged in battle.

He wets his lips and brings his hands back up, this time opening his shirt as he does. He passes his fingers over his erect nipples and taut stomach to the button on his pants. He snaps it open and pulls the zipper open just an inch, gives it a quick sharp tug and feels the tension building inside.

Angel watches on baited breath, knotted up behind the door like a carnival pretzel. Through the tiny crack in the casement, she can see Theo's hands unfasten his zipper. The clean white line of his underwear is now visible. The firelight licks at his chest, crawling up and over the divots of his stomach, catching the peaks of his nipples and casting shadows over his eyes. His hands go down again, open and spread apart, fingers digging, his biceps flexed and clenching. Angel takes a deep breath, her fingers white around the door knob.

Theo rolls his head back as his zipper reaches the bottom. He shifts up and pushes his jeans down to his knees. He traces his fingers across the bulge in his underwear. Millions of nerves stand up and salute as he does. He slips a finger beneath the lip of his elastic waistband, teasing the tender skin. He hasn't played with himself for a while. He hasn't had the luxury. Now, with Angel safely asleep in the next room and a long, dark night stretched out in front of him, he can take as long as he likes. And do whatever he likes. He thinks about that opulent shower just a few steps away. Or the luxurious bed beneath the window. Or he could go out in the hall. The idea sends prickles of excitement through his body. He could go outside and do it in the hall. He's rented out the whole top floor. There wouldn't be anyone out there.

The idea sends him over the edge and he knows he won't even make it off the couch. He pushes his underwear frantically down to his knees and then thumps back against the couch.

Angel exhales, her eyes rapt on the swollen organ under the control of its master. It's exactly as she imagined it. Exactly. Size, width, even texture and color. She runs her tongue along her lower lip and bites down on it. She's burning, unbearably so. She considers joining him in this private dance but is too enamored to move a muscle. Only her eyes can still move and they dart from his face, to his chest, to that thick agent between his legs getting hammered by his firmly gripped fingers.

Theo starts by stroking the veiny length. Then he holds his hands still and moves his hips up into his fingers. He imagines Angel is his guardian, that she watches from just inches away. He imagines her breath on it, her open lips poised just above his shaft. "Fuck," he whispers as the couch begins to creak more urgently beneath him. His breath is coming faster now, his mouth now open and his eyes beginning to roll. "Fuck," he says again as those tiny orgasmic beads begin to bloom in his hips. It won't be long now.

Angel watches, her eyes wide, her mouth dry. At first, he seemed in command of it, but now it has him under control. Fondling turns to drudgery, a hard and constant rhythmic action. His whole body begins to swell and heave, his hips now rising and leaving the safety of the couch. His stomach, his ass, his thighs, all his muscles gathered toward a common goal. He begins to call out, his chest tightening, his cock like a piston threading through his taught fist. His beats become shorter and faster and she knows the end is near. She holds the doorknob tighter, getting uncomfortably wet. She should just go in to him. Why doesn't she just go in to him? She could take that beautiful thing into her own hands. Surprise him. And then let him pump that piston inside her. But then she sees something that changes everything. Beside him, on the couch, are the wrestling magazines.

Calling out to a god he no longer believes in, Theo's hips slowly return to the sofa. He rests his head back on the couch, gasping, his eyes still closed. He's adrift now, his body encased in a mother's womb, his mind roving on a midnight sea. He keeps his cock in his good hand, smoothing his thumb over the swollen head. There is nothing but pleasure bleating through his body. With his free hand, he flips through the magazines, thinking about Daniel. Then he hears a soft click. He rises quickly to his feet. Then he hears another soft thump. It's Angel's door closing across the hall. He sits down slowly, then stands again and lifts up his pants. Was Angel there? Did she see him? He's not as worried about the masturbation as he is about the magazines he used to do it. He goes to the door and creaks it open. There is no one in the hall and no sign that she had been here. But he heard the click. He closes the door behind him to discover that the clicking sound is identical. He crosses the hall and poises his fist at the door. He has to explain. But how can he tell Ryder's story without exposing her? And what if she doesn't like that he's bisexual? What if it scares her away?

He turns back quietly. He can't do this right now. Maybe he imagined the click. It could've been a crack from the fire. It could've been anything. Uneasily, he returns to his room and closes the door. He considers locking it but that would send Angel the wrong message. So he leaves it unlocked and crawls into bed.

Angel launches into the bathroom and slams the door behind her. Her pants are around her ankles even before her dog wakes up from the loud bang the door made. She rocks against her hands, her eyes turned up, her mouth open. Seeing Theo touch himself was the single most erotic experience of her life. She gasps out a few breaths, remembering his hands massaging over his cock. And how big that thing was and how he looked when he touched it. She thumps her head back against the door, her eyes rolling back in her head. She gasps a few times and orgasms before she even realizes it's coming. Once it's done, she raises her hands above her head and stretches her naked body across the door imagining Theo up against her. Only then does she think about the fact that he might have seen her spying on him. She jerked back when she saw him reach for the magazine and forgot she was holding the door. It snapped shut but she isn't sure how loudly. She fled as fast as she could at that point.

She's so hungry for him now. Why did she run away? Would he have been embarrassed? Because she'd pay good money to see that show again. She wants to go back. She wants to ask him about the magazines. How can she just let this moment go? She looks back in the direction of his room. Should she go look again? Maybe he's waiting on the couch for her. Maybe he's waiting naked. And she can just crawl right on top of him and get started. She's never had sex before, at least not with someone else. Would he be able to tell? Would he be disappointed by her inexperience? Does he even want to sleep with her?

She lowers her hands and pulls up her pants. She should just go to bed and try to get some sleep. It's almost one in the morning. She leaves the bathroom then thinks about her bag again. That's why she originally went into the room. She needed her bag. It would be a perfect excuse to return. And if she's wrong about everything, then she could just pick up the bag and pretend like that's all she came for. She hesitates, looking at the door, her heart beating very loudly in her chest.

Terrified, she leaves her room and crosses the hall. She stands in front of his door for a few seconds, listening. It's very quiet inside. She taps lightly on the door, probably only loud enough for her dog to hear. When Theo doesn't respond, she taps a bit louder. The door clicks open. Angel straightens, bracing herself to see him, but the door only opens a few centimeters and then stalls there. She pushes it open a bit more and sees Theo asleep in his bed, the fire burning down to ashes. The door mustn't have been latched.

Disappointed, and a bit relieved, she enters the room quietly and reaches down for her bag. The magazines are rolled up and back inside. Was he really reading them? Or maybe he was just reading a magazine she'd mistaken for her own. After all, it just doesn't make sense that he'd be looking at Daniel's magazines and getting aroused. Unless he was like Daniel. She looks up at him asleep in the bed. Could he be gay? Then a word seems to come into her ears. Or bisexual? Daniel wasn't gay; he was bisexual. He liked Anna and Nicholas. He was phoenix desire wrapped in white plastic. Is that what Theo is too? Is that how he knew Daniel? Then an even more alarming idea comes into her mind. What if Theo was bisexual *with* Daniel? She drops her bag at the thought of it and crouches down as its contents tumble out onto the floor. She glances up at the bed but Theo's form remains still. She reaches down to gather up her things but those magazines are open again. And in the spread she sees two men, very much like Theo and Daniel, engaged in a hot battle. Theo and Daniel together? Could it really be true?

She rises without her bag and looks over at Theo's sleeping form. She takes a few steps towards the bed. Theo lies on his back with one hand over his head and one across his chest. The blanket swoops low across his hips and she can see almost everything. Almost. She twists her hands together, her eyes flickering between his face and his hips. Making her decision, she reaches for the blanket. Standing at the foot of the bed, she cautiously tugs the blanket an inch down, then another inch. Then, seeing that he is undisturbed, she pulls the covers all the way down to the floor. Stretched out across the bed is her naked Adonis. She nibbles on her lower lip, staring at him. Theo is asleep. Dead asleep. Maybe she could touch herself in front of him and not even wake him. The idea of playing with herself in the same room as Theo sends a hot flush over her whole body. Glancing at his sleeping form, at his slowly rising chest, she begins to unbutton her shirt. A log in the fire goes off behind her. There is a huge snap and then a shower of sparks. Her hand stalls on her top button, her eyes going quickly to his. He is not waking. Swallowing hard, she continues to open her shirt and then looking to his resting face, she opens it up, her breasts pointed hard towards him. Drowning in lust, she slips the shirt off one shoulder and then the next and then lets it fall to the floor. It lands with a soft thump behind her heels. Breathing harder now, she reaches for the pants. There is no underwear, she didn't bother grabbing those when she dressed in the bathroom, so when she unzips the fly, she is completely exposed. Her eyes drifting down to his cock, she hooks her thumbs in her jeans and slides them down. She rises in front of him naked. She closes her eyes and rolls her head back while she slides her hand across the back of her neck. And then another hand joins hers and she's pulled back against a hard, familiar body.

"Angel, my love," she hears and she opens her eyes. The fire is burning brighter now and in her shadow which lays beside Theo on the bed, are the outline of wings. She falls back with a gasp against Ryder's body and his hands move around her waist to catch her. He is naked behind her. "So you've figured out our secret?"

"You and Theo?" she whispers.

"Yes," he says and brushes his hands over her chest. Then he takes her arms and stretches them out to the sides as if she's being crucified. He holds her open at the wrists while he moves his mouth to the crook of her neck. Angel gasps and mews, her hips swaying in soft little circles.

"Like in the magazines?" she says, her breath coming hard now.

"Yes," he says against her neck, stretching her arms out further. "I've had a taste of Theodore Duncan, but Angel, you had him first. Are you ready to remember?"

Theo creaks his eyes open, his limbs and joints frozen, his mouth thick and swollen. He feels like he's been sleeping for weeks but it is still dark out. The fire he lit when first arriving is still burning brightly. But shouldn't it be burned out by now?

He tries to lift his head but sore muscles won't allow it. Instead, he rolls his head across the pillow and sees Angel on the bed beside him. She is stretched across the sheets and she is naked. He tries to speak her name but no sound comes out. That's when he realizes there is another person in the room. He turns his head to see his raven haired Eros kneeling over him. He is naked too.

Angel turns her gaze on the two men, her mind wonderfully slow. She has been in this place so many times before but the only memory was inside her unconsciousness. Her beautiful Daniel. Her beautiful Theo. And now they are here together.

Theo stares up at his old master turned guardian. He looks different with death between them, bigger, stronger. He kneels over Theo's hips, his bare thighs pressed against his own. Theo sits up and Ryder leans down to whisper in his ear.

"She wants to see us together."

Angel's fingers rise to her lips. She runs them across the soft flesh, staring first at Theo then up at Ryder who straddles him. Yes, she wants to see them together. She wants to see their bodies up against each other. She wants to see them touch each other.

Theo stirs to his old lover. He rises on his knees to face Ryder on the bed. They never had a moment like this, where they were safe and controlled and had all the time in the world. Their affair on the Reserve was always on the run. He misses running. The thrill of his feet pounding against the earth, of his muscles jolting with each step, of chasing and being chased.

Angel watches as Theo rises on his knees to meet Ryder. Two hard hips come face to face, plunging their shadows together. The men whisper each other's name and exchange a smile. One man is lean, dark, wiry with the wings of Greek god mounted on his back. The other is longer, tougher, with veined arms and the dark workings of an elaborate tattoo on his back. The man, who she remembers as the mentor, touches the face of his student. The student touches the face of the teacher. Their faces move closer and Angel's fingers dive down between her legs. She arches and moans as men's mouths come together, as their hips get nearer, as their cocks get harder. They kiss with experienced passion, with knowledge, hands moving quicker and bolder the longer they are together. During the undulations of their bodies, the moonlight thunders down between them and she can see the acquaintance of two silken rods, each hardened by the other, each moving against the other, yielding, resolving, blending, growing. The sight of it makes her wild with yearning. She touches herself with unabashed pleasure, even presents herself to them as an alternate ending. They enjoy the diversion, turning slightly, their bodies still closely entwined. They touch each other while they look at her, Ryder examining the length of Theo with a strong and unusually large hand. Angel puts her thumb in her mouth, bites down on it as Ryder's hand pulls and strokes. Unable to contain herself any longer, she rises to kneel with them. They bring her into the fold, mouths moving from man to woman then back to man again. Then Ryder moves behind her. His hands come around to the front, holding her around the waist and breasts. He holds her as Theo moves in. Angel stares helplessly at Theo's hot throbbing monster, a monster awakened by her. She gasps out a breath, leaning back against Ryder. Ryder moves his fingers across her hard tipped breast and touches his tongue to her neck. Then he looks up at Theo.

Theo approaches on his knees. From this angle it looks as if Ryder's wings are hers. She is a glorious visage, a raven haired cherub, pulsing Light energy in waves across the bed. She opens her mouth, breathing out in small gasps as one of Ryder's hands begins to move down. Theo's eyes fix on those heaven bound fingers slowly sliding down to her rolling hips. Angel rocks wildly as contact is made, throwing her head back over Ryder's shoulder. She turns her head his way and they kiss each other on the mouth. Where jealously intervened just a few days earlier, only arousal beckons him forward now. The hands of his mentor on the hands of his lover drive his ecstasy to all new levels.

Angel, lost from behind in delirious bliss, receives an unexpected knock at the front door. She unlocks her mouth from Ryder's to find another man eager for access. Ryder's fingers trail back from her thigh, and lightly pinch her backside. Haughty and prepared for battle, Theo moves closer to her. Angel inhales him, moving her hands forward to touch his firm chest, his thick arms and then to his neck where she pulls him against her, where old lover's lips finally meet. An injection of fierce recollections charges in from above, about nights long forgotten, about the first angel she ever loved. There is nowhere to go. There is nowhere to run. Ryder rises like a wall behind her, and Theo like a dam in front. Both express their love for her, for each other, through her and all around her. She cries out for rescue but is hoping that none will ever come.

Simmering in a hot pot of pent up want and desire, Angel pushes her hips against Theo's. Ryder's hands come in between them. Looking over Angel's shoulder, Ryder takes Theo by the shaft and guides him into port. Angel shudders back as her new guardian helps her old one inside. Theo enters her slick hallway slowly, her hot, tight viscera encircling every inch of him. Theo gasps over her shoulder as he reaches the top and then Ryder's lips touch his own. He tastes his mentor's mouth while slowly thrusting into his charge. Ryder uses Angel as an extension of himself, uses his hips to move hers forward while Theo plunges in with silky and succulent strokes. Angel shudders out her breaths now, hissing through clenched teeth, pushing Theo's chest back so she can watch him in action. His delivery is swift and prompt, the room now silent but for the smack of their eager hips and the gasps of anxious breaths. Behind her, Ryder is rigid and rubbing against the slit of her backside. The men meet in the middle, running ripples over hollows, touching loving hands that love each other, loving her. Their hands intertwine over her, clenching and kneading and spreading. She rolls her head back until she is seeing double. She's wet as ice cream on a south summer porch, left there to be poked and prodded by two ruthless August suns breaking their heavenly vows so they can harvest her ripe fruits. Yes, she says, yes, yes, and her hands rise behind her head. Men bucking from both sides, she rains down all over them, a jinn-possessed orgasm, satisfaction from dual incubi. Theo digs in one last time, as if trying to reach Ryder on the other side. Ryder responds in kind, shooting fiery devotion halfway up her back. Like three cars on a train track, they slowly chug to a halt, billows of steam releasing as the engine runs down. Angel collapses into the arms of her lovers times two, one at each side lowering her gently to the bed. Raw and red and barely able to keep her eyes open, she looks from one to the other in brazen delight.

"Sleep," Ryder says from just off her left ear. He looks hotly across the bed to where Theo is situated as Angel's eyes slowly close. "Sleep," he says to the both of them.

Chapter 46ॐ

Angel takes in a breath, eyes cracking open like a creature first emerging from its egg. First, she sees sky, the deepest blue with slivers of easy white clouds passing through it. Then her focus widens to see the mountains situated happily below, then the window that frames the whole scene. Then she sees the bed where her aching body is resting on and then Theo beneath the covers beside her. They slept together last night, a wild, erotic affair, many parts of it blacked out in her memory. She looks over at him, her body feeling uncommonly sticky and dirty. The bed reeks of sweat, of sex, of last night's frivolities that seemed to start with no beginning and conclude with no ending. She feels like she's still encased in that fragrant dream. But then she stretches her arms over her head and sees her scars visible in the light of day. Glancing in Theo's direction, she turns as quietly as possible and finds a shirt thrown off the side of the bed. She pulls it on and rolls the sleeves down over her wrists. Feeling a little edgy, she turns on her side, trying to re-engage her dreamlike state. She struggles to remember the details of the encounter. It was like the night at the cemetery where she woke up with an impression of what happened but few details. Everything is so fuzzy with her imagination confusing reality with fantasy. It wasn't just Theo last night, but she imagined her and Ryder and all of them together. And it was so real. Like the dreams she used to have before Bea died. And, even though he is right beside her, she can hardly believe that Theo is real too. And here beside her sharing this bed. It's all just too good to be true.

Theo wakes long before his body does. He remains sheathed in dark chocolate, his tongue smooth like milk in his mouth. Sex, is all he can think of, the smell of it, the feel of it, the taste of it. Awareness of his lower extremities comes next. He's aching and sore in all kinds of places. He remembers so many hands on his body, not just hers but Ryder's too. But like Angel, it is hard to sort out the events of the night before. He opens his eyes and sees her watching him. She is wearing his shirt on top but nothing down below.

Angel stares at him as he stares at her. Theo reaches a hand for her and intertwines their fingers. Angel takes a deep breath, looking down where those strong fingers hold her so tightly. Denial has been her very best friend for such a long time, even as Theo came into her life, it continued it's faithful union. But she can deny her feelings for him no longer. He is everything to her. He has saved her in every possible way and she will do everything and anything to stay by his side from now on. Even if this is all a lie, some incredibly elaborate plan concocted by bullies barely clever enough to tie their own shoes, she'll follow it through until the bitter end; she'll die to keep this alive.

Her old life seems so far away now, like her former life was the dream and this is the reality. All those feelings of desperation have faded so fast, her past a distant and dark memory. Stealing food, hiding in the science lab hallway, and that horrible, horrible house is all so far away. She thought she would never escape it; she believed there was no hope for love after Ambrose left. But she has barely even thought of the boy who used to consume her thoughts day and night. He is just a passing fancy compared to Theo. So much has changed in such a short amount of time; it's so hard to believe it's real. So long she has been alone and now there is companionship, another heartbeat in the bed.

Theo closes his eyes, trying to stay awake but feels himself fading again. He is exhausted. He remembers how he spent those first few weeks as Angel's guardian. How hard he resisted temptation. But she was always too strong for him. He can see it now as well. Once she is at full power, he will be struggling to keep up. She'll be hiking two miles ahead of him for the rest of his life. He hopes she will be happy with him, that he will be enough. She is so strong, so wild, so free. Life with her will be a constant adventure.

"Theo?" Angel whispers, her throat sore and scratchy.

"Hmmm?" Theo says in reply, his fingers moving lazily towards hers.

"Are you awake?" Angel asks, happily entwining her fingers in his.

Theo peers an eyelid open. "Not yet."

Angel smiles. She's tired too but doesn't want to sleep through anything anymore. She wants to be awake every second she is with him.

"What do you want to do today?" Theo mumbles, a weary dawn erection throbbing with the morning sun.

"I don't know. Nothing?" Angel says, tucking her free hand beneath her cheek and continuing to watch him as he struggles to stay awake.

"Like that plan." Theo yawns and rubs his bad hand across his chest. He recollects Ryder's hands doing the same thing last night. The thought of his old mentor makes him smile. He is so present in his mind this morning. Also on is mind is the coming trial, the Yu's, and what's been going on with Romeo since he left. "I'll have to go back sometime," he says, thinking of the trial.

Angel experiences a cold jolt. "Go back where?"

"Back to the apartment. I need to pack a few things."

Uncertainty creeps in again. Is he leaving? Was this all a ruse to score her virginity and then run away? Is this what happened with Bea? Is this how they got her?

"You don't need to come," he continues, unaware of her change in temperament. "You can just go hiking with Xavier or something until I get back."

Anxiety eats away at her. It's a perfect opportunity to ditch her. She stays with Xavier and Theo runs back to dish out all the dirty details to Romeo and company. She closes her eyes, feigning exhaustion, trying to fight off her unhappy reverie. She's ninety-nine percent certain this is not a trick but it's that one percent that has her entire focus. That tiny little chance has her paralyzed with fear once again.

"Angel?" Theo asks, thinking she has fallen asleep.

Angel's eyes flutter open. She's too scared to let him go alone. It's petty, she knows it is, but she can't let him out of her sight until she feels more secure with him. "I'd like to come," she says, trying to sound cheery.

"You don't have to," Theo says, hoping she would stay here instead. He'd feel better if she did, feel safer if she was here with Xavier instead of going back to that old town. Save the Date is creeping closer and closer and though Angel seems happy and content now, he is still nervous about that deadline.

"There's a few things I'd like to get out of my old place too." Angel lies, forcing a smile. "It would be good for me too."

Angel stares out the side mirror as the mountains fade on the horizon. Beside her, trees and empty fields speed by, devoid of all humanity. She doesn't want to go back to her old town, not ever again. Maybe she was being too paranoid this morning. After all, Romeo is busy preparing for the trial, a trial which Theo orchestrated. This just can't be a trick. Romeo would never allow it to go this far.

She sighs, wrestling with her anxiety. This could all be real. Theo could be in her life now. And somewhere out there is the land he bought for her. He wants to build a house on it. Anything she wants. She tries to imagine herself in the quiet countryside, a small stream at the edge of the property, her dog running freely out in the yard, but is scared to believe. She has such a tenuous hold on her happiness as it is. And it all depends on him, on Theodore Duncan. If he leaves, her whole world falls apart.

Returning her gaze forward, she stares at the nasty little dot approaching in the distance, her old town. Her anxiety only heightens at the thought of returning to the place that has been her prison her whole life. Just because Romeo isn't involved, doesn't mean Theo can't leave her. He can have anyone he wants; why would he want her? In fact, returning with him may make things even worse because if he leaves her there, she will be trapped in that town all over again. At least if she stayed in the mountains, she would have Xavier and Alice and the rest to console her. Maybe she could survive without him there. Maybe.

As the town unfolds on the horizon, her stomach begins to twist and grind. That place represents so much misery for her. There's nothing left there but horrible memories. Closer and closer her past approaches until the memories are as indistinguishable as the buildings in the distance. She didn't realize how miserable she was until Theo took her away. Now it is coming back to her tenfold.

"Are you okay?" Theo asks her, glancing over.

Angel nods even though she is not. "Be glad when we never see this place again."

"Double for me," Theo nods and turns up the music.

She looks over at him as he nods his head to the thunderous beat. How quickly her hero could become her tormentor. How quickly all the beautiful experiences he's built for her could sour if they were constructed in deceit. He could poison the one place she thought she could find freedom: the mountains. Going there was always the second last resort before suicide. Without it, there is only death and despair.

Theo parks the car in front of his apartment. Like Angel, he wishes this visit were over even before it's begun. There are things he has to pick up here. He can't leave his laptop, his medication, or the files for the Yu's. In fact he has notes here on Angel that he wouldn't want falling in to the wrong hands. It might be good to destroy them right now before he leaves.

"I'm going to walk back to the house," Angel says, her mood dropping even more. She is nauseous at the thought of returning to the old place but it's the reason she gave for coming with him. She will have to follow through or he will suspect her real reason for tailing him here.

"To the house?" Theo says, his heart jolting a bit. "I can drive you over if you need to get a few things."

Angel looks over and sees worry in his face. Will she ever be able to fully trust him? Or anyone else after what she's been through? She thought that if she found someone to love, then everything would be okay. But it is much more complicated than that. Her issues are internal, perhaps her misery as well. Maybe no one can resolve it except for her.

"I can walk," she says, keeping her voice even. "It's a nice day."

"Take the car then." Theo passes Angel the keys, deciding that his visit here will be much shorter than intended. Even though Romeo is tied up in legalities, he still doesn't want to leave Angel alone. To his surprise, she refuses, saying that it would be good to get the dog out for a walk. Theo kisses her by the car and then watches her leave, feeling anxious about her departure. He supposes he'll have to get over his own issues of control and fear with Angel. He can't be with her every moment. He can't protect her from everything.

Angel takes the long road home. She struggles to regain the optimism she felt just a few hours ago waking up next to Theo. She is just so scared of losing him and cannot comprehend why he is with her in the first place. Maybe going home will straighten her head out. Maybe she needs to remember where she was to appreciate how far she's come.

She walks vigorously until highway turns to gravel and the descent towards her old homestead begins. The houses get smaller, the yards messier, and just a few hundred meters past the city limits, her home comes into view. It's more of a shed now that she's had a little taste of the good life. Just a two room hut unfit for even a prisoner to live in. No water, no power and with very few working utilities. As she passes by the wood fence, buried waist deep in seeded grasses, a painful pit forms in her stomach. She hates this place. It was torture before her family left and even worse after they were gone. She couldn't find happiness here no matter what the circumstance. This place and this life would've killed her eventually.

She enters the creaky gate and lets the dog in. He races up to the front door excitedly. He was happy here; he was always grateful. She took him from a dirty alley and gave him a roof over his head and a place to sleep. She wishes she could be as content as her dog. She passes through the worn trail between old tractor parts and truck tires, past the leaking water pump and then to the broken porch. The house looks like it's ready to fall in and she's surprised no one has thrown her out of it. She supposes if she were inside city limits, they would. How much she's hated this place and now she feels sorry for it. After all, it's not the house's fault that it ended up such a mess; it was just so poorly taken care of that it fell into disrepair. If it had better caretakers, it might have thrived. She feels bad leaving it behind after all it's been through. Now it will just fall into ruins. Probably be vandalized and gossiped about for generations to come.

She enters the front door and the dog bounds in, sniffing everything in sight. Angel covers her nose, the smell much worse than she remembers. The rotting food, the old water in the sink, the carpet that hasn't been vacuumed for years. She's embarrassed that Theo ever saw this place. Just the smell makes her feel unwell. Maybe part of her depression was illness, airborne bacteria from the condition of her home. This place is repulsive. Standing here, in the filth and remains of her life, all she wants to do is burn it to the ground. Make it so it never existed. Let the house rest in peace. It wouldn't take much, the house being as old and dried out as it is. She could start the fire in the bedroom, in the bed. By the time anyone knew what was happening, the place would be burned to the ground. And with it all her bad memories would be burned to ash as well.

Crossing the hall, she enters the bedroom. As soon as she walks in, she wants to cry. What tortures she went through here, what agony. Her sad little bed remains where she left it with covers strewn across a deflated mattress the Yu's gave her after Romeo urinated on her old one. Bea was always there when something went wrong. Cussing Romeo out and running to her parents for help. She feels great guilt over not having contacted the Yu's after the funeral. After all, they were probably the closest she'll ever come to having real parents.

She goes to the corner of the room and turns up the carpet where her secret compartment is hidden. There she finds her suicide note carefully set between the old shotgun and some stolen CD's. She holds the note in her hands like it is a delicate, dried-up old flower and any sudden movement could shattered the fragile thing to pieces. This could be all that was left of her. Just this note. Just like Daniel. Except his note never made it to its recipient. His last words remained unspoken. He left only confused silence in the wake of his suicide. There would be no confusion left in the wake of hers. Only hatred and loathing for what she did to all those *poor, helpless children*. Poor, helpless, malicious, cruel, uncaring children who took her best friend's life and posted a video online as if it was some form of entertainment. Sure, they are finally facing their punishment, but that doesn't bring her best friend back. Beatrice Yu will remain underground forever. Whatever she was going to become was extinguished by teenage pranksters.

Angel wakes up a while later after crying herself to sleep. She feels a little better now that she's cried it out. Maybe coming back was what she needed to help her clear her head. She was so trapped here. All she wanted was someone to care, to hear her pain, to acknowledge that she was alive. And even if Theo turns out to be a fraud, she still has the mountains and Xavier and her new friends. She could've left this place at any point but just didn't see the door that was open right in front of her. She sets her suicide note with her gun beneath the floorboards where it will be forgotten with the rest of her old secrets. Even though it was painful to come back, she's glad she did. She feels better, hopeful and eager to meet up with Theo and leave this place forever. Save the Date is over. This house is over. This town is over. It is all over.

She hears a knock on the door and looks over excitedly. Theo's here and he couldn't have had better timing. She straightens herself and rushes to the door. The dog is there too, waiting excitedly and wagging his tail. Angel can't wait to see him again. She feels like they've been apart for weeks instead of hours. She flings the door open and her smile slowly fades. Her eyes go over the haggard old man standing at the door. He looks sickly, underweight, thinning strands of stringy hair pasted to his forehead. His eyes are bloodshot and stinging with hot tears. She backs up a few unsteady steps as the man enters her house.

"You're not even going to say hello?" he asks, gruffly.

Angel continues to back step, her mind racing. She's not sure but she thinks this man is her father.

"Come here," he says extending his arms forward. Heart racing, Angel remains still. The man stumbles forward and embraces her and she is assaulted by a familiar stench of sweat and alcohol. She can hardly breathe and is more scared than she's ever been in her life. She has no doubt now who he is now. She could never forget that smell. Her father's arms come around her back and pull her in very tight. He even lifts her slightly off the ground as he squeezes her.

"We're coming home," he says into her ear. "We're going to be a family again. You and me and your mother."

Angel swallows hard, forcibly gripped to her father's burly chest, her hands extended out in tense, little fists behind his back. He's breathing very hard and his face is so sweaty against her cheek. She stares out at an old truck parked on the street. Are the rest of them there? Where is her mother? Where is her sister?

Like he can read her mind, her father says, "Don't wait for that sister of yours. All I do for you girls and this is how I'm repaid? I give you everything I have and you girls are never satisfied. Is it too much to ask for a little respect? Now your sister thinks she is so much better than the rest of us. She runs off with her boyfriend with not even a note left behind. No thanks. No manners. We had nothing growing up. Nothing! You ungrateful kids these days think you deserve to live like kings."

Angel breaths in short, little gasps, staring desperately out the door towards freedom. She has to get away. His smell is all over her and it brings back every horrible memory she's tried so hard to forget. Life was bad after they left, but this reminds her of the absolute fear of living with a time bomb. She remembers him drinking in his corner, a spring trap ready to snap. And the rest of them stroking his fragile ego and being forced to agree with every insane thing he came up with. Father ruled this house and his rules were absolute. Drunk, disorderly rules that changed from day to day, sometimes from hour to hour.

Her father releases his grip on her, but as she steps back, he grabs her wrist. "Let's have a look at you," he says in a disconcerting way. He never touched her, only to hit her, but her sister was another story. His eyes go up and then go down and then come up and now he's angry. "Say something! Don't just stand there like your stupid mother! Speak!"

Angel flushes red hot and she quickly says, "Where's mom?"

With one hand holding her wrist, her father reaches back and pushes the door closed, locking it. The dog glances up from the porch as he's left outside. "She'll be along, soon. You know your mother. She seems to think that the world revolves around her schedule."

The dog comes to the door and starts scratching at it, barking excitedly. Angel tenses, certain that he'll turn on her dog but he doesn't seem to notice.

"What is this?" her father says, his eyes going around the room.

"What?" she replies very quietly, her father's fingers burning into her wrist.

"What? *What*? You know how I hate that word. Disrespectful, little...what? How about a *pardon me*? How about an *excuse me*? *What*, Angel, is look at this place! Look at it!" He forces Angel around until they face the living room together. Now beside her, his breath wafts over her face, hot and sour. He seemed so much smaller when she saw him standing in the door, almost unrecognizable against the bully erected in her memory. First impressions denied, she now remembers the feeling of being trapped, dominated and intimidated by someone who was supposed to love her. Selfish, stupid man, only concerned about his problems, his emotions, his everything. He ran that boy over and dragged him for sixteen blocks. Had he not been caught, Angel thinks it is likely he would never have shed a tear. Perhaps, he wouldn't have even known, so slovenly drunk that he couldn't even hear a ten year old boy being torn to pieces beneath his pickup truck. It's the same truck parked outside. He's still driving it. Angel and her mom had to take it to the wash and clean it up afterwards. Her father never saw the boy or the carnage left behind. But she did. She remembers that blood running down the drain in the car wash as her mother hurrying to make it all disappear. Her father never really paid for what he did. In the end he made everyone else accountable for his own actions.

He lets her go with a shove and then begins to pace. Seeing an opportunity, Angel turns and sprints for the door. She flings it open, nearly breaking it off its hinges and runs out into the yard. He could be just inches behind her but she doesn't look back. She runs faster than she's ever run in her life and reaches the gate before she hears the scream. She turns around to see her father up on the porch. He has her dog by the ear.

"No," she whispers as he twists the dog's ear making him scream again. He's trapped there, his sad little puppy eyes trailing after her.

"Get back in this house," her father growls, pointing back inside.

Angel stares desperately at her dog in the hands of the only real monster she's ever known. There is an ocean of yard between her and the porch and, turning back, it takes just as long as the real one to cross. He always knew how to beat her. He knew what her weaknesses were. She can see nothing has changed as she falls back into her old pattern as submissive child under abusive father. It's a cycle too long standing to break. She says nothing as she returns. She knows that a plea of 'don't hurt him' will only garnish the opposite results. She must play this through until she can find an escape route for both her and her dog.

"That's right," her father says, sounding extremely satisfied as she nears the house. "In this house, you live under my rules and you will do as you're told. No disrespect. I am the boss here." He backs in, continuing to drag the dog by his ear. He lures Angel back in the house as well, demanding that she close and lock the front door. "Now clean it," he says. "This place will be spic and span by the time your mother returns."

"But, I..." Angel begins without thinking.

"Excuse me? *Excuse me?* I didn't hear that?" He pulls down on the dog's ear again and Angel loses it. She lunges forward trying to get the animal free from her father's cruel grasp. They fight, briefly, with Angel trying to push him off her dog while defending herself from his swings. It ends with a good stern slap to her face that knocks her off her feet.

"Do you think this is easy for me Angel?" he shouts, looming over her. Angel rolls over to get up, but he's suddenly on top of her, pushing her face into the carpet. Sticky, hard bristles come up between her teeth and into her eyes as he holds a fistful of hair and forces her face down into the filthy carpet. His voice is high-pitched and strained now. He's crossed that invisible line; the one that only he knows the boundaries of. "We're living in that shit-hole truck struggling to keep what's left of this family alive and all you have to do is take care of this place while we're gone. What sixteen year old girl gets a whole house to herself? What sixteen year old girl gets a car to do with what she wishes? What sixteen year old girl gets to lounge around and do whatever she wants? You tell me, Angel, because I want to know why you think that little yellow friend of yours has it so much better than you." He gasps in a shallow breath. "You think I'm a failure, Angel?"

There's a pause and Angel realizes he's waiting for an answer. "No," she says into the dirty carpet.

"Oh I'm sure you don't!" He yells back towards the dog who is now barking angrily. "Why is there a dog in this house? Do you know how upset your mother will be when she sees there's some dirty animal living here? You may enjoy squatting in filth but the rest of us prefer to live like civilized human beings. Clean it up." He shoves her face down one last time to emphasize his point. "Clean it up."

Angel begins the arduous task of returning their ransacked house to the pristine image that only exists in her father's fractured mind. He's locked the dog in the bathroom and now he's pacing the hall, drinking. She won't leave without the dog, not even to get help because her father will kill him by the time she returns. Her only hope is that Theo will show up at the door. She doesn't know if he could fight her father off, but the distraction would be enough for her and her dog to escape.

Not allowed to leave the house, she stacks garbage beside the front door, making sure there's still a clear path to run when the times comes. Even as she cleans, she looks for something she can use as a weapon. Romeo took everything the last time he broke in. She struggles to find even the smallest item that might provide her some meager protection. The gun is in the bedroom. The gun would get her out and she hasn't discounted that solution yet. But with her father in the hallway, she doesn't dare risk that option yet.

"So sick of this shit," her father murmurs from the hall. Perhaps alcohol will be her ally rather than enemy. If she just waits until he gets drunk enough and passes out, she can leave without further incident. She moves to the kitchen, unable to face the living room any longer. Her father walks to the end of the hall, watching her every move. She stacks the dishes to the side of the sink and then begins to put the broken ones by the door. When she's done, she empties the sink of the putrid water and returns the dishes inside.

"Wash them," her father says, leaning sloppily against the wall.

"I can't," she replies softly, her back turned away from him, her shoulders high and tense.

"I'm sorry?" he snaps.

"There's no water," she whispers.

"No water?" he cries. "Have you tried turning on the taps? Just turn them on and water will come out. Do I have to do everything for you girls?" He comes over, bumping Angel to the side and twists one tap on and the next. He does it three or four times as if he expects the plumbing to submit to his bullying as well. "Oh, that's great, Angel, now you've broken it. Perfect. How much this is going to cost me? I haven't been here for five minutes and already you're pinching my wallet. Do you think I've got money to throw around?"

A horrible sweat breaks down Angel's back. This seems like more than her father's usual drunk raving. He's excessively unhinged. And he seems to think that no time has passed since he's left. He seems to think that she's still sixteen. She's worried he might have lost his mind.

"There's no water," she repeats quietly. "I can't wash them."

"And whose fault is that? Who let this house fall apart?"

"I did," Angel answers obediently.

"So wash up these dishes."

Angel turns and stares at her father's sweat stained chest. "But there's..." She doesn't even see the punch coming for her.

Angel wakes up in her bedroom. She's not sure how much time has passed. She sits up groggily, feeling a crusty patch that must be blood on the back of her head. She has no memory of what happened, just that she's in great danger and she has to escape. She sits up and sees her father seated across the room looking about as hung-over as she feels.

"You're right, Angel," he says, dropping the bottle beside him. "You're always right and I'm always wrong."

Angel lowers her head, unable to respond. There was always a cycle before. First the anger, and then the remorse, and after that will come the resentment because her father let himself be vulnerable in a moment of weakness. And then resentment will breed anger and anger will start the drinking all over again.

"At least you stayed. Not like your ungrateful sister. Where are you going to go? You don't have anyone. You don't have any friends. Nobody loves you, Angel. Nobody cares about you. This family is all you've got. We're all you've got in this whole wide world."

Just a glimmer of hope bleeds in. That's not true anymore. She has Theo. She has her friends up in the resort town. She has people who care now.

"What are you smiling about? You find this amusing?" He stumbles towards her, struggling to keep his balance. He grabs her by the chin and forces her head up. "You listen to me," he says, his speech heavily slurred. "I love you. I love *you*. I don't know why you never believe me," he says with a wry twist of his mouth. "Who else is going to love someone like you, Angel? No one. People like us, we're outside and no one wants us. And we don't want them neither. The only man you can trust is your father. Do you understand?"

Angel nods tensely, her eyes brimming with tears.

"Some people have and some people have not. You and me, we're the nots. We don't get breaks. We don't get opportunities. That's why we have to stay together. Come hell or high-water, this family is all we got." He pauses then smiles. "You've become a very beautiful girl, Angel."

Angel closes her eyes, trembling, as he runs a few fingers through her hair. She knows exactly where this is going. Everyone knew what was happening with her sister behind closed doors. She must escape now. But when she opens her eyes, he is suddenly upon her. He pushes her back to the bed and sits across her waist.

"No," Angel cries, suddenly frantically pushing him away, "Please, don't."

Her father chuckles and pins her hands over her head. "Does Angel like to be tickled? Does she?" he says, using his free hand to poke at her stomach. Angel twists beneath him, terrified. He growls with laughter, shoving his fat fingers painfully in her stomach. Then he suddenly stops, a new and more frightening look on his face. Still holding her hands above her head, he begins to descend. Angel takes in a deep breath like she's about to be thrust underwater for a very long time. But then her father stops, looking repulsed.

"What have you done to yourself?" he says, pushing back. The look on his face is of absolute repulsion. Like she's diseased, contagious, disgusting. She realizes he has seen the scars on her arms.

"Filthy bitch," he says as he stumbles away. "What good are you to me now? What good are you to anyone?"

Angel lies on the bed for what feels like hours. Of all the things her father has ever done, his reaction to her scars was the most painful. Is that how Theo will react when he sees them? She was a fool to believe that anything in her life could change. Her father is right. She's stuck here. She's nobody. It would have been better for everyone if she had never met Theodore Duncan.

To make matters worse, her father has just found a poem she was sketching out about Theo. He now paces the hall, pausing every so often to pound the bathroom door when the dog gets too loud. "Who the fuck is Theodore Duncan?" he keeps saying, mumbling his name over and over again. Then he twists his voice up to a high pitched squeal as if to imitate the pathetic shrill to Angel's voice as she writes, "Theodore Duncan is a dream. He is the knight I first thought him to be and for some reason he has decided to rescue me." He snorts and then laughs and then continues to read silently. Angel shudders each time he passes by the open doorway, mocking her precious and private passages dedicated to the only real man she's ever known. Her fears about Theo seem like a distant memory now. He *is* that knight coming in to rescue her. He has saved her in every way possible. How could she ever doubt him? He is a dream compared to the life she used to live. She's assaulted by the past, of things she's been trying to forget. How can she ever hope to be normal again after everything she's been through? Her first plan was the right plan. Suicide *is* her destiny. But this time she's taking someone different with her. This time she's taking the one who really deserves to die.

Her father stomps to the far end and tears up the letter she'd been writing about Theo. He's building up now, the way the clouds start charging before a thunderstorm. She has to make a move now. She scurries over to the corner of the bedroom and pulls out the gun from beneath the floorboards. Two shots will do it. One for him and one for herself, then this whole nightmare will finally be over. Theo will be upset...for a while. He'll find someone else soon enough. Any girl would be lucky to have him. It would've never worked anyway. One day he will see her scars and she will see that same look on his face that she just did on her father's. This is the way it ends. She was a fool to think it would end any other way.

Chapter 47☙

Theo leaves the Yu's feeling completely revived. Romeo is being crucified in the trial. Angel may not even need to testify because so many people have come forward to stand against Ramirez and his friends. Her testifying will be her own decision. The videos the kids posted online are the most damning evidence at all. They are time stamped and posted for all eyes to see. They clearly map out the design of the plan to court Beatrice Yu. Their intent was malicious; they meant to hurt her for fun. But now their boasting has backfired. They're about to be hanged and they brought their own gallows and cable to the tribunal.

Theo steps out on to the street on the most perfect summer day. Angel should be back at his apartment now. They'll grab some food and be back at the resort before midnight. From there, the future is completely open to them.

He gets in his car and begins his drive home, so distracted he nearly drives over a pedestrian crossing the road. Waving and grimacing, he slows down a bit. But, turning the corner, he also nearly hits a dog out on the road. He steers around the old thing, looking at the side window at it. That's when he realizes it's Angel's dog.

He stops the car immediately and rushes out. The dog is walking very slowly, with one front paw drawn up to its chest. It looks like he's been run over. He must have gotten away from Angel and got hit by a car. Theo struggles to pick him up and carry him back to the car. He drives straight to the vet, pounding on the front counter until a staff member appears. Together, they take the dog inside and call the vet over. Waiting, Theo hunches down over the dog and says, "Hey buddy. You're okay now. Help's coming."

"Did you run him over?" the assistant asks, injecting something into the dog to make him calm down.

"No, I found him."

The man frowns. "This isn't your dog?"

"No, yes, no, it is. He's my girlfriend's dog. He must have run away."

Theo paces the waiting room as the vet takes the dog back for x-rays. Angel must be worried sick. Why hasn't he given her a cell phone yet? She's impossible to reach without it. He tries calling his apartment in case she's waiting there but gets no answer. She's probably out looking for the dog. He wishes he could let her know that the dog is with him.

The vet comes out. "He'll be all right," he says and Theo releases a heavy sigh, but the vet isn't finished. "You said this is your girlfriend's dog?"

"He's a stray. She found him a few months ago." He notices the look on the vet's face. "Is something wrong?"

The vet glances at his assistant. "This dog hasn't been run over; he's been beaten."

"Beaten?' Theo says, confused.

"He has broken ribs and a torn ear. It looks like someone did this to him on purpose."

"On purpose?" Theo says, his mind racing. Then a horrible new thought comes to his head. "Shit! Angel!"

Theo crashes the Tombstone up on the sidewalk outside Angel's home and rushes out, leaving the car running and the driver's door open. There's an old truck parked out front. He barely notices it. All he can think is: get to Angel. Somehow he missed something, some sort of hidden danger lurking in the shadows, waiting for her to be alone. She's not popular in this town and even less so in certain circles since Romeo and the chief of police were picked up. He should never have left her alone. A million scenarios go through his head as he stumbles through the yard tripping over hidden obstacles, falling and swearing. He's not going to lose her. Not now.

He bursts through the front door and stumbles to a stop. There is a man inside, standing by the door staring back at him like he's the one who's crazy. The man is dirty, unkempt, and obviously intoxicated.

"Who the fuck are you?" the man growls.

"Where's Angel?" Theo demands.

The dirty man uses his body to block the door, folding his arms over his burly chest. "There's no one by that name living here."

Theo launches forward, his fist following closely behind. Explanations, he'll get later. Angel is his first priority. He plants a punch squarely in the man's face and continues on around the corner, not even bothering to look back. Even in Angel's pillaged house, there's sign of disturbance. Theo's heart begins to pound out of his chest as he rounds the corner to her bedroom. What if she's dead? What if her pages finally ran out? A swell of panic urges him forward and he enters the room. She's there. She's in bed, under the covers, her face hidden by her hair. He rushes to her, calling her name but she doesn't move. And then he sees blood.

"Shit!" he cries, throwing back the covers. "Angel? Angel?"

Angel groans and that's all he needs to hear. He sweeps her up in his arms and turns back into the hall. He's welling up as he leaves the room and sees the unconscious man who met him at the door. It occurs to him that this man might be her father. He is the only man in her life other than Romeo who would hurt her like this.

"He killed him," Angel cries as she gains consciousness. "He killed him."

Theo carries her out as quickly as he can. She is hysterical, weeping, and clawing at him. She has a clump of dried blood in her hair. He's out of his mind with fear, his heart like a fist pumping. He has to get her out of here and now. He has to get to the car and back to safety. He'll never forgive himself for letting this happen.

Angel stares up at the ceiling, her blood faintly pulsing through her veins. Theo is somewhere nearby, she can hear his voice as he talks to the police, but he sounds very far away. She feels nothing around her, not even the bed that must be beneath her, only her soul adrift across the chaos of her life.

Her father's words echo around her head like inside a hallow cavern. Worthless. Alone. Unlovable. Dirty. Unworthy. All things she knows to be true yet somehow she let Theo convince her otherwise. She's cracked everywhere and doesn't understand why she hasn't shattered to pieces. Is her father dead? She was going for the gun and that's the last thing she remembers. And then Theo was there. And then she woke up here.

She hears the police stomping down the stairs and then the door to the street open and closing. Then Theo's footsteps come her way. She closes her eyes, pretending to sleep. She can't deal with him right now. She can't deal with anything. All she wants is to be left alone. But then he touches her and she cringes back violently. She knows this is over now. She can't say here with him. He can't know what she really is. He deserves better than her.

"Don't touch me," she whispers and recoils further. Something has fractured inside her head. Something that can't be repaired. There is no hope for recovery. She wants to die. She wants this to be over and done with. The pain is too much to deal with any longer.

"Angel, was that your father?" Theo asks, sitting a careful distance away.

"My father is dead," she says, her eyes distant. Theo's arms suddenly come up under her. She screams and begins to fight furiously but he won't let go. Threats turn to pleas, then to cries, and then she finally submits. She collapses into his arms, but knows it is only temporary. She'll never feel safe again.

Angel wakes up in Theo's arms that afternoon. She's seated with her back against his chest, his arms drawn around her front. It's quiet now. She stares down at her feet side by side with his, bathed in the warm light coming across the bed. The bathroom door is slightly ajar. A few of his dresser drawers are open. From the mirror over the dresser, she can see just the top of their heads, hers slightly lower than his and therefore hardly visible at all.

She's numb now, some of her more frightening feelings shouting a little less loudly now. She still hasn't eaten or drank since she left the resort this morning. She can hardly believe the life she lived there. For a while, she began to believe that everything could change, that she could have friends, be loved, be happy. Now everything is lost. Her father is back and she will never be free of him. Her beautiful dog is dead, just like her best friend. Maybe she'll stay alive if Theo lets her keep the land. She'll go out there and build a small cabin and go completely feral. But even in that there is little hope.

Theo feels her stir. From his higher vantage point, he can see her face from the dresser mirror. She's bruised from her hairline down to her eye where her father must have hit her in the face. He couldn't feel worse if he'd punched her himself. The cops will want to talk to her, they'll want all the dirty details. Theo plans on having her long gone before that happens. Angel has been through enough, the last thing she needs is some hostile encounter with a corrupt police department. Her father is still out there somewhere. But he'll never find Angel again. Theo will make sure of that.

"Hey," he says, gently rubbing his thumb along her forearm. Her eyes flicker around nervously. She doesn't realize he can see her through the mirror. "Do you need anything?"

Angel swallows hard. "Water. I'm thirsty."

"All right." Theo loosens himself from behind her and lowers her gently back to the pillow. Then he brings up the covers. None of it seems to comfort her. He returns with water and helps her drink. He wants to take her to the hospital but is worried it might upset her more, so he sits by her bed like a worried housemother waiting until she feels strong enough to speak.

"I'm cold," she says, and seems to be saying it mostly to herself.

"Do you want a shower?" he asks. She's worse than he's ever seen her, set back a hundred years from just a few hours with her father. What happened in that house? He obviously beat her, but what else?

"Did I kill him?" she asks quietly.

"Who?"

"My father."

"No…unfortunately," he replies and receives a slight lift in her eyes for his dark jest. "Wish *I* had."

"I doesn't matter," Angel replies, her voice barely audible.

"It does. Angel, let's just get your dog and get the fuck out of here. We'll go back to the…"

"My dog is dead," she grumbles.

"No he isn't. I found him and took him to the vet." Theo smiles, trying to catch her elusive gaze. The dog would be dead if he hadn't found him. He's such a beast that even if someone saw him wounded, they might be too scared to approach him. But that didn't happen. Fate, it seems, intervened on her behalf for once.

Angel experiences a slight burst of hope. She glances tentatively at Theo. "He's alive?"

"He has a few broken ribs but he's okay. The vet is taking care of him right now."

Tears come to Angel's eyes. Tiny, tiny pieces of her broken heart begin to mend together, even if it is just the part that retains the love for a loyal animal. "I thought he was dead."

"Your father is a horrible man, Angel. Horrible. But he's gone now and it's just us left. I'm not leaving you. Not ever again. Not even if you want me too."

Angel's heart beats weakly for him but she's so sick, so tired. All she wants to do is get her dog and get out of here. This place is sickness. It is poison. No happiness can come in a place like this. "Can we go see him?"

"Of course." Theo rises again, going to the dresser to find a new shirt. Whatever she wants is what she's going to get, not just now, but for the rest of her life. He quickly strips off his shirt and shakes out the new one. He turns back to his bed and Angel is completely changed, white, sickly, her eyes open wide in terror.

"What…" He turns and catches himself in the mirror and sees what she just saw. Beautiful Monster tattooed from shoulder to shoulder with Angel across his scarred and burned back.

"Angel," he says, holding his hand out to her. "Wait a second. Let me explain."

Angel covers her mouth with both hands, unable to breath. "No," she whispers, thoughts going off like firecrackers behind her eyes. A trick. A ruse. Theo is a phony. Theo is a fake. She was right all along.

"No, no, don't think anything yet. Just let me explain." He comes forward, clutching his shirt against his chest.

"Don't come any closer." She shrinks back in the bed and then in the smallest voice, whispers, "It was a trick. You tricked me."

"No, no, Angel, a trick? No, Angel, just..." He drops his shirt as she tries to bolt. She reaches the door to the kitchen but he catches her at the waist.

"You lied to me!" she screams. "You *are* one of them. This was all a game. This was all a fucking game!" A tornado of feelings rips her insides to shreds. Beautiful Monster. No one could know that. No one should. It was lies. It was all lies.

"No, no, no," Theo pleads, forcibly pulling her back. "Listen to me!"

"You made it all up! It was you and Romeo. You did it to me just like you did to Bea," she screams, feeling like she might faint. She throws an elbow back hard into his stomach.

Theo recoils, losing his grip, but then reaches up and catches her sleeve. She turns back, trying to escape the shirt he holds. He can't believe what he's hearing. A trick? Romeo? What does she mean?

"You lied to me! You planned this. It was all a game to you," she cries hatefully and then furious tears come down her face. "I knew it! I knew it! How could I fucking believe that..."

"Listen to me!" he shouts. "When I first came here...before I came I was...in an accident. Last Halloween, Angel, I..."

"...you cared about me? You read my journal. You were spying on me in my house. That's how you knew. How could I be so..."

"...died. That's not what happened at all. Just let me explain, I..."

"...stupid? I'm so fucking stupid! Of course you don't like me. Why..."

701

"...love you. Don't you see? Angel listen to me. I have to..."

"...would anyone want me? Oh my god, you killed Bea. You killed Bea. And I gave up everything. I'm..."

"...tell you this. Shut up and let me tell you this!!"

"...already dead." Angel snaps her arms free from the sleeve and from his grip. She turns to run, but Theo catches her wrist. They crash down on the kitchen floor together and Angel's knees him in the crotch. Theo recoils with a wail and then she's gone.

Theo speeds through town in his Thunderbird, his hands like vice grips on the wheel. He came down the stairs right after her, hobbled really, but she was already gone. He jumped in his car without even bothering with his shoes or shirt. He has to find her. He's terrified what she'll do if she believes he betrayed her. It never even occurred to him that she might think he was employed by Romeo. How long had she been thinking that? He's sure it makes perfect sense in her head. First a man comes into Bea's life and then into hers. How could he have been so stupid? He should've explained everything to her long ago. He slams his fist on the steering wheel, running through a stop sign. He goes straight to the vet, convinced that she would get her dog and then run. They haven't seen her. And they look at the shirtless, shoeless man like he's escaped from an asylum. Next, he goes to all the places she used to go, even to the school where he circles the parking lot looking for any sign of her. All the while praying that she won't do anything desperate.

He sucks in a few breaths suddenly overwhelmed with panic. She could be anywhere never knowing how precious her life actually is. He pushes back from the steering wheel, rubbing his sore eyes. She's on foot and she's so fast. She could be anywhere. He goes back to the apartment and searches around the area, calling her name like she's a lost puppy. Then he becomes convinced that she might have stolen a car. And if she's done that, chances are he might never find her again. He rests his head on the steering wheel, his stomach churning. Every minute that passes puts her further away from him. He has to move faster. Where would she go? What places does Angel know? Thinking about Bea, he drives out to the Yu's place but finds the house dark and quiet, no sign of anyone. Then, remembering the night she played the piano, he turns his car out towards the old church. His stomach hurts. He can barely breathe. He weaves in and out of traffic, running stop signs and red lights. He has to find her.

Racing out of town, he wonders if she would go back to the mountains. Or would any place associated with him be the last place she'd go? As he's thinking, he passes by her house noticing that the cops are all gone. Here? Would she really come back here? After what her father just put her through? He brings his car to another screeching halt and runs for the front door. Her father's truck is still parked out front. He was long gone by the time the cops arrived but he has to still be in the area.

Theo enters the living room and sees the sun setting through the streaky bay window. Filtered light settles across Angel's personal prison, catching the tops of the old tractors and abandoned vehicles buried in the hopeless overgrowth beyond the window. The sun enters the cluttered front room, making even the banal seem ominous. How could anyone have left her to die in a place like this? How could anyone see her like this and look away? The sun shrinks on the horizon turning tips of metal fragments to bloody stumps. Theo's breath is suddenly taken away and a pain pinches his chest. *Angel, please be here.* He turns down the hall knowing there is only one room she ever felt a sense of safety in. He swings around the corner finding the bedroom empty, the same claret light leaking into every fusty corner. He turns in a circle, feeling like he might faint. Then he hears something. Just the faintest whimper. He spins around and runs for the closet. He pulls the door open to find her there curled up around herself looking very much like a dying animal cowering against its attacker in its last defense.

"Angel," he whispers, dropping to his knees.

"Stay away from me," Angel hisses. She had no place to go, no place to run. Even knowing her father might be here, she came back. She stumbled over the pages of her torn up poetry to hide in the only corner she had left. But Theo came right to it, found it like he knew it was there. Theo, liar, betrayer, fake. Fucking fake. She was a fool to believe anyone could love her. There is no hope for people like her, her father is right. She can't even look at Theo, can't even think of him. This is a betrayal like no other. Like nothing she could ever dream of even in her darkest and wildest fantasies. It tunnels a hole right through her guts, like acid eating her from the inside out. She sees all the things she should've seen before, all his little slip ups, all the curiosities she let slide because she wanted so very desperately to believe in him. He groomed her, he seduced her, he preyed on her, and when the time was right, he took for everything she had.

"Don't run. I will make you understand this," Theo whispers, extending his palms out. He's scared even the smallest movement might spook her and cause her to bolt. He has to convince her as quickly as he can.

Angel takes a few deep breaths, her head throbbing. She has no more tears left to shed. Her whole body has gone dry. Dried up and blown away. Why hasn't she crumbled to bits yet?

"I'm going to tell you a story," Theo says evenly, keeping his body in the doorway, blocking any exit she may attempt to make. "I want you to listen to it and then you can decide. I would never do anything to hurt you. Never." He touches his fingertips to her tense, pulsing arm.

Angel explodes, his touch like a pin to an over-inflated balloon. Theo forces himself in the tight space with her, pushing her back into the confines of the closet. Pinning her there so she can't move. "Listen to me!"

"You won't get away with this. I'll kill you. Kill me or I'll kill you!" Angel twists around like a drunken ballerina as Theo tries to partner her. He grabs her by the waist and pulls her against him. Angel throws an elbow back and catches him in the face. He lets go, just long enough for her to slip by but then he's there again. They both tumble back into the closet, Theo now seated against the wall with Angel in his lap. He has her awkwardly by the neck, her torso arched away like a gusty sail, her legs kicking in protest between his knees.

"Listen to me!!" Theo screams and the whole world seems to silence.

Angel gasps, exhaling through clenched teeth, her limbs locked angrily in his. She can't move but neither can he. "Let me go," she hisses.

"Never." Theo tightens his hold on her neck as she briefly struggles again. If he loses her this time, he is certain he will never see her again. She fights him furiously, her hands pinching down on wherever they land. He pulls her back until his mouth is right beside her ear.

"Six months ago I died."

Angel kicks out. A fish on a hook that refuses to accept its fate. Theo remains firm, taking a hit to his nose from the back of her head with quiet resolve. And when she is settled again, he continues.

"Six months ago, I died. I was hit by a car, my heart stopped, my brain stopped. I was dead."

Angel kicks out furiously, his breath hot in her ear just like her father's. The sun drops, its intense light reaching the open door of the closet. It catches a mirror leaned against the wall and reflects the light sharply back in her face. She cringes trying to turn away from it. The angle, the way it's coming in, it's blazing right into her eyes, burning her sensitive corneas, tunneling right into her brain. She's completely blinded, and hopelessly trapped. This is the end of her, she can feel it stronger than anything she's ever felt before. This is how she dies. In the arms of the man she thought she loved.

"Angel, listen to me!" Theo cries, frustrated. He has told her this story in his head a million times and in so many wonderful ways but now the words are all jammed up inside him. He struggles to remember the important bits, the details he was sure would convince her of his sincerity. "I was dead. They put me on life support but I was dead. My body was dead. My brain was dead. And while I was dead, my soul went somewhere else."

Angel slumps backwards, closing her eyes against the angles of the setting sun. It comes hot across her face, lights up her features in the dark room so that there is no flaw left unturned.

Theo holds strong, refusing to give up. This is life and death now. Her life and death. He has to fight for this. "I went to a place. Not like Heaven…like, I don't know. It was…a place and there were other people there who had died. We were…fuck! Fuck. Fuck! Angel, I died and when I died I became your guardian. I was watching over you."

Angel slumps limp like a mouse in the grips of a cat's jaw, the same way she used to submit when her father broke her down. Her eyes would unfasten and she'd go deep inside herself to a place where no one could reach her and hope the torture would end soon. She's exhausted. She hasn't eaten for days, been beaten and betrayed. Every time she thinks the world has found a new way to beat her, another contender shows up in the ring.

"I don't know, maybe I was an angel, maybe my soul was just adrift or something but somehow I ended up here with you. Think, Angel. Wasn't there something familiar about me when we first met? Didn't you feel like we've met before?" Theo does not ease his grip on her, if anything he intensifies it. The light that was solely on Angel's face now reaches his face as well. Reflected through the mirror is a vibrating yellow orb haloed in orange light so intense it leaves dark spots floating in front of his eyes. He squeezes his eyes shut and continues his plea. "Do you remember that night when you stole the car?"

Angel just hangs, her eyes closed as well. The wound on her head has reopened and she can feel blood like a tear coming down her forehead.

"I was there. You were driving. It was late at night. It was what's her name's car, that little bitch from school. You know the one. God, I hate those kids. Anyway, the cops showed up and you left the car behind and you ran. I followed you back here. I was always with you, Angel, even though you couldn't see me. I went to school with you. Those kids flattened your bike tire. You sat alone at the end of the hall. The lunch lady gave you free food. Romeo was there," his voice turns bitter, "He surrounded you by the lockers."

Angel slouches forward further, as far as he'll let her go. "You knew that because you were one of them," she breathes, her voice barely audible. "You knew that because you tricked me like you tricked Bea. Because you spied on me." She shudders and then begins to shake uncontrollably. The trickle of blood has reached her eye and is seeping in. Now when she opens her eye she sees only red lines like prison bars. Except her prison is on the inside, it's in her head, around her brain, and there's no escape from this life sentence. She feels her heart slowing, her body going limp. Could she die just from her own will? Could she stop her own heart from the inside?

Theo holds her fiercely. She's dead weight in his arms, a concrete doll folded forward in his lap. He's not even sure she's listening to him. And if she is, she's not hearing him. But he can't stop now. He has to go on. "You went to the church outside of town. You and Bea. You guys broke in through a window and ate all the food. I was there. I was sitting right beside you even though you couldn't see me. Bea gave this horrible sermon..."

A light flickers in Angel's head over the memory. She'd forgotten about Bea and the night at the church.

"I was here when you were writing in your journal." He feels her tense. He knows he's entering dangerous waters now but he has be bold to reach her. He cannot hold anything back. "You were in love with a boy from work called Ambrose."

Angel pushes as far from him as possible. "You read my journals," she weeps. "You're disgusting."

"No, I was with you. I could hear your thoughts. I could see how much you cared for him. And how much you hurt for him too." He takes a deep breath. "I know about Save the Date. I know what you were going to do to Romeo and his friends."

A tear comes down Angel's face, mixed in hot blood. All her secrets, everything exposed. She supposes they had a good laugh over it, made copies and posted it up on the internet. She supposes they got off on her fantasies, used them for their own pleasure. She's so sick and in so much pain, she just doesn't know how she can still be alive. Pain radiates through her chest and abdomen. A hot sweat covers her back. Her heart is a slow, unsteady beat now.

"I was here the night the boys broke in the house." Theo swallows hard, wincing against the mirror reflecting in his face. It's so bright, it's painful. "You hid in the bathroom. In the bathtub. You braced the door with a piece of wood."

"Shut up!" Angel cries, tears causing more blood trails down her cheek. The pain is so unbearable. He was one of the boys who broke into her house. So where are the rest of them? Are they watching this? Lying in wait so they can finish the job? She closes her eyes but the sunspots remain. Why is it taking the sun so long to set? Why can't the light just finally go out?

"I was inside the room with you. Try and remember, Angel. We have been together for so long. I've been a ghost in your life so long. Angel, the boys went away but you didn't stop." Theo feels his hold on her breaking. He's so tired; he doesn't know how much longer he can restrain her like this. Emotionally, he's wrecked. How can he make her believe? He takes a deep breath, his voice breaking. "You cut yourself. On your arms. One side says: Dead; the other side say: Loser. I know how much you hate those scars. I know."

Angel inhales a sob, collapsing forward, but Theo pulls her back against his chest.

"You wrote beautiful monster on the wall in your blood. You thought about your father and about them leaving you here alone. We both woke up together in that cold bloody bathroom. You broke the mirror but I wouldn't let you finish the job. I brought you back to this closet. I begged you to write, to do anything to make yourself feel better. I told you that if it makes you feel better, then it doesn't matter if it's real. Try and remember, Angel. I've been here for a very long time."

Pain throbs though Angel's chest. Why isn't she dying? How long can a broken heart keep pumping? What is it going to take to end this? Why is it so hard to end one insignificant life?

"Angel, I've danced with you. And when you dance, you dream. And that night you danced and dreamed you were a singer a concert."

Angel's breath catches in her throat. She opens her eyes and the sunlight burns in. How could he know that? She never wrote it down, never told anyone. That's something that happened inside her head.

"I could hear your thoughts after a while. I didn't mean to, it was just a part of the process. I wasn't here all the time. I could come and go from this place. Angel, we were so close. Try to remember. I came back for you, Angel. I turned my back against my religion because they were content to watch you die. I came back from the dead to try and save you. That's how I knew so much. Because I already knew you. You already know me too."

Angel pushes back with a painful gasp. Everything is breaking inside. Already broken. Her defenses fall away and there is nothing left behind but an open, oozing wound, a broken outer shell spilling out the inner contents of a soft centered candy. She can't understand his words. They make no sense to her. Death is her only refuge now. The light from the mirror gets brighter and brighter. It's burning right through her eyelids. The air is heavy and hard to breath. And then something moves in the light. Daniel Ryder comes out of the sun. He passes between the mirror and the reflection and suddenly he is there crouching before them, his brilliant wings spread beneath the narrow wall of the closet. He appears more wild in the light, more untamed, more stirring, more arousing. His eyes are deep wells of desire framed in the thickest, darkest lashes and gleaming like gold. His hair is sheer black, longer than before, falling across his eyes and over his shoulders. He raises his large hand to Angel's face and traces a cross on her wet forehead. "Angels and Ministers of Grace defend us," he whispers.

Angel jolts backwards as the catch on her memories releases, the memoirs of her secret life revealing like a slideshow. "Oh my god," she whispers, her eyes rolling back as wave after wave of her dream life returns. Theo in her home, in her bed, in her bath. All the time they spent together before she ever met him. The love and passion they exchanged with life and death between them. He was there the whole time, just like he said, the most impossible explanation come true. And then Ryder in the graveyard, at the resort, all the dark places of her life suddenly illuminated. Surprise after surprise is revealed to her tear stained eyes. It's not just her own memories that come flooding in, but Theo's experiences as well. She's battered by his warm impressions of her until her own self-hatred is forced to flee in shame. She sees how he first came to her, how stiff and naive he was. She sees how he broke his vows and how he believed that she was so much stronger than him. She sees him struggle and fight and Ryder, beautiful Ryder, who saved him as well. She weeps as she remembers and feels a soft kiss against her forehead. She forces her weary eyes open to see her new guardian hovering above her, knowing that her former guardian holds her from behind. They are all together in this. She is not alone and hasn't been for a very long time.

"I am in the place before you fall asleep and before you rise. That is where you will see me. I am yours, just as I was his." Ryder smiles, his teeth white against his trim beard. He plucks something out of the air. A chain with a small medallion on it. "This is the medal of Saint Christopher, for your protection. It was mine once, when I lived on this earth. Now I want you to have it." He leans forward and kisses her on the forehead again, whispering, "Eros went with her and Beautiful Desire followed her." Ryder moves aside to trace a cross on his Theo's forehead. Then kisses him too.

Theo tilts his head back as memories also come back to him. He remembers all the things that got lost in the dark. Full recollections from the Reserve and the forgotten times he spent as Angel's guardian. He also experiences Angel's impressions of him: his arrival in town, how he views her as her hero, her rescuer, how hard she fought to let him in. The whole experience washes him in love's pure light, leaving all the fear, anxiety and anger behind.

Angel stares up at her wayward guardian. In this moment they are fused, all emotion and all understanding. Where former lovers fought before, now they cling to each other. In Ryder's company, all shadows depart. Together they remember all the encounters they lost between them. Pure love. Pure sex. Such a connection formed that can never be broken. They are united, absolutely, forever, and ever more.

"For the Father knows about desire, and what the flesh needs: the flesh does not long for the soul. The joys of love are found in the love of the living, in the underworld we shall lie as dust and ashes." Ryder anoints them in his special blessing of spirit and body alike. Touching each in the way they wish. Angel more tenderly; Theo more passionately.

"Angel," Ryder says, now turning his attention solely on her.

Angel settles back against Theo's firm chest, easy tears sliding down her face. She stares up at him, this force of nature, god's rebel warrior down on one knee in front of her. His beautiful hands, so large yet so gentle come to each side of her face and she stares into the very eyes of love himself. Love with no conditions, no judgments, no limits. Daniel is love absolutely.

"Do you remember what I said in the graveyard? That you are a doorway?"

Angel answers only with her eyes, her mouth unable to respond.

"I think it is time we shut that doorway." Ryder takes a relic from the folds of his robe and presses it to her forehead. Angel feels it burning hot against her skin. Ryder pushes it against her as he speaks, his commanding voice filling the room, the house, the whole sky. "Michael, Gabriel, Uriel and Raphael, Archangels, defend us and protect us against the wickedness and snares of all evil and by the power of the Light and of the Universe; thrust into the dark all demons and evil spirits who wander through the world for the ruin of human souls. Angel, I release you from the six that hold you. I cast out Odium, Envy, Apathy, Misery, Severance, and Sadism. I bring you the Light. We are the seven holies. Let Love, Hope, Compassion, Temperance, Union, Grace, and Divinity now reside in their place. Keep my Light as your protection. You are now surrounded in the Light."

Angel pushes back against Theo feeling like something is going to burst from her chest. It's as if he is extracting all the pain and pressure like a thorn to be plucked from her body.

The demons cling to her, interwoven like a spider's web twisted around her lungs, her heart, her spine. She sees Romeo, she sees her parents, she sees the boy beneath the truck, the stealing, the lying, the dark dreams of death. The cutting, the crying, the hurting, the hunger. The pain, the fear, the anxiety, the sadness. Suddenly it all stands before her like a great wall of brick and mortar. A wall she has been banging her head against for years.

Sweat pours down Theo's face as he struggles to hold Angel, suddenly weighing twice what she did just minutes ago. Her body trembles and shakes against him. His eyes jerk up to Ryder but there is no fear in his mentor's face. He is a Goliath now, brilliant as the warrior angels, fierce as Malik and wild as Azrael. He has never seen his mentor at full power before. It shakes everything inside him.

Ryder pulls the relic from Angel's forehead and she releases one final cry. Ryder has pulled the pins from her emotional grenade, detonated it and suddenly it is all gone. Romeo is a million miles away. Her father a feather. She feels drugged, warm, spent, breathing as one with the men around her. Everything is so clear now. So clear. She doesn't have to sift through six layers of darkness to get to seven's truth anymore. It's presently there now. Her new reality.

Ryder reaches forward and places a holy kiss on each of his lover lips. "Like the winds of the sea are the ways of fate. As we voyage along through life: tis the set of a soul that decides its goal and not the calm or the strife." And as the sun sets and he begins to disappear, his voice fades with the dying of the light.

Chapter 48∞

Theo rises. It's morning. The sun is shining through the windows more grand and more brilliant than he's ever seen. He's back in his apartment with Angel in his arms but has no memory of how they returned. His body is sore from the battle in the closet but his head is clear and joyful. He looks down at Angel resting peacefully beside him. There was a connection they gained under the stairs, a brief moment when Ryder allowed them to be in each other's mind. Theo has seen himself through her. He is her hero. And she is everything to him. He hopes she can see that too now.

Angel opens her eyes and sees Theo's face above her. It is full of hope, excitement, and love. Her old life is a distant memory; those dark feelings all completely lost to her. She is everything she should've been before the world got a hold of her. She exhales a small breath and a smile spreads across Theo's face. A face more beautiful than the sun itself. He is hers now and she is his. They will run away to a life unimaginable. From now on, it will be the fantasy she always dreamed it would be. She smiles brightly, not needing to conceal the love she feels for him anymore. She knows the sentiment is completely returned.

"You ready to get out of this place?" Theo says, leaning on his elbow beside her. Angel still has blood in her hair from her father's attack and he reeks with sweat from the exorcism in the closet.

"Oh, I certainly am," she breathes, her eyes searching his. He leans down and kisses her. As he does, she reaches up and gently touches the side of his face. She has never felt so alive. She no longer yearns for Death and his chariot. It is life she seeks now.

Theo sniffs himself and grimaces. "I think I should shower."

Angel smiles. "I think I should too."

Theo rises from the bed and lifts her up with him. They stand and embrace in the rising sun. There's some clinking in the kitchen. The dog probably needs to go outside. "I'll get him," Theo says, reluctantly leaving her embrace.

"I can do it," Angel says. "You get the shower going?"

"Sure." He watches her pad out of the bedroom, his heart full and swollen. But then a cold, hard needle stabs his heart. The dog isn't here. The dog is at the vet. His eyes shoot to Angel who has stalled just outside the doorway. She is staring straight forward and not moving.

"Angel?" he asks.

Angel stares across the room at the blood shot eyes of her father, and even closer, at the double barrels of the shotgun that used to hide beneath the floorboards of her bedroom. He's standing on the other side of the kitchen with no shoes and a heavy nosebleed. His eyes are red and bleary. He looks more dangerous than she's ever seen him.

Theo takes a step towards her. He doesn't know who's in the kitchen but he has a terrible notion. He looks around for something he can use as a weapon. He does not know Angel's father is armed.

"Stay back," Angel says, with a swift jerk of her arm. She holds her palm out to Theo in an arresting motion. She's not sure her father even knows there is someone else in the apartment because when she speaks the words, she is saying them to him and not Theo.

Theo pauses until he hears another man's voice in the kitchen. Then he launches forward and comes to a quick stop beside Angel, nearly knocking her over. He grabs her arm and steps in front of her. Across the kitchen is a madman trying to kill the girl he gave life to. A madman who intends to kill his own daughter. He looks completely insane, like he's been living in the woods for years, not on the run for a few hours.

"Hold on a second," Theo says holding his hands out in front of him. "Just wait."

Angel's father sways behind the shotgun, aiming it unsteadily in their direction. "You putting your dirty hands on my little girl?"

"Just wait. You don't have to do this. Let's talk about this first." Theo continues to hold his palms up between them, not so much in surrender but in negotiation.

"I don't take orders from you," her father replies darkly, cocking the gun at Theo.

"No!" Angel screams, pulling Theo against her. Her father knows how to get her every time. Every time. First her dog and then Theo. She won't let it happen. Even if it means her own death in exchange for his. This has to stop now. She wrestles out from behind Theo so that they face her father side by side. "You don't touch him! You stay away from him!"

Her father's blistered eyes ignite. He exhales a long shaky breath, his sweaty fingers sliding over the trigger.

"No! Don't!" Angel screams, extending her arms in front of Theo. "Don't touch him. Don't hurt him. I'll do whatever you want. Do you want to go home? We can go home and wait for mom. Mom is going to be home soon. We should be there when she gets home."

Confusion registers over her father's face and he stumbles back a step. He is a doorway just like she was, except he has no guardian on his side. No one to keep his demons at bay. His pool in the Field is open and unoccupied. One of the many that have been overlooked due to lack of workforce. And her father only aggravates things with the alcohol. He puts himself in a vulnerable state and lets his evils take control. And he's so drunk right now that he might shoot them by accident while he is struggling to keep his balance.

"We can go home," Angel says again, feeling like she has struck a chord with him. "Just like it used to be. Remember? Do you remember how it used to be?"

Angel and Theo wait as her father seems to waver between fantasy and reality. But then he focuses on Angel and his resolve strengthens. "A slut like your sister," he whispers. "As long as I got something to give you girls, then you stay right beside me. But as soon as I got nothing. Nothing! You run your selfish little asses for higher ground. Fuck all of you."

"Whoa," Theo says quickly. "I can give you money. I can give you anything you want. A million dollars? You got it. Whatever you want." Theo sees the father's eyes narrow on Angel. "Not that," he warns darkly. "You can't have her."

The father's gun points back at Theo. "Can't have her? Who the fuck are you? She is already mine! She was always mine. I am her father and I own her. You are nothing. Nothing!" There is a brilliant flash and a loud bang and then Theo feels a warm sensation spread across his chest. He hears Angel scream and then he floats down to the linoleum floor soft as a feather gently touching down to the earth. He blinks back hot tears as a bubbles rise and pop from his chest. He focuses up at the ceiling, one of many he's spent admiring along his unconventional return to life.

He hears Angel's voice calling to him in the distance. He lifts his eyes to hers but finds Ryder's there instead. Those warm eyes greet him with a smile. "Welcome back, Theodore."

THE BEGINNING

Chapter 49ଔ

Angel puts on her jacket and descends the spiral staircase to the first floor. Andy and Dianna Duncan are waiting at the table in front of a full breakfast spread.

"Good-morning!" her adoptive father cries, rising to pull out a chair for her. "I hope you're hungry."

"Always!" Angel exclaims, grabbing a fork and digging in.

"Honestly," Dianne says, setting a napkin neatly in her lap. "I don't know how this girl eats so much and doesn't put on a pound."

"I've gained like ten pounds since I got here," Angel says, pausing to speak between bites. She looks between mother and father, each such a wonderful reminder of the son. Andy is more like him in looks while Dianna is more similar in nature. She has become very attached to the two since she moved in.

"What time are we meeting Buddy?" Dianna asks, sipping daintily at a cup of orange oolong tea.

"After breakfast, I think," Andy replies. "Thought we'd take the new hybrid out for a spin, hey, Angel?"

"Sounds like fun," Angel replies. "Though I have to go to the tattoo parlor at three."

"Let's have a look," Andy requests and Angel extends her arms on the table, palms up. From wrist to elbow, framed in flowers and roses are the words Beautiful Monster where Dead Loser used to reside. A lot has come to pass since Theo was shot. She hardly remembers the days that followed, every hour and minute so dreadfully painful. Just when she had thought she had found everything, her father took it all away. She was so distraught when she met Theo's parents that she could conceal nothing from them, not her life or her scars.

They took her in that very night. They vowed to finish what Theo started and began work on the house he was going to build her in the mountains. Though it seems she has no choice about the extravagant nature of the house when Theo's parents are involved. At least it doesn't have an elevator. But Angel has influenced them as well. They've put solar power in the mansion and bought a hybrid. For them it is more of a game than a necessity, but they are still playing along.

"Well it's certainly not to my taste," Dianne says, peering up over her reading glasses. "But they are doing a good job. Who is this person that is painting your arm?"

Angel smiles at Theo's mom, finding her wry and dry sense of humor much to her liking. Clearing her throat and blushing a little, she says, "Um...his name is Nathaniel Ryder."

"Oh yes," Andy says. "He is the one who did our son's tattoo."

Angel focuses back on her food. And *did* her son, she thinks, well, sort of. One of the many memories that they shared that horrible night. She is so grateful for that encounter now, for everything they experienced together. She wishes she could've appreciated him more when he was around.

"Oh my goodness, look at the time." Dianne abandons her boiled egg and sets her napkin aside. "We had better get going."

Andy rises, folding his newspaper and leaving it on his chair. He looks over his wife's head and says, "The dog is in the pool again." They all look over to see dog Theo gleefully doing laps around the backyard pool. Andy gestures to the closest staff member to go deal with the situation. Then the three of them leave the kitchen.

Angel sits in the backseat of the hybrid while Theo's parents chatter in the front seat. They remind her of parrots, each one proudly shouting out phrases but neither caring about what the other is saying. While they talk, she stares out the side window at the streets Theo used to haunt. She sleeps in his room now, bundles his clothes up under her pillow so she can smell him while she dreams. And he is always in her dreams now. Every night it is her and Theo, or Ryder, or all of them together. Every morning, she wakes up wishing she could sleep forever.

"Oh there he is! He is leaving without us," Dianna cries, indicating for her husband to pull to the sidewalk where Buddy is walking down the street, hands shoved in his pockets.

"That boy has such a crush on you," Andy calls over his shoulder at Angel.

"Andy!" Dianna scolds. "You are embarrassing the girl."

"It's all right," Angel says, the crush of no surprise to her. Buddy has been smitten since the day they met. Though Angel cannot return the sentiment, she enjoys it all the same. It's so nice to have people in her life who care about her and want to be near her.

"Like the car, Mrs. D," Buddy says, falling into the seat next to Angel. More quietly and reserved, he says, "Hi Angel."

Andy turns and winks at Angel. She only smiles in return. Her life is so easy now. No one has ever treated her the way they did back in that horrible little town. The Yu's got their retribution. Because of the video Romeo and Stacey posted online, the intent to cause Bea harm was undeniable. Did they mean to kill her? It took the jury a while to decide on that one. His case really became an example of bullying gone out of control and the media was all over it. Romeo was charged with manslaughter and Stacey got community service and probation. The chief of police was fired and the Yu's took every penny that town had left back home with them.

"So," Buddy says, rubbing his hands together nervously. "What are you doing afterwards? Do you want to go get something to eat?"

"Sorry Buddy," Andy calls from behind the wheel. "She is getting...inked." He pats himself on the back for his hip use of an urban colloquialism.

"Oh, you're getting more work done?" Buddy asks.

Angel proudly displays the tattoo again. Beautiful Monster, to match the one on Theo's back and to cover up the last vestiges of her old life. Dianna suggested cosmetic surgery but Angel ultimately decided to cover instead of rebuild. She doesn't want all the memories from her past gone. In fact, she wants to keep quite a lot of them.

"Maybe I'll get a little something someday," Dianna says, holding out her arm and trailing a manicured finger down her skin.

"Dianna!" Andy exclaims.

"Oh posh," she cries. "Just a little rose or something. Imagine what the girls in church group would say."

"Way to go, Mrs. D." Buddy raises his eyebrows at Angel.

Angel just smiles, her gaze returning out the window. She misses Theo so much. Their lives were just beginning. He came to her so quickly and she had so little time to appreciate him. How much she relives those last days with him, going over every second they spent together, every word he said to her. She knows it was a tough time too, but she can only recall good memories now. Everything about her time with him makes her smile.

They drive past the old car lot where Theo got the Thunderbird. The lot is empty now, the cars and trailer gone. All that's left is a big 'under construction' sign across the chain link fence. The story of the Ryder's and how Theo came to know them was a wonderful distraction when she first arrived to town. It was Buddy who helped her uncover it by taking her to the tattoo shop where Theo got his work done. She knew Nathaniel as soon as she met him, but did not know the stories of Gerry and the car lot. Theo saved that family too. He was a hero in so many lives.

"We're here," Andy says and then proudly points to the dashboard of the hybrid. "And look how little gas we've used."

They park the car and the four of them get out and walk slowly across the crowded parking lot. Andy and Dianna link hands, and then Dianna reaches back for Angel. She joins them happily. Andy looks back and offers his palm to Buddy. Buddy chuckles and rolls his eyes. "I pass."

"So will you be going up to see Xavier and his friends this weekend?" Andy asks.

"Maybe," Angel answers. She had so much support after Theo was shot, Xavier and company even came up to the city.

She has stayed in close contact with them ever since and Alice has become her best friend. She has so many people in her life now that she can hardly recall what it felt like to be alone.

They enter the wide glass doors of the four story building set in the middle of a paved parking lot. They continue down a clean, white hallway where a woman stands outside a room writing on a digital pad.

"Oh hello, Mr. Duncan, Mrs. Duncan," she says politely as they near.

"Any news?"

"Nothing I'm afraid. Same as yesterday."

Angel glances in the hospital room where Theo lies quietly in a coma. As his parents chatter with the nurse, Angel goes to his side. By the time the ambulance got to the apartment, he had already been dead for several minutes. His heart had stopped. His breath was gone. He had no blood left in his body. They manage to get a pulse in the hospital but his brain never came back. Machines feed him and breathe for him but he is a body with no spirit.

Angel touches his arm, his bad hand now removed. He'll be upset when he sees it gone. And she's knows he'll see it again. Because for a brief moment she shared his memories and she knows what happened the last time he died. She knows that somehow, someway, he's fighting to get back to her. And even if he doesn't make it, even if Theo cannot cheat death a second time, there is comfort knowing that he is with Ryder and that they will be together in that dream state between sleeping and awakening until she can join them on the Reserve.

She smiles, staring down at him, her guardian, her shining knight. He saved her in every way possible and, even if she spends the rest of her life trying, she will never be able to repay that debt. He gave her everything, even the pages of his own Life Book in exchange for hers. She has no doubt that if he hadn't come to her, she'd be looking at a very different future right now. Or she wouldn't have a future at all.

She glances up at her reflection in the hospital window and for a second sees a shadow of someone else standing there. As it fades, only herself remains. And for the first time in her life, she can look into that reflection without shame. She is happy now. She is loved now. Her Life Book is back on the shelves of the Reserve. Its bindings full of empty pages.

☙❧

Made in the USA
Columbia, SC
09 August 2018